Everyman, I will go with thee,
and be thy guide

THE EVERYMAN
LIBRARY

*The Everyman Library was founded by J. M. Dent
in 1906. He chose the name Everyman because he wanted
to make available the best books ever written in every
field to the greatest number of people at the cheapest possible
price. He began with Boswell's 'Life of Johnson';
his one-thousandth title was Aristotle's 'Metaphysics',
by which time sales exceeded forty million.*

*Today Everyman paperbacks remain true to
J. M. Dent's aims and high standards, with a wide range
of titles at affordable prices in editions which address
the needs of today's readers. Each new text is reset to give
a clear, elegant page and to incorporate the latest thinking
and scholarship. Each book carries the pilgrim logo,
the character in 'Everyman', a medieval mystery play,
a proud link between Everyman
past and present.*

NINETEENTH-CENTURY AMERICAN SHORT STORIES

Edited by
CHRISTOPHER BIGSBY
University of East Anglia

EVERYMAN
J. M. DENT · LONDON
CHARLES E. TUTTLE
VERMONT

First published in Everyman in 1995

J. M. Dent
Orion Publishing Group
Orion House, 5 Upper St Martin's Lane,
London WC2H 9EA
and
Charles E. Tuttle Co., Inc.
28 South Main Street,
Rutland, Vermont 05701, USA

Typeset in Sabon by Deltatype Ltd, Ellesmere Port, Cheshire
Printed in Great Britain by
The Guernsey Press Co. Ltd,
Guernsey, Channel Islands

British Library Cataloguing-in-Publication Data
is available upon request.

ISBN 0 460 87552 3

CONTENTS

NOTE ON THE EDITOR

CHRISTOPHER BIGSBY, Professor of American Studies at the University of East Anglia, is the author of more than twenty books on aspects of American culture. He has written on the literary achievement of African-Americans (*The Black American Writer; The Second Black Renaissance*); on popular culture (*Super-culture; Approaches to Popular Culture*); and on the American theatre (*Confrontation and Commitment; A Critical Introduction to 20th Century American Drama; American Drama: 1945–1990*). His books include studies of Edward Albee and David Mamet, an edition of the plays of Susan Glaspell and a collection of original essays by actors, directors, playwrights and critics called *Arthur Miller and Company*. He is a regular broadcaster with BBC radio and television and is the author and co-author of several radio and television plays. In 1994 he published *Hester*, a prequel to *The Scarlet Letter*. He is also the Director of the Arthur Miller Centre for American Studies. He lives in Norwich, England.

Year	Literary Events	Historical Events
1800	Edgeworth, *Castle Rackrent* Brown, *Arthur Mervyn* Webster, *An American Dictionary of the English Language* (–1828) Schiller, *Mary Stuart*	Washington DC becomes the capital of US The division of the Northwest territories Spain cedes Louisiana to French Italy is occupied by the French
1801	Chateaubriand, *Atala*	US at war with Tripoli Alexander I is crowned Emperor of Russia Establishment of the United Kingdom of Great Britain and Ireland
1802	de Staël, *Delphine*	Napoleon becomes President of Italian Republic Georgia cedes western territory to US
1803	Kleist, *The Schroffenstein Family*	Ohio is admitted to the Union Napoleon sells Louisiana Territory to US
1804	Blake, *Jerusalem, Milton* Schiller, *Wilhelm Tell*	12th Amendment ratified Napoleon crowned Emperor of France
1805	Wordsworth, *The Prelude* Scott, *The Lay of the Last Minstrel* Chateaubriand, *René*	US peace with Tripoli Treaty of St Petersburg Battle of Trafalgar; Battle of Austerlitz Michigan Territory is created

Year	Literary Events	Historical Events
1806	Scott, *Ballads and Lyrical Pieces*	Prussia declares war on France War between Russia and Turkey Confederation of the Rhine; end of Holy Roman Empire Continental Blockade
1807	Moore, *Irish Melodies* (1807–34); Barlow, *The Columbiad*	Slave Trade in British Empire abolished; Napoleon, with Alexander Tsar of Russia, control Europe; US Embargo Act; Fulton's steamboat in the Hudson
1808	*Salmagundi, The Whim-Whams and Opinions of Launcelot Longstaff,* Washington Irving with James Kirke Paulding and William Irving	The US frigate *Chesapeake* is fired upon by British frigate *Leopard*
1809	Irving, *A History of New York* [. . .] *by Diedrich Knickerbocker*; Tyler, *The Yankey in London*; William Cullen Bryant, *The Embargo*	Repeal of Embargo Act; James Madison President of US
1811		Battle of Albuera; Luddite Riots in England; opening of the Twelfth Congress of US
1812	Paulding, *The Diverting History of John Bull and Brother Jonathan*	Napoleon's retreat from Moscow
1813	Southey, *Life of Nelson* Shelley, *Queen Mab*; Jane Austen, *Pride and Prejudice*	
1814	Wordsworth, *The Excursion* Scott, *Waverley*	Napoleon in Elba Treaty of Ghent
1815	Peacock, *Headlong Hall* Scott, *Guy Mannering*	Battle of Waterloo; Congress of Vienna and second Peace of Paris
1816	Jane Austen, *Emma* Scott, *The Antiquary* .	Chief Justice Marshall interpreting the Constitution of the United States

Year	Literary Events	Historical Events
1817	Coleridge, *Biographia Literaria*; Byron, *Beppo*; Jane Austen and Madame de Staël died; *Edinburgh Monthly* (*Blackwood's Magazine*) founded; Moore, *Lallah Rookh*	James Monroe President of US
1818	Mary Wollstonecraft Shelley, *Frankenstein*; Peacock, *Nightmare Abbey*; Scott, *The Heart of Midlothian*; Payne, *Brutus, or, The Fall of Tarquin*; Paulding, *The Backwoodsman*; Keats, *Endymion*	
1819	Irving, *The Sketch Book of Geoffrey Crayon, Gent*; Scot, *Ivanhoe*; Shelley, *The Cenci* Birth of Whitman	Carlsbad Decree Purchase of Florida from Spain
1820	Shelley, *Prometheus Unbound* Lamb, *Essays of Elia* (1820–5)	Revolution in Italy and Spain; death of George III; George IV crowned; Missouri Compromise, about slavery in the Louisiana Territory
1821	James Mill, *Elements of Political Economy*; Scott, *Kenilworth*; De Quincey, *Confessions of an Opium-Eater*	Revolution in Piedmont, Greece and South America Death of Napoleon
1822	Irving, *Bracebridge Hall* Paulding, *A Sketch of Old England*; Byron, *Hours of Idleness*. Death of Shelley	Turkish Invasion of Greece
1823	*Westminster Review* begun by Jeremy Bentham; Scott, *Quentin Durward*	Monroe Doctrine; Congress of Verona
1824	Death of Lord Byron Irving, *Tales of a Traveller*	Mehemet Ali intervenes in Greece

Year	Literary Events	Historical Events
1825	Paulding, *John Bull in America*	First railway between Stockton and Darlington Independence of Spanish America Nicholas 1 Tsar of Russia
1826	James Fenimore Cooper, *The Last of the Mohicans*	
1827	Poe, first volume of *Poems* Stendhal, *Armance* Manzoni, *I Promessi Sposi*	
1828	Webster, *An American Dictionary of the English Language*; Scott, *The Fair Maid of Perth* Hawthorne, *Fanshawe* (published anonymously)	Russo-Turkish war
1829	Poe, *Tamerlane*; Balzac, *Les Chouans*	Swan River Settlement; Greece independent; Andrew Jackson President of US
1830	Stendhal, *Le Rouge et le Noir* Birth of Emily Dickinson	Revolution in France
1831	Hugo, *Notre-Dame de Paris* Peacock, *Crotchet Castle*	Faraday discovers electro-magnetic induction
1832	Irving, *The Alhambra* Death of Sir Walter Scott and Goethe	Electric telegraph invented by Morse; Mazzini founds 'Young Italy'
1833	Balzac, *Eugénie Grandet* Pushkin, *Eugene Onegin* Lydia Maria Child, *Appeal in Favor of [. . .] Africans*	
1834	Davy Crockett, *Narrative*	The New Poor Law Tolpuddle Martyrs; abolition of slavery in the British Empire

Year	Literary Events	Historical Events
1835	Irving, *The Crayon Miscellany*; Hoffman, *A Winter in the West*; de Tocqueville, *De la démocratie en Amerique* Lydia Maria Child, *A History of the Condition of Women*	John Quincey Adams president of US Second Seminole War
1836	Emerson, *Nature*	Texas declares Independence; Chartism in England
1837	Dickens, *Pickwick Papers* Emerson, *The American Scholar*; Hawthorne, *Twice-Told Tales*	Queen Victoria succeeds to the throne; rebellion in Canada Great Trek in South Africa Martin Van Buren President of US
1838	Poe, *Narrative of Arthur Gordon Pym of Nantucket* Whittier, *Ballads and Anti-Slavery Poems*	Afghan War; Anti Corn Law League founded; first Atlantic Steamships
1839	Poe, *Fall of the House of Usher*	Treaty of London
1840	Dana, *Two Years before the Mast* Hoffman, *Greyslaer: A Romance of the Mohawk* Poe, *Tales of the Grotesque and Arabesque*	Opium War between Britain and China
1841	Emerson, *Essays* (first series) Channing, *Works* (1841–3)	John Tyler elected president Brook Farm established
1842	Dickens, *American Notes* Longfellow, *Ballads and other Poems*	Chartists' Second Petition
1843	Prescott, *History of the Conquest of Mexico*	
1844	Emerson, *Essays* (second series)	Telegraph line, Washington to Baltimore
1845	Emerson, *Representative Men*; Poe, 'The Raven'	Admission of Texas into the Union

Year	Literary Events	Historical Events
1846	Melville, *Typee* Hawthorne, *Mosses from an Old Manse* Bryant, *The White-footed Deer and Other Poems*	Repeal of Corn Laws US at war with Mexico
1847	Melville, *Omoo* Longfellow, *Evangeline* Thackeray, *Vanity Fair* Emily Brontë, *Wuthering Heights*	Mormons settle in Utah Irish potato famine
1848		Revolutions in Europe; gold discovered in California Mexico cedes Texas to US
1849	Melville, *Redburn*; Parkman, *The Oregon Trail*; Thoreau, *A Week on the Concord and Merrimack Rivers* Irving, *A Life of Oliver Goldsmith*	Oregon Treaty; the 49th parallel of latitude became the boundary between US and Canada; California Gold Rush; Zachary Taylor elected president; Fugitive Slave Law
1850	Dickens, *David Copperfield* Hawthorne, *The Scarlet Letter* Melville, *White Jacket* Tennyson, *In Memoriam*	Death of President Taylor
1851	Melville, *Moby-Dick* Hawthorne, *The House of the Seven Gables*	Great Exhibition, London
1852	Stowe, *Uncle Tom's Cabin* Melville, *Pierre* Hawthorne, *The Blithedale Romance, The Life of Franklin Pierce* Elizabeth Drew Stoddard, *The Margesons*	Napoleon III Emperor Treaty of London; Sand River Convention
1853	Dickens, *Bleak House* Hawthorne, *Tanglewood Tales, for Girls and Boys*	Russia and Turkey at war Franklin Pierce President of US Railway from New York to Chicago

Year	Literary Events	Historical Events
1854	Irving, *Wolfert's Roost*	War declared against Russia
	Thoreau, *Walden*	by France and Britain
	Dickens, *Hard Times*	Kansas-Nebraska Act
1855	Whitman, *Leaves of Grass*	End of Crimean War
	Longfellow, *Song of*	
	Hiawatha; death of Charlotte	
	Brontë	
	Tolstoy, *Sevastopol Sketches*	
1856	Turgenev, *Rudin*	Bessemer invents process for
	Harriet Beecher Stowe, *Dred*	steel; Livingstone in Africa
	Melville, *Piazza Tales*	Peace of Paris; Britain bombs
	Emerson, *English Traits*	Canton
1857	Flaubert, *Madame Bovary*	Indian Mutiny; James
	Melville, *The Confidence-Man*	Buchanan President of
		US until 1861
1858	Longfellow, *The Courtship of*	*Great Eastern* launched
	Miles Standish; Oliver	
	Wendell Holmes, *The*	
	Autocrat at the Breakfast	
	Table	
1859	George Eliot, *Adam Bede*	Harper's ferry raid – US one
	Goncharov, *Oblomov*	step closer to civil war; De
	Turgenev, *On the Eve*	Lesseps begins the Suez Canal
1860	Hawthorne, *The Marble Faun*	
1861	Dickens, *Great Expectations*	American Civil War
	Dostoevsky, *Notes from the*	
	House of the Dead	
1862	Hugo, *Les Misérables*	
	Rebecca Harding Davis,	
	Margaret Howth	
1863	Tolstoy, *The Cossacks*	Battle of Gettysburg
	Hawthorne, *Our Old Home*	Emancipation Proclamation
1864	Goncourts, *Renée Mauperin*	
	Dostoevsky, *Notes from the*	
	Underground	
	Death of Hawthorne	
1865	Elizabeth Drew Stoddard,	American Civil War ends
	Two Men	Assassination of Lincoln

Year	Literary Events	Historical Events
1866	Greeley, *The American Conflict* Eliot, *Felix Holt* Dostoevsky, *Crime and Punishment* Elizabeth Gaskell, *Wives and Daughters*	Transatlantic cable laid Fourteenth amendment
1867	Harris, *Sut Luvingood Yarns* Elizabeth Drew Stoddard, *Temple House*	National Ku Klux Klan Reconstruction Act Purchase of Alaska
1868	Lydia Maria Child, *Appeal for the Indians* Rebecca Harding Davis, *Waiting for the Verdict* Louisa May Alcott, *Little Women*	
1869	Twain, *The Innocents Abroad* Harriet Beecher Stowe, *Oldtown Folks*	
1870	Harte, *The Luck of Roaring Camp* Rossetti, first sonnets of 'The House of Life'	Fifteenth Amendment ratified Standard Oil Company Franco-Prussian War
1871	Twain, *Roughing It* George Eliot, *Middlemarch*	
1872	Harriet Beecher Stowe, *Oldtown Fireside Stories* Spencer, *The Study of Sociology* Howells, *Their Wedding Journey*	Banking scandal in New York
1873	Twain, *The Gilded Age*	
1874	Rebecca Harding Davis, *John Andross*	
1875	James, *A Passionate Pilgrim*	

Year	Literary Events	Historical Events
1876	Louisa May Alcott, *Rose in Bloom* Twain, *Tom Sawyer* Tolstoy, *Anna Karenina* James, *Roderick Hudson*	Bell's speaking telephone Battle of Little Big Horn Centennial Exposition, Philadelphia
1877	James, *Washington Square*	
1879	James, *Daisy Miller* Ibsen, *A Doll's House*	Edison's incandescent lamp
1880		Bicycle invented
1881	James, *The Portrait of a Lady*	
1882	Howells, *A Modern Instance*	Combustion engine invented
1883	Twain, *Life on the Mississippi* Mary Wilkins Freeman, *Decorative Plaques*	Metropolitan Opera founded Brooklyn Bridge completed
1884	Sarah Orne Jewett, *A Country Doctor* Twain, *Huckleberry Finn*	
1885	Howells, *The Rise of Silas Lapham* Sarah Orne Jewett, *A Marsh Island*	Grover Cleveland elected President Statue of Liberty
1886	James, *The Bostonians* Sarah Orne Jewett, *A White Heron*	AFL founded Haymarket Riot, Chicago
1887	Mary Wilkins Freeman, *A Humble Romance*; Page, *Marse Chan*; Frederic, *Seth's Brother's Wife*	
1888	Bellamy, *Looking Backwards* Page, *Red Rock*	International Council of Women
1890	Howells, *A Hazard of New Fortunes*	

Year	Literary Events	Historical Events
1891	Adams, *Historical Essays* Bierce, *Tales of Soldiers and Civilians* Dickinson, *Poems* (post) Hardy, *Tess of the D'Urbervilles* Morris, *News from Nowhere* Mary Wilkins Freeman, *A New England Nun* Garland, *Main-Travelled Roads*	Populist Party formed
1892	Deaths of Tennyson and Whitman Charlotte Perkins Gilman, 'The Yellow Wallpaper' Garland, *Prairie Folk* and 'political' novels	Famine in Russia
1893	Mary Wilkins Freeman, *Jane Field*; Crane, *Maggie: A Girl of the Streets*	Financial panic in America
1894	Berenson, *Italian Painters of the Renaissance* (1894–1907) Sargent elected to Royal Academy Howells, *A Traveller from Altruria*; Mary Wilkins Freeman, *Pembroke* Frederic, *Marsena*	
1895	Hardy, *Jude the Obscure* James, *Guy Domville* Wilde, *An Ideal Husband* Wister, *Red Men and White* Garland, *Rose of Dutcher's Cooly*; Crane, *The Red Badge of Courage*	New York Public Library opened Cuba fights Spain for independence

Year	Literary Events	Historical Events
1896	Sarah Orne Jewett, *The Country of the Pointed Firs* Harold Frederic, *The Damnation of Theron Ware* DuBois, *The Suppression of the Slave Trade*; Dunbar, *Lyrics of Lowly Life*	Klondike gold rush
1897	Garland, *Wayside Courtships* Crane, 'The Bride Comes to Yellow Sky'	
1898	Charlotte Perkins Gilman, *Women and Economics* Wister, *Lin McLean* Crane, 'The Open Boat'	Discovery of radium
1899	Kate Chopin, *The Awakening* James, *The Awkward Age* Chesnutt, *The Conjure Woman, The Wife of His Youth*; O. Henry, 'Whistling Dick's Christmas Stocking Edith Wharton, *The Great Inclination*; DuBois, *The Philadelphia Negro*; Dunbar, *Lyrics of the Hearthside*	Boer War (1899–1902)
1900	Death of Ruskin Isadora Duncan's solo recitals in Paris Conrad, *Lord Jim* Mary Wilkins Freeman, *The Heart's Highway*; Chesnutt, *The House Behind the Cedars* Edith Wharton, *The Touchstone*	British Labour Party founded Commonwealth of Australia founded Freud, *The Interpretation of Dreams*

INTRODUCTION

Written above the study door of the Puritan divine Cotton Mather were two words: 'BE BRIEF'. Nathaniel Hawthorne believed this motto might be placed with advantage above both church pulpit and judge's bench. There were those, however, and Hawthorne was one of them, for whom such an injunction became the basis of an aesthetic, the aesthetic of the short story.

The short story writer Katherine Mansfield once confessed to her sense of the inadequacy of her chosen form. She wrote, she explained, 'only short stories; just short stories', not the 'big things'. That air of apology is a familiar one, more especially in the twentieth century when publishers increasingly came to tolerate short stories only on the grounds that they were the price to be paid for the novels that would follow. In the nineteenth century, however, particularly in Russia, France, and, eventually, America, the short story played a central role and if, to both Edgar Allan Poe and Henry James, their fellow citizens were a little slow off the mark it is now possible to see that the form proved in many ways *the* American genre.

For Edgar Allan Poe, writing in 1842, only Washington Irving and Nathaniel Hawthorne, among American authors, had achieved anything of note. By 1888, however, and despite his admiration for the French, Henry James was ready to add the names of Poe and Bret Harte to the list of distinguished American writers and to suggest that the 'short tale' now flourished. Modesty – not always his strong suit – doubtless made James omit himself from the list, though his first two books were collections of stories. Poe, likewise, omitted his own accomplishments except that in judging the ultimate achievement of story-writing to lie in tales that emphasised terror, passion and horror, he perhaps recalled to the reader's mind something of his particular claim to attention.

V. S. Pritchett once described the short story as 'something glimpsed from the corner of the eye in passing'. It is a definition that hints at a sudden significance found in the apparently marginal, the peripheral become central, the detail transformed into the substance of meaning. Raymond Carver, who, like William Sydney Porter (O. Henry), Katherine Mansfield and Jorge Luís Borges, proved that it was possible to base a career entirely on the short story, glossed V. S. Pritchett's observation by saying:

> First the glimpse. Then the glimpse given life, turned into something that will illuminate the moment and just maybe lock it indelibly into the reader's consciousness. Make it part of the reader's own experience as Hemingway so nicely put it. Forever, the writer hopes. Forever.

For Carver the essence lay in details, in facts transformed into images. It lay, too, in form. 'I love the swift leap of a good story,' he said, 'the excitement that often commences in the first sentence, the sense of beauty and mystery found in the best of them; and the fact – so crucially important to me back at the beginning and even now a consideration – that the story can be written and read in one sitting (Like poems!).' The exclamation point was a significant one for him, as it would have been, too, for Edgar Allan Poe.

For Poe the 'tale' had marked advantages over the novel and even the poem. His primary reason for believing this was that 'unity of effect and impression is of the greatest importance', and since such unity 'cannot be thoroughly preserved in productions whose perusal cannot be completed at one sitting,' the novel and the epic poem sacrificed a crucial virtue. He thus favoured stories that could be read in anything between half an hour and two hours, and he added that:

> The ordinary novel is objectionable, from its length, for reasons already stated in substance. As it cannot be read at one sitting, it deprives itself, of course, of the immense force derivable from *totality*. Worldly interests intervening during the pauses of perusal, modify, annul, or counteract, in a greater or less degree, the impressions of the book. But simple cessation in reading would, of itself, be sufficient to destroy the true unity. In the brief tale, however, the author is enabled to carry out the fullness of his intention, be it what it may. During the hour of perusal the soul of the reader is at the writer's control.

Whereas the novel is interleaved with other experiences, the short story has something of the concentrated impact of a poem.

It is also true that in the nineteenth century novels were frequently serialised so that their parts assumed something of the shape of a short story. Henry James's *The American*, for example, appeared in twelve issues of *The Atlantic Monthly*, and *The Ambassadors* was published in an equal number of issues of *The North American Review*. Yet a story is conceived both as a totality and as a concentrated experience, and for Poe and James alike and, incidentally, for Raymond Carver a century and more later, that is a crucial and defining aspect. Nor was James entirely happy, except financially, to see his novels published in this way. Certainly he affected to be pleased when *The Wings of the Dove* failed 'to see itself "serialised" ', commenting that those works determined by 'conditions of publication', have their charm qualified by the fact that 'the prescriptions here spring from a soil wholly alien to the ground of the work itself.' When not too 'blighting', he recognised that such restrictions 'often operate as a tax on ingenuity – that ingenuity of the expert craftsman which likes to be taxed very much to the same tune to which a well-bred horse likes to be saddled.' It is an ambiguous image and he would seem to admit as much in asserting that such ingenuities were apt to result less in compromise than conformity.

That still leaves us with a problem, however. What exactly is a short story? How short is it, or how long? What Irving called a sketch Poe called a tale and Henry James a short story, when he did not speak of 'brevities', 'anecdotes', 'studies on the minor scale', 'the conceit', 'the little gem', the *'morceau de vie'*, or the 'nouvelle'. There are novellas longer than novels and stories longer than novellas. Joseph Conrad's *The Heart of Darkness* is a short story, so is Hemingway's six-sentence account of the shooting of six cabinet ministers after a failed coup in his first book, *In Our Time*. Length is plainly not the determinant. The question is one of form.

For James the novel permitted digression. Certainly in its more epic form it was a 'loose baggy monster', a description, however, that fits some novels rather more precisely than others. It might suit *War and Peace*, which he instances; scarcely Jane Austen's *Emma*. In modern terms such a description would apply to Norman Mailer's *Harlot's Ghost*, but hardly to Joyce Carol Oates's *Black Water*. On the other hand a novel can expand until it defies the art of the binder. In the nineteenth century even that was no determinant as works spilled into several volumes. Stories, though, had their parameters, and historically these tended to be determined by the requirements of the magazines in which they first made their appearance. Henry James may have chafed against their restrictions but they were the restrictions which in part defined the form.

Concerned as he was with the subject of form, Henry James debated not merely the competing values of the novel and the short story but the relationship between length and effect. For him, the fairy tale (and his examples were *Cinderella* and *Little Red Riding Hood*) is 'short and sharp and single, charged more or less with the compactness of anecdote'. This he contrasts with the 'long and loose, the copious, the various, the endless' nature of a work such as *The Arabian Nights*. He preferred the former to the latter for reasons having to do with 'lucidity' and 'roundness', believing as he did that 'working out economically almost anything is the very life of the art of representation.' For him, 'to do the complicated thing with a strong brevity and lucidity – to arrive, on behalf of the multiplicity, at a certain science of control' was the very essence of short story writing.

But while delighting in 'a deep breathing economy and an organic form' James was aware, too, of the constraints and constrictions of magazine publication. The discipline of length might have its advantages – a sonnet's freedoms being unlocked by a sonnet's rigid requirements – but it also had its oppressions. Speaking of his story 'The Coxon Fund' he said, 'to get it right was to squeeze my subject into the five or six thousand words I had been invited to make it consist of', a procedure which he likened to 'the anxious effort of some warden of the insane engaged at a critical moment in making fast a victim's straight jacket'.

Accordingly, when James was offered a greater freedom, being invited to contribute to the first number of *The Yellow Book* without restriction as to length, his response was that this 'offered licence . . . opened up the millennium to the "short story".' 'One had so often known', he explained, 'the product to struggle in one's hands, under the rude prescription of brevity at any cost, with the opposition so offered to its really becoming a story, that [. . .] indifference to the arbitrary limit of length struck me [. . .] as the fruit of the finest artistic intelligence.' In his view 'shades of difference, varieties, and styles, the value above all of the idea happily *developed*', which 'languished, to extinction, under the hard and fast rule of 'from six to eight thousand words', became possible 'when, for one's benefit, the rigour was a little relaxed.' It was so relaxed for 'The Turn of the Screw', commissioned for the Christmas number of a magazine. The result was a story over a hundred pages long. And yet what was it that he wished to stress of this story? It had, he insisted, 'the small strength [. . .] of a perfect homogeneity, of being, to the very last grain of its virtue, all of a kind.' It had, in short, Poe's 'unity of effect'.

For all his twisting to and fro, James never did come up with a satisfactory definition of the short story. On the one hand he admired economy, on the other he required space. He believed in conciseness but rebelled against restriction. When approached by Henry Harper to write for his magazine he noted, 'alas, there is no inspiration or incentive whatever in writing for *Harper* save the sole pecuniary one. They want, ever, the smaller, the slighter, the safer, the inferior thing.'

James solved his problem by calling his longer works 'nouvelles', which does not so much resolve the issue as sidestep it. But, finally, the question of definition that so concerned Poe, James and others in the nineteenth century is of less significance than the variety of uses to which short fiction was put, the immense scope that writers found in works which deliberately avoided the expansive possibilities of the novel.

For Raymond Carver, writing a century after James, there was almost a philosophical difference between the novel and the short story. As he explained:

> To write a novel, it seemed to me, a writer should be living in a world that makes sense, a world that the writer can believe in [. . .] a world that will, for a time anyway, stay fixed in one place. Along with this there has to be a belief in the essential *correctness* of that world. A belief that the known world has reasons for existing, and is worth writing about, is not likely to go up in smoke in the process. This wasn't the case with the world I knew and was living in. My world was one that seemed to change gear and directions, along with its rules, every day.

Truth thus lies in fragments. The moment can be validated; that factitious coherence implied by extended narrative cannot.

This was a personal view, in part a product of Carver's own fragmented life whose coherence had been threatened by alcohol, divorce and a series of temporary careers. It is, after all, not difficult to think of novels in which the incoherence of experience is a central thematic concern and stylistic determinant, from Kafka's *The Trial* to Beckett's *Murphy*. At the same time, however, his emphasis on the authority of event, on meaning generated and contained by the discontinuous, on the epiphanic or revelatory nature of the apparently insignificant, the detail, the ordinary, is a key to the achievement of a number of both nineteenth- and twentieth-century short story writers.

It was Chesterton who suggested that,

> our modern attraction to the short story is not an accident of form; it is a sign of a real sense of fleetingness and fragility; it means that existence is only an impression, and, perhaps, only an illusion [. . .] We have no instinct of anything ultimate and enduring beyond the episode.

Seen thus, there is no choice but to look for the transcendent in the moment, until the disregarded gesture, the casual remark, the banalities of daily living, become charged with significance. The very absence of narrative space and elaborated coherence edges experience in the direction of the image, a condition that is somewhat disturbing because intensity of focus forces every fragmentary detail to render up its meaning or meanings as a photorealist's painting unnerves us precisely by its relentless, and over-precise, reproduction of surface. The photorealist painting forces background to become foreground and concentrates attention on the moment severed from its larger context, a context which could only dilute the force of that moment and sacrifice it to the illusion of a coherence born out of process or the idea of a supposed totality. Much the same could be said of the short story and Carver has implied as much in saying that,

> It's possible in a poem or short story, to write about commonplace things and objects using commonplace but precise language, and to endow these things – a chair, a window curtain, a fork, a stone, a woman's earring – with immense, even startling power. It is possible to write a line of seemingly innocuous dialogue and have it send a chill down the reader's spine.

This is the statement of a minimalist, an admirer of Hemingway, for whom precision of language is a key to understanding, a means to unlock significance. But he was also an admirer of Chekhov and found in Henry James a similar distrust of language clouded by emotion or betrayed by inaccuracy, what James himself called 'weak signification'. Carver quotes approvingly a remark by the narrator of a story by Isaac Babel. Speaking of Maupassant and the writing of fiction, he says, 'No iron can pierce the heart with such force as a period put just in the right place.' What lies behind the search for such precision is a desire to lock the reader into the story and allow no escape, no door left carelessly open through unintentional ambiguity, vagueness, confusion or error.

This is not to say that the novel is free of a responsibility towards language or that detail there, too, may not prove the key to meaning. It does, however, underscore the fact that brevity narrows the focus and increases the pressure on the writer and the reader. That is why Carver, like Poe, saw a relationship between the short story and the poem; concision and intensity become the operative principles. In Carver's words, 'Get in, get out. Don't linger.'

The short story is no less free than the novel. Its ambition can certainly be as great. By definition, however, its strategies for realising those ambitions are likely to be different. Working within a narrower scope it cannot afford elaborate digression, a too-slow unfolding of character, an over-elaborate development of plot, an over-relaxed narrative drive. Yet, in the place of these elements may come an intensity of focus, a concentration on detail and, as Poe suggested, a sense of totality (Carver notwithstanding) which, in Poe's words, can have 'an immense force'. And, despite the achievements of the nineteenth-century novel, it can be plausibly argued that, taken together, the short stories with which America amused, entertained and instructed itself, from Poe onwards, in themselves added up to a portrait of a country still about the task of self-invention, a fiction in the making.

There would be those who endeavoured to capture the epic scope of this new country by writing something which came to be known as the Great American Novel, a work whose scale and size were to be commensurate with the nation it set out to picture. But in fact the short story, or at least the succession of short stories gathered here, could be said to have accomplished something similar, exchanging for a comprehensiveness which must fall short of its objective, the telling detail, and finding in a single incident an image which, besides the light it throws on individual lives or natures, opens up a central social or cultural truth that would be lost in a work for which sheer scale may have to substitute for insight. This was perhaps what James called 'the civic use of the imagination'.

It is tempting, in other words, to see in these short stories a greater story: that of America itself. There was a self-consciousness about America in the nineteenth century as the nation explored its destiny, identity and purpose. It was hungry to create new myths and narratives springing out of its own development. But in so far as such unambiguous accounts of American triumphalism proved inadequate to a reality more profoundly ambivalent than could be contained by notions of a new Adam in a new Eden or yet of Eldorado, a victorious individualism or a new-born community of souls, the writer occupied the space that opened up between the supposed ideal and its imperfect realisation.

Washington Irving in 'Rip Van Winkle' charts a shift in the national consciousness while ironically underscoring a more subtle continuity. Hawthorne, fascinated by what he saw as the redeeming imperfections of humankind, implicitly challenged a national faith in the virtue and possibility of a reconstituted innocence. 'The Birth-mark', no less than his great novel *The Scarlet Letter*, is a challenge to a fundamental American, as well as transcendental, belief that we are born free of history and that innocence is recoverable. Stephen Crane and Hamlin Garland dramatised the fragility of a myth born out of nature, space and the free man, while Lydia Maria Child resisted progressive and positivist notions of America's settlement of the continent in her stories of Native Americans which – like the stories of black Americans written by Charles Chesnutt and Paul Laurence Dunbar –would seem to endorse the Irish short story writer Frank O'Connor's conviction that the short story 'is attracted by submerged population groups', though, for him, these extended to artists, idealists and spoiled priests. Edgar Allan Poe, by contrast, took the inside track, finding in a broken psyche an image not only of a divided self but of an anarchy that threatens social constructions, which are no more than public expressions of the myth of an integral self. For Melville, meanwhile, in 'Bartleby the Scrivener', that central debate between the rights and obligations of the individual – in a culture that celebrates the free self and yet announces the joint stock company that is the new nation – leaves his protagonist disturbingly balanced between the role of anarchic fool and solitary saint. For Mark Twain, writing late in his career, but reflecting something of the spirit of *Huckleberry Finn*, even such redeeming ambiguity was absent as, in 'The Man that Corrupted Hadleyburg', he dissected the brash entrepreneurial spirit which was to fuel a great experiment in social living and found it corrupt to its core: a spirit touched less by Hawthorne's redemptive humanity than by a greed that translated the ideal into its reverse.

It could be argued that the short story, denied the scope to elaborate social context or trace those inter-connecting causalities that tie the past to the present and thereby the individual to a moral world, is liable to focus on the self severed from society. Frank O'Connor argues as much in his study of the short story, *The Lonely Voice*, suggesting that the genre, and perhaps the characters it features, remains, consequently, 'romantic, individualistic, and intransigent'. It is tempting to agree, not least because it is easy to find evidence for this in the work of nineteenth-century American writers. On the other hand, like all attempts at definition, it proves too prescriptive since Stephen Crane, for one, was capable of satirising precisely this assumption while, looking forward into the second half of the twentieth century, John Cheever took pleasure in exposing a loneliness and spiritual isolation born not out of separation but of too complete an absorption in the social world. Yet the tendency identified by O'Connor is, perhaps, real enough.

The American writer in the nineteenth century tended to be fascinated by the inadequacy of language in the face of experience, as by the ambivalence of words that must always prove inadequate to the thing they describe. Hawthorne's *The Scarlet Letter* concerns itself in part with the attempt of a society to impose meaning through the use of an authorised text. Hester Prynne is forced to wear a scarlet letter 'A' for adultery but her life escapes such a narrow and singular definition. Melville's *Moby-Dick* begins with a spill of words, with dictionary definitions and encyclopedic descriptions of whales. The novel itself, however, shows how remote these are from the meanings generated by a fact turned symbol. When Ambrose Bierce forces us suddenly to reconsider what we have been reading, in 'An Occurrence at Owl Creek Bridge', he forces us equally to acknowledge the power of the mind to invent the world which it inhabits. And that sudden vertigo that comes with a shift of the foundations may have moral and social force. Certainly that would seem to be part of the meaning of Poe's 'Fall of the House of Usher', just as questions about the substantiality, or otherwise, of the real, and of fiction's capacity to lie in the name of that reality, are raised in subtle form by Henry James's 'The Real Thing'.

In 'The Artist of the Beautiful' Hawthorne creates an artist who regrets the necessary coarsening of an idea as it moves into the world of tangible reality. In revulsion from the brute practicalities of his society he creates a mechanical butterfly of delicacy and mechanical perfection. It is an ironic story and is, like many of his, about the flawed nature of those who seek perfection unaware of the cost of such an endeavour. But beyond that it is, perhaps, also possible to hear in the defence Hawthorne's protagonist offers of his own efforts both a justification of the form in which he chose to tell his story and an awareness that scale may be too easily confused with scope and accomplishment: 'The Beautiful Idea has no relation to size, and may be as perfectly developed in a space too minute for any but microscopic investigation, as within the ample verge that is measured by the arc of the rainbow.' The characteristic minuteness in his objects and accomplishments, however, 'made the world even more incapable, than it might otherwise have been, of appreciating [his] genius'. He is certainly not the only one to feel that size may be confused with achievement.

Herman Melville, writing of Hawthorne and his short stories, may have suggested that you 'must have plenty of sea-room to tell the Truth in', but the evidence of his own work proves otherwise. Indeed that great ocean of a book *Moby-Dick* is dedicated to proving how elusive Truth can be, even when so wide a net is cast over it, while Melville's short stories suggest how accurately he can capture the moral ambiguity of a nation, confidently announcing its unambivalent future, within the narrow scope of what may be read at a single sitting. Such, then, is the force of the short story; such the power of many of those contained within these pages.

NINETEENTH-CENTURY
AMERICAN
SHORT STORIES

Rip Van Winkle

A Posthumous Writing of Diedrich Knickerbocker

> *By Woden, God of Saxons,*
> *From whence comes Wensday, that is Wodensday,*
> *Truth is a thing that ever I will keep*
> *Unto thylke day in which I creep into*
> *My sepulchre —*
>
> CARTWRIGHT

[The following Tale was found among the papers of the late Diedrich Knickerbocker, an old gentleman of New York, who was very curious in the Dutch history of the province, and the manners of the descendants from its primitive settlers. His historical researches, however, did not lie so much among books as among men; for the former are lamentably scanty on his favorite topics; whereas he found the old burghers, and still more their wives, rich in that legendary lore so invaluable to true history. Whenever, therefore, he happened upon a genuine Dutch family, snugly shut up in its low-roofed farmhouse, under a spreading sycamore, he looked upon it as a little clapsed volume of black-letter, and studied it with the zeal of a book-worm.

The result of all these researches was a history of the province during the reign of the Dutch governors, which he published some years since. There have been various opinions as to the literary character of his work, and, to tell the truth, it is not a whit better than it should be. Its chief merit is its scrupulous accuracy, which indeed was a little questioned on its first appearance, but has since been completely established; and it is now admitted into all historical collections as a book of unquestionable authority.

The old gentleman died shortly after the publication of his work; and now that he is dead and gone, it cannot do much harm to his memory to say that his time might have been much better employed in weightier labors. He, however, was apt to ride his hobby his own way; and though it did now and then kick up the dust a little in the eyes of his neighbors, and grieve the spirit of some friends, for whom he felt the truest deference and affection, yet his errors and follies are remembered 'more in sorrow than in anger,' and it begins to be suspected that he never intended to offend. But however his memory may be appreciated by critics, it is still held dear by many folk whose good opinion is well worth having; particularly by certain biscuit-makers, who have gone so far as to imprint his likeness on their New Year cakes; and have thus given him a chance for immortality, almost equal to being stamped on a Waterloo Medal, or a Queen Anne's Farthing.]

Whoever has made a voyage up the Hudson must remember the Kaatskill mountains. They are a dismembered branch of the great Appalachian family, and are seen away to the west of the river, swelling up to a noble height, and lording it over the surrounding country. Every change of season, every change of weather, indeed, every hour of the day, produces some change in the magical hues and shapes of these mountains, and they are regarded by all the good wives, far and near, as perfect barometers. When the weather is fair and settled, they are clothed in blue and purple, and print their bold outlines on the clear evening sky; but sometimes, when the rest of the landscape is cloudless, they will gather a hood of gray vapors about their summits, which, in the last rays of the setting sun, will glow and light up like a crown of glory.

At the foot of these fairy mountains, the voyager may have descried the light smoke curling up from a village, whose shingle-roofs gleam among the trees, just where the blue tints of the upland melt away into the fresh green of the nearer landscape. It is a little village, of great antiquity, having been founded by some of the Dutch colonists in the early times of the province, just about the beginning of the government of the good Peter Stuyvesant, (may he rest in peace!) and there were some of the houses of the original settlers standing within a few years, built of small yellow bricks brought from Holland, having latticed windows and gable fronts, surmounted with weathercocks.

In that same village, and in one of these very houses (which, to tell the precise truth, was sadly time-worn and weather-beaten), there lived, many years since, while the country was yet a province of Great Britain, a simple, good-natured fellow, of the name of Rip Van Winkle. He was a descendant of the Van Winkles who figured so gallantly in the chivalrous days of Peter Stuyvesant, and accompanied him to the siege of Fort Christina. He inherited, however, but little of the martial character of his ancestors. I have observed that he was a simple, good-natured man; he was, moreover, a kind neighbor, and an obedient, henpecked husband. Indeed, to the latter circumstance might be owing that meekness of spirit which gained him such universal popularity; for those men are most apt to be obsequious and conciliating abroad, who are under the discipline of shrews at home. Their tempers, doubtless, are rendered pliant and malleable in the fiery furnace of domestic tribulation; and a curtain-lecture is worth all the sermons in the world for teaching the virtues of patience and long-suffering. A termagant wife may, therefore, in some respects, be considered a tolerable blessing; and if so, Rip Van Winkle was thrice blessed.

Certain it is, that he was a great favorite among all the good wives of the village, who, as usual with the amiable sex, took his part in all family squabbles; and never failed, whenever they talked those matters over in their evening gossipings, to lay all the blame on Dame Van Winkle. The children of the village, too, would shout with joy whenever he approached. He assisted at their sports, made their playthings, taught them to fly kites and shoot marbles, and told them long stories of ghosts, witches, and Indians. Whenever he went dodging about the village, he was surrounded by a troop of them, hanging on his skirts, clambering on his back, and playing a thousand tricks on him with impunity; and not a dog would bark at him throughout the neighborhood.

The great error in Rip's composition was an insuperable aversion to all kinds of profitable labor. It could not be from the want of assiduity or perseverance; for he would sit on a wet rock, with a rod as long and heavy as a Tartar's lance, and fish all day without a murmur, even though he should not be encouraged by a single nibble. He would carry a fowling-piece on his shoulder for hours together, trudging through woods and swamps, and up hill and down dale, to shoot a few squirrels or wild pigeons. He would never refuse to assist a neighbor even in the roughest toil, and was a foremost man at all country frolics for husking Indian corn, or building stone fences; the women of the village, too, used to employ him to run their errands, and to do such little odd jobs as their less obliging husbands would not do for them. In a word, Rip was ready to attend to anybody's business but his own; but as to doing family duty, and keeping his farm in order, he found it impossible.

In fact, he declared it was of no use to work on his farm; it was the most pestilent little piece of ground in the whole country; everything about it went wrong, and would go wrong, in spite of him. His fences were continually falling to pieces; his cow would either go astray, or get among the cabbages; weeds were sure to grow quicker in his fields than anywhere else; the rain always made a point of setting in just as he had some out-door work to do; so that though his patrimonial estate had dwindled away under his management, acre by acre, until there was little more left than a mere patch of Indian corn and potatoes, yet it was the worst conditioned farm in the neighborhood.

His children, too, were as ragged and wild as if they belonged to nobody. His son Rip, an urchin begotten in his own likeness, promised to inherit the habits, with the old clothes, of his father. He was generally seen trooping like a colt at his mother's heels, equipped in a pair of his father's cast-off galligaskins, which he had much ado to hold up with one hand, as a fine lady does her train in bad weather.

Rip Van Winkle, however, was one of those happy mortals, of foolish, well-oiled dispositions, who take the world easy, eat white bread or brown, whichever can be got with least thought or trouble, and would rather starve on a penny than work for a pound. If left to himself, he would have whistled life away in perfect contentment; but his wife kept continually dinning in his ears about his idleness, his carelessness, and the ruin he was bringing on his family. Morning, noon, and night, her tongue was incessantly going, and everything he said or did was sure to produce a torrent of household eloquence. Rip had but one way of replying to all lectures of the kind, and that, by frequent use, had grown into a habit. He shrugged his shoulders, shook his head, cast up his eyes, but said nothing. This, however, always provoked a fresh volley from his wife; so that he was fain to draw off his forces, and take to the outside of the house – the only side which, in truth, belongs to a hen-pecked husband.

Rip's sole domestic adherent was his dog Wolf, who was as much hen-pecked as his master; for Dame Van Winkle regarded them as companions in idleness, and even looked upon Wolf with an evil eye, as the cause of his master's going so often astray. True it is, in all points of spirit befitting an honorable dog, he was as courageous an animal as ever scoured the woods; but what courage can withstand the ever-enduring and all-besetting terrors of a woman's tongue? The moment Wolf entered the house his crest fell, his tail drooped to the ground, or curled between his legs, he sneaked about with a gallows air, casting many a sidelong glance at Dame Van Winkle, and at the least flourish of a broomstick or ladle he would fly to the door with yelping precipitation.

Times grew worse and worse with Rip Van Winkle as years of matrimony rolled on; a tart temper never mellows with age, and a sharp tongue is the only edged tool that grows keener with constant use. For a long while he used to console himself, when driven from home, by frequenting a kind of perpetual club of the sages, philosophers, and other idle personages of the village, which held its sessions on a bench before a small inn, designated by a rubicund portrait of His Majesty George the Third. Here they used to sit in the shade through a long, lazy summer's day, talking listlessly over village gossip, or telling endless sleepy stories about nothing. But it would have been worth any stateman's money to have heard the profound discussions that sometimes took place, when by chance an old newspaper fell into their hands from some passing traveller. How solemnly they would listen to the contents, as drawled out by Derrick Van Bummel, the schoolmaster, a dapper learned little man, who was not to be daunted by the most gigantic word in the dictionary; and how sagely they would deliberate upon public events some months after they had taken place.

The opinions of this junto were completely controlled by Nicholas Vedder, patriarch of the village, and landlord of the inn, at the door of which he took his seat from morning till night, just moving sufficiently to avoid the sun and keep in the shade of a large tree; so that the neighbors could tell the hour by his movements as accurately as by a sun-dial. It is true he was rarely heard to speak, but smoked his pipe incessantly. His adherents, however (for every great man has his adherents), perfectly understood him, and knew how to gather his opinions. When anything that was read or related displeased him, he was observed to smoke his pipe vehemently, and to send forth short, frequent, and angry puffs; but when pleased, he would inhale the smoke slowly and tranquilly, and emit it in light and placid clouds; and sometimes, taking the pipe from his mouth, and letting the fragrant vapor curl about his nose, would gravely nod his head in token of perfect approbation.

From even this stronghold the unlucky Rip was at length routed by his termagant wife, who would suddenly break in upon the tranquillity of the assemblage and call the members all to naught; nor was that august personage, Nicholas Vedder himself, sacred from the daring tongue of this terrible virago, who charged him outright with encouraging her husband in habits of idleness.

Poor Rip was at last reduced almost to despair; and his only alternative, to escape from the labor of the farm and clamor of his wife, was to take gun in hand and stroll away into the woods. Here he would sometimes seat himself at the foot of a tree, and share the contents of his wallet with Wolf, with whom he sympathized as a fellow-sufferer in persecution. 'Poor Wolf,' he would say, 'thy mistress leads thee a dog's life of it, but never mind, my lad, whilst I live thou shalt never want a friend to stand by thee!' Wolf would wag his tail, look wistfully in his master's face, and if dogs can feel pity, I verily believe he reciprocated the sentiments with all his heart.

In a long ramble of the kind on a fine autumnal day, Rip had unconsciously scrambled to one of the highest parts of the Kaatskill mountains. He was after his favorite sport of squirrel-shooting, and the still solitudes had echoed and re-echoed with the reports of his gun. Panting and fatigued, he threw himself, late in the afternoon, on a green knoll, covered with mountain herbage, that crowned the brow of a precipice. From an opening between the trees he could overlook all the lower country for many a mile of rich woodland. He saw at a distance the lordly Hudson, far, far below him, moving on its silent but majestic course, with the reflection of a purple cloud, or the sail of a lagging bark, here and there sleeping on its glassy bosom, and at last losing itself in the blue highlands.

On the other side he looked down into a deep mountain glen, wild, lonely, and shagged, the bottom filled with fragments from the impending cliffs, and scarcely lighted by the reflected rays of the setting sun. For some time Rip lay musing on this scene; evening was gradually advancing; the mountains began to throw their long blue shadows over the valleys; he saw that it would be dark long before he could reach the village, and he heaved a heavy sigh when he thought of encountering the terrors of Dame Van Winkle.

As he was about to descend, he heard a voice from a distance, hallooing, 'Rip Van Winkle, Rip Van Winkle!' He looked around, but could see nothing but a crow winging it solitary flight across the mountain. He thought his fancy must have deceived him, and turned again to descend, when he heard the same cry ring through the still evening air: 'Rip Van Winkle! Rip Van Winkle!' – at the same time Wolf bristled up his back, and giving a low growl, skulked to his master's side, looking fearfully down into the glen. Rip now felt a vague apprehension stealing over him; he looked anxiously in the same direction, and perceived a strange figure slowly toiling up the rocks, and bending under the weight of something he carried on his back. He was surprised to see any human being in this lonely and unfrequented place; but supposing it to be some one of the neighborhood in need of his assistance, he hastened down to yield it.

On nearer approach he was still more surprised at the singularity of the stranger's appearance. He was a short, square-built old fellow, with thick bushy hair, and a grizzled beard. His dress was of the antique Dutch fashion – a cloth jerkin strapped around the waist – several pair of breeches, the outer one of ample volume, decorated with rows of buttons down the sides, and bunches at the knees. He bore on his shoulders a stout keg, that seemed full of liquor, and made signs for Rip to approach and assist him with the load. Though rather shy and distrustful of this new acquaintance, Rip complied with his usual alacrity; and mutually relieving one another, they clambered up a narrow gully, apparently the dry bed of a mountain torrent. As they ascended, Rip every now and then heard long, rolling peals, like distant thunder, that seemed to issue out of a deep ravine, or rather cleft, between lofty rocks, toward which their rugged path conducted. He paused for an instant, but supposing it to be the muttering of one of those transient thunder-showers which often take place in mountain heights, he proceeded. Passing through the ravine, they came to a hollow, like a small amphitheatre, surrounded by perpendicular precipices, over the brinks of which impending trees shot their branches, so that you only caught glimpses of the azure sky and the bright evening cloud. During the whole time Rip and his companion had labored on in silence; for though the former marvelled greatly what could be the object of carrying a keg of liquor up this wild mountain, yet there was something strange and incomprehensible about the unknown, that inspired awe and checked familiarity.

On entering the amphitheatre, new objects of wonder presented themselves. On a level spot in the centre was a company of odd-looking personages playing at ninepins. They were dressed in a quaint, outlandish fashion; some wore short doublets, others jerkins, with long knives in their belts, and most of them had enormous breeches, of similar style with that of the guide's. Their visages, too, were peculiar: one had a large beard, broad face, and small piggish eyes; the face of another seemed to consist entirely of nose, and was surmounted by a white sugar-loaf hat, set off with a little red cock's tail. They all had beards, of various shapes and colors. There was one who seemed to be the commander. He was a stout old gentleman, with a weather-beaten countenance; he wore a laced doublet, broad belt and hanger, high crowned hat and feather, red stockings, and high-heeled shoes, with roses in them. The whole group reminded Rip of the figures in an old Flemish painting, in the parlour of Dominie Van Shaick, the village parson, and which had been brought over from Holland at the time of the settlement.

What seemed particularly odd to Rip was, that, though these folks were evidently amusing themselves, yet they maintained the gravest faces, the most mysterious silence, and were, withal, the most melancholy party of pleasure he had ever witnessed. Nothing interrupted the stillness of the scene but the noise of the balls, which, whenever they rolled, echoed along the mountains like rumbling peals of thunder.

As Rip and his companion approached them, they suddenly desisted from their play, and stared at him with such fixed, statue-like gaze, and such strange, uncouth, lack-lustre countenances, that his heart turned within him, and his knees smote together. His companion now emptied the contents of the keg into large flagons, and made signs to him to wait upon the company. He obeyed with fear and trembling; they quaffed the liquor in profound silence, and then returned to their game.

By degrees Rip's awe and apprehension subsided. He even ventured, when no eye was fixed upon him, to taste the beverage, which he found had much of the flavor of excellent Hollands. He was naturally a thirsty soul and was soon tempted to repeat the draught. One taste provoked another; and he reiterated his visits to the flagon so often that at length his senses were overpowered, his eyes swam in his head, his head gradually declined, and he fell into a deep sleep.

On waking, he found himself on the green knoll whence he had first seen the old man of the glen. He rubbed his eyes – it was a bright sunny morning. The birds were hopping and twittering among the bushes, and the eagle was wheeling aloft, and breasting the pure mountain breeze. 'Surely,' thought Rip, 'I have not slept here all night.' He recalled the occurrences before he fell asleep. The strange man with a keg of liquor – the mountain ravine – the wild retreat among the rocks – the woe-begone party at ninepins – the flagon – 'Oh! that flagon! that wicked flagon!' thought Rip, 'what excuse shall I make to Dame Van Winkle?'

He looked round for his gun, but in place of the clean, well-oiled fowling-piece, he found an old firelock lying by him, the barrel encrusted with rust, the lock falling off, and the stock worm-eaten. He now suspected that the grave roisters of the mountains had put a trick upon him, and, having dosed him with liquor, had robbed him of his gun. Wolf, too, had disappeared, but he might have strayed away after a squirrel or partridge. He whistled after him, and shouted his name, but all in vain; the echoes repeated his whistle and shout, but no dog was to be seen.

He determined to revisit the scene of the last evening's gambol, and if he met with any of the party, to demand his dog and gun. As he rose to walk, he found himself stiff in the joints, and wanting in his usual activity. 'These mountain beds do not agree with me,' thought Rip, 'and if this frolic should lay me up with a fit of the rheumatism, I shall have a blessed time with Dame Van Winkle.' With some difficulty he got down into the glen: he found the gully up which he and his companion had ascended the preceding evening; but to his astonishment a mountain stream was now foaming down it, leaping from rock to rock, and filling the glen with babbling murmurs. He, however, made shift to scramble up its sides, working his toilsome way through thickets of birch, sassafras, and witch-hazel, and sometimes tripped up or entangled by the wild grape-vines that twisted their coils or tendrils from tree to tree, and spread a kind of network in his path.

At length he reached to where the ravine had opened through the cliffs to the amphitheatre; but no traces of such opening remained. The rocks presented a high, impenetrable wall, over which the torrent came tumbling in a sheet of feathery foam, and fell into a broad deep basin, black from the shadows of the surrounding forest. Here, then, poor Rip was brought to a stand. He again called and whistled after his dog; he was only answered by the cawing of a flock of idle crows, sporting high in the air about a dry tree that overhung a sunny precipice; and who, secure in their elevation, seemed to look down and scoff at the poor man's perplexities. What was to be done? the morning was passing away, and Rip felt famished for want of his breakfast. He grieved to give up his dog and gun; he dreaded to meet his wife; but it would not do to starve among the mountains. He shook his head, shouldered the rusty firelock, and, with a heart full of trouble and anxiety, turned his footsteps homeward.

As he approached the village he met a number of people, but none whom he knew, which somewhat surprised him, for he had thought himself acquainted with every one in the country round. Their dress, too, was of a different fashion from that to which he was accustomed. They all stared at him with equal marks of surprise, and whenever they cast their eyes upon him, invariably stroked their chins. The constant recurrence of this gesture induced Rip, involuntarily, to do the same, when, to his astonishment, he found his beard had grown a foot long!

He had now entered the skirts of the village. A troop of strange children ran at his heels, hooting after him, and pointing at his gray beard. The dogs, too, not one of which he recognized for an old acquaintance, barked at him as he passed. The very village was altered; it was larger and more populous. There were rows of houses which he had never seen before, and those which had been his familiar haunts had disappeared. Strange names were over the doors – strange faces at the windows – everything was strange. His mind now misgave him; he began to doubt whether both he and the world around him were not bewitched. Surely this was his native village, which he had left but the day before. There stood the Kaatskill mountains – there ran the silver Hudson at a distance – there was every hill and dale precisely as it had always been. Rip was sorely perplexed. 'That flagon last night,' thought he, 'has addled my poor head sadly!'

It was with some difficulty that he found the way to his own house, which he approached with silent awe, expecting every moment to hear the shrill voice of Dame Van Winkle. He found the house gone to decay – the roof fallen in, the windows shattered, and the doors off the hinges. A half-starved dog that looked like Wolf was skulking about it. Rip called him by name, but the cur snarled, showed his teeth, and passed on. This was an unkind cut indeed. 'My very dog,' sighed poor Rip, 'has forgotten me!'

He entered the house, which to tell the truth, Dame Van Winkle had always kept in neat order. It was empty, forlorn, and apparently abandoned. This desolateness overcame all his connubial fears – he called loudly for his wife and children – the lonely chambers rang for a moment with his voice, and then all again was silence.

He now hurried forth, and hastened to his old resort, the village inn, but it too was gone. A large rickety wooden building stood in its place, with great gaping windows, some of them broken and mended with old hats and petticoats, and over the door was painted, 'The Union Hotel, by Jonathan Doolittle.' Instead of the great tree that used to shelter the quiet little Dutch inn of yore, there now was reared a tall naked pole, with something on top that looked like a red night-cap, and from it was fluttering a flag, on which was a singular assemblage of stars and stripes; – all this was strange and incomprehensible. He recognized on the sign, however, the ruby face of King George, under which he had smoked so many a peaceful pipe; but even this was singularly metamorphosed. The red coat was changed for one of blue and buff, a sword was held in the hand instead of a sceptre, the head was decorated with a cocked hat, and underneath was painted in large characters, GENERAL WASHINGTON.

There was, as usual, a crowd of folk about the door, but none that Rip recollected. The very character of the people seemed changed. There was a busy, bustling, disputatious tone about it, instead of the accustomed phlegm and drowsy tranquillity. He looked in vain for the sage Nicholas Vedder, with his broad face, double chin, and fair long pipe, uttering clouds of tobacco-smoke instead of idle speeches; or Van Bummel, the schoolmaster, doling forth the contents of an ancient newspaper. In place of these, a lean, bilious-looking fellow, with his pockets full of handbills, was haranguing vehemently about rights of citizens – elections – members of congress – liberty – Bunker's Hill – heroes of seventy-six – and other words, which were a perfect Babylonish jargon to the bewildered Van Winkle.

The appearance of Rip, with his long, grizzled beard, his rusty fowling-piece, his uncouth dress, and an army of women and children at his heels, soon attracted the attention of the tavern-politicians. They crowded round him, eying him from head to foot with great curiosity. The orator bustled up to him, and, drawing him partly aside, inquired 'On which side he voted?' Rip stared in vacant stupidity. Another short but busy little fellow pulled him by the arm, and, rising on tiptoe, inquired in his ear, 'Whether he was Federal or Democrat?' Rip was equally at a loss to comprehend the question; when a knowing, self-important old gentleman, in a sharp cocked hat, made his way through the crowd, putting them to the right and left with his elbows as he passed, and planting himself before Van Winkle, with one arm akimbo, the other resting on his cane, his keen eyes and sharp hat penetrating, as it were, into his very soul, demanded in an austere tone, 'What brought him to the election with a gun on his shoulder, and a mob at his heels; and whether he meant to breed a riot in the village?' – 'Alas! gentlemen,' cried Rip, somewhat dismayed, 'I am a poor quiet man, a native of the place, and a loyal subject of the King, God bless him!'

Here a general shout burst from the by-standers – 'A tory! a tory! a spy! a refugee! hustle him! away with him!' It was with great difficulty that the self-important man in the cocked hat restored order; and, having assumed a tenfold austerity of brow, demanded again of the unknown culprit, what he came there for, and whom he was seeking? The poor man humbly assured him that he meant no harm, but merely came there in search of some of his neighbors, who used to keep about the tavern.

'Well – who are they? name them.'

Rip bethought himself a moment, and inquired, 'Where's Nicholas Vedder?'

There was a silence for a little while, when an old man replied, in a thin piping voice, 'Nicholas Vedder! why, he is dead and gone these eighteen years! There was a wooden tombstone in that churchyard that used to tell all about him, but that's rotten and gone too.'

'Where's Brom Dutcher?'

'Oh, he went off to the army in the beginning of the war; some say he was killed at the storming of Stony Point – others say he was drowned in a squall at the foot of Antony's Nose. I don't know – he never came back again.'

'Where's Van Bummel, the schoolmaster?'

'He went off to the wars too, was a great militia general, and is now in congress.'

Rip's heart died away at hearing of these sad changes in his home and friends, and finding himself thus alone in the world. Every answer puzzled him too, by treating of such enormous lapses of time, and of matters which he could not understand: war – congress – Stony Point – he had no courage to ask after any more friends, but cried out in despair, 'Does nobody here know Rip Van Winkle?'

'Oh, Rip Van Winkle!' exclaimed two or three, 'oh, to be sure! that's Rip Van Winkle yonder, leaning against the tree.'

Rip looked, and he beheld a precise counterpart of himself, as he went up the mountain; apparently as lazy, and certainly as ragged. The poor fellow was now completely confounded. He doubted his own identity, and whether he was himself or another man. In the midst of his bewilderment, the man in the cocked hat demanded who he was, and what was his name.

'God knows,' exclaimed he, at his wit's end; 'I'm not myself – I'm somebody else – that's me yonder – no – that's somebody else got into my shoes – I was myself last night, but I fell asleep on the mountain, and they've changed my gun, and everything's changed, and I'm changed, and I can't tell what's my name, or who I am!'

The by-standers began now to look at each other, nod, wink significantly, and tap their fingers against their foreheads. There was a whisper, also, about securing the gun, and keeping the old fellow from doing mischief, at the very suggestion of which the self-important man in the cocked hat retired with some precipitation. At this critical moment a fresh, comely woman pressed through the throng to get a peep at the gray-bearded man. She had a chubby child in her arms, which, frightened at his looks, began to cry. 'Hush, Rip,' cried she, 'hush, you little fool; the old man won't hurt you.' The name of the child, the air of the mother, the tone of her voice, all awakened a train of recollections in his mind. 'What is your name, my good woman?' asked he.

'Judith Gardenier.'

'And your father's name?'

'Ah, poor man, Rip Van Winkle was his name, but it's twenty years since he went away from home with his gun, and never has been heard of since – his dog came home without him; but whether he shot himself, or was carried away by the Indians, nobody can tell. I was then but a little girl.'

Rip had but one question more to ask; but he put it with a faltering voice:

'Where's your mother?'

'Oh, she too had died but a short time since; she broke a bloodvessel in a fit of passion at a New England pedler.'

There was a drop of comfort, at least, in this intelligence. The honest man could contain himself no longer. He caught his daughter and her child in his arms. 'I am your father!' cried he – 'Young Rip Van Winkle once – old Rip Van Winkle now! Does nobody know poor Rip Van Winkle?'

All stood amazed, until an old woman, tottering out from among the crowd, put her hand to her brow, and peering under it in his face for a moment, exclaimed, 'Sure enough! it is Rip Van Winkle – it is himself! Welcome home again, old neighbor. Why, where have you been these twenty long years?'

Rip's story was soon told, for the whole twenty years had been to him but as one night. The neighbors stared when they heard it; some were seen to wink at each other, and put their tongues in their cheeks: and the self-important man in the cocked hat, who, when the alarm was over, had returned to the field, screwed down the corners of his mouth, and shook his head – upon which there was a general shaking of the head throughout the assemblage.

It was determined, however, to take the opinion of old Peter Vanderdonk, who was seen slowly advancing up the road. He was a descendant of the historian of that name, who wrote one of the earliest accounts of the province. Peter was the most ancient inhabitant of the village, and well versed in all the wonderful events and traditions of the neighborhood. He recollected Rip at once, and corroborated his story in the most satisfactory manner. He assured the company that it was a fact, handed down from his ancestor the historian, that the Kaatskill mountains had always been haunted by strange beings. That it was affirmed that the great Hendrick Hudson, the first discoverer of the river and country, kept a kind of vigil there every twenty years, with his crew of the *Half-moon*; being permitted in this way to revisit the scenes of his enterprise, and keep a guardian eye upon the river and the great city called by his name. That his father had once seen them in their old Dutch dresses playing at ninepins in a hollow of the mountain; and that he himself had heard, one summer afternoon, the sound of their balls, like distant peals of thunder.

To make a long story short, the company broke up and returned to the more important concerns of the election. Rip's daughter took him home to live with her; she had a snug, well-furnished house, and a stout, cheery farmer for a husband, whom Rip recollected for one of the urchins that used to climb upon his back. As to Rip's son and heir, who was the ditto of himself, seen leaning against the tree, he was employed to work on the farm; but evinced an hereditary disposition to attend to anything else but his business.

Rip now resumed his old walks and habits; he soon found many of his former cronies, though all rather the worse for the wear and tear of time; and preferred making friends among the rising generation, with whom he soon grew into great favor.

Having nothing to do at home, and being arrived at that happy age when a man can be idle with impunity, he took his place once more on the bench at the inn-door, and was reverenced as one of the patriarchs of the village, and a chronicle of the old times 'before the war.' It was some time before he could get into the regular track of gossip, or could be made to comprehend the strange events that had taken place during his torpor. How that there had been a revolutionary war – that the country had thrown off the yoke of old England – and that, instead of being a subject of his Majesty George the Third, he was now a free citizen of the United States. Rip, in fact, was no politician; the changes of states and empires made but little impression on him; but there was one species of despotism under which he long groaned, and that was – petticoat government. Happily that was at an end; he had got his neck out of the yoke of matrimony, and could go in and out whenever he pleased, without dreading the tyranny of Dame Van Winkle. Whenever her name was mentioned, however, he shook his head, shrugged his shoulders, and cast up his eyes; which might pass either for an expression of resignation to his fate, or joy at his deliverance.

He used to tell his story to every stranger that arrived at Mr Doolittle's hotel. He was observed, at first, to vary on some points every time he told it, which was, doubtless, owing to his having so recently awaked. It at last settled down precisely to the tale I have related, and not a man, woman, or child in the neighborhood but knew it by heart. Some always pretended to doubt the reality of it, and insisted that Rip had been out of his head, and that this was one point on which he always remained flighty. The old Dutch inhabitants, however, almost universally gave it full credit. Even to this day they never hear a thunderstorm of a summer afternoon about the Kaatskill, but they say Hendrick Hudson and his crew are at their game of ninepins; and it is a common wish of all hen-pecked husbands in the neighborhood, when life hangs heavy on their hands, that they might have a quieting draught out of Rip Van Winkle's flagon.

NOTE

The foregoing Tale, one would suspect, had been suggested to Mr Knickerbocker by a little German superstition about the Emperor Frederick *der Rothbart*, and the Kypphäuser mountain: the subjoined note, however, which he had appended to the tale, shows that it is an absolute fact, narrated with his usual fidelity.

'The story of Rip Van Winkle may seem incredible to many, but nevertheless I give it my full belief, for I know the vicinity of our old Dutch settlements to have been very subject to marvellous events and appearances. Indeed, I have heard many stranger stories than this, in the villages along the Hudson; all of which were too well authenticated to admit of a doubt. I have even talked with Rip Van Winkle myself, who, when last I saw him, was a very venerable old man, and so perfectly rational and consistent on every other point, that I think no conscientious person could refuse to take this into the bargain; nay, I have seen a certificate on the subject taken before a country justice and signed with a cross, in the justice's own handwriting. The story, therefore, is beyond the possibility of doubt.

'D.K'

POSTSCRIPT

The following are travelling notes from a memorandum-book of Mr Knickerbocker.

The Kaatsberg, or Catskill Mountains, have always been a region full of fable. The Indians considered them the abode of spirits, who influenced the weather, spreading sunshine or clouds over the landscape, and sending good or bad hunting-seasons. They were ruled by an old squaw spirit, said to be their mother. She dwelt on the highest peak of the Catskills, and had charge of the doors of day and night to open and shut them at the proper hour. She hung up the new moons in the skies, and cut up the old ones into stars. In times of drought, if properly propitiated, she would spin light summer clouds out of cobwebs and morning dew, and send them off from the crest of the mountain, flake after flake, like flakes of carded cotton, to float in the air; until, dissolved by the heart of the sun, they would fall in gentle showers, causing the grass to spring, the fruits to ripen, and the corn to grow an inch an hour. If displeased, however, she would brew up clouds black as ink, sitting in the midst of them like a bottle-bellied spider in the midst of its web; and when these clouds broke, woe betide the valleys!

In old times, say the Indian traditions, there was a kind of Manitou or Spirit, who kept about the wildest recesses of the Catskill Mountains, and took a mischievous pleasure in wreaking all kinds of evils and vexations upon the red men. Sometimes he would assume the form of a bear, a panther, or a deer, lead the bewildered hunter a weary chase through tangled forests and among ragged rocks; and then spring off with a loud ho! ho! leaving him aghast on the brink of a beetling precipice or raging torrent.

The favorite abode of this Manitou is still shown. It is a great rock or cliff on the loneliest part of the mountains, and, from the flowering vines which clamber about it, and the wild flowers which abound in its neighborhood, is known by the name of the Garden Rock. Near the foot of it is a small lake, the haunt of the solitary bittern, with water-snakes basking in the sun on the leaves of the pond-lilies which lie on the surface. This place was held in great awe by the Indians, insomuch that the boldest hunter would not pursue his game within its precincts. Once upon a time, however, a hunter who had lost his way, penetrated to the Garden Rock, where he beheld a number of gourds placed in the crotches of trees. One of these he seized and made off with it, but in the hurry of his retreat he let it fall among the rocks, when a great stream gushed forth, which washed him away and swept him down precipices, where he was dashed to pieces, and the stream made its way to the Hudson, and continues to flow to the present day; being the identical stream known by the name of the Kaaterskill.

1820

LYDIA MARIA CHILD
1802–1880

The Lone Indian

A white man, gazing on the scene,
  Would say a lovely spot was here,
And praise the lawns so fresh and green
  Between the hills so sheer.
I like it not – I would the plain
Lay in its tall old groves again.

BRYANT

Powontonamo was the son of a mighty chief. He looked on his tribe with such a fiery glance, that they called him the Eagle of the Mohawks. His eye never blinked in the sunbeam, and he leaped along the chase like the untiring waves of Niagara. Even when a little boy, his tiny arrow would hit the frisking squirrel in the ear, and bring down the humming bird on her rapid wing. He was his father's pride and joy. He loved to toss him high in his sinewy arms, and shout, 'Look, Eagle-eye, look! and see the big hunting-grounds of the Mohawks! Powontonamo will be their chief. The winds will tell his brave deeds. When men speak of him, they will not speak loud; but as if the Great Spirit had breathed in thunder.'

The prophecy was fulfilled. When Powontonamo became a man, the fame of his beauty and courage reached the tribes of Illinois; and even the distant Osage showed his white teeth with delight, when he heard the wild deeds of the Mohawk Eagle. Yet was his spirit frank, chivalrous, and kind. When the white men came to buy land, he met them with an open palm, and spread his buffalo for the traveller. The old chiefs loved the bold youth, and offered their daughters in marriage. The eyes of the young Indian girls sparkled when he looked on them. But he treated them all with the stern indifference of a warrior, until he saw Soonseetah raise her long dark eye-lash. Then his heart melted beneath the beaming glance of beauty. Soonseetah was the fairest of the Oneidas. The young men of her tribe called her the Sunny-eye. She was smaller than her nation usually are; and her slight, graceful figure was so elastic in its motions, that the tall grass would rise up and shake off its dew drops, after her pretty moccasins had pressed it. Many a famous chief had sought her love; but when they brought the choicest furs, she would smile disdainfully, and say, 'Soonseetah's foot is warm. Has not her father an arrow?' When they offered her food, according to the Indian custom, her answer was, 'Soonseetah has not seen all the warriors. She will eat with the bravest.' The hunters told the young Eagle that Sunny-eye of Oneida was beautiful as the bright birds in the hunting-land beyond the sky; but that her heart was proud, and she said the great chiefs were not good enough to dress venison for her. When Powontonamo listened to these accounts, his lip would curl slightly, as he threw back his fur-edged mantle, and placed his firm, springy foot forward, so that the beads and shells of his rich moccasin might be seen to vibrate at every sound of his tremendous war song. If there was vanity in the act, there was likewise becoming pride. Soonseetah heard of his haughty smile, and resolved in her own heart that no Oneida should sit beside her, till she had seen the chieftain of the Mohawks. Before many moons had passed away, he sought her father's wigwam, to carry delicate furs and shining shells to the young coquette of the wilderness. She did not raise her bright melting eyes to his, when he came near her; but when he said, 'Will the Sunny-eye look on the gift of a Mohawk? his barbed arrow is swift; his foot never turned from the foe;' the colour of her brown cheek was glowing as an autumnal twilight. Her voice was like the troubled note of the wren, as she answered, 'The furs of Powontonamo are soft and warm to the foot of Soonseetah. She will weave the shells in the wampum belt of the Mohawk Eagle.' The exulting lover sat by her side, and offered her venison and parched corn. She raised her timid eye, as she tasted the food; and then the young Eagle knew that Sunny-eye would be his wife.

There was feasting and dancing, and the marriage song rang merrily in Mohawk cabins, when the Oneida came among them. Powontonamo loved her as his own heart's blood. He delighted to bring her the fattest deers of the forest, and load her with ribbons and beads of the English. The prophets of his people liked it not that the strangers grew so numerous in the land. They shook their heads mournfully, and said, 'The moose and the beaver will not live within sound of the white man's gun. They will go beyond the lakes, and the Indians must follow their trail.' But the young chief laughed them to scorn. He said, 'The land is very big. The mountain eagle could not fly over it in many days. Surely the wigwams of the English will never cover it.' Yet when he held his son in his arms, as his father had done before him, he sighed to hear the strokes of the axe levelling the old trees of his forests. Sometimes he looked sorrowfully on his baby boy, and thought he had perchance done him much wrong, when he smoked a pipe in the wigwam of the stranger.

One day, he left his home before the grey mist of morning had gone from the hills, to seek food for his wife and child. The polar-star was bright in the heavens ere he returned; yet his hands were empty. The white man's gun had scared the beasts of the forest, and the arrow of the Indian was sharpened in vain. Powontonamo entered his wigwam with a cloudy brow. He did not look at Soonseetah; he did not speak to her boy; but, silent and sullen, he sat leaning on the head of his arrow. He wept not, for an Indian may not weep; but the muscles of his face betrayed the struggle within his soul. The Sunny-eye approached fearfully, and laid her little hand upon his brawny shoulder, as she asked, 'Why is the Eagle's eye on the earth? What has Soonseetah done, that her child dare not look in the face of his father?' Slowly the warrior turned his gaze upon her. The expression of sadness deepened, as he answered, 'The Eagle has taken a snake to his nest: how can his young sleep in it?' The Indian boy, all unconscious of the forebodings which stirred his father's spirit, moved to his side, and peeped up in his face with a mingled expression of love and fear.

The heart of the generous savage was full, even to bursting. His hand trembled, as he placed it on the sleek black hair of his only son. 'The Great Spirit bless thee! the Great Spirit bless thee, and give thee back the hunting ground of the Mohawk!' he exclaimed. Then folding him, for an instant, in an almost crushing embrace, he gave him to his mother, and darted from the wigwam.

Two hours he remained in the open air; but the clear breath of heaven brought no relief to his noble and suffering soul. Wherever he looked abroad, the ravages of the civilized destroyer met his eye. Where were the trees, under which he had frolicked in infancy, sported in boyhood, and rested after the fatigues of battle? They formed the English boat, or lined the English dwelling. Where were the holy sacrifice-heaps of his people? The stones were taken to fence in the land, which the intruder dared to call his own. Where was his father's grave? The stranger's road passed over it, and his cattle trampled on the ground where the mighty Mohawk slumbered. Where were his once powerful tribe? Alas, in the white man's wars they had joined with the British, in the vain hope of recovering their lost privileges. Hundreds had gone to their last home; others had joined distant tribes; and some pitiful wretches, whom he scorned to call brethren, consented to live on the white man's bounty. These were corroding reflections; and well might fierce thoughts of vengeance pass through the mind of the deserted prince; but he was powerless now; and the English swarmed, like vultures around the dying. 'It is the work of the Great Spirit,' said he. 'The Englishman's God made the Indian's heart afraid; and now he is like a wounded buffalo, when hungry wolves are on his trail.'

When Powontonamo returned to his hut, his countenance, though severe, was composed. He spoke to the Sunny-eye with more kindness than the savage generally addresses the wife of his youth; but his look told her that she must not ask the grief which had put a woman's heart within the breast of the far-famed Mohawk Eagle.

The next day, when the young chieftain went out on a hunting expedition, he was accosted by a rough, square-built farmer. 'Powow,' said he, 'your squaw has been stripping a dozen of my trees, and I don't like it over much.' It was a moment when the Indian could ill brook a white man's insolence. 'Listen, Buffalo-head!' shouted he; and as he spoke he seized the shaggy pate of the unconscious offender, and eyed him with the concentrated venom of an ambushed rattlesnake – 'Listen to the chief of the Mohawks! These broad lands are all his own. When the white man first left his cursed foot-print in the forest, the Great Bear looked down upon the big tribes of Iroquois and Abnaquis. The wigwams of the noble Delawares were thick, where the soft winds dwell. The rising sun glanced on the fierce Pequods; and the Illinois, the Miamies, and warlike tribes like the hairs of your head, marked his going down. Had the red man struck you then, your tribes would have been as dry grass to the lightning! Go – shall the Sunny-eye of Oneida ask the pale face for a basket?' He breathed out a quick, convulsive laugh, and his white teeth showed through his parted lips, as he shook the farmer from him, with the strength and fury of a raging panther.

After that, his path was unmolested, for no one dared to awaken his wrath; but a smile never again visited the dark countenance of the degraded chief. The wild beasts had fled so far from the settlements, that he would hunt days and days without success. Soonseetah sometimes begged him to join the remnant of the Oneidas, and persuade them to go far off, toward the setting sun. Powontonamo replied, 'This is the burial place of my fathers;' and the Sunny-eye dared say no more.

At last, their boy sickened and died, of a fever he had taken among the English. They buried him beneath a spreading oak, on the banks of the Mohawk, and heaped stones upon his grave, without a tear. 'He must lie near the water,' said the desolate chief, 'else the white man's horses will tread on him.'

The young mother did not weep; but her heart had received its death-wound. The fever seized her, and she grew paler and weaker every day. One morning, Powontonamo returned with some delicate food he had been seeking for her. 'Will Soonseetah eat?' said he. He spoke in a tone of subdued tenderness; but she answered not. The foot which was wont to bound forward to meet him, lay motionless and cold. He raised the blanket which partly concealed her face, and saw that the Sunny-eye was closed in death. One hand was pressed hard against her heart, as if her last moments had been painful. The other grasped the beads which the young Eagle had given her in the happy days of courtship. One heart-rending shriek was rung from the bosom of the agonized savage. He tossed his arms wildly above his head, and threw himself beside the body of her he had loved as fondly, deeply, and passionately, as ever a white man loved. After the first burst of grief had subsided, he carefully untied the necklace from her full, beautiful bosom, crossed her hands over the sacred relic, and put back the shining black hair from her smooth forehead. For hours he watched the corpse in silence. Then he arose and carried it from the wigwam. He dug a grave by the side of his lost boy; laid the head of Soonseetah toward the rising sun; heaped the earth upon it, and covered it with stones, according to the custom of his people.

Night was closing in, and still the bereaved Mohawk stood at the grave of Sunny-eye, as motionless as its cold inmate. A white man, as he passed, paused, and looked in pity on him. 'Are you sick?' asked he. 'Yes; me sick. Me very sick here,' answered Powontonamo, laying his hand upon his swelling heart. 'Will you go home?' '*Home*!' exclaimed the heart broken chief, in tones so thrilling, that the white man started. Then slowly, and with a half vacant look, he added, 'Yes; me go home. By and by me go home.' Not another word would he speak; and the white man left him, and went his way. A little while longer he stood watching the changing heavens; and then, with reluctant step, retired to his solitary wigwam.

The next day, a tree, which Soonseetah had often said was just as old as their boy, was placed near the mother and child. A wild vine was straggling among the loose stones, and Powontonamo carefully twined it around the tree. 'The young oak is the Eagle of the Mohawks,' he said; 'and now the Sunny-eye has her arms around him.' He spoke in the wild music of his native tongue; but there was none to answer. 'Yes; Powontonamo will go home,' sighed he. 'He will go where the sun sets in the ocean, and the white man's eyes have never looked upon it.' One long, one lingering glance at the graves of his kindred, and the Eagle of the Mohawks bade farewell to the land of his fathers.

For many a returning autumn, a lone Indian was seen standing at the consecrated spot we have mentioned; but, just thirty years after the death of Soonseetah, he was noticed for the last time. His step was then firm, and his figure erect, though he seemed old and way-worn. Age had not dimmed the fire of his eye, but an expression of deep melancholy had settled on his wrinkled brow. It was Powontonamo – he who had once been the Eagle of the Mohawks! He came to lie down and die beneath the broad oak, which shadowed the grave of Sunny-eye. Alas! the white man's axe had been there! The tree he had planted was dead; and the vine, which had leaped so vigorously from branch to branch, now, yellow and withering, was falling to the ground. A deep groan burst from the soul of the savage. For thirty wearisome years, he had watched that oak, with its twining tendrils. They were the only things left in the wide world for him to love, and they were gone! He looked abroad. The hunting land of his tribe was changed, like its chieftain. No light canoe now shot down the river, like a bird upon the wing. The laden boat of the white man alone broke its smooth surface. The Englishman's road wound like a serpent around the banks of the Mohawk; and iron hoofs had so beaten down the war-path, that a hawk's eye could not discover an Indian track. The last wigwam was destroyed; and the sun looked boldly down upon spots he had visited only by stealth, during thousands and thousands of moons. The few remaining trees, clothed in the fantastic mourning of autumn; the long line of heavy clouds, melting away before the coming sun; and the distant mountain, seen through the blue mist of departing twilight, alone remained as he had seen them in his boyhood. All things spoke a sad language to the heart of the desolate Indian. 'Yes,' said he, 'the young oak and the vine are like the Eagle and the Sunny-eye. They are cut down, torn, and trampled on. The leaves are falling, and the clouds are scattering, like my people. I wish I could once more see the trees standing thick, as they did when my mother held me to her bosom, and sung the warlike deeds of the Mohawks.'

A mingled expression of grief and anger passed over his face, as he watched a loaded boat in its passage across the stream. 'The white man carries food to his wife and children, and he finds them in his home,' said he. 'Where is the squaw and the papoose of the red man? They are here!' As he spoke, he fixed his eye thoughtfully upon the grave. After a gloomy silence, he again looked round upon the fair scene, with a wandering and troubled gaze. 'The pale face may like it,' murmured he; 'but an Indian cannot die here in peace.' So saying, he broke his bow string, snapped his arrows, threw them on the burial place of his fathers, and departed for ever.

None ever knew where Powontonamo laid his dying head. The hunters from the west said a red man had been among them, whose tracks were far off toward the rising sun; that he seemed like one who had lost his way, and was sick to go home to the Great Spirit. Perchance, he slept his last sleep where the distant Mississippi receives its hundred streams. Alone, and unfriended, he may have laid him down to die, where no man called him brother; and the wolves of the desert, long ere this, may have howled the death-song of the Mohawk Eagle.

1828

The Birth-mark

In the latter part of the last century, there lived a man of science – an eminent proficient in every branch of natural philosophy – who, not long before our story opens, had made experience of a spiritual affinity, more attractive than any chemical one. He had left his laboratory to the care of an assistant, cleared his fine countenance from the furnace-smoke, washed the stain of acids from his fingers, and persuaded a beautiful woman to become his wife. In those days, when the comparatively recent discovery of electricity, and other kindred mysteries of nature, seemed to open paths into the region of miracle, it was not unusual for the love of science to rival the love of woman, in its depth and absorbing energy. The higher intellect, the imagination, the spirit, and even the heart, might all find their congenial aliment in pursuits which, as some of their ardent votaries believed, would ascend from one step of powerful intelligence to another, until the philosopher should lay his hand on the secret of creative force, and perhaps make new worlds for himself. We know not whether Aylmer possessed this degree of faith in man's ultimate control over nature. He had devoted himself, however, too unreservedly to scientific studies, ever to be weaned from them by any second passion. His love for his young wife might prove the stronger of the two; but it could only be by intertwining itself with his love of science, and uniting the strength of the latter to its own.

Such a union accordingly took place, and was attended with truly remarkable consequences, and a deeply impressive moral. One day, very soon after their marriage, Aylmer sat gazing at his wife, with a trouble in his countenance that grew stronger, until he spoke.

'Georgiana,' said he, 'has it never occurred to you that the mark upon your cheek might be removed?'

'No, indeed,' said she, smiling; but perceiving the seriousness of his manner, she blushed deeply. 'To tell you the truth, it has been so often called a charm, that I was simple enough to imagine it might be so.'

'Ah, upon another face, perhaps it might,' replied her husband. 'But never on yours! No, dearest Georgiana, you came so nearly perfect from the hand of Nature, that this slightest possible defect — which we hesitate whether to term a defect or a beauty — shocks me, as being the visible mark of earthly imperfection.'

'Shocks you, my husband!' cried Georgiana, deeply hurt; at first reddening with momentary anger, but then bursting into tears. 'Then why did you take me from my mother's side? You cannot love what shocks you!'

To explain this conversation, it must be mentioned, that, in the centre of Georgiana's left check, there was a singular mark, deeply interwoven, as it were, with the texture and substance of her face. In the usual state of her complexion — a healthy, though delicate bloom — the mark wore a tint of deeper crimson, which imperfectly defined its shape amid the surrounding rosiness. When she blushed, it gradually became more indistinct, and finally vanished amid the triumphant rush of blood, that bathed the whole cheek with its brilliant glow. But, if any shifting emotion caused her to turn pale, there was the mark again, a crimson stain upon the snow, in what Aylmer sometimes deemed an almost fearful distinctness. Its shape bore not a little similarity to the human hand, though of the smallest pigmy size. Georgiana's lovers were wont to say that some fairy, at her birth-hour, had laid her tiny hand upon the infant's cheek, and left this impress there, in token of the magic endowments that were to give her such sway over all hearts. Many a desperate swain would have risked life for the privilege of pressing his lips to the mysterious hand. It must not be concealed, however, that the impression wrought by this fairy sign-manual varied exceedingly, according to the difference of temperament in the beholders. Some fastidious persons — but they were exclusively of her own sex — affirmed that the Bloody Hand, as they chose to call it, quite destroyed the effect of Georgiana's beauty, and rendered her countenance even hideous. But it would be as reasonable to say that one of those small blue stains, which sometimes occur in the purest statuary marble, would convert the Eve of Powers to a monster. Masculine observers, if the birth-mark did not heighten their admiration, contented themselves with wishing it away, that the world might possess one living specimen of ideal loveliness, without the semblance of a flaw. After his marriage — for he thought little or nothing of the matter before — Aylmer discovered that this was the case with himself.

Had she been less beautiful – if Envy's self could have found aught else to sneer at – he might have felt his affection heightened by the prettiness of this mimic hand, now vaguely portrayed, now lost, now stealing forth again, and glimmering to-and-fro with every pulse of emotion that throbbed within her heart. But, seeing her otherwise so perfect, he found this one defect grow more and more intolerable, with every moment of their united lives. It was the fatal flaw of humanity, which Nature, in one shape or another, stamps ineffaceably on all her productions, either to imply that they are temporary and finite, or that their perfection must be wrought by toil and pain. The Crimson Hand expressed the ineludible gripe, in which mortality clutches the highest and purest of earthly mould, degrading them into kindred with the lowest, and even with the very brutes, like whom their visible frames return to dust. In this manner, selecting it as the symbol of his wife's liability to sin, sorrow, decay, and death, Aylmer's sombre imagination was not long in rendering the birth-mark a frightful object, causing him more trouble and horror than ever Georgiana's beauty, whether of soul or sense, had given him delight.

At all the seasons which should have been their happiest, he invariably, and without intending it – nay, in spite of a purpose to the contrary – reverted to this one disastrous topic. Trifling as it at first appeared, it so connected itself with innumerable trains of thought, and modes of feeling, that it became the central point of all. With the morning twilight, Aylmer opened his eyes upon his wife's face, and recognized the symbol of imperfection; and when they sat together at the evening hearth, his eyes wandered stealthily to her cheek, and beheld, flickering with the blaze of the wood fire, the spectral Hand that wrote mortality, where he would fain have worshipped. Georgiana soon learned to shudder at his gaze. It needed but a glance, with the peculiar expression that his face often wore, to change the roses of her cheek into a deathlike paleness, amid which the Crimson Hand was brought strongly out, like a bas-relief of ruby on the whitest marble.

Late, one night, when the lights were growing dim, so as hardly to betray the stain on the poor wife's cheek, she herself, for the first time, voluntarily took up the subject.

'Do you remember, my dear Aylmer,' said she, with a feeble attempt at a smile – 'have you any recollection of a dream, last night, about this odious Hand?'

'None! – none whatever!' replied Aylmer, starting; but then he added in a dry, cold tone, affected for the sake of concealing the real depth of his emotion: – 'I might well dream of it; for before I fell asleep, it had taken a pretty firm hold of my fancy.'

'And you did dream of it,' continued Georgiana, hastily; for she dreaded lest a gush of tears should interrupt what she had to say – 'A terrible dream! I wonder that you can forget it. Is it possible to forget this one expression? "It is in her heart now – we must have it out!" Reflect, my husband; for by all means I would have you recall that dream.'

The mind is in a sad note, when Sleep, the all-involving, cannot confine her spectres within the dim region of her sway, but suffers them to break forth, affrighting this actual life with secrets that perchance belong to a deeper one. Aylmer now remembered his dream. He had fancied himself, with his servant Aminadab, attempting an operation for the removal of the birth-mark. But the deeper went the knife, the deeper sank the Hand, until at length its tiny grasp appeared to have caught hold of Georgiana's heart; whence, however, her husband was inexorably resolved to cut or wrench it away.

When the dream had shaped itself perfectly in his memory, Aylmer sat in his wife's presence with a guilty feeling. Truth often finds its way to the mind close-muffled in robes of sleep, and then speaks with uncompromising directness of matters in regard to which we practise an unconscious self-deception, during our waking moments. Until now, he had not been aware of the tyrannizing influence acquired by one idea over his mind, and of the lengths which he might find in his heart to go, for the sake of giving himself peace.

'Aylmer,' resumed Georgiana, solemnly, 'I know not what may be the cost to both of us, to rid me of this fatal birth-mark. Perhaps its removal may cause cureless deformity. Or, it may be, the stain goes as deep as life itself. Again, do we know that there is a possibility, on any terms, of unclasping the firm grip of this little Hand, which was laid upon me before I came into the world?'

'Dearest Georgiana, I have spent much thought upon the subject,' hastily interrupted Aylmer – 'I am convinced of the perfect practicability of its removal.'

'If there be the remotest possibility of it,' continued Georgiana, 'let the attempt be made, at whatever risk. Danger is nothing to me; for life – while this hateful mark makes me the object of your horror and disgust – life is a burthen which I would fling down with joy. Either remove this dreadful Hand, or take my wretched life! You have deep science! All the world bears witness of it. You have achieved great wonders! Cannot you remove this little, little mark, which I cover with the tips of two small fingers? Is this beyond your power, for the sake of your own peace, and to save your poor wife from madness?'

'Noblest – dearest – tenderest wife!' cried Aylmer, rapturously. 'Doubt not my power. I have already given this matter the deepest thought – thought which might almost have enlightened me to create a being less perfect than yourself. Georgiana, you have led me deeper than ever into the heart of science. I feel myself fully competent to render this dear cheek as faultless as its fellow; and then, most beloved, what will be my triumph, when I shall have corrected what Nature left imperfect, in her fairest work! Even Pygmalion, when his sculptured woman assumed life, felt not greater ecstasy than mine will be.'

'It is resolved, then,' said Georgiana, faintly smiling – 'And, Aylmer, spare me not, though you should find the birth-mark take refuge in my heart at last.'

Her husband tenderly kissed her cheek – her right cheek – not that which bore the impress of the Crimson Hand.

The next day, Aylmer apprized his wife of a plan that he had formed, whereby he might have opportunity for the intense thought and constant watchfulness, which the proposed opera-tion would require; while Georgiana, likewise, would enjoy the perfect repose essential to its success. They were to seclude themselves in the extensive apartments occupied by Aylmer as a laboratory, and where, during his toilsome youth, he had made discoveries in the elemental powers of nature, that had roused the admiration of all the learned societies in Europe. Seated calmly in this laboratory, the pale philosopher had investigated the secrets of the highest cloud-region, and of the profoundest mines; he had satisfied himself of the causes that kindled and kept alive the fires of the volcano; and had explained the mystery of fountains, and how it is that they gush forth, some so bright and pure, and others with such rich medicinal virtues, from the dark bosom of the earth. Here, too, at an earlier period, he had studied the wonders of the human frame, and attempted to fathom the very process by which Nature assimilates all her precious influences from earth and air, and from the spiritual world, to create and foster Man, her masterpiece. The latter pursuit, however, Aylmer had long laid aside, in unwilling recognition of the truth, against which all seekers sooner or later stumble, that our great creative Mother, while she amuses us with apparently working in the broadest sunshine, is yet severely careful to keep her own secrets, and, in spite of her pretended openness, shows us nothing but results. She permits us indeed, to mar, but seldom to mend, and, like a jealous patentee, on no account to make. Now, however, Aylmer resumed these half-forgotten investigations; not, of course, with such hopes or wishes as first suggested them; but because they involved much physiological truth, and lay in the path of his proposed scheme for the treatment of Georgiana.

As he led her over the threshold of the laboratory, Georgiana was cold and tremulous. Aylmer looked cheerfully into her face, with intent to reassure her, but was so startled with the intense glow of the birth-mark upon the whiteness of her cheek, that he could not restrain a strong convulsive shudder. His wife fainted.

'Aminadab! Aminadab!' shouted Alymer, stamping violently on the floor.

Forthwith, there issued from an inner apartment a man of low stature, but bulky frame, with shaggy hair hanging about his visage, which was grimed wtih the vapors of the furnace. This personage had been Aylmer's under-worker during his whole scientific career, and was admirably fitted for that office by his great mechanical readiness, and the skill with which, while incapable of comprehending a single principle, he executed all the practical details of his master's experiments. With his vast strength, his shaggy hair, his smoky aspect, and the indescribable earthiness that incrusted him, he seemed to represent man's physical nature; while Aylmer's slender figure, and pale, intellectual face, were no less apt a type of the spiritual element.

'Throw open the door of the boudoir, Aminadab,' said Aylmer, 'and burn a pastille.'

'Yes, master,' answered Aminadab, looking intently at the lifeless form of Georgiana; and then he mutted to himself: 'If she were my wfe, I'd never part with that birth-mark.'

When Georgiana recovered consciousness, she found herself breathing an atmosphere of penetrating fragrance, the gentle potency of which had recalled her from her deathlike faintness. The scene around her looked like enchantment. Aylmer had converted those smoky, dingy, sombre rooms, where he had spent his brightest years in recondite pursuits, into a series of beautiful apartments, not unfit to be the secluded abode of a lovely woman. The walls were hung with gorgeous curtains, which imparted the combination of grandeur and grace, that no other species of adornment can achieve; and as they fell from the ceiling to the floor, their rich and ponderous folds, concealing all angles and straight lines, appeared to shut in the scene from infinite space. For aught Georgiana knew, it might be a pavilion among the clouds. And Aylmer, excluding the sunshine, which would have interfered with his chemical processes, had supplied its place with perfumed lamps, emitting flames of various hue, but all uniting in a soft, empurpled radiance. He now knelt by his wife's side, watching her earnestly, but without alarm; for he was confident in his science, and felt that he could draw a magic circle round her, within which no evil might intrude.

'Where am I? Ah, I remember!' said Georgiana, faintly; and she placed her hand over her cheek, to hide the terrible mark from her husband's eyes.

'Fear not, dearest!' exclaimed he. 'Do not shrink from me! Believe me, Georgiana, I even rejoice in this single imperfection, since it will be such rapture to remove it.'

'Oh, spare me!' sadly replied his wife – 'Pray do not look at it again. I never can forget that convulsive shudder.'

In order to soothe Georgiana, and, as it were, to release her mind from the burthen of actual things, Aylmer now put in practice some of the light and playful secrets, which science had taught him among its profounder lore. Airy figures, absolutely bodiless ideas, and forms of unsubstantial beauty, came and danced before her, imprinting their momentary footsteps on beams of light. Though she had some indistinct idea of the method of these optical phenomena, still the illusion was almost perfect enough to warrant the belief, that her husband possessed sway over the spiritual world. Then again, when she felt a wish to look forth from her seclusion, immediately, as if her thoughts were answered, the procession of external existence flitted across a screen. The scenery and the figures of actual life were perfectly represented, but with that bewitching, yet indescribable difference, which always makes a picture, an image, or a shadow, so much more attractive than the original. When wearied of this, Aylmer bade her cast her eyes upon a vessel, containing a quantity of earth. She did so, with little interest at first, but was soon startled, to perceive the germ of a plant, shooting upward from the soil. Then came the slender stalk – the leaves gradually unfolded themselves – and amid them was a perfect and lovely flower.

'It is magical!' cried Georgiana, 'I dare not touch it.'

'Nay, pluck it,' answered Aylmer, 'pluck it, and inhale its brief perfume while you may. The flower will wither in a few moments, and leave nothing save its brown seed-vessels – but thence may be perpetuated a race as ephemeral as itself.'

But Georgiana had no sooner touched the flower than the whole plant suffered a blight, its leaves turning coal-black, as if by the agency of fire.

'There was too powerful a stimulus,' said Aylmer thoughtfully.

To make up for this abortive experiment, he proposed to take her portrait by a scientific process of his own invention. It was to be effected by rays of light striking upon a polished plate of metal. Georgiana assented – but, on looking at the result, was affrighted to find the features of the portrait blurred and indefinable; while the minute figure of a hand appeared where the cheek should have been. Aylmer snatched the metallic plate, and threw it into a jar of corrosive acid.

Soon, however, he forgot these mortifying failures. In the intervals of study and chemical experiment, he came to her, flushed and exhausted, but seemed invigorated by her presence, and spoke in glowing language of the resources of his art. He gave a history of the long dynasty of the Alchemists, who spent so many ages in quest of the universal solvent, by which the Golden Principle might be elicited from all things vile and base. Aylmer appeared to believe that, by the plainest scientific logic, it was altogether within the limits of possibility to discover this long-sought medium; but, he added, a philosopher who should go deep enough to acquire the power, would attain too lofty a wisdom to stoop to the exercise of it. Not less singular were his opinions in regard to the Elixir Vitæ. He more than intimated, that it was his option to concoct a liquid that should prolong life for years – perhaps interminably – but that it would produce a discord in nature, which all the world, and chiefly the quaffer of the immortal nostrum, would find cause to curse.

'Aylmer, are you in earnest?' asked Georgiana, looking at him with amazement and fear; 'it is terrible to possess such power, or even to dream of possessing it!'

'Oh, do not tremble, my love!' said her husband, 'I would not wrong either you or myself by working such inharmonious effects upon our lives. But I would have you consider how trifling, in comparison, is the skill requisite to remove this little Hand.'

At the mention of the birth-mark, Georgiana, as usual, shrank, as if a red-hot iron had touched her cheek.

Again Aylmer applied himself to his labors. She could hear his voice in the distant furnace-room, giving directions to Aminadab, whose harsh, uncouth, misshapen tones were audible in response, more like the grunt or growl of a brute than human speech. After hours of absence, Aylmer reappeared, and proposed that she should now examine his cabinet of chemical products, and natural treasures of the earth. Among the former he showed her a small vial, in which, he remarked, was contained a gentle yet most powerful fragrance, capable of impregnating all the breezes that blow across a kingdom. They were of inestimable value, the contents of that little vial; and, as he said so, he threw some of the perfume into the air, and filled the room with piercing and invigorating delight.

'And what is this?' asked Georgiana, pointing to a small crystal globe, containing a gold-coloured liquid. 'It is so beautiful to the eye, that I could imagine it the Elixir of Life.'

'In one sense it is,' replied Aylmer, 'or rather the Elixir of Immortality. It is the most precious poison that ever was concocted in this world. By its aid, I could apportion the lifetime of any mortal at whom you might point your finger. The strength of the dose would determine whether he were to linger out years, or drop dead in the midst of a breath. No king, on his guarded throne, could keep his life, if I, in my private station, should deem that the welfare of millions justified me in depriving him of it.'

'Why do you keep such a terrific drug?' inquired Georgiana in horror.

'Do not mistrust me, dearest!' said her husband, smiling; 'its virtuous potency is yet greater than its harmful one. But, see! here is a powerful cosmetic. With a few drops of this, in a vase of water, freckles may be washed away as easily as the hands are cleansed. A stronger infusion would take the blood out of the cheek, and leave the rosiest beauty a pale ghost.'

'Is it with this lotion that you intend to bathe my cheek?' asked Georgiana anxiously.

'Oh, no!' hastily replied her husband – 'this is merely superficial. Your case demands a remedy that shall go deeper.'

In his interviews with Georgiana, Aylmer generally made minute inquiries as to her sensations, and whether the confinement of the rooms, and the temperature of the atmosphere, agreed with her. These questions had such a particular drift, that Georgiana began to conjecture that she was already subjected to certain physical influences, either breathed in with the fragrant air, or taken with her food. She fancied, likewise – but it might be altogether fancy – that there was a stirring up of her system –a strange indefinite sensation creeping through her veins, and tingling, half painfully, half pleasurably, at her heart. Still, whenever she dared to look into the mirror, there she beheld herself, pale as a white rose, and with the crimson birth-mark stamped upon her cheek. Not even Aylmer now hated it so much as she.

To dispel the tedium of the hours which her husband found it necessary to devote to the processes of combination and analysis, Georgiana turned over the volumes of his scientific library. In many dark old tomes, she met with chapters full of romance and poetry. They were the works of the philosophers of the middle ages, such as Albertus Magnus, Cornelius Agrippa, Paracelsus, and the famous friar who created the prophetic Brazen Head. All these antique naturalists stood in advance of their centuries, yet were imbued with some of the credulity, and therefore were believed, and perhaps imagined themselves, to have acquired from the investigation of nature a power above nature, and from physics a sway over the spiritual world. Hardly less curious and imaginative were the early volumes of the Transactions of the Royal Society, in which the members, knowing little of the limits of natural possibility, were continually recording wonders, or proposing methods whereby wonders might be wrought.

But, to Georgiana, the most engrossing volume was a large folio from her husband's own hand, in which he had recorded every experiment of his scientific career, with its original aim, the methods adopted for its development, and its final success or failure, with the circumstances to which either event was attributable. The book, in truth, was both the history and emblem of his ardent, ambitious, imaginative, yet practical and laborious, life. He handled physical details, as if there were nothing beyond them; yet spiritualized them all, and redeemed himself from

materialism, by his strong and eager aspiration towards the
infinite. In his grasp, the veriest clod of earth assumed a soul.
Georgiana, as she read, reverenced Aylmer, and loved him more
profoundly than ever, but with a less entire dependence on his
judgment than heretofore. Much as he had accomplished, she
could not but observe that his most splendid successes were
almost invariably failures, if compared with the ideal at which he
aimed. His brightest diamonds were the merest pebbles, and felt
to be so by himself, in comparison with the inestimable gems
which lay hidden beyond his reach. The volume, rich with
achievements that had won renown for its author, was yet as
melancholy a record as ever mortal hand had penned. It was the
sad confession, and continual exemplification, of the short-
comings of the composite man – the spirit burthened with clay
and working in matter – and of the despair that assails the higher
nature, at finding itself so miserably thwarted by the earthly part.
Perhaps every man of genius, in whatever sphere, might recognize
the image of his own experience in Aylmer's journal.

So deeply did these reflections affect Georgiana, that she laid
her face upon the open volume, and burst into tears. In this
situation she was found by her husband.

'It is dangerous to read in a sorcerer's books,' said he, with a
smile, though his countenance was uneasy and displeased.
'Georgiana, there are pages in that volume, which I can scarcely
glance over and keep my senses. Take heed lest it prove as
detrimental to you!'

'It has made me worship you more than ever,' said she.

'Ah! wait for this one success,' rejoined he, 'then worship me if
you will. I shall deem myself hardly unworthy of it. But, come! I
have sought you for the luxury of your voice. Sing to me, dearest!'

So she poured out the liquid music of her voice to quench the
thirst of his spirit. He then took his leave, with a boyish
exuberance of gaiety, assuring her that her seclusion would
endure but a little longer, and that the result was already certain.
Scarcely had he departed, when Georgiana felt irresistibly impelled to follow him. She had forgotten to inform Aylmer of a
symptom, which, for two or three hours past, had begun to excite
her attention. It was a sensation in the fatal birth-mark, not
painful, but which induced a restlessness throughout her system.
Hastening after her husband, she intruded, for the first time, into
the laboratory.

The first thing that struck her eye was the furnace, that hot and feverish worker, with the intense glow of its fire, which, by the quantities of soot clustered above it, seemed to have been burning for ages. There was a distilling apparatus in full operation. Around the room were retorts, tubes, cylinders, crucibles, and other apparatus of chemical research. An electrical machine stood ready for immediate use. The atmosphere felt oppressively close, and was tainted with gaseous odors, which had been tormented forth by the processes of science. The severe and homely simplicity of the apartment, with its naked walls and brick pavement, looked strange, accustomed as Georgiana had become to the fantastic elegance of her boudoir. But what chiefly, indeed almost solely, drew her attention, was the aspect of Aylmer himself.

He was pale as death, anxious, and absorbed, and hung over the furnace as if it depended upon his utmost watchfulness whether the liquid, which it was distilling, should be the draught of immortal happiness or misery. How different from the sanguine and joyous mien that he had assumed for Georgiana's encouragement!

'Carefully now, Aminadab! Carefully, thou human machine! Carefully, thou man of clay!' muttered Aylmer, more to himself than his assistant. 'Now, if there be a thought too much or too little, it is all over!'

'Hoh! hoh!' mumbled Aminadab – 'look, master, look!'

Aylmer raised his eyes hastily, and at first reddened, then grew paler than ever, on beholding Georgiana. He rushed towards her, and seized her arm with a grip that left the print of his fingers upon it.

'Why do you come hither? Have you no trust in your husband?' cried he impetuously. 'Would you throw the blight of that fatal birth-mark over my labors? It is not well done. Go, prying woman, go!'

'Nay, Aylmer,' said Georgiana, with the firmness of which she possessed no stinted endowment, 'it is not you that have a right to complain. You mistrust your wife! You have concealed the anxiety with which you watch the development of this experiment. Think not so unworthily of me, my husband! Tell me all the risk we run; and fear not that I shall shrink, for my share in it is far less than your own!'

'No, no, Georgiana!' said Aylmer impatiently, 'it must not be.'

'I submit,' replied she calmly. 'And, Aylmer, I shall quaff whatever draught you bring me; but it will be on the same principle that would induce me to take a dose of poison, if offered by your hand.'

'My noble wife,' said Aylmer, deeply moved, 'I knew not the height and depth of your nature, until now. Nothing shall be concealed. Know, then, that this Crimson Hand, superficial as it seems, has clutched its grasp into your being, with a strength of which I had no previous conception. I have already administered agents powerful enough to do aught except to change your entire physical system. Only one thing remains to be tried. If that fail us, we are ruined!'

'Why did you hesitate to tell me this?' asked she.

'Because, Georgiana,' said Aylmer, in a low voice, 'there is danger!'

'Danger? There is but one danger – that this horrible stigma shall be left upon my cheek!' cried Georgiana. 'Remove it! remove it! – whatever be the cost – or we shall both go mad!'

'Heaven knows your words are too true,' said Aylmer, sadly. 'And now, dearest, return to your boudoir. In a little while, all will be tested.'

He conducted her back, and took leave of her with a solemn tenderness, which spoke far more than his words how much was now at stake. After his departure, Georgiana became wrapt in musings. She considered the character of Aylmer, and did it completer justice than at any previous moment. Her heart exulted, while it trembled, at his honorable love, so pure and lofty that it would accept nothing less than perfection, nor miserably make itself contented with an earthlier nature than he had dreamed of. She felt how much more precious was such a sentiment, than the meaner kind which would have borne with the imperfection for her sake, and have been guilty of treason to holy love, by degrading its perfect idea to the level of the actual. And, with her whole spirit, she prayed that, for a single moment, she might satisfy his highest and deepest conception. Longer than one moment, she well knew, it could not be; for his spirit was ever on the march – ever ascending – and each instant required something that was beyond the scope of the instant before.

The sound of her husband's footsteps aroused her. He bore a crystal goblet, containing a liquor colorless as water, but bright enough to be the draught of immortality. Aylmer was pale; but it seemed rather the consequence of a highly wrought state of mind, and tension of spirit, than of fear or doubt.

'The concoction of the draught has been perfect,' said he, in answer to Georgiana's look. 'Unless all my science have deceived me, it cannot fail.'

'Save on your account, my dearest Aylmer,' observed his wife, 'I might wish to put off this birth-mark of mortality by relinquishing mortality itself, in preference to any other mode. Life is but a sad possession to those who have attained precisely the degree of moral advancement at which I stand. Were I weaker and blinder, it might be happiness. Were I stronger, it might be endured hopefully. But, being what I find myself, methinks I am of all mortals the most fit to die.'

'You are fit for heaven without tasting death!' replied her husband. 'But why do we speak of dying? The draught cannot fail. Behold its effect upon this plant!'

On the window-seat there stood a geranium, diseased with yellow blotches, which had overspread all its leaves. Aylmer poured a small quantity of the liquid upon the soil in which it grew. In a little time, when the roots of the plant had taken up the moisture, the unsightly blotches began to be extinguished in a living verdure.

'There needed no proof,' said Georgiana, quietly. 'Give me the goblet. I joyfully stake all upon your word.'

'Drink, then, thou lofty creature!' exclaimed Aylmer, with fervid admiration. 'There is no taint of imperfection on thy spirit. Thy sensible frame, too, shall soon be all perfect!'

She quaffed the liquid, and returned the goblet to his hand.

'It is grateful,' said she, with a placid smile. 'Methinks it is like water from a heavenly fountain; for it contains I know not what of unobtrusive fragrance and deliciousness. It allays a feverish thirst, that had parched me for many days. Now, dearest, let me sleep. My earthly senses are closing over my spirit, like the leaves round the heart of a rose, at sunset.'

She spoke the last words with a gentle reluctance, as if it required almost more energy than she could command to pronounce the faint and lingering syllables. Scarcely had they loitered through her lips, ere she was lost in slumber. Aylmer sat by her side, watching her aspect with the emotions proper to a man, the whole value of whose existence was involved in the process now to be tested. Mingled with this mood, however, was the philosophic investigation, characteristic of the man of science. Not the minutest symptom escaped him. A heightened flush of the cheek – a slight irregularity of breath – a quiver of the eyelid – a hardly perceptible tremor through the frame – such were the details which, as the moments passed, he wrote down in his folio volume. Intense thought had set its stamp upon every previous page of that volume; but the thoughts of years were all concentrated upon the last.

While thus employed, he failed not to gaze often at the fatal Hand, and not without a shudder. Yet once, by a strange and unaccountable impulse, he pressed it with his lips. His spirit recoiled, however, in the very act, and Georgiana, out of the midst of her deep sleep, moved uneasily and murmured, as if in remonstrance. Again, Aylmer resumed his watch. Nor was it without avail. The Crimson Hand, which at first had been strongly visible upon the marble paleness of Georgiana's cheek now grew more faintly outlined. She remained not less pale than ever; but the birth-mark, with every breath that came and went, lost somewhat of its former distinctness. Its presence had been awful; its departure was more awful still. Watch the stain of the rainbow fading out of the sky; and you will know how that mysterious symbol passed away.

'By Heaven, it is well nigh gone!' said Aylmer to himself, in almost irrepressible ecstasy. 'I can scarcely trace it now. Success! Success! And now it is like the faintest rose-color. The slightest flush of blood across her cheek would overcome it. But she is so pale!'

He drew aside the window-curtain, and suffered the light of natural day to fall into the room, and rest upon her cheek. At the same time, he heard a gross, hoarse chuckle, which he had long known as his servant Aminadab's expression of delight.

'Ah, clod! Ah, earthly mass!' cried Aylmer, laughing in a sort of frenzy. 'You have served me well! Matter and Spirit – Earth and Heaven – have both done their part in this! Laugh, thing of senses! You have earned the right to laugh.'

These exclamations broke Georgiana's sleep. She slowly unclosed her eyes, and gazed into the mirror, which her husband had arranged for that purpose. A faint smile flitted over her lips, when she recognized how barely perceptible was now that Crimson Hand, which had once blazed forth with such disastrous brilliancy as to scare away all their happiness. But then her eyes sought Aylmer's face, with a trouble and anxiety that he could by no means account for.

'My poor Aylmer!' murmured she.

'Poor? Nay, richest! Happiest! Most favored!' exclaimed he. 'My peerless bride, it is successful! You are perfect!'

'My poor Aylmer!' she repeated, with a more than human tenderness. 'You have aimed loftily! you have done nobly! Do not repent, that, with so high and pure a feeling, you have rejected the best that earth could offer. Aylmer – dearest Aylmer – I am dying!'

Alas, it was too true! The fatal Hand had grappled with the mystery of life, and was the bond by which an angelic spirit kept itself in union with a mortal frame. As the last crimson tint of the birth-mark – that sole token of human imperfection – faded from her cheek, the parting breath of the now perfect woman passed into the atmosphere, and her soul, lingering a moment near her husband, took its heavenward flight. Then a hoarse, chuckling laugh was heard again! Thus ever does the gross Fatality of Earth exult in its invariable triumph over the immortal essence, which, in this dim sphere of half-development, demands the completeness of a higher state. Yet, had Aylmer reached a profounder wisdom, he need not thus have flung away the happiness, which would have woven his mortal life of the self-same texture with the celestial. The momentary circumstance was too strong for him; he failed to look beyond the shadowy scope of Time, and living once for all in Eternity, to find the perfect Future in the present.

1843

The Artist of the Beautiful

An elderly man, with his pretty daughter on his arm, was passing along the street, and emerged from the gloom of the cloudy evening into the light that fell across the pavement from the window of a small shop. It was a projecting window; and on the inside were suspended a variety of watches – pinchbeck, silver, and one or two of gold – all with their faces turned from the street, as if churlishly disinclined to inform the wayfarers what o'clock it was. Seated within the shop, sidelong to the window, with his pale face bent earnestly over some delicate piece of mechanism, on which was thrown the concentrated lustre of a shade-lamp, appeared a young man.

'What can Owen Warland be about?' muttered old Peter Hovenden – himself a retired watchmaker, and the former master of this same young man, whose occupation he was now wondering at. 'What can the fellow be about? These six months past, I have never come by his shop without seeing him just as steadily at work as now. It would be a flight beyond his usual foolery to seek for the Perpetual Motion. And yet I know enough of my old business to be certain, that what he is now so busy with is no part of the machinery of a watch.'

'Perhaps, father,' said Annie, without showing much interest in the question, 'Owen is inventing a new kind of time-keeper. I am sure he has ingenuity enough.'

'Poh, child! he has not the sort of ingenuity to invent anything better than a Dutch toy,' answered her father, who had formerly been put to much vexation by Owen Warland's irregular genius. 'A plague on such ingenuity! All the effect that ever I knew of it, was to spoil the accuracy of some of the best watches in my shop. He would turn the sun out of its orbit, and derange the whole course of time, if, as I said before, his ingenuity could grasp anything bigger than a child's toy!'

'Hush, father! he hears you,' whispered Annie, pressing the old man's arm. 'His ears are as delicate as his feelings, and you know how easily disturbed they are. Do let us move on.'

So Peter Hovenden and his daughter Annie plodded on, without further conversation, until, in a by-street of the town, they found themselves passing the open door of a blacksmith's shop. Within was seen the forge, now blazing up, and illuminating the high and dusky roof, and now confining its lustre to a narrow precinct of the coal-strewn floor, according as the breath of the bellows was puffed forth, or again inhaled into its vast leathern lungs. In the intervals of brightness, it was easy to distinguish objects in remote corners of the shop, and the horse-shoes that hung upon the wall; in the momentary gloom, the fire seemed to be glimmering amidst the vagueness of unenclosed space. Moving about in this red glare and alternate dusk, was the figure of the blacksmith, well worthy to be viewed in so picturesque an aspect of light and shade, where the bright blaze struggled with the black night, as if each would have snatched his comely strength from the other. Anon, he drew a white-hot bar of iron from the coals, laid it on the anvil, uplifted his arm of might, and was soon enveloped in the myriads of sparks which the strokes of his hammer scattered into the surrounding gloom.

'Now, that is a pleasant sight,' said the old watchmaker. 'I know what it is to work in gold, but give me the worker in iron, after all is said and done. He spends his labor upon a reality. What say you, daughter Annie?'

'Pray don't speak so loud, father,' whispered Annie. 'Robert Danforth will hear you.'

'And what if he should hear me?' said Peter Hovenden; 'I say again, it is a good and a wholesome thing to depend upon main strength and reality, and to earn one's bread with the bare and brawny arm of a blacksmith. A watchmaker gets his brain puzzled by his wheels within a wheel, or loses his health or the nicety of his eyesight, as was my case; and finds himself, at middle age, or a little after, past labor at his own trade, and fit for nothing else, yet too poor to live at his ease. So, I say once again, give me main strength for my money. And then, how it takes the nonsense out of a man! Did you ever hear of a blacksmith being such a fool as Owen Warland, yonder?'

'Well said, uncle Hovenden!' shouted Robert Danforth, from the forge, in a full, deep, merry voice, that made the roof re-echo. 'And what says Miss Annie to that doctrine? She, I suppose, will think it a genteeler business to tinker up a lady's watch, than to forge a horse-shoe or make a gridiron!'

Annie drew her father onward, without giving him time for reply.

But we must return to Owen Warland's shop, and spend more meditation upon his history and character than either Peter Hovenden, or probably his daughter Annie, or Owen's old schoolfellow, Robert Danforth, would have thought due to so slight a subject. From the time that his little fingers could grasp a pen-knife, Owen had been remarkable for a delicate ingenuity, which sometimes produced pretty shapes in wood, principally figures of flowers and birds, and sometimes seemed to aim at the hidden mysteries of mechanism. But it was always for purposes of grace, and never with any mockery of the useful. He did not, like the crowd of schoolboy artizans, construct little windmills on the angle of a barn, or watermills across the neighboring brook. Those who discovered such peculiarity in the boy, as to think it worth their while to observe him closely, sometimes saw reason to suppose that he was attempting to imitate the beautiful movements of Nature, as exemplified in the flight of birds or the activity of little animals. It seemed, in fact, a new development of the love of the Beautiful, such as might have made him a poet, a painter, or a sculptor, and which was as completely refined from all utilitarian coarseness, as it could have been in either of the fine arts. He looked with singular distaste at the stiff and regular processes of ordinary machinery. Being once carried to see a steam-engine, in the expectation that his intuitive comprehension of mechanical principles would be gratified, he turned pale, and grew sick, as if something monstrous and unnatural had been presented to him. This horror was partly owing to the size and terrible energy of the Iron Laborer; for the character of Owen's mind was microscopic, and tended naturally to the minute, in accordance with his diminutive frame, and the marvellous smallness and delicate power of his fingers. Not that his sense of beauty was thereby diminished into a sense of prettiness. The Beautiful Idea has no relation to size, and may be as perfectly developed in a space too minute for any but microscopic investigation, as within the ample verge that is measured by the arc of the rainbow. But, at all events, this characteristic minuteness in his objects and accomplishments made the world even more incapable, than it might otherwise have been, of appreciating Owen Warland's genius. The boy's relatives saw nothing better to be done – as perhaps there was not – than to bind him apprentice to a watchmaker, hoping that his strange ingenuity might thus be regulated, and put to utilitarian purposes.

Peter Hovenden's opinion of his apprentice has already been expressed. He could make nothing of the lad. Owen's apprehension of the professional mysteries, it is true, was inconceivably quick. But he altogether forgot or despised the grand object of a watchmaker's business, and cared no more for the measurement of time than if it had been merged into eternity. So long, however, as he remained under his old master's care, Owen's lack of sturdiness made it possible, by strict injunctions and sharp oversight, to restrain his creative eccentricity within bounds. But when his apprenticeship was served out, and he had taken the little shop which Peter Hovenden's failing eyesight compelled him to relinquish, then did people recognize how unfit a person was Owen Warland to lead old blind Father Time along his daily course. One of his most rational projects was, to connect a musical operation with the machinery of his watches, so that all the harsh dissonances of life might be rendered tuneful, and each flitting moment fall into the abyss of the Past in golden drops of harmony. If a family-clock was entrusted to him for repair – one of those tall, ancient clocks that have grown nearly allied to human nature, by measuring out the lifetime of many generations – he would take upon himself to arrange a dance or funeral procession of figures, across its venerable face, representing twelve mirthful or melancholy hours. Several freaks of this kind quite destroyed the young watchmaker's credit with that steady and matter-of-fact class of people who hold the opinion that time is not to be trifled with, whether considered as the medium of advancement and prosperity in this world, or preparation for the next. His custom rapidly diminished – a misfortune, however, that was probably reckoned among his better accidents by Owen Warland, who was becoming more and more absorbed in a secret occupation, which drew all his science and manual dexterity into itself, and likewise gave full employment to the characteristic tendencies of his genius. This pursuit had already consumed many months.

After the old watchmaker and his pretty daughter had gazed at him, out of the obscurity of the street, Owen Warland was seized with a fluttering of the nerves, which made his hand tremble too violently to proceed with such delicate labor as he was now engaged upon.

'It was Annie herself!' murmured he. 'I should have known it, by this throbbing of my heart, before I heard her father's voice. Ah, how it throbs! I shall scarcely be able to work again on this exquisite mechanism tonight. Annie – dearest Annie – thou shouldst give firmness to my heart and hand, and not shake them thus; for if I strive to put the very spirit of Beauty into form, and give it motion, it is for thy sake alone. Oh, throbbing heart, be quiet! If my labor be thus thwarted, there will come vague and unsatisfied dreams, which will leave me spiritless to-morrow.'

As he was endeavoring to settle himself again to his task, the shop-door opened, and gave admittance to no other than the stalwart figure which Peter Hovenden had paused to admire, as seen amid the light and shadow of the blacksmith's shop. Robert Danforth had brought a little anvil of his own manufacture, and peculiarly constructed, which the young artist had recently bespoken. Owen examined the article, and pronounced it fashioned according to his wish.

'Why, yes,' said Robert Danforth, his strong voice filling the shop as with the sound of a bass-viol, 'I consider myself equal to anything in the way of my own trade; though I should have made but a poor figure at yours, with such a fist as this,' – added he, laughing, as he laid his vast hand beside the delicate one of Owen. 'But what then? I put more main strength into one blow of my sledge-hammer, than all that you have expended since you were a 'prentice. Is not that the truth?'

'Very probably,' answered the low and slender voice of Owen. 'Strength is an earthly monster. I make no pretensions to it. My force, whatever there may be of it, is altogether spiritual.'

'Well; but, Owen, what are you about!' asked his old school-fellow, still in such a hearty volume of tone that it made the artist shrink; especially as the question related to a subject so sacred as the absorbing dream of his imagination. 'Folks do say, that you are trying to discover the Perpetual Motion.'

'The Perpetual Motion? nonsense!' replied Owen Warland, with a movement of digust; for he was full of little petulances. 'It can never be discovered! It is a dream that may delude men whose brains are mystified with matter, but not me. Besides, if such a discovery were possible, it would not be worth my while to make it, only to have the secret turned to such purposes as are now effected by steam and water-power. I am not ambitious to be honored with the paternity of a new kind of cotton-machine.'

'That would be droll enough!' cried the blacksmith, breaking out into such an uproar of laughter, that Owen himself, and the bell-glasses on his work-board, quivered in unison. 'No, no, Owen! No child of yours will have iron joints and sinews. Well, I won't hinder you any more. Good night, Owen, and success; and if you need any assistance, so far as a downright blow of hammer upon anvil will answer the purpose, I'm your man!'

And with another laugh, the man of main strength left the shop.

'How strange it is,' whispered Owen Warland to himself, leaning his head upon his hand, 'that all my musings, my purposes, my passion for the Beautiful, my consciousness of power to create it – a finer, more ethereal power, of which this earthly giant can have no conception – all, all, look so vain and idle, whenever my path is crossed by Robert Danforth! He would drive me mad, were I to meet him often. His hard, brute force darkens and confuses the spiritual element within me. But I, too, will be strong in my own way. I will not yield to him!'

He took from beneath a glass, a piece of minute machinery, which he set in the condensed light of his lamp, and, looking intently at it through a magnifying glass, proceeded to operate with a delicate instrument of steel. In an instant, however, he fell back in his chair, and clasped his hands, with a look of horror on his face, that made its small features as impressive as those of a giant would have been.

'Heaven! What have I done!' exclaimed he. 'The vapor! the influence of that brute force! it has bewildered me, and obscured my perception. I have made the very stroke – the fatal stroke – that I have dreaded from the first! It is all over – the toil of months – the object of my life! I am ruined!'

And there he sat, in strange despair, until his lamp flickered in the socket, and left the Artist of the Beautiful in darkness.

Thus it is, that ideas which grow up within the imagination, and appear so lovely to it, and of a value beyond whatever men call valuable, are exposed to be shattered and annihilated by contact with the Practical. It is requisite for the ideal artist to possess a force of character that seems hardly compatible with its delicacy; he must keep his faith in himself, while the incredulous world assails him with its utter disbelief; he must stand up against mankind and be his own sole disciple, both as respects his genius, and the objects to which it is directed.

For a time, Owen Warland succumbed to this severe, but inevitable test. He spent a few sluggish weeks, with his head so continually resting in his hands, that the townspeople had scarcely an opportunity to see his countenance. When, at last, it was again uplifted to the light of day, a cold, dull, nameless change was perceptible upon it. In the opinion of Peter Hovenden, however, and that order of sagacious understandings who think that life should be regulated, like clockwork, with leaden weights, the alteration was entirely for the better. Owen now indeed, applied himself to business with dogged industry. It was marvellous to witness the obtuse gravity with which he would inspect the wheels of a great, old silver watch; thereby delighting the owner, in whose fob it had been worn till he deemed it a portion of his own life, and was accordingly jealous of its treatment. In consequence of the good report thus acquired, Owen Warland was invited by the proper authorities to regulate the clock in the church-steeple. He succeeded so admirably in this matter of public interest, that the merchants gruffly acknowledged his merits on 'Change; the nurse whispered his praises, as she gave the potion in the sick-chamber; the lover blessed him at the hour of appointed interview; and the town in general thanked Owen for the punctuality of dinner-time. In a word, the heavy weight upon his spirits kept everything in order, not merely within his own system, but wheresoever the iron accents of the church-clock were audible. It was a circumstance, though minute, yet characteristic of his present state, that, when employed to engrave names or initials on silver spoons, he now wrote the requisite letters in the plainest possible style; omitting a variety of fanciful flourishes, that had heretofore distinguished his work in this kind.

One day, during the era of this happy transformation, old Peter Hovenden came to visit his former apprentice.

'Well, Owen,' said he, 'I am glad to hear such good accounts of you from all quarters; and especially from the town-clock yonder, which speaks in your commendation every hour of the twenty-four. Only get rid altogether of your nonsensical trash about the Beautiful – which I, nor nobody else, nor yourself to boot, could never understand – only free yourself of that, and your success in life is as sure as daylight. Why, if you go in this way, I should even venture to let you doctor this precious old watch of mine; though, except my daughter Annie, I have nothing else so valuable in the world.'

'I should hardly dare touch it, sir,' replied Owen in a depressed tone; for he was weighed down by his old master's presence.

'In time,' said the latter, 'in time, you will be capable of it.'

The old watchmaker, with the freedom naturally consequent on his former authority, went on inspecting the work which Owen had in hand at the moment, together with other matters that were in progress. The artist, meanwhile, could scarcely lift his head. There was nothing so antipodal to his nature as this man's cold, unimaginative sagacity, by contact with which everything was converted into a dream, except the densest matter of the physical world. Owen groaned in spirit, and prayed fervently to be delivered from him.

'But what is this?' cried Peter Hovenden abruptly, taking up a dusty bell-glass, beneath which appeared a mechanical something, as delicate and minute as the system of a butterfly's anatomy. 'What have we here! Owen, Owen! there is witchcraft in these little chains, and wheels, and paddles! See! with one pinch of my finger and thumb, I am going to deliver you from all future peril.'

'For Heaven's sake,' screamed Owen Warland, springing up with wonderful energy, 'as you would not drive me mad – do not touch it! The slightest pressure of your finger would ruin me for ever.'

'Aha, young man! And is it so?' said the old watchmaker, looking at him with just enough of penetration to torture Owen's soul with the bitterness of wordly criticism. 'Well; take your own course. But I warn you again, that in this small piece of mechanism lives your evil spirit. Shall I exorcise him?'

'You are my Evil Spirit,' answered Owen, much excited – 'you, and the hard, coarse world! The leaden thoughts and the despondency that you fling upon me are my clogs. Else, I should long ago have achieved the task that I was created for.'

Peter Hovenden shook his head, with the mixture of contempt and indignation which mankind, of whom he was partly a representative, deem themselves entitled to feel towards all simpletons who seek other prizes than the dusty ones along the highway. He then took his leave with an uplifted finger, and a sneer upon his face that haunted the artist's dreams for many a night afterwards. At the time of his old master's visit, Owen was probably on the point of taking up the relinquished task; but, by this sinister event, he was thrown back into the state whence he had been slowly emerging.

But the innate tendency of his soul had only been accumulating fresh vigor, during its apparent sluggishness. As the summer advanced, he almost totally relinquished his business, and permitted Father Time, so far as the old gentleman was represented by the clocks and watches under his control, to stray at random through human life, making infinite confusion among the train of bewildered hours. He wasted the sunshine, as people said, in wandering through the woods and fields, and along the banks of streams. There, like a child, he found amusement in chasing butterflies, or watching the motions of water-insects. There was something truly mysterious in the intentness with which he contemplated these living playthings, as they sported on the breeze; or examined the structure of an imperial insect whom he had imprisoned. The chase of butterflies was an apt emblem of the ideal pursuit in which he had spent so many golden hours. But, would the Beautiful Idea ever be yielded to his hand, like the butterfly that symbolized it? Sweet, doubtless, were these days, and congenial to the artist's soul. They were full of bright conceptions, which gleamed through his intellectual world, as the butterflies gleamed through the outward atmosphere, and were real to him for the instant, without the toil, and perplexity, and many disappointments, of attempting to make them visible to the sensual eye. Alas, that the artist, whether in poetry or whatever other material, may not content himself with the inward enjoyment of the Beautiful, but must chase the flitting mystery beyond the verge of his ethereal domain, and crush its frail being in seizing it with a material grasp! Owen Warland felt the impulse to give external reality to his ideas, as irresistibly as any of the poets or painters, who have arrayed the world in a dimmer and fainter beauty, imperfectly copied from the richness of their visions.

The night was now his time for the slow process of recreating the one Idea, to which all his intellectual activity referred itself. Always at the approach of dusk, he stole into the town, locked himself within his shop, and wrought with patient delicacy of touch, for many hours. Sometimes he was startled by the rap of the watchman, who, when all the world should be asleep, had caught the gleam of lamp-light through the crevices of Owen Warland's shutters. Daylight, to the morbid sensibility of his mind, seemed to have an intrusiveness that interfered with his pursuits. On cloudy and inclement days, therefore, he sat with his head upon his hands, muffling, as it were, his sensitive brain in a mist of indefinite musings; for it was a relief to escape from the sharp distinctness with which he was compelled to shape out his thoughts, during his nightly toil.

From one of these fits of torpor, he was aroused by the entrance of Annie Hovenden, who came into the shop with the freedom of a customer, and also with something of the familiarity of a childish friend. She had worn a hole through her silver thimble, and wanted Owen to repair it.

'But I don't know whether you will condescend to such a task,' said she, laughing, 'now that you are so taken up with the notion of putting spirit into machinery.'

'Where did you get that idea, Annie?' said Owen, starting in surprise.

'Oh, out of my own head,' answered she, 'and from something that I heard you say, long ago, when you were but a boy, and I a little child. But, come! will you mend this poor thimble of mine?'

'Anything for your sake, Annie,' said Owen Warland – 'anything; even were it to work at Robert Danforth's forge.'

'And that would be a pretty sight!' retorted Annie, glancing with imperceptible slightness at the artist's small and slender frame. 'Well; here is the thimble.'

'But that is a strange idea of yours,' said Owen, 'about the spiritualization of matter!'

And then the thought stole into his mind, that this young girl possessed the gift to comprehend him, better than all the world beside. And what a help and strength would it be to him, in his lonely toil, if he could gain the sympathy of the only being whom he loved! To persons whose pursuits are insulated from the common business of life – who are either in advance of mankind, or apart from it – there often comes a sensation of moral cold, that makes the spirit shiver, as if it had reached the frozen solitudes around the pole. What the prophet, the poët, the reformer, the criminal, or any other man, with human yearnings, but separated from the multitude by a peculiar lot, might feel, poor Owen Warland felt.

'Annie,' cried he, growing pale as death at the thought, 'how gladly would I tell you the secret of my pursuit! You, methinks, would estimate it rightly. You, I know, would hear it with a reverence that I must not expect from the harsh, material world.'

'Would I not? to be sure I would!' replied Annie Hovenden, lightly laughing. 'Come; explain to me quickly what is the meaning of this little whirligig, so delicately wrought that it might be a plaything for Queen Mab. See; I will put it in motion.'

'Hold,' exclaimed Owen, 'hold!'

Annie had but given the slightest possible touch, with the point of a needle, to the same minute portion of complicated machinery which has been more than once mentioned, when the artist seized her by the wrist with a force that made her scream aloud. She was affrighted at the convulsion of intense rage and anguish that writhed across his features. The next instant he let his head sink upon his hands.

'Go, Annie,' murmured he, 'I have deceived myself, and must suffer for it. I yearned for sympathy – and thought – and fancied – and dreamed – that you might give it me. But you lack the talisman, Annie, that should admit you into my secrets. That touch has undone the toil of months, and the thought of a lifetime! It was not your fault, Annie – but you have ruined me!'

Poor Owen Warland! He had indeed erred, yet pardonably; for if any human spirit could have sufficiently reverenced the processes so sacred in his eyes, it must have been a woman's. Even Annie Hovenden, possibly, might not have disappointed him, had she been enlightened by the deep intelligence of love.

The artist spent the ensuing winter in a way that satisfied any persons, who had hitherto retained a hopeful opinion of him, that he was, in truth, irrevocably doomed to inutility as regarded the world, and to an evil destiny on his own part. The decease of a relative had put him in possession of a small inheritance. Thus freed from the necessity of toil, and having lost the steadfast influence of a great purpose – great, at least to him – he abandoned himself to habits from which, it might have been supposed, the mere delicacy of his organization would have availed to secure him. But when the ethereal portion of a man of genius is obscured, the earthly part assumes an influence the more uncontrollable, because the character is now thrown off the balance to which Providence had so nicely adjusted it, and which, in coarser natures, is adjusted by some other method. Owen Warland made proof of whatever show of bliss may be found in riot. He looked at the world through the golden medium of wine, and contemplated the visions that bubble up so gaily around the brim of the glass, and that people the air with shapes of pleasant madness, which so soon grow ghostly and forlorn. Even when this dismal and inevitable change had taken place, the young man might still have continued to quaff the cup of enchantments, though its vapor did but shroud life in gloom, and fill the gloom with spectres that mocked at him. There was a certain irksomeness of spirit, which, being real, and the deepest sensation of which the artist was now conscious, was more intolerable than any fantastic miseries and horrors that the abuse of wine could summon up. In the latter case, he could remember, even out of the midst of his trouble, that all was but a delusion; in the former, the heavy anguish was his actual life.

From this perilous state, he was redeemed by an incident which more than one person witnessed, but of which the shrewdest could not explain nor conjecture the operation on Owen Warland's mind. It was very simple. On a warm afternoon of spring, as the artist sat among his riotous companions, with a glass of wine before him, a splendid butterfly flew in at the open window, and fluttered about his head.

'Ah!' exclaimed Owen, who had drank freely, 'Are you alive again, child of the sun, and playmate of the summer breeze, after your dismal winter's nap! Then it is time for me to be at work!'

And leaving his unemptied glass upon the table, he departed, and was never known to sip another drop of wine.

And now, again, he resumed his wanderings in the woods and fields. It might be fancied that the bright butterfly, which had come so spiritlike into the window, as Owen sat with the rude revellers, was indeed a spirit, commissioned to recall him to the pure, ideal life that had so etherealized him among men. It might be fancied, that he went forth to seek this spirit, in its sunny haunts; for still, as in the summer-time gone by, he was seen to steal gently up, wherever a butterfly had alighted, and lose himself in contemplation of it. When it took flight, his eyes followed the winged vision, as if its airy track would show the path to heaven. But what could be the purpose of the unseasonable toil, which was again resumed, as the watchman knew by the lines of lamp-light through the crevices of Owen Warland's shutters? The townspeople had one comprehensive explanation of all these singularities. Owen Warland had gone mad! How universally efficacious – how satisfactory, too, and soothing to the injured sensibility of narrowness and dullness – is this easy method of accounting for whatever lies beyond the world's most ordinary scope! From Saint Paul's days, down to our poor little Artist of the Beautiful, the same talisman has been applied to the elucidation of all mysteries in the words or deeds of men, who spoke or acted too wisely or too well. In Owen Warland's case, the judgment of his townspeople may have been correct. Perhaps he was mad. The lack of sympathy – that contrast between himself and his neighbors, which took away the restraint of example – was enough to make him so. Or, possibly, he had caught just so much of ethereal radiance as served to bewilder him, in an earthly sense, by its intermixture with the common daylight.

One evening, when the artist had returned from a customary ramble, and had just thrown the lustre of his lamp on the delicate piece of work, so often interrupted, but still taken up again, as if his fate were embodied in its mechanism, he was surprised by the entrance of old Peter Hovenden. Owen never met this man without a shrinking of the heart. Of all the world, he was most terrible, by reason of a keen understanding, which saw so distinctly what it did see, and disbelieved so uncompromisingly in what it could not see. On this occasion, the old watchmaker had merely a gracious word or two to say.

'Owen, my lad,' said he, 'we must see you at my house to-morrow night.'

The artist began to mutter some excuse.

'Oh, but it must be so,' quoth Peter Hovenden, 'for the sake of the days when you were one of the household. What, my boy, don't you know that my daughter Annie is engaged to Robert Danforth? We are making an entertainment, in our humble way, to celebrate the event.'

'Ah!' said Owen.

That little monosyllable was all he uttered; its tone seemed cold and unconcerned, to an ear like Peter Hovenden's; and yet there was in it the stifled outcry of the poor artist's heart, which he compressed within him like a man holding down an evil spirit. One slight outbreak, however, imperceptible to the old watchmaker, he allowed himself. Raising the instrument with which he was about to begin his work, he let it fall upon the little system of machinery that had, anew, cost him months of thought and toil. It was shattered by the stroke!

Owen Warland's story would have been no tolerable representation of the troubled life of those who strive to create the Beautiful, if, amid all other thwarting influences, love had not interposed to steal the cunning from his hand. Outwardly, he had been no ardent or enterprising lover; the career of his passion had confined its tumults and vicissitudes so entirely within the artist's imagination, that Annie herself had scarcely more than a woman's intuitive perception of it. But, in Owen's view, it covered the whole field of his life. Forgetful of the time when she had shown herself incapable of any deep response, he had persisted in connecting all his dreams of artistical success with Annie's image; she was the visible shape in which the spiritual power that he worshipped, and on whose altar he hoped to lay a not unworthy offering, was made manifest to him. Of course he had deceived himself; there were no such attributes in Annie Hovenden as his imagination had endowed her with. She, in the aspect which she wore to his inward vision, was as much a creation of his own, as the mysterious piece of mechanism would be were it ever realized. Had he become convinced of his mistake through the medium of successful love; had he won Annie to his bosom, and there beheld her fade from angel into ordinary woman, the disappointment might have driven him back, with concentrated energy, upon his sole remaining object. On the other hand, had he found Annie what he fancied, his lot would have been so rich in beauty, that, out of its mere redundancy, he might have wrought the Beautiful into many a worthier type than he had toiled for. But the guise in which his sorrow came to him, the sense that the angel of his life had been snatched away and given to a rude man of earth and iron, who could neither need nor appreciate her ministrations; this was the very perversity of fate, that makes human existence appear too absurd and contradictory to be the scene of one other hope or one other fear. There was nothing left for Owen Warland but to sit down like a man that had been stunned.

He went through a fit of illness. After his recovery, his small and slender frame assumed an obtuser garniture of flesh than it had ever before worn. His thin cheeks became round; his delicate little hand, so spiritually fashioned to achieve fairy task-work, grew plumper than the hand of a thriving infant. His aspect had a childishness, such as might have induced a stranger to pat him on the head – pausing, however, in the act, to wonder what manner of child was here. It was as if the spirit had gone out of him, leaving the body to flourish in a soft of vegetable existence. Not that Owen Warland was idiotic. He could talk, and not irrationally. Somewhat of a babbler, indeed, did people begin to think him; for he was apt to discourse at wearisome length, of marvels of mechanism that he had read about in books, but which he had learned to consider as absolutely fabulous. Among them he enumerated the Man of Brass, constructed by Albertus Magnus, and the Brazen Head of Friar Bacon; and, coming down to later times, the automata of a little coach and horses, which, it was pretended, had been manufactured for the Dauphin of France; together with an insect that buzzed about the ear like a living fly, and yet was but a contrivance of minute steel springs. There was a story, too, of a duck that waddled, and quacked, and ate; though, had any honest citizen purchased it for dinner, he would have found himself cheated with the mere mechanical apparition of a duck.

'But all these accounts,' said Owen Warland, 'I am now satisfied, are mere impositions.'

Then, in a mysterious way, he would confess that he once thought differently. In his idle and dreamy days, he had considered it possible, in a certain sense, to spiritualize machinery; and to combine with the new species of life and motion, thus produced, a beauty that should attain to the ideal which Nature has proposed to herself, in all her creatures, but has never taken pains to realize. He seemed, however, to retain no very distinct perception either of the process of achieving this object, or of the design itself.

'I have thrown it all aside now,' he would say. 'It was a dream, such as young men are always mystifying themselves with. Now that I have acquired a little common sense, it makes me laugh to think of it.'

Poor, poor, and fallen Owen Warland! These were the symptoms that he had ceased to be an inhabitant of the better sphere that lies unseen around us. He had lost his faith in the invisible, and now prided himself, as such unfortunates invariably do, in the wisdom which rejected much that even his eye could see, and trusted confidently in nothing but what his hand could touch. This is the calamity of men whose spiritual part dies out of them, and leaves the grosser understanding to assimilate them more and more to the things of which alone it can take cognizance. But, in Owen Warland, the spirit was not dead, nor past away; it only slept.

How it awoke again, is not recorded. Perhaps, the torpid slumber was broken by a convulsive pain. Perhaps, as in a former instance, the butterfly came and hovered about his head, and reinspired him – as, indeed, this creature of the sunshine had always a mysterious mission for the artist – reinspired him with the former purpose of his life. Whether it were pain or happiness that thrilled through his veins, his first impulse was to thank Heaven for rendering him again the being of thought, imagination, and keenest sensibility, that he had long ceased to be.

'Now for my task,' said he. 'Never did I feel such strength for it as now.'

Yet, strong as he felt himself, he was incited to toil the more diligently, by an anxiety lest death should surprise him in the midst of his labors. This anxiety, perhaps, is common to all men who set their hearts upon anything so high, in their own view of it, that life becomes of importance only as conditional to its accomplishment. So long as we love life for itself, we seldom dread the losing it. When we desire life for the attainment of an object, we recognize the frailty of its texture. But, side by side with this sense of insecurity, there is a vital faith in our invulnerability to the shaft of death, while engaged in any task that seems assigned by Providence as our proper thing to do, and which the world would have cause to mourn for, should we leave it unaccomplished. Can the philosopher, big with the inspiration of an idea that is to reform mankind, believe that he is to be beckoned from this sensible existence, at the very instant when he is mustering his breath to speak the word of light? Should he perish so, the weary ages may pass away – the world's whole life-sand may fall, drop by drop – before another intellect is prepared to develop the truth that might have been uttered then. But history affords many an example, where the most precious spirit, at any particular epoch manifested in human shape, has gone hence untimely, without space allowed him, so far as mortal judgment could discern, to perform his mission on the earth. The prophet dies; and the man of torpid heart and sluggish brain lives on. The poet leaves his song half sung, or finishes it, beyond the scope of mortal ears, in a celestial choir. The painter – as Allston did – leaves half his conception on the canvas, to sadden us with its imperfect beauty, and goes to picture forth the whole, if it be no irreverence to say so, in the hues of Heaven. But, rather, such incomplete designs of this life will be perfected nowhere. This so frequent abortion of man's dearest projects must be taken as a proof, that the deeds of earth, however etherealized by piety or genius, are without value, except as exercises and manifestations of the spirit. In Heaven, all ordinary thought is higher and more melodious than Milton's song. Then, would he add another verse to any strain that he had left unfinished here?

But to return to Owen Warland. It was his fortune, good or ill, to achieve the purpose of his life. Pass we over a long space of intense thought, yearning effort, minute toil, and wasting anxiety, succeeded by an instant of solitary triumph; let all this be imagined; and then behold the artist, on a winter evening, seeking admittance to Robert Danforth's fireside circle. There he found the Man of Iron, with his massive substance thoroughly warmed and attempered by domestic influences. And there was Annie, too, now transformed into a matron, with much of her husband's plain and sturdy nature, but imbued, as Owen Warland still believed, with a finer grace, that might enable her to be the interpreter between Strength and Beauty. It happened, likewise, that old Peter Hovenden was a guest, this evening, at his daughter's fireside; and it was his well-remembered expression of keen, cold criticism, that first encounted the artist's glance.

'My old friend Owen!' cried Robert Danforth, starting up, and compressing the artist's delicate fingers within a hand that was accustomed to grip bars of iron. 'This is kind and neighborly, to come to us at last! I was afraid your Perpetual Motion had bewitched you out of the remembrance of old times.'

'We are glad to see you!' said Annie, while a blush reddened her matronly cheek. 'It was not like a friend, to stay from us so long.'

'Well, Owen,' inquired the old watchmaker, as his first greeting, 'how comes on the Beautiful? Have you created it at last?'

The artist did not immediately reply, being startled by the apparition of a young child of strength, that was tumbling about on the carpet; a little personage who had come mysteriously out of the infinite, but with something so sturdy and real in his composition that he seemed moulded out of the densest substance which earth could supply. This hopeful infant crawled towards the new-comer, and setting himself on end – as Robert Danforth expressed the posture – stared at Owen with a look of such sagacious observation, that the mother could not help exchanging a proud glance with her husband. But the artist was disturbed by the child's look, as imagining a resemblance between it and Peter Hovenden's habitual expression. He could have fancied that the old watchmaker was compressed into this baby-shape, and was looking out of those baby-eyes, and repeating – as he now did – the malicious question:

'The Beautiful, Owen! How comes on the Beautiful? Have you succeeded in creating the Beautiful?'

'I have succeeded,' replied the artist, with a momentary light of triumph in his eyes, and a smile of sunshine, yet steeped in such depth of thought that it was almost sadness. 'Yes, my friends, it is the truth. I have succeeded!'

'Indeed!' cried Annie, a look of maiden mirthfulness peeping out of her face again. 'And is it lawful, now, to inquire what the secret is?'

'Surely; it is to disclose it, that I have come,' answered Owen Warland. 'You shall know, and see, and touch, and possess, the secret! For Annie – if by that name I may still address the friend of my boyish years – Annie, it is for your bridal gift that I have wrought this spiritualized mechanism, this harmony of motion, this Mystery of Beauty! It comes late, indeed; but it is as we go onward in life, when objects begin to lose their freshness of hue, and our souls their delicacy of perception, that the spirit of Beauty is most needed. If – forgive me, Annie – if you know how to value this gift, it can never come too late!'

He produced, as he spoke, what seemed a jewel-box. It was carved richly out of ebony by his own hand, and inlaid with a fanciful tracery of pearl, representing a boy in pursuit of a butterfly, which, elsewhere, had become a winged spirit, and was flying heavenward; while the boy, or youth, had found such efficacy in his strong desire, that he ascended from earth to cloud, and from cloud to celestial atmosphere, to win the Beautiful. This case of ebony the artist opened, and bade Annie place her finger on its edge. She did so, but almost screamed, as a butterfly fluttered forth, and alighting on her finger's tip, sat waving the ample magnificence of its purple and gold-speckled wings, as if in prelude to a flight. It is impossible to express by words the glory, the splendor, the delicate gorgeousness, which were softened into the beauty of this object. Nature's ideal butterfly was here realized in all its perfection; not in the pattern of such faded insects as flit among earthly flowers, but of those which hover across the meads of Paradise, for child-angels and the spirits of departed infants to disport themselves with. The rich down was visible upon its wings; the lustre of its eyes seemed instinct with spirit. The firelight glimmered around this wonder – the candles gleamed upon it – but it glistened apparently by its own radiance, and illuminated the finger and outstretched hand on which it rested, with a white gleam like that of precious stones. In its perfect beauty, the consideration of size was entirely lost. Had its wings overarched the firmament, the mind could not have been more filled or satisfied.

'Beautiful! Beautiful!' exclaimed Annie. 'Is it alive? Is it alive?'

'Alive? To be sure it is,' answered her husband. 'Do you suppose any mortal has skill enough to make a butterfly – or would put himself to the trouble of making one, when any child may catch a score of them in a summer's afternoon? Alive? Certainly! But this pretty box is undoubtedly of our friend Owen's manufacture; and really it does him credit.'

At this moment, the butterfly waved its wings anew, with a motion so absolutely lifelike that Annie was startled, and even awe-stricken; for, in spite of her husband's opinion, she could not satisfy herself whether it was indeed a living creature, or a piece of wondrous mechanism.

'Is it alive?' she repeated, more earnestly than before.

'Judge for yourself,' said Owen Warland, who stood gazing in her face with fixed attention.

The butterfly now flung itself upon the air, fluttered round Annie's head, and soared into a distant region of the parlor, still making itself perceptible to sight by the starry gleam in which the motion of its wings enveloped it. The infant on the floor, followed its course with his sagacious little eyes. After flying about the room, it returned, in a spiral curve, and settled again on Annie's finger.

'But is it alive?' exclaimed she again; and the finger, on which the gorgeous mystery had alighted, was so tremulous that the butterfly was forced to balance himself with his wings. 'Tell me if it be alive, or whether you created it?'

'Wherefore ask who created it, so it be beautiful?' replied Owen Warland. 'Alive? Yes, Annie; it may well be said to possess life, for it absorbed my own being into itself; and in the secret of that butterfly, and in its beauty — which is not merely outward, but deep as its whole system — is represented the intellect, the imagination, the sensibility, the soul, of an Artist of the Beautiful! Yes, I created it. But' — and here his countenance somewhat changed — 'this butterfly is not now to me what it was when I beheld it afar off, in the day-dreams of my youth.'

'Be it what it may, it is a pretty plaything,' said the blacksmith, grinning with childlike delight. 'I wonder whether it would condescend to alight on such a great clumsy finger as mine? Hold it hither, Annie!'

By the artist's direction, Annie touched her finger's tip to that of her husband; and, after a momentary delay, the butterfly fluttered from one to the other. It preluded a second flight by a similar, yet not precisely the same waving of wings, as in the first experiment; then, ascending from the blacksmith's stalwart finger, it rose in a gradually enlarging curve to the ceiling, made one wide sweep around the room, and returned with an undulating movement to the point whence it had started.

'Well, that does beat all nature!' cried Robert Danforth, bestowing the heartiest praise that he could find expression for; and, indeed, had he paused there, a man of finer words and nicer perception, could not easily have said more. 'That goes beyond me, I confess! But what then? There is more real use in one downright blow of my sledge-hammer, than in the whole five years' labor that our friend Owen has wasted on this butterfly!'

Here the child clapped his hands, and made a great babble of indistinct utterance, apparently demanding that the butterfly should be given him for a plaything.

Owen Warland, meanwhile, glanced sidelong at Annie, to discover whether she sympathized in her husband's estimate of the comparative value of the Beautiful and the Practical. There was, amid all her kindness towards himself, amid all the wonder and admiration with which she contemplated the marvelous work of his hands, and incarnation of his idea, a secret scorn; too secret, perhaps, for her own consciousness, and perceptible only to such intuitive discernment as that of the artist. But Owen, in the latter stages of his pursuit, had risen out of the region in which such a discovery might have been torture. He knew that the world, and Annie as the representative of the world, whatever praise might be bestowed, could never say the fitting word, nor feel the fitting sentiment which should be the perfect recompense of an artist who, symbolizing a lofty moral by a material trifle – converting what was earthly, to spiritual gold – had won the Beautiful into his handiwork. Not at this latest moment, was he to learn that the reward of all high performance must be sought within itself, or sought in vain. There was, however, a view of the matter, which Annie, and her husband, and even Peter Hovenden, might fully have understood, and which would have satisfied them that the toil of years had here been worthily bestowed. Owen Warland might have told them, that this butterfly, this plaything, this bridal-gift of a poor watchmaker to a blacksmith's wife, was, in truth, a gem of art that a monarch would have purchased with honors and abundant wealth, and have treasured it among the jewels of his kingdom, as the most unique and wondrous of them all! But the artist smiled, and kept the secret to himself.

'Father,' said Annie, thinking that a word of praise from the old watchmaker might gratify his former apprentice, 'do come and admire this pretty butterfly!'

'Let us see,' said Peter Hovenden, rising from his chair, with the sneer upon his face that always made people doubt, as he himself did, in everything but a material existence. 'Here is my finger for it to alight upon. I shall understand it better when once I have touched it.'

But, to the increased astonishment of Annie, when the tip of her father's finger was pressed against that of her husband, on which the butterfly still rested, the insect drooped its wings, and seemed on the point of falling to the floor. Even the bright spots of gold upon its wings and body, unless her eyes deceived her, grew dim, and the glowing purple took a dusky hue, and the starry lustre that gleamed around the blacksmith's hand, became faint, and vanished.

'It is dying! it is dying!' cried Annie, in alarm.

'It has been delicately wrought,' said the artist calmly. 'As I told you, it has imbibed a spiritual essence – call it magnetism, or what you will. In an atmosphere of doubt and mockery, its exquisite susceptibility suffers torture, as does the soul of him who instilled his own life into it. It has already lost its beauty; in a few moments more, its mechanism would be irreparably injured.'

'Take away your hand, father!' entreated Annie, turning pale. 'Here is my child; let it rest on his innocent hand. There, perhaps, its life will revive, and its colors grow brighter than ever.'

Her father, with an acrid smile, withdrew his finger. The butterfly then appeared to recover the power of voluntary motion; while its hues assumed much of their original lustre, and the gleam of starlight, which was its most ethereal attribute, again formed a halo round about it. At first, when transferred from Robert Danforth's hand to the small finger of the child, this radiance grew so powerful that it positively threw the little fellow's shadow back against the wall. He, meanwhile, extended his plump hand as he had seen his father and mother do, and watched the waving of the insect's wings, with infantine delight. Nevertheless, there was a certain odd expression of sagacity, that made Owen Warland feel as if here were old Peter Hovenden, partially, and but partially, redeemed from his hard scepticisim into childish faith.

'How wise the little monkey looks!' whispered Robert Danforth to his wife.

'I never saw such a look on a child's face,' answered Annie, admiring her own infant, and with good reason, far more than the artistic butterfly. 'The darling knows more of the mystery than we do.'

As if the butterfly, like the artist, were conscious of something not entirely congenial in the child's nature, it alternately sparkled and grew dim. At length, it arose form the small hand of the infant with an airy motion, that seemed to bear it upward without an effort; as if the ethereal instincts, with which its master's spirit had endowed it, impelled this fair vision involuntarily to a higher sphere. Had there been no obstruction, it might have soared into the sky, and grown immortal. But its lustre gleamed upon the ceiling; the exquisite texture of its wings brushed against that earthly medium; and a sparkle or two, as of star-dust, floated downward and lay glimmering on the carpet. Then the butterfly came fluttering down, and instead of returning to the infant, was apparently attracted towards the artist's hand.

'Not so, not so!' murmured Owen Warland, as if his handiwork could have understood him. 'Thou hast gone forth out of thy master's heart. There is no return for thee!'

With a wavering movement, and emitting a tremulous radiance, the butterfly struggled, as it were, towards the infant, and was about to alight upon his finger. But, while it still hovered in the air, the little Child of Strength, with his grandsire's sharp and shrewd expression in his face, made a snatch at the marvellous insect, and compressed it in his hand. Annie screamed! Old Peter Hovenden burst into a cold and scornful laugh. The blacksmith, by main force, unclosed the infant's hand, and found within the palm a small heap of glittering fragments, whence the Mystery of Beauty had fled for ever. And as for Owen Warland, he looked placidly at what seemed the ruin of his life's labor, and which was yet no ruin. He had caught a far other butterfly than this. When the artist rose high enough to achieve the Beautiful, the symbol by which he made it perceptible to mortal senses became of little value in his eyes, while his spirit possessed itself in the enjoyment of the Reality.

1844

EDGAR ALLAN POE
1809–1849

The Fall of The House of Usher

Son cœur est un luth suspendu;
Sitôt qu'on le touche il résonne.
DE BÉRANGER

During the whole of a dull, dark, and soundless day in the autumn of the year, when the clouds hung oppressively low in the heavens, I had been passing alone, on horseback, through a singularly dreary tract of country, and at length found myself, as the shades of the evening drew on, within view of the melancholy House of Usher. I know not how it was – but, with the first glimpse of the building, a sense of insufferable gloom pervaded my spirit. I say insufferable; for the feeling was unrelieved by any of that half-pleasurable, because poetic, sentiment with which the mind usually receives even the sternest natural images of the desolate or terrible. I looked upon the scene before me – upon the mere house, and the simple landscape features of the domain – upon the bleak walls – upon the vacant eye-like windows – upon a few rank sedges – and upon a few white trunks of decayed trees – with an utter depression of soul which I can compare to no earthly sensation more properly than to the after-dream of the reveller upon opium – the bitter relapse into every-day life – the hideous dropping off of the veil. There was an iciness, a sinking, a sickening of the heart – an unredeemed dreariness of thought which no goading of the imagination could torture into aught of the sublime. What was it – I paused to think – what was it that so unnerved me in the contemplation of the House of Usher? It was a mystery all insoluble; nor could I grapple with the shadowy fancies that crowded upon me as I pondered. I was forced to fall back upon the unsatisfactory conclusion, that while, beyond doubt, there *are* combinations of very simple natural objects which have the power of thus affecting us, still the analysis of this power lies among considerations beyond our depth. It was possible, I reflected, that a mere different arrangement of the particulars of the scene, of the details of the picture, would be sufficient to modify, or perhaps to annihilate its capacity for sorrowful impression; and, acting upon this idea, I reined my horse to the precipitous brink of a black and lurid tarn that lay in unruffled lustre by the dwelling, and gazed down – but with a shudder even more thrilling than before – upon the remodelled and inverted images of the gray sedge, and the ghastly tree-stems, and the vacant and eye-like windows.

Nevertheless, in this mansion of gloom I now proposed to myself a sojourn of some weeks. Its proprietor, Roderick Usher, had been one of my boon companions in boyhood; but many years had elapsed since our last meeting. A letter, however, had lately reached me in a distant part of the country – a letter from him – which, in its wildly importunate nature, had admitted of no other than a personal reply. The MS. gave evidence of nervous agitation. The writer spoke of acute bodily illness – of a mental disorder which oppressed him – and of an earnest desire to see me, as his best and indeed his only personal friend, with a view of attempting, by the cheerfulness of my society, some alleviation of his malady. It was the manner in which all this, and much more, was said – it was the apparent *heart* that went with his request – which allowed me no room for hesitation; and I accordingly obeyed forthwith what I still considered a very singular summons.

Although, as boys, we had been even intimate associates, yet I really knew little of my friend. His reserve had been always excessive and habitual. I was aware, however, that his very ancient family had been noted, time out of mind, for a peculiar sensibility of temperament, displaying itself, through long ages, in many works of exalted art, and manifested, of late, in repeated deeds of munificent yet unobtrusive charity, as well as in a passionate devotion to the intricacies, perhaps even more than to the orthodox and easily recognizable beauties, of musical science. I had learned, too, the very remarkable fact, that the stem of the Usher race, all time-honoured as it was, had put forth, at no period, any enduring branch; in other words, that the entire family lay in the direct line of descent; and had always, with very trifling and very temporary variation, so lain. It was this deficiency, I considered, while running over in thought the perfect keeping of the character of the premises with the accredited character of the people, and while speculating upon the possible influence which the one, in the long lapse of centuries, might have exercised upon the other – it was this deficiency, perhaps, of collateral issue, and the consequent undeviating transmission, from sire to son, of the patrimony with the name, which had, at length, so identified the two as to merge the original title of the estate in the quaint and equivocal appellation of the 'House of Usher' – an appellation which seemed to include, in the minds of the peasantry who used it, both the family and the family mansion.

I have said that the sole effect of my somewhat childish experiment – that of looking down within the tarn – had been to deepen the first singular impression. There can be no doubt that the consciousness of the rapid increase of my superstition – for why should I not so term it? served mainly to accelerate the increase itself. Such, I have long known, is the paradoxical law of all sentiments having terror as a basis. And it might have been for this reason only, that, when I again uplifted my eyes to the house itself, from its image in the pool, there grew in my mind a strange fancy – a fancy so ridiculous, indeed, that I but mention it to show the vivid force of the sensations which oppressed me. I had so worked upon my imagination as really to believe that about the whole mansion and domain there hung an atmosphere peculiar to themselves and their immediate vicinity – an atmosphere which had no affinity with the air of heaven, but which had reeked up from the decayed trees, and the gray wall, and the silent tarn – a pestilent and mystic vapour, dull, sluggish, faintly discernible, and leaden-hued.

Shaking off from my spirit what *must* have been a dream, I scanned more narrowly the real aspect of the building. Its principal feature seemed to be that of an excessive antiquity. The discoloration of ages had been great. Minute fungi overspread the whole exterior, hanging in a fine tangled web-work from the eaves. Yet all this was apart from any extraordinary dilapidation. No portion of the masonry had fallen; and there appeared to be a wild inconsistency between its still perfect adaptation of parts, and the crumbling condition of the individual stones. In this there was much that reminded me of the specious totality of old woodwork which has rotted for long years in some neglected vault, with no disturbance from the breath of the external air. Beyond this indication of extensive decay, however, the fabric gave little token of instability. Perhaps the eye of a scrutinizing observer might have discovered a barely perceptible fissure, which, extending from the roof of the building in front, made its way down the wall in a zigzag direction, until it became lost in the sullen waters of the tarn.

Noticing these things, I rode over a short causeway to the house. A servant in waiting took my horse, and I entered the Gothic archway of the hall. A valet, of stealthy step, thence conducted me, in silence, through many dark and intricate passages in my progress to the *studio* of his master. Much that I encountered on the way contributed, I know not how, to heighten the vague sentiments of which I have already spoken. While the objects around me – while the carvings of the ceilings, the sombre tapestries of the walls, the ebon blackness of the floors, and the phantasmagoric armorial trophies which rattled as I strode, were but matters to which, or to such as which, I had been accustomed from my infancy – while I hesitated not to acknowledge how familiar was all this – I still wondered to find how unfamiliar were the fancies which ordinary images were sttirring up. On one of the staircases, I met the physician of the family. His countenance, I thought, wore a mingled expression of low cunning and perplexity. He accosted me with trepidation and passed on. The valet now threw open a door and ushered me into the presence of his master.

The room in which I found myself was very large and lofty. The windows were long, narrow, and pointed, and at so vast a distance from the black oaken floor as to be altogether inaccessible from within. Feeble gleams of encrimsoned light made their way through the trellissed panes, and served to render sufficiently distinct the more prominent objects around; the eye, however, struggled in vain to reach the remoter angles of the chamber, or the recesses of the vaulted and fretted ceiling. Dark draperies hung upon the walls. The general furniture was profuse, comfortless, antique, and tattered. Many books and musical instruments lay scattered about, but failed to give any vitality to the scene. I felt that I breathed an atmosphere of sorrow. An air of stern, deep, and irredeemable gloom hung over and pervaded all.

Upon my entrance, Usher arose from a sofa on which he had been lying at full length, and greeted me with a vivacious warmth which had much in it, I at first thought, of an overdone cordiality – of the constrained effort of the *ennuyé* man of the world. A glance, however, at his countenance convinced me of his perfect sincerity. We sat down; and for some moments, while he spoke not, I gazed upon him with a feeling half of pity, half of awe. Surely, man had never before so terribly altered, in so brief a period, as had Roderick Usher! It was with difficulty that I could bring myself to admit the identity of the wan being before me with the companion of my early boyhood. Yet the character of his face had been at all times remarkable. A cadaverousness of complexion; an eye large, liquid, and luminous beyond comparison; lips somewhat thin and very pallid, but of a surprisingly beautiful curve; a nose of a delicate Hebrew model, but with a breadth of nostril unusual in similar formations; a finely moulded chin, speaking, in its want of prominence, of a want of moral energy; hair of a more than web-like softness and tenuity; these features, with an inordinate expansion above the regions of the temple, made up altogether a countenance not easily to be forgotten. And now in the mere exaggeration of the prevailing character of these features, and of the expression they were wont to convey, lay so much of change that I doubted to whom I spoke. The now ghastly pallor of the skin, and the now miraculous lustre of the eye, above all things startled and even awed me. The silken hair, too, had been suffered to grow all unheeded, and as, in its wild gossamer texture, it floated rather than fell about the face. I could not, even with effort, connect its Arabesque expression with any idea of simply humanity.

In the manner of my friend I was at once struck with an incoherence – an inconsistency; and I soon found this to arise from a series of feeble and futile struggles to overcome an habitual trepidancy – an excessive nervous agitation. For something of this nature I had indeed been prepared, no less by his letter, than by reminiscences of certain boyish traits, and by conclusions deduced from his peculiar physical conformation and temperament. His action was alternatively vivacious and sullen. His voice varied rapidly from a tremulous indecision (when the animal spirits seemed utterly in abeyance) to that species of energetic concision – that abrupt, weighty, unhurried, and hollow-sounding enunciation – that leaden, self-balanced, and perfectly modulated guttural utterance, which may be observed in the lost drunkard, or the irreclaimable eater of opium, during the periods of his most intense excitement.

It was thus that he spoke of the object of my visit, of his earnest desire to see me, and of the solace he expected me to afford him. He entered, at some length, into what he conceived to be the nature of his malady. It was, he said, a constitutional and a family evil, and one for which he despaired to find a remedy — a mere nervous affection, he immediately added, which would undoubtedly soon pass off. It displayed itself in a host of unnatural sensations. Some of these, as he detailed them, interested and bewildered me; although, perhaps, the terms and the general manner of their narration had their weight. He suffered much from a morbid acuteness of the senses; the most insipid food was alone endurable; he could wear only garments of certain texture; the odours of all flowers were oppressive; his eyes were tortured by even a faint light; and there were but peculiar sounds, and these from stringed instruments, which did not inspire him with horror.

To an anomalous species of terror I found him a bounden slave. 'I shall perish,' said he, 'I *must* perish in this deplorable folly. Thus, thus, and not otherwise, shall I be lost. I dread the events of the future, not in themselves, but in their results. I shudder at the thought of any, even, the most trivial, incident, which may operate upon this intolerable agitation of soul. I have, indeed, no abhorrence of danger, except in its absolute effect — in terror. In this unnerved — in this pitiable condition — I feel that the period will sooner or later arrive when I must abandon life and reason together, in some struggle with the grim phantasm, FEAR.'

I learned, moreover, at intervals, and through broken and equivocal hints, another singular feature of his mental condition. He was enchained by certain superstitious impressions in regard to the dwelling which he tenanted, and whence, for many years, he had never ventured forth — in regard to an influence whose supposititious force was conveyed in terms too shadowy here to be re-stated — an influence which some peculiarities in the mere form and substance of his family mansion had, by dint of long sufferance, he said, obtained over his spirit — an effect which the *physique* of the gray walls and turrets, and of the dim tarn into which they all looked down, had, at length, brought about upon the *morale* of his existence.

He admitted, however, although with hesitation, that much of the peculiar gloom which thus afflicted him could be traced to a more natural and far more palpable origin — to the severe and long-continued illness — indeed to the evidently approaching dissolution — of a tenderly beloved sister, his sole companion for long years, his last and only relative on earth. 'Her decease,' he said, with a bitterness which I can never forget, 'would leave him

(him, the hopeless and the frail) the last of the ancient race of the Ushers.' While he spoke, the lady Madeline (for so was she called) passed slowly through a remote portion of the apartment, and, without having noticed my presence, disappeared. I regarded her with an utter astonishment not unmingled with dread; and yet I found it impossible to account for such feelings. A sensation of stupor oppressed me, as my eyes followed her retreating steps. When a door, at length, closed upon her, my glance sought instinctively and eagerly the countenance of her brother – but he had buried his face in his hands, and I could only perceive that a far more than ordinary wanness had overspread the emaciated fingers through which trickled many passionate tears.

The disease of the lady Madeline had long baffled the skill of her physicians. A settled apathy, a gradual wasting away of the person, and frequent although transient affections of a partially cataleptical character were the unusual diagnosis. Hitherto she had steadily borne up against the pressure of her malady, and had not betaken herself finally to bed; but on the closing in of the evening of my arrival at the house, she succumbed (as her brother told me at night with inexpressible agitation) to the prostrating power of the destroyer; and I learned that the glimpse I had obtained of her person would thus probably be the last I should obtain – that the lady, at least while living, would be seen by me no more.

For several days ensuing, her name was unmentioned by either Usher or myself: and during this period I was busied in earnest endeavours to alleviate the melancholy of my friend. We painted and read together, or I listened, as if in a dream, to the wild improvisations of his speaking guitar. And thus, as a closer and still closer intimacy admitted me more unreservedly into the recesses of his spirit, the more bitterly did I perceive the futility of all attempt at cheering a mind from which darkness, as if an inherent positive quality, poured forth upon all objects of the moral and physical universe in one unceasing radiation of gloom.

I shall ever bear about me a memory of the many solemn hours I thus spent alone with the master of the House of Usher. Yet I should fail in any attempt to convey an idea of the exact character of the studies, or of the occupations, in which he involved me, or led me the way. An excited and highly distempered ideality threw a sulphureous lustre over all. His long improvised dirges will ring forever in my ears. Among other things, I hold painfully in mind a

certain singular perversion and amplification of the wild air of the
last waltz of Von Weber. From the paintings over which his
elaborate fancy brooded, and which grew, touch by touch, into
vaguenesses at which I shuddered the more thrillingly, because I
shuddered knowing not why; from these paintings (vivid as their
images now are before me) I would in vain endeavour to educe
more than a small portion which should lie within the compass of
merely written words. By the utter simplicity, by the nakedness of
his designs, he arrested and overawed attention. If ever mortal
painted an idea, that mortal was Roderick Usher. For me at least,
in the circumstances then surrounding me, there arose out of the
pure abstractions which the hypochondriac contrived to throw
upon his canvas, an intensity of intolerable awe, no shadow of
which felt I ever yet in the contemplation of the certainly glowing
yet too concrete reveries of Fuseli.

One of the phantasmagoric conceptions of my friend, partak-
ing not so rigidly of the spirit of abstraction, may be shadowed
forth, although feebly, in words. A small picture presented the
interior of an immensely long and rectangular vault or tunnel,
with low walls, smooth, white, and without interruption or
device. Certain accessory points of the design served well to
convey the idea that this excavation lay at an exceeding depth
below the surface of the earth. No outlet was observed in any
portion of its vast extent, and no torch or other artificial source of
light was discernible; yet a flood of intense rays rolled throughout,
and bathed the whole in a ghastly and inappropriate splendour.

I have just spoken of that morbid condition of the auditory
nerve which rendered all music intolerable to the sufferer, with
the exception of certain effects of stringed instruments. It was,
perhaps, the narrow limits to which he thus confined himself upon
the guitar which gave birth, in great measure, to the fantastic
character of his performances. But the fervid *facility* of his
impromptus could not be so accounted for. They must have been,
and were, in the notes, as well as in the words of his wild fantasias
(for he not unfrequently accompanied himself with rhymed verbal
improvisations), the result of that intense mental collectedness
and concentration to which I have previously alluded as observable only in particular moments of the highest artificial excitement. The words of one of these rhapsodies I have easily
remembered. I was, perhaps, the more forcibly impressed with it
as he gave it, because, in the under or mystic current of its

meaning, I fancied that I perceived, and for the first time, a full consciousness on the part of Usher of the tottering of his lofty reason upon her throne. The verses, which were entitled 'The Haunted Palace,' ran very nearly, if not accurately, thus:

I

In the greenest of our valleys,
 By good angels tenanted,
Once a fair and stately palace –
 Radiant palace – reared its head.
In the monarch Thought's dominion –
 It stood there!
Never seraph spread a pinion
 Over fabric half so fair.

II

Banners yellow, glorious, golden,
 On its roof did float and flow
(This – all this – was in the olden
 Time long ago)
And every gentle air that dallied,
 In that sweet day,
Along the ramparts plumed and pallid,
 A winged odour went away.

III

Wanderers in that happy valley
 Through two luminous windows saw
Spirits moving musically
 To a lute's well-tuned law,
Round about a throne, where sitting
 (Porphyrogene!)
In state his glory well befitting,
 The ruler of the realm was seen.

IV

And all with pearl and ruby glowing
 Was the fair palace door,
Through which came flowing, flowing, flowing
 And sparkling evermore,
A troop of Echoes whose sweet duty
 Was but to sing,

In voices of surpassing beauty,
The wit and wisdom of their king.

V

But evil things, in robes of sorrow,
    Assailed the monarch's high estate;
(Ah, let us mourn, for never morrow
    Shall dawn upon him, desolate!)
And, round about his home, the glory
    That blushed and bloomed
Is but a dim-remembered story
    Of the old time entombed.

VI

And travellers now within that valley,
    Through the red-litten windows see
Vast forms that move fantastically
    To a discordant melody;
While, like a rapid ghastly river,
    Through the pale door,
A hideous throng rush out forever,
    And laugh – but smile no more.

I well remember that suggestions arising from this ballad, led us
into a train of thought, wherein there became manifest an opinion
of Usher's which I mention not so much on account of its novelty,
(for other men have thought thus,) as on account of the
pertinacity with which he maintained it. This opinion, in its
general form, was that of the sentience of all vegetable things. But,
in his disordered fancy, the idea had assumed a more daring
character, and trespassed, under certain conditions, upon the
kingdom of inorganization. I lack words to express the full extent,
or the earnest *abandon* of his persuasion. The belief, however,
was connected (as I have previously hinted) with the gray stones
of the home of his forefathers. The conditions of the sentience had
been here, he imagined, fulfilled in the method of collocation of
these stones – in the order of their arrangement, as well as in that
of the many *fungi* which overspread them, and of the decayed
trees which stood around – above all, in the long undisturbed
endurance of this arrangement, and in its reduplication in the still
waters of the tarn. Its evidence – the evidence of the sentience –
was to be seen, he said (and I here started as he spoke), in the

gradual yet certain condensation of an atmosphere of their own about the waters and the walls. The result was discoverable, he added, in that silent yet importunate and terrible influence which for centuries had moulded the destinies of his family, and which made *him* what I now saw him – what he was. Such opinions need no comment, and I will make none.

Our books – the books which, for years, had formed no small portion of the mental existence of the invalid – were, as might be supposed, in strict keeping with this character of phantasm. We pored together over such works as the Ververt et Chartreuse of Gresset; the Belphegor of Machiavelli; the Heaven and Hell of Swedenborg; the Subterranean Voyage of Nicholas Klimm of Holberg; the Chiromancy of Robert Flud, of Jean D'Indaginé, and of De la Chambre; the Journey into the Blue Distance of Tieck; and the City of the Sun of Campanella. One favourite volume was a small octavo edition of the *Directorium Inquisitorum*, by the Dominican Eymeric de Gironne; and there were passages in Pomponius Mela, about the old African Satyrs and (Œgipans, over which Usher would sit dreaming for hours. His chief delight, however, was found in the perusal of an exceedingly rare and curious book in quarto Gothic – the manual of a forgotten church – the *Vigiliæ Mortuorum secundum Chorum Ecclesiæ Maguntinæ*.

I could not help thinking of the wild ritual of this work, and of its probable influence upon the hypochondriac, when, one evening, having informed me abruptly that the lady Madeline was no more, he stated his intention of preserving her corpse for a fortnight, (previously to its final interment,) in one of the numerous vaults within the main walls of the building. The worldly reason, however, assigned for this singular proceeding, was one which I did not feel at liberty to dispute. The brother had been led to his resolution (so he told me) by consideration of the unusual character of the malady of the deceased, of certain obtrusive and eager inquiries on the part of her medical men, and of the remote and exposed situation of the burial-ground of the family. I will not deny that when I called to mind the sinister countenance of the person whom I met upon the staircase, on the day of my arrival at the house, I had no desire to oppose what I regarded as at best but a harmless, and by no means an unnatural, precaution.

At the request of Usher, I personally aided him in the

arrangements for the temporary entombment. The body having been encoffined, we two alone bore it to its rest. The vault in which we placed it (and which had been so long unopened that our torches, half smothered in its oppressive atmosphere, gave us little opportunity for investigation) was small, damp, and entirely without means of admission for light; lying, at great depth, immediately beneath that portion of the building in which was my own sleeping apartment. It had been used, apparently, in remote feudal times, for the worst purposes of a donjon-keep, and, in later days, as a place of deposit for powder, or some other highly combustible substance, as a portion of its floor, and the whole interior of a long archway through which we reached it, were carefully sheathed with copper. The door, of massive iron, had been, also, similarly protected. Its immense weight caused an unusually sharp grating sound, as it moved upon its hinges.

Having deposited our mournful burden upon tressels within this region of horror, we partially turned aside the yet unscrewed lid of the coffin, and looked upon the face of the tenant. A striking similitude between the brother and sister now first arrested my attention; and Usher, divining, perhaps, my thoughts, murmured out some few words from which I learned that the deceased and himself had been twins, and that sympathies of a scarcely intelligible nature had always existed between them. Our glances, however, rested not long upon the dead — for we could not regard her unawed. The disease which had thus entombed the lady in the maturity of youth, had left, as usual in all maladies of a strictly cataleptical character, the mockery of a faint blush upon the bosom and the face, and that suspiciously lingering smile upon the lip which is so terrible in death. We replaced and screwed down the lid, and, having secured the door of iron, made our way, with toil, into the scarcely less gloomy apartments of the upper portion of the house.

And now, some days of bitter grief having elapsed, an observable change came over the features of the mental disorder of my friend. His ordinary manner had vanished. His ordinary occupations were neglected or forgotten. He roamed from chamber to chamber with hurried, unequal, and objectless step. The pallor of his countenance had assumed, if possible, a more ghastly hue — but the luminousness of his eye had utterly gone out. The once occasional huskiness of his tone was heard no more; and a tremulous quaver, as if of extreme terror, habitually characterized his utterance. There were times, indeed, when I thought his unceasingly agitated mind was labouring with some oppressive secret, to divulge which he struggled for the necessary courage. At times, again, I was obliged to resolve all into the mere inexplicable vagaries of madness, for I beheld him gazing upon vacancy for long hours, in an attitude of the profoundest attention, as if listening to some imaginary sound. It was no wonder that his condition terrified – that it infected me. I felt creeping upon me, by slow yet certain degrees, the wild influences of his own fantastic yet impressive superstitions.

It was, especially, upon retiring to bed late in the night of the seventh or eighth day after the placing of the lady Madeline within the donjon, that I experienced the full power of such feelings. Sleep came not near my couch – while the hours waned and waned away. I struggled to reason off the nervousness which had dominion over me. I endeavoured to believe that much, if not all of what I felt was due to the bewildering influence of the gloomy furniture of the room – of the dark and tattered draperies, which, tortured into motion by the breath of a rising tempest, swayed fitfully to and fro upon the walls, and rustled uneasily about the decorations of the bed. But my efforts were fruitless. An irrepressible tremour gradually pervaded my frame; and, at length, there sat upon my very heart an incubus of utterly causeless alarm. Shaking this off with a gasp and a struggle, I uplifted myself upon the pillows, and, peering earnestly within the intense darkness of the chamber, hearkened – I know not why, except that an instinctive spirit prompted me – to certain low and indefinite sounds which came, through the pauses of the storm, at long intervals, I knew not whence. Overpowered by an intense sentiment of horror, unaccountable yet unendurable, I threw on my clothes with haste, (for I felt that I should sleep no more during the night,) and endeavoured to arouse myself from the pitiable condition into which I had fallen, by pacing rapidly to and fro through the apartment.

I had taken but few turns in this manner, when a light step on an adjoining staircase arrested my attention. I presently recognised it as that of Usher. In an instant afterward he rapped, with a gentle touch, at my door, and entered, bearing a lamp. His countenance was, as usual, cadaverously wan – but, moreover, there was a species of mad hilarity in his eyes – an evidently restrained *hysteria* in his whole demeanour. His air appalled me – but anything was preferable to the solitude which I had so long endured, and I even welcomed his presence as a relief.

'And you have not seen it?' he said abruptly, after having stared about him for some moments in silence – 'you have not then seen it? but, stay! you shall.' Thus speaking, and having carefully shaded his lamp, he hurried to one of the casements, and threw it freely open to the storm.

The impetuous fury of the entering gust nearly lifted us from our feet. It was, indeed, a tempestuous yet sternly beautiful night, and one wildly singular in its terror and its beauty. A whirlwind had apparently collected its force in our vicinity; for there were frequent and violent alterations in the direction of the wind; and the exceeding density of the clouds (which hung so low as to press upon the turrets of the house) did not prevent our perceiving the life-like velocity with which they flew careering from all points against each other, without passing away into the distance. I say that even their exceeding density did not prevent our perceiving this – yet we had no glimpse of the moon or stars – nor was there any flashing forth of the lightning. But the under surfaces of the huge masses of agitated vapour, as well as all terrestrial objects immediately around us, were glowing in the unnatural light of a faintly luminous and distinctly visible gaseous exhalation which hung about and enshrouded the mansion.

'You must not – you shall not behold this!' said I, shuddering, to Usher, as I led him, with a gentle violence, from the window to a seat. 'These appearances, which bewilder you, are merely electrical phenomena not uncommon – or it may be that they have their ghastly origin in the rank miasma of the tarn. Let us close this casement – the air is chilling and dangerous to your frame. Here is one of your favourite romances. I will read, and you shall listen – and so we will pass away this terrible night together.'

The antique volume which I had taken up was the 'Mad Trist' of Sir Launcelot Canning; but I had called it a favourite of Usher's more in sad jest than in earnest; for, in truth, there is little in its uncouth and unimaginative prolixity which could have had interest for the lofty and spiritual ideality of my friend. It was, however, the only book immediately at hand; and I indulged a vague hope that the excitement which now agitated the hypochondriac, might find relief (for the history of mental disorder is full of similar anomalies) even in the extremeness of the folly which I should read. Could I have judged, indeed, by the wild overstrained air of vivacity with which he hearkened, or apparently hearkened, to the words of the tale, I might well have congratulated myself upon the success of my design.

I had arrived at that well-known portion of the story where Ethelred, the hero of the Trist, having sought in vain for peaceable admission into the dwelling of the hermit, proceeds to make good an entrance by force. Here, it will be remembered, the words of the narrative run thus:.

'And Ethelred, who was by nature of a doughty heart, and who was now mighty withal, on account of the powerfulness of the wine which he had drunken, waited no longer to hold parley with the hermit, who, in sooth, was of an obstinate and maliceful turn, but, feeling the rain upon his shoulders, and fearing the rising of the tempest, uplifted his mace outright, and, with blows, made quickly room in the plankings of the door for his gauntleted hand; and now pulling therewith sturdily, he so cracked, and ripped, and tore all asunder, that the noise of the dry and hollow-sounding wood alarumed and reverberated throughout the forest.'

At the termination of this sentence I started and, for a moment, paused; for it appeared to me (although I at once concluded that my excited fancy had deceived me) — it appeared to me that, from some very remote portion of the mansion, there came, indistinctly, to my ears, what might have been, in its exact similarity of character, the echo (but a stifled and dull one certainly) of the very cracking and ripping sound which Sir Launcelot had so particularly described. It was, beyond doubt, the coincidence alone which had arrested my attention; for, amid the rattling of the sashes of the casements, and the ordinary commingled noises of the still increasing storm, the sound, in itself, had nothing, surely, which should have interested or disturbed me. I continued the story:

'But the good champion Ethelred, now entering within the door, was sore enraged and amazed to perceive no signal of the maliceful hermit; but, in the stead thereof, a dragon of a scaly and prodigious demeanour, and of a fiery tongue, which sate in guard before a palace of gold, with a floor of silver; and upon the wall there hung a shield of shining brass with this legend enwritten —

> Who entereth herein, a conqueror hath bin;
> Who slayeth the dragon, the shield he shall win.

And Ethelred uplifted his mace, and struck upon the head of the dragon, which fell before him, and gave up his pesty breath, with a shriek so horrid and harsh, and withal so piercing, that Ethelred had fain to close his ears with his hands against the dreadful noise of it, the like whereof was never before heard.'

Here again I paused abruptly, and now with a feeling of wild amazement – for there could be no doubt whatever that, in this instance, I did actually hear (although from what direction it proceeded I found it impossible to say) a low and apparently distant, but harsh, protracted, and most unusual screaming or grating sound – the exact counterpart of what my fancy had already conjured up for the dragon's unnatural shriek as described by the romancer.

Oppressed, as I certainly was, upon the occurrence of this second and most extraordinary coincidence, by a thousand conflicting sensations, in which wonder and extreme terror were predominant, I still retained sufficient presence of mind to avoid exciting, by any observation, the sensitive nervousness of my companion. I was by no means certain that he had noticed the sounds in question; although, assuredly, a strange alteration had, during the last few minutes, taken place in his demeanour. From a position fronting my own, he had gradually brought round his chair, so as to sit with his face to the door of the chamber; and thus I could but partially perceive his features, although I saw that his lips trembled as if he were murmuring inaudibly. His head had dropped upon his breast – yet I knew that he was not asleep, from the wide and rigid opening of the eye as I caught a glance of it in profile. The motion of his body, too, was at variance with this idea – for he rocked from side to side with a gentle yet constant and uniform sway. Having rapidly taken notice of all this I resumed the narrative of Sir Launcelot, which thus proceeded:

'And now, the champion, having escaped from the terrible fury of the dragon, bethinking himself of the brazen shield, and of the breaking up of the enchantment which was upon it, removed the carcass from out of the way before him, and approached valorously over the silver pavement of the castle to where the shield was upon the wall; which in sooth tarried not for his full coming, but fell down at his feet upon the silver floor, with a mighty great and terrible ringing sound.'

No sooner had these syllables passed my lips, than – as if a shield of brass had indeed, at the moment, fallen heavily upon a floor of silver – I became aware of a distinct, hollow, metallic, and clangorous, yet apparently muffled, reverberation. Completely unnerved, I leaped to my feet; but the measured rocking movement of Usher was undisturbed. I rushed to the chair in which he sat. His eyes were bent fixedly before him, and throughout his whole countenance there reigned a stony rigidity. But, as I placed my hand upon his shoulder, there came a strong shudder over his whole person; a sickly smile quivered about his lips; and I saw that he spoke in a low, hurried, and gibbering murmur, as if unconscious of my presence. Bending closely over him, I at length drank in the hideous import of his words.

'Not hear it? – yes, I hear it, and *have* heard it. Long – long – long – many minutes, many hours, many days, have I heard it – yet I dared not – oh, pity me, miserable wretch that I am! I dared not – I *dared* not speak! *We have put her living in the tomb!* Said I not that my senses were acute? I *now* tell you that I heard her first feeble movements in the hollow coffin. I heard them – many, many days ago – yet I dared not – I *dared not speak!* And now – tonight – Ethelred – ha! ha! the breaking of the hermit's door, and the death-cry of the dragon, and the clangour of the shield! – say, rather, the rending of her coffin, and the grating of the iron hinges of her prison, and her struggles within the coppered archway of the vault! Oh whither shall I fly? Will she not be here anon? Is she not hurrying to upbraid me for my haste? Have I not heard her footstep on the stair? Do I not distinguish that heavy and horrible beating of her heart? MADMAN!' – here he sprang furiously to his feet, and shrieked out his syllables, as if in the effort he were giving up his soul – 'MADMAN! I TELL YOU THAT SHE NOW STANDS WITHOUT THE DOOR!'

As if in the superhuman energy of his utterance there had been found the potency of a spell, the huge antique panels to which the speaker pointed threw slowly back, upon the instant, their ponderous and ebony jaws. It was the work of the rushing gust – but then without those doors there DID stand the lofty and enshrouded figure of the lady Madeline of Usher. There was blood upon her white robes, and the evidence of some bitter struggle upon every portion of her emaciated frame. For a moment she remained trembling and reeling to and fro upon the threshold, then, with a low moaning cry, fell heavily inward upon the person of her brother, and in her violent and now final death-agonies, bore him to the floor a corpse, and a victim to the terrors he had anticipated.

From that chamber, and from that mansion, I fled aghast. The storm was still abroad in all its wrath as I found myself crossing the old causeway. Suddenly there shot along the path a wild light, and I turned to see whence a gleam so unusual could have issued; for the vast house and its shadows were alone behind me. The radiance was that of the full, setting, and blood-red moon, which now shone vividly through that once barely discernible fissure, of which I have before spoken as extending from the roof of the building, in zigzag direction, to the base. While I gazed, this fissure rapidly widened – there came a fierce breath of the whirlwind – the entire orb of the satellite burst at once upon my sight – my brain reeled as I saw the mighty walls rushing asunder – there was a long tumultuous shouting sound like the voice of a thousand waters – and the deep and dank tarn at my feet closed sullenly and silently over the fragments of the 'HOUSE OF USHER.'

1839

HARRIET BEECHER STOWE
1811–1896

The Ghost in the Cap'n Brown House

'Now, Sam, tell us certain true, is there any such things as ghosts?'

'Be there ghosts?' said Sam, immediately translating into his vernacular grammar: 'wal, now, that are's jest the question, ye see.'

'Well, grandma thinks there are, and Aunt Lois thinks it's all nonsense. Why, Aunt Lois don't even believe the stories in Cotton Mather's "Magnalia." '

'Wanter know?' said Sam, with a tone of slow, languid meditation.

We were sitting on a bank of the Charles River, fishing. The soft melancholy red of evening was fading off in streaks on the glassy water, and the houses of Oldtown were beginning to loom through the gloom, solemn and ghostly. There are times and tones and moods of nature that make all the vulgar, daily real seem shadowy, vague, and supernatural, as if the outlines of this hard material present were fading into the invisible and unknown. So Oldtown, with its elm-trees, its great square white houses, its meeting-house and tavern and blacksmith's shop and mill, which at high noon seem as real and as commonplace as possible, at this hour of the evening were dreamy and solemn. They rose up blurred, indistinct, dark; here and there winking candles sent long lines through the shadows, and little drops of unforeseen rain rippled the sheeny darkness of the water.

'Wal, you see, boys, in them things it's jest as well to mind your granny. There's a consid'able sight o' gumption in grandmas. You look at the folks that's allus tellin' you what they don't believe – they don't believe this, and they don't believe that – and what sort o' folks is they? Why, like yer Aunt Lois, sort o' stringy and dry. There ain't no 'sorption got out o' not believin' nothin'.

'Lord a massy! we don't know nothin' 'bout them things. We hain't ben there, and can't say that there ain't no ghosts and sich; can we, now?'

We agreed to that fact, and sat a little closer to Sam in the gathering gloom.

'Tell us about the Cap'n Brown house, Sam.'

'Ye didn't never go over the Cap'n Brown house?'

No, we had not that advantage.

'Wal, yer see, Cap'n Brown he made all his money to sea, in furrin parts, and then come here to Oldtown to settle down.

'Now, there ain't no knowin' 'bout these 'ere old ship-masters, where they's ben, or what they's ben a doin', or how they got their money. Ask me no questions, and I'll tell ye no lies, is 'bout the best philosophy for them. Wal, it didn't do no good to ask Cap'n Brown questions too close, 'cause you didn't git no satisfaction. Nobody rightly knew 'bout who his folks was, or where they come from, and, ef a body asked him, he used to say that the very fust he know'd 'bout himself he was a young man walkin' the streets in London.

'But, yer see, boys, he hed money, and that is about all folks wanter know when a man comes to settle down. And he bought that 'are place, and built that 'are house. He built it all sea-cap'n fashion, so's to feel as much at home as he could. The parlor was like a ship's cabin. The table and chairs was fastened down to the floor, and the closets was made with holes to set the casters and the decanters and bottles in, jest's they be at sea; and there was stanchions to hold on by; and they say that blowy nights the cap'n used to fire up pretty well with his grog, till he hed about all he could carry, and then he'd set and hold on, and hear the wind blow, and kind o' feel out to sea right there to hum. There wasn't no Mis' Cap'n Brown, and there didn't seem likely to be none. And whether there ever hed been one, nobody know'd. He hed an old black Guinea nigger-woman, named Quassia, that did his work. She was shaped pretty much like one o' these 'ere great crookneck-squashes. She wa'n't no gret beauty, I can tell you; and she used to wear a gret red turban and a yaller short gown and red petticoat, and a gret string o' gold beads round her neck, and gret big gold hoops in her ears, made right in the middle o' Africa among the heathen there. For all she was black, she thought a heap o' herself, and was consid'ble sort o predominative over the cap'n. Lordy massy! boys, it's allus so. Get a man and a woman together – any sort o' woman you're a mind to, don't care who 'tis – and one way or another she gets the rule over him, and he jest has to train to her fife. Some does it one way, and some does it another; some does it by jawin', and some does it by kissin', and some does it by faculty and contrivance; but one way or another they allers does it. Old Cap'n Brown was a good stout, stocky kind o' John Bull sort o' fellow, and a good judge o' sperits, and allers kep' the best in them are cupboards o' his'n; but, fust and last, things in his house went pretty much as old Quassia said.

'Folks got to kind o' respectin' Quassia. She come to meetin' Sunday regular, and sot all fixed up in red and yaller and green, with glass beads and what not, lookin' for all the world like one o' them ugly Indian idols; but she was well-behaved as any Christian. She was a master hand at cookin'. Her bread and biscuits couldn't be beat, and no couldn't her pies, and there wa'n't no such pound-cake as she made nowhere. Wal, this 'ere story I'm a goin' to tell you was told me by Cinthy Pendleton. There ain't a more respectable gal, old or young, than Cinthy nowheres. She lives over to Sherburne now, and I hear tell she's sot up a manty-makin' business; but then she used to do tailorin' in Oldtown. She was a member o' the church, and a good Christian as ever was. Wal, ye see, Quassia she got Cinthy to come up and spend a week to the Cap'n Brown house, a doin' tailorin' and a fixin' over his close: 'twas along toward the fust o' March. Cinthy she sot by the fire in the front parlor with her goose and her press-board and her work: for there wa'n't no company callin', and the snow was drifted four feet deep right across the front door; so there wa'n't much danger o' any body comin' in. And the cap'n he was a perlite man to wimmen; and Cinthy she liked it jest as well not to have company, 'cause the cap'n he'd make himself entertainin' tellin' on her sea-stories, and all about his adventures among the Ammonites, and Perresites, and Jebusites, and all sorts o' heathen people he'd been among.

'Wal, that 'are week there come on the master snow-storm. Of all the snow-storms that hed ben, that 'are was the beater; and I tell you the wind blew as if 'twas the last chance it was ever goin' to hev. Wal, it's kind o' scary like to be shet up in a lone house with all natur' a kind o' breakin' out, and goin' on so, and the snow a comin' down so thick ye can't see 'cross the street, and the wind a pipin' and a squeelin' and a rumblin' and a tumblin' fust down this chimney and then down that. I tell you, it sort o' sets a feller thinkin' o' the three great things – death, judgment, and etarnaty; and I don't care who the folks is, nor how good they be, there's times when they must be feelin' putty consid'able solemn.

'Wal, Cinthy she said she kind o' felt so along, and she hed a sort o' queer feelin' come over her as if there was somebody or somethin' round the house more'n appeared. She said she sort o' felt it in the air; but it seemed to her silly, and she tried to get over it. But two or three times, she said, when it got to be dusk, she felt somebody go by her up the stairs. The front entry wa'n't very light in the day time, and in the storm, come five o'clock, it was so dark that all you could see was jest a gleam o' somethin', and two or three times when she started to go up stairs she see a soft white suthin' that seemed goin' up before her, and she stopped with her heart a beatin' like a trip-hammer, and she sort o' saw it go up and along the entry to the cap'n's door, and then it seemed to go right through, 'cause the door didn't open.

'Wal, Cinthy says she to old Quassia, says she, "Is there anybody lives in this house but us?"

' "Anybody lives here?" says Quassia: "what you mean?" says she.

'Says Cinthy, "I thought somebody went past me on the stairs last night and to-night."

'Lordy massy! how old Quassia did screech and laugh. "Good Lord!" says she, "how foolish white folks is! Somebody went past you? Was't the capt'in?"

' "No, it wa'n't the cap'n," says she: "it was somethin' soft and white, and moved very still; it was like somethin' in the air," says she.

'Then Quassia she haw-hawed louder. Says she, "It's hysterikes, Miss Cinthy; that's all it is."

'Wal, Cinthy she was kind o' 'shamed, but for all that she couldn't help herself. Sometimes evenin's she'd be a settin' with the cap'n, and she'd think she'd hear somebody a movin' in his room overhead; and she knowed it wa'n't Quassia, 'cause Quassia was ironin' in the kitchen. She took pains once or twice to find out that 'are.

'Wal, you see, the cap'n's room was the gret front upper chamber over the parlor, and then right opposite to it was the gret spare chamber where Cinthy slept. It was jest as grand as could be, with a gret four-post mahogany bedstead and damask curtains brought over from England; but it was cold enough to freeze a white bear solid – the way spare chambers allers is. Then there was the entry between, run straight through the house: one side was old Quassia's room, and the other was a sort o' storeroom, where the old cap'n kep' all sorts o' traps.

'Wal, Cinthy she kep' a hevin' things happen and a seein'

things, till she didn't railly know what was in it. Once when she come into the parlor jest at sundown, she was sure she see a white figure a vanishin' out o' the door that went towards the side entry. She said it was so dusk, that all she could see was jest this white figure, and it jest went out still as a cat as she come in.

'Wal, Cinthy didn't like to speak to the cap'n about it. She was a close woman, putty prudent, Cinthy was.

'But one night, 'bout the middle o' the week, this 'ere thing kind o' come to a crisis.

'Cinthy said she'd ben up putty late a sewin' and a finishin' off down in the parlor; and the cap'n he sot up with her, and was consid'able cheerful and entertainin', tellin' her all about things over in the Bermudys, and off to Chiny and Japan, and round the world ginerally. The storm that hed been a blowin' all the week was about as furious as ever; and the cap'n he stirred up a mess o' flip, and had it for her hot to go to bed on. He was a good-natured critter, and allers had feelin's for lone women; and I s'pose he knew 'twas sort o' desolate for Cinthy.

'Wal, takin' the flip so right the last thing afore goin' to bed, she went right off to sleep as sound as a nut, and slep' on till somewhere about mornin', when she said somethin' waked her broad awake in a minute. Her eyes flew wide open like a spring, and the storm hed gone down and the moon come out: and there, standin' right in the moonlight by her bed, was a woman jest as white as a sheet, with black hair hangin' down to her waist, and the brightest, mourn-fullest black eyes you ever see. She stood there lookin' right at Cinthy; and Cinthy thinks that was what waked her up; 'cause, you know, ef anybody stands and looks steady at folks asleep it's apt to wake 'em.

'Any way, Cinthy said she felt jest as ef she was turnin' to stone. She couldn't move nor speak. She lay a minute, and then she shut her eyes, and begun to say her prayers; and a minute after she opened 'em, and it was gone.

'Cinthy was a sensible gal, and one that allers hed her thoughts about her; and she jest got up and put a shawl round her shoulders, and went first and looked at the doors, and they was both on 'em locked jest as she left 'em when she went to bed. Then she looked under the bed and in the closet, and felt all round the room: where she couldn't see she felt her way, and there wa'n't nothin' there.

'Wal, next mornin' Cinthy got up and went home, and she kep'

it to herself a good while. Finally, one day when she was workin'
to our house she told Hepsy about it, and Hepsy she told me.'

'Well, Sam,' we said, after a pause, in which we heard only the
rustle of leaves and the ticking of branches against each other,
'what do you suppose it was?'

'Wal, there 'tis; you know jest as much about it as I do. Hepsy
told Cinthy it might 'a' ben a dream; so it might, but Cinthy she
was sure it wa'n't a dream, 'cause she remembers plain hearin' the
old clock on the stairs strike four while she had her eyes open
lookin' at the woman; and then she only shet 'em a minute, jest to
say "Now I lay me," and opened 'em and she was gone.

'Wal, Cinthy told Hepsy, and Hepsy she kep' it putty close. She
didn't tell it to nobody expect Aunt Sally Dickerson and the
Widder Bije Smith and your Grandma Badger and the minister's
wife and they every one o' 'em 'greed it ought to be kep close,
'cause it would make talk. Wal, come spring somehow or other it
seemed to 'a' got all over Oldtown. I heard on 't to the store and
up to the tavern; and Jake Marshall he says to me one day,
"What's this 'ere about the cap'n's house?" And the Widder
Loker she says to me, "There's ben a ghost seen in the cap'n's
house;" and I heard on 't clear over to Needham and Sherburne.

'Some o' the women they drew themselves up putty stiff and
proper. Your Aunt Lois was one on 'em.

' "Ghost," says she; "don't tell me! Perhaps it would be best ef
'twas a ghost," says she. She didn't think there ought to be no sich
doin's in nobody's house; and your grandma she shet her up, and
told her she didn't oughter talk so.'

'Talk how?' said I, interrupting Sam with wonder. 'What did
Aunt Lois mean?'

'Why, you see,' said Sam mysteriously, 'there allers is folks in
every town that's jest like the Sadducees in old times: they won't
believe in angel nor sperit, no way you can fix it; and ef things is
seen and done in a house, why, they say, it's 'cause there's
somebody there; there's some sort o' deviltry or trick about it.

'So the story got round that there was a woman kep' private in
Cap'n Brown's house, and that he brought her from furrin parts;
and it growed and growed, till there was all sorts o' ways o' tellin
on 't.

'Some said they'd seen her a settin at an open winder. Some said
that moonlight nights they'd see her a walkin' out in the back
garden kind o' in and out 'mong the bean-poles and squash-vines.

'You see, it come on spring and summer; and the winders o' the Cap'n Brown house stood open, and folks was all a watchin' on 'em day and night. Aunt Sally Dickerson told the minister's wife that she'd seen in plain daylight a woman a settin' at the chamber winder atween four and five o'clock in the mornin' – jist a settin' a lookin' out and a doin' nothin',' like anybody else. She was very white and pale, and had black eyes.

'Some said that it was a nun the cap'n had brought away from a Roman Catholic convent in Spain, and some said he'd got her out o' the Inquisition.

'Aunt Sally said she thought the minister ought to call and inquire why she didn't come to meetin', and who she was, and all about her: 'cause, you see, she said it might be all right enough ef folks only know'd jest how things was; but ef they didn't, why, folks will talk.'

'Well, did the minister do it?'

'What, Parson Lothrop? Wal, no, he didn't. He made a call on the cap'n in a regular way, and asked arter his health and all his family. But the cap'n he seemed jest as jolly and chipper as a spring robin, and he gin the minister some o' his old Jamaiky; and the minister he come away and said he didn't see nothin'; and no he didn't. Folks never does see nothin' when they aint' lookin' where 'tis. Fact is, Parson Lothrop wa'n't fond o' interferin'; he was a master hand to slick things over. Your grandma she used to mourn about it, 'cause she said he never gin no p'int to the doctrines; but 'twas all of a piece, he kind o' took every thing the smooth way.

'But your grandma she believed in the ghost, and so did Lady Lothrop. I was up to her house t'other day fixin' a door-knob, and says she, "Sam your wife told me a strange story about the Cap'n Brown house."

' "Yes, ma'am, she did," says I.

' "Well, what do you think of it?" says she.

' "Wal, sometimes I think, and then agin I don't know," says I. "There's Cinthy she's a member o' the church and a good pious gal," says I.

' "Yes, Sam," says Lady Lothrop, says she; "and Sam," says she, "it is jest like something that happened once to my grandmother when she was livin' in the old Province House in Bostin." Says she, "These 'ere things is the mysteries of Providence, and it's jest as well not to have 'em too much talked about."

' "Jest so," says I – "jest so. That 'are's what every woman I've talked with says; and I guess, fust and last, I've talked with twenty – good, safe church-members – and they's every one o' opinion that this 'ere oughtn't to be talked about. Why, over to the deakin's t'other night we went it all over as much as two or three hours, and we concluded that the best way was to keep quite still about it; and that's jest what they say over to Needham and Sherburne. I've been all round a hushin' this 'ere up, and I hain't found but a few people that hedn't the particulars one way or another." This 'ere was what I says to Lady Lothrop. The fact was, I never did see no report spread so, nor make sich sort o' sarchin's o' heart, as this 'ere. It railly did beat all; 'cause, ef 'twas a ghost, why there was the p'int proved, ye see. Cinthy's a church-member, and she *see* it, and got right up and sarched the room: but then agin, ef 'twas a woman, why that 'are was kind o' awful; it gives cause, ye see, for thinkin' all sorts o' things. There was Cap'n Brown, to be sure, he wa'n't a church-member; but yet he was as honest and regular a man as any goin', as fur as any on us could see. To be sure, nobody know'd where he come from but that wa'n't no reason agin' him: this 'ere might a ben a crazy sister, or some poor critter that he took out o' the best o' motives; and the Scriptur' says, "Charity hopeth all things." But then, ye see, folks will talk – that 'are's the pester o' all these things – and they did some on 'em talk consid'able strong about the cap'n; but somehow or other, there didn't nobody come to the p'int o' facin' on him down, and sayin' square out, "Cap'n Brown, have you got a woman in your house, or hain't you? or is it a ghost, or what is it?" Folks somehow never does come to that. Ye see, there was the cap'n so respectable, a settin' up every Sunday there in his pew, with his ruffles round his hands and his red broadcloth cloak and his cocked hat. Why, folk's hearts sort o' failed 'em when it come to sayin' any thing right to him. They thought and kind o whispered round that the minister or the deakins oughter do it: but Lordy massy! ministers, I s'pose, has feelin's like the rest of us; they don't want to eat all the hard cheeses that nobody else won't eat. Anyhow, there wasn't nothin' said direct to the cap'n; and jest for want o' that all the folks in Oldtown kep' a bilin' and a bilin' like a kettle o' soap, till it seemed all the time as if they'd bile over.

'Some o' the wimmen tried to get somethin' out o' Quassy. Lordy massy! you might as well 'a' tried to get it out an old tom-turkey; that'll strut and gobble and quitter, and drag his wings on the ground, and fly at you, but won't say nothin'. Quassy she screeched her queer sort o' laugh; and she told 'em that they was a makin' fools o' themselves, and that the cap'n's matters wa'n't none o' their bisness; and that was true enough. As to goin' into Quassia's room, or into any o' the store-rooms or closets she kep' the keys of, you might as well hev gone into a lion's den. She kep' all her places locked up tight; and there was no gettin' at nothin' in the Cap'n Brown house, else I believe some o' the wimmen would 'a' sent a search-warrant.'

'Well,' said I, 'what came of it? Didn't anybody ever find out?'

'Wal,' said Sam, 'it come to an end sort o', and didn't come to an end. It was jest this 'ere way. You see, along in October, jest in the cider-makin' time, Abel Flint he was took down with dysentery and died. You 'member the Flint house: it stood on a little rise o' ground jest lookin' over towards the Brown house. Wal, there was Aunt Sally Dickerson and the Widder Bije Smith, they set up with the corpse. He was laid out in the back chamber, you see, over the milk-room and kitchen; but there was cold victuals and sich in the front chamber where the watchers sot. Wal, now, Aunt Sally she told me that between three and four o'clock she heard wheels a rumblin', and she went to the winder, and it was clear starlight; and she see a coach come up to the Cap'n Brown house; and she see the cap'n come out bringin' a woman all wrapped in a cloak, and old Quassy came arter with her arms full o' bundles; and he put her into the kerridge, and shet her in, and it driv off; and she see old Quassy stand lookin' over the fence arter it. She tried to wake up the widder, but 'twas towards mornin', and the widder allers was a hard sleeper; so there wa'n't no witness but her.'

'Well, then, it wasn't a ghost,' said I, 'after all, and it *was* a woman.'

'Wal, there 'tis, you see. Folks don't know that 'are yit, 'cause there it's jest as broad as 'tis long. Now, look at it. There's Cinthy, she's a good, pious gal: she locks her chamber doors, both on 'em, and goes to bed, and wakes up in the night, and there's a woman there. She jest shets her eyes, and the woman's gone. She gits up and looks, and both doors is locked jest as she left 'em. That 'ere woman wa'n't flesh and blood now, no way – not such flesh and blood as we knows on; but then they say Cinthy might hev dreamed it!

'Wal, now, look at it t'other way. There's Aunt Sally Dickerson;

she's a good woman and a church-member: wal, she sees a woman in a cloak with all her bundles brought out o' Cap'n Brown's house, and put into a kerridge, and driv off, atween three and four o'clock in the mornin'. Wal, that 'ere shows there must 'a' ben a real live woman kep' there privately, and so what Cinthy saw wasn't a ghost.

'Wal, now, Cinthy says Aunt Sally might 'a' dreamed it – that she got her head so full o' stories about the Cap'n Brown house, and watched it till she got asleep, and hed this 'ere dream; and, as there didn't nobody else see it, it might 'a' ben, you know. Aunt Sally's clear she didn't dream, and then agin Cinthy's clear *she* didn't dream; but which on 'em was awake, or which on 'em was asleep, is what ain't settled in Oldtown yet.'

1872

HERMAN MELVILLE
1819–1891

Bartleby The Scrivener

A Story of Wall Street

I am a rather elderly man. The nature of my avocations for the last thirty years has brought me into more than ordinary contact with what would seem an interesting and somewhat singular set of men, of whom as yet nothing that I know of has ever been written – I mean the law-copyists or scriveners. I have known very many of them, professionally and privately, and if I pleased, could relate divers histories, at which good-natured gentlemen might smile, and sentimental souls might weep. But I waive the biographies of all other scriveners for a few passages in the life of Bartleby, who was a scrivener the strangest I ever saw or heard of. While of other law-copyists I might write the complete life, of Bartleby nothing of that sort can be done. I believe that no materials exist for a full and satisfactory biography of this man. It is an irreparable loss to literature. Bartleby was one of those beings of whom nothing is ascertainable, except from the original sources, and in his case those are very small. What my own astonished eyes saw of Bartleby, *that* is all I know of him, except, indeed, one vague report which will appear in the sequel.

Ere introducing the scrivener, as he first appeared to me, it is fit I make some mention of myself, my *employés*, my business, my chambers, and general surroundings; because some such description is indispensable to an adequate understanding of the chief character about to be presented.

Imprimis: I am a man who, from his youth upward, has been filled with a profound conviction that the easiest way of life is the best. Hence, though I belong to a profession proverbially energetic and nervous, even to turbulence, at times, yet nothing of that sort have I ever suffered to invade my peace. I am one of those unambitious lawyers who never addresses a jury, or in any way draws down public applause; but in the cool tranquillity of a snug retreat, do a snug business among rich men's bonds and mortgages and title-deeds. All who know me, consider me an eminently *safe* man. The late John Jacob Astor, a personage little given to poetic enthusiasm, had no hesitation in pronouncing my first grand point to be prudence; my next, method. I do not speak it in vanity, but simply record the fact, that I was not unemployed in my profession by the late John Jacob Astor; a name which, I admit, I love to repeat, for it hath a rounded and orbicular sound to it, and rings like unto bullion. I will freely add, that I was not insensible to the late John Jacob Astor's good opinion.

Some time prior to the period at which this little history begins, my avocations had been largely increased. The good old office, now extinct in the State of New York, of a Master in Chancery, had been conferred upon me. It was not a very arduous office, but very pleasantly remunerative. I seldom lose my temper; much more seldom indulge in dangerous indignation at wrongs and outrages; but I must be permitted to be rash here and declare, that I consider the sudden and violent abrogation of the office of Master in Chancery, by the new Constitution, as a — premature act; inasmuch as I had counted upon a life-lease of the profits, whereas I only received those of a few short years. But this is by the way.

My chambers were upstairs at No. — Wall Street. At one end they looked upon the white wall of the interior of a spacious sky-light shaft, penetrating the building from top to bottom. This view might have been considered rather tame than otherwise, deficient in what landscape painters call 'life'. But if so, the view from the other end of my chambers offered, at least, a contrast, if nothing more. In that direction my windows commanded an unobstructed view of a lofty brick wall, black by age and everlasting shade; which wall required no spy-glass to bring out its lurking beauties, but for the benefit of all near-sighted spectators, was pushed up to within ten feet of my window panes. Owing to the great height of the surrounding buildings, and my chambers being on the second floor, the interval between this wall and mine not a little resembled a huge square cistern.

At the period just preceding the advent of Bartleby, I had two persons as copyists in my employment, and a promising lad as an office-boy. First, Turkey; second, Nippers; third, Ginger Nut. These may seem names, the like of which are not usually found in the Directory. In truth they were nicknames, mutually conferred upon each other by my three clerks, and were deemed expressive of their respective persons or characters. Turkey was a short, pursy Englishman of about my own age, that is, somewhere not far from sixty. In the morning, one might say, his face was of a fine florid hue, but after twelve o'clock, meridian – his dinner hour – it blazed like a grate full of Christmas coals; and continued blazing – but, as it were, with a gradual wane – till 6 o'clock P.M. or thereabouts, after which I saw no more of the proprietor of the face, which, gaining its meridian with the sun, seemed to set with it, to rise, culminate, and decline the following day, with the like regularity and undiminished glory. There are many singular coincidences I have known in the course of my life, not the least among which was the fact, that exactly when Turkey displayed his fullest beams from his red and radiant countenance, just then, too, at that critical moment, began the daily period when I considered his business capacities as seriously disturbed for the remainder of the twenty-four hours. Not that he was absolutely idle, or averse to business then; far from it. The difficulty was, he was apt to be altogether too energetic. There was a strange, inflamed, flurried, flighty recklessness of activity about him. He would be incautious in dipping his pen into his inkstand. All his blots upon my documents, were dropped there after twelve o'clock, meridian. Indeed, not only would he be reckless and sadly given to making blots in the afternoon, but some days he went further, and was rather noisy. At such times, too, his face flamed with augmented blazonry, as if cannel coal had been heaped on anthracite. He made an unpleasant racket with his chair; spilled his sand-box; in mending his pens, impatiently split them all to pieces, and threw them on the floor in a sudden passion; stood up and leaned over his table, boxing his papers about in a most indecorous manner, very sad to behold in an elderly man like him. Nevertheless, as he was in many ways a most valuable person to me, and all the time before twelve o'clock, meridian, was the quickest, steadiest creature, too, accomplishing a great deal of work in a style not easy to be matched – for these reasons, I was willing to overlook his eccentricities, though indeed, occasionally, I remonstrated with him. I did this very gently, however, because, though the civilest, nay, the blandest and most reverential of men in the morning, yet in the afternoon he was disposed, upon provocation, to be slightly rash with his tongue, in fact, insolent. Now, valuing his morning services as I did, and resolving not to lose them – yet, at the same time, made uncomfortable by his inflamed ways after twelve o'clock; and being a man of peace, unwilling by my admonitions to call forth unseemly retorts from him – I took upon me, one Saturday noon (he was always worse on Saturdays), to hint to him, very kindly, that perhaps now that he was growing old, it might be well to abridge his labours; in short, he need not come to my chambers after twelve o'clock, but, dinner over, had best go home to his lodgings and rest himself till tea-time. But no; he insisted upon his afternoon devotions. His countenance became intolerably fervid, as he oratorically assured me – gesticulating, with a long ruler, at the other side of the room – that if his services in the morning were useful, how indispensable, then, in the afternoon?

'With submission, sir,' said Turkey on this occasion, 'I consider myself your right-hand man. In the morning I but marshal and deploy my columns; but in the afternoon I put myself at their head, and gallantly charge the foe, thus!' – and he made a violent thrust with the ruler.

'But the blots, Turkey,' intimated I.

'True – but, with submission, sir, behold these hairs! I am getting old. Surely, sir, a blot or two of a warm afternoon is not to be severely urged against grey hairs. Old age – even if it blot the page – is honourable. With submission, sir, we *both* are getting old.'

This appeal to my fellow-feeling was hardly to be resisted. At all events, I saw that go he would not. So I made up my mind to let him stay, resolving, nevertheless, to see to it, that during the afternoon he had to do with my less important papers.

Nippers, the second on my list, was a whiskered, sallow, and, upon the whole, rather piratical-looking young man of about five and twenty. I always deemed him the victim of two evil powers – ambition and indigestion. The ambition was evinced by a certain impatience of the duties of a mere copyist – an unwarrantable usurpation of strictly professional affairs, such as the original drawing up of legal documents. The indigestion seemed betokened in the occasional nervous testiness and grinning irritability, causing the teeth to audibly grind together over mistakes committed in copying; unnecessary maledictions, hissed, rather than spoken, in the heat of business; and especially by a continual discontent with the height of the table where he worked. Though of a very ingenious mechanical turn, Nippers could never get this table to suit him. He put chips under it, blocks of various sorts, bits of pasteboard, and at last went so far as to attempt an exquisite adjustment by final pieces of folded blotting-paper. But no invention would answer. If, for the sake of easing his back, he brought the table lid at a sharp angle well up toward his chin, and wrote there like a man using the steep roof of a Dutch house for his desk – then he declared that it stopped the circulation in his arms. If now he lowered the table to his waistbands, and stooped over it in writing, then there was a sore aching in his back. In short, the truth of the matter was, Nippers knew not what he wanted. Or, if he wanted anything, it was to be rid of a scrivener's table altogether. Among the manifestations of his diseased ambition was a fondness he had for receiving visits from certain ambiguous-looking fellows in seedy coats, whom he called his clients. Indeed I was aware that not only was he, at times, considerable of a ward-politician, but he occasionally did a little business at the Justices' courts, and was not unknown on the steps of the Tombs. I have good reason to believe, however, that one individual who called upon him at my chambers, and who, with a grand air, he insisted was his client, was no other than a dun, and the alleged title-deed, a bill. But with all his failings, and the annoyances he caused me, Nippers, like his compatriot Turkey, was a very useful man to me; wrote a neat, swift hand; and, when he chose, was not deficient in a gentlemanly sort of deportment. Added to this, he always dressed in a gentlemanly sort of way; and so, incidentally, reflected credit upon my chambers. Whereas with respect to Turkey, I had much ado to keep him from being a reproach to me. His clothes were apt to look oily and smell of eating-houses. He wore his pantaloons very loose and baggy in summer. His coats were execrable; his hat not to be handled. But while the hat was a thing of indifference to me, inasmuch as his natural civility and deference, as a dependent Englishman, always led him to doff it the moment he entered the room, yet his coat was another matter. Concerning his coats, I reasoned with him; but with no effect. The truth was, I suppose, that a man with so small an income, could not afford to sport such a lustrous face and a lustrous coat at one and the same time. As Nippers once observed, Turkey's money went chiefly for red ink. One winter day I presented Turkey with a highly-respectable looking coat of my own, a padded grey coat, of a most comfortable warmth, and which buttoned straight up from the knee to the neck. I thought Turkey would appreciate the favour, and abate his rashness and obstreperousness of afternoons. But no. I verily believe that buttoning himself up in so downy and blanket-like a coat had a pernicious effect upon him; upon the same principle that too much oats are bad for horses. In fact, precisely as a rash, restive horse is said to feel his oats, so Turkey felt his coat. It made him insolent. He was a man whom prosperity harmed.

Though concerning the self-indulgent habits of Turkey I had my own private surmises, yet touching Nippers I was well persuaded that whatever might be his faults in other respects, he was, at least, a temperate young man. But, indeed, nature herself seemed to have been his vintner, and at his birth charged him so thoroughly with an irritable, brandy-like disposition, that all subsequent potations were needless. When I consider how, amid the stillness of my chambers, Nippers would sometimes impatiently rise from his seat, and stooping over his table, spread his arms wide apart, seize the whole desk, and move it, and jerk it, with a grim, grinding motion on the floor, as if the table were a perverse voluntary agent, intent on thwarting and vexing him; I plainly perceive that for Nippers, brandy and water were altogether superfluous.

It was fortunate for me that, owing to its peculiar cause – indigestion – the irritability and consequent nervousness of Nippers, were mainly observable in the morning, while in the afternoon he was comparatively mild. So that Turkey's paroxysms only coming on about twelve o'clock, I never had to do with their eccentricities at one time. Their fits relieved each other like guards. When Nipper's was on, Turkey's was off; and *vice versa*. This was a good natural arrangement under the circumstances.

Ginger Nut, the third on my list, was a lad some twelve years old. His father was a carman, ambitious of seeing his son on the bench instead of a cart, before he died. So he sent him to my office as student at law, errand boy, and cleaner and sweeper, at the rate of one dollar a week. He had a little desk to himself, but he did not use it much. Upon inspection the drawer exhibited a great array of the shells of various sorts of nuts. Indeed, to this quick-witted youth the whole noble science of the law was contained in a nutshell. Not the least among the employments of Ginger Nut, as well as one which he discharged with the most alacrity, was his duty as cake and apple purveyor for Turkey and Nippers. Copying law papers being proverbially a dry, husky sort of business, my two scriveners were fain to moisten their mouths very often with Spitzenbergs to be had at the numerous stalls nigh the Custom House and Post Office. Also, they sent Ginger Nut very frequently for that peculiar cake — small, flat, round, and very spicy — after which he had been named by them. Of a cold morning, when business was but dull, Turkey would gobble up scores of these cakes, as if they were mere wafers — indeed they sell them at the rate of six or eight for a penny — the scrape of his pen blending with the crunching of the crisp particles in his mouth. Of all the fiery afternoon blunders and flurried rashness of Turkey, was his once moistening a ginger-cake between his lips, and clapping it on to a mortgage for a seal. I came within an ace of dismissing him then. But he mollified me by making an oriental bow and saying — 'With submission, sir, it was generous of me to find you in stationery on my own account.'

Now my original business — that of a conveyancer and title hunter, and drawer-up of recondite documents of all sorts — was considerably increased by receiving the master's office. There was now great work for scriveners. Not only must I push the clerks already with me, but I must have additional help. In answer to my advertisement, a motionless young man one morning stood upon my office threshold, the door being open, for it was summer. I can see that figure now — pallidly neat, pitiably respectable, incurably forlorn! It was Bartleby.

After a few words touching his qualifications, I engaged him, glad to have among my corps of copyists a man of so singularly sedate an aspect, which I thought might operate beneficially upon the flighty temper of Turkey, and the fiery one of Nippers.

I should have stated before that ground glass folding-doors divided my premises into two parts, one of which was occupied by my scriveners, the other by myself. According to my humour I threw open these doors, or closed them. I resolved to assign Bartleby a corner by the folding-doors, but on my side of them, so as to have this quiet man within easy call, in case any trifling thing was to be done. I placed his desk close up to a small side-window in that part of the room, a window which originally had afforded a lateral view of certain grimy back-yards and bricks, but which, owing to subsequent erections, commanded at present no view at all, though it gave some light. Within three feet of the panes was a wall, and the light came down from far above, between two lofty buildings, as from a very small opening in a dome. Still further to a satisfactory arrangement, I procured a high green folding screen, which might entirely isolate Bartleby from my sight, though not remove him from my voice. And thus, in a manner, privacy and society was conjoined.

At first Bartleby did an extraordinary quantity of writing. As if long famishing for something to copy, he seemed to gorge himself on my documents. There was no pause for digestion. He ran a day and night line, copying by sun-light and by candle-light. I should have been quite delighted with his application, had he been cheerfully industrious. But he wrote on silently, palely, mechanically.

It is, of course, an indispensable part of a scrivener's business to verify the accuracy of his copy, word by word. Where there are two or more scriveners in an office, they assist each other in this examination, one reading from the copy, the other holding the original. It is a very dull, wearisome, and lethargic affair. I can readily imagine that to some sanguine temperaments it would be altogether intolerable. For example, I cannot credit that the mettlesome poet Byron would have contentedly sat down with Bartleby to examine a law document of, say five hundred pages, closely written in a crimpy hand.

Now and then, in the haste of business, it had been my habit to assist in comparing some brief document myself, calling Turkey or Nippers for this purpose. One object I had in placing Bartleby so handy to me behind the screen, was to avail myself of his services on such trivial occasions. It was on the third day, I think, of his being with me, and before any necessity had arisen for having his own writing examined, that, being much hurried to complete a small affair I had in hand, I abruptly called to Bartleby. In my haste and natural expectancy of instant compliance, I sat with my head bent over the original on my desk, and my right hand sideways, and somewhat nervously extended with the copy, so that immediately upon emerging from his retreat, Bartleby might snatch it and proceed to business without the least delay.

In this very attitude did I sit when I called to him, rapidly stating what it was I wanted him to do – namely, to examine a small paper with me. Imagine my surprise, nay, my consternation, when without moving from his privacy, Bartleby in a singularly mild, firm voice, replied, 'I would prefer not to.'

I sat awhile in perfect silence, rallying my stunned faculties.

Immediately it occurred to me that my ears had deceived me, or Bartleby had entirely misunderstood my meaning. I repeated my request in the clearest tone I could assume. But in quite as clear a one came the previous reply, 'I would prefer not to.'

'Prefer not to,' echoed I, rising in high excitement, and crossing the room with a stride. 'What do you mean? Are you moonstruck? I want you to help me compare this sheet here – take it,' and I thrust it toward him.

'I would prefer not to,' said he.

I looked at him steadfastly. His face was leanly composed; his grey eye dimly calm. Not a wrinkle of agitation rippled him. Had there been at least uneasiness, anger, impatience or impertinence in his manner; in other words, had there been anything ordinarily human about him; doubtless I should have violently dismissed him from the premises. But as it was, I should have as soon thought of turning my pale plaster-of-paris bust of Cicero out of doors. I stood gazing at him awhile, as he went on with his own writing, and then reseated myself at my desk. This is very strange, thought I. What had one best do? But my business hurried me. I concluded to forget the matter for the present, reserving it for my future leisure. So calling Nippers from the other room, the paper was speedily examined.

A few days after this, Bartleby concluded four lengthy documents, being quadruplicates of a week's testimony taken before me in my High Court of Chancery. It became necessary to examine them. It was an important suit, and great accuracy was imperative. Having all things arranged, I called Turkey, Nippers and Ginger Nut from the next room, meaning to place the four copies in the hands of my four clerks, while I should read from the original. Accordingly Turkey, Nippers and Ginger Nut had taken their seats in a row, each with his document in hand, when I called to Bartleby to join this interesting group.

'Bartleby! quick, I am waiting.'

I heard a slow scrape of his chair legs on the uncarpeted floor, and soon he appeared standing at the entrance of his hermitage.

'What is wanted?' said he mildly.

'The copies, the copies,' said I hurriedly. 'We are going to examine them. There' – and I held toward him the fourth quadruplicate.

'I would prefer not to,' he said, and gently disappeared behind the screen.

For a few moments I was turned into a pillar of salt, standing at the head of my seated column of clerks. Recovering myself, I advanced toward the screen, and demanded the reason for such extraordinary conduct.

'*Why* do you refuse?'

'I would prefer not to.'

With any other man I should have flown outright into a dreadful passion, scorned all further words, and thrust him ignominiously from my presence. But there was something about Bartleby that not only strangely disarmed me, but in a wonderful manner touched and disconcerted me. I began to reason with him.

'These are your own copies we are about to examine. It is labour saving to you, because one examination will answer for your four papers. It is common usage. Every copyist is bound to help examine his copy. Is it not so? Will you not speak? Answer!'

'I prefer not to,' he replied in a flute-like tone. It seemed to me that while I had been addressing him, he carefully revolved every statement that I made; fully comprehended the meaning; could not gainsay the irresistible conclusion; but, at the same time, some paramount consideration prevailed with him to reply as he did.

'You are decided, then, not to comply with my request — a request made according to common usage and common sense?'

He briefly gave me to understand that on that point my judgment was sound. Yes: his decision was irreversible.

It is not seldom the case that when a man is browbeaten in some unprecedented and violently unreasonable way, he begins to stagger in his own plainest faith. He begins, as it were, vaguely to surmise that, wonderful as it may be, all the justice and all the reason are on the other side. Accordingly, if any disinterested persons are present, he turns to them for some reinforcement for his own faltering mind.

'Turkey,' said I, 'what do you think of this? Am I not right?'

'With submission, sir,' said Turkey, with his blandest tone, 'I think that you are.'

'Nippers,' said I, 'what do *you* think of it?'

'I think I should kick him out of the office.'

(The reader of nice perceptions will here perceive that, it being morning, Turkey's answer is couched in polite and tranquil terms but Nipper's reply in ill-tempered ones. Or, to repeat a previous sentence, Nipper's ugly mood was on duty, and Turkey's off.)

'Ginger Nut,' said I, willing to enlist the smallest suffrage in my behalf, 'what do *you* think of it?'

'I think, sir, he's a little *luny*,' replied Ginger Nut, with a grin.

'You hear what they say,' said I, turning towards the screen, 'come forth and do your duty.'

But he vouchsafed no reply. I pondered a moment in sore perplexity. But once more business hurried me. I determined again to postpone the consideration of this dilemma to my future leisure. With a little trouble we made out to examine the papers without Bartleby, though at every page or two, Turkey deferentially dropped his opinion that this proceeding was quite out of the common; while Nippers, twitching in his chair with a dyspeptic nervousness, ground out between his set teeth occasional hissing maledictions against the stubborn oaf behind the screen. And for his (Nipper's) part, this was the first and the last time he would do another man's business without pay.

Meanwhile Bartleby sat in his hermitage, oblivious to everything but his own peculiar business there.

Some days passed, the scrivener being employed upon another lengthy work. His late remarkable conduct led me to regard his ways narrowly. I observed that he never went to dinner; indeed that he never went any where. As yet I had never of my personal knowledge known him to be outside of my office. He was a perpetual sentry in the corner. At about eleven o'clock though, in the morning, I noticed that Ginger Nut would advance towards the opening in Bartleby's screen, as if silently beckoned thither by a gesture invisible to me where I sat. The boy would then leave the office jingling a few pence, and reappear with a handful of ginger-nuts which he delivered in the hermitage, receiving two of the cakes for his trouble.

He lives, then, on ginger-nuts, thought I; never eats a dinner, properly speaking; he must be a vegetarian then; but no; he never eats even vegetables, he eats nothing but ginger-nuts. My mind then ran on in reveries concerning the probable effects upon the human constitution of living entirely on ginger-nuts. Ginger-nuts are so called because they contain ginger as one of their peculiar constituents, and the final flavouring one. Now what was ginger? A hot, spicy thing. Was Bartleby hot and spicy? Not at all. Ginger, then, had no effect upon Bartleby. Probably he preferred it should have none.

Nothing so aggravates an earnest person as a passive resistance. If the individual so resisted be of a not inhumane temper, and the resisting one perfectly harmless in his passivity; then, in the better moods of the former, he will endeavour charitably to construe to his imagination what proves impossible to be solved by his judgment. Even so, for the most part, I regarded Bartleby and his ways. Poor fellow! thought I, he means no mischief; it is plain he intends no insolence; his aspect sufficiently evinces that his eccentricities are involuntary. He is useful to me. I can get along with him. If I turn him away, the chances are he will fall in with some less indulgent employer, and then he will be rudely treated, and perhaps driven forth miserably to starve. Yes. Here I can cheaply purchase a delicious self-approval. To befriend Bartleby; to humour him in his strange wilfulness, will cost me little or nothing, while I lay up in my soul what will eventually prove a sweet morsel for my conscience. But this mood was not invariable with me. The passiveness of Bartleby sometimes irritated me. I felt strangely goaded on to encounter him in new opposition, to elicit some angry spark from him answerable to my own. But indeed I might as well have essayed to strike fire with my knuckles against a bit of Windsor soap. But one afternoon the evil impulse in me mastered me, and the following little scene ensued:

'Bartleby,' said I, 'when those papers are all copied, I will compare them with you.'

'I would prefer not to.'

'How? Surely you do not mean to persist in that mulish vagary?'

No answer.

I threw open the folding-doors near by, and turning upon Turkey and Nippers, exclaimed in an excited manner:

'He says, a second time, he won't examine his papers. What do you think of it, Turkey?'

It was afternoon, be it remembered. Turkey sat glowing like a brass boiler, his bald head steaming, his hands reeling among his blotted papers.

'Think of it?' roared Turkey; 'I think I'll just step behind his screen, and black his eyes for him!'

So saying, Turkey rose to his feet and threw his arms into a pugilistic position. He was hurrying away to make good his promise, when I detained him, alarmed at the effect of incautiously rousing Turkey's combativeness after dinner.

'Sit down, Turkey,' said I, 'and hear what Nippers has to say. What do you think of it, Nippers? Would I not be justified in immediately dismissing Bartleby?'

'Excuse me, that is for you to decide, sir. I think his conduct quite unusual, and indeed unjust, as regards Turkey and myself. But it may only be a passing whim.'

'Ah,' exclaimed I, 'you have strangely changed your mind then – you speak very gently of him now.'

'All beer,' cried Turkey; 'gentleness is effects of beer – Nippers and I dined together to-day. You see how gentle *I* am, sir. Shall I go and black his eyes?'

'You refer to Bartleby, I suppose. No, not to-day, Turkey,' I replied; 'pray, put up your fists.'

I closed the doors, and again advanced towards Bartleby. I felt additional incentives tempting me to my fate. I burned to be rebelled against again. I remembered that Bartleby never left the office.

'Bartleby,' said I, 'Ginger Nut is away; just step round to the Post Office, won't you? (it was but a three minutes' walk), and see if there is anything for me.'

'I would prefer not to.'

'You *will* not?'

'I *prefer* not.'

I staggered to my desk, and sat there in a deep study. My blind inveteracy returned. Was there any other thing in which I could procure myself to be ignominiously repulsed by this lean, penniless wight? my hired clerk? What added thing is there, perfectly reasonable, that he will be sure to refuse to do?

'Bartleby!'

No answer.

'Bartleby,' in a louder tone.

No answer.

'Bartleby,' I roared.

Like a very ghost, agreeably to the laws of magical invocation, at the third summons, he appeared at the entrance of his hermitage.

'Go to the next room, and tell Nippers to come to me.'

'I prefer not to,' he respectfully and slowly said, and mildly disappeared.

'Very good, Bartleby,' said I, in a quiet sort of serenely severe self-possessed tone, intimating the unalterable purpose of some terrible retribution very close at hand. At the moment I half intended something of the kind. But upon the whole, as it was drawing towards my dinner-hour, I thought it best to put on my hat and walk home for the day, suffering much from perplexity and distress of mind.

Shall I acknowledge it? The conclusion of this whole business was, that it soon became a fixed fact of my chambers, that a pale young scrivener, by the name of Bartleby, had a desk there; that he copied for me at the usual rate of four cents a folio (one hundred words); but he was permanently exempt from examining the work done by him, that duty being transferred to Turkey and Nippers, out of compliment doubtless to their superior acuteness; moreover, said Bartleby was never on any account to be despatched on the most trivial errand of any sort; and that even if entreated to take upon him such a matter, it was generally understood that he would prefer not to – in other words, that he would refuse point-blank.

As days passed on, I became considerably reconciled to Bartleby. His steadiness, his freedom from all dissipation, his incessant industry (except when he chose to throw himself into a standing revery behind his screen), his great stillness, his unalterableness of demeanour under all circumstances, made him a valuable acquisition. One prime thing was this – *he was always there* – first in the morning, continually through the day, and the last at night. I had a singular confidence in his honesty. I felt my most precious papers perfectly safe in his hands. Sometimes to be sure I could not, for the very soul of me, avoid falling into sudden spasmodic passions with him. For it was exceeding difficult to bear in mind all the time those strange peculiarities, privileges, and unheard of exemptions, forming the tacit stipulations on Bartleby's part under which he remained in my office. Now and then, in the eagerness of despatching pressing business, I would inadvertently summon Bartleby, in a short, rapid tone, to put his finger, say, on the incipient tie of a bit of red tape with which I was about compressing some papers. Of course, from behind the screen the usual answer, 'I prefer not to,' was sure to come; and then, how could a human creature with the common infirmities of our nature, refrain from bitterly exclaiming upon such perverseness – such unreasonableness. However, every added repulse of this sort which I received only tended to lessen the probability of my repeating the inadvertence.

Here it must be said, that according to the custom of most legal gentlemen occupying chambers in densely-populated law buildings, there were several keys to my door. One was kept by a woman residing in the attic, which person weekly scrubbed and daily swept and dusted my apartments. Another was kept by Turkey for convenience sake. The third I sometimes carried in my own pocket. The fourth I knew not who had.

Now, one Sunday morning I happened to go to Trinity Church, to hear a celebrated preacher, and finding myself rather early on the ground, I thought I would walk round to my chambers for awhile. Luckily I had my key with me; but upon applying it to the lock, I found it resisted by something inserted from the inside. Quite surprised, I called out; when to my consternation a key was turned from within; and thrusting his lean visage at me, and holding the door ajar, the apparition of Bartleby appeared, in his shirt sleeves, and otherwise in a strangely tattered dishabille, saying quietly that he was sorry, but he was deeply engaged just then, and – preferred not admitting me at present. In a brief word or two, he moreover added, that perhaps I had better walk round the block two or three times, and by that time he would probably have concluded his affairs.

Now, the utterly unsurmised appearance of Bartleby, tenanting my law-chambers of a Sunday morning, with his cadaverously gentlemanly *nonchalance*, yet withal firm and self-possessed, had such a strange effect upon me, that incontinently I slunk away from my own door, and did as desired. But not without sundry twinges of impotent rebellion against the mild effrontery of this unaccountable scrivener. Indeed, it was his wonderful mildness, chiefly, which not only disarmed me, but unmanned me, as it were. For I consider that one, for the time, is in a way unmanned when he tranquilly permits his hired clerk to dictate to him, and order him away from his own premises. Furthermore, I was full of uneasiness as to what Bartleby could possibly be doing in my office in his shirt sleeves, and in an otherwise dismantled condition of a Sunday morning. Was anything amiss going on? Nay, that was out of the question. It was not to be thought of for a moment that Bartleby was an immoral person. But what could he be doing there – copying? Nay again, whatever might be his eccentricities, Bartleby was an eminently decorous person. He would be the last man to sit down to his desk in any state approaching to nudity. Besides, it was Sunday; and there was something about Bartleby that forbade the supposition that he would by any secular occupation violate the proprieties of the day.

Nevertheless, my mind was not pacified; and full of a restless curiosity, at last I returned to the door. Without hindrance I inserted my key, opened it, and entered. Bartleby was not to be seen. I looked round anxiously, peeped behind his screen; but it was very plain that he was gone. Upon more closely examining the place, I surmised that for an indefinite period Bartleby must have ate, dressed, and slept in my office, and that too without plate, mirror, or bed. The cushioned seat of a ricketty old sofa in one corner bore the faint impress of a lean, reclining form. Rolled away under his desk, I found a blanket; under the empty grate, a blacking box and brush; on a chair, a tin basin, with soap and a ragged towel; in a newspaper a few crumbs of ginger-nuts and a morsel of cheese. Yes, thought I, it is evident enough that Bartleby has been making his home here, keeping bachelor's hall all by himself. Immediately then the thought came sweeping across me, What miserable friendlessness and loneliness are here revealed! His poverty is great; but his solitude, how horrible! Think of it. Of a Sunday, Wall Street is deserted as Petra; and every night of every day it is an emptiness. This building too, which of week-days hums with industry and life, at nightfall echoes with sheer vacancy, and all through Sunday is forlorn. And here Bartleby makes his home; sole spectator of a solitude which he has seen all populous – a sort of innocent and transformed Marius brooding among the ruins of Carthage!

For the first time in my life a feeling of overpowering stinging melancholy seized me. Before, I had never experienced aught but a not-unpleasing sadness. The bond of a common humanity now drew me irresistibly to gloom. A fraternal melancholy! For both I and Bartleby were sons of Adam. I remembered the bright silks and sparkling faces I had seen that day, in gala trim, swan-like sailing down the Mississippi of Broadway; and I contrasted them with the pallid copyist, and thought to myself, Ah, happiness courts the light, so we deem the world is gay; but misery hides aloof, so we deem that misery there is none. These sad fancyings – chimeras, doubtless, of a sick and silly brain – led on to other and more special thoughts, concerning the eccentricities of Bartleby.

Presentiments of strange discoveries hovered round me. The scrivener's pale form appeared to me laid out, among uncaring strangers, in its shivering winding sheet.

Suddenly I was attracted by Bartleby's closed desk, the key in open sight left in the lock.

I mean no mischief, seek the gratification of no heartless curiosity, thought I; besides, the desk is mine, and its contents, too, so I will make bold to look within. Everything was methodically arranged, the papers smoothly placed. The pigeon holes were deep, and, removing the files of documents, I groped into their recesses. Presently I felt something there, and dragged it out. It was an old bandana handkerchief, heavy and knotted. I opened it, and saw it was a savings' bank.

I now recalled all the quiet mysteries which I had noted in the man. I remembered that he never spoke but to answer; that though at intervals he had considerable time to himself, yet I had never seen him reading – no, not even a newspaper; that for long periods he would stand looking out, at his pale window behind the screen, upon the dead brick wall; I was quite sure he never visited any refectory or eating-house; while his pale face clearly indicated that he never drank beer like Turkey, or tea and coffee even, like other men; that he never went anywhere in particular that I could learn; never went out for a walk, unless indeed that was the case at present; that he had declined telling who he was, or whence he came, or whether he had any relatives in the world; that though so thin and pale, he never complained of ill health. And more than all, I remembered a certain unconscious air of pallid – how shall I call it? – of pallid haughtiness, say, or rather an austere reserve about him, which had positively awed me into my tame compliance with his eccentricities, when I had feared to ask him to do the slightest incidental thing for me, even though I might know, from his long-continued motionlessness, that behind his screen he must be standing in one of those dead-wall reveries of his.

Revolving all these things, and coupling them with the recently discovered fact that he made my office his constant abiding place and home, and not forgetful of his morbid moodiness; revolving all these things, a prudential feeling began to steal over me. My first emotions had been those of pure melancholy and sincerest pity; but just in proportion as the forlornness of Bartleby grew and grew to my imagination, did that same melancholy merge into fear, that pity into repulsion. So true it is, and so terrible, too, that up to a certain point the thought or sight of misery enlists our best affections; but, in certain special cases, beyond that point it does not. They err who would assert that invariably this is owing to the inherent selfishness of the human heart. It rather proceeds from a certain hopelessness of remedying excessive and organic ill. To a sensitive being, pity is not seldom pain. And when at last it is perceived that such pity cannot lead to effectual succour, common sense bids the soul be rid of it. What I saw that morning persuaded me that the scrivener was the victim of innate and incurable disorder. I might give alms to his body; but his body did not pain him; it was his soul that suffered, and his soul I could not reach.

I did not accomplish the purpose of going to Trinity Church that morning. Somehow, the things I had seen disqualified me for the time from church-going. I walked homeward, thinking what I would do with Bartleby. Finally, I resolved upon this: I would put certain calm questions to him the next morning, touching his history, etc., and if he declined to answer them openly and unreservedly (and I supposed he would prefer not), then to give him a twenty dollar bill over and above whatever I might owe him, and tell him his services were no longer required; but that if in any other way I could assist him, I would be happy to do so, especially if he desired to return to his native place, wherever that might be, I would willingly help to defray the expenses. Moreover, if, after reaching home, he found himself at any time in want of aid, a letter from him would be sure of a reply.

The next morning came.

'Bartleby,' said I, gently calling to him behind his screen.

No reply.

'Bartleby,' said I, in a still gentler tone, 'come here; I am not going to ask you to do anything you would prefer not to do — I simply wish to speak to you.'

Upon this he noiselessly slid into view.

'Will you tell me, Bartleby, where you were born?'

'I would prefer not to.'

'Will you tell me *anything* about yourself?'

'I would prefer not to.'

'But what reasonable objection can you have to speak to me? I feel friendly towards you.'

He did not look at me while I spoke, but kept his glance fixed upon my bust of Cicero, which, as I then sat, was directly behind me, some six inches above my head.

'What is your answer, Bartleby?' said I, after waiting a considerable time for a reply, during which his countenance remained immovable, only there was the faintest conceivable tremor of the white attenuated mouth.

'At present I prefer to give no answer,' he said, and retired into his hermitage.

It was rather weak in me I confess, but his manner on this occasion nettled me. Not only did there seem to lurk in it a certain calm disdain, but his perverseness seemed ungrateful, considering the undeniable good usage and indulgence he had received from me.

Again I sat ruminating what I should do. Mortified as I was at his behaviour, and resolved as I had been to dismiss him when I entered my office, nevertheless I strangely felt something super-stitious knocking at my heart, and forbidding me to carry out my purpose, and denouncing me for a villain if I dared to breathe one bitter word against this forlornest of mankind. At last, familiarly drawing my chair behind his screen, I sat down and said: 'Bartleby, never mind then about revealing your history; but let me entreat you, as a friend, to comply as far as may be with the usages of this office. Say now you will help to examine papers to-morrow or next day: in short, say now that in a day or two you will begin to be a little reasonable: say so Bartleby.'

'At present I would prefer not to be a little reasonable,' was his mildly cadaverous reply.

Just then the folding-doors opened, and Nippers approached. He seemed suffering from an unusually bad night's rest, induced by severer indigestion than common. He overheard those final words of Bartleby.

'*Prefer not*, eh?' gritted Nippers – 'I'd *prefer* him, if I were you, sir,' addressing me – 'I'd *prefer* him; I'd give him preferences, the stubborn mule! What is it, sir, pray, that he *prefers* not to do now?'

Bartleby moved not a limb.

'Mr Nippers,' said I, 'I'd prefer that you would withdraw for the present.'

Somehow, of late I had got into the way of involuntarily using this word 'prefer' upon all sorts of not exactly suitable occasions. And I trembled to think that my contact with the scrivener had already and seriously affected me in a mental way. And what further and deeper aberration might it not yet produce? This apprehension had not been without efficacy in determining me to summary means.

As Nippers, looking very sour and sulky, was departing, Turkey blandly and deferentially approached.

'With submission, sir,' said he, 'yesterday I was thinking about Bartleby here, and I think that if he would but prefer to take a quart of good ale every day, it would do much towards mending him, and enabling him to assist in examining his papers.'

'So you have got the word, too,' said I, slightly excited.

'With submission, what word, sir,' asked Turkey, respectfully crowding himself into the contracted space behind the screen, and by so doing, making me jostle the scrivener. 'What word, sir?'

'I would prefer to be left alone here,' said Bartleby, as if offended at being mobbed in his privacy.

'*That's* the word, Turkey,' said I – '*that's* it.'

'Oh, *prefer*? oh, yes – queer word. I never use it myself. But, sir, as I was saying, if he would but prefer – '

'Turkey,' interrupted I, 'you will please withdraw.'

'Oh certainly, sir, if you prefer that I should.'

As he opened the folding-door to retire, Nippers at his desk caught a glimpse of me, and asked whether I would prefer to have a certain paper copied on blue paper or white. He did not in the least roguishly accent the word prefer. It was plain that it involuntarily rolled from his tongue. I thought to myself, surely I must get rid of a demented man, who already has in some degree turned the tongues, if not the heads, of myself and clerks. But I thought it prudent not to break the dismission at once.

The next day I noticed that Bartleby did nothing but stand at his window in his dead-wall revery. Upon asking him why he did not write, he said that he had decided upon doing no more writing.

'Why, how now? what next?' exclaimed I, 'do no more writing?'

'No more.'

'And what is the reason?'

'Do you not see the reason for yourself?' he indifferently replied.

I looked steadfastly at him, and perceived that his eyes looked dull and glazed. Instantly it occurred to me, that his unexampled diligence in copying by his dim window for the first few weeks of his stay with me might have temporarily impaired his vision.

I was touched. I said something in condolence with him. I hinted that, of course he did wisely in abstaining from writing for a while, and urged him to embrace that opportunity of taking wholesome exercise in the open air. This, however, he did not do. A few days after this, my other clerks being absent, and being in a great hurry to despatch certain letters by the mail, I thought that, having nothing else earthly to do, Bartleby would surely be less inflexible than usual, and carry these letters to the Post Office. But he blankly declined. So, much to my inconvenience, I went myself.

Still added days went by. Whether Bartleby's eyes improved or not, I could not say. To all appearance, I thought they did. But when I asked him if they did, he vouchsafed no answer. At all events, he would do no copying. At last, in reply to my urgings, he informed me that he had permanently given up copying.

'What!' exclaimed I; 'suppose your eyes should get entirely well – better than ever before – would you not copy then?'

'I have given up copying,' he answered and slid aside.

He remained, as ever, a fixture in my chamber. Nay – if that were possible – he became still more of a fixture than before. What was to be done? He would do nothing in the office: why should he stay there? In plain fact, he had now become a millstone to me, not only useless as a necklace, but afflictive to bear. Yet I was sorry for him. I speak less than truth when I say that, on his own account, he occasioned me uneasiness. If he would but have named a single relative or friend, I would instantly have written, and urged their taking the poor fellow away to some convenient retreat. But he seemed alone, absolutely alone in the universe. A bit of wreckage in the mid-Atlantic. At length, necessities connected with my business tyrannized over all other considerations. Decently as I could, I told Bartleby that in six days' time he must unconditionally leave the office. I warned him to take measures, in the interval, for procuring some other abode. I offered to assist him in this endeavour, if he himself would but take the first step towards a removal. 'And when you finally quit me, Bartleby,' added I, 'I shall see that you go away not entirely unprovided. Six days from this hour, remember.'

At the expiration of that period, I peeped behind the screen, and lo! Bartleby was there.

I buttoned up my coat, balanced myself; advanced slowly towards him, touched his shoulder, and said, 'The time has come; you must quit this place; I am sorry for you; here is money; but you must go.'

'I would prefer not,' he replied, with his back still towards me.

'You *must*.'

He remained silent.

Now I had an unbounded confidence in this man's common honesty. He had frequently restored to me sixpences and shillings carelessly dropped upon the floor, for I am apt to be very reckless in such shirt-button affairs. The proceeding then which followed will not be deemed extraordinary.

'Bartleby,' said I, 'I owe you twelve dollars on account; here are thirty-two; the odd twenty are yours – Will you take it?' and I handed the bills towards him.

But he made no motion.

'I will leave them here then,' putting them under a weight on the table. Then taking my hat and cane and going to the door, I tranquilly turned and added – 'After you have removed your things from these offices, Bartleby, you will of course lock the door – since every one is now gone for the day but you – and if you please, slip your key underneath the mat, so that I may have it in the morning. I shall not see you again; so good-bye to you. If hereafter in your new place of abode I can be of any service to you, do not fail to advise me by letter. Good-bye, Bartleby, and fare you well.'

But he answered not a word; like the last column of some ruined temple, he remained standing mute and solitary in the middle of the otherwise deserted room.

As I walked home in a pensive mood, my vanity got the better of my pity. I could not but highly plume myself on my masterly management in getting rid of Bartleby. Masterly I call it, and such it must appear to any dispassionate thinker. The beauty of my procedure seemed to consist in its perfect quietness. There was no vulgar bullying, no bravado of any sort, no choleric hectoring, no striding to and fro across the apartment, jerking out vehement commands for Bartleby to bundle himself off with his beggarly traps. Nothing of the kind. Without loudly bidding Bartleby depart – as an inferior genius might have done – I *assumed* the ground that depart he must; and upon that assumption built all I had to say. The more I thought over my procedure, the more I was charmed with it. Nevertheless, next morning upon awakening, I had my doubts – I had somehow slept off the fumes of vanity. One of the coolest and wisest hours a man has, is just after he awakes in the morning. My procedure seemed as sagacious as ever – but only in theory. How it would prove in practice – there was a rub. It was truly a beautiful thought to have assumed Bartleby's departure; but, after all, that assumption was simply my own, and none of Bartleby's. The great point was, not whether I had assumed that he would quit me, but whether he would prefer so to do. He was more a man of preferences than assumptions.

After breakfast, I walked down town, arguing the probabilities *pro* and *con*. One moment I thought it would prove a miserable failure, and Bartleby would be found all alive at my office as usual; the next moment it seemed certain that I should see his chair empty. And so I kept veering about. At the corner of Broadway and Canal Street, I saw quite an excited group of people standing in earnest conversation.

'I'll take odds he doesn't!' said a voice as I passed.

'Doesn't go? done!' said I, 'put up your money.'

I was instinctively putting my hand in my pocket to produce my own, when I remembered that this was an election day. The words I had overheard bore no reference to Bartleby, but to the success or non-success of some candidate for the mayoralty. In my intent frame of mind, I had, as it were, imagined that all Broadway shared in my excitement, and were debating the same question with me. I passed on, very thankful that the uproar of the street screened my momentary absent-mindedness.

As I had intended, I was earlier than usual at my office door. I stood listening for a moment. All was still. He must be gone. I tried the knob. The door was locked. Yes, my procedure had worked to a charm; he indeed must be vanished. Yet a certain melancholy mixed with this: I was almost sorry for my brilliant success. I was fumbling under the door mat for the key, which Bartleby was to have left there for me, when accidentally my knee knocked against a panel, producing a summoning sound, and in response a voice came to me from within – 'Not yet; I am occupied.'

It was Bartleby.

I was thunderstruck. For an instant I stood like the man who, pipe in mouth, was killed one cloudless afternoon long ago in Virginia, by summer lightning; at his own warm open window he was killed, and remained leaning out there upon the dreamy afternoon, till some one touched him, and he fell.

'Not gone!' I murmured at last. But again obeying that wondrous ascendency which the inscrutable scrivener had over me – and from which ascendency, for all my chafing, I could not completely escape – I slowly went down stairs and out into the street, and while walking round the block, considered what I should next do in this unheard-of perplexity. Turn the man out by an actual thrusting I could not; to drive him away by calling him hard names would not do; calling in the police was an unpleasant idea; and yet, permit him to enjoy his cadaverous triumph over me – this too I could not think of. What was to be done? or, if nothing could be done, was there anything further that I could *assume* in the matter? Yes, as before I had prospectively assumed that Bartleby would depart, so now I might retrospectively assume that departed he was. In the legitimate carrying out of this assumption, I might enter my office in a great hurry, and pretending not to see Bartleby at all, walk straight against him as if he were air. Such a proceeding would in a singular degree have the appearance of a home-thrust. It was hardly possible that Bartleby could withstand such an application of the doctrine of assumptions. But, upon second thought, the success of the plan seemed rather dubious. I resolved to argue the matter over with him again.

'Bartleby,' said I, entering the office, with a quietly severe expression, 'I am seriously displeased. I am pained, Bartleby. I had thought better of you. I had imagined you of such a gentlemanly organization, that in any delicate dilemma a slight hint would suffice – in short, an assumption; but it appears I am deceived. Why,' I added, unaffectedly starting, 'you have not even touched that money yet,' pointing to it, just where I had left it the evening previous.

He answered nothing.

'Will you, or will you not, quit me?' I now demanded in a sudden passion, advancing close to him.

'I would prefer *not* to quit you,' he replied, gently emphasizing the *not*.

'What earthly right have you to stay here? Do you pay any rent? Do you pay my taxes? Or is this property yours?'

He answered nothing.

'Are you ready to go on and write now? Are your eyes

recovered? Could you copy a small paper for me this morning? or help examine a few lines? or step round to the Post Office? In a word, will you do any thing at all, to give a colouring to your refusal to depart the premises?'

He silently retired into his hermitage.

I was now in such a state of nervous resentment that I thought it but prudent to check myself, at present, from further demonstrations. Bartleby and I were alone. I remembered the tragedy of the unfortunate Adams and the still more unfortunate Colt in the solitary office of the latter; and how poor Colt, being dreadfully incensed by Adams, and imprudently permitting himself to get wildly excited, was at unawares hurried into his fatal act – an act which certainly no man could possibly deplore more than the actor himself. Often it had occurred to me in my ponderings upon the subject, that had that altercation taken place in the public street, or at a private residence, it would not have terminated as it did. It was the circumstance of being alone in a solitary office, upstairs, of a building entirely unhallowed by humanizing domestic associations – an uncarpeted office, doubtless, of a dusty, haggard sort of appearance; this it must have been, which greatly helped to enhance the irritable desperation of the hapless Colt.

But when this old Adam of resentment rose in me and tempted me concerning Bartleby, I grappled him and threw him. How? Why, simply by recalling the divine injunction: 'A new commandment give I unto you, that ye love one another.' Yes, this it was that saved me. Aside from higher considerations, charity often operates as a vastly wise and prudent principle – a great safeguard to its possessor. Men have committed murder for jealousy's sake, and anger's sake, and hatred's sake, and selfishness' sake, and spiritual pride's sake; but no man that ever I heard of, ever committed a diabolical murder for sweet charity's sake. Mere self-interest, then, if no better motive can be enlisted, should, especially with high-tempered men, prompt all beings to charity and philanthropy. At any rate, upon the occasion in question, I strove to drown my exasperated feelings toward the scrivener by benevolently construing his conduct. Poor fellow, poor fellow! thought I, he doesn't mean any thing; and besides, he has seen hard times, and ought to be indulged.

I endeavoured also immediately to occupy myself, and at the same time to comfort my despondency. I tried to fancy that in the course of the morning, at such time as might prove agreeable to him, Bartleby, of his own free accord, would emerge from his hermitage, and take up some decided line of march in the direction of the door. But no. Half-past twelve o'clock came; Turkey began to glow in the face, overturn his inkstand, and become generally obstreperous; Nippers abated down into quietude and courtesy; Ginger Nut munched his noon apple; and Bartleby remained standing at his window in one of his profoundest dead-wall reveries. Will it be credited? Ought I to acknowledge it? That afternoon I left the office without saying one further word to him.

Some days now passed, during which at leisure intervals I looked a little into *Edwards on the Will*, and *Priestley on Necessity*. Under the circumstances, those books induced a salutary feeling. Gradually I slid into the persuasion that these troubles of mine, touching the scrivener, had been all predestinated from eternity, and Bartleby was billeted upon me for some mysterious purpose of an all-wise Providence, which it was not for a mere mortal like me to fathom. Yes, Bartleby, stay there behind your screen, thought I; I shall persecute you no more; you are harmless and noiseless as any of these old chairs; in short, I never feel so private as when I know you are here. At least I see it, I feel it; I penetrate to the predestinated purpose of my life. I am content. Others may have loftier parts to enact; but my mission in this world, Bartleby, is to furnish you with office room for such period as you may see fit to remain.

I believe that this wise and blessed frame of mind would have continued with me had it not been for the unsolicited and uncharitable remarks obtruded upon me by my professional friends who visited the rooms. But thus it often is, that the constant friction of illiberal minds wears out at last the best resolves of the more generous. Though to be sure, when I reflected upon it, it was not strange that people entering my office should be struck by the peculiar aspect of the unaccountable Bartleby, and so be tempted to throw out some sinister observations concerning him. Sometimes an attorney having business with me, and calling at my office, and finding no one but the scrivener there, would undertake to obtain some sort of precise information from him touching my whereabouts; but without heeding his idle talk, Bartleby would remain standing immovable in the middle of the room. So, after contemplating him in that position for a time, the attorney would depart, no wiser than he came.

Also, when a Reference was going on, and the room full of lawyers and witnesses and business was driving fast, some deeply occupied legal gentleman present, seeing Bartleby wholly un-employed, would request him to run round to his (the legal gentleman's) office and fetch some papers for him. Thereupon, Bartleby would tranquilly decline, and yet remain idle as before. Then the lawyer would give a great stare, and turn to me. And what could I say? At last I was made aware that all through the circle of my professional acquaintance, a whisper of wonder was running round, having reference to the strange creature I kept at my office. This worried me very much. And as the idea came upon me of his possibly turning out a long-lived man, and keep occupying my chambers, and denying my authority; and perplex-ing my visitors; and scandalizing my professional reputation; and casting a general gloom over the premises; keeping soul and body together to the last upon his savings (for doubtless he spent but half a dime a day), and in the end perhaps outlive me, and claim possession of my office by right of his perpetual occupancy: as all these dark anticipations crowded upon me more and more, and my friends continually intruded their relentless remarks upon the apparition in my room, a great change was wrought in me. I resolved to gather all my faculties together, and for ever rid me of this intolerable incubus.

Ere revolving any complicated project, however, adapted to this end, I first simply suggested to Bartleby the propriety of his permanent departure. In a calm and serious tone, I commended the idea to his careful and mature consideration. But having taken three days to meditate upon it, he apprised me that his original determination remained the same; in short, that he still preferred to abide with me.

What shall I do? I now said to myself, buttoning up my coat to the last button. What shall I do? what ought I to do? what does conscience say I *should* do with this man, or rather ghost? Rid myself of him, I must; go, he shall. But how? You will not thrust him, the poor, pale, passive mortal — you will not thrust such a helpless creature out of your door? you will not dishonour yourself by such cruelty? No, I will not, I cannot do that. Rather would I let him live and die here, and then mason up his remains in the wall. What then will you do? For all your coaxing, he will not budge. Bribes he leaves under your own paper-weight on your table; in short, it is quite plain that he prefers to cling to you.

Then something severe, something unusual must be done. What! surely you will not have him collared by a constable, and commit his innocent pallor to the common jail? And upon what ground could you procure such a thing to be done? – a vagrant, is he? What! he a vagrant, a wanderer, who refuses to budge? It is because he will *not* be a vagrant, then, that you seek to count him *as* a vagrant. That is too absurd. No visible means of support: there I have him. Wrong again: for indubitably he *does* support himself, and that is the only unanswerable proof that any man can show of his possessing the means so to do. No more then. Since he will not quit me, I must quit him. I will change my offices; I will move elsewhere, and give him fair notice, that if I find him on my new premises I will then proceed against him as a common trespasser.

Acting accordingly, next day I thus addressed him: 'I find these chambers too far from the City Hall; the air is unwholesome. In a word, I propose to remove my offices next week, and shall no longer require your services. I tell you this now, in order that you may seek another place.'

He made no reply, and nothing more was said.

On the appointed day I engaged carts and men, proceeded to my chambers, and having but little furniture, everything was removed in a few hours. Throughout all, the scrivener remained standing behind the screen, which I directed to be removed the last thing. It was withdrawn; and being folded up like a huge folio, left him the motionless occupant of a naked room. I stood in the entry watching him a moment, while something from within me upbraided me.

I re-entered – with my hand in my pocket – and – and my heart in my mouth.

'Good-bye, Bartleby; I am going – good-bye, and God some way bless you; and take that,' slipping something in his hand. But it dropped upon the floor and then – strange to say – I tore myself from him whom I had so longed to be rid of.

Established in my new quarters, for a day or two I kept the door locked, and started at every footfall in the passages. When I returned to my rooms after any little absence, I would pause at the threshold for an instant, and attentively listen, ere applying my key. But these fears were needless. Bartleby never came nigh me.

I thought all was going well, when a perturbed looking stranger visited me, inquiring whether I was the person who had recently occupied rooms at No. — Wall Street.

Full of forebodings, I replied that I was.

'Then sir,' said the stranger, who proved a lawyer, 'you are responsible for the man you left there. He refuses to do any copying, he refuses to do anything; and he says he prefers not to; and he refuses to quit the premises.'

'I am very sorry, sir,' said I, with assumed tranquillity, but an inward tremor, 'but, really, the man you allude to is nothing to me – he is no relation or apprentice of mine, that you should hold me responsible for him.'

'In mercy's name, who is he?'

'I certainly cannot inform you. I know nothing about him. Formerly I employed him as a copyist; but he has done nothing for me now for some time past.'

'I shall settle him then – good morning, sir.'

Several days passed, and I heard nothing more; and though I often felt a charitable prompting to call at the place and see poor Bartleby, yet a certain squeamishness of I know not what withheld me.

All is over with him, by this time, thought I at last, when through another week no further intelligence reached me. But coming to my room the day after, I found several persons waiting at my door in a high state of nervous excitement.

'That's the man – here he comes,' cried the foremost one, whom I recognized as the lawyer who had previously called upon me alone.

'You must take him away, sir, at once,' cried a portly person among them, advancing upon me, and whom I knew to be the landlord of No. — Wall Street. 'These gentlemen, my tenants, cannot stand it any longer; Mr. B —,' pointing to the lawyer, 'has turned him out of his room, and he now persists in haunting the building generally, sitting upon the banisters of the stairs by day, and sleeping in the entry by night. Everybody here is concerned; clients are leaving the offices; some fears are entertained of a mob; something you must do, and that without delay.'

Aghast at this torrent, I fell back before it, and would fain have locked myself in my new quarters. In vain I persisted that Bartleby was nothing to me – no more than to any one else there. In vain – I was the last person known to have anything to do with him, and they held me to the terrible account. Fearful then of being exposed in the papers (as one person present obscurely threatened) I considered the matter, and at length said, that if the lawyer would give me a confidential interview with the scrivener, in his (the lawyer's) own room, I would that afternoon strive my best to rid them of the nuisance they complained of.

Going up stairs to my old haunt, there was Bartleby silently sitting upon the banister at the landing.

'What are you doing here, Bartleby?' said I.

'Sitting upon the banister,' he mildly replied.

I motioned him into the lawyer's room, who then left us.

'Bartleby,' said I, 'are you aware that you are the cause of great tribulation to me, by persisting in occupying the entry after being dismissed from the office?'

No answer.

'Now one of two things must take place. Either you must do something, or something must be done to you. Now what sort of business would you like to engage in? Would you like to re-engage in copying for some one?'

'No; I would prefer not to make any change.'

'Would you like a clerkship in a dry-goods store?'

'There is too much confinement about that. No, I would not like a clerkship; but I am not particular.'

'Too much confinement,' I cried, 'why you keep yourself confined all the time!'

'I would prefer not to take a clerkship,' he rejoined, as if to settle that little item at once.

'How would a bartender's business suit you? There is no trying of the eyesight in that.'

'I would not like it at all; though, as I said before, I am not particular.'

His unwonted wordiness inspirited me. I returned to the charge.

'Well then, would you like to travel through the country collecting bills for the merchants? That would improve your health.'

'No, I would prefer to be doing something else.'

'How then would going as a companion to Europe to entertain some young gentleman with your conversation – how would that suit you?'

'Not at all. It does not strike me that there is anything definite about that. I like to be stationary. But I am not particular.'

'Stationary you shall be then,' I cried, now losing all patience, and for the first time in all my exasperating connection with him fairly flying into a passion. 'If you do not go away from these premises before night, I shall feel bound – indeed I *am* bound – to – to – to quit the premises myself!' I rather absurdly concluded, knowing not with what possible threat to try to frighten his immobility into compliance. Despairing of all further efforts, I was precipitately leaving him, when a final thought occurred to me – one which had not been wholly unindulged before.

'Bartleby,' said I, in the kindest tone I could assume under such exciting circumstances, 'will you go home with me now – not to my office, but my dwelling – and remain there till we can conclude upon some convenient arrangement for you at our leisure? Come, let us start now, right away.'

'No: at present I would prefer not to make any change at all.'

I answered nothing; but effectually dodging every one by the suddenness and rapidity of my flight, rushed from the building, ran up Wall street toward Broadway, and then jumping into the first omnibus was soon removed from pursuit. As soon as tranquillity returned I distinctly perceived that I had now done all that I possibly could, both in respect to the demands of the landlord and his tenants, and with regard to my own desire and sense of duty, to benefit Bartleby, and shield him from rude persecution. I now strove to be entirely care-free aned quiescent; and my conscience justified me in the attempt; though indeed it was not so successful as I could have wished. So fearful was I of being again hunted out by the incensed landlord and his exasperated tenants, that, surrendering my business to Nippers, for a few days I drove about the upper part of the town and through the suburbs, in my rockaway; crossed over to Jersey City and Hoboken, and paid fugitive visits to Manhattanville and Astoria. In fact I almost lived in my rockaway for the time.

When again I entered my office, lo, a note from the landlord lay upon the desk. I opened it with trembling hands. It informed me that the writer had sent to the police, and had Bartleby removed to the Tombs as a vagrant. Moreover, since I knew more about him than any one else, he wished me to appear at that place, and make a suitable statement of the facts. These tidings had a conflicting effect upon me. At first I was indignant; but at last almost approved. The landlord's energetic, summary disposition had led him to adopt a procedure which I do not think I would have decided upon myself; and yet as a last resort, under such peculiar circumstances, it seemed the only plan.

As I afterwards learned, the poor scrivener, when told that he must be conducted to the Tombs, offered not the slightest obstacle, but in his own pale, unmoving way silently acquiesced.

Some of the compassionate and curious bystanders joined the party; and headed by one of the constables, arm-in-arm with Bartleby the silent procession filed its way through all the noise, and heat, and joy of the roaring thoroughfares at noon.

The same day I received the note I went to the Tombs, or, to speak more properly, the Halls of Justice. Seeking the right officer, I stated the purpose of my call, and was informed that the individual I described was indeed within. I then assured the functionary that Bartleby was a perfectly honest man, and greatly to be a compassionated (however unaccountable) eccentric. I narrated all I knew, and closed by suggesting the idea of letting him remain in as indulgent confinement as possible till something less harsh might be done – though indeed I hardly knew what. At all events, if nothing else could be decided upon, the alms-house must receive him. I then begged to have an interview.

Being under no disgraceful charge, and quite serene and harmless in all his ways, they had permitted him freely to wander about the prison, and especially in the inclosed grass-platted yards thereof. And so I found him there, standing all alone in the quietest of the yards, his face toward a high wall – while all around, from the narrow slits of the jail windows, I thought I saw peering out upon him the eyes of murderers and thieves.

'Bartleby!'

'I know you,' he said, without looking round – 'and I want nothing to say to you.'

'It was not I that brought you here, Bartleby,' said I, keenly pained at his implied suspicion. 'And to you, this should not be so vile a place. Nothing reproachful attaches to you by being here. And see, it is not so sad a place as one might think. Look, there is the sky and here is the grass.'

'I know where I am,' he replied, but would say nothing more, and so I left him.

As I entered the corridor again a broad, meat-like man in an

apron accosted me, and jerking his thumb over his shoulder said –
'Is that your friend?'

'Yes.'

'Does he want to starve? If he does, let him live on the prison fare, that's all.'

'Who are you?' asked I, not knowing what to make of such an unofficially speaking person in such a place.

'I am the grub-man. Such gentlemen as have friends here, hire me to provide them with something good to eat.'

'Is this so?' said I, turning to the turnkey.

He said it was.

'Well then,' said I, slipping some silver into the grub-man's hands (for so they called him), 'I want you to give particular attention to my friend there; let him have the best dinner you can get. And you must be as polite to him as possible.'

'Introduce me, will you?' said the grub-man, looking at me with an expression which seemed to say he was all impatience for an opportunity to give a specimen of his breeding.

Thinking it would prove of benefit to the scrivener, I acquiesced; and asking the grub-man his name, went up with him to Bartleby.

'Bartleby, this is Mr Cutlets; you will find him very useful to you.'

'Your sarvant, sir, your sarvant,' said the grub-man, making a low salutation behind his apron. 'Hope you find it pleasant here, sir – spacious grounds – cool apartments, sir – hope you'll stay with us some time – try to make it agreeable. May Mrs Cutlets and I have the pleasure of your company to dinner, sir, in Mrs Cutlets' private room?'

'I prefer not to dine to-day,' said Bartleby, turning away. 'It would disagree with me; I am unused to dinners.' So saying, he slowly moved to the other side of the inclosure and took up a position fronting the dead-wall.

'How's this?' said the grub-man, addressing me with a stare of astonishment. 'He's odd, ain't he?'

'I think he is a little deranged,' said I, sadly.

'Deranged? deranged is it? Well now, upon my word, I thought that friend of yourn was a gentleman forger; they are always pale and genteel-like, them forgers. I can't help pity 'em – can't help it, sir. Did you know Monroe Edwards?' he added touchingly, and paused. Then, laying his hand pityingly on my shoulder, sighed, 'he died of the consumption at Sing-Sing. So you weren't acquainted with Monroe?'

'No, I was never socially acquainted with any forgers. But I cannot stop longer. Look to my friend yonder. You will not lose by it. I will see you again.'

Some few days after this, I again obtained admission to the Tombs, and went through the corridors in quest of Bartleby; but without finding him.

'I saw him coming from his cell not long ago,' said a turnkey, 'maybe he's gone to loiter in the yards.'

So I went in that direction.

'Are you looking for the silent man?' said another turnkey passing me. 'Yonder he lies – sleeping in the yard there. 'Tis not twenty minutes since I saw him lie down.'

The yard was entirely quiet. It was not accessible to the common prisoners. The surrounding walls, of amazing thickness, kept off all sounds behind them. The Egyptian character of the masonry weighed upon me with its gloom. But a soft imprisoned turf grew under foot. The heart of the eternal pyramids, it seemed, wherein by some strange magic, through the clefts grass-seed, dropped by birds, had sprung.

Strangely huddled at the base of the wall – his knees drawn up, and lying on his side, his head touching the cold stones – I saw the wasted Bartleby. But nothing stirred. I paused; then went close up to him; stooped over, and saw that his dim eyes were open; otherwise he seemed profoundly sleeping. Something prompted me to touch him. I felt his hand, when a tingling shiver ran up my arm and down my spine to my feet.

The round face of the grub-man peered upon me now. 'His dinner is ready. Won't he dine to-day, either? Or does he live without dining?'

'Lives without dining,' said I, and closed the eyes.

'Eh – He's asleep, ain't he?'

'With kings and counsellors,' murmured I.

There would seem little need for proceeding further in this history. Imagination will readily supply the meagre recital of poor Bartleby's interment. But ere parting with the reader, let me say, that if this little narrative has sufficiently interested him, to awaken curiosity as to who Bartleby was, and what manner of life he led prior to the present narrator's making his acquaintance, I can only reply, that in such curiosity I fully share – but am wholly unable to gratify it. Yet here I hardly know whether I should divulge one little item of rumour, which came to my ear a few months after the scrivener's decease. Upon what basis it rested, I could never ascertain; and hence, how true it is I cannot now tell. But inasmuch as this vague report has not been without a certain strange suggestive interest to me, however sad, it may prove the same with some others; and so I will briefly mention it. The report was this: that Bartleby had been a subordinate clerk in the Dead Letter Office at Washington, from which he had been suddenly removed by a change in the administration. When I think over this rumour I cannot adequately express the emotions which seize me. Dead letters! does it not sound like dead men? Conceive a man by nature and misfortune prone to a pallid hopelessness: can any business seem more fitted to heighten it than that of continually handling these dead letters, and assorting them for the flames? For by the cartload they are annually burned. Sometimes from out the folded paper the pale clerk takes a ring: the finger it was meant for, perhaps, moulders in the grave; a bank-note sent in swiftest charity: he whom it would relieve, nor eats nor hungers any more; pardon for those who died despairing; hope for those who died unhoping; good tidings for those who died stifled by unrelieved calamities. On errands of life, these letters speed to death.

Ah Bartleby! Ah humanity!

1856

The Prescription

The Doctor said that change of air would do me good, and that the farther I went from home the better. It would be wise to go, he thought, beyond the reach of daily newspapers and Adams Express; an irregular mail would be advisable. 'Choose a village,' he added, 'where there is no railroad, no telegraph wires, no barrack hotel, and no Gothic meeting-house.'

'How long must she stay?' my husband asked.

The Doctor eyed him a moment, as if a reply was rising in his mind which he would like to give utterance to, but had a doubt whether it was best to do so. He answered presently, that I must stay out of the city till I was in a different condition from the one I was in at present.

When this conversation happened on a summer afternoon in my chamber, a torn Zouave jacket of white Marseilles was lying on the sofa where the Doctor sat. A few minutes before his arrival my husband, Gérard Fuller, entered the room and came to the table where I was drawing, and being very tall and very near-sighted bent his head over my shoulder: the gleam of the gilt buttons on the said jacket, which I had on, must have caught his eye, for he started back with the exclamation:

'Haven't I told you never to wear these things? Fast women only should wear them.'

Before I could put my pencil down he cut the jacket open with his penknife, pulled it from my arms, tore it across and tossed it over on the sofa. I replaced it with a drab-coloured barege, and seated myself at a distance from the table where Gérard stood contemplating my sketch, to await further demonstration from him, when a rap came on the door and the Doctor bustled in. It is possible that there might have been an unusual expression in our faces, for he only gave a queer 'hem,' and referred to his memorandum-book. After perusing it a while he remarked that he had been looking over, in his carriage, a clever little book by a Frenchman, who said, 'that a woman may be loved for three things: for her superior intellect – a love serious but rare; for her beauty – a love vulgar and brief; for the qualities of her heart – a love lasting but monotonous.' His eyes then dropped on the torn jacket, and without waiting for any comment on his quotation he asked me how I felt, and proposed change of air for me.

'Milk-and-water will be good for her, I suppose, in the out-of-the-way place you suggest,' continued Gérard.

'Unless she finds the milk of human kindness there,' the Doctor replied.

'Good, Doctor, but said by Grimaldi thirty years ago; and I believe he added something about the cream of the joke.'

'I dare say, Mrs Fuller,' and the Doctor turned toward me, putting his fingers on my wrist, 'when can you leave home?'

Gérard answered hastily that I could go any day, but he could not accompany me. Gérard is a cloth importer, and mid-summer is his busiest time; the Doctor knew this fact.

'I sent a patient,' he said, 'two years ago to a little town famous for its bad air, its disagreeable scenery, and the stupidity of its inhabitants. I wish you would allow your wife to go there' (here his eyes rested on the jacket again). 'I am sure she can get in the same house where my patient boarded; and if you say so, I will write to my old friend, John Bowman, ancient mariner, who lives in it, and engage a room.'

'Oh,' said Gérard, in his roughest way, 'I do not believe it is necessary to write your friend; he will be glad to take a boarder, and Caroline can go tomorrow if she chooses.'

'Just so,' answered the Doctor, rising. 'It is understood then, Mrs Fuller, that you will follow my directions.'

'You had better make them more explicit,' I answered.

'I'll drop in tomorrow to see how you are, and give you my final say.'

'Where is that happy village?' inquired Gérard.

'Eighteen miles from the small city of Berford, on the sea-coast; its name is Marlow. Good-day.'

Gérard left me immediately, and, naturally, I looked in the glass as soon as I was alone. I saw no difference in my appearance, and could not account for the Doctor's penetration; for I was convinced that he knew Gérard had torn off the jacket from me. Upon second thought, I remembered that he had shown the same manner once before. It was when Gérard happened to come home one day, in the beginning of my illness, with a carriage, to take me out with him. The Doctor, perceiving that I did not wish to go, said that I had better stay at home that day. Gérard flung about in wrath, and finally rushed out of the room and went off with the carriage. The Doctor asked me, suddenly, if I was nervous before I was married. 'No,' I said.

'Your grandmother,' he remarked, 'must have been an old muff.'

As Gérard had said the same thing frequently of her, I supposed it must be true that she was; but I was impressed with an idea that the Doctor had a different reason for thinking so from what Gérard had. I was not left alone much, was I? the Doctor questioned. What individual tastes or employments had I? Did I ever feel hemmed in by circumstances? He had often noticed that dyspeptic people felt that way. These, with many more strange questions, he asked, and I believe I answered him coherently, though, while I think of it now, I wonder that I was not embarrassed.

He came the next day after the episode of the jacket, and told me that he had already written to Mr Bowman, who would be ready to receive me as soon as the letter reached him. He also gave me a prescription in a sealed envelope, adding that I need not open it till I had arrived in Marlow, for there was an apothecary's shop there.

'The Doctor has left nothing for me to arrange, I conclude,' said Gérard, when he returned home that evening.

'He has even provided for me after I get there, in giving me a sealed prescription.'

'Give it to me at once.'

I offered it to him in silence.

'Take it,' he said, after looking at it a moment; 'do you imagine I wish to break the seal?'

I did imagine it, but did not say so.

'You will obey him, of course?'

'Shall I not?'

He shrugged his shoulders for reply.

It was several days before my traveling-dress came home and I was ready to go. Gérard continually wondered why the Doctor did not come to pack my trunk and order a carriage. He also begged me not to indulge in any sentimental twaddle on his account; which was entirely satirical on his part — for I never indulged in any thing of the kind in regard to him — and endeavored to torment me after the old fashion. He remained at home the day of my departure, but said little. He appeared interested in a novel, but I noticed that he was not so absorbed in it as to prevent his following me over the house, pursuing me from room to room with his book in his hand. He filled my purse, and a new carpet-bag was silently presented to me with various useful nicknacks in it, for which I expressed my gratitude. He accompanied me to the boat, and we had the pleasure of looking out from the opposite windows of the carriage on the drive thither. Depositing my carpet-bag and shawl on the cabin floor, he obtained a chair for me, and then stood before me in a rigid attitude. I untied my bonnet, pinned it to a berth curtain, took off my gloves, and fanned myself. He stared at my hands, oblivious of the crowd of people who hurried to and fro past us, till a man cried out, 'All ashore that's going!' He pushed away my fan then, and whispered.

'It's a pity we are married.'

In lieu of a reply I fanned myself with violence, for I did not know what reply to make.

'I love you, and I am tired of you; you fatigue me.'

I fanned on.

'I wish the devil had that fan.'

I shut it up. 'Do you think it would cool him, Gérard?'

'Placid wit!'

'I am afraid the boat will start.'

'Of course you are. I am going. Won't you say any thing? – send a message to your grandmother?'

I put out my hand without a word; he grasped it till I nearly cried out with pain, and was gone.

Before I had time to start a train of reflection upon the novelty of my situation the boat started; the stewardess put a bit of paper in my hand marked '37', and informed me that it was my berth; the Captain, perambulating the cabin, stopped and asked me if I would go down to supper; and a lady, with a cushion in a leather strap, asked me to exchange berths with her, as she preferred mine to hers. By this time the boat was rocking unpleasantly, my head ached, and I was glad to retire to '35', having at once given up 37 to the lady of the cushion. At sunrise we arrived in port. A train was waiting to convey passengers to different towns by a circuitous route. At the Berford station I alighted, and discovering there the Marlow mail wagon took passage therein.

'Mr Bowman told me to look out for a lady,' said the driver, 'and I expect you are the invalid, or convalescent, or something of that sort of boarder, ain't you?'

Somehow I felt that I had suddenly lost the claim to invalidism, and so I said that I was a convalescent.

'The air is strong in Marlow,' he continued, 'and no mistake; it kills or cures strangers. Mostly kills the folks that live there, too, before they get to old age. Old Bowman, though, is seventy; he's tough. Ever introduced to him? He is a first-rate man, and no mistake; he'll do what's right by you. As for myself, speaking of health, I am twenty-four, and I have had typhus fever, dysentery, inflammatory rheumatism, and no end of stoppages; but I calculate to enjoy myself for all that.'

His loquacity continued and amused me till we reached John Bowman's house.

'There he is,' said the driver, 'a walking up and down in the sun.'

'Hi yi!' said the old man, when the driver stopped; 'have you brought somebody here, Ike?'

'That ere boarder, you know.'

He approached the wagon, and lifting a white beaver hat, said: 'Your servant, marm.'

'Bear a hand, will you,' said the driver, 'and unlash the trunk?'

Mr Bowman propped his gold-headed cane against the paling, turned up the cuffs of his blue cloth jacket, and proceeded to unfasten the trunk. I observed that, in spite of his handsome beaver hat and gold-headed cane, he wore coarse gray trousers, patched at the knees, and cow-hide shoes; and that he had a noble head, pale, dignified features, long gray hair rising from his forehead like a crown, and a diminutive figure. He interested me, and I felt no surprise at the fact of his being a friend of Doctor Brown's. I looked at the house before I entered it. It had been long built, and never painted; the martins were flying round the squat chimneys; and on the ridge-pole of the low porch several pigeons were daintily stepping to and fro. There was an iron knocker on the door, and before it a brick pavement, in the cracks of which tufts and seams of grass grew. The house interested me also.

'Now, then,' said Mr Bowman, smiting the dust from his hands, 'we are ready, marm. Will you walk in? Mrs Bowman's dinner is ready.'

He opened the door softly, and preceding me, entered a room, where a tall, Roman-nosed old lady sat reading a green flannel-covered book, which I found afterward was Baxter's *Saint's*

Rest. Mr Bowman waved his hand and said, 'This is she,' and Mrs Bowman rose, addressing me with a few precise words.

'Dinner, mother,' he interrupted her with.

'Don't be impatient, father; let her get her things off.'

He took my bonnet and shawl away, and placed me at the table. Mrs Bowman went out, and returned with two covered dishes and a tea-pot, and we began dinner. She conversed during the meal; but her husband was silent for the most part, with the exception of a few 'yi-hi's' and 'pooh-pooh's', which did not seem to produce much effect upon her.

'What is the nature of your complaint?' she asked.

'Her complaint is going so fast she can't recall its name,' he said.

'Father is so confident always,' she remarked, with a smile of pity.

'Pooh! nonsense, mother.'

'You remember what the Psalmist says, father?'

For answer he buried his face in a large mug which contained cold coffee, his constant drink, and draining it, rose from the table with twinkling eyes and went out. She gave a smiling sigh of superiority as he disappeared, and proceeded in a deliberate way to clear the table. I became interested in her performances, and declined her proposal that I should go to bed till tea-time. The remains of the dinner she disposed of in various bowls, and carried to the 'cellar-way' to keep cool. She also prepared a hash for supper, and washed the dishes. I followed her into the kitchen to witness the final touch at her mid-day work, which was to scour the hooks and trammels which were already hanging on the crane as bright as steel. All this made me unmindful of the lapse of time, and I was surprised when Mr Bowman came back with the announcement that it was going on for five o'clock.

'Hasn't she been upstairs yet, mother?' he exclaimed.

'No,' she answered; 'she said she was not tired.'

'I will go now, Mr Bowman, if you will show me the way,' I said.

'I hope you won't mind the smell of the seaweed when the tide is out,' Mrs Bowman remarked.

The tide! What could that have to do with my going upstairs? I remembered catching a glimpse of a bay as we turned into the street where the house was situated, but there was no view of it in front.

'Nothing would tempt me,' she continued, 'to do my work or to stay in the back part of this house; but it is father's whim to stay here, with the butment all crumbled away, and he will stay till the underpinning goes.'

He thumped the floor gently with his cane to attract my attention, and said:

'She's here for sea-weed, and the creek, and all. Don't Doctor Brown know what he is about, mother?'

He opened the door before she could reply, and I followed him. The stairs dividing on a platform about midway, we turned to the left, went up a few steps into a narrow passage, at the end of which was a door painted light blue. It was the door of my room.

'You'll like it,' he said, as we entered, 'because there is such a prospect from the window. It will do you good. *I* look out of it at odd times, and my mind goes out on my old voyages to Amsterdam, Leghorn, and Liverpool. I think you will like the prospect, I say.'

I looked from the open window.

'Why, Mr Bowman,' I exclaimed, 'your house is built on the sand!'

'Isn't it?' he chuckled, 'and the floods don't wash it away either. Put your head out; streets in front of the house, seas behind; was there ever such a situation besides?'

I put my head out, and obtained a novel view. The house stood on the upper end of a marsh, half of its foundation on the border of it, and half on the solid ground of the street. A wide creek flowed past the underpinning of piles, whose channel had been divested by the 'butment' now crumbling apart, but which still kept the creek from making further inroads into the spongy yards of the neighbors who lived higher up the street. Below the creek stretched the beautiful bay of Marlow, and beyond that rolled the ocean, over which Mr Bowman's mind went on his old voyages.

'This is almost Venetian, Mr Bowman; colorless Venice without architecture.'

'I never went there; they have strange craft in that place I am told; the natives paddle their boats under the girls' windows. I went to St Petersburg once, in the time of the Emperor Paul. Nothing will disturb you here, unless Gil Jones comes up in his punt at high tide to steal oysters. You'll hear the water splash sometimes; that's pleasant.'

I must have looked tired or abstracted, for he made a hasty exit on tip-toe, without another word. I was weary; the sight of my unpacked trunk was discouraging. How could Gérard have allowed me to leave home alone? What occupation was I to find in this queer, lonely house with these strange, lonely old people?

After tea I unlocked my trunk, shook out my dresses, and looked over my stock of fineries. All at once I felt in better spirits; my clothes seemed to belong to me more than they had for a long time, and a strange sense of freedom stole over me when I recollected that I could keep the candle burning as long as I pleased, and sit up all night if I saw fit.

A sheet of dull, unbroken light hung before the shutterless window when I woke next morning. A mild silvery mist hid land and sea; immediately beneath the window I could see little pools of black water, and a bed of stones covered with a web of green viscous weeds. The tide was out. A faint breeze touched my face with dampness when I raised the sash, and a cloud of delicate mist edged itself into the room.

How different it was at noon!

Mr Bowman was going across the bay to fish and so we dined early; by twelve o'clock he was hoisting sail at the one wharf Marlow could boast of. Mrs Bowman went to a funeral several miles distant, and the house was left to me. I shut the windows below, bolted the outside doors, and betook myself to my room. Outside there was no shade; the pale marsh grass scorched in the sun, and the beach glittered as if every pebble was a precious stone. The water along the shore and at the mouth of the creek lay still and white, untouched by the breeze which ruffled the waters of the bay; its outlet spreading under the horizon was smooth and white also. It allured me like a magic mirror. If I should look steadfastly at it some strange mystery would be revealed to me.

It occurred to me while I stood gazing seaward to get the doctor's prescription. I opened the envelope and found on a bit of paper the following words:

'Comprehend yourself, then you will be able to comprehend others; to do this is necessary in your case.'

My case! Was it pictured in yonder magic mirror and so reflected upon my mind, or were my mental eyes opening at last?

I passed several days in thinking that I was deep in thought, but I was simply in a chaos of feeling which made my brain turbid. I sat much by my window, and continually dropped into vague emotional dreams which produced as apparently a purposeless and futile agitation in my mind as the wind produces on the sea, stirring it up within its limits, but not able to move it an inch beyond. But the chaos was a process I was unaware of till it was completed by slight influences independent of my own will. One evening a tempest came up from the north, and I stayed downstairs with the old people. For the most part we were silent, but as its lulls grew longer Mr Bowman raised his voice, and his wife removed her finger from the place in the green flannel-covered book. When the tempest ceased, and all sounds had died away in the darkness of night, she remarked that she must take in the tubs she had put out to catch rain-water, and go round the house to wipe up the puddles that had leaked in.

'You are gaining, my dear,' said Mr Bowman, when she had gone.

'What am I gaining?'

'That is the secret of the sea. I knew you would go on just so, if you had the chance. I hadn't when I was young. I went hither and thither, on this voyage and that, doing the business of other men; do you think I minded that I was doing, hi yi? No, I didn't look into the sea, and the sea didn't look into me; but when the time of action was past, when my owners wanted younger captains and I sat me down here, my ships gone, my crews gone, then I looked into the sea, and the sea looked into me, and I learned what it is to live – late to be sure. You are alone for the first time in your life, I take it, for you are a young thing, and you are gaining. I knew you would like the prospect. Mother can't abear it; there's nothing of Baxter in it.'

He laughed so loud that she was drawn back to the room to inquire if he had hysterics. I went to my room smiling too, but I felt as if there were tears in his eyes, for they were rising in mine. A band of moonlight crossed the floor, a portion of that which crossed the sea, and shimmered in long lines to the verge of the horizon.

'It is true,' I reflected, 'that I have been living and not thinking; nineteen years of unconscious doing what I had been directed to do. My biography is short, comprised in two facts. I lived with grandmother, and married Gérard Fuller; there is little need to look into the sea in order to expatiate on these topics. But the sea looks into me, and reminds me of my eight months of married life. There is little to account for before that. We have always known Gérard; he is thirty years old; I remember him a grown man when

I was a little girl. I always had to mind him. Grandmother wished me to marry him because he is the son of her old friend, for whom she still wears a mourning ring. Gérard was the only man ever intimate at our house. He was devoted to her, though she sometimes quarreled with him. He worried her into a consent to our marriage against her judgment, for she had a theory that a woman should not be married till she was twenty-five. We had not been married a month before he told me that he wished I had her character, and wondered if my marriage had really arrested my development. From that moment I felt myself the automaton he believed me to be. He began a series of experiments with me, ranging from the lively to the severe, always ending in the severe. I never retaliated, never showed anger, never remonstrated; I have more than once endeavored to pacify him, and have shaped my course entirely by his demands. His first experiment was melodramatic. His own friend, Ned Conover, happened to admire the way my hair was arranged one day. He had hardly left us when Gérard took my comb out, and pulled out the hair-pins, saying that he could not bear the way my hair was dressed. I remarked that he was hurting me, he replied that, as I was not thin-skinned, he did not believe it. But when he came home the next evening and saw that I had dressed my hair another way, he scowled and did not address a word to me for twenty-four hours. We were living with grandmother then, and I mentioned the incident to her; she looked aghast, but said nothing. Soon afterward he bought a house, and furnished it without consulting me: he supposed, he observed, that my tastes were the same as his, and that he need not trouble me. Grandmother was disappointed at our leaving her; but Gérard said that young people had better be by themselves, and she made no objection. She had several skirmishes with him, however, before we moved, and I was glad when the time came for us to go. He did not alter his behavior toward me when we lived alone. He was away from home more than formerly. Sometimes when he returned there was an inquiring expression in his face; he always went away again immediately when he wore that expression. There were times more pleasant, rare times though, when he asked me to read to him while he smoked in my chamber; I never took my eyes from my book that I did not find him perusing my face with a strange intentness. When he took me to the opera, and forgot almost that I was his wife, or to the theatre, where we could not fail to have the same chord of appreciation struck. Two months ago my health began to decline. Gérard said it was the coffee, and ordered tea for breakfast; but I did not improve. Then he said it was because I read too much, and I stopped reading. It must be sewing, he concluded, want of exercise, air, and fifty other things. But I grew worse, and Doctor Brown was called. He said little at first, and the medicine he gave was so mild that I am inclined to think it was sweetened water. Gérard stormed at him, maligned him, but succumbed to all he proposed; indeed, he carried out his directions with nervous haste. He watched me more closely than ever; how many times have I opened my eyes to see his face close to mine, full of eager anxiety! But how sullen he was if I spoke to him! At last I kept my eyes shut when I knew he bent over my pillow. It was irksome to suffer this espionage. Was it wise?'

The moon was setting behind the light-house across the bay, and the sea darkened. Whether I had been wise or foolish, it was time to go to bed.

The day after the tempest Mr Bowman handed me a letter from Gérard.

'What has Brown's prescription done for you?' it abruptly opened with. 'You are impatient to return, I know; but why should you be? you have the society that always suffices you — yourself.'

I laid the letter aside without finishing it. 'He is a brute,' I said; 'let me be free of him. I am free.'

'Mr Bowman,' I said, when I went downstairs, 'men are brutes.'

'Yes, my dear, except when women tyrannize over them.'

'What are they then, father?' his wife asked.

'Transformed into meek angels and saints. But why do you say so now particularly, my dear; did you hear me swearing at mother?'

'The old story-books on the shelves in the passage say so.'

'So they do, my dear; hi yi, those stories went on more than one voyage with me.'

'Poor kind of bread to cast on the waters, father,' Mrs Bowman observed.

'It returned though.'

I left them arguing the point. It was evident that she did not consider Mr Bowman one of the saved; but I knew that she thought him one of the wisest of men, and was happy with him.

I determined not to answer Gérard.

Within a week after the arrival of the letter I received one from Doctor Brown, which was more pithy even than Gérard's. It contained the following advice:

'*Pursue your studies; I am inclined to believe that my prescription was a happy one. Let me know how you are. Physicians love intricate cases; besides, an account of the Bowmans will not come amiss. Is Bowman satisfied with your progress? If he is, I shall be. Be sure to stay till the September rains come on.*'

I divined that Gérard had applied to the Doctor to write me, and decided not to answer the second letter also. But the two letters stirred my impulses: I began to wish the monotony of my life broken into by something tangible. I opened my port-folio, desiring to write to somebody, but what correspondent could I appeal to? I must write to myself – I would start a Diary. I commenced at once, with a motto, of course:

'Seldom should the morning's gold
On the waters be unrolled;
Or the troubled queen of night
Lift her misty veil of light.
Neither wholly dark nor bright,
Gray by day and gray by night,
That's the light, the sky for me,
By the margent of the sea.'

(Page first.)
The above motto is singularly inappropriate. It was in the vivid sunshine and clear moonlight which reigned over the sea that I tried to render, the thoughts to the sea which it gave. In its light I saw images – not fantastic, airy shapes – but those of a plain man and woman named Gérard and Caroline. When will –
(Interruption.)
(Resume.)
Mr. Bowman came in to ask me to walk in the best street of Marlow, which has two rows of linden trees, short, thick, and vigorous in growth, in spite of the sea-wind, which gives them in

infancy a slight slant to the northwest. Was glad to get back to my beloved Diary. How delightful it is to be able to express one's thoughts freely!

(Third page.)

I choose a new leaf each time I return to my Diary, because I do not feel that I have made a right beginning. I long to say something which is really important, and should never be seen by human eye. Some days have passed since I last wrote here. We have had rainy, dull weather. I stayed downstairs, and sewed on Mrs Bowman's patch-work, of the 'Job's trouble' pattern, in red, yellow, and white calico. She has promised it for my bed next summer. Next summer! Shall I revisit these haunts again?

Today it is clear, and Mr Bowman is going to take me across the harbor in the *Polly*. What if I should be drowned? I think Gérard—

When we came back from our sail who should I see walking up and down the wharf but Gérard?

'Who upon 'arth is that?' queried Mr Bowman.

'It looks like my husband.'

'We are going to have a rush of strangers in Marlow,' he said, embarrassed at his own surprise at the unexpected appearance of my husband. As the boat grated against the side of the wharf he stepped on the cap log, and extended his hand for the rope, which Mr Bowman tossed toward him with, 'Your servant, Sir; we are all right.'

As Gérard turned it round a post he looked down at me with a curious expression, which indicated that he would wait for me to make a move, although he doubted whether I could do any thing original under his eye. Outwardly I was as calm as the water round the wharf, inwardly in a whirl. I contrived, however, by the time I put my foot on the gunwale to disentangle one idea, and that was, to take no pains to conceal the character of the relation between us; just as he was should he appear, as far as it lay in me to allow the truth to become apparent. I therefore took his hand to assist myself ashore, and dropped it immediately to walk in advance of him. Half-way up the wharf Mr Bowman overtook me, and walked nimbly beside me with his basket of fish, while Gérard lingered behind, looking to the right and the left in admiration of the landscape.

'Does he read the *Saint's Rest*?' Mr Bowman slyly whispered. I shook my head, and the old man looked puzzled.

'For form's sake, Caroline,' growled Gérard, on the other side, 'you had better introduce me to your fisherman.'

'For form's sake, Mr Bowman, I introduce you to Mr Fuller, but you already know him.'

Gérard looked suspiciously at me.

'No occasion for an introduction,' Mr Bowman answered; 'I knew him from his resemblance to you.'

'Is it so striking?' I laughed, scanning Gérard with a nonchalant air, and meeting his eyes, which were filled with astonishment and a certain expression which disturbed me, for it denoted approbation! He started a lively conversation on fish, which lasted till we reached our door. A large valise on the step met my view, and led my thoughts to speculate on the length of his stay. He must have come with an intention to remain. He seemed to understand my thoughts; for as we went in he said, with a meaning smile.

'You know how fond I am of fishing.'

'It is too late in the season for that,' I answered.

'Walk in, Sir,' said Mr Bowman. 'This is my wife. Supper, mother.'

For a wonder Mrs Bowman was reading a pictorial newspaper, which served Gérard for a topic of talk with her. She grew lively in his presence. I saw at once that she would side with him if any contention should appear. I looked at Mr Bowman, and detected a shade of sadness in his face. That he would sympathize with me I was sure. I put my hand on his brown fist as it lay beside his plate like a lump of brown bread. 'My dear,' he answered, with vivacity, 'you are not well enough to go home yet.'

'I am not going home.'

Gérard raised his eyebrows.

'Father not having any children of his own alive is fond of young folks,' Mrs Bowman remarked.

'Yes,' he replied, simply, 'I love Mrs Fuller.'

'Don't you love children, ma'am?' Gérard asked, with some sharpness.

'I have been a mother.'

'Do you love them, Gérard?' I asked, under my breath.

'Yes, but not the childish.'

Had the sea told me all it might have told me? Or had it revealed but a one-sided story?

I slipped upstairs while he was engaged with the subject of the herring-fishery, and in my room saw the large valise again – the precursor of the coming of my lord and master. I took up my Diary and wrote in large letters the date of Gérard's arrival and these words—

'*End of my Diary.*'

I then seated myself by the window. A breeze had sprung up since sunset, and the waves were lifting up their many voices in a melancholy dirge. The moon was not up, the stars were few, and the bay was hemmed in with darkness.

I heard Gérard's quick step along the passage; he opened my door.

'Shut that window,' were his first words.

For reply I put my head tolerably far outside of it. After a moment's silence he began to unpack his valise, and laid out on the chairs a stock of shirts, handkerchiefs, and collars. He also approached my little table with an apparatus for shaving. The Diary caught his eye, and he deliberately read it.

'Equal to Miss Julia Mills's Diary,' he commented. 'But why do you end it?'

'Because you have come and would read whatever I might write.'

He came toward me and offered his hand.

'Pooh, Gérard! what nonsense it is for me to take your hand.'

He was silent again for a moment, and then ordered me once more to shut the window. It was damp, but I rose and left it open. As I walked across the room the impulse seized me to leave it to him; but he anticipated my thought, and caught me just as I put my hand on the latch.

'I dare say you will keep me here,' I said, 'but what will my staying avail you?'

'You are my wife; why shouldn't I compel you to stay?' and he favored me with Petruchio's opinions:

> 'She is my goods, my chattels, she is my house,
> My household stuff, my field, my barn,
> My horse, my ox, my ass, my any thing.'

'He forgot to say aught about the *soul* of the shrew, didn't he?'

Cool enough to quote Shakspeare as he was, I saw that he was deeply agitated. I went on:

'Do you know that facts are no longer stubborn to me? I shall fight them, and conquer.'

'What do you mean?'

'I mean there shall be something ideal in my life to live for – an ideal man, maybe.'

'Where will you find him?'

'Yonder,' I answered vaguely, looking toward the window.

'Did you ever have an ideal, Caroline, that you were disappointed in utterly?'

I never had, I said, but his question disturbed me. What if I were in fault somehow?

'Madam, I will leave you. There seems to be a lack of sofas in the house for one to sleep on, but I think I can manage the night.'

'Before you go, let me give you a text to discourse upon. Doctor Brown sent me from under your tyranny.'

'The tyranny of love,' he said to himself.

'You nearly extinguished me.'

'Did I?'

'I can't love you in your way.'

'No?'

'And you wouldn't let me love in my way.'

'Had you any way?'

'I might have had.'

He darted out like an arrow, and I fell to crying.

When I opened my door the next morning he was beside it, leaning against the wall, very pale. My impulse was to stop; but I did not follow it, and walked downstairs. We entered the room, however, at the same time. Mr Bowman looked at me over his spectacles till I felt uncomfortable; but he was uncommonly 'chipper', to use his own expression, during breakfast.

The day ended as it began. Several days passed like it. I watched Gérard, and he watched me. It was strange, but I was obliged to acknowledge that I was making his acquaintance in this silent way. He was not the man I had known as my husband. His eyes often sought mine; perhaps he was making the same mental comments.

Mr Bowman informed us one day that he was on the point of being very sick, and begged us to take care of him. I asked him what the matter was. He replied that the foolishness of two young people of his acquaintance was killing him by inches.

I believe I turned pale and looked weak; for Gérard dropped the book he was reading, and rushed toward me, exclaiming:

'It is not you who are foolish, Caroline; it is I!'

'No, it is not you, Gérard, it is me.'

'Can you love a brute?'

'Brute!' Mr Bowman exclaimed. 'She knows the universal truth that Nature did not turn us out handsomely; reptile and four-legged rudiments cling to us yet.'

'Caroline!'

'Gérard!'

'Now isn't this enough to make me down sick?' cried the old man. 'Kiss each other and do better, and give my love to Brown.'

Gérard told me afterward, with a queer smile, that his first night in Marlow was spent in looking for my 'ideal man.'

'And you found him,' I answered.

1864

REBECCA HARDING DAVIS
1831–1910

Life in the Iron-Mills

Is this the end?
O Life, as futile, then, as frail!
What hope of answer or redress?

A cloudy day: do you know what that is in a town of iron-works?
The sky sank down before dawn, muddy, flat, immovable. The air
is thick, clammy with the breath of crowded human beings. It
stifles me. I open the window, and, looking out, can scarcely see
through the rain the grocer's shop opposite, where a crowd of
drunken Irishmen are puffing Lynchburg tobacco in their pipes. I
can detect the scent through all the foul smells ranging loose in the
air.

The idiosyncrasy of this town is smoke. It rolls sullenly in slow
folds from the great chimneys of the iron-foundries, and settles
down in black, slimy pools on the muddy streets. Smoke on the
wharves, smoke on the dingy boats, on the yellow river – clinging
in a coating of greasy soot to the house-front, the two faded
poplars, the faces of the passers-by. The long train of mules,
dragging masses of pig-iron through the narrow street, have a foul
vapor hanging to their reeking sides. Here, inside, is a little broken
figure of an angel pointing upward from the mantel-shelf; but
even its wings are covered with smoke, clotted and black. Smoke
everywhere! A dirty canary chirps desolately in a cage beside me.
Its dream of green fields and sunshine is a very old dream – almost
worn out, I think.

From the back-window I can see a narrow brick-yard sloping
down to the river-side, strewed with rain-butts and tubs. The
river, dull and tawny colored, (*la belle rivière!*) drags itself
sluggishly along, tired of the heavy weight of boats and coal-
barges. What wonder? When I was a child, I used to fancy a look
of weary, dumb appeal upon the face of the negro-like river
slavishly bearing its burden day after day. Something of the same
idle notion comes to me today, when from the street-window I

look on the slow stream of human life creeping past, night and morning, to the great mills. Masses of men, with dull, besotted faces bent to the ground, sharpened here and there by pain or cunning; skin and muscle and flesh begrimed with smoke and ashes; stooping all night over boiling caldrons of metal, laired by day in dens of drunkenness and infamy; breathing from infancy to death an air saturated with fog and grease and soot, vileness for soul and body. What do you make of a case like that, amateur psychologist? You call it an altogether serious thing to be alive: to these men it is a drunken jest, a joke – horrible to angels perhaps, to them commonplace enough. My fancy about the river was an idle one: it is no type of such a life. What if it be stagnant and slimy here? It knows that beyond there waits for it odorous sunlight – quaint old gardens, dusky with soft, green foliage of apple-trees, and flushing crimson with roses – air, and fields, and mountains. The future of the Welsh puddler passing just now is not so pleasant. To be stowed away, after his grimy work is done, in a hole in the muddy graveyard, and after that – *not* air, nor green fields, nor curious roses.

Can you see how foggy the day is? As I stand here, idly tapping the window-pane, and looking out through the rain at the dirty back-yard and the coalboats below, fragments of an old story float up before me – a story of this old house into which I happened to come today. You may think it a tiresome story enough, as foggy as the day, sharpened by no sudden flashes of pain or pleasure. I know: only the outline of a dull life, that long since, with thousands of dull lives like its own, was vainly lived and lost: thousands of them – massed vile, slimy lives, like those of the torpid lizards in yonder stagnant water-butt. Lost? There is a curious point for you to settle, my friend, who study psychology in a lazy, *dilettante* way. Stop a moment. I am going to be honest. This is what I want you to do. I want you to hide your disgust, take no heed to your clean clothes, and come right down with me – here, into the thickest of the fog and mud and foul effluvia. I want you to hear this story. There is a secret down there, in this nightmare fog, that has lain dumb for centuries: I want to make it a real thing to you. You, Egoist, or Pantheist, or Arminian, busy in making straight paths for your feet on the hills, do not see it clearly – this terrible question which men here have gone mad and died trying to answer. I dare not put this secret into words. I told you it was dumb. These men, going by with drunken faces and brains full of unawakened power, do not ask it of Society or of God. Their lives ask it; their deaths ask it. There is no reply. I will tell you plainly that I have a great hope; and I bring it to you to be tested. It is this: that this terrible dumb question is its own reply; that it is not the sentence of death we think it, but, from the very extremity of its darkness, the most solemn prophecy which the world has known of the Hope to come. I dare make my meaning no clearer, but will only tell my story. It will, perhaps, seem to you as foul and dark as this thick vapor about us, and as pregnant with death; but if your eyes are free as mine are to look deeper, no perfume-tinted dawn will be so fair with promise of the day that shall surely come.

My story is very simple – only what I remember of the life of one of these men – a furnace-tender in one of Kirby & John's rolling-mills – Hugh Wolfe. You know the mills? They took the great order for the Lower Virginia railroads there last winter; run usually with about a thousand men. I cannot tell why I choose the half-forgotten story of this Wolfe more than that of myriads of these furnace-hands. Perhaps because there is a secret underlying sympathy between that story and this day with its impure fog and thwarted sunshine – or perhaps simply for the reason that this house is the one where the Wolfes lived. There were the father and son – both hands, as I said, in one of Kirby & John's mills for making railroad-iron – and Deborah, their cousin, a picker in some of the cotton-mills. The house was rented then to half a dozen families. The Wolfes had two of the cellar-rooms. The old man, like many of the puddlers and feeders of the mills, was Welsh – had spent half of his life in the Cornish tin-mines. You may pick the Welsh emigrants, Cornish miners, out of the throng passing the windows, any day. They are a trifle more filthy; their muscles are not so brawny; they stoop more. When they are drunk, they neither yell, nor shout, nor stagger, but skulk along like beaten hounds. A pure, unmixed blood, I fancy; shows itself in the slight angular bodies and sharply-cut facial lines. It is nearly thirty years since the Wolfes lived here. Their lives were like those of their class: incessant labor, sleeping in kennel-like rooms, eating rank pork and molasses, drinking – God and the distillers only know what; with an occasional night in jail, to atone for some drunken excess. Is that all of their lives? of the portion given to them and these their duplicates swarming the streets today? nothing beneath? all? So many a political reformer will tell you – and many a private reformer, too, who has gone among them with a heart tender with Christ's charity, and come out outraged, hardened.

One rainy night, about eleven o'clock, a crowd of half-clothed women stopped outside the cellar-door. They were going home from the cotton-mill.

'Good-night, Deb,' said one, a mulatto, steadying herself against the gas-post. She needed the post to steady her. So did more than one of them.

'Dah's a ball to Miss Potts' tonight. Ye'd best come.'

'Inteet, Deb, if hur'll come, hur'll hef fun,' said a shrill Welsh voice in the crowd.

Two or three dirty hands were thrust out to catch the gown of the woman, who was groping for the latch of the door.

'No.'

'No? Where's Kit Small, then?'

'Begorra! on the spools. Alleys behint, though we helped her, we dud. An wid ye! Let Deb alone! It's ondacent frettin' a quite body. Be the powers, an' we'll have a night of it! there'll be lashin's o' drink – the Vargent be blessed and praised for 't!'

They went on, the mulatto inclining for a moment to show fight, and drag the woman Wolfe off with them; but, being pacified, she staggered away.

Deborah groped her way into the cellar, and, after considerable stumbling, kindled a match, and lighted a tallow dip, that sent a yellow glimmer over the room. It was low, damp – the earthen floor covered with a green, slimy moss – a fetid air smothering the breath. Old Wolfe lay asleep on a heap of straw, wrapped in a torn horse-blanket. He was a pale, meek little man, with a white face and red rabbit-eyes. The woman Deborah was like him; only her face was even more ghastly, her lips bluer, her eyes more watery. She wore a faded cotton gown and a slouching bonnet. When she walked, one could see that she was deformed, almost a hunchback. She trod softly, so as not to waken him, and went through into the room beyond. There she found by the half-extinguished fire an iron saucepan filled with cold boiled potatoes, which she put upon a broken chair with a pint-cup of ale. Placing the old candlestick beside this dainty repast, she untied her bonnet, which hung limp and wet over her face, and prepared to eat her supper. It was the first food that had touched her lips since morning. There was enough of it, however: there is not always. She was hungry –

one could see that easily enough – and not drunk, as most of her companions would have been found at this hour. She did not drink, this woman – her face told that, too – nothing stronger than ale. Perhaps the weak, flaccid wretch had some stimulant in her pale life to keep her up – some love or hope, it might be, or urgent need. When that stimulant was gone, she would take to whiskey. Man cannot live by work alone. While she was skinning the potatoes, and munching them, a noise behind her made her stop.

'Janey!' she called, lifting the candle and peering into the darkness. 'Janey, are you there?'

A heap of ragged coats was heaved up, and the face of a young girl emerged, staring sleepily at the woman.

'Deborah,' she said, at last, 'I'm here the night.'

'Yes, child. Hur's welcome,' she said, quietly eating on.

The girl's face was haggard and sickly; her eyes were heavy with sleep and hunger: real Milesian eyes they were, dark, delicate blue, glooming out from black shadows with a pitiful fright.

'I was alone,' she said, timidly.

'Where's the father?' asked Deborah, holding out a potato, which the girl greedily seized.

'He's beyant – wid Haley – in the stone house.' (Did you ever hear the word *jail* from an Irish mouth?) 'I came here. Hugh told me never to stay melone.'

'Hugh?'

'Yes.'

A vexed frown crossed her face. The girl saw it, and added quickly –

'I have not seen Hugh the day, Deb. The old man says his watch lasts till the mornin'.'

The woman sprang up, and hastily began to arrange some bread and flitch in a tin pail, and to pour her own measure of ale into a bottle. Tying on her bonnet, she blew out the candle.

'Lay ye down, Janey dear,' she said, gently, covering her with the old rags. 'Hur can eat the potatoes, if hur's hungry.'

'Where are ye goin', Deb? The rain's sharp.'

'To the mill, with Hugh's supper.'

'Let him bide till th' morn. Sit ye down.'

'No, no,' – sharply pushing her off. 'The boy'll starve.'

She hurried from the cellar, while the child wearily coiled herself up for sleep. The rain was falling heavily, as the woman, pail in hand, emerged from the mouth of the alley, and turned down the narrow street, that stretched out, long and black, miles before her. Here and there a flicker of gas lighted an uncertain space of muddy footwalk and gutter; the long rows of houses, except an occasional lager-bier shop, were closed; now and then she met a band of millhands skulking to or from their work.

Not many even of the inhabitants of a manufacturing town know the vast machinery of system by which the bodies of workmen are governed, that goes on unceasingly from year to year. The hands of each mill are divided into watches that relieve each other as regularly as the sentinels of an army. By night and day the work goes on, the unsleeping engines groan and shriek, the fiery pools of metal boil and surge. Only for a day in the week, in half-courtesy to public censure, the fires are partially veiled; but as soon as the clock strikes midnight, the great furnaces break forth with renewed fury, the clamor begins with fresh, breathless vigor, the engines sob and shriek like 'gods in pain'.

As Deborah hurried down through the heavy rain, the noise of these thousand engines sounded through the sleep and shadow of the city like far-off thunder. The mill to which she was going lay on the river, a mile below the city-limits. It was far, and she was weak, aching from standing twelve hours at the spools. Yet it was her almost nightly walk to take this man his supper, though at every square she sat down to rest, and she knew she should receive small word of thanks.

Perhaps, if she had possessed an artist's eye, the picturesque oddity of the scene might have made her step stagger less, and the path seem shorter; but to her the mills were only 'summit deilish to look at by night.'

The road leading to the mills had been quarried from the solid rock, which rose abrupt and bare on one side of the cinder-covered road, while the river, sluggish and black, crept past on the other. The mills for rolling iron are simply immense tent-like roofs, covering acres of ground, open on every side. Beneath these roofs Deborah looked in on a city of fires, that burned hot and fiercely in the night. Fire in every horrible form: pits of flame waving in the wind; liquid metal-flames writhing in tortuous streams through the sand; wide caldrons filled with boiling fire, over which bent ghastly wretches stirring the strange brewing; and through all, crowds of half-clad men, looking like revengeful ghosts in the red light, hurried, throwing masses of glittering fire.

It was like a street in Hell. Even Deborah muttered, as she crept through, ' 'T looks like t' Devil's place!' It did – in more ways than one.

She found the man she was looking for, at last, heaping coal on a furnace. He had not time to eat his supper; so she went behind the furnace, and waited. Only a few men were with him, and they noticed her only by a 'Hyur comes t' hunchback, Wolfe.'

Deborah was stupid with sleep; her back pained her sharply; and her teeth chattered with cold, with the rain that soaked her clothes and dripped from her at every step. She stood, however, patiently holding the pail, and waiting.

'Hout, woman! ye look like a drowned cat. Come near to the fire' – said one of the men, approaching to scrape away the ashes.

She shook her head. Wolfe had forgotten her. He turned, hearing the man, and came closer.

'I did no' think; gi' me my supper, woman.'

She watched him eat with a painful eagerness. With a woman's quick instinct, she saw that he was not hungry – was eating to please her. Her pale, watery eyes began to gather a strange light.

'Is't good, Hugh? T' ale was a bit sour, I feared.'

'No, good enough.' He hesitated a moment. 'Ye 're tired, poor lass! Bide here till I go. Lay down there on that heap of ash, and go to sleep.'

He threw her an old coat for a pillow, and turned to his work. The heap was the refuse of the burnt iron, and was not a hard bed; the half-smothered warmth, too, penetrated her limbs, dulling their pain and cold shiver.

Miserable enough she looked, lying there on the ashes like a limp, dirty rag – yet not an unfitting figure to crown the scene of hopeless discomfort and veiled crime: more fitting, if one looked deeper into the heart of things – at her thwarted woman's form, her colorless life, her waking stupor that smothered pain and hunger – even more fit to be a type of her class. Deeper yet if one could look, was there nothing worth reading in this wet, faded thing, half-covered with ashes? no story of a soul filled with groping passionate love, heroic unselfishness, fierce jealousy? of years of weary trying to please the one human being whom she loved, to gain one look of real heart-kindness from him? If anything like this were hidden beneath the pale, bleared eyes, and dull, washed-out-looking face, no one had ever taken the trouble to read its faint signs: not the half-clothed furnace-tender, Wolfe, certainly. Yet he was kind to her: it was his nature to be kind, even to the very rats that swarmed in the cellar: kind to her in just the same way. She knew that. And it might be that very knowledge had given to her face its apathy and vacancy more than her low, torpid life. One sees that dead, vacant look steal sometimes over the rarest, finest of women's faces – in the very midst, it may be, of their warmest summer's day; and then one can guess at the secret of intolerable solitude that lies hid beneath the delicate laces and brilliant smile. There was no warmth, no brilliancy, no summer for this woman; so the stupor and vacancy had time to gnaw into her face perpetually. She was young, too, though no one guessed it; so the gnawing was the fiercer.

She lay quiet in the dark corner, listening, through the monotonous din and uncertain glare of the works, to the dull plash of the rain in the far distance – shrinking back whenever the man Wolfe happened to look towards her. She knew, in spite of all his kindness, that there was that in her face and form which made him loathe the sight of her. She felt by instinct, although she could not comprehend it, the finer nature of the man, which made him among his fellow-workmen something unique, set apart. She knew, that, down under all the vileness and coarseness of his life, there was a groping passion for whatever was beautiful and pure –that his soul sickened with disgust at her deformity, even when his words were kindest. Through this dull consciousness, which never left her, came, like a sting, the recollection of the dark blue eyes and lithe figure of the little Irish girl she had left in the cellar. The recollection struck through even her stupid intellect with a vivid glow of beauty and of grace. Little Janey, timid, helpless, clinging to Hugh as her only friend: that was the sharp thought, the bitter thought, that drove into the glazed eyes a fierce light of pain. You laugh at it? Are pain and jealousy less savage realities down here in this place I am taking you to than in your own house or your own heart – your heart, which they clutch at sometimes? The note is the same, I fancy, be the octave high or low.

If you could go into this mill where Deborah lay, and drag out from the hearts of these men the terrible tragedy of their lives, taking it as a symptom of the disease of their class, no ghost Horror would terrify you more. A reality of soul-starvation, of living death, that meets you every day under the besotted faces on the street – I can paint nothing of this, only give you the outside outlines of a night, a crisis in the life of one man: whatever muddy depth of soul-history lies beneath you can read according to the eyes God has given you.

Wolfe, while Deborah watched him as a spaniel its master, bent over the furnace with his iron pole, unconscious of her scrutiny, only stopping to receive orders. Physically, Nature had promised the man but little. He had already lost the strength and instinct vigor of a man, his muscles were thin, his nerves weak, his face (a meek, woman's face) haggard, yellow with consumption. In the mill he was known as one of the girl-men: 'Molly Wolfe' was his *sobriquet*. He was never seen in the cockpit, did not own a terrier, drank but seldom; when he did, desperately. He fought sometimes, but was always thrashed, pommelled to a jelly. The man was game enough, when his blood was up: but he was no favorite in the mill; he had the taint of school-learning on him —not to a dangerous extent, only a quarter or so in the free-school in fact, but enough to ruin him as a good hand in a fight.

For other reasons, too, he was not popular. Not one of themselves, they felt that, though outwardly as filthy and ash-covered; silent, with foreign thoughts and longings breaking out through his quietness in innumerable curious ways: this one, for instance. In the neighboring furnace-buildings lay great heaps of the refuse from the ore after the pig-metal is run. *Korl* we call it here: a light, porous substance, of a delicate, waxen, flesh-colored tinge. Out of the blocks of this *korl*, Wolfe, in his off-hours from the furnace, had a habit of chipping and moulding figures — hideous, fantastic enough, but sometimes strangely beautiful: even the mill-men saw that, while they jeered at him. It was a curious fancy in the man, almost a passion. The few hours for rest he spent hewing and hacking with his blunt knife, never speaking, until his watch came again — working at one figure for months, and, when it was finished, breaking it to pieces perhaps, in a fit of disappointment. A morbid, gloomy man, untaught, unled, left to feed his soul in grossness and crime, and hard, grinding labor.

I want you to come down and look at this Wolfe, standing there among the lowest of his kind, and see him just as he is, that you may judge him justly when you hear the story of this night. I want you to look back, as he does every day, at his birth in vice, his starved infancy; to remember the heavy years he has groped through as boy and man — the slow, heavy years of constant, hot work. So long ago he began, that he thinks sometimes he has worked there for ages. There is no hope that it will ever end. Think that God put into this man's soul a fierce thirst for beauty – to know it, to create it; to *be* – something, he knows not what – other than he is. There are moments when a passing cloud, the sun glinting on the purple thistles, a kindly smile, a child's face, will rouse him to a passion of pain – when his nature starts up with a mad cry of rage against God, man, whoever it is that has forced this vile, slimy life upon him. With all this groping, this mad desire, a great blind intellect stumbling through wrong, a loving poet's heart, the man was by habit only a coarse, vulgar laborer, familiar with sights and words you would blush to name. Be just: when I tell you about this night, see him as he is. Be just – not like man's law, which seizes on one isolated fact, but like God's judging angel, whose clear, sad eye saw all the countless cankering days of this man's life, all the countless nights, when, sick with starving, his soul fainted in him, before it judged him for this night, the saddest of all.

I called this night the crisis of his life. If it was, it stole on him unawares. These great turning-days of life cast no shadow before, slip by unconsciously. Only a trifle, a little turn of the rudder, and the ship goes to heaven or hell.

Wolfe, while Deborah watched him, dug into the furnace of melting iron with his pole, dully thinking only how many rails the lump would yield. It was late – nearly Sunday morning; another hour, and the heavy work would be done – only the furnaces to replenish and cover for the next day. The workmen were growing more noisy, shouting, as they had to do, to be heard over the deep clamor of the mills. Suddenly they grew less boisterous – at the far end, entirely silent. Something unusual had happened. After a moment, the silence came nearer; the men stopped their jeers and drunken choruses. Deborah, stupidly lifting up her head, saw the cause of the quiet. A group of five or six men were slowly approaching, stopping to examine each furnace as they came. Visitors often came to see the mills after night: except by growing less noisy, the men took no notice of them. The furnace where Wolfe worked was near the bounds of the works; they halted there hot and tired: a walk over one of these great foundries was no trifling task. The woman, drawing out of sight, turned over to sleep. Wolfe, seeing them stop, suddenly roused from his indifferent stupor, and watched them keenly. He knew some of them: the overseer, Clarke – a son of Kirby, one of the mill-owners – and a Doctor May, one of the town-physicians. The other two were strangers. Wolfe came closer. He seized eagerly every chance that brought him into contact with this mysterious class that shone down on him perpetually with the glamour of another order of being. What made the difference between them? That was the mystery of his life. He had a vague notion that perhaps tonight he could find it out. One of the strangers sat down on a pile of bricks, and beckoned young Kirby to his side.

'This *is* hot, with a vengeance. A match, please?' – lighting his cigar. 'But the walk is worth the trouble. If it were not that you must have heard it so often, Kirby, I would tell you that your works look like Dante's Inferno.'

Kirby laughed.

'Yes. Yonder is Farinata himself in the burning tomb,' – pointing to some figure in the shimmering shadows.

'Judging from some of the faces of your men,' said the other, 'they bid fair to try the reality of Dante's vision, some day.'

Young Kirby looked curiously around, as if seeing the faces of his hands for the first time.

'They're bad enough, that's true. A desperate set, I fancy. Eh, Clarke?'

The overseer did not hear him. He was talking of net profits just then – giving, in fact, a schedule of the annual business of the firm to a sharp peering little Yankee, who jotted down notes on a paper laid on the crown of his hat: a reporter for one of the city-papers, getting up a series of reviews of the leading manufactories. The other gentlemen had accompanied them merely for amusement. They were silent until the notes were finished, drying their feet at the furnaces, and sheltering their faces from the intolerable heat. At last the overseer concluded with—

'I believe that is a pretty fair estimate, Captain.'

'Here, some of you men!' said Kirby, 'bring up those boards. We may as well sit down, gentlemen, until the rain is over. It cannot last much longer at this rate.'

'Pig-metal,' – mumbled the reporter – 'um! coal facilities – um! hands employed, twelve hundred – bitumen – um! all right, I believe, Mr Clarke; sinking-fund – what did you say was your sinking-fund?'

'Twelve hundred hands?' said the stranger, the young man who had first spoken. 'Do you control their votes, Kirby?'

'Control? No.' The young man smiled complacently. 'But my father brought seven hundred votes to the polls for his candidate last November. No forcework, you understand – only a speech or two, a hint to form themselves into a society, and a bit of red and blue bunting to make them a flag. The Invincible Roughs – I believe that is their name. I forget the motto: "Our country's hope," I think.'

There was a laugh. The young man talking to Kirby sat with an amused light in his cool gray eye, surveying critically the half-clothed figures of the puddlers, and the slow swing of their brawny muscles. He was a stranger in the city – spending a couple of months in the borders of a Slave State, to study the institutions of the South – a brother-in-law of Kirby's – Mitchell. He was an amateur gymnast – hence his anatomical eye; a patron, in a *blasé* way, of the prize-ring; a man who sucked the essence out of a science or philosophy in an indifferent, gentlemanly way; who took Kant, Novalis, Humboldt, for what they were worth in his own scales; accepting all, despising nothing, in heaven, earth, or hell, but one-idead men; with a temper yielding and brilliant as summer water, until his Self was touched, when it was ice, though brilliant still. Such men are not rare in the States.

As he knocked the ashes from his cigar, Wolfe caught with a quick pleasure the contour of the white hand, the blood-glow of a red ring he wore. His voice, too, and that of Kirby's, touched him like music – low, even, with chording cadences. About this man Mitchell hung the impalpable atmosphere belonging to the thoroughbred gentleman. Wolfe, scraping away the ashes beside him, was conscious of it, did obeisance to it with his artist sense, unconscious that he did so.

The rain did not cease. Clarke and the reporter left the mills; the others, comfortably seated near the furnace, lingered, smoking and talking in a desultory way. Greek would not have been more unintelligible to the furnace-tenders, whose presence they soon forgot entirely. Kirby drew out a newspaper from his pocket and read aloud some article, which they discussed eagerly. At every sentence, Wolfe listened more and more like a dumb, hopeless animal, with a duller, more stolid look creeping over his face, glancing now and then at Mitchell, marking acutely every smallest sign of refinement, then back to himself, seeing as in a mirror his filthy body, his more stained soul.

Never! He had no words for such a thought, but he knew now, in all the sharpness of the bitter certainty, that between them there was a great gulf never to be passed. Never!

The bell of the mills rang for midnight. Sunday morning had dawned. Whatever hidden message lay in the tolling bells floated past these men unknown. Yet it was there. Veiled in the solemn music ushering the risen Saviour was a key-note to solve the darkest secrets of a world gone wrong – even this social riddle which the brain of the grimy puddler grappled with madly tonight.

The men began to withdraw the metal from the caldrons. The mills were deserted on Sundays, except by the hands who fed the fires, and those who had no lodgings and slept usually on the ash-heaps. The three strangers sat still during the next hour, watching the men cover the furnaces, laughing now and then at some jest of Kirby's.

'Do you know,' said Mitchell, 'I like this view of the works better than when the glare was fiercest? These heavy shadows and the amphitheatre of smothered fires are ghostly, unreal. One could fancy these red smouldering lights to be the half-shut eyes of wild beasts, and the spectral figures their victims in the den.'

Kirby laughed. 'You are fanciful. Come, let us get out of the den. The spectral figures, as you call them, are a little too real for me to fancy a close proximity in the darkness – unarmed, too.'

The others rose, buttoning their overcoats, and lighting cigars.

'Raining, still,' said Doctor May, 'and hard. Where did we leave the coach, Mitchell?'

'At the other side of the works. Kirby, what's that?'

Mitchell stared back, half-frightened, as, suddenly turning a corner, the white figure of a woman faced him in the darkness – a woman, white, of giant proportions, crouching on the ground, her arms flung out in some wild gesture of warning.

'Stop! Make that fire burn there!' cried Kirby, stopping short.

The flame burst out, flashing the gaunt figure into bold relief.

Mitchell drew a long breath.

'I thought it was alive,' he said, going up curiously.

The others followed.

'Not marble, eh?' asked Kirby, touching it.

One of the lower overseers stopped.

'Korl, Sir.'

'Who did it?'

'Can't say. Some of the hands; chipped it out in off-hours.'

'Chipped to some purpose, I should say. What a flesh-tint the stuff has! Do you see, Mitchell?'

'I see.'

He had stepped aside where the light fell boldest on the figure, looking at it in silence. There was not one line of beauty or grace in it: a nude woman's form, muscular, grown coarse with labor, the powerful limbs instinct with some one poignant longing. One idea: there it was in the tense, rigid muscles, the clutching hands, the wild, eager face, like that of a starving wolf's. Kirby and Doctor May walked around it, critical, curious. Mitchell stood aloof, silent. The figure touched him strangely.

'Not badly done,' said Doctor May. 'Where did the fellow learn that sweep of the muscles in the arm and hand? Look at them! They are groping – do you see? clutching: the peculiar action of a man dying of thirst.'

'They have ample facilities for studying anatomy,' sneered Kirby, glancing at the half-naked figures.

'Look,' continued the Doctor, 'at this bony wrist, and the strained sinews of the instep! A working-woman – the very type of her class.'

'God forbid!' muttered Mitchell.

'Why?' demanded May. 'What does the fellow intend by the figure? I cannot catch the meaning.'

'Ask him,' said the other, dryly. 'There he stands,' – pointing to Wolfe, who stood with a group of men, leaning on his ash-rake.

The Doctor beckoned him with the affable smile which kind-hearted men put on, when talking to these people.

'Mr Mitchell has picked you out as the man who did this – I'm sure I don't know why. But what did you mean by it?'

'She be hungry.'

Wolfe's eyes answered Mitchell, not the Doctor.

'Oh-h! But what a mistake you have made, my fine fellow! You have given no sign of starvation to the body. It is strong – terribly strong. It has the mad, half-despairing gesture of drowning.'

Wolfe stammered, glanced appealingly at Mitchell, who saw the soul of the thing, he knew. But the cool, probing eyes were turned on himself now – mocking, cruel, relentless.

'Not hungry for meat,' the furnace-tender said at last.

'What then? Whiskey?' jeered Kirby, with a coarse laugh.

Wolfe was silent a moment, thinking.

'I dunno,' he said, with a bewildered look. 'It mebbe. Summat to make her live, I think – like you. Whiskey ull do it, in a way.'

The young man laughed again. Mitchell flashed a look of disgust somewhere – not at Wolfe.

'May,' he broke out impatiently, 'are you blind? Look at that woman's face! It asks questions of God, and says, "I have a right to know." Good God, how hungry it is!'

They looked a moment; then May turned to the mill-owner:

'Have you many such hands as this? What are you going to do with them? Keep them at puddling iron?'

Kirby shrugged his shoulders. Mitchell's look had irritated him.

'*Ce n'est pas mon affaire.* I have no fancy for nursing infant geniuses. I suppose there are some stray gleams of mind and soul among these wretches. The Lord will take care of his own; or else they can work out their own salvation. I have heard you call our American system a ladder which any man can scale. Do you doubt it? Or perhaps you want to banish all social ladders, and put us all on a flat table-land – eh, May?'

The Doctor looked vexed, puzzled. Some terrible problem lay hid in this woman's face, and troubled these men. Kirby waited for an answer, and, receiving none, went on, warming with his subject.

'I tell you, there's something wrong that no talk of "*Liberté*" or "*Égalité*" will do away. If I had the making of men, these men who do the lowest part of the world's work should be machines – nothing more – hands. It would be kindness. God help them! What are taste, reason, to creatures who must live such lives as that?' He pointed to Deborah, sleeping on the ash-heap. 'So many nerves to sting them to pain. What if God had put your brain, with all its agony of touch, into your fingers, and bid you work and strike with that?'

'You think you could govern the world better?' laughed the Doctor.

'I do not think at all.'

'That is true philosophy. Drift with the stream, because you cannot dive deep enough to find bottom, eh?'

'Exactly,' rejoined Kirby. 'I do not think. I wash my hands of all social problems – slavery, caste, white or black. My duty to my operatives has a narrow limit – the pay-hour on Saturday night. Outside of that, if they cut korl, or cut each other's throats, (the more popular amusement of the two,) I am not responsible.'

The Doctor sighed – a good honest sigh, from the depths of his stomach.

'God help us! Who is responsible?'

'Not I, I tell you,' said Kirby, testily. 'What has the man who pays them money to do with their souls' concerns, more than the grocer or butcher who takes it?'

'And yet,' said Mitchell's cynical voice, 'look at her! How hungry she is!'

Kirby tapped his boot with his cane. No one spoke. Only the dumb face of the rough image looking into their faces with the awful question, 'What shall we do to be saved?' Only Wolfe's face, with its heavy weight of brain, its weak, uncertain mouth, its desperate eyes, out of which looked the soul of his class – only Wolfe's face turned towards Kirby's. Mitchell laughed – a cool, musical laugh.

'Money has spoken!' he said, seating himself lightly on a stone with the air of an amused spectator at a play. 'Are you answered?' – turning to Wolfe his clear, magnetic face.

Bright and deep and cold as Arctic air, the soul of the man lay tranquil beneath. He looked at the furnace-tender as he had looked at a rare mosaic in the morning; only the man was the more amusing study of the two.

'Are you answered? Why, May, look at him! "*De profundis clamavi.*" Or, to quote in English, "Hungry and thirsty, his soul faints in him." And so Money sends back its answer into the depths through you, Kirby! Very clear the answer, too! I think I remember reading the same words somewhere: washing your hands in Eau de Cologne, and saying, "I am innocent of the blood of this man. See ye to it!" '

Kirby flushed angrily.

'You quote Scripture freely.'

'Do I not quote correctly? I think I remember another line, which may amend my meaning? "Inasmuch as ye did it unto one of the least of these, ye did it unto me." Deist? Bless you, man, I was raised on the milk of the Word. Now, Doctor, the pocket of the world having uttered its voice, what has the heart to say? You are a philanthropist, in a small way – *n'est ce pas?* Here, boy, this gentleman can show you how to cut korl better – or your destiny. Go on, May!'

'I think a mocking devil possesses you tonight,' rejoined the Doctor, seriously.

He went to Wolfe and put his hand kindly on his arm. Something of a vague idea possessed the Doctor's brain that much good was to be done here by a friendly word or two: a latent genius to be warmed into life by a waited-for sunbeam. Here it was: he had brought it. So he went on complacently:

'Do you know, boy, you have it in you to be a great sculptor, a great man? do you understand?' (talking down to the capacity of his hearer: it is a way people have with children, and men like Wolfe) – 'to live a better, stronger life than I, or Mr Kirby here? A man may make himself anything he chooses. God has given you stronger powers than many men – me, for instance.'

May stopped, heated, glowing with his own magnanimity. And it was magnanimous. The puddler had drunk in every word, looking through the Doctor's flurry, and generous heat, and self-approval, into his will, with those slow, absorbing eyes of his.

'Make yourself what you will. It is your right.'

'I know,' quietly. 'Will you help me?'

Mitchell laughed again. The Doctor turned now, in a passion –

'You know, Mitchell, I have not the means. You know, if I had, it is in my heart to take this boy and educate him for' –

'The glory of God, and the glory of John May.'

May did not speak for a moment; then, controlled, he said –

'Why should one be raised, when myriads are left? I have not the money, boy,' to Wolfe, shortly.

'Money?' He said it over slowly, as one repeats the guessed answer to a riddle, doubtfully. 'That is it? Money?'

'Yes, money – that is it,' said Mitchell, rising, and drawing his furred coat about him. 'You've found the cure for all the world's diseases. Come, May, find your good-humor, and come home. This damp wind chills my very bones. Come and preach your Saint Simonian doctrines tomorrow to Kirby's hands. Let them have a clear idea of the rights of the soul, and I'll venture next week they'll strike for higher wages. That will be the end of it.'

'Will you send the coach-driver to this side of the mills?' asked Kirby, turning to Wolfe.

He spoke kindly: it was his habit to do so. Deborah, seeing the puddler go, crept after him. The three men waited outside. Doctor May walked up and down, chafed. Suddenly he stopped.

'Go back, Mitchell! You say the pocket and the heart of the world speak without meaning to these people. What has its head to say? Taste, culture, refinement? Go!'

Mitchell was leaning against a brick wall. He turned his head indolently, and looked into the mills. There hung about the place a thick, unclean odor. The slightest motion of his hand marked that he perceived it, and his insufferable disgust. That was all. May said nothing, only quickened his angry tramp.

'Besides,' added Mitchell, giving a corollary to his answer, 'it would be of no use. I am not one of them.'

'You do not mean' – said May, facing him.

'Yes, I mean just that. Reform is born of need, not pity. No vital movement of the people's has worked down, for good or evil; fermented, instead, carried up the heaving, cloggy mass. Think back through history, and you will know it. What will this lowest deep – thieves, Magdalens, negroes – do with the light filtered through ponderous Church creeds, Baconian theories, Goethe schemes? Some day, out of their bitter need will be thrown up their own light-bringer – their Jean Paul, their Cromwell, their Messiah.'

'Bah!' was the Doctor's inward criticism. However, in practice, he adopted the theory; for, when, night and morning, afterwards, he prayed that power might be given these degraded souls to rise, he glowed at heart, recognizing an accomplished duty.

Wolfe and the woman had stood in the shadow of the works as the coach drove off. The Doctor had held out his hand in a frank, generous way, telling him to 'take care of himself, and to remember it was his right to rise.' Mitchell had simply touched his hat, as to an equal, with a quiet look of thorough recognition. Kirby had thrown Deborah some money, which she found, and clutched eagerly enough. They were gone now, all of them. The man sat down on the cinder-road, looking up into the murky sky.

' 'T be late, Hugh. Wunnot hur come?'

He shook his head doggedly, and the woman crouched out of his sight against the wall. Do you remember rare moments when a sudden light flashed over yourself, your world, God? when you stood on a mountain-peak, seeing your life as it might have been, as it is? one quick instant, when custom lost its force and everyday usage? when your friend, wife, brother, stood in a new light? your soul was bared, and the grave – a foretaste of the nakedness of the Judgment-Day? So it came before him, his life, that night. The slow tides of pain he had borne gathered themselves up and surged against his soul. His squalid daily life, the brutal coarseness eating into his brain, as the ashes into his skin: before, these things had been a dull aching into his consciousness; tonight, they were reality. He gripped the filthy red shirt that clung, stiff with soot, about him, and tore it savagely from his arm. The flesh beneath was muddy with grease and ashes – and the heart beneath that! And the soul? God knows.

Then flashed before his vivid poetic sense the man who had left him – the pure face, the delicate, sinewy limbs, in harmony with all he knew of beauty or truth. In his cloudy fancy he had pictured a Something like this. He had found it in this Mitchell, even when he idly scoffed at his pain: a Man all-knowing, all-seeing, crowned by Nature, reigning – the keen glance of his eye falling like a sceptre on other men. And yet his instinct taught him that he too – He! He looked at himself with sudden loathing, sick, wrung his hands with a cry, and then was silent. With all the phantoms of his heated, ignorant fancy, Wolfe had not been vague in his ambitions. They were practical, slowly built up before him out of his knowledge of what he could do. Through years he had day by day made this hope a real thing to himself – a clear, projected figure of himself, as he might become.

Able to speak, to know what was best, to raise these men and women working at his side up with him: sometimes he forgot this defined hope in the frantic anguish to escape – only to escape – out of the wet, the pain, the ashes, somewhere, anywhere, – only for one moment of free air on a hill-side, to lie down and let his sick soul throb itself out in the sunshine. But tonight he panted for life. The savage strength of his nature was roused; his cry was fierce to God for justice.

'Look at me!' he said to Deborah, with a low, bitter laugh, striking his puny chest savagely. 'What am I worth, Deb? Is it my fault that I am no better? My fault? My fault?'

He stopped, stung with a sudden remorse, seeing her hunchback shape writhing with sobs. For Deborah was crying thankless tears, according to the fashion of women.

'God forgi' me, woman! Things go harder wi' you nor me. It's a worse share.'

He got up and helped her to rise; and they went doggedly down the muddy street, side by side.

'It's all wrong,' he muttered, slowly – 'all wrong! I dunnot understan'. But it'll end some day.'

'Come home, Hugh!' she said, coaxingly; for he had stopped, looking around bewildered.

'Home – and back to the mill!' He went on saying this over to himself, as if he would mutter down every pain in this dull despair.

She followed him through the fog, her blue lips chattering with cold. They reached the cellar at last. Old Wolfe had been drinking since she went out, and had crept nearer the door. The girl Janey slept heavily in the corner. He went up to her, touching softly the worn white arm with his fingers. Some bitterer thought stung him, as he stood there. He wiped the drops from his forehead, and went into the room beyond, livid, trembling. A hope, trifling, perhaps, but very dear, had died just then out of the poor puddler's life, as he looked at the sleeping, innocent girl – some plan for the future, in which she had borne a part. He gave it up that moment, then and forever. Only a trifle, perhaps, to us: his face grew a shade paler – that was all. But, somehow, the man's soul, as God and the angels looked down on it, never was the same afterwards.

Deborah followed him into the inner room. She carried a candle, which she placed on the floor, closing the door after her. She had seen the look on his face, as he turned away: her own grew deadly. Yet, as she came up to him, her eyes glowed. He was seated on an old chest, quiet, holding his face in his hands.

'Hugh!' she said, softly.

He did not speak.

'Hugh, did hur hear what the man said – him with the clear voice? Did hur hear? Money, money – that it wud do all?'

He pushed her away – gently, but he was worn out; her rasping tone fretted him.

'Hugh!'

The candle flared a pale yellow light over the cobwebbed brick walls, and the woman standing there. He looked at her. She was young, in deadly earnest; her faded eyes, and wet, ragged figure caught from their frantic eagerness a power akin to beauty.

'Hugh, it is true! Money ull do it! Oh, Hugh, boy, listen till me! He said it true! It is money!'

'I know. Go back! I do not want you here.'

'Hugh, it is t' last time. I'll never worrit hur again.'

There were tears in her voice now, but she choked them back.

'Hear till me only tonight! If one of t' witch people wud come, them we heard of t' home, and gif hur all hur wants, what then? Say, Hugh!!'

'What do you mean?'

'I mean money.'

Her whisper shrilled through his brain.

'If one of t' witch dwarfs wud come from t' lane moors tonight, and gif hur money, to go out – *out*, I say – out, lad, where t' sun shines, and t' heath grows, and t' ladies walk in silken gownds, and God stays all t' time – where t' man lives that talked to us tonight – Hugh knows – Hugh could walk there like a king!'

He thought the woman mad, tried to check her, but she went on, fierce in her eager haste.

'If *I* were t' witch dwarf, if I had t' money, wud hur thank me? Wud hur take me out o' this place wid hur and Janey? I wud not come into the gran' house hur wud build, to vex hur wid t' hunch – only at night, when t' shadows were dark, stand far off to see hur.'

Mad? Yes! Are many of us mad in this way?

'Poor Deb! poor Deb!' he said, soothingly.

'It is here,' she said, suddenly, jerking into his hand a small roll. 'I took it! I did it! Me, me! not hur! I shall be hanged, I shall be burnt in hell, if anybody knows I took it! Out of his pocket, as he leaned against t' bricks. Hur knows?'

She thrust it into his hand, and then, her errand done, began to gather chips together to make a fire, choking down hysteric sobs.

'Has it come to this?'

That was all he said. The Welsh Wolfe blood was honest. The roll was a small green pocket-book containing one or two gold pieces, and a check for an incredible amount, as it seemed to the poor puddler. He laid it down, hiding his face again in his hands.

'Hugh, don't be angry wud me! It's only poor Deb – hur knows?'

He took the long skinny fingers kindly in his.

'Angry? God help me, no! Let me sleep. I am tired.'

He threw himself heavily down on the wooden bench, stunned with pain and weariness. She brought some old rags to cover him.

It was late on Sunday evening before he awoke. I tell God's truth, when I say he had then no thought of keeping this money. Deborah had hid it in his pocket. He found it there. She watched him eagerly, as he took it out.

'I must gif it to him,' he said, reading her face.

'Hur knows,' she said with a bitter sign of disappointment. 'But it is hur right to keep it.'

His right! The word struck him. Doctor May had used the same. He washed himself, and went out to find this man Mitchell. His right! Why did this chance word cling to him so obstinately? Do you hear the fierce devils whisper in his ear, as he went slowly down the darkening street?

The evening came on, slow and calm. He seated himself at the end of an alley leading into one of the larger streets. His brain was clear tonight, keen, intent, mastering. It would not start back, cowardly, from any hellish temptation, but meet it face to face. Therefore the great temptation of his life came to him veiled by no sophistry, but bold, defiant, owning its own vile name, trusting to one bold blow for victory.

He did not deceive himself. Theft! That was it. At first the word sickened him; then he grappled with it. Sitting there on a broken cart-wheel, the fading day, the noisy groups, the church-bells' tolling passed before him like a panorama, while the sharp struggle went on within. This money! He took it out, and looked at it. If he gave it back, what then? He was going to be cool about it.

People going by to church saw only a sickly mill-boy watching them quietly at the alley's mouth. They did not know that he was mad, or they would not have gone by so quietly: mad with hunger; stretching out his hands to the world, that had given so much to them, for leave to live the life God meant him to live. His soul within him was smothering to death; he wanted so much, thought so much, and *knew* – nothing. There was nothing of which he was certain, except the mill and things there. Of God and heaven he had heard so little, that they were to him what fairy-land is to a child: something real, but not here; very far off. His brain, greedy, dwarfed, full of thwarted energy and unused powers, questioned these men and women going by, coldly, bitterly, that night. Was it not his right to live as they – a pure life, a good, true-hearted life, full of beauty and kind words? He only wanted to know how to use the strength within him. His heart warmed, as he thought of it. He suffered himself to think of it longer. If he took the money?

Then he saw himself as he might be, strong, helpful, kindly. The night crept on, as this one image slowly evolved itself from the crowd of other thoughts and stood triumphant. He looked at it. As he might be! What wonder, if it blinded him to delirium – the madness that underlies all revolution, all progress, and all fall?

You laugh at the shallow temptation? You see the error underlying its argument so clearly – that to him a true life was one of full development rather than self-restraint? that he was deaf to the higher tone in a cry of voluntary suffering for truth's sake than in the fullest flow of spontaneous harmony? I do not plead his cause. I only want to show you the mote in my brother's eye: then you can see clearly to take it out.

The money – there it lay on his knee, a little blotted slip of paper, nothing in itself; used to raise him out of the pit, something straight from God's hand. A thief! Well, what was it to be a thief? He met the question at last, face to face, wiping the clammy drops of sweat from his forehead. God made this money – the fresh air, too – for his children's use. He never made the difference between poor and rich. The Something who looked down on him that moment through the cool gray sky had a kindly face, he knew – loved his children alike. Oh, he knew that!

There were times when the soft floods of color in the crimson and purple flames, or the clear depth of amber in the water below the bridge, had somehow given him a glimpse of another world than this – of an infinite depth of beauty and of quiet somewhere, somewhere, a depth of quiet and rest and love. Looking up now, it became strangely real. The sun had sunk quite below the hills, but his last rays struck upward, touching the zenith. The fog had risen, and the town and river were steeped in its thick, gray damp; but overhead, the sun-touched smoke-clouds opened like a cleft ocean – shifting, rolling seas of crimson mist, waves of billowy silver veined with blood-scarlet, inner depths unfathomable of glancing light. Wolfe's artist-eye grew drunk with color. The gates of that other world! Fading, flashing before him now! What, in that world of Beauty, Content, and Right, were the petty laws, the mine and thine, of mill-owners and mill hands?

A consciousness of power stirred within him. He stood up. A man – he thought, stretching out his hands – free to work, to live, to love! Free! His right! He folded the scrap of paper in his hand. As his nervous fingers took it in, limp and blotted, so his soul took in the mean temptation, lapped it in fancied rights, in dreams of improved existences, drifting and endless as the cloud-seas of color. Clutching it, as if the tightness of his hold would strengthen his sense of possession, he went aimlessly down the street. It was his watch at the mill. He need not go, need never go again, thank God! shaking off the thought with unspeakable loathing.

Shall I go over the history of the hours of that night? how the man wandered from one to another of his old haunts, with a half-consciousness of bidding them farewell – lanes and alleys and backyard where the mill-hands lodged – noting, with a new eagerness, the filth and drunkenness, the pig-pens, the ash-heaps covered with potato-skins, the bloated, pimpled women at the doors – with a new disgust, a new sense of sudden triumph, and, under all, a new, vague dread, unknown before, smothered down, kept under, but still there? It left him but once during the night, when, for the second time in his life, he entered a church. It was a sombre Gothic pile, where the stained light lost itself in far-retreating arches; built to meet the requirements and sympathies of a far other class than Wolfe's. Yet it touched, moved him uncontrollably. The distances, the shadows, the still, marble figures, the mass of silent kneeling worshippers, the mysterious music, thrilled, lifted his soul with a wonderful pain. Wolfe forgot himself, forgot the new life he was going to live, the mean terror gnawing underneath. The voice of the speaker strengthened the charm; it was clear, feeling, full, strong. An old man, who had lived much, suffered much; whose brain was keenly alive, dominant; whose heart was summer-warm with charity. He taught it tonight. He held up Humanity in its grand total; showed the great world-cancer to his people. Who could show it better? He was a Christian reformer; he studied the age thoroughly; his outlook at man had been free, world-wide, over all time. His faith stood sublime upon the Rock of Ages; his fiery zeal guided vast schemes by which the gospel was to be preached to all nations. How did he preach it tonight? In burning, light-laden words he painted the incarnate Life, Love, the universal Man: words that became reality in the lives of these people – that lived again in beautiful words and actions, trifling, but heroic. Sin, as he defied it, was a real foe to them; their trials, temptations, were his. His words passed far over the furnace-tender's grasp, toned to suit another class of culture; they sounded in his ears a very pleasant song in an unknown tongue. He meant to cure this world-cancer with a steady eye that had never glared with hunger, and a hand that neither poverty nor strychnine-whiskey had taught to shake. In this morbid, distorted heart of the Welsh puddler he had failed.

Wolfe rose at last, and turned from the church down the street. He looked up; the night had come on foggy, damp; the golden mists had vanished, and the sky lay dull and ash-colored. He wandered again aimlessly down the street, idly wondering what had become of the cloud-sea of crimson and scarlet. The trial-day of this man's life was over, and he had lost the victory. What followed was mere drifting circumstance – a quicker walking over the path – that was all. Do you want to hear the end of it? You wish me to make a tragic story out of it? Why, in the police reports of the morning paper you can find a dozen such tragedies: hints of shipwrecks unlike any that ever befell on the high seas; hints that here a power was lost to heaven – that there a soul went down where no tide can ebb or flow. Commonplace enough the hints are – jocose sometimes, done up in rhyme.

Doctor May, a month after the night I have told you of, was reading to his wife at breakfast from this fourth column of the morning-paper: an unusual thing – these police-reports not being, in general, choice reading for ladies; but it was only one item he read.

'Oh, my dear! You remember that man I told you of, that we saw at Kirby's mill? that was arrested for robbing Mitchell? Here he is; just listen: "Circuit Court. Judge Day. Hugh Wolfe, operative in Kirby & John's Loudon Mills. Charge, grand larceny. Sentence, nineteen years hard labor in penitentiary." Scoundrel! Serves him right! After all our kindness that night! Picking Mitchell's pocket at the very time!'

His wife said something about the ingratitude of that kind of people, and then they began to talk of something else.

Nineteen years! How easy that was to read! What a simple word for Judge Day to utter! Nineteen years! Half a lifetime!

Hugh Wolfe sat on the window-ledge of his cell, looking out. His ankles were ironed. Not usual in such cases; but he had made two desperate efforts to escape. 'Well,' as Haley, the jailer said, 'small blame to him! Nineteen years' imprisonment was not a pleasant thing to look forward to.' Haley was very good-natured about it, though Wolfe had fought him savagely.

'When he was first caught,' the jailer said afterwards, in telling the story, 'before the trial, the fellow was cut down at once – laid there on that pallet like a dead man, with his hands over his eyes. Never saw a man so cut down in my life. Time of the trial, too, came the queerest dodge of any customer I ever had. Would choose no lawyer. Judge gave him one, of course. Gibson it was. He tried to prove the fellow crazy; but it wouldn't go. Thing was plain as daylight: money found on him. 'T was a hard sentence – all the law allows; but it was for 'xample's sake. These mill-hands are gettin' onbearable. When the sentence was read, he just looked up, and said the money was his by rights, and that all the world had gone wrong. That night, after the trial, a gentleman came to see him here, name of Mitchell – him as he stole from.

Talked to him for an hour. Thought he came for curiosity, like. After he was gone, thought Wolfe was remarkable quiet, and went into his cell. Found him very low; bed all bloody. Doctor said he had been bleeding at the lungs. He was as weak as a cat; yet if ye'll b'lieve me, he tried to get a-past me and get out. I just carried him like a baby, and threw him on the pallet. Three days after, he tried it again: that time reached the wall. Lord help you! he fought like a tiger – giv' some terrible blows. Fightin' for life, you see; for he can't live long, shut up in the stone crib down yonder. Got a death-cough now. 'T took two of us to bring him down that day; so I just put the irons on his feet. There he sits, in there. Goin' tomorrow, with a batch more of 'em. That woman, hunchback, tried with him – you remember? she's only got three years. 'Complice. But *she's* a woman, you know. He's been quiet ever since I put on irons: giv' up, I suppose. Looks white, sick-lookin'. It acts different on 'em, bein' sentenced. Most of 'em gets reckless, devilish-like. Some prays awful, and sings them vile songs of the mills, all in a breath. That woman, now, she's desper't'. Been beggin' to see Hugh, as she calls him, for three days. I'm a-goin' to let her in. She don't go with him. Here she is in the next cell. I'm a-goin' now to let her in.'

He let her in. Wolfe did not see her. She crept into a corner of the cell, and stood watching him. He was scratching the iron bars of the window with a piece of tin which he had picked up, with an idle, uncertain, vacant stare, just as a child or idiot would do.

'Tryin' to get out, old boy?' laughed Haley. 'Them irons will need a crow-bar beside your tin, before you can open 'em.'

Wolfe laughed, too, in a senseless way.

'I think I'll get out,' he said.

'I believe his brain's touched,' said Haley, when he came out.

The puddler scraped away with the tin for half an hour. Still Deborah did not speak. At last she ventured nearer, and touched his arm.

'Blood?' she said, looking at some spots on his coat with a shudder.

He looked up at her. 'Why, Deb!' he said, smiling – such a bright, boyish smile, that it went to poor Deborah's heart directly, and she sobbed and cried out loud.

'Oh, Hugh, lad! Hugh! dunnot look at me, when it wur my fault! To think I brought hur to it! And I loved hur so! Oh, lad, I dud!'

The confession, even in this wretch, came with the woman's blush through the sharp cry.

He did not seem to hear her – scraping away diligently at the bars with the bit of tin.

Was he going mad? She peered closely into his face. Something she saw there made her draw suddenly back – something which Haley had not seen, that lay beneath the pinched, vacant look it had caught since the trial, or the curious gray shadow that rested on it. That gray shadow – yes, she knew what that meant. She had often seen it creeping over women's faces for months, who died at last of slow hunger or consumption. That meant death, distant, lingering: but this – Whatever it was the woman saw, or thought she saw, used as she was to crime and misery, seemed to make her sick with a new horror. Forgetting her fear of him, she caught his shoulders, and looked keenly, steadily, into his eyes.

He sat on the side of the low pallet, thinking. Whatever was the mystery which the woman had seen on his face, it came out now slowly, in the dark there, and became fixed – a something never seen on his face before. The evening was darkening fast. The market had been over for an hour; the rumbling of the carts over the pavement grew more infrequent: he listened to each, as it passed, because he thought it was to be for the last time. For the same reason, it was, I suppose, that he strained his eyes to catch a glimpse of each passer-by, wondering who they were, what kind of homes they were going to, if they had children – listening eagerly to every chance word in the street, as if – (God be merciful to the man! what strange fancy was this?) – as if he never should hear human voices again.

It was quite dark at last. The street was a lonely one. The last passenger, he thought, was gone. No – there was a quick step: Joe Hill, lighting the lamps. Joe was a good old chap; never passed a fellow without some joke or other. He remembered once seeing the place where he lived with his wife. 'Granny Hill' the boys called her. Bedridden she was; but so kind as Joe was to her! kept the room so clean! and the old woman, when he was there, was laughing at 'some of t' lad's foolishness.' The step was far down the street; but he could see him place the ladder, run up, and light the gas. A longing seized him to be spoken to once more.

'Joe!' he called, out of the grating. 'Good-bye, Joe!'

The old man stopped a moment, listening uncertainly; then hurried on. The prisoner thrust his hand out of the window, and called again, louder; but Joe was too far down the street. It was a little thing; but it hurt him – this disappointment.

'Good-bye, Joe!' he called, sorrowfully enough.

'Be quiet!' said one of the jailers, passing the door, striking on it with his club.

Oh, that was the last, was it?

There was an inexpressible bitterness on his face, as he lay down on the bed, taking the bit of tin, which he had rasped to a tolerable degree of sharpness, in his hand – to play with, it may be. He bared his arms, looking intently at their corded veins and sinews. Deborah, listening in the next cell, heard a slight clicking sound, often repeated. She shut her lips tightly, that she might not scream; the cold drops of sweat broke over her, in her dumb agony.

'Hur knows best,' she muttered at last, fiercely clutching the boards where she lay.

If she could have seen Wolfe, there was nothing about him to frighten her. He lay quite still, his arms outstretched, looking at the pearly stream of moonlight coming into the window. I think in that one hour that came then he lived back over all the years that had gone before. I think that all the low, vile life, all his wrongs, all his starved hopes, came then, and stung him with a farewell poison that made him sick unto death. He made neither moan nor cry, only turned his worn face now and then to the pure light, that seemed so far off, as one that said, 'How long, O Lord? how long?'

The hour was over at last. The moon, passing over her nightly path, slowly came nearer, and threw the light across his bed on his feet. He watched it steadily, as it crept up, inch by inch, slowly. It seemed to him to carry with it a great silence. He had been so hot and tired there always in the mills! The years had been so fierce and cruel! There was coming now quiet and coolness and sleep. His tense limbs relaxed, and settled in a calm languor. The blood ran fainter and slow from his heart. He did not think now with a savage anger of what might be and was not; he was conscious only of deep stillness creeping over him. At first he saw a sea of faces: the mill-men – women he had known, drunken and bloated – Janeys timid and pitiful – poor old Debs: then they floated together like a mist, and faded away, leaving only the clear, pearly moonlight.

Whether, as the pure light crept up the stretched-out figure, it brought with it calm and peace, who shall say? His dumb soul was alone with God in judgment. A Voice may have spoken for it from far-off Calvary, 'Father, forgive them, for they know not what they do!' Who dare say? Fainter and fainter the heart rose and fell, slower and slower the moon floated from behind a cloud, until, when at last its full tide of white splendor swept over the cell, it seemed to wrap and fold into a deeper stillness the dead figure that never should move again. Silence deeper than the Night! Nothing that moved, save the black, nauseous stream of blood dripping slowly from the pallet to the floor!

There was outcry and crowd enough in the cell the next day. The coroner and his jury, the local editors, Kirby himself, and boys with their hands thrust knowingly into their pockets and heads on one side, jammed into the corners. Coming and going all day. Only one woman. She came late, and outstayed them all. A Quaker, or Friend, as they call themselves. I think this woman was known by that name in heaven. A homely body, coarsely dressed in gray and white. Deborah (for Haley had let her in) took notice of her. She watched them all — sitting on the end of the pallet, holding his head in her arms — with the ferocity of a watch-dog, if any of them touched the body. There was no meekness, no sorrow, in her face; the stuff out of which murderers are made, instead. All the time Haley and the woman were laying straight the limbs and cleaning the cell, Deborah sat still, keenly watching the Quaker's face. Of all the crowd there that day, this woman alone had not spoken to her — only once or twice had put some cordial to her lips. After they all were gone, the woman, in the same still, gentle way, brought a vase of wood-leaves and berries, and placed it by the pallet, then opened the narrow window. The fresh air blew in, and swept the woody fragrance over the dead face. Deborah looked up with a quick wonder.

'Did hur know my boy wud like it? Did hur know Hugh?'

'I know Hugh now.'

The white fingers passed in a slow, pitiful way over the dead, worn face. There was a heavy shadow in the quiet eyes.

'Did hur know where they'll bury Hugh?' said Deborah in a shrill tone, catching her arm.

This had been the question hanging on her lips all day.

'In t' town-yard? Under t' mud and ash? T' lad 'll smother, woman! He wur born in t' lane moor, where t' air is frick and strong. Take hur out, for God's sake, take hur out where t' air blows!'

The Quaker hesitated, but only for a moment. She put her strong arm around Deborah and led her to the window.

'Thee sees the hills, friend, over the river? Thee sees how the light lies warm there, and the winds of God blow all the day? I live there – where the blue smoke is, by the trees. Look at me.' She turned Deborah's face to her own, clear and earnest. 'Thee will believe me? I will take Hugh and bury him there tomorrow.'

Deborah did not doubt her. As the evening wore on, she leaned against the iron bars, looking at the hills that rose far off, through the thick sodden clouds, like a bright, unattainable calm. As she looked, a shadow of their solemn repose fell on her face; its fierce discontent faded into a pitiful, humble quiet. Slow, solemn tears gathered in her eyes: the poor weak eyes turned so hopelessly to the place where Hugh was to rest, the grave heights looking higher and brighter and more solemn than ever before. The Quaker watched her keenly. She came to her at last, and touched her arm.

'When thee comes back,' she said, in a low, sorrowful tone, like one who speaks from a strong heart deeply moved with remorse or pity, 'thee shall begin thy life again – there on the hills. I came too late; but not for thee – by God's help, it may be.'

Not too late. Three years after, the Quaker began her work. I end my story here. At evening-time it was light. There is no need to tire you with the long years of sunshine, and fresh air, and slow, patient Christ-love, needed to make healthy and hopeful this impure body and soul. There is a homely pine house, on one of these hills, whose windows overlook broad, wooded slopes and clover-crimsoned meadows – niched into the very place where the light is warmest, the air freest. It is the Friends' meeting-house. Once a week they sit there, in their grave, earnest way, waiting for the Spirit of Love to speak, opening their simple hearts to receive His words: There is a woman, old, deformed, who takes a humble place among them: waiting like them: in her gray dress, her worn face, pure and meek, turned now and then to the sky. A woman much loved by these silent, restful people; more silent than they, more humble, more loving. Waiting: with her eyes turned to hills higher and purer than these on which she lives – dim and far off now, but to be reached some day. There may be in her heart some latent hope to meet there the love denied her here – that she shall find him whom she lost, and that then she will not be all-unworthy. Who blames her? Something is lost in the passage of every soul from one eternity to the other – something pure and beautiful, which might have been and was not: a hope, a talent, a love, over which the soul mourns, like Esau deprived of his birthright. What blame to the meek Quaker, if she took her lost hope to make the hills of heaven more fair?

Nothing remains to tell that the poor Welsh puddler once lived, but this figure of the mill-woman cut in korl. I have it here in a corner of my library. I keep it hid behind a curtain – it is such a rough, ungainly thing. Yet there are about it touches, grand sweeps of outline, that show a master's hand. Sometimes – to-night, for instance – the curtain is accidentally drawn back, and I see a bare arm stretched out imploringly in the darkness, and an eager, wolfish face watching mine: a wan, woeful face, through which the spirit of the dead korl-cutter looks out, with its thwarted life, its mighty hunger, its unfinished work. Its pale, vague lips seem to tremble with a terrible question.

'Is this the End?' they say – 'nothing beyond? no more?' Why, you tell me you have seen that look in the eyes of dumb brutes – horses dying under the lash. I know.

The deep of the night is passing while I write. The gas-light wakens from the shadows here and there the objects which lie scattered through the room: only faintly, though; for they belong to the open sunlight. As I glance at them, they each recall some task or pleasure of the coming day. A half-moulded child's head; Aphrodite; a bough of forest-leaves; music, work; homely fragments, in which lie the secrets of all eternal truth and beauty. Prophetic all! Only this dumb, woeful face seems to belong to and end with the night. I turn to look at it. Has the power of its desperate need commanded the darkness away? While the room is yet steeped in heavy shadow, a cool, gray light suddenly touches its head like a blessing hand, and its groping arm points through the broken cloud to the far East, where, in the flickering, nebulous crimson, God has set the promise of the Dawn.

1861

The Man That Corrupted Hadleyburg

1

It was many years ago. Hadleyburg was the most honest and upright town in all the region around about. It had kept that reputation unsmirched during three generations, and was prouder of it than of any other of its possessions. It was so proud of it, and so anxious to insure its perpetuation, that it began to teach the principles of honest dealing to its babies in the cradle, and made the like teachings the staple of their culture thenceforward through all the years devoted to their education. Also, throughout the formative years temptations were kept out of the way of the young people, so that their honesty could have every chance to harden and solidify, and become a part of their very bone. The neighboring towns were jealous of this honorable supremacy, and affected to sneer at Hadleyburg's pride in it and call it vanity; but all the same they were obliged to acknowledge that Hadleyburg was in reality an incorruptible town; and if pressed they would also acknowledge that the mere fact that a young man hailed from Hadleyburg was all the recommendation he needed when he went forth from his natal town to seek for responsible employment.

But at last, in the drift of time, Hadleyburg had the ill luck to offend a passing stranger – possibly without knowing it, certainly without caring, for Hadleyburg was sufficient unto itself, and cared not a rap for strangers or their opinions. Still, it would have been well to make an exception in this one's case, for he was a bitter man and revengeful. All through his wanderings during a whole year he kept his injury in mind, and gave all his leisure moments to trying to invent a compensating satisfaction for it. He contrived many plans, and all of them were good, but none of them was quite sweeping enough; the poorest of them would hurt a great many individuals, but what he wanted was a plan which would comprehend the entire town, and not let so much as one person escape unhurt. At last he had a fortunate idea, and when it fell into his brain it lit up his whole head with an evil joy. He began

to form a plan at once, saying to himself, 'That is the thing to do –
I will corrupt the town.'

Six months later he went to Hadleyburg, and arrived in a buggy
at the house of the old cashier of the bank about ten at night. He
got a sack out of the buggy, shouldered it, and staggered with it
through the cottage yard, and knocked at the door. A woman's
voice said 'Come in,' and he entered, and set his sack behind the
stove in the parlor, saying politely to the old lady who sat reading
the *Missionary Herald* by the lamp:

'Pray keep your seat, madam, I will not disturb you. There –
now it is pretty well concealed; one would hardly know it was
there. Can I see your husband a moment, madam?'

No, he was gone to Brixton, and might not return before
morning.

'Very well, madam, it is no matter. I merely wanted to leave that
sack in his care, to be delivered to the rightful owner when he shall
be found. I am a stranger; he does not know me; I am merely
passing through the town tonight to discharge a matter which
has been long in my mind. My errand is now completed, and I go
pleased and a little proud, and you will never see me again. There
is a paper attached to the sack which will explain everything.
Good night, madam.'

The old lady was afraid of the mysterious big stranger, and was
glad to see him go. But her curiosity was roused, and she went
straight to the sack and brought away the paper. It began as
follows:

TO BE PUBLISHED; or, the right man sought out by private
inquiry – either will answer. This sack contains gold coin
weighing a hundred and sixty pounds four ounces –

'Mercy on us, and the door not locked!'

Mrs Richards flew to it all in a tremble and locked it, then
pulled down the window-shades and stood frightened, worried,
and wondering if there was anything else she could do toward
making herself and the money more safe. She listened awhile for
burglars, then surrendered to curiosity and went back to the lamp
and finished reading the paper:

I am a foreigner, and am presently going back to my own
country, to remain there permanently. I am grateful to America
for what I have received at her hands during my long stay under

her flag; and to one of her citizens – a citizen of Hadleyburg – I am especially grateful for a great kindness done me a year or two ago. Two great kindnesses, in fact. I will explain. I was a gambler. I say I WAS. I was a ruined gambler. I arrived in this village at night, hungry and without a penny. I asked for help – in the dark; I was ashamed to beg in the light. I begged of the right man. He gave me twenty dollars – that is to say, he gave me life, as I considered it. He also gave me fortune; for out of that money I have made myself rich at the gaming-table. And finally, a remark which he made to me has remained with me to this day, and has at last conquered me; and in conquering has saved the remnant of my morals; I shall gamble no more. Now I have no idea who that man was, but I want him found, and I want him to have this money, to give away, throw away, or keep, as he pleases. It is merely my way of testifying my gratitude to him. If I could stay, I would find him myself; but no matter, he will be found. This is an honest town, an incorruptible town, and I know I can trust it without fear. This man can be identified by the remark which he made to me; I feel persuaded that he will remember it.

And now my plan is this: If you prefer to conduct the inquiry privately, do so. Tell the contents of this present writing to any one who is likely to be the right man. If he shall answer, 'I am the man; the remark I made was so-and-so,' apply the test – to wit: open the sack, and in it you will find a sealed envelope containing the remark. If the remark mentioned by the candidate tallies with it, give him the money, and ask no further questions, for he is certainly the right man.

But if you shall prefer a public inquiry, then publish this present writing in the local paper – with these instructions added, to wit: Thirty days from now, let the candidate appear at the town-hall at eight in the evening (Friday), and hand his remark, in a sealed envelope, to the Rev. Mr Burgess (if he will be kind enough to act); and let Mr Burgess there and then destroy the seals of the sack, open it, and see if the remark is correct; if correct, let the money be delivered, with my sincere gratitude, to my benefactor thus identified.

Mrs Richards sat down, gently quivering with excitement, and was soon lost in thinkings – after this pattern: 'What a strange thing it is! . . . And what a fortune for that kind man who set his bread afloat upon the waters! . . . If it had only been my husband that did it! – for we are so poor, so old and poor!. . .' Then, with a sigh – 'But it was not my Edward; no, it was not he that gave a stranger twenty dollars. It is a pity, too; I see it now . . .' Then with a shudder – 'But it is *gambler's* money! the wages of sin: we couldn't take it; we couldn't touch it. I don't like to be near it; it seems a defilement.' She moved to a farther chair . . . 'I wish Edward would come and take it to the bank; a burglar might come at any moment; it is dreadful to be here all alone with it.'

At eleven Mr Richards arrived, and while his wife was saying, 'I am *so* glad you've come!' he was saying. 'I'm so tired – tired clear out; it is dreadful to be poor, and have to make these dismal journeys at my time of life. Always at the grind, grind, grind, on a salary – another man's slave, and he sitting at home in his slippers, rich and comfortable.'

'I am so sorry for you, Edward, you know that; but be comforted: we have our livelihood; we have our good name –'

'Yes, Mary, and that is everything. Don't mind my talk – it's just a moment's irritation and doesn't mean anything. Kiss me – there, it's all gone now, and I am not complaining any more. What have you been getting? What's in the sack?'

Then his wife told him the great secret. It dazed him for a moment; then he said:

'It weighs a hundred and sixty pounds? Why, Mary, it's for-ty thousand dollars – think of it – a whole fortune! Not ten men in this village are worth that much. Give me the paper.'

He skimmed through it and said:

'Isn't it an adventure! Why, it's a romance, it's like the impossible things one reads about in books, and never sees in life.' He was well stirred up now; cheerful, even gleeful. He tapped his old wife on the cheek, and said, humorously, 'Why, we're rich, Mary, rich; all we've got to do is to bury the money and burn the papers. If the gambler ever comes to inquire, we'll merely look coldly upon him and say: "What is this nonsense you are talking? We have never heard of you and your sack of gold before"; and then he would look foolish, and—'

'And in the mean time, while you are running on with your jokes, the money is still here, and it is fast getting along toward burglar-time.'

'True. Very well, what shall we do – make the inquiry private? No, not that: it would spoil the romance. The public method is better. Think what a noise it will make! And it will make all the other towns jealous; for no stranger would trust such a thing to any town but Hadleyburg, and they know it. It's a great card for us. I must get to the printing-office now, or I shall be too late.'

'But stop – stop – don't leave me here with it, Edward!'

But he was gone. For only a little while, however. Not far from his own house he met the editor-proprietor of the paper, and gave him the document, and said, 'Here is a good thing for you, Cox – put it in.'

'It may be too late, Mr Richards, but I'll see.'

At home again he and his wife sat down to talk the charming mystery over; they were in no condition for sleep. The first question was, Who could the citizen have been who gave the stranger the twenty dollars? It seemed a simple one; both answered it in the same breath:

'Barclay Goodson.'

'Yes,' said Richards, 'He could have done it, and it would have been like him, but there's not another in the town.'

'Everybody will grant that, Edward – grant it privately, anyway. For six months, now, the village has been its own proper self once more – honest, narrow, self-righteous, and stingy.'

'It is what he always called it, to the day of his death – said it right out publicly, too.'

'Yes, and he was hated for it.'

'Oh, of course; but he didn't care. I reckon he was the best-hated man among us, except the Reverend Burgess.'

'Well, Burgess deserves it – he will never get another congregation here. Mean as the town is, it knows how to estimate *him*. Edward, doesn't it seem odd that the stranger should appoint Burgess to deliver the money?'

'Well, yes – it does. That is – that is—'

'Why so much that-*is*-ing? Would *you* select him?'

'Mary, maybe the stranger knows him better than this village does.'

'Much *that* would help Burgess!'

The husband seemed perplexed for an answer; the wife kept a steady eye upon him, and waited. Finally Richards said, with the hesitancy of one who is making a statement which is likely to encounter doubt:

'Mary, Burgess is not a bad man.'

His wife was certainly surprised.

'Nonsense!' she exclaimed.

'He is not a bad man. I know. The whole of his unpopularity

had its foundation in that one thing – the thing that made so much noise.'

'That "one thing," indeed! As if that "one thing" wasn't enough, all by itself.'

'Plenty. Plenty. Only he wasn't guilty of it.'

'How you talk! Not guilty of it! Everybody knows he *was* guilty.'

'Mary, I give you my word – he was innocent.'

'I can't believe it, and I don't. How do you know?'

'It is a confession. I am ashamed, but I will make it. I was the only man who knew he was innocent. I could have saved him, and – and – well, you know how the town was wrought up – I hadn't the pluck to do it. It would have turned everybody against me. I felt mean, ever so mean; but I didn't dare; I hadn't the manliness to face that.'

Mary looked troubled, and for a while was silent. Then she said, stammeringly:

'I – I don't think it would have done for you to – to – One mustn't – er – public opinion – one has to be so careful – so–' It was a difficult road, and she got mired; but after a little she got started again. 'It was a great pity, but – Why, we couldn't afford it, Edward – we couldn't indeed. Oh, I wouldn't have had you do it for anything!'

'It would have lost us the good will of so many people, Mary; and then – and then –'

'What troubles me now is, what *he* thinks of us, Edward.'

'He? *He* doesn't suspect that I could have saved him.'

'Oh,' exclaimed the wife, in a tone of relief, 'I am glad of that! As long as he doesn't know that you could have saved him, he – he – well, that makes it a great deal better. Why, I might have known he didn't know, because he is always trying to be friendly with us, as little encouragement as we give him. More than once people have twitted me with it. There's the Wilsons, and the Wilcoxes, and the Harknesses, they take a mean pleasure in saying, "*Your friend* Burgess," because they know it pesters me. I wish he wouldn't persist in liking us so; I can't think why he keeps it up.'

'I can explain it. It's another confession. When the thing was new and hot, and the town made a plan to ride him on a rail, my conscience hurt me so that I couldn't stand it, and I went privately and gave him notice, and he got out of the town and stayed out till it was safe to come back.'

'Edward! If the town had found it out –'

'*Don't*! It scares me yet, to think of it. I repented of it the minute it was done; and I was even afraid to tell you, lest your face might betray it to somebody. I didn't sleep any that night, for worrying. But after a few days I saw that no one was going to suspect me, and after that I got to feeling glad I did it. And I feel glad yet, Mary – glad through and through.'

'So do I, now, for it would have been a dreadful way to treat him. Yes, I'm glad; for really you did owe him that, you know. But, Edward, suppose it should come out yet, some day!'

'It won't.'

'Why?'

'Because everybody thinks it was Goodson.'

'Of course they would!'

'Certainly. And of course *he* didn't care. They persuaded poor old Sawlsberry to go and charge it on him, and he went blustering over there and did it. Goodson looked him over, like as if he was hunting for a place on him that he could despise the most, then he says, "So you are the Committe of Inquiry, are you?" Sawlsberry said that was about what he was. "Hm. Do they require particulars, or do you reckon a kind of a *general* answer will do?' If they require particulars, I will come back, Mr Goodson; I will take the general answer first." "Very well, then, tell them to go to hell – I reckon that's general enough. And I'll give you some advice, Sawlsberry; when you come back for the particulars, fetch a basket to carry the relics of yourself home in." '

'Just like Goodson; it's got all the marks. He had only one vanity: he thought he could give advice better than any other person.'

'It settled the business, and saved us, Mary. The subject was dropped.'

'Bless you, I'm not doubting *that*.'

Then they took up the gold-sack mystery again, with strong interest. Soon the conversation began to suffer breaks – interruptions caused by absorbed thinkings. The breaks grew more and more frequent. At last Richards lost himself wholly in thought. He sat long, gazing vacantly at the floor, and by and by he began to punctuate his thoughts with little nervous movements of his hands that seemed to indicate vexation. Meantime his wife too had relapsed into a thoughtful silence, and her movements were beginning to show a troubled discomfort. Finally Richards got up and strode aimlessly about the room, plowing his hands through his hair, much as a somnambulist might do who was having a bad dream. Then he seemed to arrive at a definite purpose; and without a word he put on his hat and passed quickly out of the house. His wife sat brooding, with a drawn face, and did not seem to be aware that she was alone. Now and then she murmured, 'Lead us not into t— . . . but – but – we are so poor, so poor! . . . Lead us not into . . . Ah, who would be hurt by it? – and no one would ever know . . . Lead us . . .' The voice died out in mumblings. After a little she glanced up and muttered in a half-frightened, half-glad way:

'He is gone! But, oh dear, he may be too late – too late . . . Maybe not – maybe there is still time.' She rose and stood thinking, nervously clasping and unclasping her hands. A slight shudder shook her frame, and she said, out of a dry throat, 'God forgive me – it's awful to think such things – but . . . Lord, how we are made – how strangely we are made!'

She turned the light low, and slipped stealthily over and kneeled down by the sack and felt of its ridgy sides with her hands, and fondled them lovingly; and there was a gloating light in her poor old eyes. She fell into fits of absence; and came half out of them at times to mutter, 'If we had only waited – oh, if we had only waited a little, and not been in such a hurry!'

Meantime Cox had gone home from his office and told his wife all about the strange thing that had happened, and they had talked it over eagerly, and guessed that the late Goodson was the only man in the town who could have helped a suffering stranger with so noble a sum as twenty dollars. Then there was a pause, and the two became thoughtful and silent. And by and by nervous and fidgety. At last the wife said, as if to herself:

'Nobody knows this secret but the Richardses . . . and us . . . nobody.'

The husband came out of his thinkings with a slight start, and gazed wistfully at his wife, whose face was become very pale; then he hesitatingly rose, and glanced furtively at his hat, then at his wife – a sort of mute inquiry. Mrs Cox swallowed once or twice, with her hand at her throat, then in place of speech she nodded her head. In a moment she was alone, and mumbling to herself.

And now Richards and Cox were hurrying through the deserted streets, from opposite directions. They met, panting, at the foot of the printing-office stairs; by the night light there they read each other's face. Cox whispered:

'Nobody knows about this but us?'

The whispered answer was,

'Not a soul – on honor, not a soul!'

'If it isn't too late to—'

The men were starting upstairs; at this moment they were overtaken by a boy, and Cox asked:

'Is that you, Johnny?'

'Yes, sir.'

'You needn't ship the early mail – nor *any* mail; wait till I tell you.'

'It's already gone, sir.'

'*Gone?*' It had the sound of an unspeakable disappointment in it.

'Yes, sir. Time-table for Brixton and all the towns beyond changed today, sir – had to get the papers in twenty minutes earlier than common. I had to rush; if I had been two minutes later—'

The men turned and walked slowly away, not waiting to hear the rest. Neither of them spoke during ten minutes; then Cox said, in a vexed tone:

'What possessed you to be in such a hurry, *I* can't make out.'

The answer was humble enough:

'I see it now, but somehow I never thought, you know, until it was too late. But the next time—'

'Next time be hanged! It won't come in a thousand years.'

Then the friends separated without a good night, and dragged themselves home with the gait of mortally stricken men. At their homes their wives sprang up with an eager 'Well?' – then saw the answer with their eyes and sank down sorrowing, without waiting for it to come in words. In both houses a discussion followed of a heated sort – a new thing; there had been discussions before, but not heated ones, not ungentle ones. The discussions tonight were a sort of seeming plagiarisms of each other. Mrs Richards said,

'If you had only waited, Edward – if you had only stopped to think; but no, you must run straight to the printing-office and spread it all over the world.'

'It *said* publish it.'

'That is nothing; it also said do it privately, if you liked. There, now – is that true, or not?'

'Why, yes — yes, it is true; but when I thought what a stir it would make, and what a compliment it was to Hadleyburg that a stranger should trust it so—'

'Oh, certainly, I know all that; but if you had only stopped to think, you would have seen that you *couldn't* find the right man, because he is in his grave, and hasn't left chick nor child nor relation behind him; and as long as the money went to somebody that awfully needed it, and nobody would be hurt by it, and — and—'

She broke down, crying. Her husband tried to think of some comforting thing to say, and presently came out with this:

'But after all, Mary, it must be for the best — it *must* be; we know that. And we must remember that it was so ordered—'

'Ordered! Oh, everything's *ordered*, when a person has to find some way out when he has been stupid. Just the same, it was *ordered* that the money should come to us in this special way, and it was you that must take it on yourself to go meddling with the designs of Providence — and who gave you the right? It was wicked, that is what it was — just blasphemous presumption, and no more becoming to a meek and humble professor of—'

'But, Mary, you know how we have been trained all our lives long, like the whole village, till it is absolutely second nature to us to stop not a single moment to think when there's an honest thing to be done—'

'Oh, I know it, I know it — it's been one everlasting training and training and training in honesty — honesty shielded, from the very cradle, against every possible temptation, and so it's *artificial* honesty, and weak as water when temptation comes, as we have seen this night. God knows I never had shade nor shadow of a doubt of my petrified and indestructible honesty until now — and now, under the very first big and real temptation, I — Edward, it is my belief that this town's honesty is as rotten as mine is; as rotten as yours is. It is a mean town, a hard, stingy town, and hasn't a virtue in the world but this honesty it is so celebrated for and so conceited about; and so help me, I do believe that if ever the day comes that its honesty falls under great temptation, its grand reputation will go to ruin like a house of cards. There, now, I've made confession, and I feel better; I am a humbug, and I've been one all my life, without knowing it. Let no man call me honest again — I will not have it.'

'I — well, Mary, I feel a good deal as you do; I certainly do. It

seems strange, too, so strange. I never could have believed it –
never.'

A long silence followed; both were sunk in thought. At last the
wife looked up and said:

'I know what you are thinking, Edward.'

Richards had the embarrassed look of a person who is caught.

'I am ashamed to confess it, Mary, but –'

'It's no matter, Edward, I was thinking the same question
myself.'

'I hope so. State it.'

'You were thinking, if a body could only guess out *what the
remark was* that Goodson made to the stranger.'

'It's perfectly true. I feel guilty and ashamed. And you?'

'I'm past it. Let us make a pallet here; we've got to stand watch
till the bank vault opens in the morning and admits the sack . . .
Oh dear, oh dear – if we hadn't made the mistake!'

The pallet was made, and Mary said:

'The open seasame – what could it have been? I do wonder
what that remark could have been? But come; we will get to bed
now.'

'And sleep?'

'No: think.'

'Yes, think.'

By this time the Coxes too had completed their spat and their
reconciliation, and were turning in – to think, to think, and toss,
and fret, and worry over what the remark could possibly have
been which Goodson made to the stranded derelict; that golden
remark; that remark worth forty thousand dollars, cash.

The reason that the village telegraph-office was open later than
usual that night was this: The foreman of Cox's paper was the
local representative of the Associated Press. One might say its
honorary representative, for it wasn't four times a year that he
could furnish thirty words that would be accepted. But this time it
was different. His despatch stating what he had caught got an
instant answer:

Send the whole thing – all the details – twelve hundred words.

A colossal order! The foreman filled the bill; and he was the
proudest man in the State. By breakfast-time the next morning the
name of Hadleyburg the Incorruptible was on every lip in
America, from Montreal to the Gulf, from the glaciers of Alaska

to the orange-groves of Florida; and millions and millions of people were discussing the stranger and his money-sack, and wondering if the right man would be found, and hoping some more news about the matter would come soon – right away.

2

Hadleyburg village woke up world-celebrated – astonished – happy – vain. Vain beyond imagination. Its nineteen principal citizens and their wives went about shaking hands with each other, and beaming, and smiling, and congratulating, and saying *this* thing adds a new word to the dictionary – *Hadleyburg*, synonym for *incorruptible* – destined to live in dictionaries forever! And the minor and unimportant citizens and their wives went around acting in much the same way. Everybody ran to the bank to see the gold-sack; and before noon grieved and envious crowds began to flock in from Brixton and all neighboring towns; and that afternoon and next day reporters began to arrive from everywhere to verify the sack and its history and write the whole thing up anew, and make dashing free-hand pictures of the sack, and of Richards's house, and the bank, and the Presbyterian church, and the Baptist church, and the public square, and the town-hall where the test would be applied and the money delivered; and damnable portraits of the Richardses, and Pinkerton the banker, and Cox, and the foreman, and Reverend Burgess, and the postmaster – and even of Jack Halliday, who was the loafing, good-natured, no-account, irreverent fisherman, hunter, boys' friend, stray-dogs' friend, typical 'Sam Lawson' of the town. The little mean, smirking, oily Pinkerton showed the sack to all comers, and rubbed his sleek palms together pleasantly, and enlarged upon the town's fine old reputation for honesty and upon this wonderful endorsement of it, and hoped and believed that the example would now spread far and wide over the American world, and be epoch-making in the matter of moral regeneration. And so on, and so on.

By the end of a week things had quieted down again; the wild intoxication of pride and joy had sobered to a soft, sweet, silent delight – a sort of deep, nameless, unutterable content. All faces bore a look of peaceful, holy happiness.

Then a change came. It was a gradual change: so gradual that its beginnings were hardly noticed; maybe were not noticed at all, except by Jack Halliday, who always noticed everything; and always made fun of it, too, no matter what it was. He began to throw out chaffing remarks about people not looking quite so happy as they did a day or two ago; and next he claimed that the new aspect was deepening to positive sadness; next, that it was taking on a sick look; and finally he said that everybody was become so moody, thoughtful, and absent-minded that he could rob the meanest man in town of a cent out of the bottom of his breeches pocket and not disturb his revery.

At this stage – or at about this stage – a saying like this was dropped at bedtime – with a sigh, usually – by the head of each of the nineteen principal households: 'Ah, what *could* have been the remark that Goodson made?'

And straightway – with a shudder – came this, from the man's wife:

'Oh, *don't*! What horrible thing are you mulling in your mind? Put it away from you, for God's sake!'

But that question was wrung from those men again the next night – and got the same retort. But weaker.

And the third night the men uttered the question yet again – with anguish, and absently. This time – and the following night – the wives fidgeted feebly, and tried to say something. But didn't.

And the night after that they found their tongues and responded – longingly:

'Oh, if we *could* only guess!'

Halliday's comments grew daily more and more sparklingly disagreeable and disparaging. He went diligently about, laughing at the town, individually and in mass. But his laugh was the only one left in the village; it fell upon a hollow and mournful vacancy and emptiness. Not even a smile was findable anywhere. Halliday carried a cigar-box around on a tripod, playing that it was a camera, and halted all passers and aimed the thing and said, 'Ready! – now look pleasant, please,' but not even this capital joke could surprise the dreary faces into any softening.

So three weeks passed – one week was left. It was Saturday evening – after supper. Intead of the aforetime Saturday-evening flutter and bustle and shopping and larking, the streets were empty and desolate. Richards and his old wife sat apart in their little parlor – miserable and thinking. This was become their evening habit now: the lifelong habit which had preceded it, of reading, knitting, and contented chat, or receiving or paying neighborly calls, was dead and gone and forgotten, ages ago – two or three weeks ago; nobody talked now, nobody read, nobody visited – the whole village sat at home, sighing, worrying, silent. Trying to guess out that remark.

The postman left a letter. Richards glanced listlessly at the superscription and the postmark – unfamiliar, both – and tossed the letter on the table and resumed his might-have-beens and his hopeless dull miseries where he had left them off. Two or three hours later his wife got wearily up and was going away to bed without a good night – custom now – but she stopped near the letter and eyed it awhile with a dead interest, then broke it open, and began to skim it over. Richards, sitting there with his chair tilted back against the wall and his chin between his knees, heard something fall. It was his wife. He sprang to her side, but she cried out:

'Leave me alone, I am too happy. Read the letter – read it!'

He did. He devoured it, his brain reeling. The letter was from a distant state, and it said:

I am a stranger to you, but no matter: I have something to tell. I have just arrived home from Mexico, and learned about that episode. Of course you do not know who made that remark, but I know, and I am the only person living who does know. It was GOODSON. I knew him well, many years ago. I passed through your village that very night, and was his guest till the midnight train came along. I overheard him make that remark to the stranger in the dark – it was in Hale Alley. He and I talked of it the rest of the way home, and while smoking in his house. He mentioned many of your villagers in the course of his talk – most of them in a very uncomplimentary way, but two or three favorably; among these latter yourself. I say 'favorably' – nothing stronger. I remember his saying he did not actually LIKE any person in the town – not one; but that you – I THINK he said you – am almost sure – had done him a very great service once, possibly without knowing the full value of it, and he wished he had a fortune, he would leave it to you when he died, and a curse apiece for the rest of the citizens. Now, then, if it was you that did him that service, you are his legitimate heir, and entitled to the sack of gold. I know that I can trust to your honor and honesty, for in a citizen of Hadleyburg these virtues are an unfailing inheritance, and so I am going to reveal to you the remark, well satisfied that if you are not the right man you will seek and find the right one and see that poor Goodson's debt of gratitude for the service referred to is paid. This is the remark: 'YOU ARE FAR FROM BEING A BAD MAN: GO, AND REFORM.'

HOWARD L. STEPHENSON

'Oh, Edward, the money is ours, and I am so grateful, *oh*, so grateful – kiss me, dear, it's forever since we kissed – and we needed it so – the money – and now you are free of Pinkerton and his bank, and nobody's slave any more; it seems to me I could fly for joy.'

It was a happy half-hour that the couple spent there on the settee caressing each other; it was the old days come again – days that had begun with their courtship and lasted without a break till the stranger brought the deadly money. By and by the wife said:

'Oh, Edward, how lucky it was you did him that grand service, poor Goodson! I never liked him, but I love him now. And it was fine and beautiful of you never to mention it or brag about it.' Then, with a touch of reproach, 'But you ought to have told *me*, Edward, you ought to have told your wife, you know.'

'Well, I – er – well, Mary, you see—'

'Now stop hemming and hawing, and tell me about it, Edward. I always loved you, and now I'm proud of you. Everybody believes there was only one good generous soul in this village, and now it turns out that you – Edward, why don't you tell me?'

'Well – er – er – Why, Mary, I can't!'

'You *can't*? *Why* can't you?'

'You see, he – well, he – he made me promise I wouldn't.'

The wife looked him over, and said, very slowly:

'Made – you – promise? Edward, what do you tell me that for?'

'Mary, do you think I would lie?'

She was troubled and silent for a moment, then she laid her hand within his and said:

'No . . . no. We have wandered far enough from our bearings – God spare us that! In all your life you have never uttered a lie. But now – now that the foundations of things seem to be crumbling from under us, we – we –' She lost her voice for a moment, then said, brokenly, 'Lead us not into temptation . . . I think you made the promise, Edward. Let it rest so. Let us keep away from that ground. Now – that is all gone by; let us be happy again; it is no time for clouds.'

Edward found it something of an effort to comply, for his mind kept wandering – trying to remember what the service was that he had done Goodson.

The couple lay awake the most of the night, Mary happy and busy, Edward busy but not so happy. Mary was planning what she would do with the money. Edward was trying to recall that service. At first his conscience was sore on account of the lie he had told Mary – if it was a lie. After much reflection – suppose it *was* a lie? What then? Was it such a great matter? Aren't we always *acting* lies? Then why not *tell* them? Look at Mary – look what she had done. While he was hurrying off on his honest errand, what was she doing? Lamenting because the papers hadn't been destroyed and the money kept! Is theft better than lying?

That point lost its sting – the lie dropped into the background and left comfort behind it. The next point came to the front: *Had* he rendered that service? Well, here was Goodson's own evidence as reported in Stephenson's letter; there could be no better evidence than that – it was even *proof* that he had rendered it. Of course. So that point was settled . . . No, not quite. He recalled with a wince that this unknown Mr Stephenson was just a trifle unsure as to whether the performer of it was Richards or some other – and, oh dear, he had put Richards on his honor! He must himself decide whither that money must go – and Mr Stephenson was not doubting that if he was the wrong man he would go honorably and find the right one. Oh, it was odious to put a man in such a situation – ah, why couldn't Stephenson have left out that doubt! What did he want to intrude that for?

Further reflection. How did it happen that *Richards's* name remained in Stephenson's mind as indicating the right man, and not some other man's name? That looked good. Yes, that looked very good. In fact, it went on looking better and better, straight along – until by and by it grew into positive *proof*. And then Richards put the matter at once out of his mind, for he had a private instinct that a proof once established is better left so.

He was feeling reasonably comfortable now, but there was still one other detail that kept pushing itself on his notice: of course he had done that service – that was settled; but what *was* the service? He must recall it – he would not go to sleep till he had recalled it; it would make his peace of mind perfect. And so he thought and thought. He thought of a dozen things – possible services, even probable services – but none of them seemed adequate, none of them seemed large enough, none of them seemed worth the money – worth the fortune Goodson had wished he could leave in his will. And besides, he couldn't remember having done them, anyway. Now, then – now, then – what *kind* of a service would it be that would make a man so inordinately grateful? Ah – the saving of his soul! That must be it. Yes, he could remember, now, how he once set himself the task of converting Goodson, and labored at it as much as – he was going to say three months; but upon closer examination it shrunk to a month, then to a week, then to a day, then to nothing. Yes, he remembered now, and with unwelcome vividness, that Goodson had told him to go to thunder and mind his own business – *he* wasn't hankering to follow Hadleyburg to heaven!

So that solution was a failure – he hadn't saved Goodson's soul. Richards was discouraged. Then after a little came another idea: had he saved Goodson's property? No, that wouldn't do – he hadn't any. His life? That is it! Of course. Why, he might have thought of it before. This time he was on the right track, sure. His imagination-mill was hard at work in a minute, now.

Thereafter during a stretch of two exhausting hours he was busy saving Goodson's life. He saved it in all kinds of difficult and perilous ways. In every case he got it saved satisfactorily up to a certain point; then, just as he was beginning to get well persuaded that it had really happened, a troublesome detail would turn up which made the whole thing impossible. As in the matter of drowning, for instance. In that case he had swum out and tugged Goodson ashore in an unconscious state with a great crowd looking on and applauding, but when he had got it all thought out and was just beginning to remember all about it, a whole swarm of disqualifying details arrived on the ground: the town would have known of the circumstance, Mary would have known of it, it would glare like a limelight in his own memory instead of being an inconspicuous service which he had possibly rendered 'without knowing its full value.' And at this point he remembered that he couldn't swim, anyway.

Ah – *there* was a point which he had been overlooking from the start: it had to be a service which he had rendered 'possibly without knowing the full value of it.' Why, really, that ought to be an easy hunt – much easier than those others. And sure enough, by and by he found it. Goodson, years and years ago, came near marrying a very sweet and pretty girl, named Nancy Hewitt, but in some way or other the match had been broken off; the girl died, Goodson remained a bachelor, and by and by became a soured one and a frank despiser of the human species. Soon after the girl's death the village found out, or thought it had found out, that she carried a spoonful of negro blood in her veins. Richards worked at these details a good while, and in the end he thought he remembered things concerning them which must have gotten mislaid in his memory through long neglect. He seemed to dimly remember that it was *he* that found out about the negro blood; that it was he that told the village; that the village told Goodson where they got it; that he thus saved Goodson from marrying the tainted girl; that he had done him this great service 'without knowing the full value of it', in fact without knowing that he *was* doing it; but that Goodson knew the value of it, and what a narrow escape he had had, and so went to his grave grateful to his benefactor and wishing he had a fortune to leave him. It was all clear and simple now, and the more he went over it the more luminous and certain it grew; and at last, when he nestled to sleep satisfied and happy, he remembered the whole thing just as if it had been yesterday. In fact, he dimly remembered Goodson's *telling* him his gratitude once. Meantime Mary had spent six thousand dollars on a new house for herself and a pair of slippers for her pastor, and then had fallen peacefully to rest.

That same Saturday evening the postman had delivered a letter to each of the other principal citizens – nineteen letters in all. No two of the envelopes were alike, and no two of the superscriptions were in the same hand, but the letters inside were just like each other in every detail but one. They were exact copies of the letter received by Richards – handwriting and all – and were all signed by Stephenson, but in place of Richards's name each receiver's own name appeared.

All night long eighteen principal citizens did what their caste-brother Richards was doing at the same time – they put in their energies trying to remember what notable service it was that they had unconsciously done Barclay Goodson. In no case was it a holiday job; still they succeeded.

And while they were at this work, which was difficult, their wives put in the night spending the money, which was easy. During that one night the nineteen wives spent an average of seven thousand dollars each out of the forty thousand in the sack – a hundred and thirty-three thousand altogether.

Next day there was a surprise for Jack Halliday. He noticed that the faces of the nineteen chief citizens and their wives bore that expression of peaceful and holy happiness again. He could not understand it, neither was he able to invent any remarks about it that could damage it or disturb it. And so it was his turn to be dissatisfied with life. His private guesses at the reasons for the happiness failed in all instances, upon examination. When he met Mrs Wilcox and noticed the placid ecstasy in her face, he said to himself, 'Her cat has had kittens' – and went and asked the cook: it was not so; the cook had detected the happiness, but did not know the cause. When Halliday found the duplicate ecstasy in the face of 'Shadbelly' Billson (village nickname), he was sure some neighbor of Billson's had broken his leg, but inquiry showed that this had not happened. The subdued ecstasy in Gregory Yates's face could mean but one thing – he was a mother-in-law short; it was another mistake. 'And Pinkerton – Pinkerton – he has collected ten cents that he thought he was going to lose.' And so on, and so on. In some cases the guesses had to remain in doubt, in the others they proved distinct errors. In the end Halliday said to himself, 'Anyway it foots up that there's nineteen Hadleyburg families temporily in heaven: I don't know how it happened; I only know Providence is off duty today.'

An architect and builder from the next state had lately ventured to set up a small business in this unpromising village, and his sign had now been hanging out a week. Not a customer yet; he was a discouraged man, and sorry he had come. But his weather changed suddenly now. First one and then another chief citizen's wife said to him privately:

'Come to my house Monday week – but say nothing about it for the present. We think of building.'

He got eleven invitations that day. That night he wrote his daughter and broke off her match with her student. He said she could marry a mile higher than that.

Pinkerton the banker and two or three other well-to-do men planned country-seats – but waited. That kind don't count their chickens until they are hatched.

The Wilsons devised a grand new thing – a fancy-dress ball. They made no actual promises, but told all their acquaintanceship in confidence that they were thinking the matter over and thought they should give it – 'and if we do, you will be invited, of course.' People were surprised, and said, one to another, 'Why, they are crazy, those poor Wilsons, they can't afford it.' Several among the nineteen said privately to their husbands, 'It is a good idea: we will keep still till their cheap thing is over, then *we* will give one that will make it sick.'

The days drifted along, and the bill of future squanderings rose higher and higher, wilder and wilder, more and more foolish and reckless. It began to look as if every member of the nineteen would not only spend his whole forty thousand dollars before receiving-day, but be actually in debt by the time he got the money. In some cases light-headed people did not stop with planning to spend, they really spent – on credit. They bought land, mortgages, farms, speculative stocks, fine clothes, horses, and various other things, paid down the bonus, and made themselves liable for the rest – at ten days. Presently the sober second thought came, and Halliday noticed that a ghastly anxiety was beginning to show up in a good many faces. Again he was puzzled, and didn't know what to make of it. 'The Wilcox kittens aren't dead, for they weren't born; nobody's broken a leg; there's no shrinkage in mother-in-laws; *nothing* has happened – it is an unsolvable mystery.'

There was another puzzled man, too – the Rev. Mr Burgess. For days, wherever he went, people seemed to follow him or to be watching out for him; and if he ever found himself in a retired spot, a member of the nineteen would be sure to appear, thrust an envelope privately into his hand, whisper 'To be opened at the town-hall Friday evening,' then vanish away like a guilty thing. He was expecting that there might be one claimant for the sack – doubtful, however, Goodson being dead – but it never occurred to him that all this crowd might be claimants. When the great Friday came at last, he found that he had nineteen envelopes.

3

The town-hall had never looked finer. The platform at the end of it was backed by a showy draping of flags; at intervals along the walls were festoons of flags; the gallery fronts were clothed in flags; the supporting columns were swathed in flags; all this was to impress the stranger, for he would be there in considerable force, and in a large degree he would be connected with the press. The house was full. The 412 fixed seats were occupied; also the 68 extra chairs which had been packed into the aisles; the steps of the platform were occupied; some distinguished strangers were given seats on the platform; at the horseshoe of tables which fenced the front and sides of the platform sat a strong force of special correspondents who had come from everywhere. It was the best-dressed house the town had ever produced. There were some tolerably expensive toilets there, and in several cases the ladies who wore them had the look of being unfamiliar with that kind of clothes. At least the town thought they had that look, but the notion could have arisen from the town's knowledge of the fact that these ladies had never inhabited such clothes before.

The gold-sack stood on a little table at the front of the platform where all the house could see it. The bulk of the house gazed at it with a burning interest, a mouth-watering interest, a wistful and pathetic interest; a minority of nineteen couples gazed at it tenderly, lovingly, proprietarily, and the male half of this minority kept saying over to themselves the moving little impromptu speeches of thankfulness for the audience's applause and congratulations which they were presently going to get up and deliver. Every now and then one of these got a piece of paper out of his vest pocket and privately glanced at it to refresh his memory.

Of course there was a buzz of conversation going on – there always is; but at last when the Rev. Mr Burgess rose and laid his hand on the sack he could hear his microbes gnaw, the place was so still. He related the curious history of the sack, then went on to speak in warm terms of Hadleyburg's old and well-earned reputation for spotless honesty, and of the town's just pride in this reputation. He said that this reputation was a treasure of priceless value; that under Providence its value had now become inestimably enhanced, for the recent episode had spread this fame far and wide, and thus had focused the eyes of the American world upon this village, and made its name for all time, as he hoped and believed, a synonym for commercial incorruptibility. [*Applause.*] 'And who is to be the guardian of this noble treasure – the community as a whole? No! The responsibility is individual, not communal. From this day forth each and every one of you is in his own person its special guardian, and individually responsible that no harm shall come to it. Do you – does each of you – accept this great trust? [*Tumultuous assent.*] Then all is well. Transmit it to your children and to your children's children. Today your purity is beyond reproach – see to it that it shall remain so. Today there is not a person in your community who could be beguiled to touch a penny not his own – see to it that you abide in this grace. ['*We will! we will!*'] This is not the place to make comparisons between ourselves and other communities – some of them ungracious toward us; they have their ways, we have ours; let us be content. [*Applause.*] I am done. Under my hand, my friends, rests a stranger's eloquent recognition of what we are; through him the world will always henceforth know what we are. We do not know who he is, but in your name I utter your gratitude, and ask you to raise your voices in endorsement.'

The house rose in a body and made the walls quake with the thunders of its thankfulness for the space of a long minute. Then it sat down, and Mr Burgess took an envelope out of his pocket. The house held its breath while he slit the envelope open and took from it a slip of paper. He read its contents – slowly and impressively – the audience listening with tranced attention to this magic document, each of whose words stood for an ingot of gold:

' "The remark which I made to the distressed stranger was this: 'You are very far from being a bad man: go, and reform.' " '

Then he continued:

'We shall know in a moment whether the remark here quoted corresponds with the one concealed in the sack; and if that shall prove to be so – and it undoubtedly will – this sack of gold belongs to a fellow-citizen who will henceforth stand before the nation as the symbol of the special virtue which has made our town famous throughout the land – Mr Billson!'

The house had gotten itself all ready to burst into the proper tornado of applause; but instead of doing it, it seemed stricken with a paralysis; there was a deep hush for a moment or two, then a wave of whispered murmurs swept the place – of about this tenor: '*Billson!* oh, come, this is *too* thin! Twenty dollars to a stranger – or *anybody* – *Billson*! tell it to the marines!' And now at this point the house caught its breath all of a sudden in a new access of astonishment, for it discovered that whereas in one part of the hall Deacon Billson was standing up with his head meekly bowed, in another part of it Lawyer Wilson was doing the same. There was a wondering silence now for a while.

Everybody was puzzled, and nineteen couples were surprised and indignant.

Billson and Wilson turned and stared at each other. Billson asked, bitingly:

'Why do *you* rise, Mr Wilson?'

'Because I have a right to. Perhaps you will be good enough to explain to the house why *you* rise?'

'With great pleasure. Because I wrote that paper.'

'It is an impudent falsity! I wrote it myself.'

It was Burgess's turn to be paralyzed. He stood looking vacantly at first one of the men and then the other, and did not seem to know what to do. The house was stupefied. Lawyer Wilson spoke up, now, and said,

'I ask the Chair to read the name signed to that paper.'

That brought the Chair to itself, and it read out the name:

' "John Wharton *Billson*." '

'There!' shouted Billson, 'what have you got to say for yourself, now? And what kind of apology are you going to make to me and to this insulted house for the imposture which you have attempted to play here?'

'No apologies are due, sir; and as for the rest of it, I publicly charge you with pilfering my note from Mr Burgess and substituting a copy of it signed with your own name. There is no other way by which you could have gotten hold of the test-remark; I alone, of living men, possessed the secret of its wording.'

There was likely to be a scandalous state of things if this went on; everybody noticed with distress that the short-hand scribes were scribbling like mad; many people were crying 'Chair, Chair! Order! Order!' Burgess rapped with his gavel, and said:

'Let us not forget the proprieties due. There has evidently been a mistake somewhere, but surely that is all. If Mr Wilson gave me an envelope – and I remember now that he did – I still have it.'

He took one out of his pocket, opened it, glanced at it, looked surprised and worried, and stood silent a few moments. Then he waved his hand in a wandering and mechanical way, and made an effort or two to say something, then gave it up, despondently. Several voices cried out:

'Read it! Read it! What is it?'

So he began in a dazed and sleep-walker fashion:

' "*The remark which I made to the unhappy stranger was this: "You are far from being a bad man.* [The house gazed at him, marveling.] *Go, and reform.*' " [*Murmurs*: 'Amazing! what can this mean?'] This one,' said the chair, 'is signed Thurlow G. Wilson.'

'There!' cried Wilson. 'I reckon that settles it! I knew perfectly well my note was purloined.'

'Purloined!' retorted Billson. 'I'll let you know that neither you nor any man of your kidney must venture to—'

THE CHAIR 'Order, gentlemen, order! Take your seats, both of you, please.'

They obeyed, shaking their heads and grumbling angrily. The house was profoundly puzzled; it did not know what to do with this curious emergency. Presently Thompson got up. Thompson was the hatter. He would have liked to be a Nineteener; but such was not for him: his stock of hats was not considerable enough for the position. He said:

'Mr Chairman, if I may be permitted to make a suggestion, can both of these gentlemen be right? I put it to you, sir, can both have happened to say the same words to the stranger? It seems to me—'

The tanner got up and interrupted him. The tanner was a disgruntled man, he believed himself entitled to be a Nineteener, but he couldn't get recognition. It made him a little unpleasant in his ways and speech. Said he:

'Sho, *that's* not the point! *That* could happen – twice in a hundred years – but not the other thing. *Neither* of them gave the twenty dollars!'

[*A ripple of applause.*]

BILLSON '*I* did!'

WILSON '*I* did!'

Then each accused the other of pilfering.

THE CHAIR 'Order! Sit down, if you please – both of you. Neither of the notes has been out of my possession at any moment.'

A VOICE 'Good – that settles *that*!'

THE TANNER 'Mr Chairman, one thing is now plain: one of these men has been eavesdropping under the other one's bed, and filching family secrets. If it is not unparliamentary to suggest it, I will remark that both are equal to it. [*The Chair.* 'Order! order!'] I withdraw the remark, sir, and will confine myself to suggesting that *if* one of them has overheard the other reveal the test-remark to his wife, we shall catch him now.'

A VOICE 'How?'

THE TANNER 'Easily. The two have not quoted the remark in exactly the same words. You would have noticed that, if there hadn't been a considerable stretch of time and an exciting quarrel inserted between the two readings.'

A VOICE 'Name the difference.'

THE TANNER 'The word *very* is in Billson's note, and not in the other.'

MANY VOICES 'That's so – he's right!'

THE TANNER 'And so, if the Chair will examine the test-remark in the sack, we shall know which of these two frauds – [*The Chair.* 'Order!'] – which of these two adventurers – [*The Chair.* 'Order! order!'] – which of these two gentlemen – [*laughter and applause*] – is entitled to wear the belt as being the first dishonest blatherskite ever bred in this town – which he has dishonored, and which will be a sultry place for him from now out!' [*Vigorous applause.*]

MANY VOICES 'Open it! open the sack!'

Mr Burgess made a slit in the sack, slid his hand in and brought out an envelope. In it were a couple of folded notes. He said:

'One of these is marked, "Not to be examined until all written communications which have been addressed to the Chair – if any – shall have been read." The other is marked *"The Test."* Allow me. It is worded – to wit:

' "I do not require that the first half of the remark which was made to me by my benefactor shall be quoted with exactness, for it was not striking, and could be forgotten; but its closing fifteen words are quite striking, and I think easily rememberable; unless *these* shall be accurately reproduced, let the applicant be regarded as an impostor. My benefactor began by saying he seldom gave advice to any one, but that it always bore the hall-mark of high value when he did give it. Then he said this – and it has never faded from my memory: '*You are far from being a bad man—*' " '

FIFTY VOICES 'That settles it – the money's Wilson's! Wilson! Wilson! Speech! Speech!'

People jumped up and crowded around Wilson, wringing his hand and congratulating fervently – meantime the Chair was hammering with the gavel and shouting:

'Order, gentlemen! Order! Order! Let me finish reading, please.' When quiet was restored, the reading was resumed – as follows:

' " '*Go, and reform – or, mark my words – some day, for your sins, you will die and go to hell or Hadleyburg –* TRY AND MAKE IT THE FORMER.' " '

A ghastly silence followed. First an angry cloud began to settle darkly upon the faces of the citizenship; after a pause the cloud began to rise, and a tickled expression tried to take its place; tried so hard that it was only kept under with great and painful difficulty; the reporters, the Brixtonites, and other strangers bent their heads down and shielded their faces with their hands, and managed to hold in by main strength and heroic courtesy. At this most inopportune time burst upon the stillness the roar of a solitary voice – Jack Halliday's:

'*That's* got the hall-mark on it!'

Then the house let go, strangers and all. Even Mr Burgess's gravity broke down presently, then the audience considered itself officially absolved from all restraint, and it made the most of its privilege. It was a good long laugh, and a tempestuously whole-hearted one, but it ceased at last – long enough for Mr Burgess to try to resume, and for the people to get their eyes partially wiped; then it broke out again; and afterward yet again; then at last Burgess was able to get out these serious words:

'It is useless to try to disguise the fact – we find ourselves in the presence of a matter of grave import. It involves the honor of your town, it strikes at the town's good name. The difference of a single word between the test-remarks offered by Mr Wilson and Mr Billson was itself a serious thing, since it indicated that one or the other of these gentlemen had committed a theft—'

The two men were sitting limp, nerveless, crushed; but at these words both were electrified into movement, and started to get up –

'Sit down!' said the Chair, sharply, and they obeyed. 'That, as I have said, was a serious thing. And it was – but for only one of them. But the matter has become graver; for the honor of *both* is now in formidable peril. Shall I go even further, and say in inextricable peril? *Both* left out the crucial fifteen words.' He paused. During several moments he allowed the pervading stillness to gather and deepen its impressive effects, then added: 'There would seem to be but one way whereby this could happen. I ask these gentlemen – Was there *collusion – agreement*?'

A low murmur sifted through the house; its import was, 'He's got them both.'

Billson was not used to emergencies; he sat in a helpless collapse. But Wilson was a lawyer. He struggled to his feet, pale and worried, and said:

'I ask the indulgence of the house while I explain this most painful matter. I am sorry to say what I am about to say, since it must inflict irreparable injury upon Mr Billson, whom I have

always esteemed and respected until now, and in whose invulnerability to temptation I entirely believed – as did you all. But
for the preservation of my own honor I must speak – and with
frankness. I confess with shame – and I now beseech your pardon
for it – that I said to the ruined stranger all of the words contained
in the test-remark, including the disparaging fifteen. [*Sensation.*]
When the late publication was made I recalled them, and I
resolved to claim the sack of coin, for by every right I was entitled
to it. Now I will ask you to consider this point, and weigh it well:
that stranger's gratitude to me that night knew no bounds; he said
himself that he could find no words for it that were adequate, and
that if he should ever be able he would repay me a thousandfold.
Now, then, I ask you this: Could I expect – could I believe – could
I even remotely imagine – that, feeling as he did, he would do so
ungrateful a thing as to add those quite unnecessary fifteen words
to his test? – set a trap for me? – expose me as a slanderer of my
own town before my own people assembled in a public hall? It
was preposterous; it was impossible. His test would contain only
the kindly opening clause of my remark. Of that I had no shadow
of doubt. You would have thought as I did. You would not have
expected a base betrayal from one whom you had befriended and
against whom you had committed no offense. And so, with
perfect confidence, perfect trust, I wrote on a piece of paper the
opening words – ending with "Go, and reform," – and signed it.
When I was about to put it in an envelope I was called into my
back office, and without thinking I left the paper lying open on my
desk.' He stopped, turned his head slowly toward Billson, waited
a moment, then added: 'I ask you to note this: when I returned, a
little later, Mr Billson was retiring by my street door.' [*Sensation.*]
    In a moment Billson was on his feet and shouting:
    'It's a lie! It's an infamous lie!'
    THE CHAIR 'Be seated, sir! Mr Wilson has the floor.'
    Billson's friends pulled him into his seat and quieted him, and
Wilson went on:
    'Those are the simple facts. My note was now lying in a
different place on the table from where I had left it. I noticed that,
but attached no importance to it, thinking a draught had blown it
there. That Mr Billson would read a private paper was a thing
which could not occur to me; he was an honorable man, and he
would be above that. If you will allow me to say it, I think his extra
word "*very*" stands explained; it is attributable to a defect of

memory. I was the only man in the world who could furnish here any detail of the test-remark — by *honorable* means. I have finished.'

There is nothing in the world like a persuasive speech to fuddle the mental apparatus and upset the convictions and debauch the emotions of an audience not practised in the tricks and delusions of oratory. Wilson sat down victorious. The house submerged him in tides of approving applause; friends swarmed to him and shook him by the hand and congratulated him, and Billson was shouted down and not allowed to say a word. The Chair hammered and hammered with its gavel, and kept shouting:

'But let us proceed, gentlemen, let us proceed!'

At last there was a measurable degree of quiet, and the hatter said:

'But what is there to proceed with, sir, but to deliver the money?'

VOICES 'That's it! That's it! Come forward, Wilson!'

THE HATTER 'I move three cheers for Mr Wilson, Symbol of the special virtue which—'

The cheers burst forth before he could finish; and in the midst of them — and in the midst of the clamor of the gavel also — some enthusiasts mounted Wilson on a big friend's shoulder and were going to fetch him in triumph to the platform. The Chair's voice now rose above the noise —

'Order! To your places! You forget that there is still a document to be read.' When quiet had been restored he took up the document, and was going to read it, but laid it down again, saying, 'I forgot; this is not to be read until all written communications received by me have first been read.' He took an envelope out of his pocket, removed its enclosure, glanced at it — seemed astonished — held it out and gazed at it — stared at it.

Twenty or thirty voices cried out:

'What is it! Read it! read it!'

And he did — slowly, and wondering:

' "*The remark which I made to the stranger* — [*Voices.* 'Hello! how's this?'] — *was this:* '*You are far from being a bad man.* [*Voices.* 'Great Scott!'] *Go, and reform*' ", [*Voices.* 'Oh, saw my leg off!'] Signed by Mr. Pinkerton, the banker.'

The pandemonium of delight which turned itself loose now was of a sort to make the judicious weep. Those whose withers were unwrung laughed till the tears ran down; the reporters, in throes of laughter, set down disordered pot-hooks which would never in the world be decipherable; and a sleeping dog jumped up, scared out of its wits, and barked itself crazy at the turmoil. All manner of cries were scattered through the din: 'We're getting rich – *two* Symbols of Incorruptibility! – without counting Billson!' '*Three*! – count Shadbelly in – we can't have too many!' 'All right – Billson's elected!' 'Alas, poor Wilson – victim of *two* thieves!'

A POWERFUL VOICE 'Silence! The Chair's fished up something more out of its pocket.'

VOICES 'Hurrah! Is it something fresh? Read it! read! read!'

THE CHAIR [*reading*] ' "*The remark which I made,*" ' etc.: " '*You are far from being a bad man. Go,*" ' etc. Signed, "Gregory Yates." '

TORNADO OF VOICES 'Four Symbols!' ' 'Rah for Yates!' 'Fish again!'

The house was in a roaring humor now, and ready to get all the fun out of the occasion that might be in it. Several Nineteeners, looking pale and distressed, got up and began to work their way toward the aisles, but a score of shouts went up:

'The doors, the doors – close the doors; no Incorruptible shall leave this place! Sit down, everybody!'

The mandate was obeyed.

'Fish again! Read! read!'

The Chair fished again, and once more the familiar words began to fall from its lips – ' "*You are far from being a bad man.*" '

'Name! name! What's his name?'

' "L. Ingoldsby Sargent." '

'Five elected! Pile up the Symbols! Go on, go on!'

' "*You are far from being a bad—*" '

'Name! name!'

' "Nicholas Whitworth." '

'Hooray! hooray! it's a symbolical day!'

Somebody wailed in, and began to sing this rhyme (leaving out 'it's') to the lovely 'Mikado' tune of 'When a man's afraid, a beautiful maid—'; the audience joined in, with joy;) then, just in time, somebody contributed another line –

And don't you this forget—

The house roared it out. A third line was at once furnished –

Corruptibles far from Hadleyburg are—

The house roared that one too. As the last note died, Jack Halliday's voice rose high and clear, freighted with a final line –

But the Symbols are here, you bet!

That was sung, with booming enthusiasm. Then the happy house started in at the beginning and sang the four lines through twice, with immense swing and dash, and finished up with a crashing three-times-three and a tiger for 'Hadleyburg the Incorruptible and all Symbols of it which we shall find worthy to receive the hall-mark tonight.'

Then the shoutings at the Chair began again, all over the place:

'Go on! go on! Read! read some more! Read all you've got!'

'That's it – go on! We are winning eternal celebrity!'

A dozen men got up now and began to protest. They said that this farce was the work of the abandoned joker, and was an insult to the whole community. Without a doubt these signatures were all forgeries—

'Sit down! sit down! Shut up! You are confessing. We'll find *your* names in the lot.'

'Mr. Chairman, how many of those envelopes have you got?'

The Chair counted.

'Together with those that have been already examined, there are nineteen.'

A storm of derisive applause broke out.

'Perhaps they all contain the secret. I move that you open them all and read every signature that is attached to a note of that sort – and read also the first eight words of the note.

'Second the motion!'

It was put and carried – uproariously. Then poor old Richards got up, and his wife rose and stood at his side. Her head was bent down, so that none might see that she was crying. Her husband gave her his arm, and so supporting her, he began to speak in a quavering voice:

'My friends, you have known us two – Mary and me – all our lives, and I think you have liked us and respected us—'

The Chair interrupted him:

'Allow me. It is quite true – that which you are saying, Mr Richards: this town *does* know you two; it *does* like you; it *does* respect you; more – it honors you and *loves* you—'

Halliday's voice rang out:

'That's the hall-marked truth, too! If the Chair is right, let the house speak up and say it. Rise! Now, then – hip! hip! hip! – all together!'

The house rose in mass, faced toward the old couple eagerly, filled the air with a snow-storm of waving handkerchiefs, and delivered the cheers with all its affectionate heart.

The Chair then continued:

'What I was going to say is this: We know your good heart, Mr Richards, but this is not a time for the exercise of charity toward offenders. [*Shouts of 'Right! right!'*] I see your generous purpose in your face, but I cannot allow you to plead for these men—'

'But I was going to—'

'Please take your seat, Mr Richards. We must examine the rest of these notes – simple fairness to the men who have already been exposed requires this. As soon as that has been done – I give you my word for this – you shall be heard.'

MANY VOICES 'Right! – the Chair is right – no interruption can be permitted at this stage! Go on! – the names! the names! – according to the terms of the motion!'

The old couple sat reluctantly down, and the husband whispered to the wife, 'It is pitifully hard to have to wait; the shame will be greater than ever when they find we were only going to plead for *ourselves*.'

Straightway the jollity broke loose again with the reading of the names.

' "You are far from being a bad man—" Signature, "Robert J. Titmarsh."

' "You are far from being a bad man—" Signature, "Eliphalet Weeks."

' "You are far from being a bad man—" Signature, "Oscar B. Wilder." '

At this point the house lit upon the idea of taking the eight words out of the Chairman's hands. He was not unthankful for that. Thenceforward he held up each note in its turn, and waited. The house droned out the eight words in a massed and measured and musical deep volume of sound (with a daringly close resemblance to a well-known church chant) – ' "You are f-a-r from being a b-a-a-a-d man." ' Then the Chair said, 'Signature, "Archibald Wilcox." ' And so on, and so on, name after name, and everybody had an increasingly and gloriously good time except the wretched Nineteen. Now and then, when a particularly shining name was called, the house made the Chair wait while it chanted the whole of the test-remark from the beginning to the closing words, 'And go to hell or Hadleyburg – try and make it the for-or-m-e-r!' and in these special cases they added a grand and agonized and imposing 'A-a-a-a-*men!*'

The list dwindled, dwindled, dwindled, poor old Richards keeping tally of the count, wincing when a name resembling his own was pronounced, and waiting in miserable suspense for the time to come when it would be his humiliating privilege to rise with Mary and finish his plea, which he was intending to word thus: '. . . for until now we have never done any wrong thing, but have gone our humble way unreproached. We are very poor, we are old, and have no chick nor child to help us; we were sorely tempted, and we fell. It was my purpose when I got up before to make confession and beg that my name might not be read out in this public place, for it seemed to us that we could not bear it; but I was prevented. It was just; it was our place to suffer with the rest. It has been hard for us. It is the first time we have ever heard our name fall from any one's lips – sullied. Be merciful – for the sake of the better days; make our shame as light to bear as in your charity you can.' At this point in his revery Mary nudged him, perceiving that his mind was absent. The house was chanting, 'You are f-a-r,' etc.

'Be ready,' Mary whispered, 'Your name comes now; he has read eighteen.'

The chant ended.

'Next! next! next!' came volleying from all over the house.

Burgess put his hand into his pocket. The old couple, trembling, began to rise. Burgess fumbled a moment, then said,

'I find I have read them all.'

Faint with joy and surprise, the couple sank into their seats, and Mary whispered:

'Oh, bless God, we are saved! – he has lost ours – I wouldn't give this for a hundred of those sacks!'

The house burst out with its 'Mikado' travesty, and sang it three times with ever-increasing enthusiasm, rising to its feet when it reached for the third time the closing line –

But the Symbols are here, you bet!

and finishing up with cheers and a tiger for 'Hadleyburg purity and our eighteen immortal representatives of it.'

Then Wingate, the saddler, got up and proposed cheers, 'for the cleanest man in town, the one solitary important citizen in it who didn't try to steal the money – Edward Richards.'

They were given with great and moving heartiness; then somebody proposed that Richards be elected sole guardian and Symbol of the now Sacred Hadleyburg Tradition, with power and right to stand up and look the whole sarcastic world in the face.

Passed, by acclamation; they sang the 'Mikado' again, and ended it with:

And there's one Symbol left, you bet!

There was a pause; then –

A VOICE 'Now, then, who's to get the sack?'

THE TANNER (*with bitter sarcasm*) 'That's easy. The money has to be divided among the eighteen Incorruptibles. They gave the suffering stranger twenty dollars apiece – and that remark – each in his turn – it took twenty-two minutes for the procession to move past. Staked the stranger – total contribution, $360. All they want is just the loan back – and interest – forty thousand dollars altogether.'

MANY VOICES [*derisively*] 'That's it! Divvy! divvy! Be kind to the poor – don't keep them waiting!'

THE CHAIR 'Order! I now offer the stranger's remaining document. It says: "If no claimant shall appear [*grand chorus of groans*] I desire that you open the sack and count out the money to the principal citizens of your town, they to take it in trust [*cries of 'Oh! Oh! Oh!'*], and use it in such ways as to them shall seem best for the propagation and preservation of your community's noble reputation for incorruptible honesty [*more cries*] – a reputation to which their names and their efforts will add a new and far-reaching luster." [*Enthusiastic outburst of sarcastic applause.*] That seems to be all. No – here is a postscript:

"P.S. – CITIZENS OF HADLEYBURG: There is no test-remark – nobody made one. [*Great sensation.*] There wasn't any pauper stranger, nor any twenty-dollar contribution, nor any accompanying benediction and compliment – these are all inventions. [*General buzz and hum of astonishment and delight.*] Allow me to tell my story – it will take but a word or two. I passed through your town at a certain time, and received a deep offense which I had not earned. Any other man would have been content to kill one or two of you and call it square, but to me that would have been a trivial revenge, and inadequate; for the dead do not suffer. Besides, I could not kill you all – and, anyway, made as I am, even that would not have satisfied me. I wanted to damage every man in the place, and every woman – and not in their bodies or in their estate, but in their vanity – the place where feeble and foolish people are most vulnerable. So I disguised myself and came back and studied you. You were easy game. You had an old and lofty reputation for honesty, and naturally you were proud of it – it was your treasure of treasures, the very apple of your eye. As soon as I found out that you carefully and vigilantly kept yourself and your children *out of temptation*, I knew how to proceed. Why, you simple creatures, the weakest of all weak things is a virtue which has not been tested in the fire. I laid a plan, and gathered a list of names. My project was to corrupt Hadleyburg the Incorruptible. My idea was to make liars and thieves of nearly half a hundred smirchless men and women who had never in their lives uttered a lie or stolen a penny. I was afraid of Goodson. He was neither born nor reared in Hadleyburg. I was afraid that if I started to operate my scheme by getting my letter laid before you, you would say to yourselves, 'Goodson is the only man among us who would give away twenty dollars to a poor devil' – and then you might not bite at my bait. But Heaven took Goodson; then I knew I was safe, and I set my trap and baited it, It may be that I shall not catch all the men to whom I mailed the pretended test secret, but I shall catch the most of them, if I know Hadleyburg nature. [*Voices:* 'Right – *he got every last one of them.*'] I believe they will even steal ostensible *gamble*-money, rather than miss, poor, tempted, and mistrained fellows. I am hoping to eternally and everlastingly squelch your vanity and give Hadleyburg a new renown – one that will *stick* – and spread far. If I have succeeded, open the sack and summon the Committee on Propagation and Preservation of the Hadleyburg Reputation."

A CYCLONE OF VOICES 'Open it! Open it! The Eighteen to the front! Committee on Propagation of the Tradition! Forward – the Incorruptibles!'

The Chair ripped the sack wide, and gathered up a handful of bright, broad, yellow coins, shook them together, then examined them –

'Friends, they are only gilded disks of lead!'

There was a crashing outbreak of delight over this news, and when the noise had subsided, the tanner called out:

'By right of apparent seniority in this busines, Mr Wilson is Chairman of the Committee on Propagation of the Tradition. I suggest that he step forward on behalf of his pals, and receive in trust the money.'

A HUNDRED VOICES 'Wilson! Wilson! Wilson! Speech! Speech!'

WILSON [*in a voice trembling with anger*] 'You will allow me to say, and without apologies for my language, *damn* the money!'

A VOICE 'Oh, and him a Baptist!'

A VOICE 'Seventeen Symbols left! Step up, gentlemen, and assume your trust!'

There was a pause – no response.

THE SADDLER 'Mr Chairman, we've got *one* clean man left, anyway, out of the late aristocracy: and he needs money, and deserves it. I move that you appoint Jack Halliday to get up there and auction off that sack of gilt twenty-dollar pieces, and give the result to the right man – the man whom Hadleyburg delights to honor – Edward Richards.'

This was received with great enthusiasm, the dog taking a hand again; the saddler started the bids at a dollar, the Brixton folk and Barnum's representative fought hard for it, the people cheered every jump that the bids made, the excitement climbed moment by moment higher and higher, the bidders got on their mettle and grew steadily more and more daring, more and more determined, the jumps went from a dollar up to five, then to ten, then to twenty, then fifty, then to a hundred, then –

At the beginning of the auction Richards whispered in distress to his wife: 'O Mary, can we allow it? It – it you see, it is an honor-reward, a testimonial to purity of character, and – and – can we allow it? Hadn't I better get up and – O Mary, what ought we to do? – what do you think we – [*Halliday's voice. 'Fifteen I'm bid! – fifteen for the sack! – twenty! – ah, thanks! – thirty – thanks again! Thirty, thirty, thirty! – do I hear forty? – forty it is! Keep the ball rolling, gentlemen, keep it rolling! – fifty! thanks, noble Roman! going at fifty, fifty, fifty! – seventy! – ninety! – splendid! – a hundred! – pile it up, pile it up! – hundred and twenty – forty! – just in time! – hundred and fifty! – TWO hundred! – superb! Do I hear two h— thanks! two hundred and fifty! –*]

'It is another temptation, Edward – I'm all in a tremble – but, oh, we've escaped *one* temptation, and that ought to warn us to – ['*Six did I hear? – thanks! – six-fifty, six-f—* SEVEN *hundred!*'] And yet, Edward, when you think – nobody susp— ['*Eight hundred dollars! – hurrah! – make it nine! – Mr Parsons, did I hear you say – thanks – nine! – this noble sack of virgin lead going at only nine hundred dollars, gilding and all – come! do I hear – a thousand! – gratefully yours! – did some one say eleven? – a sack which is going to be the most celebrated in the whole Uni—* '] O Edward' (beginning to sob), 'we are *so* poor! – but – but – do as you think best – do as you think best.'

Edward fell – that is, he sat still; sat with a conscience which was not satisfied but which was overpowered by circumstances.

Meantime a stranger, who looked like an amateur detective gotten up as an impossible English earl, had been watching the evening's proceedings with manifest interest, and with a contented expression in his face; and he had been privately commenting to himself. He was now soliloquizing somewhat like this: 'None of the Eighteen are bidding; that is not satisfactory; I must change that – the dramatic unities require it; they must buy the sack they tried to steal; they must pay a heavy price, too – some of them are rich. And another thing, when I make a mistake in Hadleyburg nature the man that puts that error upon me is entitled to a high honorarium, and some one must pay it. This poor old Richards has brought my judgment to shame; he is an honest man: I don't understand it, but I acknowledge it. Yes, he saw my deuces *and* with a straight flush, and by rights the pot is his. And it shall be a jack-pot, too, if I can manage it. He disappointed me, but let that pass.'

He was watching the bidding. At a thousand, the market broke; the prices tumbled swiftly. He waited – and still watched. One competitor dropped out; then another, and another. He put in a bid or two, now. When the bids had sunk to ten dollars, he added a five; some one raised him a three; he waited a moment, then flung in a fifty-dollar jump, and the sack was his – at $1,282. The house broke out in cheers – then stopped; for he was on his feet, and had lifted his hand. He began to speak.

'I desire to say a word, and ask a favor. I am a speculator in rarities, and I have dealings with persons interested in numismatics all over the world. I can make a profit on this purchase, just as it stands; but there is a way, if I can get your approval, whereby

I can make every one of these laden twenty-dollar pieces worth its
face in gold, and perhaps more. Grant me that approval, and I will
give part of my gains to your Mr Richards, whose invulnerable
probity you have so justly and so cordially recognized tonight;
his share shall be ten thousand dollars, and I will hand him the
money tomorrow. [*Great applause from the house.* But the
'invulnerable probity' made the Richardses blush prettily; however, it went for modesty, and did no harm.] If you will pass my
proposition by a good majority – I would like a two-thirds vote – I
will regard that as the town's consent, and that is all I ask. Rarities
are always helped by any device which will rouse curiosity and
compel remark. Now if I may have your permission to stamp
upon the faces of each of these ostensible coins the names of the
eighteen gentlemen who –'

Nine-tenths of the audience were on their feet in a moment –
dog and all – and the proposition was carried with a whirlwind of
approving applause and laughter.

They sat down, and all the Symbols except 'Dr' Clay Harkness
got up, violently protesting against the proposed outrage, and
threatening to –

'I beg you not to threaten me,' said the stranger, calmly. 'I know
my legal rights, and am not accustomed to being frightened at
bluster.' [*Applause.*] He sat down. 'Dr' Harkness saw an opportunity here. He was one of the two very rich men of the place, and
Pinkerton was the other. Harkness was proprietor of a mint; that
is to say, a popular patent medicine. He was running for the
legislature on one ticket, and Pinkerton on the other. It was a close
race and a hot one, and getting hotter every day. Both had strong
appetites for money; each had bought a great tract of land, with a
purpose; there was going to be a new railway, and each wanted to
be in the legislature and help locate the route to his own
advantage; a single vote might make the decision, and with it two
or three fortunes. The stake was large, and Harkness was a daring
speculator. He was sitting close to the stranger. He leaned over
while one or another of the other Symbols was entertaining the
house with protests and appeals, and asked, in a whisper.

'What is your price for the sack?'

'Forty thousand dollars.'

'I'll give you twenty.'

'No.'

'Twenty-five.'

'No.'

'Say thirty.'

'The price is forty thousand dollars; not a penny less.'

'All right, I'll give it. I will come to the hotel at ten in the morning. I don't want it known: will see you privately.'

'Very good.' Then the stranger got up and said to the house:

'I find it late. The speeches of these gentlemen are not without merit, not without interest, not without grace; yet if I may be excused I will take my leave. I thank you for the great favor which you have shown me in granting my petition. I ask the Chair to keep the sack for me until tomorrow, and to hand these three five-hundred-dollar notes to Mr Richards.' They were passed up to the Chair. 'At nine I will call for the sack, and at eleven will deliver the rest of the ten thousand to Mr Richards in person, at his home. Good night.'

Then he slipped out, and left the audience making a vast noise, which was composed of a mixture of cheers, the 'Mikado' song, dog-disapproval, and the chant, 'You are f-a-r from being a b-a-a-d man – a-a-a-a-men!'

4

At home the Richardses had to endure congratulations and compliments until midnight. Then they were left to themselves. They looked a little sad, and they sat silent and thinking. Finally Mary sighed and said,

'Do you think we are to blame, Edward – *much* to blame?' and her eyes wandered to the accusing triplet of big bank-notes lying on the table, where the congratulators had been gloating over them and reverently fingering them. Edward did not answer at once; then he brought out a sigh and said, hesitatingly:

'We – we couldn't help it, Mary. It – well, it was ordered. *All* things are.'

Mary glanced up and looked at him steadily, but he didn't return the look. Presently she said:

'I thought congratulations and praises always tasted good. But – it seems to me, now – Edward?'

'Well?'

'Are you going to stay in the bank?'

'N-no.'

'Resign?'

'In the morning – by note.'

'It does seem best.'

Richards bowed his head in his hands and muttered:

'Before, I was not afraid to let oceans of people's money pour through my hands, but – Mary, I am so tired, so tired –'

'We will go to bed.'

At nine in the morning the stranger called for the sack and took it to the hotel in a cab. At ten Harkness had a talk with him privately. The stranger asked for and got five checks on a metropolitan bank – drawn to 'Bearer' – four for $1,500 each, and one for $34,000. He put one of the former in his pocketbook, and the remainder, representing $38,500, he put in an envelope, and with these he added a note, which he wrote after Harkness was gone. At eleven he called at the Richards house and knocked. Mrs Richards peeped through the shutters, then went and received the envelope, and the stranger disappeared without a word. She came back flushed and a little unsteady on her legs, and gasped out:

'I am sure I recognized him! Last night it seemed to me that maybe I had seen him somewhere before.'

'He is the man that brought the sack here?'

'I am almost sure of it.'

'Then he is the ostensible Stephenson, too, and sold every important citizen in this town with his bogus secret. Now if he has sent checks instead of money, we are sold, too, after we thought we had escaped. I was beginning to feel fairly comfortable once more, after my night's rest, but the look of that envelope makes me sick. It isn't fat enough; $8,500 in even the largest bank-notes makes more bulk than that.'

'Edward, why do you object to checks?'

'Checks signed by Stephenson! I am resigned to take the $8,500 if it could come in bank-notes – for it does seem that it was so ordered, Mary – but I have never had much courage, and I have not the pluck to try to market a check signed with that disastrous name. It would be a trap. That man tried to catch me; we escaped somehow or other; and now he is trying a new way. If it is checks –'

'Oh, Edward, it is *too* bad!' and she held up the checks and began to cry.

'Put them in the fire! quick! we mustn't be tempted. It is a trick to make the world laugh at *us*, along with the rest, and – Give them to *me*, since you can't do it!' He snatched them and tried to hold his grip till he could get to the stove; but he was human, he was a cashier, and he stopped a moment to make sure of the signature. Then he came near to fainting.

'Fan me, Mary, fan me! They are the same as gold!'

'Oh, how lovely, Edward! Why?'

'Signed by Harkness. What can the mystery of that be, Mary?'

'Edward, do you think—'

'Look here – look at this! Fifteen – fifteen – fifteen – thirty-four. Thirty-eight thousand five hundred! Mary, the sack isn't worth twelve dollars, and Harkness – apparently – has paid about par for it.'

'And does it all come to us, do you think – instead of the ten thousand?'

'Why, it looks like it. And the checks are made to "Bearer", too.'

'Is that good, Edward? What is it for?'

'A hint to collect them at some distant bank, I reckon. Perhaps Harkness doesn't want the matter known. What is that – a note?'

'Yes. It was with the checks.'

It was in the 'Stephenson' handwriting, but there was no signature. It said:

'I am a disappointed man. Your honesty is beyond the reach of temptation. I had a different idea about it, but I wronged you in that, and I beg pardon, and do it sincerely. I honor you – and that is sincere too. This town is not worthy to kiss the hem of your garment. Dear sir, I made a square bet with myself that there were nineteen debauchable men in your self-righteous community. I have lost. Take the whole pot, you are entitled to it.'

Richards drew a deep sigh, and said:

'It seems written with fire – it burns so. Mary – I am miserable again.'

'I, too. Ah, dear, I wish –'

'To think, Mary – he *believes* in me.'

'Oh, don't, Edward – I can't bear it.'

'If those beautiful words were deserved, Mary – and God knows I believed I deserved them once – I think I could give the forty thousand dollars for them. And I would put that paper away, as representing more than gold and jewels, and keep it always. But now – We could not live in the shadow of its accusing presence, Mary.'

He put it in the fire.

A messenger arrived and delivered an envelope.

Richards took from it a note and read it; it was from Burgess.

'You saved me, in a difficult time. I saved you last night. It was at a cost of a lie, but I made the sacrifice freely, and out of a grateful heart. None in this village knows so well as I know how brave and good and noble you are. At bottom you cannot respect me, knowing as you do of that matter of which I am accused, and by the general voice condemned; but I beg that you will at least believe that I am a grateful man; it will help me to bear my burden.'

[Signed]

BURGESS

'Saved, once more. And on such terms!' He put the note in the fire. 'I – I wish I were dead, Mary, I wish I were out of it all.'

'Oh, these are bitter, bitter days, Edward. The stabs, through their very generosity, are so deep – and they come so fast!'

Three days before the election each of two thousand voters suddenly found himself in possession of a prized memento – one of the renowned bogus double-eagles. Around one of its faces was stamped these words: 'THE REMARK I MADE TO THE POOR STRANGER WAS –' Around the other face was stamped these: 'GO, AND REFORM. [SIGNED] PINKERTON.' Thus the entire remaining refuse of the renowned joke was emptied upon a single head, and with calamitous effect. It revived the recent vast laugh and concentrated it upon Pinkerton; and Harkness's election was a walkover.

Within twenty-four hours after the Richardses had received their checks their consciences were quieting down, discouraged; the old couple were learning to reconcile themselves to the sin which they had committed. But they were to learn, now, that a sin takes on new and real terrors when there seems a chance that it is going to be found out. This gives it a fresh and most substantial and important aspect. At church the morning sermon was of the usual pattern; it was the same old things said the same old way; they had heard them a thousand times and found them innocuous, next to meaningless, and easy to sleep under; but now it was different: the sermon seemed to bristle with accusations; it seemed aimed straight and specially at people who were concealing deadly sins. After church they got away from the mob of congratulators as soon as they could, and hurried homeward, chilled to the bone at they did not know what – vague, shadowy, indefinite fears. And by chance they caught a glimpse of Mr Burgess as he turned a corner. He paid no attention to their nod of recognition! He hadn't seen it; but they did not know that. What could his conduct mean? It might mean – it might mean –oh, a dozen dreadful things. Was it possible that he knew that Richards could have cleared him of guilt in that bygone time, and had been silently waiting for a chance to even up accounts? At home, in their distress they got to imagining that their servant might have been in the next room listening when Richards revealed the secret to his wife that he knew of Burgess's innocence; next, Richards began to imagine that he had heard the swish of a gown in there at that time; next, he was sure he *had* heard it. They would call Sarah in, on a pretext, and watch her face: if she had been betraying them to Mr Burgess, it would show in her manner. They asked her some questions – questions which were so random and incoherent and seemingly purposeless that the girl felt sure that the old people's minds had been affected by their sudden good fortune; the sharp and watchful gaze which they bent upon her frightened her, and that completed the business. She blushed, she became nervous and confused, and to the old people these were plain signs of guilt – guilt of some fearful sort or other – without doubt she was a spy and a traitor. When they were alone again they began to piece many unrelated things together and get horrible results out of the combination. When things had got about to the worst, Richards was delivered of a sudden gasp, and his wife asked:

'Oh, what is it – what is it?'

'The note – Burgess's note! Its language was sarcastic, I see it now.' He quoted: ' "At bottom you cannot respect me, *knowing*, as you do, of *that matter* of which I am accused" – oh, it is perfectly plain, now, God help me! He knows that I know! You see the ingenuity of the phrasing. It was a trap – and like a fool, I walked into it. And Mary –?'

'Oh, it is dreadful – I know what you are going to say – he didn't return your transcript of the pretended test-remark.'

'No – kept it to destroy us with. Mary, he has exposed us to some already. I know it – I know it well. I saw it in a dozen faces after church. Ah, he wouldn't answer our nod of recognition – *he* knew what he had been doing!'

In the night the doctor was called. The news went around in the morning that the old couple were rather seriously ill – prostrated by the exhausting excitement growing out of their great windfall, the congratulations, and the late hours, the doctor said. The town was sincerely distressed; for these old people were about all it had left to be proud of, now.

Two days later the news was worse. The old couple were delirious, and were doing strange things. By witness of the nurses, Richards had exhibited checks – for $8,500? No – for an amazing sum – $38,500! What could be the explanation of this gigantic piece of luck?

The following day the nurses had more news – and wonderful. They had concluded to hide the checks, lest harm come to them; but when they searched they were gone from under the patient's pillow – vanished away. The patient said:

'Let the pillow alone; what do you want?'

'We thought it best that the checks—'

'You will never see them again – they are destroyed. They came from Satan. I saw the hell-brand on them, and I knew they were sent to betray me to sin.' Then he fell to gabbling strange and dreadful things which were not clearly understandable, and which the doctor admonished them to keep to themselves.

Richards was right; the checks were never seen again.

A nurse must have talked in her sleep, for within two days the forbidden gabblings were the property of the town; and they were of a surprising sort. They seemed to indicate that Richards had been a claimant for the sack himself, and that Burgess had concealed that fact and then maliciously betrayed it.

Burgess was taxed with this and stoutly denied it. And he said it was not fair to attach weight to the chatter of a sick old man who was out of his mind. Still, suspicion was in the air, and there was much talk.

After a day or two it was reported that Mrs Richards's delirious deliveries were getting to be duplicates of her husband's. Suspicion flamed up into conviction, now, and the town's pride in the purity of its one undiscredited important citizen began to dim down and flicker toward extinction.

Six days passed, then came more news. The old couple were dying. Richards's mind cleared in his latest hour, and he sent for Burgess. Burgess said:

'Let the room be cleared. I think he wishes to say something in privacy.'

'No!' said Richards: 'I want witnesses. I want you all to hear my

confession, so that I may die a man, and not a dog. I was clean –
artifically – like the rest; and like the rest I fell when temptation
came. I signed a lie, and claimed the miserable sack. Mr Burgess
remembered that I had done him a service, and in gratitude (and
ignorance) he supressed my claim and saved me. You know the
thing that was charged against Burgess years ago. My testimony,
and mine alone, could have cleared him, and I was a coward, and
left him to suffer disgrace –'

'No – no – Mr. Richards, you—'

'My servant betrayed my secret to him—'

'No one has betrayed anything to me—'

– 'and then he did a natural and justifiable thing, he repented of
the saving kindness which he had done me, and he *exposed* me –
as I deserved—'

'Never! – I make oath—'

'Out of my heart I forgive him.'

Burgess's impassioned protestations fell upon deaf ears; the
dying man passed away without knowing that once more he had
done poor Burgess a wrong. The old wife died that night.

The last of the sacred Nineteen had fallen prey to the fiendish
sack; the town was stripped of the last rag of its ancient glory. Its
mourning was not showy, but it was deep.

By act of the Legislature – upon prayer and petition –
Hadleyburg was allowed to change its name to (never mind what
– I will not give it away), and leave one word out of the motto that
for many generations had graced the town's official seal.

It is an honest town once more, and the man will have to rise
early that catches it napping again.

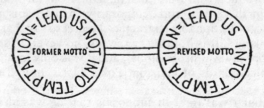

1899

The Outcasts of Poker Flat

As Mr John Oakhurst, gambler, stepped into the main street of Poker Flat on the morning of the twenty-third of November, 1850, he was conscious of a change in its moral atmosphere since the preceding night. Two or three men, conversing earnestly together, ceased as he approached, and exchanged significant glances. There was a Sabbath lull in the air, which, in a settlement unused to Sabbath influences, looked ominous.

Mr Oakhurst's calm, handsome face betrayed small concern in these indications. Whether he was conscious of any predisposing cause was another question. 'I reckon they're after somebody,' he reflected; 'likely it's me.' He returned to his pocket the handkerchief with which he had been whipping away the red dust of Poker Flat from his neat boots, and quietly discharged his mind of any further conjecture.

In point of fact. Poker Flat was 'after somebody.' It had lately suffered the loss of several thousand dollars, two valuable horses, and a prominent citizen. It was experiencing a spasm of virtuous reaction, quite as lawless and ungovernable as any of the acts that had provoked it. A secret committee had determined to rid the town of all improper persons. This was done permanently in regard of two men who were then hanging from the boughs of a sycamore in the gulch, and temporarily in the banishment of certain other objectionable characters. I regret to say that some of these were ladies. It is but due to the sex, however, to state that their impropriety was professional, and it was only in such easily established standards of evil that Poker Flat ventured to sit in judgment.

Mr Oakhurst was right in supposing that he was included in this category. A few of the committee had urged hanging him as a possible example, and a sure method of reimbursing themselves from his pockets of the sums he had won from them. 'It's agin justice,' said Jim Wheeler, 'to let this yer young man from Roaring

Camp – an entire stranger – carry away our money.' But a crude sentiment of equity residing in the breasts of those who had been fortunate enough to win from Mr Oakhurst overruled this narrower local prejudice.

Mr Oakhurst received his sentence with philosophic calmness, none the less coolly that he was aware of the hesitation of his judges. He was too much of a gambler not to accept Fate. With him, life was at best an uncertain game, and he recognized the usual percentage in favour of the dealer.

A body of armed men accompanied the deported wickedness of Poker Flat to the outskirts of the settlement. Besides Mr Oakhurst, who was known to be a coolly desperate man, and for whose intimidation the armed escort was intended, the expatriated party consisted of a young woman, familiarly known as 'The Duchess'; another, who had won the title of 'Mother Shipton'; and 'Uncle Billy,' a suspected sluice-robber and confirmed drunkard. The cavalcade provoked no comments from the spectators, nor was any word uttered by the escort. Only when the gulch which marked the uttermost limit of Poker Flat was reached, the leader spoke briefly, and to the point. The exiles were forbidden to return, at the peril of their lives.

As the escort disappeared, their pent-up feelings found vent in a few hysterical tears from the Duchess, some bad language from Mother Shipton, and a Parthian volley of expletives from Uncle Billy. The philosophic Oakhurst alone remained silent. He listened calmly to Mother Shipton's desire to cut somebody's heart out, to the repeated statements of the Duchess that she would die in the road, and to the alarming oaths that seemed to be bumped out of Uncle Billy as he rode forward. With the easy good-humour characteristic of his class, he insisted upon exchanging his own riding-horse, 'Five Spot,' for the sorry mule which the Duchess rode. But even this act did not draw the party into any closer sympathy. The young woman readjusted her somewhat draggled plumes with a feeble, faded coquetry; Mother Shipton eyed the possessor of 'Five Spot' with malevolence; and Uncle Billy included the whole party in one sweeping anathema.

The road to Sandy Bar – a camp that, not having as yet experienced the regenerating influences of Poker Flat, consequently seemed to offer some invitation to the emigrants – lay over a steep mountain range. It was distant a day's severe travel. In that advanced season, the party soon passed out of the moist, temperate regions of the foot-hills into the dry, cold, bracing air of the Sierras. The trail was narrow and difficult. At noon the Duchess, rolling out of her saddle upon the ground, declared her intention of going no farther, and the party halted.

The spot was singularly wild and impressive. A wooded amphitheatre, surrounded on three sides by precipitous cliffs of naked granite, sloped gently toward the crest of another precipice that overlooked the valley. It was, undoubtedly the most suitable spot for a camp, had camping been advisable. But Mr Oakhurst knew that scarcely half the journey to Sandy Bar was accomplished, and the party were not equipped or provisioned for delay. This fact he pointed out to his companions curtly, with a philosophic commentary on the folly of 'throwing up their hand before the game was played out.' But they were furnished with liquor, which in this emergency stood them in place of food, fuel, rest, and prescience. In spite of his remonstrances, it was not long before they were more or less under its influence. Uncle Billy passed rapidly from a bellicose state into one of stupor, the Duchess became maudlin, and Mother Shipton snored. Mr Oakhurst alone remained erect, leaning against a rock, calmly surveying them.

Mr Oakhurst did not drink. It interfered with a profession which required coolness, impassiveness, and presence of mind, and, in his own language, he 'couldn't afford it.' As he gazed at his recumbent fellow-exiles, the loneliness begotten of his pariah-trade, his habits of life, his very vices, for the first time seriously oppressed him. He bestirred himself in dusting his black clothes, washing his hands and face, and other acts characteristic of his studiously neat habits, and for a moment forgot his annoyance. The thought of deserting his weaker and more pitiable companions never perhaps occurred to him. Yet he could not help feeling the want of that excitement which, singularly enough, was most conducive to that calm equanimity for which he was notorious. He looked at the gloomy walls that rose a thousand feet sheer above the circling pines around him; at the sky, ominously clouded; at the valley below, already deepening into shadow. And, doing so, suddenly he heard his own name called.

A horseman slowly ascended the trail. In the fresh, open face of the new-comer Mr Oakhurst recognized Tom Simson, otherwise known as 'The Innocent' of Sandy Bar. He had met him some months before over a 'little game,' and had, with perfect equanimity, won the entire fortune – amounting to some forty dollars – of that guileless youth. After the game was finished, Mr Oakhurst drew the youthful speculator behind the door, and thus addressed him: 'Tommy, you're a good little man, but you can't gamble worth a cent. Don't try it over again.' He then handed him his money back, pushed him gently from the room, and so made a devoted slave of Tom Simson.

There was a remembrance of this in his boyish and enthusiastic greeting of Mr Oakhurst. He had started, he said, to go to Poker Flat to seek his fortune. 'Alone?' No, not exactly alone; in fact (a giggle), he had run away with Piney Woods. Didn't Mr Oakhurst remember Piney? She that used to wait on the table at the Temperance House? They had been engaged a long time, but old Jake Woods had objected; and so they had run away, and were going to Poker Flat to be married, and here they were. And they were tired out, and how lucky it was they had found a place to camp and company. All this the Innocent delivered rapidly, while Piney, a stout, comely damsel of fifteen, emerged from behind the pine-tree where she had been blushing unseen, and rode to the side of her lover.

Mr Oakhurst seldom troubled himself with sentiment, still less with propriety; but he had a vague idea that the situation was not fortunate. He retained, however, his presence of mind sufficiently to kick Uncle Billy, who was about to say something, and Uncle Billy was sober enough to recognize in Mr Oakhurst's kick a superior power that would not bear trifling. He then endeavoured to dissuade Tom Simson from delaying further, but in vain. He even pointed out the fact that there was no provision, nor means of making a camp. But, unluckily, the Innocent met this objection by assuring the party that he was provided with an extra mule loaded with provisions, and by the discovery of a rude attempt at a loghouse near the trail. 'Piney can stay with Mrs Oakhurst,' said the Innocent, pointing to the Duchess, 'and I can shift for myself.'

Nothing but Mr Oakhurst's admonishing foot saved Uncle Billy from bursting into a roar of laughter. As it was, he felt compelled to retire up the cañon until he could recover his gravity. There he confided the joke to the tall pine-trees, with many slaps of his leg, contortions of his face, and the usual profanity. But when he returned to the party, he found them seated by a fire – for the air had grown strangely chill and the sky overcast – in apparently amicable conversation. Piney was actually talking in an impulsive, girlish fashion to the Duchess, who was listening with an interest and animation she had not shown for many days. The Innocent was holding forth, apparently with equal effect, to Mr Oakhurst and Mother Shipton, who was actually relaxing into amiability. 'Is this yer a d——d picnic?' said Uncle Billy, with inward scorn, as he surveyed the sylvan group, the glancing firelight, and the tethered animals in the foreground. Suddenly an idea mingled with the alcoholic fumes that disturbed his brain. It was apparently of a jocular nature, for he felt impelled to slap his leg again and cram his fist into his mouth.

As the shadows crept slowly up the mountain, a slight breeze rocked the tops of the pine-trees, and moaned through their long and gloomy aisles. The ruined cabin, patched and covered with pine-boughs, was set apart for the ladies. As the lovers parted, they unaffectedly exchanged a kiss, so honest and sincere that it might have been heard above the swaying pines. The frail Duchess and the malevolent Mother Shipton were probably too stunned to remark upon this last evidence of simplicity, and so turned without a word to the hut. The fire was replenished, the men lay down before the door, and in a few minutes were asleep.

Mr Oakhurst was a light sleeper. Toward morning he awoke, benumbed and cold. As he stirred the dying fire, the wind which was now blowing strongly, brought to his cheek that which caused the blood to leave it – snow.

He started to his feet with the intention of awakening the sleepers, for there was no time to lose. But turning to where Uncle Billy had been lying, he found him gone. A suspicion leaped to his brain and a curse to his lips. He ran to the spot where the mules had been tethered; they were no longer there. The tracks were already rapidly disappearing in the snow.

The momentary excitement brought Mr Oakhurst back to the fire with his usual calm. He did not waken the sleepers. The Innocent slumbered peacefully, with a smile on his good-humoured, freckled face; the virgin Piney slept beside her frailer sisters as sweetly as though attended by celestial guardians, and Mr Oakhurst, drawing his blanket over his shoulders, stroked his moustache and waited for the dawn. It came slowly in a whirling mist of snowflakes, that dazzled and confused the eye. What could be seen of the landscape appeared magically changed. He looked over the valley, and summed up the present and future in two words – 'snowed in!'

A careful inventory of the provisions, which, fortunately for the party, had been stored within the hut, and so escaped the felonious fingers of Uncle Billy, disclosed the fact that with care and prudence they might last ten days longer. 'That is,' said Mr Oakhurst, *sotto voce* to the Innocent, 'if you're willing to board us. If you ain't – and perhaps you'd better not – you can wait till Uncle Billy gets back with provisions.' For some occult reason, Mr Oakhurst could not bring himself to disclose Uncle Billy's rascality, and so offered the hypothesis that he had wandered from the camp, and had accidentally stampeded the animals. He dropped a warning to the Duchess and Mother Shipton, who of course knew the facts of their associate's defection. 'They'll find out the truth about us *all* when they find out anything,' he added, significantly, 'and there's no good frightening them now.'

Tom Simson not only put all his worldly store at the disposal of Mr Oakhurst, but seemed to enjoy the prospect of their enforced seclusion. 'We'll have a good camp for a week, and then the snow'll melt, and we'll all go back together.' The cheerful gaiety of the young man and Mr Oakhurst's calm infected the others. The Innocent, with the aid of pine-boughs, extemporised a thatch for the roofless cabin, and the Duchess directed Piney in the rearrangement of the interior with a taste and tact that opened the blue eyes of that provincial maiden to their fullest extent. 'I reckon now you're used to fine things at Poker Flat,' said Piney. The Duchess turned away sharply to conceal something that reddened her cheek through its professional tint, and Mother Shipton requested Piney not to 'chatter'. But when Mr Oakhurst returned from a weary search for the trail, he heard the sound of happy laughter echoed from the rocks. He stopped in some alarm, and his thoughts first naturally reverted to the whisky, which he had prudently *cachéd*. 'And yet it don't somehow sound like whisky,' said the gambler. It was not until he caught sight of the blazing fire through the still blinding storm, and the group around it, that he settled to the conviction that it was 'square fun'.

Whether Mr Oakhurst had *cachéd* his cards with the whisky, as something debarred the free access of the community, I cannot say. It was certain that, in Mother Shipton's words, he 'didn't say cards once' during that evening. Happily, the time was beguiled by an accordion, produced somewhat ostentatiously by Tom Simson from his pack. Notwithstanding some difficulties attending the manipulation of this instrument, Piney Woods managed to pluck several reluctant melodies from its keys, to an accompaniment by the Innocent on a pair of bone castanets. But the crowning festivity of the evening was reached in a rude camp-meeting hymn, which the lovers, joining hands, sang with great earnestness and vociferation. I fear that a certain defiant tone and Covenanter's swing to its chorus, rather than any devotional quality, caused it speedily to infect the others, who at last joined in the refrain:

> ' "I'm proud to live in the service of the Lord,
>   And I'm bound to die in His army." '

The pines rocked, the storm eddied and whirled above the miserable group, and the flames of their altar leaped heavenward, as if in token of the vow.

At midnight the storm abated, the rolling clouds parted, and the stars glittered keenly above the sleeping camp. Mr Oakhurst, whose professioanl habits had enabled him to live on the smallest possible amount of sleep, in dividing the watch with Tom Simson, somehow managed to take upon himself the greater part of that duty. He excused himself to the Innocent by saying that he had 'often been a week without sleep.'

'Doing what?' asked Tom.

'Poker!' replied Oakhurst, sententiously; 'when a man gets a streak of luck – nigger-luck – he don't get tired. The luck gives in first. Luck,' continued the gambler, reflectively, 'is a mighty queer thing. All you know about it for certain is that's it's bound to change. And it's finding out when it's going to change that makes you. We've had a streak of bad luck since we left Poker Flat – you come along, and slap you get into it, too. If you can hold your cards right along, you're all right. For,' added the gambler, with cheerful irrelevance –

> ' "I'm proud to live in the service of the Lord,
>   And I'm bound to die in His army." '

The third day came, and the sun, looking through the white-curtained valley, saw the outcasts divide their slowly decreasing store of provisions for the morning meal. It was one of the peculiarities of that mountain climate that its rays diffused a kindly warmth over the wintry landscape, as if in regretful commiseration of the past. But it revealed drift on drift of snow piled high around the hut – a hopeless, unchartered, trackless sea of white lying below the rocky shores to which the castaways still clung. Through the marvellously clear air the smoke of the pastoral village of Poker Flat rose miles away. Mother Shipton saw it, and from a remote pinnacle of her rocky fastness hurled in that direction a final malediction. It was her last vituperative attempt, and perhaps for that reason was invested with a certain degree of sublimity. It did her good, she privately informed the Duchess. 'Just you go out there and cuss, and see.' She then set herself to the task of amusing 'the child,' as she and the Duchess were pleased to call Piney. Piney was no chicken, but it was a soothing and original theory of the pair thus to account for the fact that she didn't swear and wasn't improper.

When night crept up again through the gorges, the reedy notes of the accordion rose and fell in fitful spasms and long-drawn gasps by the flickering camp-fire. But music failed to fill entirely the aching void left by insufficient food, and a new diversion was proposed by Piney — story-telling. Neither Mr Oakhurst nor his female companions caring to relate their personal experiences, this plan would have failed too, but for the Innocent. Some months before he had chanced upon a stray copy of Mr Pope's ingenious translation of the *Iliad*. He now proposed to narrate the principal incidents of that poem — having thoroughly mastered the argument and fairly forgotten the words — in the current vernacular of Sandy Bar. And so for the rest of the night the Homeric demi-gods again walked the earth. Trojan bully and wily Greek wrestled in the winds, and the great pines in the cañon seemed to bow to the wrath of the son of Peleus. Mr Oakhurst listened with quiet satisfaction. Most especially was he interested in the fate of 'Ash-heels,' as the Innocent persisted in denominating the 'swift-footed Achilles'.

So with small food and much of Homer and the accordion, a week passed over the heads of the outcasts. The sun again forsook them, and again from leaden skies the snowflakes were sifted over the land. Day by day closer around them drew the snowy circle, until at last they looked from their prison over drifted walls of dazzling white that towered twenty feet above their heads. It became more and more difficult to replenish their fires, even from the fallen trees beside them, now half hidden in the drifts. And yet no one complained. The lovers turned from the dreary prospect, and looked into each other's eyes, and were happy. Mr Oakhurst settled himself coolly to the losing game before him. The Duchess, more cheerful than she had been, assumed the care of Piney. Only Mother Shipton – once the strongest of the party – seemed to sicken and fade. At midnight on the tenth day she called Oakhurst to her side.

'I'm going,' she said, in a voice of querulous weakness, 'but don't say anything about it. Don't waken the kids. Take the bundle from under my head and open it.'

Mr Oakhurst did so. It contained Mother Shipton's rations for the last week, untouched.

'Give 'em to the child,' she said, pointing to the sleeping Piney.

'You've starved yourself,' said the gambler.

'That's what they call it,' said the women, querulously, as she lay down again, and, turning her face to the wall, passed quietly away.

The accordion and the bones were put aside that day, and Homer was forgotten. When the body of Mother Shipton had been committed to the snow, Mr Oakhurst took the Innocent aside, and showed him a pair of snow-shoes, which he had fashioned from the old pack-saddle.

'There's one chance in a hundred to save her yet,' he said, pointing to Piney; 'but it's there,' he added, pointing toward Poker Flat. 'If you can reach there in two days, she's safe.'

'And you?' asked Tom Simson.

'I'll stay here,' was the curt reply.

The lovers parted with a long embrace.

'You are not going too?' said the Duchess, as she saw Mr Oakhurst apparently waiting to accompany him.

'As far as the cañon,' he replied. He turned suddenly, and kissed the Duchess, leaving her pallid face aflame, and her trembling limbs rigid with amazement.

Night came, but not Mr Oakhurst. It brought the storm again and the whirling snow. Then the Duchess, feeding the fire, found that some one had quietly piled beside the hut enough fuel to last a few days longer. The tears rose to her eyes, but she hid them from Piney.

The women slept but little. In the morning, looking into each other's faces, they read their fate. Neither spoke; but Piney, accepting the position of the stronger, drew near and placed her arm around the Duchess's waist. They kept this attitude for the rest of the day. That night the storm reached its greatest fury, and, rending asunder the protecting pines, invaded the very hut.

Toward morning they found themselves unable to feed the fire, which gradually died away. As the embers slowly blackened, the Duchess crept closer to Piney, and broke the silence of many hours: 'Piney, can you pray?'

'No, dear,' said Piney, simply.

The Duchess, without knowing exactly why, felt relieved, and, putting her head upon Piney's shoulder, spoke no more. And so reclining, the younger and purer pillowing the head of her soiled sister upon her virgin breast, they fell asleep.

The wind lulled as if it feared to waken them. Feathery drifts of snow, shaken from the long pine-boughs, flew like white-winged birds, and settled about them as they slept. The moon through the rifted clouds looked down upon what had been the camp. But all human stain, all trace of earthly travail, was hidden beneath the spotless mantle mercifully flung from above.

They slept all that day and the next, nor did they waken when voices and footsteps broke the silence of the camp. And when pitying fingers brushed the snow from their wan faces, you could scarcely have told, from the equal peace that dwelt upon them, which was she that had sinned. Even the law of Poker Flat recognized this, and turned away, leaving them still locked in each other's arms.

But at the head of the gulch, on one of the largest pine-trees, they found the deuce of clubs pinned to the bark with a bowie-knife. It bore the following, written in pencil, in a firm hand:

BENEATH THIS TREE
LIES THE BODY
OF
JOHN OAKHURST,
WHO STRUCK A STREAK OF BAD LUCK
ON THE 23RD OF NOVEMBER, 1850,
AND
HANDED IN HIS CHECKS
ON THE 7TH DECEMBER, 1850.

And pulseless and cold, with a derringer by his side and a bullet in his heart, though still calm as in life, beneath the snow lay he who was at once the strongest and yet the weakest of the outcasts of Poker Flat.

1870

AMBROSE BIERCE

1842–1913?

An Occurrence at Owl Creek Bridge

1

A man stood upon a railroad bridge in northern Alabama, looking down into the swift water twenty feet below. The man's hands were behind his back, the wrists bound with a cord. A rope closely encircled his neck. It was attached to a stout cross-timber above his head and the slack fell to the level of his knees. Some loose boards laid upon the sleepers supporting the metals of the railway supplied a footing for him and his executioners – two private soldiers of the Federal army, directed by a sergeant who in civil life may have been a deputy sheriff. At a short remove upon the same temporary platform was an officer in the uniform of his rank, armed. He was a captain. A sentinel at each end of the bridge stood with his rifle in the position known as 'support,' that is to say, vertical in front of the left shoulder, the hammer resting on the forearm thrown straight across the chest – a formal and unnatural position, enforcing an erect carriage of the body. It did not appear to be the duty of these two men to know what was occurring at the centre of the bridge; they merely blockaded the two ends of the foot planking that traversed it.

Beyond one of the sentinels nobody was in sight; the railroad ran straight away into a forest for a hundred yards, then, curving, was lost to view. Doubtless, there was an outpost farther along. The other bank of the stream was open ground – a gentle acclivity topped with a stockade of vertical tree trunks, loop-holed for rifles, with a single embrasure through which protruded the muzzle of a brass cannon commanding the bridge. Midway of the slope between bridge and fort were the spectators – a single company of infantry in line, at 'parade rest', the butts of the rifles on the ground, the barrels inclining slightly backward against the right shoulder, the hands crossed upon the stock. A lieutenant stood at the right of the line, the point of his sword upon the ground, his left hand resting upon his right. Excepting the group of four at the centre of the bridge, not a man moved. The company faced the bridge, staring stonily, motionless. The sentinels, facing the banks of the stream, might have been statues to adorn the bridge. The captain stood with folded arms, silent, observing the work of his subordinates, but making no sign. Death is a dignitary who when he comes announced is to be received with formal manifestations of respect, even by those most familiar with him. In the code of military etiquette silence and fixity are forms of deference.

The man who was engaged in being hanged was apparently about thirty-five years of age. He was a civilian, if one might judge from his habit, which was that of a planter. His features were good – a straight nose, firm mouth, broad forehead, from which his long, dark hair was combed straight back, falling behind his ears to the collar of his well-fitting frock-coat. He wore a moustache and pointed beard, but no whiskers; his eyes were large and dark grey, and had a kindly expression which one would hardly have expected in one whose neck was in the hemp. Evidently this was no vulgar assassin. The liberal military code makes provision for hanging many kinds of persons, and gentlemen are not excluded.

The preparations being complete, the two private soldiers stepped aside and each drew away the plank upon which he had been standing. The sergeant turned to the captain, saluted and placed himself immediately behind that officer, who in turn moved apart one pace. These movements left the condemned man and the sergeant standing on the two ends of the same plank, which spanned three of the cross-ties of the bridge. The end upon which the civilian stood almost, but not quite, reached a fourth. This plank had been held in place by the weight of the captain; it was now held by that of the sergeant. At a signal from the former the latter would step aside, the plank would tilt and the condemned man go down between two ties. The arrangement commended itself to his judgment as simple and effective. His face had not been covered nor his eyes bandaged. He looked a moment at his 'unsteadfast footing,' then let his gaze wander to the swirling water of the stream racing madly beneath his feet. A piece of dancing driftwood caught his attention and his eyes followed it down the current. How slowly it appeared to move! What a sluggish stream!

He closed his eyes in order to fix his last thoughts upon his wife and children. The water, touched to gold by the early sun, the brooding mists under the banks at some distance down the stream, the fort, the soldiers, the piece of drift – all had distracted him. And now he became conscious of a new disturbance. Striking through the thought of his dear ones was a sound which he could neither ignore nor understand, a sharp, distinct, metallic percussion like the stroke of a blacksmith's hammer upon the anvil; it had the same ringing quality. He wondered what it was, and whether immeasurably distant or near by – it seemed both. Its recurrence was regular, but as slow as the tolling of a death-knell. He awaited each stroke with impatience and – he knew not why – apprehension. The intervals of silence grew progressively longer; the delays became maddening. With their greater infrequency the sounds increased in strength and sharpness. They hurt his ear like the thrust of a knife; he feared he would shriek. What he heard was the ticking of his watch.

He unclosed his eyes and saw again the water below him. 'If I could free my hands,' he thought, 'I might throw off the noose and spring into the stream. By diving I could evade the bullets and, swimming vigorously, reach the bank, take to the woods and get away home. My home, thank God, is as yet outside their lines; my wife and little ones are still beyond the invader's farthest advance.'

As these thoughts, which have here to be set down in words, were flashed into the doomed man's brain rather than evolved from it, the captain nodded to the sergeant. The sergeant stepped aside.

2

Peyton Farquhar was a well-to-do planter, of an old and highly respected Alabama family. Being a slave owner, and like other slave owners a politician, he was naturally an original secessionist and ardently devoted to the Southern cause. Circumstances of an imperious nature, which it is unnecessary to relate here, had prevented him from taking service with the gallant army that had fought the disastrous campaigns ending with the fall of Corinth, and he chafed under the inglorious restraint, longing for the release of his energies, the larger life of the soldier, the opportunity for distinction. The opportunity, he felt, would come, as it comes to all in war time. Meanwhile he did what he could. No service was too humble for him to perform in aid of the South, no adventure too perilous for him to undertake if consistent with the character of a civilian who was at heart a soldier, and who in good faith and without too much qualification assented to at least a part of the frankly villainous dictum that all is fair in love and war.

One evening while Farquhar and his wife were sitting on a rustic bench near the entrance to his grounds, a grey-clad soldier rode up to the gate and asked for a drink of water. Mrs. Farquhar was only too happy to serve him with her own white hands. While she was fetching the water her husband approached the dusty horseman and inquired eagerly for news from the front.

'The Yanks are repairing the railroads,' said the man, 'and are getting ready for another advance. They have reached the Owl Creek bridge, put it in order and built a stockade on the north bank. The commandant has issued an order, which is posted everywhere, declaring that any civilian caught interfering with the railroad, its bridges, tunnels or trains will be summarily hanged. I saw the order.'

'How far is it to the Owl Creek bridge?' Farquhar asked.

'About thirty miles.'

'Is there no force on this side the creek?'

'Only a picket post half a mile out, on the railroad, and a single sentinel at this end of the bridge.'

'Suppose a man – a civilian and student of hanging – should elude the picket post and perhaps get the better of the sentinel,' said Farquhar, smiling, 'what could he accomplish?'

The soldier reflected. 'I was there a month ago,' he replied. 'I observed that the flood of last winter had lodged a great quantity of driftwood against the wooden pier at this end of the bridge. It is now dry and would burn like tow.'

The lady had now brought the water, which the soldier drank. He thanked her ceremoniously, bowed to her husband and rode away. An hour later, after nightfall, he repassed the plantation, going northward in the direction from which he had come. He was a Federal scout.

3

As Peyton Farquhar fell straight downward through the bridge he lost consciousness and was as one already dead. From this state he was awakened – ages later, it seemed to him – by the pain of a sharp pressure upon his throat, followed by a sense of suffocation. Keen, poignant agonies seemed to shoot from his neck downward

through every fibre of his body and limbs. These pains appeared
to flash along well-defined lines of ramification and to beat with
an inconceivably rapid periodicity. They seemed like streams of
pulsating fire heating him to an intolerable temperature. As to his
head, he was conscious of nothing but a feeling of fullness – of
congestion. These sensations were unaccompanied by thought.
The intellectual part of his nature was already effaced; he had
power only to feel, and feeling was torment. He was conscious of
motion. Encompassed in a luminous cloud, of which he was now
merely the fiery heart, without material substance, he swung
through unthinkable arcs of oscillation, like a vast pendulum.
Then all at once, with terrible suddenness, the light about him
shot upward with the noise of a loud plash; a frightful roaring was
in his ears, and all was cold and dark. The power of thought was
restored; he knew that the rope had broken and he had fallen into
the stream. There was no additional strangulation: the noose
about his neck was already suffocating him and kept the water
from his lungs. To die of hanging at the bottom of a river! – the
idea seemed to him ludicrous. He opened his eyes in the darkness
and saw above him a gleam of light, but how distant, how
inaccessible! He was still sinking, for the light became fainter and
fainter until it was a mere glimmer. Then it began to grow and
brighten, and he knew that he was rising toward the surface –
knew it with reluctance, for he was now very comfortable. 'To be
hanged and drowned,' he thought 'that is not so bad; but I do not
wish to be shot. No, I will not be shot; that is not fair.'

He was not conscious of an effort, but a sharp pain in his wrist
apprised him that he was trying to free his hands. He gave the
struggle his attention, as an idler might observe the feat of a
juggler, without interest in the outcome. What splendid effort! –
what magnificent, what superhuman strength! Ah, that was a fine
endeavour! Bravo! The cord fell away; his arms parted and
floated upward, the hands dimly seen on each side in the growing
light. He watched them with a new interest as first one and then
the other pounced upon the noose at his neck. They tore it away
and thrust it fiercely aside, its undulations resembling those of a
water-snake. 'Put it back, put it back!' He thought he shouted
these words to his hands, for the undoing of the noose had been
succeeded by the direst pang that he had yet experienced. His neck
ached horribly; his brain was on fire; his heart, which had been
fluttering faintly, gave a great leap, trying to force itself out at his

mouth. His whole body was racked and wrenched with an insupportable anguish! But his disobedient hands gave no heed to the command. They beat the water vigorously with quick, downward strokes, forcing him to the surface. He felt his head emerge; his eyes were blinded by the sunlight; his chest expanded convulsively, and with a supreme and crowning agony his lungs engulfed a great draught of air, which instantly he expelled in a shriek!

He was now in full possession of his physical senses. They were, indeed, preternaturally keen and alert. Something in the awful disturbance of his organic sytem had so exalted and refined them that they made record of things never before perceived. He felt the ripples upon his face and heard their separate sounds as they struck. He looked at the forest on the bank of the stream, saw the individual trees, the leaves and the veining of each leaf – saw the very insects upon them: the locusts, the brilliant-bodied flies, the grey spiders stretching their webs from twig to twig. He noted the prismatic colours in all the dewdrops upon a million blades of grass. The humming of the gnats that danced above the eddies of the stream, the beating of the dragon-flies' wings, the strokes of the water-spiders' legs, like oars which had lifted their boat – all these made audible music. A fish slid along beneath his eyes and he heard the rush of its body parting the water.

He had come to the surface facing down the stream; in a moment the visible world seemed to wheel slowly round, himself the pivotal point, and he saw the bridge, the fort, the soldiers upon the bridge, the captain, the sergeant, the two privates, his executioners. They were in silhouette against the blue sky. They shouted and gesticulated, pointing at him. The captain had drawn his pistol, but did not fire; the others were unarmed. Their movements were grotesque and horrible, their forms gigantic.

Suddenly he heard a sharp report and something struck the water smartly within a few inches of his head, spattering his face with spray. He heard a second report, and saw one of the sentinels with his rifle at his shoulder, a light cloud of blue smoke rising from the muzzle. The man in the water saw the eye of the man on the bridge gazing into his own through the sights of the rifle. He observed that it was a grey eye and remembered having read that grey eyes were keenest, and that all famous marksmen had them. Nevertheless, this one had missed.

A counter-swirl had caught Farquhar and turned him half round; he was again looking into the forest on the bank opposite the fort. The sound of a clear, high voice in a monotonous singsong now rang out behind him and came across the water with a distinctness that pierced and subdued all other sounds, even the beating of the ripples in his ears. Although no soldier, he had frequented camps enough to know the dread significance of that deliberate, drawling, aspirated chant; the lieutenant on shore was taking a part in the morning's work. How coldly and pitilessly – with what an even, calm intonation, presaging, and enforcing tranquillity in the men – with what accurately measured intervals fell those cruel words:

'Attention company! . . . Shoulder arms! . . . Ready! . . . Aim! . . . Fire!'

Farquhar dived – dived as deeply as he could. The water roared in his ears like the voice of Niagara, yet he heard the dulled thunder of the volley and, rising again toward the surface, met shining bits of metal, singularly flattened, oscillating slowly downward. Some of them touched him on the face and hands, then fell away, continuing their descent. One lodged between his collar and neck; it was uncomfortably warm and he snatched it out.

As he rose to the surface, gasping for breath, he saw that he had been a long time under water; he was perceptibly further downstream – nearer to safety. The soldiers had almost finished reloading; the metal ramrods flashed all at once in the sunshine as they were drawn from the barrels, turned in the air, and thrust into their sockets. The two sentinels fired again, independently and ineffectually.

The hunted man saw all this over his shoulder; he was now swimming vigorously with the current. His brain was as energetic as his arms and legs; he thought with the rapidity of lightning.

'The officer,' he reasoned, 'will not make that martinet's error a second time. It is as easy to dodge a volley as a single shot. He has probably already given the command to fire at will. God help me, I cannot dodge them all!'

An appalling plash within two yards of him was followed by a loud, rushing sound, *diminuendo*, which seemed to travel back through the air to the fort and died in an explosion, which stirred the very river to its deeps! A rising sheet of water curved over him, fell down upon him, blinded him, strangled him! The cannon had taken a hand in the game. As he shook his head free from the commotion of the smitten water he heard the deflected shot humming through the air ahead, and in an instant it was cracking and smashing the branches in the forest beyond.

'They will not do that again,' he thought; 'the next time they will use a charge of grape. I must keep my eye upon the gun; the smoke will apprise me – the report arrives too late; it lags behind the missile. That is a good gun.'

Suddenly he felt himself whirled round and round – spinning like a top. The water, the banks, the forests, the now distant bridge, fort and men – all were commingled and blurred. Objects were represented by their colours only; circular horizontal streaks of colour – that was all he saw. He had been caught in a vortex and was being whirled on with a velocity of advance and gyration that made him giddy and sick. In a few moments he was flung upon the gravel at the foot of the left bank of the stream – the southern bank – and behind a projecting point which concealed him from his enemies. The sudden arrest of his motion, the abrasion of one of his hands on the gravel, restored him, and he wept with delight. He dug his fingers into the sand, threw it over himself in handfuls and audibly blessed it. It looked like diamonds, rubies, emeralds; he could think of nothing beautiful which it did not resemble. The trees upon the bank were giant garden plants; he noted a definite order in their arrangement, inhaled the fragrance of their blooms. A strange, roseate light shone through the spaces among their trunks and the wind made in their branches the music of æolian harps. He had no wish to perfect his escape – was content to remain in that enchanting spot until retaken.

A whiz and rattle of grapeshot among the branches high above his head roused him from his dream. The baffled cannoneer had fired him a random farewell. He sprang to his feet, rushed up the sloping bank, and plunged into the forest.

All that day he travelled, laying his course by the rounding sun. The forest seemed interminable; nowhere did he discover a break in it, not even a woodman's road. He had not known that he lived in so wild a region. There was something uncanny in the revelation.

By nightfall he was fatigued, footsore, famishing. The thought of his wife and children urged him on. At last he found a road which led him in what he knew to be the right direction. It was as wide and straight as a city street, yet it seemed untravelled. No fields bordered it, no dwelling anywhere. Not so much as the barking of a dog suggested human habitation. The black bodies of the trees formed a straight wall on both sides, terminating on the horizon in a point, like a diagram in a lesson in perspective. Overhead, as he looked up through this rift in the wood, shone great golden stars looking unfamiliar and grouped in strange constellations. He was sure they were arranged in some order which had a secret and malign significance. The wood on either side was full of singular noises, among which – once, twice, and again – he distinctly heard whispers in an unknown tongue.

His neck was in pain and lifting his hand to it he found it horribly swollen. He knew that it had a circle of black where the rope had bruised it. His eyes felt congested; he could no longer close them. His tongue was swollen with thirst; he relieved its fever by thrusting it forward from between his teeth into the cold air. How softly the turf had carpeted the untravelled avenue – he could no longer feel the roadway beneath his feet!

Doubtless, despite his suffering, he had fallen asleep while walking, for now he sees another scene – perhaps he has merely recovered from a delirium. He stands at the gate of his own home. All is as he left it, and all bright and beautiful in the morning sunshine. He must have travelled the entire night. As he pushes open the gate and passes up the wide white walk, he sees a flutter of female garments; his wife, looking fresh and cool and sweet, steps down from the veranda to meet him. A the bottom of the steps she stands waiting, with a smile of ineffable joy, an attitude of matchless grace and dignity. Ah, how beautiful she is! He springs forward with extended arms. As he is about to clasp her he feels a stunning blow upon the back of his neck; a blinding white light blazes all about him with a sound like the shock of a cannon – then all is darkness and silence!

Peyton Farquhar was dead; his body, with a broken neck, swung gently from side to side beneath the timbers of the Owl Creek bridge.

1890

HENRY JAMES
1843–1916

The Real Thing

I

When the porter's wife (she used to answer the house-bell) announced 'A gentleman – with a lady, sir,' I had as I often had in those days, for the wish was father to the thought, an immediate vision of sitters. Sitters my visitors in this case proved to be; but not in the sense I should have preferred. However, there was nothing at first to indicate that they might not have come for a portrait. The gentleman, a man of fifty, very high and very straight, with a moustache slightly grizzled and a dark grey walking-coat admirably fitted, both of which I noted professionally – I don't mean as a barber or yet as a tailor – would have struck me as a celebrity if celebrities often were striking. It was a truth of which I had for some time been conscious that a figure with a good deal of frontage was, as one might say, almost never a public institution. A glance at the lady helped to remind me of this paradoxical law: she also looked too distinguished to be a 'personality'. Moreover one would scarcely come across two variations together.

Neither of the pair spoke immediately – they only prolonged the preliminary gaze which suggested that each wished to give the other a chance. They were visibly shy; they stood there letting me take them in – which, as I afterwards perceived, was the most practical thing they could have done. In this way their embarrassment served their cause. I had seen people painfully reluctant to mention that they desired anything so gross as to be represented on canvas; but the scruples of my new friends appeared almost insurmountable. Yet the gentleman might have said 'I should like a portrait of my wife,' and the lady might have said 'I should like a portrait of my husband.' Perhaps they were not husband and wife – this naturally would make the matter more delicate. Perhaps they wished to be done together – in which case they ought to have brought a third person to break the news.

'We come from Mr Rivet,' the lady said at last, with a dim smile which had the effect of a moist sponge passed over a 'sunk' piece of painting, as well as of a vague allusion to vanished beauty. She was as tall and straight, in her degree, as her companion, and with ten years less to carry. She looked as sad as a woman could look whose face was not charged with expression; that is her tinted oval mask showed friction as an exposed surface shows it. The hand of time had played over her freely, but only to simplify. She was slim and stiff, and so well-dressed, in dark blue cloth, with lappets and pockets and buttons, that it was clear she employed the same tailor as her husband. The couple had an indefinable air of prosperous thrift – they evidently got a good deal of luxury for their money. If I was to be one of their luxuries it would behove me to consider my terms.

'Ah, Claude Rivet recommended me?' I inquired; and I added that it was very kind of him, though I could reflect that, as he only painted landscape, this was not a sacrifice.

The lady looked very hard at the gentleman, and the gentleman looked round the room. Then staring at the floor a moment and stroking his moustache, he rested his pleasant eyes on me with the remark: 'He said you were the right one.'

'I try to be, when people want to sit.'

'Yes, we should like to,' said the lady anxiously.

'Do you mean together?'

My visitors exchanged a glance. 'If you could do anything with *me*, I suppose it would be double,' the gentleman stammered.

'Oh yes, there's naturally a higher charge for two figures than for one.'

'We should like to make it pay,' the husband confessed.

'That's very good of you,' I returned, appreciating so unwonted a sympathy – for I supposed he meant pay the artist.

A sense of strangeness seem to dawn on the lady. 'We mean for the illustrations – Mr Rivet said you might put one in.'

'Put one in – an illustration?' I was equally confused.

'Sketch her off, you know,' said the gentleman, colouring.

It was only then that I understood the service Claude Rivet had rendered me; he had told them that I worked in black and white, for magazines, for story-books, for sketches of contemporary life, and consequently had frequent employment for models. These things were true, but it was not less true (I may confess it now – whether because the aspiration was to lead to everything or to nothing I leave the reader to guess), that I couldn't get the honours, to say nothing of the emoluments, of a great painter of portraits out of my head. My 'illustrations' were my pot-boilers; I looked to a different branch of art (far and away the most interesting it had always seemed to me) to perpetuate my fame. There was no shame in looking to it also to make my fortune; but that fortune was by so much further from being made from the moment my visitors wished to be 'done' for nothing. I was disappointed; for in the pictorial sense I had immediately *seen* them. I had seized their type – I had already settled what I would do with it. Something that wouldn't absolutely have pleased them, I afterwards reflected.

'Ah, you're – you're – a –?' I began, as soon as I had mastered my surprise. I couldn't bring out the dingy word 'models'; it seemed to fit the case so little.

'We haven't had much practice,' said the lady.

'We've got to *do* something, and we've thought that an artist in your line might perhaps make something of us,' her husband threw off. He further mentioned that they didn't know many artists and that they had gone first, on the off-chance (he painted views of course, but sometimes put in figures – perhaps I remembered), to Mr Rivet, whom they had met a few years before at a place in Norfolk where he was sketching.

'We used to sketch a little ourselves,' the lady hinted.

'It's very awkward, but we absolutely *must* do something,' her husband went on.

'Of course, we're not so *very* young,' she admitted, with a wan smile.

With the remark that I might as well know something more about them, the husband had handed me a card extracted from a neat new pocket-book (their appurtenances were all of the freshest) and inscribed with the words 'Major Monarch'. Impressive as these words were they didn't carry my knowledge much further; but my visitor presently added: 'I've left the army, and we've had the misfortune to lose our money. In fact our means are dreadfully small.'

'It's an awful bore,' said Mrs Monarch.

They evidently wished to be discreet – to take care not to swagger because they were gentlefolks. I perceived they would have been willing to recognise this as something of a drawback, at the same time that I guessed at an underlying sense – their

consolation in adversity – that they *had* their points. They
certainly had; but these advantages struck me as preponderantly
social; such for instance as would help to make a drawing-room
look well. However, a drawing-room was always, or ought to be,
a picture.

In consequence of his wife's allusion to their age Major
Monarch observed: 'Naturally, it's more for the figure that we
thought of going in. We can still hold ourselves up.' On the instant
I saw that the figure was indeed their strong point. His 'naturally'
didn't sound vain, but it lighted up the question. '*She* has got the
best,' he continued, nodding at his wife, with a pleasant after-
dinner absence of circumlocution. I could only reply, as if we were
in fact sitting over our wine, that this didn't prevent his own from
being very good; which led him in turn to rejoin: 'We thought that
if you ever have to do people like us, we might be something like it.
She, particularly – for a lady in a book, you know.'

I was so amused by them that, to get more of it, I did my best to
take their point of view; and though it was an embarrassment to
find myself appraising physically, as if they were animals on hire
or useful blacks, a pair whom I should have expected to meet only
in one of the relations in which criticism is tacit, I looked at Mrs
Monarch judicially enough to be able to exclaim, after a moment,
with conviction: 'Oh yes, a lady in a book!' She was singularly like
a bad illustration.

'We'll stand up, if you like,' said the Major; and he raised
himself before me with a really grand air.

I could take his measure at a glance – he was six feet two and a
perfect gentleman. It would have paid any club in process of
formation and in want of a stamp to engage him at a salary to
stand in the principal window. What struck me immediately was
that in coming to me they had rather missed their vocation; they
could surely have been turned to better account for advertising
purposes. I couldn't of course see the thing in detail, but I could
see them make someone's fortune – I don't mean their own. There
was something in them for a waistcoat-maker, an hotel-keeper or
a soap-vendor. I could imagine 'We always use it' pinned on their
bosoms with the greatest effect; I had a vision of the promptitude
with which they would launch a table d'hôte.

Mrs Monarch sat still, not from pride but from shyness, and
presently her husband said to her: 'Get up, my dear, and show
how smart you are.' She obeyed, but she had no need to get up to

show it. She walked to the end of the studio, and then she came back blushing, with her fluttered eyes on her husband. I was reminded of an incident I had accidentally had a glimpse of in Paris – being with a friend there, a dramatist about to produce a play – when an actress came to him to ask to be intrusted with a part. She went through her paces before him, walked up and down as Mrs Monarch was doing. Mrs. Monarch did it quite as well, but I abstained from applauding. It was very odd to see such people apply for such poor pay. She looked as if she had ten thousand a year. Her husband had used the word that described her: she was, in the London current jargon, essentially and typically 'smart'. Her figure was, in the same order of ideas, conspicuously and irreproachably 'good'. For a woman of her age her waist was surprisingly small; her elbow moreover had the orthodox crook. She held her head at the conventional angle; but why did she come to *me*? She ought to have tried on jackets at a big shop. I feared my visitors were not only destitute, but 'artistic' – which would be a great complication. When she sat down again I thanked her, observing that what a draughtsman most valued in his model was the faculty of keeping quiet.

'Oh, *she* can keep quiet,' said Major Monarch. Then he added, jocosely: 'I've always kept her quiet.'

'I'm not a nasty fidget, am I?' Mrs Monarch appealed to her husband.

He addressed his answer to me. 'Perhaps it isn't out of place to mention – because we ought to be quite business-like, oughtn't we? – that when I married her she was known as the Beautiful Statue.'

'Oh dear!' said Mrs Monarch, ruefully.

'Of course I should want a certain amount of expression,' I rejoined.

'Of *course*!' they both exclaimed.

'And then I suppose you know that you'll get awfully tired.'

'Oh, we *never* get tired!' they eagerly cried.

'Have you had any kind of practice?'

They hesitated – they looked at each other. 'We've been photographed, *immensely*,' said Mrs Monarch.

'She means the fellows have asked us,' added the Major.

'I see – because you're so good-looking.'

'I don't know what they thought, but they were always after us.'

'We always got our photographs for nothing,' smiled Mrs Monarch.

'We might have brought some, my dear,' her husband remarked.

'I'm not sure we have any left. We've given quantities away,' she explained to me.

'With our autographs and that sort of thing,' said the Major.

'Are they to be got in the shops?' I inquired, as a harmless pleasantry.

'Oh, yes; *hers* – they used to be.'

'Not now,' said Mrs Monarch, with her eyes on the floor.

2

I could fancy the 'sort of thing' they put on the presentation-copies of their photographs, and I was sure they wrote a beautiful hand. It was odd how quickly I was sure of everything that concerned them. If they were now so poor as to have to earn shillings and pence, they never had had much of a margin. Their good looks had been their capital, and they had good-humouredly made the most of the career that this resource marked out for them. It was in their faces, the blankness, the deep intellectual repose of the twenty years of country-house visiting which had given them pleasant intonations. I could see the sunny drawing-rooms, sprinkled with periodicals she didn't read, in which Mrs Monarch had continuously sat; I could see the wet shrubberies in which she had walked, equipped to admiration for either exercise. I could see the rich covers the Major had helped to shoot and the wonderful garments in which, late at night, he repaired to the smoking-room to talk about them. I could imagine their leggings and waterproofs, their knowing tweeds and rugs, their rolls of sticks and cases of tackle and neat umbrellas; and I could evoke the exact appearance of their servants and the compact variety of their luggage on the platforms of country stations.

They gave small tips, but they were liked; they didn't do anything themselves but they were welcome. They looked so well everywhere; they gratified the general relish for stature, complexion and 'form'. They knew it without fatuity or vulgarity, and they respected themselves in consequence. They were not superficial; they were thorough and kept themselves up – it had been their line. People with such a taste for activity had to have some line. I could feel how, even in a dull house, they could have been

counted upon for cheerfulness. At present something had happened – it didn't matter what, their little income had grown less, it
had grown least – and they had to do something for pocket-
money. Their friends liked them, but didn't like to support them.
There was something about them that represented credit – their
clothes, their manners, their type; but if credit is a large empty
pocket in which an occasional chink reverberates, the chink at
least must be audible. What they wanted of me was to help to
make it so. Fortunately they had no children – I soon divined that.
They would also perhaps wish our relations to be kept secret: this
was why it was 'for the figure' – the reproduction of the face
would betray them.

I liked them – they were so simple; and I had no objection to
them if they would suit. But, somehow, with all their perfections I
didn't easily believe in them. After all they were amateurs, and the
ruling passion of my life was the detestation of the amateur.
Combined with this was another perversity – an innate preference
for the represented subject over the real one: the defect of the real
one was so apt to be a lack of representation. I liked things that
appeared; then one was sure. Whether they *were* or not was a
subordinate and almost always a profitless question. There were
other considerations, the first of which was that I already had two
or three people in use, notably a young person with big feet, in
alpaca, from Kilburn, who for a couple of years had come to me
regularly for my illustrations and with whom I was still – perhaps
ignobly – satisfied. I frankly explained to my visitors how the case
stood; but they had taken more precautions than I supposed.
They had reasoned out their opportunity, for Claude Rivet had
told them of the projected *édition de luxe* of one of the writers of
our day – the rarest of the novelists – who, long neglected by the
multitudinous vulgar and dearly prized by the attentive (need I
mention Philip Vincent?) had had the happy fortune of seeing, late
in life, the dawn and then the full light of a higher criticism – an
estimate in which, on the part of the public, there was something
really of expiation. The edition in question, planned by a
publisher of taste, was practically an act of high reparation; the
woodcuts with which it was to be enriched were the homage of
English art to one of the most independent representatives of
English letters. Major and Mrs Monarch confessed to me that
they had hoped I might be able to work *them* into my share of the
enterprise. They knew I was to do the first of the books, *Rutland*

Ramsay, but I had to make clear to them that my participation in the rest of the affair – this first book was to be a test – was to depend on the satisfaction I should give. If this should be limited my employers would drop me without a scruple. It was therefore a crisis for me, and naturally I was making special preparations, looking about for new people, if they should be necessary, and securing the best types. I admitted however that I should like to settle down to two or three good models who would do for everything.

'Should we have often to – a – put on special clothes?' Mrs Monarch timidly demanded.

'Dear, yes – that's half the business.'

'And should we be expected to supply our own costumes?'

'Oh, no; I've got a lot of things. A painter's models put on – or put off – anything he likes.'

'And do you mean – a – the same?'

'The same?'

Mrs Monarch looked at her husband again.

'Oh, she was just wondering,' he explained, 'if the costumes are in *general* use.' I had to confess that they were, and I mentioned further that some of them (I had a lot of genuine, greasy last-century things) had served their time, a hundred years ago, on living, world-stained men and women. 'We'll put on anything that *fits*,' said the Major.

'Oh, I arrange that – they fit in the pictures.'

'I'm afraid I should do better for the modern books. I would come as you like,' said Mrs Monarch.

'She has got a lot of clothes at home: they might do for contemporary life,' her husband continued.

'Oh, I can fancy scenes in which you'd be quite natural.' And indeed I could see the slipshod rearrangements of stale properties – the stories I tried to produce pictures for without the exasperation of reading them – whose sandy tracts the good lady might help to people. But I had to return to the fact that for this sort of work – the daily mechanical grind – I was already equipped; the people I was working with were fully adequate.

'We only thought we might be more like *some* characters,' said Mrs Monarch mildly, getting up.

Her husband also rose; he stood looking at me with a dim wistfulness that was touching in so fine a man. 'Wouldn't it be rather a pull sometimes to have – a – to have –?' He hung fire; he

wanted me to help him by phrasing what he meant. But I couldn't
— I didn't know. So he brought it out, awkwardly: 'The *real* thing;
a gentleman, you know, or a lady.' I was quite ready to give a
general assent — I admitted that there was a great deal in that. This
encouraged Major Monarch to say, following up his appeal with
an unacted gulp: 'It's awfully hard — we've tried everything.' The
gulp was communicative; it proved too much for his wife. Before I
knew it Mrs Monarch had dropped again upon a divan and burst
into tears. Her husband sat down beside her, holding one of her
hands; whereupon she quickly dried her eyes with the other, while
I felt embarrassed as she looked up at me. 'There isn't a
confounded job I haven't applied for — waited for — prayed for.
You can fancy we'd be pretty bad first. Secretaryships and that
sort of thing? You might as well ask for a peerage. I'd be *anything*, —
I'm strong; a messenger or a coalheaver. I'd put on a gold-laced
cap and open carriage-doors in front of the haberdasher's; I'd
hang about a station, to carry portmanteaus; I'd be a postman.
But they won't *look* at you; there are thousands, as good as
yourself, already on the ground. *Gentlemen*, poor beggars, who
have drunk their wine, who have kept their hunters!'

I was as reassuring as I knew how to be, and my visitors were
presently on their feet again while, for the experiment, we agreed
on an hour. We were discussing it when the door opened and Miss
Churm came in with a wet umbrella. Miss Churm had to take the
omnibus to Maida Vale and then walk half-a-mile. She looked a
trifle blowsy and slightly splashed. I scarcely ever saw her come in
without thinking afresh how odd it was that, being so little in
herself, she should yet be so much in others. She was a meagre
little Miss Churm, but she was an ample heroine of romance. She
was only a freckled cockney, but she could represent everything,
from a fine lady to a shepherdess; she had the faculty, as she might
have had a fine voice or long hair. She couldn't spell, and she loved
beer, but she had two or three 'points', and practice, and a knack,
and mother-wit, and a kind of whimsical sensibility, and a love of
the theatre, and seven sisters, and not an ounce of respect,
especially for the *h*. The first thing my visitors saw was that her
umbrella was wet, and in their spotless perfection they visibly
winced at it. The rain had come on since their arrival.

'I'm all in a soak; there *was* a mess of people in the 'bus. I wish
you lived near a stytion,' said miss Churm. I requested her to get
ready as quickly as possible, and she passed into the room in

which she always changed her dress. But before going out she asked me what she was to get into this time.

'It's the Russian princess, don't you know?' I answered; 'the one with the "golden eyes", in black velvet, for the long thing in the *Cheapside*.'

'Golden eyes? I *say*!' cried Miss Churm, while my companions watched her with intensity as she withdrew. She always arranged herself, when she was late, before I could turn round; and I kept my visitors a little, on purpose, so that they might get an idea, from seeing her, what would be expected of themselves. I mentioned that she was quite my notion of an excellent model – she was really very clever.

'Do you think she looks like a Russian princess?' Major Monarch asked, with lurking alarm.

'When I make her, yes.'

'Oh, if you have to *make* her—!' he reasoned acutely.

'That't the most you can ask. There are so many that are not makeable.'

'Well now, *here's* a lady' – and with a persuasive smile he passed his arm into his wife's – 'who's already made!'

'Oh, I'm not a Russian princess,' Mrs Monarch protested, a little coldly. I could see that she had known some and didn't like them. There, immediately, was a complication of a kind that I never had to fear with Miss Churm.

This young lady came back in black velvet – the gown was rather rusty and very low on her lean shoulders – and with a Japanese fan in her red hands. I reminded her that in the scene I was doing she had to look over someone's head. 'I forget whose it is; but it doesn't matter. Just look over a head.'

'I'd rather look over a stove,' said Miss Churm; and she took her station near the fire. She fell into position, settled herself into a tall attitude, gave a certain backward inclination to her head and a certain forward droop to her fan, and looked, at least to my prejudiced sense, distinguished and charming, foreign and dangerous. We left her looking so, while I went downstairs with Major and Mrs Monarch.

'I think I could come about as near it as that,' said Mrs Monarch.

'Oh, you think she's shabby, but you must allow for the alchemy of art.'

However, they went off with an evident increase of comfort,

founded on their demonstrable advantage in being the real thing. I could fancy them shuddering over Miss Churm. She was very droll about them when I went back, for I told her what they wanted.

'Well, if *she* can sit I'll tyke to bookkeeping,' said my model.

'She's very lady-like,' I replied, as an innocent form of aggravation.

'So much the worse for *you*. That means she can't turn round.'

'She'll do for the fashionable novels.'

'Oh yes, she'll *do* for them!' my model humorously declared. 'Ain't they bad enough without her?' I had often sociably denounced them to Miss Churm.

3

It was for the elucidation of a mystery in one of these works that I first tried Mrs Monarch. Her husband came with her, to be useful if necessary – it was sufficiently clear that as a general thing he would prefer to come with her. At first I wondered if this were for 'propriety's' sake – if he were going to be jealous and meddling. The idea was too tiresome, and if it had been confirmed it would speedily have brought our acquaintance to a close. But I soon saw there was nothing in it and that if he accompanied Mrs Monarch it was (in addition to the chance of being wanted) simply because he had nothing else to do. When she was away from him his occupation was gone – she never *had* been away from him. I judged, rightly, that in their awkward situation their close union was their main comfort and that this union had no weak spot. It was a real marriage, an encouragement to the hesitating, a nut for pessimists to crack. Their address was humble (I remember afterwards thinking it had been the only thing about them that was really professional), and I could fancy the lamentable lodgings in which the Major would have been left alone. He could bear them with his wife – he couldn't bear them without her.

He had too much tact to try and make himself agreeable when he couldn't be useful; so he simply sat and waited, when I was too absorbed in my work to talk. But I liked to make him talk – it made my work, when it didn't interrupt it, less sordid, less special. To listen to him was to combine the excitement of going out with the economy of staying at home. There was only one hindrance: that I seemed not to know any of the people he and his wife had known. I think he wondered extremely, during the term of our intercourse, whom the deuce I *did* know. He hadn't a stray sixpence of an idea to fumble for, so we didn't spin it very fine – we confined ourselves to questions of leather and even of liquor (saddlers and breeches-makers and how to get good claret cheap), and matters like 'good trains' and the habits of small game. His lore on these last subjects was astonishing, he managed to interweave the stationmaster with the ornithologist. When he couldn't talk about greater things he could talk cheerfully about smaller, and since I couldn't accompany him into reminiscences of the fashionable world he could lower the conversation without a visible effort to my level.

So earnest a desire to please was touching in a man who could so easily have knocked one down. He looked after the fire and had an opinion on the draught of the stove, without my asking him, and I could see that he thought many of my arrangements not half clever enough. I remember telling him that if I were only rich I would offer him a salary to come and teach me how to live. Sometimes he gave a random sigh, of which the essence was: 'Give me even such a bare old barrack as *this*, and I'd do something with it!' When I wanted to use him he came alone; which was an illustration of the superior courage of women. His wife could bear her solitary second floor, and she was in general more discreet; showing by various small reserves that she was alive to the propriety of keeping our relations markedly professional – not letting them slide into sociability. She wished it to remain clear that she and the Major were employed, not cultivated, and if she approved of me as a superior, who could be kept in his place, she never thought me quite good enough for an equal.

She sat with great intensity, giving the whole of her mind to it, and was capable of remaining for an hour almost as motionless as if she were before a photographer's lens. I could see she had been photographed often, but somehow the very habit that made her good for that purpose unfitted her for mine. At first I was extremely pleased with her lady-like air, and it was a satisfaction, on coming to follow her lines, to see how good they were and how far they could lead the pencil. But after a few times I began to find her too insurmountably stiff; do what I would with it my drawing looked like a photograph or a copy of a photograph. Her figure had no variety of expression – she herself had no sense of variety. You may say that this was my business, was only a question of placing her. I placed her in every conceivable position, but she managed to obliterate their differences. She was always a lady certainly, and into the bargain was always the same lady. She was the real thing, but always the same thing. There were moments when I was oppressed by the serenity of her confidence that she *was* the real thing. All her dealings with me and all her husband's were an implication that this was lucky for *me*. Meanwhile I found myself trying to invent types that approached her own, instead of making her own transform itself – in the clever way that was not impossible, for instance, to poor Miss Churm. Arrange as I would and take the precautions I would, she always, in my pictures, came out too tall – landing me in the dilemma of having represented a fascinating woman as seven feet high, which, out of respect perhaps to my own very much scantier inches, was far from my idea of such a personage.

The case was worse with the Major – nothing I could do would keep *him* down, so that he became useful only for the representation of brawny giants. I adored variety and range, I cherished human accidents, the illustrative note; I wanted to characterise closely, and the thing in the world I most hated was the danger of being ridden by a type. I had quarrelled with some of my friends about it – I had parted company with them for maintaining that one *had* to be, and that if the type was beautiful (witness Raphael and Leonardo), the servitude was only a gain. I was neither Leonardo nor Raphael; I might only be a presumptuous young modern searcher, but I held that everything was to be sacrificed sooner than character. When they averred that the haunting type in question could easily *be* character, I retorted, perhaps superficially: 'Whose?' It couldn't be everybody's – it might end in being nobody's.

After I had drawn Mrs Monarch a dozen times I perceived more clearly than before that the value of such a model as Miss Churm resided precisely in the fact that she had no positive stamp, combined of course with the other fact that what she did have was a curious and inexplicable talent for imitation. Her usual appearance was like a curtain which she could draw up at request for a capital performance. This performance was simply suggestive; but it was a word to the wise – it was vivid and pretty. Sometimes, even, I thought it, though she was plain herself, too insipidly pretty; I made it a reproach to her that the figures drawn from her were monotonously (*bêtement*, as we used to say) graceful. Nothing made her more angry: it was so much her pride to feel that she could sit for characters that had nothing in common with each other. She would accuse me at such moments of taking away her 'reputytion'.

It suffered a certain shrinkage, this queer quantity, from the repeated visits of my new friends. Miss Churm was greatly in demand, never in want of employment, so I had no scruple in putting her off occasionally, to try them more at my ease. It was certainly amusing at first to do the real thing – it was amusing to do Major Monarch's trousers. They *were* the real thing, even if he did come out colossal. It was amusing to do his wife's back hair (it was so mathematically neat), and the particular 'smart' tension of her tight stays. She lent herself especially to positions in which the face was somewhat averted or blurred; she abounded in lady-like back views and *profils perdus*. When she stood erect she took naturally one of the attitudes in which court-painters represent queens and princesses; so that I found myself wondering whether, to draw out this accomplishment, I couldn't get the editor of the *Cheapside* to publish a really royal romance, 'A Tale of Buckingham Palace'. Sometimes, however, the real thing and the make-believe came into contact; by which I mean that Miss Churm, keeping an appointment or coming to make one on days when I had much work in hand, encountered her invidious rivals. The encounter was not on their part, for they noticed her no more than if she had been the housemaid; not from intentional loftiness, but simply because, as yet, professionally, they didn't know how to fraternise, as I could guess that they would have liked – or at least that the Major would. They couldn't talk about the omnibus – they always walked, and they didn't know what else to try – she wasn't interested in good trains or cheap claret. Besides, they must have felt – in the air – that she was amused at them, secretly derisive of their ever knowing how. She was not a person to conceal her scepticism if she had had a chance to show it. On the other hand Mrs Monarch didn't think her tidy; for why else did she take pains to say to me (it was going out of the way, for Mrs Monarch) that she didn't like dirty women?

One day when my young lady happened to be present with my other sitters (she even dropped in, when it was convenient, for a chat), I asked her to be so good as to lend a hand in getting tea – a service with which she was familiar and which was one of a class that, living as I did in a small way, with slender domestic resources, I often appealed to my models to render. They liked to lay hands on my property, to break the sitting, and sometimes the china – I made them feel Bohemian. The next time I saw Miss Churm after this incident she surprised me greatly by making a scene about it – she accused me of having wished to humiliate her. She had not resented the outrage at the time, but had seemed obliging and amused, enjoying the comedy of asking Mrs Monarch, who sat vague and silent, whether she would have cream and sugar, and putting an exaggerated simper into the question. She had tried intonations – as if she too wished to pass for the real thing; till I was afraid my other visitors would take offence.

Oh, *they* were determined not to do this; and their touching patience was the measure of their great need. They would sit by the hour, uncomplaining, till I was ready to use them; they would come back on the chance of being wanted, and would walk away cheerfully if they were not. I used to go to the door with them to see in what magnificent order they retreated. I tried to find other employment for them – I introduced them to several artists. But they didn't 'take', for reasons I could appreciate, and I became conscious, rather anxiously, that after such disappointments they fell back upon me with a heavier weight. They did me the honour to think that it was I who was most *their* form. They were not picturesque enough for the painters, and in those days there were not so many serious workers in black and white. Besides, they had an eye to the great job I had mentioned to them – they had secretly set their hearts on supplying the right essence for my pictorial vindication of our fine novelist. They knew that for this undertaking I should want no costume-effects, none of the frippery of past ages – that it was a case in which everything would be contemporary and satirical and, presumably, genteel. If I could work them into it their future would be assured, for the labour would of course be long and the occupation steady.

One day Mrs Monarch came without her husband – she explained his absence by his having had to go to the City. While she sat there in her usual anxious stiffness there came, at the door, a knock which I immediately recognised as the subdued appeal of a model out of work. It was followed by the entrance of a young man whom I easily perceived to be a foreigner and who proved in fact an Italian acquainted with no English word but my name, which he uttered in a way that made it seem to include all others. I had not then visited his country, nor was I proficient in his tongue;

but as he was not so meanly constituted – what Italian is? – as to depend only on that member for expression he conveyed to me, in familiar but graceful mimicry, that he was in search of exactly the employment in which the lady before me was engaged. I was not struck with him at first, and while I continued to draw I emitted rough sounds of discouragement and dismissal. He stood his ground, however, not importunately, but with a dumb, dog-like fidelity in his eyes which amounted to innocent impudence – the manner of a devoted servant (he might have been in the house for years), unjustly suspected. Suddenly I saw that this very attitude and expression made a picture, whereupon I told him to sit down and wait till I should be free. There was another picture in the way he obeyed me, and I observed as I worked that there were others still in the way he looked wonderingly, with his head thrown back, about the high studio. He might have been crossing himself in St Peter's. Before I finished I said to myself: 'The fellow's a bankrupt orange-monger, but he's a treasure.'

When Mrs Monarch withdrew he passed across the room like a flash to open the door for her, standing there with the rapt, pure gaze of the young Dante spellbound by the young Beatrice. As I never insisted, in such situations, on the blankness of the British domestic, I reflected that he had the making of a servant (and I needed one, but couldn't pay him to be only that), as well as of a model; in short I made up my mind to adopt my bright adventurer if he would agree to officiate in the double capacity. He jumped at my offer, and in the event my rashness (for I had known nothing about him) was not brought home to me. He proved a sympathetic though a desultory ministrant, and had in a wonderful degree the *sentiment de la pose*. It was uncultivated, instinctive; a part of the happy instinct which had guided him to my door and helped him to spell out my name on the card nailed to it. He had had no other introduction to me than a guess, from the shape of my high north window, seen outside, that my place was a studio and that as a studio it would contain an artist. He had wandered to England in search of fortune, like other itinerants, and had embarked, with a partner and a small green hand-cart, on the sale of penny ices. The ices had melted away and the partner had dissolved in their train. My young man wore tight yellow trousers with reddish stripes and his name was Oronte. He was sallow but fair, and when I put him into some old clothes of my own he looked like an Englishman. He was as good as Miss Churm, who could look, when required, like an Italian.

4

I thought Mrs Monarch's face slightly convulsed when, on her coming back with her husband, she found Oronte installed. It was strange to have to recognise in a scrap of a lazzarone a competitor to her magnificent Major. It was she who scented danger first, for the Major was anecdotically unconscious. But Oronte gave us tea, with a hundred eager confusions (he had never seen such a queer process), and I think she thought better of me for having at last an 'establishment.' They saw a couple of drawings that I had made of the establishment, and Mrs Monarch hinted that it never would have struck her that he had sat for them. 'Now the drawings you make from *us*, they look exactly like us,' she reminded me, smiling in triumph; and I recognised that this was indeed just their defect. When I drew the Monarchs I couldn't, somehow, get away from them – get into the character I wanted to represent; and I had not the least desire my model should be discoverable in my picture. Miss Churm never was, and Mrs Monarch thought I hid her, very properly, because she was vulgar; whereas if she was lost it was only as the dead who go to heaven are lost – in the gain of an angel the more.

By this time I had got a certain start with *Rutland Ramsay*, the first novel in the great projected series; that is I had produced a dozen drawings, several with the help of the Major and his wife, and I had sent them in for approval. My understanding with the publishers, as I have already hinted, had been that I was to be left to do my work, in this particular case, as I liked, with the whole book committed to me; but my connection with the rest of the series was only contingent. There were moments when, frankly, it *was* a comfort to have the real thing under one's hand; for there were characters in *Rutland Ramsay* that were very much like it. There were people presumably as straight as the Major and women of as good a fashion as Mrs Monarch. There was a great deal of country-house life – treated, it is true, in a fine, fanciful, ironical, generalised way – and there was a considerable implication of knickerbockers and kilts. There were certain things I had to settle at the outset; such things for instance as the exact appearance of the hero, the particular bloom of the heroine. The author of course gave me a lead, but there was a margin for interpretation. I took the Monarchs into my confidence, I told them frankly what I was about, I mentioned my embarrassments and alternatives. 'Oh, take *him*!' Mrs Monarch murmured sweetly, looking at her husband; and 'What could you want better than my wife?' the Major inquired, with the comfortable candour that now prevailed between us.

I was not obliged to answer these remarks – I was only obliged to place my sitters. I was not easy in mind, and I postponed, a little timidly perhaps, the solution of the question. The book was a large canvas, the other figures were numerous, and I worked off at first some of the episodes in which the hero and the heroine were not concerned. When once I had set *them* up I should have to stick to them – I couldn't make my young man seven feet high in one place and five feet nine in another. I inclined on the whole to the latter measurement, though the Major more than once reminded me that *he* looked about as young as anyone. It was indeed quite possible to arrange him, for the figure, so that it would have been difficult to detect his age. After the spontaneous Oronte had been with me a month, and after I had given him to understand several different times that his native exuberance would presently constitute an insurmountable barrier to our further intercourse, I waked to a sense of his heroic capacity. He was only five feet seven, but the remaining inches were latent. I tried him almost secretly at first, for I was really rather afraid of the judgment my other models would pass on such a choice. If they regarded Miss Churm as little better than a snare, what would they think of the representation by a person so little the real thing as an Italian street-vendor of a protagonist formed by a public school?

If I went a little in fear of them it was not because they bullied me, because they had got an oppressive foothold, but because in their really pathetic decorum and mysteriously permanent new-ness they counted on me so intensely. I was therefore very glad when Jack Hawley came home: he was always of such good counsel. He painted badly himself, but there was no one like him for putting his finger on the place. He had been absent from England for a year; he had been somewhere – I don't remember where – to get a fresh eye. I was in a good deal of dread of any such organ, but we were old friends; he had been away for months and a sense of emptiness was creeping into my life. I hadn't dodged a missile for a year.

He came back with a fresh eye, but with the same old black velvet blouse, and the first evening he spent in my studio we smoked cigarettes till the small hours. He had done no work himself, he had only got the eye; so the field was clear for the production of my little things. He wanted to see what I had done for the *Cheapside*, but he was disappointed in the exhibition. That at least seemed the meaning of two or three comprehensive groans which, as he lounged on my big divan, on a folded leg, looking at my latest drawings, issued from his lips with the smoke of the cigarette.

'What's the matter with you?' I asked.

'What's the matter with *you*?'

'Nothing save that I'm mystified.'

'You are indeed. You're quite off the hinge. What's the meaning of this new fad?' And he tossed me, with visible irreverence, a drawing in which I happened to have depicted both my majestic models. I asked if he didn't think it good, and he replied that it struck him as execrable, given the sort of thing I had always represented myself to him as wishing to arrive at; but I let that pass, I was so anxious to see exactly what he meant. The two figures in the picture looked colossal, but I supposed this was *not* what he meant, inasmuch as, for aught he knew to the contrary, I might have been trying for that. I maintained that I was working exactly in the same way as when he last had done me the honour to commend me. 'Well, there's a big hole somewhere,' he answered; 'wait a bit and I'll discover it.' I depended upon him to do so: where else was the fresh eye? But he produced at last nothing more luminous than 'I don't know – I don't like your types.' This was lame, for a critic who had never consented to discuss with me anything but the question of execution, the direction of strokes and the mystery of values.

'In the drawings you've been looking at I think my types are very handsome.'

'Oh, they won't do!'

'I've had a couple of new models.'

'I see you have. *They* won't do.'

'Are you very sure of that?'

'Absolutely – they're stupid.'

'You mean *I* am – for I ought to get round that.'

'You *can't* – with such people. Who are they?'

I told him, as far as was necessary, and he declared, heartlessly: '*Ce sont des gens qu'il faut mettre à la porte.*'

'You've never seen them; they're awfully good,' I compassionately objected.

'Not seen them? Why, all this recent work of yours drops to pieces with them. It's all I want to see of them.'

'No one else has said anything against it – the *Cheapside* people are pleased.'

'Everyone else is an ass, and the *Cheapside* people the biggest asses of all. Come, don't pretend, at this time of day, to have pretty illusions about the public, especially about publishers and editors. It's not for *such* animals you work – it's for those who know, *coloro che sanno*; so keep straight for *me* if you can't keep straight for yourself. There's a certain sort of thing you tried for from the first – and a very good thing it is. But this twaddle isn't *in* it.' When I talked with Hawley later about *Rutland Ramsay* and its possible successors he declared that I must get back into my boat again or I would go to the bottom. His voice in short was the voice of warning.

I noted the warning, but I didn't turn my friends out of doors. They bored me a good deal; but the very fact that they bored me admonished me not to sacrifice them – if there was anything to be done with them – simply to irritation. As I look back at this phase they seem to me to have pervaded my life not a little. I have a vision of them as most of the time in my studio, seated, against the wall, on an old velvet bench to be out of the way, and looking like a pair of patient courtiers in a royal ante-chamber. I am convinced that during the coldest weeks of the winter they held their ground because it saved them fire. Their newness was losing its gloss, and it was impossible not to feel that they were objects of charity. Whenever Miss Churm arrived they went away, and after I was fairly launched in *Rutland Ramsay* Miss Churm arrived pretty often. They managed to express to me tacitly that they supposed I wanted her for the low life of the book, and I let them suppose it, since they had attempted to study the work – it was lying about the studio – without discovering that it dealt only with the highest circles. They had dipped into the most brilliant of our novelists without deciphering many passages. I still took an hour from them, now and again, in spite of Jack Hawley's warning: it would be time enough to dismiss them, if dismissal should be necessary, when the rigour of the season was over. Hawley had made their acquaintance – he had met them at my fireside – and thought them a ridiculous pair. Learning that he was a painter they tried to approach him, to show him too that they were the real thing; but he looked at them, across the big room, as if they were miles away: they were a compendium of everything that he most objected to in the social system of his country. Such people as that, all convention and patent-leather, with ejaculations that stopped conversation, had no business in a studio. A studio was a place to learn to see, and how could you see through a pair of feather beds?

The main inconvenience I suffered at their hands was that, at first, I was shy of letting them discover how my artful little servant had begun to sit to me for *Rutland Ramsay*. They knew that I had been odd enough (they were prepared by this time to allow oddity to artists) to pick a foreign vagabond out of the streets, when I might have had a person with whiskers and credentials; but it was some time before they learned how high I rated his accomplishments. They found him in an attitude more than once, but they never doubted I was doing him as an organ-grinder. There were several things they never guessed, and one of them was that for a striking scene in the novel, in which a footman briefly figured, it occurred to me to make use of Major Monarch as the menial. I kept putting this off, I didn't like to ask him to don the livery – besides the difficulty of finding a livery to fit him. At last, one day late in the winter, when I was at work on the despised Oronte (he caught one's idea in an instant), and was in the glow of feeling that I was going very straight, they came in, the Major and his wife, with their society laugh about nothing (there was less and less to laugh at), like country-callers – they always reminded me of that – who have walked across the park after church and are presently persuaded to stay to luncheon. Luncheon was over, but they could stay to tea – I knew they wanted it. The fit was on me, however, and I couldn't let my ardour cool and my work wait, with the fading daylight, while my model prepared it. So I asked Mrs Monarch if she would mind laying it out – a request which, for an instant, brought all the blood to her face. Her eyes were on her husband's for a second, and some mute telegraphy passed between them. Their folly was over the next instant; his cheerful shrewdness put an end to it. So far from pitying their wounded pride, I must add, I was moved to give it as complete a lesson as I could. They bustled about together and got out the cups and saucers and made the kettle boil. I know they felt as if they were waiting on my servant, and when the tea was prepared I said: 'He'll have a cup, please – he's tired.' Mrs Monarch brought him one where he stood, and he took it from her as if he had been a gentleman at a party, squeezing a crush-hat with his elbow.

Then it came over me that she had made a great effort for me – made it with a kind of nobleness – and that I owed her compensation. Each time I saw her after this I wondered what the compensation could be. I couldn't go on doing the wrong thing to oblige them. Oh, it *was* the wrong thing, the stamp of the work for which they sat – Hawley was not the only person to say it now. I sent in a large number of the drawings I had made for *Rutland Ramsay*, and I received a warning that was more to the point than Hawley's. The artistic adviser of the house for which I was working was of opinion that many of my illustrations were not what had been looked for. Most of these illustrations were the subjects in which the Monarchs had figured. Without going into the question of what *had* been looked for, I saw at this rate I shouldn't get the other books to do. I hurled myself in despair upon Miss Churm, I put her through all her paces. I not only adopted Oronte publicly as my hero, but one morning when the Major looked in to see if I didn't require him to finish a figure for the *Cheapside*, for which he had begun to sit the week before, I told him that I had changed my mind – I would do the drawing from my man. At this my visitor turned pale and stood looking at me. 'Is *he* your idea of an English gentleman?' he asked.

I was disappointed, I was nervous, I wanted to get on with my work; so I replied with irritation: 'Oh, my dear Major – I can't be ruined for *you*!'

He stood another moment; then, without a word, he quitted the studio. I drew a long breath when he was gone, for I said to myself that I shouldn't see him again. I had not told him definitely that I was in danger of having my work rejected, but I was vexed at his not having felt the catastrophe in the air, read with me the moral of our fruitless collaboration, the lesson that, in the deceptive atmosphere of art, even the highest respectability may fail of being plastic.

I didn't owe my friends money, but I did see them again. They re-appeared together, three days later, and under the circumstances there was something tragic in the fact. It was a proof to me that they could find nothing else in life to do. They had threshed the matter out in a dismal conference – they had digested the bad news that they were not in for the series. If they were not useful to me even for the *Cheapside* their function seemed difficult to determine, and I could only judge at first that they had come, forgivingly, decorously, to take a last leave. This made me rejoice in secret that I had little leisure for a scene; for I had placed both my other models in position together and I was pegging away at a drawing from which I hoped to derive glory. It had been suggested by the passage in which Rutland Ramsay, drawing up a chair to Artemisia's piano-stool, says extraordinary things to her while she ostensibly fingers out a difficult piece of music. I had done Miss Churm at the piano before – it was an attitude in which she knew how to take on an absolutely poetic grace. I wished the two figures to 'compose' together, intensely, and my little Italian had entered perfectly into my conception. The pair were vividly before me, the piano had been pulled out; it was a charming picture of blended youth and murmured love, which I had only to catch and keep. My visitors stood and looked at it, and I was friendly to them over my shoulder.

They made no response, but I was used to silent company and went on with my work, only a little disconcerted (even though exhilarated by the sense that *this* was at least the ideal thing) at not having got rid of them after all. Presently I heard Mrs Monarch's sweet voice beside, or rather above me: 'I wish her hair was a little better done.' I looked up and she was staring with a strange fixedness at Miss Churm, whose back was turned to her. 'Do you mind my just touching it?' she went on – a question which made me spring up for an instant, as with the instinctive fear that she might do the young lady a harm. But she quieted me with a glance I shall never forget – I confess I should like to have been able to paint *that* – and went for a moment to my model. She spoke to her softly, laying a hand upon her shoulder and bending over her; and as the girl, understanding, gratefully assented, she disposed her rough curls, with a few quick passes, in such a way as to make Miss Churm's head twice as charming. It was one of the most heroic personal services I had ever seen rendered. Then Mrs Monarch turned away with a low sigh and, looking about her as if for something to do, stooped to the floor with a noble humility and picked up a dirty rag that had dropped out of my paint-box.

The Major meanwhile had also been looking for something to do and, wandering to the other end of the studio, saw before him my breakfast things, neglected, unremoved. 'I say, can't I be useful *here*?' he called out to me with an irrepressible quaver. I assented with a laugh that I fear was awkward and for the next ten minutes, while I worked, I heard the light clatter of china and the tinkle of spoons and glass. Mrs Monarch assisted her husband – they washed up my crockery, they put it away. They wandered off into my little scullery, and I afterwards found that they had cleaned my knives and that my slender stock of plate had an unprecedented surface. When it came over me, the latent eloquence of what they were doing, I confess that my drawing was blurred for a moment – the picture swam. They had accepted their failure, but they couldn't accept their fate. They had bowed their heads in bewilderment to the perverse and cruel law in virtue of which the real thing could be so much less precious than the unreal; but they didn't want to starve. If my servants were my models, my models might be my servants. They would reverse the parts – the others would sit for the ladies and gentlemen, and *they* would do the work. They would still be in the studio – it was an intense dumb appeal to me not to turn them out. 'Take us on,' they wanted to say – 'we'll do *anything*.'

When all this hung before me the *afflatus* vanished – my pencil dropped from my hand. My sitting was spoiled and I got rid of my sitters, who were also evidently rather mystified and awestruck. Then, alone with the Major and his wife, I had a most uncomfortable moment. He put their prayer into a single sentence: 'I say, you know – just let *us* do for you, can't you?' I couldn't – it was dreadful to see them emptying my slops; but I pretended I could, to oblige them, for about a week. Then I gave them a sum of money to go away; and I never saw them again. I obtained the remaining books, but my friend Hawley repeats that Major and Mrs Monarch did me a permanent harm, got me into a second-rate trick. If it be true I am content to have paid the price – for the memory.

1893

GEORGE WASHINGTON CABLE

1844–1925

Café des Exilés

That which in 1835 – I think he said thirty-five – was a reality in
the Rue Burgundy – I think he said Burgundy – is now but a
reminiscence. Yet so vividly was its story told me that at this
moment the old Café des Exilés appears before my eye, floating in
the clouds of reverie, and I doubt not I see it just as it was in the old
times.

An antiquated story-and-a-half Creole cottage sitting right
down on the banquette, as do the Choctaw squaws who sell bay
and sassafras and life everlasting, with a high, close board fence
shutting out of view the diminutive garden on the southern side.
An ancient willow droops over the roof of round tiles, and partly
hides the discolored stucco, which keeps dropping off into the
garden as though the old café was stripping for the plunge into
oblivion – disrobing for its execution. I see, well up in the angle of
the broad side gable, shaded by its rude awning of clapboards, as
the eyes of an old dame are shaded by her wrinkled hand, the
window of Pauline. Oh, for the image of the maiden, were it but
for one moment, leaning out of the casement to hang her
mockingbird and looking down into the garden – where, above
the barrier of old boards, I see the top of the fig tree, the pale green
clump of bananas, the tall palmetto with its jagged crown,
Pauline's own two orange trees holding up their hands toward the
window, heavy with the promises of autumn; the broad, crimson
mass of the many-stemmed oleander, and the crisp boughs of the
pomegranate loaded with freckled apples, and with here and there
a lingering scarlet blossom.

The Café des Exilés, to use a figure, flowered, bore fruit, and
dropped it long ago – or rather Time and Fate, like some uncursed
Adam and Eve, came side by side and cut away its clusters, as we
sever the golden burden of the banana from its stem; then, like a
banana which has borne its fruit, it was razed to the ground and
made way for newer, brighter growth. I believe it would set every
tooth on edge should I go by there now – now that I have heard the

story – and see the old site covered by the 'Shoo-fly Coffeehouse'. Pleasanter far to close my eyes and call to view the unpretentious portals of the old café, with her children – for such those exiles seem to me – dragging their rocking chairs out and sitting in their wonted group under the long, outreaching eaves which shaded the banquette of the Rue Burgundy.

It was in 1835 that the Café des Exilés was, as one might say, in full blossom. Old M. D'Hemecourt, father of Pauline and host of the café, himself a refugee from Santo Domingo, was the cause –at least the human cause – of its opening. As its white-curtained, glazed doors expanded, emitting a little puff of his own cigarette smoke, it was like the bursting of catalpa blossoms, and the exiles came like bees, pushing into the tiny room to sip its rich variety of tropical syrups, its lemonades, its orangeades, its orgeats, its barley waters, and its outlandish wines, while they talked of dear home – that is to say, of Barbados, of Martinique, of Santo Domingo, and of Cuba.

There were Pedro and Benigno, and Fernandez and Francisco, and Benito. Benito was a tall, swarthy man, with immense gray mustachios, and hair as harsh as tropical grass and gray as ashes. When he could spare his cigarette from his lips, he would tell you in a cavernous voice, and with a wrinkled smiled, that he was 'a-t-thorty-seveng.'

There was Martinez of Santo Domingo, yellow as a canary, always sitting with one leg curled under him and holding the back of his head in his knitted fingers against the back of his rocking chair. Father, mother, brother, sisters, all, had been massacred in the struggle of '21 and '22; he alone was left to tell the tale, and told it often, with that strange, infantile insensibility to the solemnity of his bereavement so peculiar to Latin people.

But, besides these, and many who need no mention, there were two in particular, around whom all the story of the Café des Exilés, of old M. D'Hemecourt and of Pauline, turns as on a double center. First, Manuel Mazaro, whose small, restless eyes were as black and bright as those of a mouse, whose light talk became his dark girlish face, and whose redundant locks curled so prettily and so wonderfully black under the fine white brim of his jaunty Panama. He had the hands of a woman, save that the nails were stained with the smoke of cigarettes. He could play the guitar delightfully, and wore his knife down behind his coat collar.

The second was 'Major' Galahad Shaughnessy. I imagine I can see him, in his white duck, brass-buttoned roundabout, with his saberless belt peeping out beneath, all his boyishness in his sea-blue eyes, leaning lightly against the doorpost of the Café des Exilés as a child leans against his mother, running his fingers over a basketful of fragrant limes and watching his chance to strike some solemn Creole under the fifth rib with a good old Irish joke.

Old D'Hemecourt drew him close to his bosom. The Spanish Creoles were, as the old man termed it, both cold and hot, but never warm. Major Shaughnessy was warm, and it was no uncommon thing to find those two apart from the others, talking in an undertone, and playing at *confidantes* like two schoolgirls. The kind old man was at this time drifting close up to his sixtieth year. There was much he could tell of Santo Domingo, whither he had been carried from Martinique in his childhood, whence he had become a refugee to Cuba, and thence to New Orleans in the flight of 1809.

It fell one day to Manuel Mazaro's lot to discover, by sauntering within earshot, that to Galahad Shaughnessy only, of all the children of the Café des Exilés, the good host spoke long and confidentially concerning his daughter. The words, half-heard and magnified like objects seen in a fog, meaning Manuel Mazaro knew not what, but made portentous by his suspicious nature, were but the old man's recital of the grinding he had got between the millstones of his poverty and his pride, in trying so long to sustain, for little Pauline's sake, that attitude before society which earns respect from a surface-viewing world. It was while he was telling this that Manuel Mazaro drew near; the old man paused in an embarrassed way; the Major, sitting sidewise in his chair, lifted his cheek from its resting place on his elbow; and Mazaro, after standing an awkward moment, turned away with such an inward feeling as one may guess would arise in a heart full of Cuban blood, not unmixed with Indian.

As he moved off, M. D'Hemecourt resumed: that in a last extremity he had opened, partly from dire want, partly for very love to homeless souls, the Café des Exilés. He had hoped that, as strong drink and high words were to be alike unknown to it, it might not prejudice sensible people; but it had. He had no doubt they said among themselves, 'She is an excellent and beautiful girl and deserving all respect'; and respect they accorded, but their *respects* they never came to pay.

'A café is a café,' said the old gentleman. 'It is nod possib' to ezcape him, aldough de Café des Exilés is differen' from de rez.'

'It's different from the Café des Réfugiés,' suggested the Irishman.

'Differen' as possib',' replied M. D'Hemecourt. He looked about upon the walls. The shelves were luscious with ranks of cooling syrups which he alone knew how to make. The expression of his face changed from sadness to a gentle pride, which spoke without words, saying – and let our story pause a moment to hear it say:

'If any poor exile, from any island where guavas or mangoes or plantains grow, wants a draught which will make him see his home among the cocoa palms, behold the Café des Exilés ready to take the poor child up and give him the breast! And if gold or silver he has them not, why Heaven and Santa Maria and Saint Christopher bless him! It makes no difference. Here is a rocking chair, here a cigarette, and here a light from the host's own tinder. He will pay when he can.'

As this easily pardoned pride said, so it often occurred; and if the newly come exile said his father was a Spaniard – Come!' old M. D'Hemecourt would cry; 'another glass; it is an innocent drink; my mother was a Castilian.' But, if the exile said his mother was a Frenchwoman, the glasses would be forthcoming all the same, for 'My father,' the old man would say, 'was a Frenchman of Martinique, with blood as pure as that wine and a heart as sweet as this honey; come, a glass of orgeat' – and he would bring it himself in a quart tumbler.

Now, there are jealousies and jealousies. There are people who rise up quickly and kill, and there are others who turn their hot thoughts over silently in their minds as a brooding bird turns her eggs in the nest. Thus did Manuel Mazaro, and took it ill that Galahad should see a vision in the temple while he and all the brethren tarried without. Pauline had been to the Café des Exilés in some degree what the image of the Virgin was to their churches at home; and for her father to whisper her name to one and not to another was, it seemed to Mazaro, as if the old man, were he a sacristan, should say to some single worshipper, 'Here, you may have this madonna; I make it a present to you.' Or, if such was not the handsome young Cuban's feeling, such, at least, was the disguise his jealousy put on. If Pauline was to be handed down from her niche, why, then, farewell Café des Exilés. She was its preserving influence, she made the place holy; she was the burning candles on the altar. Surely the reader will pardon the pen that lingers in the mention of her.

And yet I know not how to describe the forbearing unspoken tenderness with which all these exiles regarded the maiden. In the balmy afternoons, as I have said, they gathered about their mother's knee, that is to say, upon the banquette outside the door. There, lolling back in their rocking chairs, they would pass the evening hours with oft-repeated tales of home; and the moon would come out and glide among the clouds like a silver barge among islands wrapped in mist, and they loved the silently gliding orb with a sort of worship, because from her soaring height she looked down at the same moment upon them and upon their homes in the far Antilles. It was somewhat thus that they looked upon Pauline as she seemed to them held up halfway to heaven, they knew not how. Ah, those who have been pilgrims; who have wandered out beyond harbor and light; whom fate hath led in lonely paths strewn with thorns and briars not of their own sowing; who, homeless in a land of homes, see windows gleaming and doors ajar, but not for them – it is they who well understand what the worship is that cries to any daughter of our dear mother Eve whose footsteps chance may draw across the path, the silent, beseeching cry, 'Stay a little instant that I may look upon you. Oh, woman, beautifier of the earth! Stay till I recall the face of my sister; stay yet a moment while I look from afar, with helpless-hanging hands, upon the softness of thy cheek, upon the folded coils of thy shining hair; and my spirit shall fall down and say those prayers which I may never again – God knoweth – say at home.'

She was seldom seen; but sometimes, when the lounging exiles would be sitting in their afternoon circle under the eaves, and some old man would tell his tale of fire and blood and capture and escape, and the heads would lean forward from the chairbacks and a great stillness would follow the ending of the story, old M. D'Hemecourt would all at once speak up and say, laying his hands upon the narrator's knee, 'Comrade, your throat is dry, here are fresh limes; let my dear child herself come and mix you a lemonade.' Then the neighbors over the way, sitting about their doors, would by and by softly say, 'See, see! there is Pauline!' and all the exiles would rise from their rocking chairs, take off their hats, and stand as men stand in church, while Pauline came out like the moon from a cloud, descended the three steps of the café door, and stood with water and glass, a new Rebecca with her pitcher, before the swarthy wanderer.

What tales that would have been tear-compelling, nay, heart-rending, had they not been palpable inventions, the pretty, womanish Mazaro from time to time poured forth, in the ever-ungratified hope that the goddess might come down with a draught of nectar for him, it profiteth not to recount; but I should fail to show a family feature of the Café des Exilés did I omit to say that these make-believe adventures were heard with every mark of respect and credence; while, on the other hand, they were never attempted in the presence of the Irishman. He would have moved an eyebrow, or made some barely audible sound, or dropped some seemingly innocent word, and the whole company, in spite of themselves, would have smiled. Wherefore, it may be doubted whether at any time the curly-haired young Cuban had that playful affection for his Celtic comrade, which a habit of giving little velvet taps to Galahad's cheek made a show of.

Such was the Café des Exilés, such its inmates, such its guests, when certain apparently trivial events began to fall around it as germs of blight fall upon corn, and to bring about that end which cometh to all things.

The little seed of jealousy, dropped into the heart of Manuel Mazaro, we have already taken into account.

Galahad Shaughnessy began to be especially active in organizing a society of Spanish-Americans, the design of which, as set forth in its manuscript constitution, was to provide proper funeral honors to such of their membership as might be overtaken by death; and, whenever it was practicable, to send their ashes to their native land. Next to Galahad in this movement was an elegant old Mexican physician, Dr— – his name escapes me – whom the Café des Exilés sometimes took upon her lap – that is to say doorstep – but whose favorite resort was the old Café des Refugiés in the Rue Royale (Royal Street, as it was beginning to be called). Manuel Mazaro was made secretary.

It was for some reason thought judicious for the society to hold its meetings in various places, now here, now there; but the most frequent rendezvous was the Café des Exilés; it was quiet; those Spanish Creoles, however they may afterward cackle, like to lay their plans noiselessly, like a hen in a barn. There was a very general confidence in this old institution, a kind of inward assurance that 'mother wouldn't tell'; though, after all, what great secrets could there be connected with a mere burial society?

Before the hour of the meeting, the Café des Exilés always sent away her children and closed the door. Presently they would commence returning, one by one, as a flock of wild fowl will do, that has been startled up from its accustomed haunt. Frequenters of the Café des Refugiés also would appear. A small gate in the close garden fence let them into a room behind the café proper, and by and by the apartment would be full of dark-visaged men conversing in the low, courteous tone common to their race. The shutters of doors and windows were closed and the chinks stopped with cotton; some people are so jealous of observation.

On a certain night after one of those meetings had dispersed in its peculiar way, the members retiring two by two at intervals, Manuel Mazaro and M. D'Hemecourt were left alone, sitting close together in the dimly lighted room, the former speaking, the other, with no pleasant countenance, attending. It seemed to the young Cuban a proper precaution – he was made of precautions –to speak in English. His voice was barely audible.

'– Sayce to me, "Manuel, she t-theeing I want-n to marry hor." Señor, you shouth 'ave see' him laugh!'

M. D'Hemecourt lifted up his head and laid his hand upon the young man's arm.

'Manuel Mazaro,' he began, 'iv dad w'ad you say is nod–'

The Cuban interrupted.

'If is no' t-thrue you will keel Manuel Mazaro? – a' r-r-right-a!'

'No,' said the tender old man, 'no, bud h-I am positeef dad de Madjor will shood you.'

Mazaro nodded, and lifted one finger for attention.

'–sayce to me, "Manuel, you goin' tell-a Señor D'Hemecourt, I fin'- a you some nigh' an' cut-a you' heart ou'." An' I sayce to heem-a, "Boat-a if Señor D'Hemecourt he fin'-in' ou' frone Pauline"—'

'Silence!' fiercely cried the old man. 'My God! 'Sieur Mazaro, neider you, neider somebody helse s'all h'use de nem of me daughter. It is nod possib' dad you s'all spick him! I cannot pearmid thad.'

While the old man was speaking these vehement words, the Cuban was emphatically nodding approval.

'Co-rect-a, co-rect-a, Señor,' he replied. 'Señor, you' r-r-r-right-a; escuse-a me, Señor, escuse-a me. Señor D'Hemecourt,

Mayor Shaughness', when he talkin' wi' me he usin' hor-a name o the t-thime-a!'

'My fren',' said M. D'Hemecourt, rising and speaking with labored control, 'I muz tell you good nighd. You 'ave sooprise me a verry gred deal. I s'all *in*vestigade doze ting; an', Manuel Mazaro, h-I am a hole man; bud I will requez you, iv dad wad you say is nod de true – my God! – not to h-ever ritturn again ad de Café des Exilés.'

Mazaro smiled and nodded. His host opened the door into the garden, and, as the young man stepped out, noticed even then how handsome was his face and figure, and how the odor of the night jasmine was filling the air with an almost insupporting sweetness. The Cuban paused a moment, as if to speak, but checked himself, lifted his girlish face, and looked up to where the daggers of the palmetto tree were crossed upon the face of the moon, dropped his glance, touched his Panama, and silently followed by the bareheaded old man, drew open the little garden gate, looked cautiously out, said good night, and stepped into the street.

As M. D'Hemecourt returned to the door through which he had come, he uttered an ejaculation of astonishment. Pauline stood before him. She spoke hurriedly in French.

'Papa, Papa, it is not true.'

'No, my child,' he responded, 'I am sure it is not true; I am sure it is all false; but why do I find you out of bed so late, little bird? The night is nearly gone.'

He laid his hand upon her cheek.

'Ah, Papa, I cannot deceive you. I thought Manuel would tell you something of this kind, and I listened.'

The father's face immediately betrayed a new and deeper distress.

'Pauline, my child,' he said with tremulous voice, 'if Manuel's story is all false, in the name of Heaven how could you think he was going to tell it?'

He unconsciously clasped his hands. The good child had one trait which she could not have inherited from her father; she was quick-witted and discerning; yet now she stood confounded.

'Speak, my child,' cried the alarmed old man; 'speak! Let me live, and not die.'

'Oh, Papa,' she cried, 'I do not know!'

The old man groaned.

'Papa, Papa,' she cried again, 'I felt it; I know not how; something told me.'

'Alas!' exclaimed the old man. 'If it was your conscience!'

'No, no, no, Papa,' cried Pauline, 'but I was afraid of Manuel Mazaro, and I think he hates him – and I think he will hurt him in any way he can – and I *know* he will even try to kill him. Oh, my God!'

She struck her hands together above her head and burst into a flood of tears. Her father looked upon her with such sad sternness as his tender nature was capable of. He laid hold of one of her arms to draw a hand from the face whither both hands had gone.

'You know something else,' he said; 'you know that the Major loves you, or you think so: is it not true?'

She dropped both hands and, lifting her streaming eyes that had nothing to hide straight to his, suddenly said:

'I would give worlds to think so!' and sunk upon the floor.

He was melted and convinced in one instant.

'Oh, my child, my child,' he cried, trying to lift her. 'Oh, my poor little Pauline, your Papa is not angry. Rise, my little one; so; kiss me; Heaven bless thee. Pauline, treasure, what shall I do with thee? Where shall I hide thee?'

'You have my counsel already, Papa.'

'Yes, my child, and you were right. The Café des Exilés never should have been opened. It is no place for you; no place at all.'

'Let us leave it,' said Pauline.

'Ah, Pauline, I would close it tomorrow if I could, but now it is too late; I cannot.'

'Why?' asked Pauline pleadingly.

She had cast an arm about his neck. Her tears sparkled with a smile.

'My daughter, I cannot tell you; you must go now to bed; good night – or good morning; God keep you!'

'Well, then, Papa,' she said, 'have no fear; you need not hide me; I have my prayer book, and my altar, and my garden, and my window; my garden is my fenced city, and my window my watchtower; do you see?'

'Ah, Pauline,' responded the father, 'but I have been letting the enemy in and out at pleasure.'

'Good night,' she answered, and kissed him three times on either cheek; 'the blessed Virgin will take care of us; good night; *he* never said those things; not he; good night.'

The next evening Galahad Shaughnessy and Manuel Mazaro met at that 'very different' place, the Café des Réfugiés. There was much free talk going on about Texan annexation, about chances of war with Mexico, about Santo Domingan affairs, about Cuba and many et ceteras. Galahad was in his usual gay mood. He strode about among a mixed company of Louisianais, Cubans, and *Américains*, keeping them in a great laugh with his account of one of Ole Bull's concerts, and how he had there extorted an invitation from M. and Mme Devoti to attend one of their famous children's fancy dress balls.

'Halloo!' said he as Mazaro approached, 'heer's the etheerial Angelica herself. Look-ut heer, sissy, why ar'n't ye in the maternal arms of the Café des Exilés?'

Mazaro smiled amiably and sat down. A moment after, the Irishman, stepping away from his companions, stood before the young Cuban and asked, with a quiet business air:

'D'ye want to see me, Mazaro?'

The Cuban nodded, and they went aside. Mazaro, in a few quick words, looking at his pretty foot the while, told the other on no account to go near the Café des Exilés, as there were two men hanging about there, evidently watching for him, and—

'Wut's the use o' that?' asked Galahad; 'I say, wut's the use o' that?'

Major Shaughnessy's habit of repeating part of his words arose from another, of interrupting any person who might be speaking.

'They must know – I say they must know that whenever I'm nowhurs else I'm heer. What do they want?'

Mazaro made a gesture, signifying caution and secrecy, and smiled, as if to say, 'You ought to know.'

'Aha!' said the Irishman softly. 'Why don't they come here?'

'Z-afrai',' said Mazaro; 'd'they frai' to do an'teen een d-these-a crowth.'

'That's so,' said the Irishman; 'I say, that's so. If I don't feel very much like go-un, I'll not go; I say, I'll not go. We've no business tonight, eh, Mazaro?'

'No, Señor.'

A second evening was much the same, Mazaro repeating his warning. But when, on the third evening, the Irishman again repeated his willingness to stay away from the Café des Exilés unless he should feel strongly impelled to go, it was with the mental reservation that he did feel very much in that humor, and, unknown to Mazaro, should thither repair, if only to see whether some of those deep old fellows were not contriving a practical joke.

'Mazaro,' said he, 'I'm go-un around the caurnur a bit; I want ye to wait heer till I come back. I say I want ye to wait heer till I come back; I'll be gone about three-quarters of an hour.'

Mazaro assented. He saw with satisfaction the Irishman start in a direction opposite that in which lay the Café des Exilés, tarried fifteen or twenty minutes, and then, thinking he could step around to the Café des Exilés and return before the expiration of allotted time, hurried out.

Meanwhile that peaceful habitation sat in the moonlight with her children about her feet. The company outside the door was somewhat thinner than common. M. D'Hemecourt was not among them, but was sitting in the room behind the café. The long table which the burial society used at their meetings extended across the apartment, and a lamp had been placed upon it. M. D'Hemecourt sat by the lamp. Opposite him was a chair, which seemed awaiting an expected occupant. Beside the old man sat Pauline. They were talking in cautious undertones, and in French.

'No,' she seemed to insist; 'we do not know that he refuses to come. We only know that Manuel says so.'

The father shook his head sadly. 'When has he ever stayed away three nights together before?' he asked. 'No, my child; it is intentional. Manuel urges him to come, but he only sends poor excuses.'

'But,' said the girl, shading her face from the lamp and speaking with some suddenness, 'why have you not send word to him by some other person?'

M. D'Hemecourt looked up at his daughter a moment, and then smiled at his own simplicity.

'Ah!' he said. 'Certainly; and that is what I will – run away, Pauline. There is Manuel, now, ahead of time!'

A step was heard outside the café. The maiden, though she knew the step was not Mazaro's, rose hastily, opened the nearest door, and disappeared. She had barely closed it behind her when Galahad Shaughnessy entered the apartment.

D'Hemecourt rose up, both surprised and confused.

'Good evening, Munsher D'Himecourt,' said the Irishman. 'Munsher D'Himecourt, I know it's against rules – I say, I know it's against rules to come in here, but' – smiling – 'I want to have a private wurd with ye. I say, I want to have a private wurd with ye.'

In the closet of bottles the maiden smiled triumphantly. She also wiped the dew from her forehead, for the place was very close and warm.

With her father was no triumph. In him sadness and doubt were so mingled with anger that he dared not lift his eyes, but gazed at the knot in the wood of the table, which looked like a caterpillar curled up. Mazaro, he concluded, had really asked the Major to come.

'Mazaro tol' you?' he asked.

'Yes,' answered the Irishman. 'Mazaro told me I was watched, and asked—'

'Madjor,' unluckily interrupted the old man, suddenly looking up and speaking with subdued fervor, 'for w'y – iv Mazaro tol' you – for w'y you din come more sooner? Dad is one 'eavy charge again' you.'

'Didn't Mazaro tell ye why I didn't come?' asked the other, beginning to be puzzled at his host's meaning.

'Yez,' replied M. D'Hemecourt, 'bud one brev zhenteman should not be afraid of—'

The young man stopped him with a quiet laugh. 'Munsher D'Himecourt,' said he, 'I'm nor afraid of any two men living – I say I'm nor afraid of any two men living, and certainly not of the two that's bean a-watchin' me lately, if they're the two I think they are.'

M. D'Hemecourt flushed in a way quite incomprehensible to the speaker, who nevertheless continued:

'It was the charges,' he said, with some slyness in his smile. 'They *are* heavy, as ye say, and that's the very reason – I say that's the very reason why I stayed away, ye see, eh? I say that's the very reason I stayed away.'

Then, indeed, there was a dew for the maiden to wipe from her brow, unconscious that every word that was being said bore a different significance in the mind of each of the three. The old man was agitated.

'Bud, sir,' he began, shaking his head and lifting his hand.

'Bless yer soul, Munsher D'Himecourt,' interrupted the Irishman. 'Wut's the use o' grapplin' two cutthroats, when—'

'Madjor Shaughnessy!' cried M. D'Hemecourt, losing all self-control. 'H-I am nod a cud-troad, Madjor Shaughnessy, h-an I 'ave a r-r-righd to wadge you.'

The Major rose from his chair.

'What d'ye mean?' he asked vacantly, and then: 'Look-ut here, Munsher D'Himecourt, one of uz is crazy. I say one—'

'No, sar-r-r!' cried the other, rising and clenching his trembling fist. 'H-I am nod crezzy. I 'ave de righd to wadge dad man wad mague rimark aboud me dotter.'

'I never did no such a thing.'

'You did.'

'I never did no such a thing.'

'Bud you 'ave jus hacknowledge'—'

'I never did no such a *thing*, I tell ye, and the man that's told ye so is a liur.'

'Ah-h-h-h!' said the old man, wagging his finger. 'Ah-h-h-h! You call Manuel Mazaro one liar?'

The Irishman laughed out.

'Well, I should say so!'

He motioned the old man into his chair, and both sat down again.

'Why, Munsher D'Himecourt, Mazaro's been keepin' me away from heer with a yarn about two Spaniards watchin' for me. That's what I came in to ask ye about. My dear sur, do ye s'pose I wud talk about the goddess—I mean, yer daughter—to the likes o' Mazaro—I say to the likes o' Mazaro?'

To say the old man was at sea would be too feeble an expression —he was in the trough of the sea, with a hurricane of doubts and fears whirling around him. Somebody had told a lie, and he, having struck upon its sunken surface, was dazed and stunned. He opened his lips to say he knew not what, when his ear caught the voice of Manuel Mazaro, replying to the greeting of some of his comrades outside the front door.

'He is comin'!' cried the old man. 'Mague you'sev hide, Madjor; do not led 'im kedge you, *Mon Dieu!*'

The Irishman smiled.

'You little yellow wretch!' said he quietly, his blue eyes dancing. 'I'm goin' to catch *him*.'

A certain hidden hearer instantly made up her mind to rush out between the two young men and be a heroine.

'*Non, non!*' exclaimed M. D'Hemecourt excitedly. 'Nod in de Café des Exilés—nod now, Madjor. Go in dad door, hif you pliz, Madjor. You will heer 'im w'at he 'ave to say. Mague you'sev de troub'. Nod dad door—diz one.'

The Major laughed again and started toward the door indicated, but in an instant stopped.

'I can't go in theyre,' he said. 'That's yer daughter's room.'

'*Oui, oui, mais!*' cried the other softly, but Mazaro's step was near.

'I'll just slip in heer,' and the amused Shaughnessy tripped lightly to the closet door, drew it open in spite of a momentary resistance from within which he had no time to notice, stepped into a small recess full of shelves and bottles, shut the door, and stood face to face – the broad moonlight shining upon her through a small, high-grated opening on one side – with Pauline. At the same instant the voice of the young Cuban sounded in the room.

Pauline was in a great tremor. She made as if she would have opened the door and fled, but the Irishman gave a gesture of earnest protest and reassurance. The re-opened door might make the back parlor of the Café des Exilés a scene of blood. Thinking of this, what could she do? She stayed.

'You goth a heap-a thro-vle, Señor,' said Manuel Mazaro, taking the seat so lately vacated. He had patted M. D'Hemecourt tenderly on the back and the old gentleman had flinched; hence the remark, to which there was no reply.

'Was a bee crowth a' the Café the Réfugiés,' continued the young man.

'Bud, w'ere dad Madjor Shaughnessy?' demanded M. D'Hemecourt, with the little sternness he could command.

'Mayor Shaughness' – yez-a; was there; boat-a,' with a disparaging smile and shake of the head, '*he* woon-a come-a to you, Señor. Oh, no.'

The old man smiled bitterly.

'*Non?*' he asked.

'Oh, no, Señor!' Mazaro drew his chair closer. 'Señor' – he paused – 'eez a-vary bath-a fore-a you thaughter, eh?'

'W'at?' asked the host, snapping like a tormented dog.

'D-theze talkin' 'bou',' answered the young man; 'd-theze coffee howces noth a goo' plaze-a fore hor, eh?'

The Irishman and the maiden looked into each other's eyes an instant, as people will do when listening; but Pauline's immediately fell, and when Mazaro's words were understood, her blushes became visible even by moonlight.

'He's r-right!' emphatically whispered Galahad.

She attempted to draw back a step, but found herself against the shelves. M. D'Hemecourt had not answered. Mazaro spoke again.

'Boat-a you canno' help-a, eh? I know, 'out-a she gettin' marry, eh?'

Pauline trembled. Her father summoned all his force and rose as if to ask his questioner to leave him; but the handsome Cuban motioned him down with a gesture that seemed to beg for only a moment more.

'Señor, if a-was one man whath lo-va you' thauther, all is possiblee to lo-va.'

Pauline, nervously braiding some bits of wire which she had unconsciously taken from a shelf, glanced up – against her will – into the eyes of Galahad. They were looking so steadily down upon her that with a great leap of the heart for joy she closed her own and half-turned away. But Mazaro had not ceased.

'All is possiblee to lo-va, Señor, you shouth-a let marry hor an' tak'n 'way frone d'these plaze, Señor.'

'Manuel Mazaro,' said M. D'Hemecourt, again rising, 'you 'ave say enough.'

'No, no, Señor; no, no; I want tell-a you – is a-one man – *whath lo-va* you' thaughter; an' I *knowce* him!'

Was there no cause for quarrel, after all? Could it be that Mazaro was about to speak for Galahad?

'Madjor Shaughnessy?'

Mazaro smiled mockingly.

'Mayor Shaughness',' he said; 'oh, no; not Mayor Shaughness'!'

Pauline could stay no longer; escape she must, though it be in Manuel Mazaro's very face. Turning again and looking up into Galahad's face in a great fright, she opened her lips to speak, but—

'Mayor Shaughness',' continued the Cuban; '*he* nev'r-a lo-va you' thaughter.'

Galahad was putting the maiden back from the door with his hand.

'Pauline,' he said, 'it's a lie!'

'An', Señor,' pursued the Cuban, 'if a was possiblee you' thaughter to lo-va heem, a-wouth-a be worse-a kine in worlt; but, Señor, I—'

M. D'Hemecourt made a majestic sign for silence. He had resumed his chair, but he rose up once more, took the Cuban's hat from the table, and tendered it to him.

'Manuel Mazaro, you 'ave—'

'Señor, I goin' tell you—'

'Manuel Mazaro, you—'

'Boat-a, Señor—'

'Bud, Manuel Maz—'

'Señor, escuse-a me—'

'Huzh!' cried the old man. 'Manuel Mazaro, you 'ave desceive' me! You 'ave *mocque* me, Manu—'

'Señor,' cried Mazaro, 'I swear-a to you that all-a what I sayin' ees-a—'

He stopped aghast. Galahad and Pauline stood before him.

'Is what?' asked the blue-eyed man, with a look of quiet delight on his face, such as Mazaro instantly remembered to have seen on it one night when Galahad was being shot at in the Sucking Calf Restaurant in St Peter Street.

The table was between them, but Mazaro's hand went upward toward the back of his coat collar.

'Ah, ah!' cried the Irishman, shaking his head with a broader smile and thrusting his hand threateningly into his breast; 'don't ye do that! Just finish yer speech.'

'Was-a notthin',' said the Cuban, trying to smile back.

'Yer a liur,' said Galahad.

'No,' said Mazaro, still endeavoring to smile through his agony; 'z-was on'y tellin' Señor D'Hemecourt someteen z-was t-thrue.'

'And I tell ye,' said Galahad, 'ye'r a liur, and to be so kind an' get yersel' to the front stoop, as I'm desiruz o' kickin' ye before the crowd.'

'Madjor!' cried D'Hemecourt—

'Go,' said Galahad, advancing a step toward the Cuban.

Had Manuel Mazaro wished to impersonate the prince of darkness, his beautiful face had the correct expresson for it. He slowly turned, opened the door into the café, sent one glowering look behind, and disappeared.

Pauline laid her hand upon her lover's arm.

'Madjor,' began her father.

'Oh, Madjor and Madjor,' said the Irishman; 'Munsher D'Hemecourt, just say "Madjor, heer's a gude wife fur ye," and I'll let the little serpent go.'

Thereupon, sure enough, both M. D'Hemecourt and his daughter, rushing together, did what I have been hoping all along, for the reader's sake, they would have dispensed with; they burst into tears; whereupon the Major, with his Irish appreciation of the ludicrous, turned away to hide his smirk and began good-humoredly to scratch himself first on the temple and then on the thigh.

Mazaro passed silently through the group about the doorsteps, and not many minutes afterward, Galahad Shaughnessy, having taken a place among the exiles, rose with the remark that the old gentleman would doubtless be willing to tell them good night. Good night was accordingly said, the Café des Exilés closed her windows, then her doors, winked a moment or two through the cracks in the shutters, and then went fast asleep.

The Mexican physician, at Galahad's request, told Mazaro that at the next meeting of the burial society he might and must occupy his accustomed seat without fear of molestation; and he did so.

The meeting took place some seven days after the affair in the back parlor, and on the same ground. Business being finished, Galahad, who presided, stood up, looking, in his white duck suit among his darkly clad companions, like a white sheep among black ones, and begged leave to order 'dlasses' from the front room. I say among black sheep; yet, I suppose, than that double row of languid, effeminate faces, one would have been taxed to find a more harmless-looking company. The glasses were brought and filled.

'Gentlemen,' said Galahad, 'comrades, this may be the last time we ever meet together an unbroken body.'

Martinez of Santo Domingo, he of the horrible experience, nodded with a lurking smile, curled a leg under him, and clasped his fingers behind his head.

'Who knows,' continued the speaker, 'but Señor Benito, though strong and sound and har'ly thirty-seven' – here all smiled – 'may be taken ill tomorrow?'

Martinez smiled across to the tall, gray Benito on Galahad's left, and he, in turn, smilingly showed to the company a thin, white line of teeth between his moustachios like distant reefs.

'Who knows,' the young Irishman proceeded to inquire, 'I say, who knows but Pedro, theyre, may be struck wid a fever?'

Pedro, a short, compact man of thoroughly mixed blood, and with an eyebrow cut away, whose surname no one knew, smiled his acknowledgments.

'Who knows?' resumed Galahad, when those who understood

English had explained in Spanish to those who did not, 'but they may soon need the services not only of our good doctor heer, but of our society; and that Fernandez and Benigno, and Gonzalez and Dominguez, may not be chosen to see, on that very schooner lying at the Picayune Tier just now, their beloved remains and so forth safely delivered into the hands and lands of their people. I say, who knows bur it may be so!'

The company bowed graciously as who should say, 'Well-turned phrases, Señor – well-turned.'

'And *amigos*, if so be that such is their approoching fate, I will say:'

He lifted his glass, and the rest did the same.

'I say, I will say to them, Creoles, countrymen, and lovers, boun voyadge an' good luck to ye's.'

For several moments there was much translating, bowing and murmured acknowledgments; Mazaro said: '*Bueno!*' and all around among the long double rank of moustachioed lips amiable teeth were gleaming, some white, some brown, some yellow, like bones in the grass.

'And now, gentlemen,' Galahad recommenced, 'fellow-exiles, once more. Munsher D'Himecourt, it was yer practice, until lately, to reward a good talker with a dlass from the hands o yer daughter.' (*Si, si!*) 'I'm bur a poor speaker.' (*Si, si, Señor, z-a-fine-a kin'-a can be; si!*) 'However, I'll ask ye, not knowun bur it may be the last time we all meet together, if ye will not let the goddess of the Café des Exilés grace our company with her presence for just about one minute?' (*Yez-a, Señor; si; yez-a-oui.*)

Every head was turned toward the old man, nodding the echoed request.

'Ye see, friends,' said Galahad in a true Irish whisper, as M. D'Hemecourt left the apartment, 'her poseetion has been a-growin' more and more embarrassin' daily, and the operaytions of our society were likely to make it wurse in the future; wherefore I have lately taken steps – I say I tuke steps this morn to relieve the old gentleman's distresses and his daughter's—'

He paused. M. D'Hemecourt entered with Pauline, and the exiles all rose up. Ah! But why say again she was lovely?

Galahad stepped forward to meet her, took her hand, led her to the head of the board, and, turning to the company, said:

'Friends and fellow patriots, Mishtress Shaughnessy.'

There was no outburst of astonishment – only the same old

bowing, smiling, and murmuring of compliment. Galahad turned with a puzzled look to M. D'Hemecourt, and guessed the truth. In the joy of an old man's heart he had already that afternoon told the truth to each and every man separately, as a secret too deep for them to reveal, but too sweet for him to keep. The Major and Pauline were man and wife.

The last laugh that was ever heard in the Café des Exilés sounded softly through the room.

'Lads,' said the Irishman. 'Fill yer dlasses. Here's to the Café des Exilés, God bless her!'

And the meeting slowly adjourned.

Two days later, signs and rumors of sickness began to find place about the Café des Réfugiés, and the Mexican physician made three calls in one day. It was said by the people around that the tall Cuban gentleman named Benito was very sick in one of the back rooms. A similar frequency of the same physician's calls was noticed about the Café des Exilés.

'The man with one eyebrow,' said the neighbors, 'is sick. Pauline left the house yesterday to make room for him.

'Ah! Is it possible?'

'Yes, it is really true; she and her husband. She took her mockingbird with her; he carried it; he came back alone.'

On the next afternoon the children about the Café des Réfugiés enjoyed the spectacle of the invalid Cuban moved on a trestle to the Café des Exilés, although he did not look so deathly sick as they could have liked to see him, and on the fourth morning the doors of the Café des Exilés remained closed. A black-bordered funeral notice, veiled with crepe, announced that the great Caller-home of exiles had served his summons upon Don Pedro Hernandez (surname borrowed for the occasion), and Don Carlos Mendez y Benito.

The hour for the funeral was fixed at 4 P.M. It never took place. Down at the Picayune Tier on the riverbank there was, about two o'clock that same day, a slight commotion, and those who stood aimlessly about a small, neat schooner, said she was 'seized.' At four there suddenly appeared before the Café des Exilés a squad of men with silver crescents on their breasts – police officers. The old cottage sat silent with closed doors, the crepe hanging heavily over the funeral notice like a widow's veil, the little unseen garden sending up odors from its hidden censers, and the old weeping willows bending over all.

'Nobody here?' asks the leader.

The crowd which has gathered stares without answering.

As quietly and peaceably as possible the officers pry open the door. They enter, and the crowd pushes in after. There are the two coffins, looking very heavy and solid, lying in state but unguarded.

The crowd draws a breath of astonishment. 'Are they going to wrench the tops off with hatchet and chisel?'

Rap, rap, rap; wrench, rap, wrench. Ah! The cases come open.

'Well kept?' asks the leader flippantly.

'Oh yes,' is the reply. And then all laugh.

One of the lookers on pushes up and gets a glimpse within.

'What is it?' ask the other idlers.

He tells one quietly.

'What did he say?' ask the rest, one of another.

'He says they are not dead men, but new muskets—'

'Here, clear out!' cries an officer, and the loiterers fall back and by and by straggle off.

The exiles? What became of them, do you ask? Why, nothing; they were not troubled, but they never all came together again. Said a chief of police to Major Shaughnessy years afterward:

'Major, there was only one thing that kept your expedition from succeeding – you were too sly about it. Had you come out flat and said what you were doing, we'd never a-said a word to you. But that little fellow gave us the wink, and then we had to stop you.'

And was no one punished? Alas, one was. Poor, pretty, curly-headed, traitorous Mazaro! He was drawn out of the Carondelet Canal – cold, dead! And when his wounds were counted – they were just the number of the Café des Exilés' children, less Galahad. But the mother – that is, the old café – did not see it; she had gone up the night before in a chariot of fire.

In the files of the old *Picayune* and *Price-Current* of 1837 may be seen the mention of Galahad Shaughnessy among the merchants –'our enterprising and accomplished fellow towns-man,' and all that. But old M. D'Hemecourt's name is cut in marble, and his citizenship is in 'a city whose maker and builder is God.'

Only yesterday I dined with the Shaughnessys – fine old couple and handsome. Their children sat about them and entertained me most pleasantly. But there isn't one can tell a tale as their father can — 'twas he told me this one, though here and there my enthusiasm may have taken liberties. He knows the history of every old house in the French Quarter; or, if he happens not to know a true one, he can make one up as he goes along.

1879

SARAH ORNE JEWETT
1849–1909

Poor Joanna

One evening my ears caught a mysterious allusion which Mrs Todd made to Shell-heap Island. It was a chilly night of cold northeasterly rain, and I made a fire for the first time in the Franklin stove in my room, and begged my two housemates to come in and keep me company. The weather had convinced Mrs Todd that it was time to make a supply of cough-drops, and she had been bringing forth herbs from dark and dry hiding-places, until now the pungent dust and odor of them had resolved themselves into one mighty flavor of spearmint that came from a simmering caldron of syrup in the kitchen. She called it done, and well done, and had ostentatiously left it to cool, and taken her knitting-work because Mrs Fosdick was busy with hers. They sat in the two rocking-chairs, the small woman and the large one, but now and then I could see that Mrs Todd's thoughts remained with the cough-drops. The time of gathering herbs was nearly over, but the time of syrups and cordials had begun.

The heat of the open fire made us a little drowsy, but something in the way Mrs Todd spoke of Shell-heap Island waked my interest. I waited to see if she would say any more, and then took a roundabout way back to the subject by saying what was first in my mind: that I wished the Green Island family were there to spend the evening with us – Mrs Todd's mother and her brother William.

Mrs Todd smiled, and drummed on the arm of the rocking-chair. 'Might scare William to death,' she warned me; and Mrs Fosdick mentioned her intention of going out to Green Island to stay two or three days, if this wind didn't make too much sea.

'Where is Shell-heap Island?' I ventured to ask, seizing the opportunity.

'Bears nor'east somewheres about three miles from Green Island; right off-shore, I should call it about eight miles out,' said Mrs Todd. 'You never was there, dear; 't is off the thoroughfares, and a very bad place to land at best.'

'I should think 't was,' agreed Mrs Fosdick, smoothing down her black silk apron. ' 'T is a place worth visitin' when you once get there. Some o' the old folks was kind o' fearful about it. 'T was 'counted a great place in old Indian times; you can pick up their stone tools 'most any time if you hunt about. There's a beautiful spring o' water, too. Yes, I remember when they used to tell queer stories about Shell-heap Island. Some said 't was a great bangeing-place for the Indians, and an old chief resided there once that ruled the winds; and others said they'd always heard that once the Indians come down from up country an' left a captive there without any bo't, an' 't was too far to swim across to Black Island, so called, an' he lived there till he perished.'

'I've heard say he walked the island after that, and sharp-sighted folks could see him an' lose him like one o' them citizens Cap'n Littlepage was acquainted with up to the north pole,' announced Mrs Todd grimly. 'Anyway, there was Indians – you can see their shell-heap that named the island; and I've heard myself that 't was one o' their cannibal places, but I never could believe it. There never was no cannibals on the coast o' Maine. All the Indians o' these regions are tame-looking folks.'

'Sakes alive, yes!' exclaimed Mrs Fosdick. 'Ought to see them painted savages I've seen when I was young out in the South Sea Islands! That was the time for folks to travel, 'way back in the old whalin' days!'

'Whalin' must have been dull for a lady, hardly ever makin' a lively port, and not takin' any mixed cargoes,' said Mrs Todd. 'I never desired to go a whalin' v'y'ge myself.'

'I used to return feelin' very slack an' behind the times, 't is true,' explained Mrs Fosdick, 'but 't was excitin', an' we always done extra well, and felt rich when we did get ashore. I liked the variety. There, how times have changed; how few seafarin' families there are left! What a lot o' queer folks there used to be about here, anyway, when we was young, Almiry. Everybody's just like everybody else, now; nobody to laugh about, and nobody to cry about.'

It seemed to me that there were peculiarities of character in the region of Dunnet Landing yet, but I did not like to interrupt.

'Yes,' said Mrs Todd after a moment of meditation, 'there was certain a good many curiosities of human natur' in this neighbor-hood years ago. There was more energy then, and in some the energy took a singular turn. In these days the young folks is all copy-cats, 'fraid to death they won't be all just alike; as for the old folks, they pray for the advantage o' bein' a little different.'

'I ain't heard of a copy-cat this great many years,' said Mrs Fosdick laughing; ' 't was a favorite term o' my grandmother's. No, I wa'n't thinking o' those things, but of them strange straying creatur's that used to rove the country. You don't see them now, or the ones that used to hive away in their own houses with some strange notion or other.'

I thought again of Captain Littlepage, but my companions were not reminded of his name; and there was brother William at Green Island, whom we all three knew.

'I was talking o' poor Joanna the other day. I had n't thought of her for a great while,' said Mrs Fosdick abruptly. 'Mis' Brayton an' I recalled her as we sat together sewing. She was one o' your peculiar persons, wa'n't she? Speaking of such persons,' she turned to explain to me, 'there was a sort of a nun or hermit person lived out there for years all alone on Shell-heap Island. Miss Joanna Todd, her name was – a cousin o' Almiry's late husband.'

I expressed my interest, but as I glanced at Mrs Todd I saw that she was confused by sudden affectionate feeling and unmistakable desire for reticence.

'I never want to hear Joanna laughed about,' she said anxiously. _VIRGIN_

'Nor I,' answered Mrs Fosdick reassuringly. 'She was crossed in love – that was all the matter to begin with; but as I look back, I can see that Joanna was doomed from the first fall into a melancholy. She retired from the world for good an' all, though she was a well-off woman. All she wanted was to get away from folks; she thought she wasn't fit to live with anybody, and wanted to be free. Shell-heap Island come to her from her father, and first thing folks knew she'd gone off out there to live, and left word she didn't want no company. 'T was a bad place to get to, unless the wind an' tide were just right; 't was hard work to make a landing.'

'What time of year was this?' I asked.

'Very late in the summer,' said Mrs Fosdick. 'No, I never could laugh at Joanna, as some did. She set everything by the young man, an' they were going to marry in about a month, when he got bewitched by a girl 'way up the bay, and married her, and went off to Massachusetts. He wasn't well thought of – there were those who thought Joanna's money was what had tempted him; but she'd given him her whole heart, an' she wa'n't so young as she had been. All her hopes were built on marryin', an' havin' a real home and somebody to look to; she acted just like a bird when its nest is spoilt. The day after she heard the news she was in dreadful woe, but the next she came to herself very quiet, and took the horse and wagon, and drove fourteen miles to the lawyer's, and signed a paper givin' her half of the farm to her brother. They never had got along very well together, but he didn't want to sign it, till she acted so distressed that he gave in. Edward Todd's wife was a good woman, who felt very bad indeed, and used every argument with Joanna; but Joanna took a poor old boat that had been her father's and lo'ded in a few things, and off she put all alone, with a good land breeze, right out to sea. Edward Todd ran down to the beach, an' stood there cryin' like a boy to see her go, but she was out o' hearin'. She never stepped foot on the mainland again long as she lived.'

'How large an island is it? How did she manage in winter?' I asked.

'Perhaps thirty acres, rocks and all,' answered Mrs Todd, taking up the story gravely. 'There can't be much of it that the salt spray don't fly over in storms. No, 't is a dreadful small place to make a world of; it has a different look from any of the other islands, but there's a sheltered cove on the south side, with mud-flats across one end of it at low water where there's excellent clams, and the big shell-heap keeps some o' the wind off a little house her father took the trouble to build when he was a young man. They said there was an old house built o' logs there before that, with a kind of natural cellar in the rock under it. He used to stay out there days to a time, and anchor a little sloop he had, and dig clams to fill it, and sail up to Portland. They said the dealers always gave him an extra price, the clams were so noted. Joanna used to go out and stay with him. They were always great companions, so she knew just what 't was out there. There was a few sheep that belonged to her brother an' her, but she bargained for him to come and get them on the edge o' cold weather. Yes, she desired him to come for the sheep; an' his wife thought perhaps Joanna 'd return, but he said no, an' lo'ded the bo't with warm things an' what he thought she'd need through the winter. He come home with the sheep an' left the other things by the house, but she never so much as looked out o' the window. She done it for a penance. She must have wanted to see Edward by that time.'

Mrs Fosdick was fidgeting with eagerness to speak.

'Some thought the first cold snap would set her ashore, but she always remained,' concluded Mrs Todd soberly.

'Talk about the men not having any curiosity!' exclaimed Mrs Fosdick scornfully. 'Why, the waters round Shell-heap Island were white with sails all that fall. 'T was never called no great of a fishin'-ground before. Many of 'em made excuse to go ashore to get water at the spring; but at last she spoke to a bo't-load, very dignified and calm, and said that she'd like it better if they'd make a practice of getting water to Black Island or somewheres else and leave her alone, except in case of accident or trouble. But there was one man who had always set everything by her from a boy. He'd have married her if the other had n't come about an' spoilt his chance, and he used to get close to the island, before light, on his way out fishin', and throw a little bundle 'way up the green slope front o' the house. His sister told me she happened to see, the first time, what a pretty choice he made o' useful things that a woman would feel lost without. He stood off fishin', and could see them in the grass all day, though sometimes she'd come out and walk right by them. There was other bo'ts near, out after mackerel. But early next morning his present was gone. He did n't presume too much, but once he took her a nice firkin o' things he got up to Portland, and when spring come he landed her a hen and chickens in a nice little coop. There was a good many old friends had Joanna on their minds.'

'Yes,' said Mrs Todd, losing her sad reserve in the growing sympathy of these reminiscences. 'How everybody used to notice whether there was smoke out of the chimney! The Black Island folks could see her with a spy-glass, and if they'd ever missed getting some sign o' life they'd have sent notice to her folks. But after the first year or two Joanna was more and more forgotten as an every-day charge. Folks lived very simple in those days, you know,' she continued, as Mrs Fosdick's knitting was taking much thought at the moment. 'I expect there was always plenty of driftwood thrown up, and a poor failin' patch of spruces covered all the north side of the island, so she always had something to burn. She was very fond of workin' in the garden ashore, and that first summer she began to till the little field out there, and raised a nice parcel o' potatoes. She could fish, o' course, and there was all her clams an' lobsters. You can always live well in any wild place by the sea when you'd starve to death up country, except 't was berry time. Joanna had berries out there, blackberries at least, and there was a few herbs in case she needed them. Mullein in great quantities and a plant o' wormwood I remember seeing once when I stayed there, long before she fled out to Shell-heap. Yes, I recall the wormwood, which is always a planted herb, so there must have been folks there before the Todds' day. A growin' bush makes the best gravestone; I expect that wormwood always stood for somebody's solemn monument. Catnip, too, is a very endurin' herb about an old place.'

'But what I want to know is what she did for other things,' interrupted Mrs Fosdick. 'Almiry, what did she do for clothin' when she needed to replenish, or risin' for her bread, or the piece-bag that no woman can live long without?'

'Or company,' suggested Mrs Todd. 'Joanna was one that loved her friends. There must have been a terrible sight o' long winter evenin's that first year.'

'There was her hens,' suggested Mrs Fosdick, after reviewing the melancholy situation. 'She never wanted the sheep after that first season. There wa'n't no proper pasture for sheep after the June grass was past, and she ascertained the fact and couldn't bear to see them suffer; but the chickens done well. I remember sailin' by one spring afternoon, an' seein' the coops out front o' the house in the sun. How long was it before you went out with the minister? You were the first ones that ever really got ashore to see Joanna.'

I had been reflecting upon a state of society which admitted such personal freedom and a voluntary hermitage. There was something mediæval in the behavior of poor Joanna Todd under a disappointment of the heart. The two women had drawn closer together, and were talking on, quite unconscious of the listener.

'Poor Joanna!' said Mrs Todd again, and sadly shook her head as if there were things one could not speak about. ——

'I called her a great fool,' declared Mrs Fosdick, with spirit, 'but I pitied her then, and I pity her far more now. Some other minister would have been a great help to her – one that preached self-forgetfulness and doin' for others to cure our own ills; but Parson Dimmick was a vague person, well meanin', but very numb in his feelin's. I don't suppose at that troubled time Joanna could think of any way to mend her troubles except to run off and hide.'

'Mother used to say she didn't see how Joanna lived without

having nobody to do for, getting her own meals and tending her own poor self day in an' day out,' said Mrs Todd sorrowfully.

'There was the hens,' repeated Mrs Fosdick kindly. 'I expect she soon came to makin' folks o' them. No, I never went to work to blame Joanna, as some did. She was full o' feeling, and her troubles hurt her more than she could bear. I see it all now as I couldn't when I was young.'

'I suppose in old times they had their shut-up convents for just such folks,' said Mrs Todd, as if she and her friend had disagreed about Joanna once, and were now in happy harmony. She seemed to speak with new openness and freedom. 'Oh yes, I was only too pleased when the Reverend Mr Dimmick invited me to go out with him. He hadn't been very long in the place when Joanna left home and friends. 'T was one day that next summer after she went, and I had been married early in the spring. He felt that he ought to go out and visit her. She was a member of the church, and might wish to have him consider her spiritual state. I wa'n't so sure o' that, but I always liked Joanna, and I'd come to be her cousin by marriage. Nathan an' I had conversed about goin' out to pay her a visit, but he got his chance to sail sooner 'n he expected. He always thought everything of her, and last time he come home, knowing nothing of her change, he brought her a beautiful coral pin from a port he'd touched at somewheres up the Mediterranean. So I wrapped the little box in a nice piece of paper and put it in my pocket, and picked her a bunch of fresh lemon balm, and off we started.'

Mrs Fosdick laughed. 'I remember hearin' about your trials on the v'y'ge,' she said.

'Why, yes,' continued Mrs Todd in her company manner. 'I picked her the balm, an' we started. Why, yes, Susan, the minister liked to have cost me my life that day. He would fasten the sheet, though I advised against it. He said the rope was rough an' cut his hand. There was a fresh breeze, an' he went on talking rather high flown, an' I felt some interested. All of a sudden there come up a gust, and he give a screech and stood right up and called for help, 'way out there to sea. I knocked him right over into the bottom o' the bo't, getting by to catch hold of the sheet an' untie it. He wasn't but a little man; I helped him right up after the squall passed, and made a handsome apology to him, but he did act kind o' offended.'

'I do think they ought not to settle them landlocked folks in parishes where they're liable to be on the water,' insisted Mrs Fosdick. 'Think of the families in our parish that was scattered all about the bay, and what a sight o' sails you used to see, in Mr Dimmick's day, standing across to the mainland on a pleasant Sunday morning, filled with church-going folks, all sure to want him some time or other! You couldn't find no doctor that would stand up in the boat and screech if a flaw struck her.'

'Old Dr Bennett had a beautiful sailboat, didn't he?' responded Mrs Todd. 'And how well he used to brave the weather! Mother always said that in time o' trouble that tall white sail used to look like an angel's wing comin' over the sea to them that was in pain. Well, there's a difference in gifts. Mr Dimmick was not without light.'

' 'T was light o' the moon, then,' snapped Mrs Fosdick; 'he was pompous enough, but I never could remember a single word he said. There, go on, Mis' Todd; I forget a great deal about that day you went to see poor Joanna.'

'I felt she saw us coming, and knew us a great way off; yes, I seemed to feel it within me,' said our friend, laying down her knitting. 'I kept my seat, and took the bo't inshore without saying a word; there was a short channel that I was sure Mr Dimmick wasn't acquainted with, and the tide was very low. She never came out to warn us off nor anything, and I thought, as I hauled the bo't up on a wave and let the Reverend Mr Dimmick step out, that it was somethin' gained to be safe ashore. There was a little smoke out o' the chimney o' Joanna's house, and it did look sort of homelike and pleasant with wild mornin'-glory vines trained up; an' there was a plot o' flowers under the front window, portulacas and things. I believe she'd made a garden once, when she was stopping there with her father, and some things must have seeded in. It looked as if she might have gone over to the other side of the island. 'T was neat and pretty all about the house, and a lovely day in July. We walked up from the beach together very sedate, and I felt for poor Nathan's little pin to see if 't was safe in my dress pocket. All of a sudden Joanna come right to the fore door and stood there, not sayin' a word.'

My companions and I had been so intent upon the subject of the conversation that we had not heard any one open the gate, but at this moment, above the noise of the rain, we heard a loud knocking. We were all startled as we sat by the fire, and Mrs Todd rose hastily and went to answer the call, leaving her rocking-chair in violent motion. Mrs Fosdick and I heard an anxious voice at the door speaking of a sick child, and Mrs Todd's kind, motherly voice inviting the messenger in: then we waited in silence. There was a sound of heavy dropping of rain from the eaves, and the distant roar and undertone of the sea. My thoughts flew back to the lonely woman on her outer island; what separation from humankind she must have felt, what terror and sadness, even in a summer storm like this!

'You send right after the doctor if she ain't better in half an hour,' said Mrs Todd to her worried customer as they parted; and I felt a warm sense of comfort in the evident resources of even so small a neighborhood, but for the poor hermit Joanna there was no neighbor on a winter night.

'How did she look?' demanded Mrs Fosdick, without preface, as our large hostess returned to the little room with a mist about her from standing long in the wet doorway, and the sudden draught of her coming beat out the smoke and flame from the Franklin stove. 'How did poor Joanna look?'

'She was the same as ever, except I thought she looked smaller,' answered Mrs Todd after thinking a moment; perhaps it was only a last considering thought about her patient. 'Yes, she was just the same, and looked very nice, Joanna did. I had been married since she left home, an' she treated me like her own folks. I expected she'd look strange, with her hair turned gray in a night or somethin', but she wore a pretty gingham dress I'd often seen her wear before she went away; she must have kept it nice for best in the afternoons. She always had beautiful, quiet manners. I remember she waited till we were close to her, and then kissed me real affectionate, and inquired for Nathan before she shook hands with the minister, and then she invited us both in. 'T was the same little house her father had built him when he was a bachelor, with one livin'-room, and a little mite of a bedroom out of it where she slept, but 't was neat as a ship's cabin. There was some old chairs, an' a seat made of a long box that might have held boat tackle an' things to lock up in his fishin' days, and a good enough stove so anybody could cook and keep warm in cold weather. I went over once from home and stayed 'most a week with Joanna when we was girls, and those young happy days rose up before me. Her father was busy all day fishin' or clammin'; he was one o' the pleasantest men in the world, but Joanna's mother had the grim streak, and never knew what 't was to be happy. The first minute my eyes fell upon Joanna's face I saw how she had grown to look like Mis' Todd. 'T was the mother right over again.'

'Oh dear me!' said Mrs Fosdick.

'Joanna had done one thing very pretty. There was a little piece o' swamp on the island where good rushes grew plenty, and she'd gathered 'em, and braided some beautiful mats for the floor and a thick cushion for the long bunk. She'd showed a good deal of invention; you see there was a nice chance to pick up pieces o' wood and boards that drove ashore, and she'd made good use o' what she found. There wasn't no clock, but she had a few dishes on a shelf, and flowers set about in shells fixed to the walls, so it did look sort of homelike, though so lonely and poor. I couldn't keep the tears out o' my eyes, I felt so sad. I said to myself, I must get mother to come over an' see Joanna; the love in mother's heart would warm her, an' she might be able to advise.'

'Oh no, Joanna was dreadful stern,' said Mrs Fosdick.

'We were all settin' down very proper, but Joanna would keep stealin' glances at me as if she was glad I come. She had but little to say; she was real polite an' gentle, and yet forbiddin'. The minister found it hard,' confessed Mrs Todd; 'he got embarrassed, an' when he put on his authority and asked her if she felt to enjoy religion in her present situation, an' she replied that she must be excused from answerin', I thought I should fly. She might have made it easier for him; after all, he was the minister and had taken some trouble to come out, though 't was kind of cold an' unfeelin' the way he inquired. I thought he might have seen the little old Bible a-layin' on the shelf close by him, an' I wished he knew enough just to lay his hand on it an' read somethin' kind an' fatherly 'stead of accusin' her, an' then given poor Joanna his blessin' with the hope she might be led to comfort. He did offer prayer, but 't was all about hearin' the voice o' God out o' the whirlwind; and I thought while he was goin' on that anybody that had spent the long cold winter all alone out on Shell-heap Island knew a good deal more about those things than he did. I got so provoked I opened my eyes and stared right at him.

'She didn't take no notice, she kep' a nice respectful manner towards him, and when there come a pause she asked if he had any interest about the old Indian remains, and took down some queer stone gouges and hammers off of one of her shelves and showed them to him same 's if he was a boy. He remarked that he'd like to walk over an' see the shell-heap; so she went right to the door and pointed him the way. I see then that she'd made her some kind o' sandal-shoes out o' the fine rushes to wear on her feet; she stepped light an' nice in 'em as shoes.'

Mrs Fosdick leaned back in her rocking-chair and gave a heavy sigh.

'I didn't move at first, but I'd held out just as long as I could,' said Mrs Todd, whose voice trembled a little. 'When Joanna returned from the door, an' I could see that man's stupid back departin' among the wild rose bushes, I just ran to her an' caught her in my arms. I wasn't so big as I be now, and she was older than me, but I hugged her tight, just as if she was a child. "Oh, Joanna dear," I says, "won't you come ashore an' live 'long o' me at the Landin', or go over to Green Island to mother's when winter comes? Nobody shall trouble you, an' mother finds it hard bein' alone. I can't bear to leave you here" – and I burst right out crying. I'd had my own trials, young as I was, an' she knew it. Oh, I did entreat her; yes, I entreated Joanna.'

'What did she say then?' asked Mrs Fosdick, much moved.

'She looked the same way, sad an' remote through it all,' said Mrs Todd mournfully. She took hold of my hand, and we sat down close together; 't was as if she turned round an' made a child of me. "I haven't got no right to live with folks no more," she said. "You must never ask me again, Almiry: I've done the only thing I could do, and I've made my choice. I feel a great comfort in your kindness, but I don't deserve it. I have committed the unpardonable sin; you don't understand," says she humbly. "I was in great wrath and trouble, and my thoughts was so wicked towards God that I can't expect ever to be forgiven. I have come to know what it is to have patience, but I have lost my hope. You must tell those that ask how 't is with me," she said, "an' tell them I want to be alone." I could n't speak; no, there wa'n't anything I could say, she seemed so above everything common. I was a good deal younger then than I be now, and I got Nathan's little coral pin out o' my pocket and put it into her hand; and when she saw it and I told her where it come from, her face did really light up for a minute, sort of bright an' pleasant. "Nathan an' I was always good friends; I'm glad he don't think hard of me," says she. "I want you to have it, Almiry, an' wear it for love o' both o' us," and she handed it back to me. "You give my love to Nathan – he's a dear good man," she said; "an' tell your mother, if I should be sick she mustn't wish I could get well, but I want her to be the one to come." Then she seemed to have said all she wanted to, as if she was done with the world, and we sat there a few minutes longer together. It was real sweet and quiet except for a good many birds and the sea rollin' up on the beach; but at last she rose, an' I did too, and she kissed me and held my hand in hers a minute, as if to say good-by; then she turned and went right away out o' the door and disappeared.

'The minister come back pretty soon, and I told him I was ready, and we started down to the bo't. He had picked up some round stones and things and was carrying them in his pocket-handkerchief; an' he sat down amidships without making any question, and let me take the rudder an' work the bo't, an' made no remarks for some time, until we sort of eased it off speaking of the weather, an' subjects that arose as we skirted Black Island, where two or three families lived belongin' to the parish. He preached next Sabbath as usual, somethin' high soundin' about creation, and I couldn't help thinkin' he might never get no further; he seemed to know no remedies, but he had a great use of words.'

Mrs Fosdick sighed again. 'Hearin' you tell about Joanna brings the time right back as if 't was yesterday,' she said. 'Yes, she was one o' them poor things that talked about the great sin; we don't seem to hear nothing about the unpardonable sin now, but you may say't was not uncommon then.'

'I expect that if it had been in these days, such a person would be plagued to death with idle folks,' continued Mrs Todd, after a long pause. 'As it was, nobody trespassed on her; all the folks about the bay respected her an' her feelings; but as time wore on, after you left here, one after another ventured to make occasion to put somethin' ashore for her if they went that way. I know mother used to go to see her sometimes, and send William over now and then with something fresh an' nice from the farm. There is a point on the sheltered side where you can lay a boat close to shore an' land anything safe on the turf out o' reach o' the water. There were one or two others, old folks, that she would see, and now an' then she'd hail a passin' boat an' ask for somethin'; and mother got her to promise that she would make some sign to the Black Island folk if she wanted help. I never saw her myself to speak to after that day.'

'I expect nowadays, if such a thing happened, she'd have gone out West to her uncle's folks or up to Massachusetts and had a change, an' come home good as new. The world's bigger an' freer than it used to be,' urged Mrs Fosdick.

'No,' said her friend. ' 'T is like bad eyesight, the mind of such a person: if your eyes don't see right there may be a remedy, but there's no kind of glasses to remedy the mind. No, Joanna was Joanna, and there she lays on her island where she lived and did her poor penance. She told mother the day she was dyin' that she always used to want to be fetched inshore when it come to the last; but she'd thought it over, and desired to be laid on the island, if 't was thought right. So the funeral was out there, a Saturday afternoon in September. 'Twas a pretty day, and there wa'n't hardly a boat on the coast within twenty miles that didn't head for Shell-heap cram-full o' folks, an' all real respectful, same 's if she'd always stayed ashore and held her friends. Some went out o' mere curiosity, I don't doubt – there's always such to every funeral; but most had real feelin', and went purpose to show it. She'd got most o' the wild sparrows as tame as could be, livin' out there so long among 'em, and one flew right in and lit on the coffin an' began to sing while Mr Dimmick was speakin'. He was put out by it, an' acted as if he didn't know whether to stop or go on. I may have been prejudiced, but I wa'n't the only one thought the poor little bird done the best of the two.'

'What became o' the man that treated her so, did you ever hear?' asked Mrs Fosdick. 'I know he lived up to Massachusetts for a while. Somebody who came from the same place told me that he was in trade there an' doin' very well, but that was years ago.'

'I never heard anything more than that; he went to the war in one o' the early rigiments. No, I never heard any more of him,' answered Mrs Todd. 'Joanna was another sort of person, and perhaps he showed good judgment in marryin' somebody else, if only he'd behaved straightforward and manly. He was a shifty-eyed, coaxin' sort of man, that got what he wanted out o' folks, an' only gave when he wanted to buy, made friends easy and lost 'em without knowin' the difference. She'd had a piece o' work tryin' to make him walk accordin' to her right ideas, but she'd have had too much variety ever to fall into a melancholy. Some is meant to be the Joannas in this world, an' 't was her poor lot.'

1896

A Shameful Affair

Mildred Orme, seated in the snuggest corner of the big front porch of the Kraummer farmhouse, was as content as a girl need hope to be.

This was no such farm as one reads about in humorous fiction. Here were swelling acres where the undulating wheat gleamed in the sun like a golden sea. For silver there was the Meramec – or, better, it was pure crystal, for here and there one might look clean through it down to where the pebbles lay like green and yellow gems. Along the river's edge trees were growing to the very water, and in it, sweeping it when they were willows.

The house itself was big and broad, as country houses should be. The master was big and broad, too. The mistress was small and thin, and it was always she who went out at noon to pull the great clanging bell that called the farmhands to dinner.

From her agreeable corner where she lounged with her Browning or her Ibsen, Mildred watched the woman do this every day. Yet when the clumsy farmhands all came tramping up the steps and crossed the porch in going to their meal that was served within, she never looked at them. Why should she? Farmhands are not so very nice to look at, and she was nothing of an anthropologist. But once when the half dozen men came along, a paper which she had laid carelessly upon the railing was blown across their path. One of them picked it up, and when he had mounted the steps restored it to her. He was young, and brown, of course, as the sun had made him. He had nice blue eyes. His fair hair was dishevelled. His shoulders were broad and square and his limbs strong and clean. A not unpicturesque figure in the rough attire that bared his throat to view and gave perfect freedom to his every motion.

Mildred did not make these several observations in the half second that she looked at him in courteous acknowledgment. It took her as many days to note them all. For she signaled him out each time that he passed her, meaning to give him a condescending little smile, as she knew how. But he never looked at her. To be sure, clever young women of twenty, who are handsome, besides, who have refused their half dozen offers and are settling down to the conviction that life is a tedious affair, are not going to care a straw whether farmhands look at them or not. And Mildred did not care, and the thing would not have occupied her a moment if Satan had not intervened, in offering the employment which natural conditions had failed to supply. It was summer time; she was idle; she was piqued, and that was the beginning of the shameful affair.

'Who are these men, Mrs Kraummer, that work for you? Where do you pick them up?'

'Oh, ve picks 'em up everyvere. Some is neighbors, some is tramps, and so.'

'And that broad-shouldered young fellow – is he a neighbor? The one who handed me my paper the other day – you remember?'

'Gott, no! You might yust as well say he vas a tramp. Aber he vorks like a steam ingine.'

'Well, he's an extremely disagreeable-looking man. I should think you'd be afraid to have him about, not knowing him.'

'Vat you vant to be 'fraid for?' laughed the little woman. 'He don't talk no more un ven he vas deef und dumb. I didnt t'ought you vas sooch a baby.'

'But, Mrs Kraummer, I don't want you to think I'm a baby, as you say – a coward, as you mean. Ask the man if he will drive me to church tomorrow. You see, I'm not so very much afraid of him,' she added with a smile.

The answer which this unmannerly farmhand returned to Mildred's request was simply a refusal. He could not drive her to church because he was going fishing.

'Aber,' offered good Mrs Kraummer, 'Hans Platzfeldt will drive you to church, oder vereever you vants. He vas a goot boy vat you can trust, dat Hans.'

'Oh, thank him very much. But I find I have so many letters to write tomorrow, and it promises to be hot, too. I shan't care to go to church after all.'

She could have cried for vexation. Snubbed by a farmhand! a tramp, perhaps. She, Mildred Orme, who ought really to have been with the rest of the family at Narragansett – who had come to seek in this retired spot the repose that would enable her to follow exalted lines of thought. She marvelled at the problematic nature of farmhands.

After sending her the uncivil message already recorded, and as he passed beneath the porch where she sat, he did look at her finally, in a way to make her positively gasp at the sudden effrontery of the man.

But the inexplicable look stayed with her. She could not banish it.

2

It was not so very hot after all, the next day, when Mildred walked down the long narrow footpath that led through the bending wheat to the river. High above her waist reached the yellow grain. Mildred's brown eyes filled with a reflected golden light as they caught the glint of it, as she heard the trill that it answered to the gentle breeze. Anyone who has walked through the wheat in midsummer-time knows that sound.

In the woods it was sweet and solemn and cool. And there beside the river was the wretch who had annoyed her, first, with his indifference, then with the sudden boldness of his glance.

'Are you fishing?' she asked politely and with kindly dignity, which she supposed would define her position toward him. The inquiry lacked not pertinence, seeing that he sat motionless, with a pole in his hand and his eyes fixed on a cork that bobbed aimlessly on the water.

'Yes, madam,' was his brief reply.

'It won't disturb you if I stand here a moment, to see what success you will have?'

'No, madam.'

She stood very still, holding tight to the book she had brought with her. Her straw hat had slipped disreputably to one side, over the wavy bronze-brown bang that half covered her forehead. Her cheeks were ripe with color that the sun had coaxed there; so were her lips.

All the other farmhands had gone forth in Sunday attire. Perhaps this one had none better than these working clothes that he wore. A feminine commiseration swept her at the thought. He spoke never a word. She wondered how many hours he could sit there, so patiently waiting for fish to come to his hook. For her part, the situation began to pall, and she wanted to change it at last.

'Let me try a moment, please? I have an idea—'

'Yes, madam.'

'The man is surely an idiot, with his monosyllables,' she commented inwardly. But she remembered that monosyllables belong to a boor's equipment.

She laid her book carefully down and took the pole gingerly that he came to place in her hands. Then it was his turn to stand back and look respectfully and silently on at the absorbing performance.

'Oh!' cried the girl, suddenly, seized with excitement upon seeing the line dragged deep in the water.

'Wait, wait! Not yet.'

He sprang to her side. With his eyes eagerly fastened on the tense line, he grasped the pole to prevent her drawing it, as her intention seemed to be. That is, he meant to grasp the pole, but instead, his brown hand came down upon Mildred's white one.

He started violently at finding himself so close to a bronze-brown tangle that almost swept his chin – to a hot cheek only a few inches away from his shoulder, to a pair of young, dark eyes that gleamed for an instant unconscious things into his own.

Then, why it ever happened, or how ever it happened, his arms were holding Mildred and he kissed her lips. She did not know if it was ten times or only once.

She looked around – her face milk-white – to see him disappear with rapid strides through the path that had brought her there. Then she was alone.

Only the birds had seen, and she could count on their discretion. She was not wildly indignant, as many would have been. Shame stunned her. But through it she gropingly wondered if she should tell the Kraummers that her chaste lips had been rifled of their innocence. Publish her own confusion? No! Once in her room she would give calm thought to the situation, and determine then how to act. The secret must remain her own: a hateful burden to bear alone until she could forget it.

3

And because she feared not to forget it, Mildred wept that night. All day long a hideous truth had been thrusting itself upon her that made her ask herself if she could be mad. She feared it. Else why was that kiss the most delicious thing she had known in her twenty years of life? The sting of it had never left her lips since it was pressed into them. The sweet trouble of it banished sleep from her pillow.

But Mildred would not bend the outward conditions of her life to serve any shameful whim that chanced to visit her soul, like an ugly dream. She would avoid nothing. She would go and come as always.

In the morning she found in her chair upon the porch the book she had left by the river. A fresh indignity! But she came and went as she intended to, and sat as usual upon the porch amid her familiar surroundings. When the Offender passed her by she knew it, though her eyes were never lifted. Are there only sight and sound to tell such things? She discerned it by a wave that swept her with confusion and she knew not what besides.

She watched him furtively, one day, when he talked with Farmer Kraummer out in the open. When he walked away she remained like one who has drunk much wine. Then unhesitatingly she turned and began her preparations to leave the Kraummer farmhouse.

When the afternoon was far spent they brought letters to her. One of them read like this:

'My Mildred, deary! I am only now at Narragansett, and so broke up not to find you. So you are down at that Kraummer farm, on the Iron Mountain. Well! What do you think of that delicious crank, Fred Evelyn? For a man must be a crank who does such things. Only fancy! Last year he chose to drive an engine back and forth across the plains. This year he tills the soil with laborers. Next year it will be something else as insane – because he likes to live more lives than one kind, and other Quixotic reasons. We are great chums. He writes me he's grown as strong as an ox. But he hasn't mentioned that you are there. I know you don't get on with him, for he isn't a bit intellectual – detests Ibsen and abuses Tolstoi. He doesn't read "in books" – says they are spectacles for the short-sighted to look at life through. Don't snub him, dear, or be too hard on him; he has a heart of gold, if he is the first crank in America.'

Mildred tried to think – to feel that the intelligence which this letter brought to her would take somewhat of the sting from the shame that tortured her. But it did not. She knew that it could not.

In the gathering twilight she walked again through the wheat that was heavy and fragrant with dew. The path was very long and very narrow. When she was midway she saw the Offender

coming toward her. What could she do? Turn and run, as a little
child might? Spring into the wheat, as some frightened four-
footed creature would? There was nothing but to pass him with
the dignity which the occasion clearly demanded.

But he did not let her pass. He stood squarely on the pathway
before her, hat in hand, a perturbed look upon his face.

'Miss Orme,' he said, 'I have wanted to say to you, every hour
of the past week, that I am the most consummate hound that
walks the earth.'

She made no protest. Her whole bearing seemed to indicate that
her opinion coincided with his own.

'If you have a father, or brother, or any one, in short, to whom
you may say such things—'

'I think you aggravate the offense, sir, by speaking of it. I shall
ask you never to mention it again. I want to forget that it ever
happened. Will you kindly let me by.'

'Oh,' he ventured eagerly, 'you want to forget it! Then, maybe,
since you are willing to forget, you will be generous enough to
forgive the offender some day?'

'Some day,' she repeated, almost inaudibly, looking seemingly
through him, but not at him – 'some day – perhaps; when I shall
have forgiven myself.'

He stood motionless, watching her slim, straight figure lessen-
ing by degrees as she walked slowly away from him. He was
wondering what she meant. Then a sudden, quick wave came
beating into his brown throat and staining it crimson, when he
guessed what it might be.

1893

The Storm

1

The leaves were so still that even Bibi thought it was going to rain. Bibinôt, who was accustomed to converse on terms of perfect equality with his little son, called the child's attention to certain sombre clouds that were rolling with sinister intention from the west, accompanied by a sullen, threatening roar. They were at Friedheimer's store and decided to remain there till the storm had passed. They sat within the door on two empty kegs. Bibi was four years old and looked very wise.

'Mama'll be 'fraid, yes,' he suggested with blinking eyes.

'She'll shut the house. Maybe she got Sylvie helpin' her this evenin',' Bobinôt responded reassuringly.

'No; she ent got Sylvie. Sylvie was helpin' her yistiday,' piped Bibi.

Bobinôt arose and going across to the counter purchased a can of shrimps, of which Calixta was very fond. Then he returned to his perch on the keg and sat stolidly holding the can of shrimps while the storm burst. It shook the wooden store and seemed to be ripping great furrows in the distant field. Bibi laid his little hand on his father's knee and was not afraid.

2

Calixta, at home, felt no uneasiness for their safety. She at at a side window sewing furiously on a sewing machine. She was greatly occupied and did not notice the approaching storm. But she felt very warm and often stopped to mop her face on which the perspiration gathered in beads. She unfastened her white sacque at the throat. It began to grow dark, and suddenly realizing the situation she got up hurriedly and went about closing windows and doors.

Out on the small front gallery she had hung Bobinôt's Sunday clothes to air and she hastened out to gather them before the rain fell. As she stepped outside, Alcée Laballière rode in at the gate. She had not seen him very often since her marriage, and never alone. She stood there with Bobinôt's coat in her hands, and the big rain drops began to fall. Alcée rode his horse under the shelter of a side projection where the chickens had huddled and there were plows and a harrow piled up in the corner.

'May I come and wait on your gallery till the storm is over, Calixta?' he asked.

'Come 'long in, M'sieur Alcée.'

His voice and her own startled her as if from a trance, and she seized Bobinôt's vest. Alcée, mounting to the porch, grabbed the trousers and snatched Bibi's braided jacket that was about to be carried away by a sudden gust of wind. He expressed an intention to remain outside, but it was soon apparent that he might as well have been out in the open: the water beat in upon the boards in driving sheets, and he went inside, closing the door after him. It was even necessary to put something beneath the door to keep the water out.

'My! what a rain! It's good two years sence it rain' like that,' exclaimed Calixta as she rolled up a piece of bagging and Alcée helped her to thrust it beneath the crack.

She was a little fuller of figure than five years before when she married; but she had lost nothing of her vivacity. Her blue eyes still retained their melting quality; and her yellow hair, dishevelled by the wind and rain, kinked more stubbornly than ever about her ears and temples.

The rain beat upon the low, shingled roof with a force and clatter that threatened to break an entrance and deluge them there. They were in the dining room – the sitting room – the general utility room. Adjoining was her bedroom, with Bibi's couch alongside her own. The door stood open, and the room with its white, monumental bed, its closed shutters, looked dim and mysterious.

Alcée flung himself into a rocker and Calixta nervously began to gather up from the floor the lengths of a cotton sheet which she had been sewing.

'If this keeps up, *Dieu sait* if the levees goin' to stan' it!' she exclaimed.

'What have you got to do with the levees?'

'I got enough to do! An' there's Bobinôt with Bibi out in that storm – if he only didn' left Friedhammer's!'

'Let us hope, Calixta, that Bobinôt's got sense enough to come in out of a cyclone.'

She went and stood at the window with a greatly disturbed look on her face. She wiped the frame that was clouded with moisture. It was stiflingly hot. Alcée got up and joined her at the window, looking over her shoulder. The rain was coming down in sheets obscuring the view of far-off cabins and enveloping the distant wood in a gray mist. The playing of the lightning was incessant. A bolt struck a tall chinaberry tree at the edge of the field. It filled all visible space with a blinding glare and the crash seemed to invade the very boards they stood upon.

Calixta put her hands to her eyes, and with a cry, staggered backward. Alcée's arm encircled her, and for an instant he drew her close and spasmodically to him.

'*Bonté!*' she cried, releasing herself from his encircling arm and retreating from the window, 'the house'll go next! If I only knew w'ere Bibi was!' She would not compose herself; she would not be seated. Alcée clasped her shoulders and looked into her face. The contact of her warm, palpitating body when he had unthinkingly drawn her into his arms, had aroused all the old-time infatuation and desire for her flesh.

'Calixta,' he said, 'don't be frightened. Nothing can happen. The house is too low to be struck, with so many tall trees standing about. There! Aren't you going to be quiet? say, aren't you?' he pushed her hair back from her face that was warm and steaming. Her lips were as red and moist as pomegranate seed. Her white neck and a glimpse of her full, firm bosom disturbed him powerfully. As she glanced up at him the fear in her liquid blue eyes had given place to a drowsy gleam that unconsciously betrayed a sensuous desire. He looked down into her eyes and there was nothing for him to do but to gather her lips in a kiss. It reminded him of Assumption.

'Do you remember – in Assumption, Calixta?' he asked in a low voice broken by passion. Oh! she remembered; for in Assumption he had kissed her and kissed and kissed her; until his senses would well nigh fail, and to save her he would resort to a desperate flight. If she was not an immaculate dove in those days, she was still inviolate; a passionate creature whose very defenselessness had made her defense, against which his honor forbade him to prevail. Now – well, now – her lips seemed in a manner free to be tasted, as well as her round, white throat and her whiter breasts.

They did not heed the crashing torrents, and the roar of the elements made her laugh as she lay in his arms. She was a revelation in that dim, mysterious chamber; as white as the couch she lay upon. Her firm, elastic flesh that was knowing for the first time its birthright, was like a creamy lily that the sun invites to contribute its breath and perfume to the undying life of the world.

The generous abundance of her passion, without guile or trickery, was like a white flame which penetrated and found response in depths of his own sensuous nature that had never yet been reached.

When he touched her breasts they gave themselves up in quivering ecstasy, inviting his lips. Her mouth was a fountain of delight. And when he possessed her, they seemed to swoon together at the very borderland of life's mystery.

He stayed cushioned upon her, breathless, dazed, enervated, with his heart beating like a hammer upon her. With one hand she clasped his head, her lips lightly touching his forehead. The other hand stroked with a soothing rhythm his muscular shoulders.

The growl of the thunder was distant and passing away. The rain beat softly upon the shingles, inviting them to drowsiness and sleep. But they dared not yield.

The rain was over; and the sun was turning the glistening green world into a palace of gems. Calixta, on the gallery, watched Alcée ride away. He turned and smiled at her with a beaming face; and she lifted her pretty chin in the air and laughed aloud.

3

Bobinôt and Bibi, trudging home, stopped without at the cistern to make themselves presentable.

'My! Bibi, w'at will yo' mama say! You ought to be ashame'. You oughtn' put on those good pants. Look at 'em! An' that mud on yo' collar! How you got that mud on yo' collar, Bibi? I never saw such a boy!' Bibi was the picture of pathetic resignation. Bobinôt was the embodiment of serious solicitude as he strove to remove from his own person and his son's the signs of their tramp over heavy roads and through wet fields. He scraped the mud off Bibi's bare legs and feet with a stick and carefully removed all traces from his heavy brogans. Then, prepared for the worst – the meeting with an over-scrupulous housewife, they entered cautiously at the back door.

Calixta was preparing supper. She had set the table and was dripping coffee at the hearth. She sprang up as they came in.

'Oh, Bobinôt! You back! My! but I was uneasy. W'ere you been during the rain? An' Bibi? he ain't wet? he ain't hurt?' She had clasped Bibi and was kissing him effusively. Bobinôt's explanations and apologies which he had been composing all along the way, died on his lips as Calixta felt him to see if he were dry, and seemed to express nothing but satisfaction at their safe return.

'I brought you some shrimps, Calixta,' offered Bobinôt, hauling the can from his ample side pocket and laying it on the table.

'Shrimps! Oh, Bobinôt! you too good fo' anything!' and she gave him a smacking kiss on the cheek that resounded. '*J'vous réponds*, we'll have a feas' to night! umph-umph!'

Bobinôt and Bibi began to relax and enjoy themselves, and when the three seated themselves at the table they laughed much and so loud that anyone might have heard them as far away as Laballières.

4

Alcée Laballière wrote to his wife, Clarisse, that night. It was a loving letter, full of tender solicitude. He told her not to hurry back, but if she and the babies liked it at Biloxi, to stay a month longer. He was getting on nicely; and though he missed them, he was willing to bear the separation a while longer – realizing that their health and pleasure were the first things to be considered.

5

As for Clarisse, she was charmed upon receiving her husband's letter. She and the babies were doing well. The society was agreeable; many of her old friends and acquaintances were at the bay. And the first free breath since her marriage seemed to restore the pleasant liberty of her maiden days. Devoted as she was to her husband, their intimate conjugal life was something which she was more than willing to forego for a while.

So the storm passed and every one was happy.

1898

MARY E. WILKINS FREEMAN
1852–1930

The Revolt of 'Mother'

'Father!'

'What is it?'

'What are them men diggin' over there in the field for?'

There was a sudden dropping and enlarging of the lower part of the old man's face, as if some heavy weight had settled therein; he shut his mouth tight, and went on harnessing the great bay mare. He hustled the collar on to her neck with a jerk.

'Father!'

The old man slapped the saddle upon the mare's back.

'Look here, father, I want to know what them men are diggin' over in the field for, and I'm goin' to know.'

'I wish you'd go into the house, mother, an' 'tend to your own affairs,' the old man said then. He ran his words together, and his speech was almost as inarticulate as a growl.

But the woman understood; it was her most native tongue. 'I ain't goin' into the house till you tell me what them men are doin' over there in the field,' said she.

Then she stood waiting. She was a small woman, short and straight-waisted like a child in her brown cotton gown. Her forehead was mild and benevolent between the smooth curves of gray hair; there were meek downward lines about her nose and mouth; but her eyes, fixed upon the old man, looked as if the meekness had been the result of her own will, never of the will of another.

They were in the barn, standing before the wide open doors. The spring air, full of the smell of growing grass and unseen blossoms, came in their faces. The deep yard in front was littered with farm wagons and piles of wood; on the edges, close to the fence and the house, the grass was a vivid green, and there were some dandelions.

The old man glanced doggedly at his wife as he tightened the last buckles on the harness. She looked as immovable to him as one of the rocks in his pastureland, bound to the earth with generations of blackberry vines. He slapped the reins over the horse, and started forth from the barn.

'*Father!*' said she.

The old man pulled up. 'What is it?'

'I want to know what them men are diggin' over there in that field for.'

'They're diggin' a cellar, I s'pose, if you've got to know.'

'A cellar for what?'

'A barn.'

'A barn? You ain't goin' to build a barn over there where we was goin' to have a house, father?'

The old man said not another word. He hurried the horse into the farm wagon, and clattered out of the yard, jouncing as sturdily on his seat as a boy.

The woman stood a moment looking after him, then she went out of the barn across a corner of the yard to the house. The house, standing at right angles with the great barn and a long reach of sheds and out-buildings, was infinitesimal compared with them. It was scarcely as commodious for people as the little boxes under the barn eaves were for doves.

A pretty girl's face, pink and delicate as a flower, was looking out of one of the house windows. She was watching three men who were digging over in the field which bounded the yard near the road line. She turned quietly when the woman entered.

'What are they digging for, mother?' said she. 'Did he tell you?'

'They're diggin' for – a cellar for a new barn.'

'Oh, mother, he ain't going to build another barn?'

'That's what he says.'

A boy stood before the kitchen glass combing his hair. He combed slowly and painstakingly, arranging his brown hair in a smooth hillock over his forehead. He did not seem to pay any attention to the conversation.

'Sammy, did you know father was going to build a new barn?' asked the girl.

The boy combed assiduously.

'Sammy!'

He turned, and showed a face like his father's under his smooth crest of hair. 'Yes, I s'pose I did,' he said, reluctantly.

'How long have you known it?' asked his mother.

' 'Bout three months, I guess.'

'Why didn't you tell of it?'

'Didn't think 'twould do no good.'

'I don't see what father wants another barn for,' said the girl, in her sweet, slow voice. She turned again to the window, and stared out at the digging men in the field. Her tender, sweet face was full of a gentle distress. Her forehead was as bald and innocent as a baby's with the light hair strained back from it in a row of curl papers. She was quite large, but her soft curves did not look as if they covered muscles.

Her mother looked sternly at the boy. 'Is he goin' to buy more cows?'

The boy did not reply; he was tying his shoes.

'Sammy, I want you to tell me if he's goin' to buy more cows.'

'I s'pose he is.'

'How many?'

'Four, I guess.'

His mother said nothing more. She went into the pantry, and there was a clatter of dishes. The boy got his cap from a nail behind the door, took an old arithmetic from the shelf, and started for school. He was lightly built, but clumsy. He went out of the yard with a curious spring in the hips, that made his loose home-made jacket tilt up in the rear.

The girl went to the sink, and began to wash the dishes that were piled up there. Her mother came promptly out of the pantry, and shoved her aside. 'You wipe 'em,' said she, 'I'll wash. There's a good many this mornin'.'

The mother plunged her hands vigorously into the water, the girl wiped the plates slowly and dreamily. 'Mother,' said she, 'don't you think it's too bad father's going to build that new barn, much as we need a decent house to live in?'

Her mother scrubbed a dish fiercely. 'You ain't found out yet we're women-folks, Nanny Penn,' said she. 'You ain't seen enough of men-folks yet to. One of these days you'll find it out, an' then you'll know that we know only what men-folks think we do, so far as any use of it goes, an' how we'd ought to reckon men-folks in with Providence, an' not complain of what they do any more than we do of the weather.'

'I don't care; I don't believe George is anything like that, anyhow,' said Nanny. Her delicate face flushed pink, her lips pouted softly, as if she were going to cry.

'You wait an' see. I guess George Eastman ain't no better than other men. You hadn't ought to judge father, though. He can't help it, 'cause he don't look at things jest the way we do. An' we've been pretty comfortable here, after all. The roof don't leak – ain't never but once – that's one thing. Father's kept it shingled right up.'

'I do wish we had a parlor.'

'I guess it won't hurt George Eastman any to come to see you in a nice clean kitchen. I guess a good many girls don't have as good a place as this. Nobody's ever heard me complain.'

'I ain't complained either, mother.'

'Well, I don't think you'd better, a good father an' a good home as you've got. S'pose your father made you go out an' work for your livin'? Lots of girls have to that ain't no stronger an' better able to than you be.'

Sarah Penn washed the frying-pan with a conclusive air. She scrubbed the outside of it as faithfully as the inside. She was a masterly keeper of her box of a house. Her one living-room never seemed to have in it any of the dust which the friction of life with inanimate matter produces. She swept, and there seemed to be no dirt to go before the broom; she cleaned, and one could see no difference. She was like an artist so perfect that he has apparently no art. Today she got out a mixing bowl and a board, and rolled some pies, and there was no more flour upon her than upon her daughter who was doing finer work. Nanny was to be married in the fall, and she was sewing on some white cambric and embroidery. She sewed industriously while her mother cooked; her soft milk-white hands and wrists showed whiter than her delicate work.

'We must have the stove moved out in the shed before long,' said Mrs Penn. 'Talk about not havin' things, it's been a real blessin' to be able to put a stove up in that shed in hot weather. Father did one good thing when he fixed that stove-pipe out there.'

Sarah Penn's face as she rolled her pies had that expression of meek vigor which might have characterized one of the New Testament saints. She was making mince-pies. Her husband, Adoniram Penn, liked them better than any other kind. She baked twice a week. Adoniram often liked a piece of pie between meals. She hurried this morning. It had been later than usual when she began, and she wanted to have a pie baked for dinner. However deep a resentment she might be forced to hold against her husband, she would never fail in sedulous attention to his wants.

Nobility of character manifests itself at loop-holes when it is not provided with large doors. Sarah Penn's showed itself today in flaky dishes of pastry. So she made the pies faithfully, while across the table she could see, when she glanced up from her work, the sight that rankled in her patient and steadfast soul – the digging of the cellar of the new barn in the place where Adoniram forty years ago had promised her their new house should stand.

The pies were done for dinner. Adoniram and Sammy were home a few minutes after twelve o'clock. The dinner was eaten with serious haste. There was never much conversation at the table in the Penn family. Adoniram asked a blessing, and they ate promptly, then rose up and went about their work.

Sammy went back to school, taking soft sly lopes out of the yard like a rabbit. He wanted a game of marbles before school, and feared his father would give him some chores to do. Adoniram hastened to the door and called after him, but he was out of sight.

'I don't see what you let him go for, mother,' said he. 'I wanted him to help me unload that wood.'

Adoniram went to work out in the yard unloading wood from the wagon. Sarah put away the dinner dishes, while Nanny took down her curl papers and changed her dress. She was going down to the store to buy some more embroidery and thread.

When Nanny was gone, Mrs Penn went to the door. 'Father!' she called.

'Well, what is it!'

'I want to see you jest a minute, father.'

'I can't leave this wood nohow. I've got to git it unloaded an' go for a load of gravel afore two o'clock. Sammy had ought to helped me. You hadn't ought to let him go to school so early.'

'I want to see you jest a minute.'

'I tell ye I can't, nohow, mother.'

'Father, you come here.' Sarah Penn stood in the door like a queen; she held her head as if it bore a crown; there was that patience which makes authority royal in her voice. Adoniram went.

Mrs Penn led the way into the kitchen, and pointed to a chair. 'Sit down, father,' said she; 'I've got somethin' I want to say to you.'

He sat down heavily; his face was quite stolid, but he looked at her with restive eyes. 'Well, what is it, mother?'

'I want to know what you're buildin' that new barn for, father?'

'I ain't got nothin' to say about it.'

'It can't be you think you need another barn?'

'I tell ye I ain't got nothin' to say about it, mother; an' I ain't goin' to say nothin'.'

'Be you goin' to buy more cows?'

Adoniram did not reply; he shut his mouth tight.

'I know you be, as well as I want to. Now, father, look here' – Sarah Penn had not sat down; she stood before her husband in the humble fashion of a Scripture woman – 'I'm goin' to talk real plain to you; I never have sence I married you, but I'm goin' to now. I ain't never complained, an' I ain't goin' to complain now, but I'm goin' to talk plain. You see this room here, father; you look at it well. You see there ain't no carpet on the floor, an' you see the paper is all dirty, an' droppin' off the wall. We ain't had no new paper on it for ten year, an' then I put it on myself, an' it didn't cost but ninepence a roll. You see this room, father – it's all the one I've had to work in an' eat in an' sit in sence we was married. There ain't another woman in the whole town whose husband ain't got half the means you have but what's got better. It's all the room Nanny's got to have her company in; an' there ain't one of her mates but what's got better, an' their fathers not so able as hers is. It's all the room she'll have to be married in. What would you have thought, father, if we had had our weddin' in a room no better than this? I was married in my mother's parlor, with a carpet on the floor, an' stuffed furniture, an' a mahogany card-table. An' this is all the room my daughter will have to be married in. Look here, father!'

Sarah Penn went across the room as though it were a tragic stage. She flung open a door and disclosed a tiny bedroom, only large enough for a bed and bureau, with a path between. 'There, father,' said she – 'there's all the room I've had to sleep in forty year. All my children were born there – the two that died, an' the two that's livin'. I was sick with a fever there.'

She stepped to another door and opened it. It led into the small, ill-lighted pantry. 'Here,' said she, 'is all the buttery I've got – every place I've got for my dishes, to set away my victuals in, an' to keep my milkpans in. Father, I've been takin' care of the milk of six cows in this place, an' now you're goin' to build a new barn, an' keep more cows, an' give me more to do in it.'

She threw open another door. A narrow crooked flight of stairs wound upward from it. 'There, father,' said she, 'I want you to look at the stairs that go up to them two unfinished chambers that are all the places our son an' daughter have had to sleep in all their lives. There ain't a pretty girl in town nor a more ladylike one than Nanny, an' that's the place she has to sleep in. It ain't so good as your horse's stall; it ain't so warm an' tight.'

Sarah Penn went back and stood before her husband. 'Now, father,' said she, 'I want to know if you think you're doin' right an' accordin' to what you profess. Here, when we was married, forty year ago, you promised me faithful that we should have a new house built in that lot over in the field before the year was out. You said you had money enough, an' you wouldn't ask me to live in no such place as this. It is forty year now, an' you've been makin' more money, an' I've been savin' of it for you ever since, an' you ain't built no house yet. You've built sheds an' cow-houses an' one new barn, an' now you're goin' to build another. Father, I want to know if you think it's right. You're lodgin' your dumb beasts better than you are your own flesh an' blood. I want to know if you think it's right.'

'I ain't got nothin' to say.'

'You can't say nothin' without ownin' it ain't right, father. An' there's another thing − I ain't complained; I've got along forty year, an' I suppose I should forty more, if it wasn't for that − if we don't have another house, Nanny she can't live with us after she's married. She'll have to go somewhere else to live away from us, an' it don't seem as if I could have it so, noways, father. She wasn't ever strong. She's got considerable color, but there wasn't never any backbone to her. I've always took the heft of everything off her, an' she ain't fit to keep house an' do everything herself. She'll be all worn out inside of a year. Think of her doin' all the washin' an' ironin' an' bakin' with them soft white hands an' arms, an' sweepin'! I can't have it so, noways, father.'

Mrs Penn's face was burning; her mild eyes gleamed. She had pleaded her little cause like a Webster; she had ranged from severity to pathos; but her opponent employed that obstinate silence which makes eloquence futile with mocking echoes. Adoniram arose clumsily.

'Father, ain't you got nothin' to say?' said Mrs Penn.

'I've got to go off after that load of gravel. I can't stan' here talkin' all day.'

'Father, won't you think it over, an' have a house built there instead of a barn?'

'I ain't got nothin' to say.'

Adoniram shuffled out. Mrs Penn went into her bedroom. When she came out, her eyes were red. She had a roll of unbleached cotton cloth. She spread it out on the kitchen table, and began cutting out some shirts for her husband. The men over in the field had a team to help them this afternoon; she could hear their halloos. She had a scanty pattern for the shirts; she had to plan and piece the sleeves.

Nanny came home with her embroidery, and sat down with her needlework. She had taken down her curl papers, and there was a soft roll of fair hair like an aureole over her forehead; her face was as delicately fine and clear as porcelain. Suddenly she looked up, and the tender red flamed all over her face and neck. 'Mother,' said she.

'What say?'

'I've been thinking – I don't see how we're goin' to have any – wedding in this room. I'd be ashamed to have his folks come in if we didn't have anybody else.'

'Mebbe we can have some new paper before then; I can put it on. I guess you won't have no call to be ashamed of your belongin's.'

'We might have the wedding in the new barn,' said Nanny, with gentle pettishness. 'Why, mother, what makes you look so?'

Mrs Penn had started, and was staring at her with a curious expression. She turned again to her work, and spread out a pattern carefully on the cloth. 'Nothin',' said she.

Presently Adoniram clattered out of the yard in his two-wheeled dump cart, standing as proudly upright as a Roman charioteer. Mrs Penn opened the door and stood there a minute looking out; the halloos of the men sounded louder.

It seemed to her all through the spring months that she heard nothing but the halloos and the noises of saws and hammers. The new barn grew fast. It was a fine edifice for this little village. Men came on pleasant Sundays, in their meeting suits and clean shirt bosoms, and stood around it admiringly. Mrs Penn did not speak of it, and Adoniram did not mention it to her, although sometimes, upon a return from inspecting it, he bore himself with injured dignity.

'It's a strange thing how your mother feels about the new barn,' he said, confidentially, to Sammy one day.

Sammy only grunted after an odd fashion for a boy; he had learned it from his father.

The barn was all completed ready for use by the third week in July. Adoniram had planned to move his stock in on Wednesday; on Tuesday he received a letter which changed his plans. He came in with it early in the morning. 'Sammy's been to the post-office,' said he, 'an' I've got a letter from Hiram.' Hiram was Mrs Penn's brother, who lived in Vermont.

'Well,' said Mrs Penn, 'what does he say about the folks?'

'I guess they're all right. He says he thinks if I come up country right off there's a chance to buy jest the kind of a horse I want.' He stared reflectively out of the window at the new barn.

Mrs Penn was making pies. She went on clapping the rolling-pin into the crust, although she was very pale, and her heart beat loudly.

'I dun' know but what I'd better go,' said Adoniram. 'I hate to go off jest now, right in the midst of hayin', but the ten-acre lot's cut, an' I guess Rufus an' the others can git along without me three or four days. I can't get a horse round here to suit me, nohow, an' I've got to have another for all that wood-haulin' in the fall. I told Hiram to watch out, an' if he got wind of a good horse to let me know. I guess I'd better go.'

'I'll get out your clean shirt an' collar,' said Mrs Penn calmly.

She laid out Adoniram's Sunday suit and his clean clothes on the bed in the little bedroom. She got his shaving-water and razor ready. At last she buttoned on his collar and fastened his black cravat.

Adoniram never wore his collar and cravat except on extra occasions. He held his head high, with a rasped dignity. When he was all ready, with his coat and hat brushed, and a lunch of pie and cheese in a paper bag, he hesitated on the threshold of the door. He looked at his wife, and his manner was definitely apologetic. '*If* them cows come today, Sammy can drive 'em into the new barn,' said he; 'an' when they bring the hay up, they can pitch it in there.'

'Well,' replied Mrs Penn.

Adoniram set his shaven face ahead and started. When he had cleared the door-step, he turned and looked back with a kind of nervous solemnity. 'I shall be back by Saturday if nothin' happens,' said he.

'Do be careful, father,' returned his wife.

She stood in the door with Nanny at her elbow and watched him out of sight. Her eyes had a strange, doubtful expression in them; her peaceful forehead was contracted. She went in, and about her baking again. Nanny sat sewing. Her wedding-day was drawing nearer, and she was getting pale and thin with her steady sewing. Her mother kept glancing at her.

'Have you got that pain in your side this mornin'?' she asked.

'A little.'

Mrs Penn's face, as she worked, changed, her perplexed forehead smoothed, her eyes were steady, her lips firmly set. She formed a maxim for herself, although incoherently with her unlettered thoughts. 'Unsolicited opportunities are the guide-posts of the Lord to the new roads of life,' she repeated in effect, and she made up her mind to her course of action.

'S'posin' I *had* wrote to Hiram,' she muttered once, when she was in the pantry – 's'posin I had wrote, an' asked him if he knew of any horse? But I didn't, an' father's goin' wa'n't none of my doin'. It looks like a providence.' Her voice rang out quite loud at the last.

'What you talkin' about, mother?' called Nanny.

'Nothin'.'

Mrs Penn hurried her baking; at eleven o'clock it was all done. The load of hay from the west field came slowly down the cart track, and drew up at the new barn. Mrs Penn ran out. 'Stop!' she screamed, 'stop!'

The men stopped and looked; Sammy upreared from the top of the load, and stared at his mother.

'Stop!' she cried out again. 'Don't you put the hay in that barn; put it in the old one.'

'Why, he said to put it in here,' returned one of the haymakers, wonderingly. He was a young man, a neighbor's son, whom Adoniram hired by the year to help on the farm.

'Don't you put the hay in the new barn; there's room enough in the old one, ain't there?' said Mrs Penn.

'Room enough,' returned the hired man, in his thick, rustic tones. 'Didn't need the new barn, nohow, far as room's con-cerned. Well, I s'pose he changed his mind.' He took hold of the horses' bridles.

Mrs Penn went back to the house. Soon the kitchen windows were darkened, and a fragrance like warm honey came into the room.

Nanny laid down her work. 'I thought father wanted them to put the hay into the new barn?' she said, wonderingly.

'It's all right,' replied her mother.

Sammy slid down from the load of hay, and came in to see if dinner was ready.

'I ain't goin' to get a regular dinner today, as long as father's gone,' said his mother. 'I've let the fire go out. You can have some bread an' milk an' pie. I thought we could get along.' She set out some bowls of milk, some bread, and a pie on the kitchen table. 'You'd better eat your dinner now,' said she. 'You might jest as well get through with it. I want you to help me afterwards.'

Nanny and Sammy stared at each other. There was something strange in their mother's manner. Mrs Penn did not eat anything herself. She went into the pantry, and they heard her moving dishes while they ate. Presently she came out with a pile of plates. She got the clothes-basket out of the shed, and packed them in it. Nanny and Sammy watched. She brought out cups and saucers, and put them in with the plates.

'What you goin' to do, mother?' inquired Nanny, in a timid voice. A sense of something unusual made her tremble, as if it were a ghost. Sammy rolled his eyes over his pie.

'You'll see what I'm goin' to do,' replied Mrs Penn. 'If you're through, Nanny, I want you to go upstairs an' pack up your things; an' I want you, Sammy, to help me take down the bed in the bedroom.'

'Oh, mother, what for?' gasped Nanny.

'You'll see.'

During the next few hours a feat was performed by this simple, pious New England mother which was equal in its way to Wolfe's storming of the Heights of Abraham. It took no more genius and audacity of bravery for Wolfe to cheer his wondering soldiers up those steep precipices, under the sleeping eyes of the enemy, than for Sarah Penn, at the head of her children, to move all their little household goods into the new barn while her husband was away.

Nanny and Sammy followed their mother's instructions without a murmur; indeed, they were overawed. There is a certain uncanny and superhuman quality about all such purely original undertakings as their mother's was to them. Nanny went back and forth with her light load, and Sammy tugged with sober energy.

At five o'clock in the afternoon the little house in which the Penns had lived for forty years had emptied itself into the new barn.

Every builder builds somewhat for unknown purposes, and is in a measure a prophet. The architect of Adoniram Penn's barn, while he designed it for the comfort of four-footed animals, had planned better than he knew for the comfort of humans. Sarah Penn saw at a glance its possibilities. Those great box-stalls, with quilts hung before them, would make better bedrooms than the one she had occupied for forty years, and there was a tight carriage-room. The harness-room, with its chimney and shelves, would make a kitchen of her dreams. The great middle space would make a parlor, by-and-by, fit for a palace. Upstairs there was as much room as down. With partitions and windows, what a house would there be! Sarah looked at the row of stanchions before the allotted space for cows, and reflected that she would have her front entry there.

At six o'clock the stove was up in the harness room, the kettle was boiling, and the table set for tea. It looked almost as homelike as the abandoned house across the yard had ever done. The young hired man milked, and Sarah directed him calmly to bring the milk to the new barn. He came gaping, dropping little blots of foam from the brimming pails on the grass. Before the next morning he had spread the story of Adoniram Penn's wife moving into the new barn all over the little village. Men assembled in the store and talked it over, women with shawls over their heads scuttled into each other's houses before their work was done. Any deviation from the ordinary course of life in this quiet town was enough to stop all progress in it. Everybody paused to look at the staid, independent figure on the side track. There was a difference of opinion with regard to her. Some held her to be insane; some, of a lawless and rebellious spirit.

Friday the minister went to see her. It was in the forenoon, and she was at the barn door shelling peas for dinner. She looked up and returned his salutation with dignity, then she went on with her work. She did not invite him in. The saintly expression of her face remained fixed, but there was an angry flush over it.

The minister stood awkwardly before her, and talked. She handled the peas as if they were bullets. At last she looked up, and her eyes showed the spirit that her meek front had covered for a lifetime.

'There ain't no use talkin', Mr Hersey,' said she. 'I've thought it all over an' over, an' I believe I'm doin' what's right. I've made it the subject of prayer, an' it's betwixt me an' the Lord an' Adoniram. There ain't no call for nobody else to worry about it.'

'Well, of course, if you have brought it to the Lord in prayer, and feel satisfied that you are doing right, Mrs Penn,' said the minister, helplessly. His thin gray-bearded face was pathetic. He was a sickly man; his youthful confidence had cooled; he had to scourge himself up to some of his pastoral duties as relentlessly as a Catholic ascetic, and then he was prostrated by the smart.

'I think it's right jest as much as I think it was right for our forefathers to come over here from the old country 'cause they didn't have what belonged to 'em,' said Mrs Penn. She arose. The barn threshold might have been Plymouth Rock from her bearing. 'I don't doubt you mean well, Mr Hersey,' said she, 'but there are things people hadn't ought to interfere with. I've been a member of the church for over forty years. I've got my own mind an' my own feet, an' I'm goin' to think my own thoughts an' go my own way, an' nobody but the Lord is goin' to dictate to me unless I've a mind to have him. Won't you come in an' set down? How is Mis' Hersey?'

'She is well, I thank you,' replied the minister. He added some more perplexed apologetic remarks; then he retreated.

He could expound the intricacies of every character-study in the Scriptures, he was competent to grasp the Pilgrim Fathers and all historical innovators, but Sarah Penn was beyond him. He could deal with primal cases, but parallel ones worsted him. But, after all, although it was aside from his providence, he wondered more how Adoniram Penn would deal with his wife than how the Lord would. Everybody shared the wonder. When Adoniram's four new cows arrived, Sarah ordered three to be put in the old barn, the other in the house shed where the cooking-stove had stood. That added to the excitement. It was whispered that all four cows were domiciled in the house.

Towards sunset on Saturday, when Adoniram was expected home, there was a knot of men in the road near the new barn. The hired man had milked, but he still hung around the premises. Sarah Penn had supper all ready. There were brown bread and baked beans and custard pie; it was the supper that Adoniram loved on a Saturday night. She had on a clean calico, and she bore herself imperturbably. Nanny and Sammy kept close at her heels. Their eyes were large, and Nanny was full of nervous tremors. Still there was to them more pleasant excitement than anything else. An inborn confidence in their mother over their father asserted itself.

Sammy looked out of the harness-room window. 'There he is,' he announced, in an awed whisper. He and Nanny peeped around the casing. Mrs Penn kept on about her work. The children watched Adoniram leave the new horse standing in the drive while he went to the house door. It was fastened. Then he went around to the shed. That door was seldom locked, even when the family was away. The thought how her father would be confronted by the cow flashed upon Nanny. There was a hysterical sob in her throat. Adoniram emerged from the shed and stood looking about in a dazed fashion. His lips moved; he was saying something, but they could not hear what it was. The hired man was peeping around a corner of the old barn, but nobody saw him.

Adoniram took the new horse by the bridle and led him across the yard to the new barn. Nanny and Sammy slunk close to their mother. The barn doors rolled back, and there stood Adoniram, with the long mild face of the great Canadian farm horse looking over his shoulder.

Nanny kept behind her mother, but Sammy stepped suddenly forward, and stood in front of her.

Adoniram stared at the group. 'What are airth you all down here for?' said he. 'What's the matter over to the house?'

'We've come here to live, father,' said Sammy. His shrill voice quavered out bravely.

'What' – Adoniram sniffed – 'what is it smells like cookin'?' said he. He stepped forward and looked in the open door of the harness-room. Then he turned to his wife. His old bristling face was pale and frightened. 'What on airth does this mean, mother?' he gasped.

'You come in here, father,' said Sarah. She led the way into the harness-room and shut the door. 'Now, father,' said she, 'you needn't be scared. I ain't crazy. There ain't nothin' to be upset over. But we've come here to live, an' we're goin' to live here. We've got jest as good a right here as new horses an' cows. The house wasn't fit for us to live in any longer, an' I made up my mind I wa'n't goin' to stay there. I've done my duty by you forty year, an' I'm goin' to do it now; but I'm goin' to live here. You've got to put in some windows and partitions; an' you'll have to buy some furniture.'

'Why, mother!' the old man gasped.

'You'd better take your coat off an' get washed — there's the wash basin — an' then we'll have supper.'

'Why, mother!'

Sammy went past the window, leading the new horse to the old barn. The old man saw him, and shook his head speechlessly. He tried to take off his coat, but his arms seemed to lack the power. His wife helped him. She poured some water into the tin basin, and put in a piece of soap. She got the comb and brush, and smoothed his thin gray hair after he had washed. Then she put the beans, hot bread, and tea on the table. Sammy came in, and the family drew up. Adoniram sat looking dazedly at his plate, and they waited.

'Ain't you goin' to ask a blessin', father?' said Sarah.

And the old man bent his head and mumbled.

All through the meal he stopped eating at intervals, and stared furtively at his wife; but he ate well. The home food tasted good to him, and his old frame was too sturdily healthy to be affected by his mind. But after supper he went out, and sat down on the step of the smaller door at the right of the barn, through which he had meant his Jerseys to pass in stately file, but which Sarah designed for her front house door, and he leaned his head on his hands.

After the supper dishes were cleared away and the milk-pans washed, Sarah went out to him. The twilight was deepening. There was a clear green glow in the sky. Before them stretched the smooth level of field; in the distance was a cluster of hay-stacks like the huts of a village; the air was very cool and calm and sweet. The landscape might have been an ideal one of peace.

Sarah bent over and touched her husband on one of this thin, sinewy shoulders. 'Father!'

The old man's shoulders heaved: he was weeping.

'Why, don't do so, father,' said Sarah.

'I'll — put up the — partitions, an' — everything you — want, mother.'

Sarah put her apron up to her face; she was overcome by her own triumph.

Adoniram was like a fortress whose walls had no active resistance, and went down the instant the right besieging tools were used. 'Why, mother,' he said, hoarsely, 'I hadn't no idee you was so set on't as all this comes to.'

1890

THOMAS NELSON PAGE
1853–1922

Marse Chan

A Tale of Old Virginia

One afternoon, in the autumn of 1872, I was riding leisurely down the sandy road that winds along the top of the water-shed between two of the smaller rivers of eastern Virginia. The road I was travelling, following 'the ridge' for miles, had just struck me as most significant of the character of the race whose only avenue of communication with the outside world it had formerly been. Their once splendid mansions, now fast falling to decay, appeared to view from time to time, set back far from the road, in proud seclusion, among groves of oak and hickory, now scarlet and gold with the early frost. Distance was nothing to this people; time was of no consequence to them. They desired but a level path in life, and that they had, though the way was longer, and the outer world strode by them as they dreamed.

I was aroused from my reflections by hearing someone ahead of me calling, 'Heah! heah – whoo-oop, heah!'

Turning the curve in the road, I saw just before me a negro standing, with a hoe and a watering-pot in his hand. He had evidently just gotten over the 'worm-fence' into the road, out of the path which led zigzag across the 'old field' and was lost to sight in the dense growth of sassafras. When I rode up, he was looking anxiously back down this path for his dog. So engrossed was he that he did not even hear my horse, and I reined in to wait until he should turn around and satisfy my curiosity as to the handsome old place half a mile off from the road.

The numerous out-buildings and the large barns and stables told that it had once been the seat of wealth, and the wild waste of sassafras that covered the broad fields gave it an air of desolation that greatly excited my interest. Entirely oblivious of my proximity, the negro went on calling 'Whoo-oop, heah!' until along the path, walking very slowly and with great dignity, appeared a noble-looking old orange and white setter, gray with age, and corpulent with excessive feeding. As soon as he came in sight, his master began:

'Yes, dat you! You gittin' deaf as well as bline, I s'pose! Kyarnt heah me callin', I reckon? Whyn't yo' come on, dawg?'

The setter sauntered slowly up to the fence and stopped, without even deigning a look at the speaker, who immediately proceeded to take the rails down, talking meanwhile:

'Now, I got to pull down de gap, I s'pose! Yo' so sp'ilt yo' kyahn hardly walk. Jes' ez able to git over it as I is! Jes' like white folks – think 'cuz you's white and I's black, I got to wait on yo' all de time. Ne'm mine, I ain' gwi' do it!'

The fence having been pulled down sufficiently low to suit his dogship, he marched sedately through, and, with a hardly perceptible lateral movement of his tail, walked on down the road. Putting up the rails carefully, the negro turned and saw me.

'Sarvent, marster,' he said, taking his hat off. Then, as if apologetically for having permitted a stranger to witness what was merely a family affair, he added: 'He know I don' mean nothin' by what I sez. He's Marse Chan's dawg, an' he's so ole he kyahn git long no pearter. He know I'se jes' prod-jickin' wid 'im.'

'Who is Marse Chan?' I asked; 'and whose place is that over there, and the one a mile or two back – the place with the big gate and the carved stone pillars?'

'Marse Chan,' said the darky, 'he's Marse Channin' – my young marster; an' dem places – dis one's Weall's, an' de one back dyar wid de rock gate-pos's is ole Cun'l Chahmb'lin's. Dey don' nobody live dyar now, 'cep' niggers. Arfter de war some one or nurr bought our place, but his name done kind o' slipped me. I nuver hearn on 'im befo'; I think dey's half-strainers. I don' ax none on 'em no odds. I lives down de road heah, a little piece, an' I jes' steps down of a evenin' and looks arfter de graves.'

'Well, where is Marse Chan?' I asked.

'Hi! don' you know? Marse Chan, he went in de army. I was wid im. Yo' know he warn' gwine an' lef' Sani.'

'Will you tell me all about it?' I said, dismounting.

Instantly, and as if by instinct, the darky stepped forward and took my bridle. I demurred a little; but with a bow that would have honored old Sir Roger, he shortened the reins, and taking my horse from me, led him along.

'Now tell me about Marse Chan,' I said.

'Lawd, marster, hit's so long ago, I'd a'most forgit all about it, ef I hedn' been wid him ever sence he wuz born. Ez 'tis, I remembers it jes' like 'twuz yistiddy. Yo' know Marse Chan an' me – we wuz boys togerr. I wuz older'n he wuz, jes' de same ez he wuz whiter'n me. I wuz born plantin' corn time, de spring arfter big Jim an' de six steers got washed away at de upper ford right down dyar b'low de quarters ez he wuz a bringin' de Chris'mas things home; an' Marse Chan, he warn' born tell mos' to de harves' arfter my sister Nancy married Cun'l Chahmb'lin's Torm, 'bout eight years arfterwoods.

'Well, when Marse Chan wuz born, dey wuz de grettes' doin's at home you ever did see. De folks all hed holiday, jes' like in de Chris'mas. Ole marster (we didn' call 'im *ole* marster tell arfter Marse Chan wuz born – befo' dat he wuz jes' de marster, so) – well, ole marster, his face fyar shine wid pleasure, an' all de folks wuz mighty glad, too, 'cause dey all loved ole marster, and aldo' dey did step aroun' right peart when ole marster was lookin' at 'em, dyar warn' nyar han' on de place but what, ef he wanted anythin', would walk up to de back poach, an' say he warn' to see de marster. An' ev'ybody wuz talkin' 'bout de young marster, an' de maids an' de wimmens 'bout de kitchen wuz sayin' how 'twuz de purties' chile dey ever see; an' at dinner-time de mens (all on 'em hed holiday) come roun' de poach an' ax how de missis an' de young marster wuz, an' ole marster come out on de poach an' smile wus'n a 'possum, an' sez, "Thankee! Bofe doin' fust rate, boys;" an' den he stepped back in de house, sort o' laughin' to hisse'f, an' in a minute he come out ag'in wid de baby in he arms, all wrapped up in flannens an' things, an' sez, "Heah he is, boys." All de folks den, dey went up on de poach to look at 'im, drappin' dey hats on de steps, an' scrapin' dey feets ez dey went up. An' pres'n'y ole marster, lookin' down at we all chil'en all packed togerr down dyah like a parecel o' sheep-burrs, cotch sight o' *me* (he knowed my name, 'cause I use' to hole he hoss fur 'im sometimes; but he didn' know all de chil'en by name, dey wuz so many on 'em), an' he sez, "Come up heah." So up I goes tippin', skeered like, an' old marster sez, "Ain' you Mymie's son?" "Yass, seh," sez I. "Well," sez he, "I'm gwine to give you to yo' young Marse Channin' to be his body-servant," an' he put de baby right in my arms (it's de truth I'm tellin' yo'!), an' yo' jes' ought to a-heard de folks sayin', "Lawd! marster, dat boy'll drap dat chile!" "Naw, he won't," sez marster; "I kin trust 'im." And den he sez: "Now, Sam, from dis time you belong to yo' young Marse Channin'; I wan' you to tek keer on 'im ez long ez he lives. You are to be his boy from dis time. An' now," he sez, "carry 'im in de house." An' he walks arfter me an' opens de do's fur me, an' I kyars 'im in my arms, an' lays 'im down on de bed. An from dat time I was tooken in de house to be Marse Channin's body- servant.

'Well, you nuver see a chile grow so. Pres'n'y he growed up right big, an' ole marster sez he must have some edication. So he sont 'im to school to ole Miss Lawry down dyar, dis side o' Cun'l Chahmb'lin's, an' I use' to go 'long wid 'im an' tote he books an' we all's snacks; an' when he larnt to read an' spell right good, an' got 'bout so-o big, ole Miss Lawry she died, an' old marster said he mus' have a man to teach 'im an' trounce 'im. So we all went to Mr Hall, whar kep' de school-house beyant de creek, an' dyar we went ev'y day, 'cep Sat'd'ys of co'se, an' sich days ez Marse Chan din' warn' go, an' ole missis begged 'im off.

'Hit wuz down dyar Marse Chan fust took notice o' Miss Anne. Mr Hall, he taught gals ez well ez boys, an' Cun'l Chahmb'lin he sont his daughter (dat's Miss Anne I'm talkin' about). She wuz a leetle bit o' gal when she fust come. Yo' see, her ma wuz dead, an' ole Miss Lucy Chahmb'lin, she lived wid her brurr an' kep' house for 'im; an' he wuz so busy wid politics, hc didn' have much time to spyar, so he sont Miss Anne to Mr Hall's by a 'ooman wid a note. When she come dat day in de school-house, an' all de chil'en looked at her so hard, she tu'n right red, an' tried to pull her long curls over her eyes, an' den put bofe de backs of her little han's in her two eyes, an' begin to cry to herse'f. Marse Chan he was settin' on de een' o' de bench nigh de do', an' he jes' reached out an' put an arm roun' her an' drawed her up to 'im. An' he kep' whisperin' to her, an' callin' her name, an' coddlin' her; an' pres'n'y she took her han's down an' begin to laugh.

'Well, dey 'peared to tek' a gre't fancy to each urr from dat time. Miss Anne she warn' nuthin' but a baby hardly, an' Marse Chan he wuz a good big boy 'bout mos' thirteen years ole, I reckon. Hows'ever, dey sut'n'y wuz sot on each urr an' (yo' heah me!) ole marster an' Cun'l Chahmb'lin dey 'peared to like it 'bout well ez de chil'en. Yo' see, Cun'l Chahmb'lin's place j'ined ourn, an' it looked jes' ez natural fur dem two chil'en to marry an' mek it one plantation, ez it did fur de creek to run down de bottom from our place into Cun'l Chahmblin's. I don' rightly think de chil'en though 'bout gittin' *married*, not den, no mo'n I thought 'bout marryin' Judy when she wuz a little gal at Cun'l Chahmb'lin's, runnin' 'bout de house, huntin' fur Miss Lucy's spectacles; but dey wuz good frien's from de start. Marse Chan he use' to kyar

Miss Anne's books fur her ev'y day, an' ef de road wuz muddy or she wuz tired, he use' to tote her; an' 'twarn' hardly a day passed dat he didn' kyar her some'n' to school – apples or hick'y nuts, or some'n'. He wouldn't let none o' de chil'en tease her, nurr. Heh! One day, one o' de boys poked he finger at Miss Anne, and arfter school Marse Chan he axed 'im 'roun' hine de school-house out o' sight, an' ef he didn' whop im!

'Marse Chan, he wuz de peartes' scholar ole Mr Hall hed, an' Mr Hall he wuz mighty proud o' him. I don' think he use' to beat 'im ez much ez he did de urrs, aldo' he wuz de head in all debilment dat went on, jes' ez he wuz in sayin' he lessons.

'Heh! one day in summer, jes' fo' de school broke up, dyah come up a storm right sudden, an' riz de creek (dat one yo' cross' back yonder), an' Marse Chan he toted Miss Anne home on he back. He ve'y off'n did dat when de parf wuz muddy. But dis day when dey come to de creek, it had done washed all de logs 'way. 'Twuz still mighty high, so Marse Chan he put Miss Anne down, an' he took a pole an' waded right in. Hit took 'im long up to de shoulders. Den he waded back, an' took Miss Anne up on his head an' kyared her right over. At fust she wuz skeered; but he tol' her he could swim an' wouldn' let her git hu't, an' den she let 'im kyar her 'cross, she hol'in' his han's. I warn' 'long dat day, but he sut'n'y did dat thing.

'Ole marster he wuz so pleased 'bout it, he giv' Marse Chan a pony; an' Marse Chan rode 'im to school de day arfter he come, so proud, an' sayin' how he wuz gwine to let Anne ride behine 'im; an' when he come home dat evenin' he wuz walkin'. "Hi! where's yo' pony?" said old marster. "I give 'im to Anne," says Marse Chan. "She liked 'im, an' – I kin walk." "Yes," sez ole marster, laughin', "I s'pose you's already done giv' her yo'se'f, an' nex' thing I know you'll be givin' her this plantation and all my niggers."

'Well, about a fortnight or sich a matter arfter dat, Cun'l Chahmb'lin sont over an' invited all o' we all over to dinner, an' Marse Chan wuz 'spressly named in de note whar Ned brought; an' arfter dinner he made ole Phil, whar wuz his ker'ige-driver, bring roun' Marse Chan's pony wid a little side-saddle on 'im, an' a beautiful little hoss wid a bran'-new saddle an' bridle on 'im; an' he gits up an' meks Marse Chan a gre't speech, an' presents 'im de little hoss; an' den he calls Miss Anne, an' she comes out on de poach in a little ridin' frock, an' dey puts her on her pony, an'

Marse Chan mounts his hoss, an' dey goes to ride, while de grown folks is a-laughin' an' chattin' an' smokin' dey cigars.

'Dem wuz good ole times, marster – de bes' Sam ever see! Dey wuz, in fac'! Niggers didn' hed nothin' 't all to do – jes' hed to 'ten' to de feedin' an' cleanin' de hosses, an' doin' what de marster tell 'em to do; an' when dey wuz sick, dey had things sont 'em out de house, an' de same doctor come to see 'em whar 'ten' to de white folks when dey wuz po'ly. Dyar warn' no trouble nor nothin'.

'Well, things tuk a change arfter dat. Marse Chan he went to de bo'din' school, whar he use' to write to me constant. Ole missis use' to read me de letters, an' den I'd git Miss Anne to read 'em ag'in to me when I'd see her. He use' to write to her too, an' she use' to write to him too. Den Miss Anne she wuz sont off to school too. An' in de summer time dey'd bofe come home, an' yo' hardly knowed whether Marse Chan lived at home or over at Cun'l Chahmb'lin's. He wuz over dyah constant. 'Twuz always ridin' or fishin' down dyah in de river; or sometimes he' go over dyah, an' 'im an' she'd go out an' set in de yard onder de trees; she settin' up mekin' out she wuz knittin' some sort o' bright-cullored some'n', wid de grarss growin' all up 'g'inst her, an' her hat th'owed back on her neck, an' he readin' to her out books; an' sometimes dey'd bofe read out de same book, fust one an' den todder. I use' to see 'em! Dat wuz when dey wuz growin' up like.

'Den ole marster he run for Congress, an' ole Cun'l Chahmbl'in he wuz put up to run 'g'inst ole marster by de Dimicrats; but ole marster he beat 'im. Yo' know he wuz gwine do dat! Co'se he wuz! Dat made ole Cun'l Chahmb'lin mighty mad, and dey stopt visitin' each urr' reg'lar, like dey had been doin' all 'long. Den Cun'l Chahmb'lin he sort o' got in debt, an' sell some o' he niggers, an' dat's de way de fuss begun. Dat's whar de lawsuit cum from. Ole marster he didn' like nobody to sell niggers, an' knowin' dat Cun'l Chahmb'lin wuz sellin' o' his, he writ an' offered to buy his M'ria an' all her chil'en, 'cause she hed married our Zeek'yel. An' don' yo' think, Cun'l Chahmb'lin axed ole marster mo' 'n th'ee niggers wuz wuth fur M'ria! Befo' old marster bought her, dough, de sheriff cum an' levelled on M'ria an' a whole parecel o' urr niggers. Ole marster he went to de sale, an' bid for 'em; but Cun'l Chahmb'lin he got some one to bid 'g'inst ole marster. Dey wuz knocked out to ole marster dough, an' den dey hed a big lawsuit, an' ole marster wuz agwine to co't, off an' on, fur some years, till at lars' de co't decided dat M'ria belonged to ole marster. Ole Cun'l Chahmb'lin den wuz so mad he sued ole marster for a little strip o' lan' down dyah on de line fence, whar he said belonged to 'im. Evy'body knowed hit belonged to ole marster. Ef yo' go down dyah now, I kin show it to yo', inside de line fence, whar it hed done bin ever since long befo' Cun'l Chahmb'lin wuz born. But Cun'l Chahmb'lin wuz a mons'us perseverin' man, an' ole marster he wouldn' let nobody run over 'im. No, dat he wouldn'! So dey wuz agwine down to co't about dat, fur I don' know how long, till ole marster beat 'im.

'All dis time, yo' know, Marse Chan wuz agoin' back'ads an' for'ads to college, an' wuz growed up a ve'y fine young man. He wuz a ve'y likely gent'man! Miss Anne she hed done mos' growed up too – wuz puttin' her hyar up like ole missis use' to put hers up, an' 't wuz jes' ez bright ez de sorrel's mane when de sun cotch on it, an' her eyes wuz gre't big dark eyes, like her pa's, on'y bigger an' not so fierce, an' 'twarn' none o' de young ladies ez purty ez she wuz. She an' Marse Chan still set a heap o' sto' by one 'nurr, but I don' think dey wuz easy wid each urr ez when he used to tote her home from school on his back. Marse Chan he use' to love de ve'y groun' she walked on, dough, in my 'pinion. Heh! His face 'twould light up whenever she come into chu'ch, or anywhere, jes' like de sun hed come th'oo a chink on it suddenly.

'Den ole marster lost he eyes. D' yo' ever heah 'bout dat? Heish! Didn' yo'? Well, one night de big barn cotch fire. De stables, yo' know, wuz under de big barn, an' all de hosses wuz in dyah. Hit 'peared to me like 'twarn' no time befo' all de folks an' de neighbors dey come, an' dey wuz a-totin' water, an' a-tryin' to save de po' critters, and dey got a heap on 'em out; but de ker'ige-hosses dey wouldn' come out, an' dey wuz a-runnin' back'ads an' for'ads inside de stalls, a-nikerin' an' a-screamin', like dey knowed dey time hed come. Yo' could heah 'em so pitiful, an' pres'n'y old marster said to Ham Fisher (he wuz de ker'ige-driver), "Go in dyah an' try to save 'em; don' let 'em bu'n to death." An' Ham he went right in. An' jest arfter he got in, de shed whar it hed fus' cotch fell in, an' de sparks shot 'way up in de air; an' Ham didn' come back, an' de fire begun to lick out under de eaves over whar de ker'ige-hosses' stalls wuz, an' all of a sudden ole marster tu'ned an' kissed ole missis, who wuz standin' nigh him, wid her face jes' ez white ez a sperit's, an', befo' anybody knowed what he wuz gwine do, jumped right in de do', an' de smoke come po'in' out behine 'im. Well, seh, I nuver 'spects to heah tell Judgment sich a soun' ez de folks set up! Ole missis she jes' drapt down on her knees in de mud an' prayed out loud. Hit 'peared like her pra'r wuz heard; for in a minit, right out de same do', kyarin' Ham Fisher in his arms, come ole marster, wid his clo's all blazin'. Dey flung water on 'im, an' put 'im out; an', ef you b'lieve me, yo' wouldn' a-knowed 'twuz ole marster. Yo' see, he hed find Ham Fisher done fall down in de smoke right by the ker'ige-hoss' stalls, whar he sont him, an' he hed to tote 'im back in his arms th'oo de fire what hed done cotch de front part o' de stable, and to keep de flame from gittin' down Ham Fisher's th'ote he hed tuck off his own hat and mashed it all over Ham Fisher's face, an' he hed kep' Ham Fisher from bein' so much bu'nt; but *he* wuz bu'nt dreadful! His beard an' hyar wuz all nyawed off, an' his face an' han's an' neck wuz scorified terrible. Well, he jes' laid Ham Fisher down, an' then he kind o' staggered for'ad, an' old missis ketch' 'im in her arms. Ham Fisher, he warn' bu'nt so bad, an' he got out in a month or two; an' arfter a long time, ole marster he got well, too; but he wuz always stone blind arfter that. He nuver could see none from dat night.

'Marse Chan he comed home from college toreckly, an' he sut'n'y did nuss ole marster faithful – jes' like a 'ooman. Den he took charge of de plantation arfter dat; an' I use' to wait on 'im jes' like when we wuz boys togedder; an' sometimes we'd slip off an' have a fox-hunt, an' he'd be jes' like he wuz in ole times, befo' ole marster got bline, an' Miss Anne Chahmbl'in stopt comin' over to our house, an' settin' onder de trees, readin' out de same book.

'He sut'n'y wuz good to me. Nothin' nuver made no diffunce 'bout dat. He nuver hit me a lick in his life – an' nuver let nobody else do it, nurr.

'I 'members one day, when he wuz a leetle bit o' boy, ole marster hed done tole we all chil'en not to slide on de straw-stacks; an' one day me an' Marse Chan thought ole marster hed done gone 'way from home. We watched him git on he hoss an' ride up de road out o' sight, an' we wuz out in de field a-slidin' an' a-slidin', when up comes ole marster. We started to run; but he hed done see us, an' he called us to come back; an' sich a whuppin' ez he did gi' us!

'Fust he took Marse Chan, an' den he teched me up. He nuver hu't me, but in co'se I wuz a-hollerin' ez hard ez I could stave it, 'cause I knowed dat wuz gwine mek him stop. Marse Chan he hed'n open he mouf long ez ole marster wuz tunin' 'im; but soon ez he commence warmin' me an' I begin to holler, Marse Chan he bu'st out cryin', an' stept right in befo' ole marster, an' ketchin' de whup, sed:

' "Stop, seh! Yo' sha'n't whup 'im; he b'longs to me, an' ef you hit 'im another lick I'll set 'im free!"

'I wish yo' hed see ole marster. Marse Chan he warn' mo'n eight years ole, an' dyah dey wuz — ole marster stan'in' wid he whup raised up, an' Marse Chan red an' cryin', hol'in' on to it, an' sayin' I b'longst to 'im.

'Ole marster, he raise' de whup, an' den he drapt it, an' broke out in a smile over he face, an' he chuck' Marse Chan onder de chin, an' tu'n right roun' an' went away, laughin' to hisse'f, an' I heah' 'im tellin' ole missis dat evenin', an' laughin' 'bout it.

' 'Twan so mighty long arfter dat when dey fust got to talkin' 'bout de war. Dey wuz a-dictatin' back'ads an' for'ds 'bout it fur two or th'ee years 'fo' it come sho' nuff, you know. Ole marster, he was a Whig, an' of co'se Marse Chan he tuk after he pa. Cun'l Chahmb'lin, he wuz a Dimicrat. He wuz in favor of de war, an' ole marster and Marse Chan dey wuz agin' it. Dey wuz a-talkin' 'bout it all de time, an' purty soon Cun'l Chahmb'lin he went about ev'vywhar speakin' an' noratin' 'bout Ferginia ought to secede; an' Marse Chan he wuz picked up to talk agin' 'im. Dat wuz de way dey come to fight de duil. I sut'n'y wuz skeered fur Marse Chan dat mawnin', an' he was jes' ez cool! Yo' see, it happen so: Marse Chan he wuz a-speakin' down at de Deep Creek Tavern, an' he kind o' got de bes' of ole Cun'l Chahmb'lin. All de white folks laughed an' hoorawed, an' ole Cun'l Chahmb'lin — my Lawd! I t'ought he'd 'a' bu'st, he was so mad. Well, when it come to his time to speak, he jes' light into Marse Chan. He call 'im a traitor, an' a ab'litionis', an' I don' know what all. Marse Chan, he jes' kep' cool till de ole Cun'l light into he pa. Ez soon ez he name ole marster, I seen Marse Chan sort o' lif' up he head. D' yo' ever see a hoss rar he head up right sudden at night when he see somethin' comin' to'ds 'im from de side an' he don' know what 'tis? Ole Cun'l Chahmb'lin he went right on. He said ole marster hed taught Marse Chan; dat ole marster wuz a wuss ab'litionis' dan he son. I looked at Marse Chan, an' sez to myse'f: "Fo' Gord! old Cun'l Chahmb'lin better min'", an' I hedn' got de wuds out, when ole Cun'l Chahmb'lin 'cuse' ole marster o' cheatin' 'im out o' he niggers, an' stealin' piece o' he lan' — dat's de lan' I tole you 'bout. Well, seh, nex' thing I knowed, I heahed Marse Chan – hit all happen right 'long togerr, like lightnin' and thunder when they hit right at you – I heah 'im say:

' "Cun'l Chahmb'lin, what you say is false, an' yo' know it to be so. You have wilfully slandered one of de pures' an' nobles' men Gord ever made, an' nothin' but yo' gray hyars protects you."

'Well, ole Cun'l Chahmb'lin, he ra'ed an' he pitch'd. He said he wan' too ole, an' he'd show 'im so.

' "Ve'y well," says Marse Chan.

'De meetin' broke up den. I wuz hol'in' de hosses out dyar in de road by de een' o' de poach, an' I see Marse Chan talkin' an' talkin' to Mr Gordon an' anudder gent'man, and den he come out an' got on de sorrel an' galloped off. Soon ez he got out o' sight he pulled up, an' we walked along tell we come to de road whar leads off to'ds Mr Barbour's. He wuz de big lawyer o' de country. Dar he tu'ned off. All dis time he hedn' sed a wud, 'cep' to kind o' mumble to hisse'f now and den. When we got to Mr Barbour's, he got down an' went in. Dat wuz in de late winter; de folks wuz jes' beginnin' to plough fur corn. He stayed dyar 'bout two hours, an' when he come out Mr Barbour come out to de gate wid 'im an' shake han's arfter he got up in de saddle. Den we all rode off. 'Twuz late den – good dark; an' we rid ez hard ez we could, tell we come to de ole school-house at ole Cun'l Chahmb'lin's gate. When we got dar, Marse Chan got down an' walked right slow 'roun' de house. Arfter lookin' roun' a little while an' tryin' de do' to see ef it wuz shet, he walked down de road tell he got to de creek. He stop' dyar a little while an' picked up two or three little rocks an' frowed 'em in, an' pres'n'y he got up an' we come on home. Ez he got down, he tu'ned to me an', rubbin' de sorrel's nose, said: "Have 'em well fed, Sam; I'll want 'em early in de mawnin'."

'Dat night at supper he laugh an' talk, an' he set at de table a long time. Arfter ole marster went to bed, he went in de charmber an' set on de bed by 'im talkin' to 'im and tellin' 'im 'bout de meetin' an' e'vything; but he nuver mention ole Cun'l Chahmb'lin's name. When he got up to come out to de office in de yard, whar he slept, he stooped down an' kissed 'im jes' like he wuz a baby layin' dyar in de bed, an' he'd hardly let ole missis go at all. I knowed some'n wuz up, an' nex mawnin' I called 'im early befo' light, like he tole me, an' he dressed an' come out pres'n'y jes' like he wuz goin' to church. I had de hosses ready, an' we went out de back way to'ds de river. Ez we rode along, he said:

' "Sam, you an' I wuz boys togedder, wa'n't we?"

' "Yes," sez I, "Marse Chan, dat we wuz."

' "You have been ve'y faithful to me," sez he, "an' I have seen to it that you are well provided fur. You want to marry Judy, I know, an' you'll be able to buy her ef you want to."

'Den he tole me he wuz goin' to fight a duil, an' in case he should git shot, he had set me free and giv' me nuff to tek keer o' me an' my wife ez long ez we lived. He said he'd like me to stay an' tek keer o' ole marster an' ole missis ez long ez dey lived, an' he said it wouldn' be very long, he reckoned. Dat wuz de on'y time he voice broke – when he said dat; an' I couldn' speak a wud, my th'oat choked me so.

'When we come to de river, we tu'ned right up de bank, an' arfter ridin' 'bout a mile or sich a matter, we stopped whar dey wuz a little clearin' wid elder bushes on one side an' two big gum-trees on de urr, an' de sky wuz all red, an' de water down to'ds whar the sun wuz comin' wuz jes' like de sky.

'Pres'n'y Mr Gordon he come, wid a 'hogany box 'bout so big 'fore 'im, an' he got down, an' Marse Chan tole me to tek all de hosses an' go 'roun' behine de bushes whar I tell you 'bout – off to one side; an' 'fore I got 'roun' dar, ole Cun'l Chahmb'lin an' Mr Hennin an' Dr Call come ridin' from t'urr way, to'ds ole Cun'l Chahmb'lin's. When dey hed tied dey hosses, de urr gent'mens went up to whar Mr Gordon wuz, an' arfter some chattin' Mr Hennin step' off 'bout fur ez 'cross dis road, or mebbe it mout be a little furder; an' den I seed 'em th'oo de bushes loadin' de pistils, an' talk a little while; an' den Marse Chan an' ole Cun'l Chahmb'lin walked up wid de pistils in dey han's, an' Marse Chan he stood wid his face right to'ds de sun. I seen it shine on him jes' ez it come up over de low groun's, an' he look like he did sometimes when he come out of church. I wuz so skeered I couldn' say nothin'. Ole Cun'l Chahmb'lin could shoot fust rate, an' Marse Chan he never missed.

'Den I heard Mr Gordon say, "Gent'mens, is yo' ready?" and bofe of 'em sez, "Ready," jes' so.

'An' he sez, "Fire, one, two" – an' ez he said "one," 'ole Cun'l Chahmb'lin raised he pistil an' shot right at Marse Chan. De ball went th'oo his hat. I see he hat sort o' settle on he head ez de bullit hit it, an' *he* jes' tilted his pistil up in de a'r an' shot – *bang*; an' ez de pistil went *bang*, he sez to Cun'l Chahmb'lin, "I mek you a present to yo' fam'ly, seh!"

'Well, dey had some talkin' arfter dat. I didn' git rightly what it wuz; but it 'peared like Cun'l Chahmb'lin he warn't satisfied, an' wanted to have anurr shot. De seconds dey wuz talkin', an' pres'n'y dey put de pistils up, an' Marse Chan an' Mr Gordon shook han's wid Mr Hennin an' Dr Call, an' come an' got on dey hosses. An' Cun'l Chahmb'lin he got on his horse an' rode away wid de urr gent'mens, lookin' like he did de day befo' when all de people laughed at 'im.

'I b'lieve ole Cun'l Chahmb'lin wan' to shoot Marse Chan, anyway!

'We come on home to breakfast, I totin' de box wid de pistils befo' me on de roan. Would you b'lieve me, seh, Marse Chan he nuver said a wud 'bout it to ole marster or nobody. Ole missis didn' fin' out 'bout it for mo'n a month, an' den, Lawd! how she did cry and kiss Marse Chan; an' ole marster, aldo' he never say much, he wuz jes' ez please' ez ole missis. He call' me in de room an' made me tole 'im all 'bout it, an' when I got th'oo he gi' me five dollars an' a pyar of breeches.

'But ole Cun'l Chahmb'lin he nuver did furgive Marse Chan, an' Miss Anne she got mad too. Wimmens is mons'us onreasonable nohow. Dey's jes' like a catfish: you can n' tek hole on 'em like udder folks, an' when you gits 'm yo' can n' always hole 'em.

'What meks me think so? Heaps o' things – dis: Marse Chan he done gi' Miss Anne her pa jes' ez good ez I gi' Marse Chan's dawg sweet 'taters, an' she git mad wid 'im ez if he hed kill 'im 'stid o' sen'in' 'im back to her dat mawnin' whole an' soun'. B'lieve me! she wouldn' even speak to him arfter dat!

'Don' I 'member dat mawnin'!

'We wuz gwine fox-huntin', 'bout six weeks or sich a matter arfter de duil, an' we met Miss Anne ridin' 'long wid anurr lady an' two gent'mens whar wuz stayin' at her house. Dyar wuz always some one or nurr dyar co'ting her. Well, dat mawnin' we meet 'em right in de road. 'Twuz de fust time Marse Chan had see her sence de duil, an' he raises he hat ez he pahss, an' she looks right at 'im wid her head up in de yair like she nuver see 'im befo' in her born days; an' when she comes by me, she sez, "Good-mawnin', Sam!" Gord! I nuver see nuthin' like de look dat come on Marse Chan's face when she pahss 'im like dat. He gi' de sorrel a pull dat fotch 'im back settin' down in de san' on he hanches. He ve'y lips wuz white. I tried to keep up wid 'im, but 'twarn' no use. He sont me back home pres'n'y, an' he rid on. I sez to myself,

"Cun'l Chahmb'lin, don' yo' meet Marse Chan dis mawnin'. He ain' bin lookin' 'roun' de ole school-house, whar he an' Miss Anne use' to go to school to ole Mr Hall together, fur nuffin'. He won' stan' no prodjickin' today."

'He nuver come home dat night tell 'way late, an' ef he'd been fox-huntin' it mus' ha' been de ole red whar lives down in de greenscum mashes he'd been chasin'. De way de sorrel wuz gormed up wid sweat an' mire sut'n'y did hu't me. He walked up to de stable wid he head down all de way, an' I'se seen 'im go eighty miles of a winter day, an' prance into de stable at night ez fresh ez ef he hed jes' cantered over to ole Cun'l Chahmb'lin's to supper. I nuver seen a hoss beat so sence I knowed de fetlock from de fo'lock, an' bad ez he wuz he wan' ez bad ez Marse Chan.

'Whew! he didn' git over dat thing, seh – he nuver did git over it.

'De war come on jes' den, an Marse Chan wuz elected cap'n; but he wouldn't tek it. He said Firginia hadn't seceded, an' he wuz gwine stan' by her. Den dey 'lected Mr Gordon cap'n.

'I sut'n'y did wan' Marse Chan to tek de place, cuz I knowed he wuz gwine tek me wid 'im. He wan' gwine widout Sam. An' beside, he look so po' an' thin, I thought he wuz gwine die.

'Of co'se, ole missis she heared 'bout it, an' she met Miss Anne in de road, an' cut her jes' like Miss Anne cut Marse Chan.

'Ole missis, she wuz proud ez anybody! So we wuz mo' strangers dan ef we hadn' live' in a hunderd miles of each urr. An' Marse Chan he wuz gittin' thinner an' thinner, an' Firginia she come out, an' den Marse Chan he went to Richmond an' listed, an' come back an' sey he wuz a private, an' he didn' know whe'r he could tek me or not. He writ to Mr Gordon, hows'ever, an' 'twuz 'cided dat when he went I wuz to go 'long an' wait on him an' de cap'n too. I didn' min' dat, yo' know, long ez I could go wid Marse Chan, an' I like' Mr Gordon, anyways.

'Well, one night Marse Chan come back from de offis wid a telegram dat say, "Come at once," so he wuz to start nex' mawnin'. He uniform wuz all ready, gray wid yaller trimmin's, an' mine wuz ready too, an' he had ole marster's sword, whar de State gi' 'im in de Mexikin war; an' he trunks wuz all packed wid ev'rythin' in 'em, an' my chist was packed too, an' Jim Rasher he druv 'em over to de depo' in de waggin, an' we wuz to start nex' mawnin' 'bout light. Dis wuz 'bout de las' o' spring, you know. Dat night ole missis made Marse Chan dress up in he uniform, an' he sut'n'y did look splendid, wid he long mustache an' he wavin' hyar an' he tall figger.

'Arfter supper he come down an' sez: "Sam, I wan' you to tek dis note an' kyar it over to Cun'l Chahmb'lin's an' gi' it to Miss Anne wid yo' own han's, an' bring me wud what she sez. Don' let anyone know 'bout it, or know why you've gone." "Yes, seh," sez I.

'Yo' see, I knowed Miss Anne's maid over at ole Cun'l Chahmb'lin's – dat wuz Judy whar is my wife now – an' I knowed I could wuk it. So I tuk de roan an' rid over, an' tied 'im down de hill in de cedars, an' I wen' 'roun' to de back yard. 'Twuz a right blowy sort o' night; de moon wuz jes' risin', but de clouds wuz so big it didn' shine 'cep' th'oo a crack now an' den. I soon foun' my gal, an' arfter tellin' her two or three lies 'bout herse'f, I got her to go in an' ax Miss Anne to come to de do'. When she come, I gi' her de note, an' arfter a little while she bro't me anurr, an' I tole her goodbye, an' she gi' me a dollar, an' I come home an' gi' de letter to Marse Chan. He read it, an' tole me to have de hosses ready at twenty minits to twelve at de corner of de garden. An' jes' befo' dat he come out ez ef he wuz gwine to bed, but instid he come, an' we all struck out to'ds Cun'l Chahmb'lin's. When we got mos' to de gate, de hosses got sort o' skeered, an' I see dey wuz some'n or somebody standin' jes' inside; an' Marse Chan he jumpt off de sorrel an' flung me de bridle and he walked up.

'She spoke fust ('twus Miss Anne had done come out dyar to meet Marse Chan), an' she sez, jes' ez cold ez a chill, "Well, seh, I granted your favor. I wished to relieve myse'f of de obligations you placed me under a few months ago, when you made me a present of my father, whom you fust insulted an' then prevented from gittin' satisfaction."

'Marse Chan he didn' speak fur a minit, an' den he said: "Who is with you?" (Dat wuz ev'y wud.'

' "No one," sez she; "I came alone."

' "My God!" sez he, "you didn' come all through those woods by yourse'f at this time o' night?"

' "Yes, I'm not afraid," sez she. (An' heah dis nigger! I don' b'lieve she wuz.)

'De moon come out, an I cotch sight o' her stan'in dyar in her white dress, wid de cloak she had wrapped herse'f up in drapped off on de groun', an' she didn' look like she wuz 'feared o' nuthin'.

She wuz mons'us purty ez she stood dyar wid de green bushes behine her, an' she hed jes' a few flowers in her breas' – right hyar – and some leaves in her sorrel hyar; an' de moon come out an' shined down on her hyar an' her frock, an' 'peared like de light wuz jes' stan'in' off it ez she stood dyar lookin' at Marse Chan wid her head tho'd back, jes' like dat mawnin' when she pahss Marse Chan in de road widout speakin' to 'im, an' sez to me, "Good mawnin', Sam."

'Marse Chan, he den tole her he hed come to say goodbye to her, ez he wuz gwine 'way to de war nex' mawnin'. I wuz watchin' on her, an' I tho't, when Marse Chan tole her dat, she sort o' started an' looked up at 'im like she wuz mighty sorry, an' 'peared like she didn' stan' quite so straight arfter dat. Den Marse Chan he went on talkin' right fars' to her; an' he tole her how he had loved her ever sence she wuz a little bit o' baby mos', an' how he nuver 'membered de time when he hedn' 'spected to marry her. He tole her it wuz his love for her dat hed made 'im stan' fust at school an' collige, an' hed kep' 'im good an' pure; an' now he wuz gwine 'way, wouldn' she let it be like 'twuz in ole times, an' ef he come back from de war wouldn' she try to think on him ez she use' to do when she wuz a little guirl?

'Marse Chan he had done been talkin' so serious, he hed done tuk Miss Anne's han', an' wuz lookin' down in her face like he wuz list'nin' wid his eyes.

'Arfter a minit Miss Anne said somethin'; an' Marse Chan he cotch her urr han' an' sez:

' "But if you love me, Anne?"

'When he said dat, she tu'ned her head 'way from 'im, an' wait' a minit, an' den she said – right clear:

' "But I don' love yo'." (Jes' dem th'ee wuds!) De wuds fall right slow – like dirt falls out a spade on a coffin when yo's buryin' anybody, an' seys, "Uth to uth." Marse Chan he jes' let her hand drap, an' he stiddy hisse'f 'g'inst de gate-pos', an' he didn' speak torekly. When he did speak, all he sez wuz:

' "I mus' see you home safe."

'I 'clar, marster, I didn' know 'twuz Marse Chan's voice tell I look at 'im right good. Well, she wouldn' let 'im go wid her. She jes' wrap' her cloak 'roun' her shoulders, an' wen' 'long back by herse'f, widout doin' more'n jes' look up once at Marse Chan leanin' dyah 'g'inst de gate-pos' in he sodger clo's, wid de eyes on de groun'. She said "Goodbye" sort o' sorf, an' Marse Chan, widout lookin' up, shake han's wid her, an' she wuz done gone down de road. Soon ez she got 'mos' 'roun de curve, Marse Chan followed her, keepin' under de trees so ez not to be seen, an' I led de hosses on down de road behine 'im. He kep' 'long behine her tell she wuz safe in de house, an' den he come an' got on he hoss, an' we all come home.

'Nex' mawnin' we all come off to j'ine de army. An' dey wuz a-drillin' an' a-drillin' all 'bout for a while an' dey went 'long wid all de res' o' de army, an' I went wid Marse Chan an' clean he boots, an' look arfter de tent, an' tek keer o' him an' de hosses. An' Marse Chan, he wan' a bit like he use' to be. He wuz so solum an' moanful all de time, a leas' 'cep' when dyah wuz gwine to be a fight. Den he'd peartin' up, an' he alwuz rode at de head o' de company, 'cause he wuz tall; an' hit wan' on'y in battles whar all his company wuz dat *he* went, but he use' to volunteer whenever de cun'l wanted anybody to fine out anythin', an' 'twuz so dangersome he didn' like to mek one man go no sooner'n anurr, yo' know, an' ax'd who'd volunteer. *He* 'peared to like to go prowlin' aroun' 'mong dem Yankees, and' he use' to tek me wid 'im whenever he could. Yes, seh, he sut'n'y wuz a good sodger! He didn' mine bullets no more'n he did so many draps o' rain. But I use' to be pow'ful skeered sometimes. It jes' use' to 'pear like fun to 'im. In camp he use' to be so sorreful he'd hardly open he mouf. You'd 'a' tho't he wuz seekin', he used to look so moanful; but jes' le' 'im git into danger, an' he use' to be like ole times – jolly an' laughin' like when he wuz a boy.

'When Cap'n Gordon got he leg shot off, dey mek Marse Chan cap'n on de spot,' cause one o' de lieutenants got kilt de same day, an' turr one (named Mr Ronny) wan' no 'count, an' all de company said Marse Chan wuz de man.

'An' Marse Chan he wuz jes' de same. He didn' never mention Miss Anne's name, but I knowed he wuz thinkin' on her constant. One night he wuz settin' by de fire in camp, an' Mr Ronny – he wuz de secon' lieutenant – got to talkin' 'bout ladies, an' he say all sorts o' things 'bout 'em, an' I see Marse Chan kinder lookin' mad; an' de lieutenant mention Miss Anne's name. He hed been courtin' Miss Anne 'bout de time Marse Chan fit de duil wid her pa, an' Miss Anne hed kicked 'im, dough he wuz mighty rich, 'cause he warn' nuthin' but a half-strainer, an' 'cause she like Marse Chan, I believe, dough she didn' speak to 'im; an' Mr Ronny he got drunk, an' 'cause Cun'l Chahmb'lin tole 'im not to come dyah no more, he got mighty mad. An' dat evenin' I'se tellin' yo' 'bout, he wuz talkin', an' he mention' Miss Anne's name. I see Marse Chan tu'n he eye 'roun' on 'im an' keep it on he face, and pres'n'y Mr Ronny said he wuz gwine hev some fun dyah yit. He didn' mention her name dat time; but he said dey wuz all on 'em a parecel of stuck-up 'risticrats, an' her pa wan' no gent'man anyway, an'—I don't know what he wuz gwine say (he nuver said it), fur ez he got dat far Marse Chan riz up an' hit 'im a crack, an' he fall like he hed been hit wid a fence-rail. He challenge' Marse Chan to fight a duil, an' Marse Chan he excepted de challenge, an' dey wuz gwine fight; but some on 'em tole 'im Marse Chan wan' gwine mek a present o' him to his fam'ly, an' he got somebody to bre'k up de duil; twan' nuthin' dough, but he wuz 'fred to fight Marse Chan. An' purty soon he lef' de comp'ny.

'Well, I got one o' de gent'mens to write Judy a letter for me, an' I tole her all 'bout de fight, an' how Marse Chan knock Mr Ronny over fur speakin' discontemptuous o' Cun'l Chahmb'lin, an' I tole her how Marse Chan wuz a-dyin' fur love o' Miss Anne. An' Judy she gits Miss Anne to read de letter fur her. Den Miss Anne she tells her pa, an' — you mind, Judy tells me all dis afterwards, an' she say when Cun'l Chahmb'lin hear 'bout it, he wuz settin' on de poach, an' he set still a good while, an' den he sey to hisse'f:

' "Well, he carn' he'p bein' a Whig."

'An' den he gits up an' walks up to Miss Anne an' he looks at her right hard; an' Miss Anne she hed done tu'n away her haid an' wuz makin' out she wuz fixin' a rose-bush 'g'inst de poach; an' when her pa kep' lookin' at her, her face got jes' de color o' de roses on de bush, and pres'n'y her pa sez:

' "Anne!"

'An' she tu'ned roun', an' he sez:

' "Do yo' want 'im?"

'An' she sez, "Yes," an' put her head on he shoulder an' begin to cry; an' he sez:

' "Well, I won' stan' between yo' no longer. Write to 'im an' say so."

'We didn' know nuthin' 'bout dis den. We wuz a-fightin' an' a-fightin' all dat time; an' come one day a letter to Marse Chan, an' I see 'im start to read it in his tent, an' he face hit look so cu'ious, an' he han's trembled so I couldn' mek out what wuz de matter wid 'im. An' he fol' de letter up an' wen' out an' wen' way down 'hine de camp, an' stayed dyah 'bout nigh an hour. Well, seh, I wuz on de lookout for 'im when he come back, an', fo' Gord, ef he face didn' shine like a angel's! I say to myse'f, "Um'm! ef de glory o' Gord ain' done shine on 'im!" An' what yo' 'spose 'twuz?

'He tuk me wid 'im dat evenin', an' he tell me he hed done git a letter from Miss Anne, an' Marse Chan he eyes look like gre't big stars, an' he face wuz jes' like 'twuz dat mawnin' when de sun riz up over de low groun', an' I see 'im stan'in' dyah wid de pistil in he han', lookin' at it, an' not knowin' but what it mout be de lars' time, an' he done mek up he mine not to shoot ole Cun'l Chahmb'lin fur Miss Anne's sake, what writ 'im de letter.

'He fol' de letter wha' was in his han' up, an' put it in he inside pocket – right dyar on de lef' side; an' den he tole me he tho't mebbe we wuz gwine hev some warm wuk in de nex' two or th'ee days, an' arfter dat ef Gord speared 'im he'd git a leave o' absence fur a few days, an' we'd go home.

'Well, dat night de orders come, an' we all hed to git over to'ds Romney; an' we rid all night till 'bout light; an' we halted right on a little creek, an' wc stayed dyah till mos' breakfas' time, an' I see Marse Chan set down on de groun' 'hine a bush an' read dat letter over an' over. I watch 'im, an' de battle wuz a-goin' on, but we had orders to stay 'hine de hill, an' ev'y now an' den de bullets would cut de limbs o' de trees right over us, an' one o' dem big shells what goes "*Awhar – awhar – awhar!*" would fall right 'mong us; but Marse Chan he didn' mine it no mo'n nuthin'! Den it 'peared to git closer an' thicker, and Marse Chan he calls me, an' I crep' up, an' he sez:

' "Sam, we'se goin' to win in dis battle, an' den we'll go home an' git married; an' I'se goin' home wid a star on my collar." An' den he sez, "Ef I'm wounded, kyar me home, yo' hear?" An' I sez, "Yes, Marse Chan."

'Well, jes' den dey blowed boots an' saddles, 'an we mounted; an' de orders come to ride 'roun' de slope, an' Marse Chan's comp'ny wuz de secon', an' when we got 'roun' dyah, we wuz right in it. Hit wuz de wust place ever dis nigger got in. An' dey said, "Charge 'em!" an' my king! ef ever you see bullets fly, dey did dat day. Hit wuz jes' like hail; an' we wen' down de slope (I long wid de res') an' up de hill right to'ds de cannons an' de fire wuz so strong dyar (dey hed a whole rigiment o' infintrys layin' down dyar onder de cannons) our lines sort o' broke an' stop; de cun'l was kilt, an' I b'lieve dey wuz jes' 'bout to bre'k all to pieces, when Marse Chan rid up an' cotch hol' de fleg an' hollers, "Foller me!" an' rid strainin' up de hill 'mong de cannons. I seen 'im when he went, de sorrel four good lengths ahead o' ev'y urr hoss, jes' like he use' to be in a fox-hunt, an' de whole rigiment right arfter 'im. Yo' ain' nuver hear thunder! Fust thing I knowed, de roan roll' head over heels an' flung me up 'g'inst de bank, like yo' chuck a nubbin over 'g'inst de foot o' de corn pile. An dat's what kep' me from bein' kilt, I 'spects. Judy she say she think 'twuz Providence, but I think 'twuz de bank. O' co'se, Providence put de bank dyah, but how come Providence nuver saved Marse Chan? When I look' 'roun', de roan wuz layin' dyah by me, stone dead, wid a cannon-ball gone 'mos' th'oo him, an' our men hed done swep' dem on t'urr side from de top o' de hill. 'Twan' mo'n a minit, de sorrel come gallupin' back wid his mane flyin', an' de rein hangin' down on one side to his knee. "Dyar!" says I, "fo' Gord! I 'specks dey done kill Marse Chan, an' I promised to tek care on him."

'I jumped up an' run over de bank, an' dyar, wid a whole lot o' dead men, an' some not dead yit, onder one o' de guns wid de fleg still in he han', an' a bullet right th'oo he body, lay Marse Chan. I tu'n 'im over an' call 'im, "Marse Chan!" but 'twan' no use, he wuz done gone home, sho' 'nuff. I pick' 'im up in my arms wid de fleg still in he han', an' toted 'im back jes' like I did dat day when he wuz a baby, an' ole marster gin 'im to me in my arms, an' sez he could trus' me, an' tell me to tek keer on 'im long ez he lived. I kyar'd 'im 'way off de battlefiel' out de way o' de balls, an' I laid 'im down onder a big tree till I could git somebody to ketch de sorrel for me. He wuz cotched arfter a while, an' I hed some money, so I got some pine plank an' made a coffin dat evenin', an' wrapt Marse Chan's body up in de fleg, an' put 'im in de coffin; but I didn' nail de top on strong, 'cause I knowed ole missis wan' see 'im; an' I got a' ambulance an' set out for home dat night. We reached dyar de nex' evenin', arfter travellin' all dat night an' all nex' day.

'Hit 'peared like somethin' hed tole ole missis he wuz comin' so; for when we got home she wuz waitin' for us – done drest up in her best Sunday-clo'es, an' stan'n' at de head o' de big steps, an' ole marster settin' in his big cheer – ez we druv up de hill to'ds de house, I drivin' de ambulance an' de sorrel leadin' 'long behine wid de stirrups crost over de saddle.

'She come down to de gate to meet us. We took de coffin out de ambulance an' kyar'd it right into de big parlor wid de pictures in it, whar dey use' to dance in ole times when Marse Chan wuz a school-boy, an' Miss Anne Chahmb'lin use' to come over, an' go wid ole missis into her chamber an' tek her things off. In dyar we laid de coffin on two o' de cheers, an' ole missis nuver said a wud; she jes' looked so ole an' white.

'When I had tell 'em all 'bout it, I tu'ned right 'roun' an' rid over to Cun'l Chahmb'lin's, 'cause I knowed dat wuz what Marse Chan he'd 'a' wanted me to do. I didn' tell nobody whar I wuz gwine, 'cause yo' know none on 'em hadn' nuver speak to Miss Anne, not sence de duil, an' dey didn' know 'bout de letter.

'When I rid up in de yard, dyar wuz Miss Anne a'stan'in' on de poach watchin' me ez I rid up. I tied my hoss to de fence, an' walked up de parf. She knowed by de way I walked dyar wuz somethin' de motter, an' she wuz mighty pale. I drapt my cap down on de een' o' de steps an' went up. She nuver opened her mouf; jes' stan' right still an' keep her eyes on my face. Fust, I couldn' speak; den I cotch my voice, an' I say, "Marse Chan, he done got he furlough."

'Her face was mighty ashy, an' she sort o' shook, but she didn' fall. She tu'ned roun' an' said, "Git me de ker'ige!" Dat wuz all.

'When de ker'ige come 'roun', she hed put on her bonnet, an' wuz ready. Ez she got in, she sey to me, "Hev yo' brought him home?" an' we drove 'long, I ridin' behine.

'When we got home, she got out, an' walked up de big walk — up to de poach by herse'f. Ole missis hed done fin' de letter in Marse Chan's pocket, wid de love in it, while I wuz 'way, an' she wuz a-waitin' on de poach. Dey sey dat wuz de fust time ole missis cry when she find de letter, an' dat she sut'n'y did cry over it, pintedly.

'Well, seh, Miss Anne she walks right up de steps, mos' up to ole missis stan'in' dyar on de poach, an' jes' falls right down mos' to her, on her knees fust, an' den flat on her face right on de flo', ketchin' at ole missis' dress wid her two han's — so.

'Ole missis stood for 'bout a minit lookin' down at her, an' den she drapt down on de flo' by her, an' took her in bofe her arms.

'I couldn' see, I wuz cryin' so myse'f, an' ev'ybody wuz cryin'. But dey went in arfter a while in de parlor, an' shet de do'; an' I heahd 'em say, Miss Anne she tuk de coffin in her arms an' kissed it, an' kissed Marse Chan, an' call 'im by his name, an' her darlin', an' ole missis lef' her cryin' in dyar tell some on 'em went in, an' found her done faint on de flo'.

'Judy (she's my wife) she tell me she heah Miss Anne when she axed ole missis mout she wear mo'nin' fur 'im. I don' know how dat is; but when we buried 'im nex' day, she wuz de one whar walked arfter de coffin, holdin' ole marster, an' ole missis she walked next to 'em.

'Well, we buried Marse Chan dyar in de ole grabeyard, wid de fleg wrapped roun' 'im, an' he face lookin' like it did dat mawnin' down in de low groun's, wid de new sun shinin' on it so peaceful.

'Miss Anne she nuver went home to stay arfter dat; she stay wid ole marster an' ole missis ez long ez dey lived. Dat warn' so mighty long, 'cause ole marster he died dat fall, when dey wuz fallerin' fur wheat – I had jes' married Judy den – an' ole missis she warn' long behine him. We buried her by him next summer. Miss Anne she went in de hospitals toreckly arfter ole missis died; an' jes' fo' Richmond fell she came home sick wid de fever. Yo' nuver would 'a' knowed her fur de same ole Miss Anne. She wuz light ez a piece o' peth, an' so white, 'cep' her eyes an' her sorrel hyar, an' she kep' on gittin' whiter an' weaker. Judy she sut'n'y did nuss her faithful. But she nuver got no betterment! De fever an' Marse Chan's bein' kilt hed done strain her, an' she died jes' fo' de folks wuz sot free.

'So we buried Miss Anne right by Marse Chan, in a place whar ole missis hed tole us to leave, an' dey's bofe on 'em sleep side by side over in de ole grabeyard at home.

'An' will yo' please tell me, marster? Dey tells me dat de Bible sey dyar won' be marryin' nor givin' in marriage in heaven, but I don' b'lieve it signifies dat – does you?'

I gave him the comfort of my earnest belief in some other interpretation, together with several spare 'eighteen-pences,' as he called them, for which he seemed humbly grateful. And as I rode away I heard him calling across the fence to his wife, who was standing in the door of a small white-washed cabin, near which we had been standing for some time:

'Judy, have Marse Chan's dawg got home?'

1887

HAROLD FREDERIC
1856–1898

The Eve of the Fourth

It was well on toward evening before this Third of July all at once made itself gloriously different from other days in my mind.

There was a very long afternoon, I remember, hot and overcast, with continual threats of rain, which never came to anything. The other boys were too excited about the morrow to care for present play. They sat instead along the edge of the broad platform-stoop in front of Delos Ingersoll's grocery-store, their brown feet swinging at varying heights above the sidewalk, and bragged about the manner in which they contemplated celebrating the anniversary of their Independence. Most of the elder lads were very independent indeed; they were already secure in the parental permission to stay up all night, so that the Fourth might be ushered in with its full quota of ceremonial. The smaller urchins pretended that they also had this permission, or were sure of getting it. Little Denny Cregan attracted admiring attention by vowing that he should remain out, even if his father chased him with a policeman all around the ward, and he had to go and live in a cave in the gulf until he was grown up.

My inferiority to these companions of mine depressed me. They were allowed to go without shoes and stockings; they wore loose and comfortable old clothes, and were under no responsibility to keep them dry or clean or whole; they had their pockets literally bulging now with all sorts of portentous engines of noise and racket – huge brown 'double-enders,' bound with waxed cord; long, slim, vicious-looking 'nigger-chasers;' big 'Union torpedoes,' covered with clay, which made a report like a horse-pistol, and were invaluable for frightening farmers' horses; and so on through an extended catalogue of recondite and sinister explosives upon which I looked with awe, as their owners from time to time exhibited them with the proud simplicity of those accustomed to greatness. Several of these boys also possessed toy cannons, which would be brought forth at twilight. They spoke firmly of ramming them to the muzzle with grass, to produce a greater noise – even if it burst them and killed everybody.

By comparison, my lot was one of abasement. I was a solitary child, and a victim to conventions. A blue necktie was daily pinned under my Byron collar, and there were gilt buttons on my zouave jacket. When we were away in the pasture playground near the gulf, and I ventured to take off my foot-gear, every dry old thistle-point in the whole territory seemed to arrange itself to be stepped upon on my whitened and tender soles. I could not swim; so, while my lithe bold comrades dived out of sight under the deep water, and darted about chasing one another far beyond their depth, I paddled ignobly around the 'baby-hole' close to the bank, in the warm and muddy shallows.

Especially apparent was my state of humiliation on this July afternoon. I had no 'double-enders,' nor might hope for any. The mere thought of a private cannon seemed monstrous and unnatural to me. By some unknown process of reasoning my mother had years before reached the theory that a good boy ought to have two ten-cent packs of small fire-crackers on the Fourth of July. Four or five succeeding anniversaries had hardened this theory into an orthodox tenet of faith, with all its observances rigidly fixed. The fire-crackers were bought for me overnight, and placed on the hall table. Beside them lay a long rod of punk. When I hastened down and out in the morning, with these ceremonial implements in my hands, the hired girl would give me, in an old kettle, some embers from the wood fire in the summer kitchen. Thus furnished, I went into the front yard, and in solemn solitude fired off these crackers one by one. Those which, by reason of having lost their tails, were only fit for 'fizzes,' I saved till after breakfast. With the exhaustion of these, I fell reluctantly back upon the public for entertainment. I could see the soldiers, hear the band and the oration, and in the evening, if it didn't rain, enjoy the fireworks; but my own contribution to the patriotic noise was always over before the breakfast dishes had been washed.

My mother scorned the little paper torpedoes as flippant and wasteful things. You merely threw one of them, and it went off, she said, and there you were. I don't know that I ever grasped this objection in its entirety, but it impressed my whole childhood with its unanswerableness. Years and years afterward, when my own children asked for torpedoes, I found myself unconsciously advising against them on quite the maternal lines. Nor was it easy to budge the good lady from her position on the great two-packs issue. I seem to recall having successfully undermined it once or twice, but two was the rule. When I called her attention to the fact that our neighbor, Tom Hemingway, thought nothing of exploding a whole pack at a time inside their wash-boiler, she was not dazzled, but only replied: 'Wilful waste makes woeful want.'

Of course the idea of the Hemingways ever knowing what want meant was absurd. They lived a dozen doors or so from us, in a big white house with stately white columns rising from veranda to gable across the whole front, and a large garden, flowers and shrubs in front, fruit-trees and vegetables behind. Squire Hemingway was the most important man in our part of the town. I know now that he was never anything more than United States Commissioner of Deeds, but in those days, when he walked down the street with his gold-headed cane, his blanket-shawl folded over his arm, and his severe, dignified, close-shaven face held well up in the air, I seemed to behold a companion of Presidents.

This great man had two sons. The elder of them, De Witt Hemingway, was a man grown, and was at the front. I had seen him march away, over a year before, with a bright drawn sword, at the side of his company. The other son, Tom, was my senior by only a twelvemonth. He was by nature proud, but often consented to consort with me when the selection of other available associates was at low ebb.

It was to this Tom that I listened with most envious eagerness, in front of the grocery-store, on the afternoon of which I speak. He did not sit on the stoop with the others – no one expected quite that degree of condescension – but leaned nonchalantly against a post, whittling out a new ramrod for his cannon. He said that this year he was not going to have any ordinary fire-crackers at all; they, he added with a meaning glance at me, were only fit for girls. He might do a little in 'double-enders,' but his real point would be in 'ringers' – an incredible giant variety of cracker, Turkey-red like the other, but in size almost a rolling-pin. Some of these he would fire off singly, between volleys from his cannon. But a good many he intended to explode, in bunches say of six, inside the tin washboiler, brought out into the middle of the road for that purpose. It would doubtless blow the old thing sky-high, but that didn't matter. They could get a new one.

Even as he spoke, the big bell in the tower of the town-hall burst forth in a loud clangor of swift-repeated strokes. It was half a mile away, but the moist air brought the urgent, clamorous sounds to our ears as if the belfy had stood close above us. We sprang off the stoop and stood poised, waiting to hear the number of the ward struck, and ready to scamper off on the instant if the fire was anywhere in our part of the town. But the excited peal went on and on without a pause. It became obvious that this meant something besides a fire. Perhaps some of us wondered vaguely what that something might be, but as a body our interest had lapsed. Billy Norris, who was the son of poor parents, but could whip even Tom Hemingway, said he had been told that the German boys on the other side of the gulf were coming over to 'rush' us on the following day, and that we ought all to collect nails to fire at them from our cannon. This we pledged ourselves to do – the bell keeping up its throbbing tumult ceaselessly.

Suddenly we saw the familiar figure of Johnson running up the street toward us. What his first name was I never knew. To every one, little or big, he was just Johnson. He and his family had moved into our town after the war began; I fancy they moved away again before it ended. I do not even know what he did for a living. But he seemed always drunk, always turbulently good-natured, and always shouting out the news at the top of his lungs. I cannot pretend to guess how he found out everything as he did, or why, having found it out, he straightway rushed homeward, scattering the intelligence as he ran. Most probably Johnson was moulded by Nature as a town-crier, but was born by accident some generations after the race of bellmen had disappeared. Our neighborhood did not like him; our mothers did not know Mrs Johnson, and we boys behaved with snobbish roughness to his children. He seemed not to mind this at all, but came up unwearyingly to shout out the tidings of the day for our benefit.

'Vicksburg's fell! Vicksburg's fell!' was what we heard him yelling as he approached.

Delos Ingersoll and his hired boy ran out of the grocery. Doors opened along the street and heads were thrust inquiringly out.

'Vicksburg's fell!' he kept hoarsely proclaiming, his arms waving in the air, as he staggered along at a dog-trot past us, and went into the saloon next to the grocery.

I cannot say how definite an idea these tidings conveyed to our boyish minds. I have a notion that at the time I assumed that Vicksburg had something to do with Gettysburg, where I knew, from the talk of my elders, that an awful fight had been proceeding since the middle of the week. Doubtless this confusion was aided by the fact that an hour or so later, on that same wonderful day, the wire brought us word that this terrible battle on Pennsylvanian soil had at last taken the form of a Union victory. It is difficult now to see how we could have known both these things on the Third of July – that is to say, before the people actually concerned seemed to have been sure of them. Perhaps it was only inspired guesswork, but I know that my town went wild over the news, and that the clouds overhead cleared away as if by magic.

The sun did well to spread that summer sky at eventide with all the pageantry of color the spectrum knows. It would have been preposterous that such a day should slink off in dull, Quaker drabs. Men were shouting in the streets now. The old cannon left over from the Mexican war had been dragged out on to the rickety covered river-bridge, and was frightening the fishes, and shaking the dry worm-eaten rafters, as fast as the swab and rammer could work. Our town bandsmen were playing as they had never played before, down in the square in front of the post-office. The management of the Universe could not hurl enough wild fire-works into the exultant sunset to fit our mood.

The very air was filled with the scent of triumph – the spirit of conquest. It seemed only natural that I should march off to my mother and quite collectedly tell her that I desired to stay out all night with the other boys. I had never dreamed of daring to prefer such a request in other years. Now I was scarcely conscious of surprise when she gave her permission, adding with a smile that I would be glad enough to come in and go to bed before half the night was over.

I steeled my heart after supper with the proud resolve that if the night turned out to be as protracted as one of those Lapland winter nights we read about in geography, I still would not surrender.

The boys outside were not so excited over the tidings of my unlooked-for victory as I had expected them to be. They received the news, in fact, with a rather mortifying stoicism. Tom Hemingway, however, took enough interest in the affair to suggest that, instead of spending my twenty cents in paltry fire-crackers, I might go downtown and buy another can of powder for his cannon. By doing so, he pointed out, I would be a part-proprietor, as it were, of the night's performance, and would be entitled to occasionally touch the cannon off. This generosity affected me, and I hastened down the long hill-street to show myself worthy of it, repeating the instruction of 'Kentucky Bear-Hunter-coarse-grain' over and over again to myself as I went.

Half-way on my journey I overtook a person whom, even in the gathering twilight, I recognized as Miss Stratford, the school-teacher. She also was walking down the hill and rapidly. It did not need the sight of a letter in her hand to tell me that she was going to the post-office. In those cruel war-days everybody went to the post-office. I myself went regularly to get our mail, and to exchange shin-plasters for one-cent stamps with which to buy yeast and other commodities that called for minute fractional currency.

Although I was very fond of Miss Stratford – I still recall her gentle eyes, and pretty, rounded, dark face, in its frame of long, black curls, with tender liking – I now coldly resolved to hurry past, pretending not to know her. It was a mean thing to do; Miss Stratford had always been good to me, shining in that respect in brilliant contrast to my other teachers, whom I hated bitterly. Still, the 'Kentucky Bear-Hunter-coarse-grain' was too important a matter to wait upon any mere female friendships, and I quickened my pace into a trot, hoping to scurry by unrecognized.

'Oh, Andrew! is that you?' I heard her call out as I ran past. For the instant I thought of rushing on, quite as if I had not heard. Then I stopped and walked beside her.

'I am going to stay up all night: mother says I may; and I am going to fire off Tom Hemingway's big cannon every fourth time, straight through till breakfast time,' I announced to her loftily.

'Dear me! I ought to be proud to be seen walking with such an important citizen,' she answered, with kindly playfulness. She added more gravely, after a moment's pause: 'Then Tom is out playing with the other boys, is he?'

'Why, of course!' I responded. 'He always lets us stand around when he fires off his cannon. He's got some "ringers" this year too.'

I heard Miss Stratford murmur an impulsive 'Thank God!' under her breath.

Full as the day had been of surprises, I could not help wondering that the fact of Tom's ringers should stir up such profound emotions in the teacher's breast. Since the subject so interested her, I went on with a long catalogue of Tom's other pyrotechnic possessions, and from that to an account of his almost supernatural collection of postage-stamps. In a few minutes more I am sure I should have revealed to her the great secret of my life, which was my determination, in case I came to assume the victorious rôle and rank of Napoleon, to immediately make Tom a Marshal of the Empire.

But we had reached the post-office square. I had never before seen it so full of people.

Even to my boyish eyes the tragic line of division which cleft this crowd in twain was apparent. On one side, over by the Seminary, the youngsters had lighted a bonfire, and were running about it – some of the bolder ones jumping through it in frolicsome recklessness. Close by stood the band, now valiantly thumping out 'John Brown's Body' upon the noisy night air. It was quite dark by this time, but the musicians knew the tune by heart. So did the throng about them, and sang it with lusty fervor. The doors of the saloon toward the corner of the square were flung wide open. Two black streams of men kept in motion under the radiance of the big reflector-lamp over these doors – one going in, one coming out. They slapped one another on the back as they passed, with exultant screams and shouts. Every once in a while, when movement was for the instant blocked, some voice lifted above the others would begin. 'Hip-hip-hip-hip—' and then would come a roar that fairly drowned the music.

On the post-office side of the square there was no bonfire. No one raised a cheer. A densely packed mass of men and women stood in front of the big square stone building, with its closed doors, and curtained windows upon which, from time to time, the shadow of some passing clerk, bareheaded and hurried, would be momentarily thrown. They waited in silence for the night mail to be sorted. If they spoke to one another, it was in whispers – as if they had been standing with uncovered heads at a funeral service in a graveyard. The dim light reflected over from the bonfire, or down from the shaded windows of the post-office, showed solemn, hard-lined, anxious faces. Their lips scarcely moved when they muttered little low-toned remarks to their neighbours. They spoke from the side of the mouth, and only on one subject.

'He went all through Fredericksburg without a scratch –'

'He looks so much like me – General Palmer told my brother he'd have known his hide in a tanyard – '

'He's been gone – let's see – it was a year some time last April – '

'He was counting on a furlough the first of this month. I suppose nobody got one as things turned out – '

'He said, "No: it ain't my style. I'll fight as much as you like, but I won't be nigger-waiter for no man, captain or no captain" – '

Thus I heard the scattered murmurs among the grown-up heads above me, as we pushed into the outskirts of the throng, and stood there, waiting for the rest. There was no sentence without a 'he' in it. A stranger might have fancied that they were all talking of one man. I knew better. They were the fathers and mothers, the sisters, brothers, wives of the men whose regiments had been in that horrible three days' fight at Gettysburg. Each was thinking and speaking of his own, and took it for granted the others would understand. For that matter, they all did understand. The town knew the name and family of every one of the twelve-score sons she had in this battle.

It is not very clear to me now why people all went to the post-office to wait for the evening papers that came in from the nearest big city. Nowadays they would be brought in bulk and sold on the street before the mail-bags had reached the post-office. Apparently that had not yet been thought of in our slow old town.

The band across the square had started up afresh with 'Annie Lisle' – the sweet old refrain of 'Wave willows, murmur waters,' comes back to me now after a quarter-century of forgetfulness – when all at once there was a sharp forward movement of the crowd. The doors had been thrown open, and the hallway was on the instant filled with a swarming multitude. The band had stopped as suddenly as it began, and no more cheering was heard. We could see whole troops of dark forms scudding toward us from the other side of the square.

'Run in for me – that's a good boy – ask for Dr Stratford's mail,' the teacher whispered, bending over me.

It seemed an age before I finally got back to her, with the paper in its postmarked wrapper buttoned up inside my jacket. I had never been in so fierce and determined a crowd before, and I emerged from it at last, confused in wits and panting for breath. I was still looking about through the gloom in a foolish way for Miss Stratford, when I felt her hand laid sharply on my shoulder.

'Well – where is it? – did nothing come?' she asked, her voice trembling with eagerness, and the eyes which I had thought so soft and dove-like flashing down upon me as if she were Miss Pritchard, and I had been caught chewing gum in school.

I drew the paper out from under my roundabout, and gave it to her. She grasped it, and thrust a finger under the cover to tear it off. Then she hesitated for a moment, and looked about her. 'Come where there is some light,' she said, and started up the street. Although she seemed to have spoken more to herself than to me, I followed her in silence, close to her side.

For a long way the sidewalk in front of every lighted store-window was thronged with a group of people clustered tight about someone who had a paper, and was reading from it aloud. Besides broken snatches of this monologue, we caught, now groans of sorrow and horror, now exclamations of proud approval, and even the beginnings of cheers, broken in upon by a general ' 'Sh-h!' as we hurried past outside the curb.

It was under a lamp in the little park nearly half-way up the hill that Miss Stratford stopped, and spread the paper open. I see her still, white-faced, under the flickering gaslight, her black curls making a strange dark bar between the pale-straw hat and the white of her shoulder shawl and muslin dress, her hands trembling as they held up the extended sheet. She scanned the columns swiftly, skimmingly for a time, as I could see by the way she moved her round chin up and down. Then she came to a part which called for closer reading. The paper shook perceptibly now, as she bent her eyes upon it. Then all at once it fell from her hands, and without a sound she walked away.

I picked the paper up and followed her along the gravelled path. It was like pursuing a ghost, so weirdly white did her summer attire now look to my frightened eyes, with such a swift and deathly silence did she move. The path upon which we were described a circle touching the four sides of the square. She did not quit it when the intersection with our street was reached, but followed straight round again toward the point where we had entered the park. This, too, in turn, she passed, gliding noiselessly forward under the black arches of the overhanging elms. The suggestion that she did not know she was going round and round in a ring startled my brain. I would have run up to her now if I had dared.

Suddenly she turned, and saw that I was behind her. She sank slowly into one of the garden-seats, by the path, and held out for a moment a hesitating hand toward me. I went up at this and looked into her face. Shadowed as it was, the change I saw there chilled my blood. It was like the face of someone I had never seen before, with fixed, wide-open, staring eyes which seemed to look beyond me through the darkness, upon some terrible sight no other could see.

'Go – run and tell – Tom – to go home! His brother – his brother has been killed,' she said to me, choking over the words as if they hurt her throat, and still with the same strange dry-eyed, far-away gaze covering yet not seeing me.

I held out the paper for her to take, but she made no sign, and I gingerly laid it on the seat beside her. I hung about for a minute or two longer, imagining that she might have something else to say – but no word came. Then, with a feebly inopportune 'Well, good-bye,' I started off alone up the hill.

It was a distinct relief to find that my companions were congregated at the lower end of the common, instead of their accustomed haunt farther up near my home, for the walk had been a lonely one, and I was deeply depressed by what had happened. Tom, it seems, had been called away some quarter of an hour before. All the boys knew of the calamity which had befallen the Hemingways. We talked about it, from time to time, as we loaded and fired the cannon which Tom had obligingly turned over to my friends. It had been out of deference to the feelings of the stricken household that they had betaken themselves and their racket off to the remote corner of the common. The solemnity of the occasion silenced ciriticism upon my conduct in forgetting to buy the powder. 'There would be enough as long as it lasted,' Billy Norris said, with philosophic decision.

We speculated upon the likelihood of De Witt Hemingway's being given a military funeral. These mournful pageants had by this time become such familiar things to us that the prospect of one more had no element of excitement in it, save as it involved a gloomy sort of distinction for Tom. He would ride in the first mourning-carriage with his parents, and this would associate us, as we walked along ahead of the band, with the most intimate aspects of the demonstration. We regretted now that the soldier company which we had so long projected remained still un-organized. Had it been otherwise we would probably have been awarded the right of the line in the procession. Someone suggested that it was not too late – and we promptly bound ourselves to meet after breakfast next day to organize and begin drilling. If we worked at this night and day, and our parents instantaneously provided us with uniforms and guns, we should be in time. It was also arranged that we should be called the De Witt C. Hemingway Fire Zouaves, and that Billy Norris should be side captain. The chief command would, of course, be reserved for

Tom. We would specially salute him as he rode past in the closed carriage, and then fall in behind, forming his honorary escort.

None of us had known the dead officer closely, owing to his advanced age. He was seven or eight years older than even Tom. But the more elderly among our group had seen him play baseball in the academy nine, and our neighbourhood was still alive with legends of his early audacity and skill in collecting barrels and dry-goods boxes at night for election bonfires. It was remembered that once he carried away a whole front-stoop from the house of a little German tailor on one of the back streets. As we stood around the heated cannon, in the great black solitude of the common, our fancies pictured this redoubtable young man once more among us – not in his blue uniform, with crimson sash and sword laid by his side, and the gauntlets drawn over his lifeless hands, but as a taller and glorified Tom, in a roundabout jacket and copper-toed boots, giving the law on this his playground. The very cannon at our feet had once been his. The night air became peopled with ghosts of his contemporaries – handsome boys who had grown up before us, and had gone away to lay down their lives in far-off Virginia or Tennessee.

These heroic shades brought drowsiness in their train. We lapsed into long silences, punctuated by yawns, when it was not our turn to ram and touch off the cannon. Finally some of us stretched ourselves out on the grass, in the warm darkness, to wait comfortably for his turn to come.

What did come instead was daybreak – finding Billy and myself alone constant to our all-night vow. We sat up and shivered as we rubbed our eyes. The morning air had a chilling freshness that went to my bones – and these, moreover, were filled with those novel aches and stiffnesses which beds were invented to prevent. We stood up, stretching out our arms, and gaping at the pearl-and-rose beginnings of the sunrise in the eastern sky. The other boys had all gone home, and taken the cannon with them. Only scraps of torn paper and tiny patches of burnt grass marked the site of our celebration.

My first weak impulse was to march home without delay, and get into bed as quickly as might be. But Billy Norris looked so finely resolute and resourceful that I hesitated to suggest this, and said nothing, leaving the initiative to him. One could see, by the most casual glance, that he was superior to mere considerations of unseasonableness in hours. I remembered now that he was one of that remarkable body of boys, the paper-carriers, who rose when all others were asleep in their warm nests, and trudged about long before breakfast distributing the *Clarion* among the well-to-do households. This fact had given him his position in our neighbourhood as quite the next in leadership to Tom Hemingway.

He presently outlined his plans to me, after having tried the centre of light on the horizon, where soon the sun would be, by an old brass compass he had in his pocket – a process which enabled him, he said, to tell pretty well what time it was. The paper wouldn't be out for nearly two hours yet – and if it were not for the fact of a great battle, there would have been no paper at all on this glorious anniversary – but he thought we would go downtown and see what was going on around about the newspaper office. Forthwith we started. He cheered my faint spirits by assuring me that I would soon cease to be sleepy, and would, in fact, feel better than usual. I dragged my feet along at his side, waiting for this revival to come, and meantime furtively yawning against my sleeve.

Billy seemed to have dreamed a good deal, during our nap on the common, about the De Witt C. Hemingway Fire Zouaves. At least he had now in his head a marvellously elaborated system of organization, which he unfolded as we went along. I felt that I had never before realized his greatness, his born genius for command. His scheme halted nowhere. He allotted offices with discriminating firmness; he treated the question of uniforms and guns as a trivial detail which would settle itself; he spoke with calm confidence of our offering our services to the Republic in the autumn; his clear vision saw even the materials for a fife-and-drum corps among the German boys in the back streets. It was true that I appeared personally to play a meagre part in these great projects; the most that was said about me was that I might make a fair third-corporal. But Fate had thrown in my way such a wonderful chance of becoming intimate with Billy that I made sure I should swiftly advance in rank – the more so as I discerned in the background of his thoughts, as it were, a grim determination to make short work of Tom Hemingway's aristocratic pretensions, once the funeral was over.

We were forced to make a detour of the park on our way down, because Billy observed some half-dozen Irish boys at play with a cannon inside, whom he knew to be hostile. If there had been only four, he said, he would have gone in and routed them. He could whip any two of them, he added, with one hand tied behind his back. I listened with admiration. Billy was not tall, but he possessed great thickness of chest and length of arm. His skin was so dark that we canvassed the theory from time to time of his having Indian blood. He did not discourage this, and he admitted himself that he was double-jointed.

The streets of the business part of the town, into which we now made our way, were quite deserted. We went around into the yard behind the printing-office, where the carrier-boys were wont to wait for the press to get to work; and Billy displayed some impatience at discovering that here too there was no one. It was now broad daylight, but through the windows of the composing-room we could see some of the printers still setting type by kerosene lamps.

We seated ourselves at the end of the yard on a big, flat, smooth-faced stone, and Billy produced from his pocket a number of 'em' quads, so he called them, and with which the carriers had learned from the printers' boys to play a very beautiful game. You shook the pieces of metal in your hands and threw them on the stone; your score depended upon the number of nicked sides that were turned uppermost. We played this game in the interest of good-fellowship for a little. Then Billy told me that the carriers always played it for pennies, and that it was unmanly for us to do otherwise. He had no pennies at that precise moment, but would pay at the end of the week what he had lost; in the meantime there was my twenty cents to go on with. After this Billy threw so many nicks uppermost that my courage gave way, and I made an attempt to stop the game; but a single remark from him as to the military destiny which he was reserving for me, if I only displayed true soldierly nerve and grit, sufficed to quiet me once more, and the play went on. I had now only five cents left.

Suddenly a shadow interposed itself between the sunlight and the stone. I looked up, to behold a small boy with bare arms and a blackened apron standing over me, watching our game. There was a great deal of ink on his face and hands, and a hardened, not to say rakish expression in his eye.

'Why don't you "jeff" with somebody of your own size?' he demanded of Billy after having looked me over critically.

He was not nearly so big as Billy, and I expected to see the latter instantly rise and crush him, but Billy only laughed and said we were playing for fun; he was going to give me all my money back. I was rejoiced to hear this, but still felt surprised at the propitiatory manner Billy adopted toward this diminutive inky boy. It was not the demeanor befitting a side-captain – and what made it worse was that the strange boy loftily declined to be cajoled by it. He sniffed when Billy told him about the military company we were forming; he coldly shook his head, with a curt 'Nixie!' when invited to join it; and he laughed aloud at hearing the name our organization was to bear.

'He ain't dead at all – that De Witt Hemingway,' he said, with jeering contempt.

'Hain't he though!' exclaimed Billy. 'The news come last night. Tom had to go home – his mother sent for him – on account of it!'

'I'll bet you a quarter he ain't dead,' responded the practical inky boy. 'Money up, though!'

'I've only got fifteen cents. I'll bet you that, though,' rejoined Billy, producing my torn and dishevelled shin-plasters.

'All right! Wait here!' said the boy, running off to the building and disappearing through the door. There was barely time for me to learn from my companion that this printer's apprentice was called 'the devil,' and could not only whistle between his teeth and crack his fingers, but chew tobacco, when he reappeared, with a long narrow strip of paper in his hand. This he held out for us to see, indicating with an ebon forefinger the special paragraph we were to read. Billy looked at it sharply, for several moments in silence. Then he said to me: 'What does it say there? I must 'a' got some powder in my eyes last night.'

I read this paragraph aloud, not without an unworthy feeling that the inky boy would now respect me deeply:

'CORRECTION. Lieutenant De Witt C. Hemingway, of Company A, —th New York, reported in earlier despatches among the killed, is uninjured. The officer killed is Lieut Carl Heinninge, Company F, same regiment.'

Billy's face visibly lengthened as I read this out, and he felt us both looking at him. He made a pretence of examining the slip of paper again, but in a half-hearted way. Then he ruefully handed over the fifteen cents and, rising from the stone, shook himself.

'Them Dutchmen never was no good!' was what he said.

The inky boy had put the money in the pocket under his apron, and grinned now with as much enjoyment as dignity would permit him to show. He did not seem to mind any longer the original source of his winnings, and it was apparent that I could not with decency recall it to him. Some odd impulse prompted me, however, to ask him if I might have the paper he had in his hand. He was magnanimous enough to present me with the proof-sheet on the spot. Then with another grin he turned and left us.

Billy stood sullenly kicking with his bare toes into a sandheap by the stone. He would not answer me when I spoke to him. It flashed across my perceptive faculties that he was not such a great man, after all, as I had imagined. In another instant or two it became quite clear to me that I had no admiration for him whatever. Without a word I turned on my heel and walked determinedly out of the yard and into the street, homeward bent.

All at once I quickened my pace; something had occurred to me. The purpose thus conceived grew so swiftly that soon I found myself running. Up the hill I sped, and straight through the park. If the Irish boys shouted after me I knew it not, but dashed on heedless of all else save the one idea. I only halted, breathless and panting, when I stood on Dr Stratford's door-step, and heard the night-bell inside jangling shrilly in response to my excited pull.

As I waited, I pictured to myself the old doctor as he would presently come down, half-dressed and pulling on his coat as he advanced. He would ask, eagerly, 'Who is sick? Where am I to go?' and I would calmly reply that he unduly alarmed himself, and that I had a message for his daughter. He would, of course, ask me what it was, and I, politely but firmly, would decline to explain to any one but the lady in person. Just what might ensue was not clear – but I beheld myself throughout commanding the situation, at once benevolent, polished, and inexorable.

The door opened with unlooked-for promptness, while my self-complacent vision still hung in mid-air. Instead of the bald and spectacled old doctor, there confronted me a white-faced, solemn-eyed lady in a black dress, whom I did not seem to know. I stared at her, tongue-tied, till she said, in a low grave voice, 'Well, Andrew, what is it?'

Then of course I saw that it was Miss Stratford, my teacher, the person whom I had come to see. Some vague sense of what the sleepless night had meant in this house came to me as I gazed confusedly at her mourning, and heard the echo of her sad tones in my ears.

'Is someone ill?' she asked again.

'No; someone – someone is very well!' I managed to reply, lifting my eyes again to her wan face. The spectacle of its drawn lines and pallor all at once assailed my wearied and over-taxed nerves with crushing weight. I felt myself beginning to whimper, and rushing tears scalded my eyes. Something inside my breast seemed to be dragging me down through the stoop.

I have now only the recollection of Miss Stratford's kneeling by my side, with a supporting arm around me, and of her thus unrolling and reading the proof-paper I had in my hand. We were in the hall now, instead of on the stoop, and there was a long silence. Then she put her head on my shoulder and wept. I could hear and feel her sobs as if they were my own.

'I – I didn't think you'd cry – that you'd be so sorry,' I heard myself saying, at last, in despondent self-defence.

Miss Stratford lifted her head and, still kneeling as she was, put a finger under my chin to make me look in her face. Lo! the eyes were laughing through their tears; the whole countenance was radiant once more with the light of happy youth and with that other glory which youth knows only once.

'Why, Andrew, boy,' she said, trembling, smiling, sobbing, beaming all at once, 'didn't you know that people cry for very joy sometimes?'

And as I shook my head she bent down and kissed me.

1894

CHARLES CHESNUTT
1858–1932

The Wife of his Youth

Mr Ryder was going to give a ball. There were several reasons why this was an opportune time for such an event.

Mr Ryder might aptly be called the dean of the Blue Veins. The original Blue Veins were a little society of colored persons organized in a certain Northern city shortly after the war. Its purpose was to establish and maintain correct social standards among a people whose social condition presented almost unlimited room for improvement. By accident, combined perhaps with some natural affinity, the society consisted of individuals who were, generally speaking, more white than black. Some envious outsider made the suggestion that no one was eligible for membership who was not white enough to show blue veins. The suggestion was readily adopted by those who were not of the favored few, and since that time the society, though possessing a longer and more pretentious name, had been known far and wide as the 'Blue Vein Society,' and its members as the 'Blue Veins.'

The Blue Veins did not allow that any such requirement existed for admission to their circle, but, on the contrary, declared that character and culture were the only things considered; and that if most of their members were light-colored, it was because such persons, as a rule, had had better opportunities to qualify themselves for membership. Opinions differed, too, as to the usefulness of the society. There were those who had been known to assail it violently as a glaring example of the very prejudice from which the colored race had suffered most; and later, when such critics had succeeded in getting on the inside, they had been heard to maintain with zeal and earnestness that the society was a lifeboat, an anchor, a bulwark and a shield – a pillar of cloud by day and of fire by night, to guide their people through the social wilderness. Another alleged prerequisite for Blue Vein membership was that of free birth; and while there was really no such requirement, it is doubtless true that very few of the members would have been unable to meet it if there had been. If there were one or two of the older members who had come up from the South and from slavery, their history presented enough romantic circumstances to rob their servile origin of its grosser aspects.

While there were no such tests of eligibility, it is true that the Blue Veins had their notions on these subjects, and that not all of them were equally liberal in regard to the things they collectively disclaimed. Mr Ryder was one of the most conservative. Though he had not been among the founders of the society, but had come in some years later, his genius for social leadership was such that he had speedily become its recognized adviser and head, the custodian of its standards, and the preserver of its traditions. He shaped its social policy, was active in providing for its entertainment, and when the interest fell off, as it sometimes did, he fanned the embers until they burst again into a cheerful flame.

There were still other reasons for his popularity. While he was not as white as some of the Blue Veins, his appearance was such as to confer distinction upon them. His features were of a refined type, his hair was almost straight; he was always neatly dressed; his manners were irreproachable, and his morals above suspicion. He had come to Groveland a young man, and obtaining employment in the office of a railroad company as messenger had in time worked himself up to the position of stationery clerk, having charge of the distribution of the office supplies for the whole company. Although the lack of early training had hindered the orderly development of a naturally fine mind, it had not prevented him from doing a great deal of reading or from forming decidedly literary tastes. Poetry was his passion. He could repeat whole pages of the great English poets; and if his pronunciation was sometimes faulty, his eye, his voice, his gestures, would respond to the changing sentiment with a precision that revealed a poetic soul and disarmed criticism. He was economical, and had saved money; he owned and occupied a very comfortable house on a respectable street. His residence was handsomely furnished, containing among other things a good library, especially rich in poetry, a piano, and some choice engravings. He generally shared his house with some young couple, who looked after his wants and were company for him; for Mr Ryder was a single man. In the early days of his connection with the Blue Veins he had been regarded as quite a catch, and young ladies and their mothers had manœuvred with much ingenuity to capture him. Not, however, until Mrs Molly

Dixon visited Groveland had any woman ever made him wish to change his condition to that of a married man.

Mrs Dixon had come to Groveland from Washington in the spring, and before the summer was over she had won Mr Ryder's heart. She possessed many attractive qualities. She was much younger than he; in fact, he was old enough to have been her father, though no one knew exactly how old he was. She was whiter than he, and better educated. She had moved in the best colored society of the country, at Washington, and had taught in the schools of that city. Such a superior person had been eagerly welcomed to the Blue Vein Society, and had taken a leading part in its activities. Mr Ryder had at first been attracted by her charms of person, for she was very good looking and not over twenty-five; then by her refined manners and the vivacity of her wit. Her husband had been a government clerk, and at his death had left a considerable life insurance. She was visiting friends in Groveland, and, finding the town and the people to her liking, had prolonged her stay indefinitely. She had not seemed displeased at Mr Ryder's attentions, but on the contrary had given him every proper encouragement; indeed, a younger and less cautious man would long since have spoken. But he had made up his mind, and had only to determine the time when he would ask her to be his wife. He decided to give a ball in her honor, and at some time during the evening of the ball to offer her his heart and hand. He had no special fears about the outcome, but, with a little touch of romance, he wanted the surroundings to be in harmony with his own feelings when he should have received the answer he expected.

Mr Ryder resolved that this ball should mark an epoch in the social history of Groveland. He knew, of course – no one could know better, the entertainments that had taken place in past years, and what must be done to surpass them. His ball must be worthy of the lady in whose honor it was to be given, and must, by the quality of its guests, set an example for the future. He had observed of late a growing liberality, almost a laxity, in social matters, even among members of his own set, and had several times been forced to meet in a social way persons whose complexions and callings in life were hardly up to the standard which he considered proper for the society to maintain. He had a theory of his own.

'I have no race prejudice,' he would say, 'but we people of

mixed blood are ground between the upper and the nether millstone. Our fate lies between absorption by the white race and extinction in the black. The one doesn't want us yet, but may take us in time. The other would welcome us, but it would be for us a backward step. "With malice towards none, with charity for all," we must do the best we can for ourselves and those who are to follow us. Self-preservation is the first law of nature.'

His ball would serve by its exclusiveness to counteract leveling tendencies, and his marriage with Mrs Dixon would help to further the upward process of absorption he had been wishing and waiting for.

2

The ball was to take place on Friday night. The house had been put in order, the carpets covered with canvas, the halls and stairs decorated with palms and potted plants; and in the afternoon Mr Ryder sat on his front porch, which the shade of a vine running up over a wire netting made a cool and pleasant lounging place. He expected to respond to the toast 'The Ladies' at the supper, and from a volume of Tennyson – his favorite poet – was fortifying himself with apt quotations. The volume was open at 'A Dream of Fair Women.' His eyes fell on these lines, and he read them aloud to judge better of their effect:

> 'At length I saw a lady within call,
>   Stiller than chisell'd marble, standing there;
> A daughter of the gods, divinely tall,
>   And most divinely fair.'

He marked the verse, and turning the page read the stanza beginning,

> 'O sweet pale Margaret,
>   O rare pale Margaret.'

He weighed the passage a moment, and decided that it would not do. Mrs Dixon was the palest lady he expected at the ball, and she was of a rather ruddy complexion, and of lively disposition and buxom build. So he ran over the leaves until his eye rested on the description of Queen Guinevere:

> 'She seem'd a part of joyous Spring:
> A gown of grass-green silk she wore,

Buckled with golden clasps before;
A light-green tuft of plumes she bore
Closed in a golden ring.

*   *   *   *   *   *

She look'd so lovely, as she sway'd
The rein with dainty finger-tips,
A man had given all other bliss,
And all his worldly worth for this,
To waste his whole heart in one kiss
Upon her perfect lips.'

As Mr Ryder murmured these words audibly, with an appreciative thrill, he heard the latch of his gate click, and a light footfall sounding on the steps. He turned his head, and saw a woman standing before his door.

She was a little woman, not five feet tall, and proportioned to her height. Although she stood erect, and looked around her with very bright and restless eyes, she seemed quite old; for her face was crossed and recrossed with a hundred wrinkles, and around the edges of her bonnet could be seen protruding here and there a tuft of short gray wool. She wore a blue calico gown of ancient cut, a little red shawl fastened around her shoulders with an old-fashioned brass brooch, and a large bonnet profusely ornamented with faded red and yellow artificial flowers. And she was very black – so black that her toothless gums, revealed when she opened her mouth to speak, were not red, but blue. She looked like a bit of the old plantation life, summoned up from the past by the wave of a magician's wand, as the poet's fancy had called into being the gracious shapes of which Mr Ryder had just been reading.

He rose from his chair and came over to where she stood.

'Good afternoon, madam,' he said.

'Good evenin', suh,' she answered, ducking suddenly with a quaint curtsy. Her voice was shrill and piping, but softened somewhat by age. 'Is dis yere whar Mistuh Ryduh lib, suh?' she asked, looking around her doubtfully, and glancing into the open windows, through which some of the preparations for the evening were visible.

'Yes,' he replied, with an air of kindly patronage, unconsciously flattered by her manner, 'I am Mr Ryder. Did you want to see me?'

'Yas, suh, ef I ain't 'sturbin' of you too much.'

'Not at all. Have a seat over here behind the vine, where it is cool. What can I do for you?'

' 'Scuse me, suh,' she continued, when she had sat down on the edge of a chair, ' 'scuse me, suh, I's lookin' for my husban'. I heerd you wuz a big man an' had libbed heah a long time, an' I 'lowed you would n't min' ef I'd come roun' an' ax you ef you'd ever heerd of a merlatter man by de name er Sam Taylor 'quirin' roun' in de chu'ches ermongs' de people fer his wife 'Liza Jane?'

Mr Ryder seemed to think for a moment.

'There used to be many such cases right after the war,' he said, 'but it has been so long that I have forgotten them. There are very few now. But tell me your story, and it may refresh my memory.'

She sat back farther in her chair so as to be more comfortable, and folded her withered hands in her lap.

'My name's 'Liza,' she began, ' 'Liza Jane. W'en I wuz young I us'ter b'long ter Marse Bob Smif, down in ole Missoura. I wuz bawn down dere. W'en I wuz a gal I wuz married ter a man named Jim. But Jim died, an' after dat I married a merlatter man named Sam Taylor. Sam wuz free-bawn, but his mammy and daddy died, an' de w'ite folks 'prenticed him ter my marster fer ter work fer 'im 'tel he wuz growed up. Sam worked in de fiel', an' I wuz de cook. One day Ma'y Ann, ole miss's maid, came rushin' out ter de kitchen, an' says she, " 'Liza Jane, ole marse gwine sell yo' Sam down de ribber."

' "Go way f'm yere," says I; "my husban's free!"

' "Don' make no diff'ence. I heerd ole marse tell ole miss he wuz gwine take yo' Sam 'way wid 'im ter-morrow, fer he needed money, an' he knowed whar he could git a t'ousan' dollars fer Sam an' no questions axed."

'W'en Sam come home f'm de fiel' dat night, I tole him 'bout ole marse gwine steal 'im, an' Sam run erway. His time wuz mos' up, an' he swo' dat w'en he wuz twenty-one he would come back an' he'p me run erway, er else save up de money ter buy my freedom. An' I know he'd 'a' done it, fer he thought a heap er me, Sam did. But w'en he come back he did n' fin' me, fer I wuz n' dere. Ole marse had heerd dat I warned Sam, so he had me whip' an' sol' down de ribber.

'Den de wah broke out, an' w'en it wuz ober de cullud folks wuz scattered. I went back ter de ole home; but Sam wuz n' dere, an' I could n' l'arn nuffin' 'bout 'im. But I knowed he'd be'n dere to look fer me an' had n' foun' me, an' had gone erway ter hunt fer me.

'I's be'n lookin' fer 'im eber sence,' she added simply, as though

twenty-five years were but a couple of weeks, 'an' I knows he's
be'n lookin' fer me. Fer he sot a heap er sto' by me, Sam did, an' I
know he's be'n huntin' fer me all dese years — 'less'n he's be'n sick
er sump'n, so he could n' work, er out'n his head, so he could n'
'member his promise. I went back down de ribber, fer I 'lowed
he'd gone down dere lookin' fer me. I's be'n ter Noo Orleens, an'
Atlanty, an' Charleston, an' Richmon'; an' we'en I'd be'n all ober
de Souf I come ter de Norf. Fer I knows I'll fin' 'im some er dese
days,' she added softly, 'er he'll fin' me, an' den we'll bofe be as
happy in freedom as we wuz in de ole days befo' de wah.' A smile
stole over her withered countenance as she paused a moment, and
her bright eyes softened into a far-away look.

This was the substance of the old woman's story. She had
wandered a little here and there. Mr Ryder was looking at her
curiously when she finished.

'How have you lived all these years?' he asked.

'Cookin', suh. I's a good cook. Does you know anybody w'at
needs a good cook, suh? I's stoppin' wid a cullud fam'ly roun' de
corner yonder 'tel I kin git a place.'

'Do you really expect to find your husband? He may be dead
long ago.'

She shook her head emphatically. 'Oh no, he ain' dead. De signs
an' de tokens tells me. I dremp three nights runnin' on'y dis las'
week dat I foun' him.'

'He may have married another woman. Your slave marriage
would not have prevented him, for you never lived with him after
the war, and without that your marriage doesn't count.'

'Would n' make no diff'ence wid Sam. He would n' marry no
yuther 'ooman 'tel he foun' out 'bout me. I knows it,' she added.
'Sump'n's be'n tellin' me all dese years dat I's gwine fin' Sam 'fo' I
dies.'

'Perhaps he's outgrown you, and climbed up in the world where
he wouldn't care to have you find him.'

'No, indeed, suh,' she replied, 'Sam ain' dat kin' er man. He wuz
good ter me, Sam wuz, but he wuz n' much good ter nobody e'se,
fer he wuz one er de triflin'es' han's on de plantation. I 'spec's ter
haf ter suppo't 'im w'en I fin' 'im, fer he nebber would work 'less'n
he had ter. But den he wuz free, an' he did n' git no pay fer his
work, an' I don' blame 'im much. Mebbe he's done better sence he
run erway, but I ain' 'spectin' much.'

'You may have passed him on the street a hundred times during the twenty-five years, and not have known him; time works great changes.'

She smiled incredulously. 'I'd know 'im 'mongs' a hund'ed men. Fer day wuz n' no yuther merlatter man like my man Sam, an' I could n' be mistook. I 's toted his picture roun' wid me twenty-five years.'

'May I see it?' asked Mr Ryder. 'It might help me to remember whether I have seen the original.'

As she drew a small parcel from her bosom he saw that it was fastened to a string that went around her neck. Removing several wrappers, she brought to light an old-fashioned daguerreotype in a black case. He looked long and intently at the portrait. It was faded with time, but the features were still distinct, and it was easy to see what manner of man it had represented.

He closed the case, and with a slow movement handed it back to her.

'I don't know of any man in town who goes by that name,' he said, 'nor have I heard of anyone making such inquiries. But if you will leave me your address, I will give the matter some attention, and if I find out anything I will let you know.'

She gave him the number of a house in the neighborhood, and went away, after thanking him warmly.

He wrote the address on the fly-leaf of the volume of Tennyson, and, when she had gone, rose to his feet and stood looking after her curiously. As she walked down the street with mincing step, he saw several persons whom she passed turn and look back at her with a smile of kindly amusement. When she had turned the corner, he went upstairs to his bedroom, and stood for a long time before the mirror of his dressing-case, gazing thoughtfully at the reflection of his own face.

3

At eight o'clock the ballroom was a blaze of light and the guests had begun to assemble; for there was a literary programme and some routine business of the society to be gone through with before the dancing. A black servant in evening dress waited at the door and directed the guests to the dressing-rooms.

The occasion was long memorable among the colored people of the city; not alone for the dress and display, but for the high average of intelligence and culture that distinguished the gathering as a whole. There were a number of school-teachers, several young doctors, three or four lawyers, some professional singers, an editor, a lieutenant in the United States army spending his furlough in the city, and others in various polite callings; these were colored, though most of them would not have attracted even a casual glance because of any marked difference from white people. Most of the ladies were in evening costume, and dress coats and dancing pumps were the rule among the men. A band of string music, stationed in an alcove behind a row of palms, played popular airs while the guests were gathering.

The dancing began at half past nine. At eleven o'clock supper was served. Mr Ryder had left the ballroom some little time before the intermission, but reappeared at the supper-table. The spread was worthy of the occasion, and the guests did full justice to it. When the coffee had been served, the toast-master, Mr Solomon Sadler, rapped for order. He made a brief introductory speech, complimenting host and guests, and then presented in their order the toasts of the evening. They were responded to with a very fair display of after-dinner wit.

'The last toast,' said the toast-master, when he reached the end of the list, 'is one which must appeal to us all. There is no one of us of the sterner sex who is not at some time dependent upon woman – in infancy for protection, in manhood for companionship, in old age for care and comforting. Our good host has been trying to live alone, but the faces I see around me tonight prove that he too is largely dependent upon the gentler sex for most that makes life worth living – the society and love of friends – and rumor is at fault if he does not soon yield entire subjection to one of them. Mr Ryder will now respond to the toast, The Ladies.'

There was a pensive look in Mr Ryder's eyes as he took the floor and adjusted his eye-glasses. He began by speaking of woman as the gift of Heaven to man, and after some general observations on the relations of the sexes he said: 'But perhaps the quality which most distinguishes woman is her fidelity and devotion to those she loves. History is full of examples, but has recorded none more striking than one which only today came under my notice.'

He then related, simply but effectively, the story told by his visitor of the afternoon. He gave it in the same soft dialect, which came readily to his lips, while the company listened attentively and sympathetically. For the story had awakened a responsive thrill in many hearts. There were some present who had seen, and others who had heard their fathers and grandfathers tell, the wrongs and sufferings of this past generation, and all of them still felt, in their darker moments, the shadow hanging over them. Mr Ryder went on:

'Such devotion and confidence are rare even among women. There are many who would have searched a year, some who would have waited five years, a few who might have hoped ten years; but for twenty-five years this woman has retained her affection for and her faith in a man she has not seen or heard of in all that time.

'She came to me today in the hope that I might be able to help her find this long-lost husband. And when she was gone I gave my fancy rein, and imagined a case I will put to you.

'Suppose that this husband, soon after his escape, had learned that his wife had been sold away, and that such inquiries as he could make brought no information of her whereabouts. Suppose that he was young, and she much older than he; that he was light, and she was black; that their marriage was a slave marriage, and legally binding only if they chose to make it so after the war. Suppose, too, that he made his way to the North, as some of us have done, and there, where he had larger opportunities, had improved them, and had in the course of all these years grown to be as different from the ignorant boy who ran away from fear of slavery as the day is from the night. Suppose, even, that he had qualified himself, by industry, by thrift, and by study, to win the friendship and be considered worthy of the society of such people as these I see around me tonight, gracing my board and filling my heart with gladness; for I am old enough to remember the day when such a gathering would not have been possible in this land. Suppose, too, that, as the years went by, this man's memory of the past grew more and more indistinct, until at last it was rarely, except in his dreams, that any image of this bygone period rose before his mind. And then suppose that accident should bring to his knowledge the fact that the wife of his youth, the wife he had left behind him – not one who had walked by his side and kept pace with him in his upward struggle, but one upon whom advancing years and a laborious life had set their mark – was alive and seeking him, but that he was absolutely safe from recognition or discovery, unless he chose to reveal himself. My friends, what would the man do? I will presume that he was one who loved honor, and tried to deal justly with all men. I will even carry the case further, and suppose that perhaps he had set his heart upon another, whom he had hoped to call his own. What would he do, or rather what ought he to do, in such a crisis of a lifetime?

'It seemed to me that he might hesitate, and I imagined that I was an old friend, a near friend, and that he had come to me for advice; and I argued the case with him. I tried to discuss it impartially. After we had looked upon the matter from every point of view, I said to him, in words that we all know:

> "This above all: to thine own self be true,
> And it must follow, as the night the day,
> Thou canst not then be false to any man."

Then, finally, I put the question to him, "Shall you acknowledge her?"

'And now, ladies and gentlemen, friends and companions, I ask you, what should he have done?'

There was something in Mr Ryder's voice that stirred the hearts of those who sat around him. It suggested more than mere sympathy with an imaginary situation; it seemed rather in the nature of a personal appeal. It was observed, too, that his look rested more especially upon Mrs Dixon, with a mingled expression of renunciation and inquiry.

She had listened, with parted lips and streaming eyes. She was the first to speak: 'He should have acknowledged her.'

'Yes,' they all echoed, 'he should have acknowledged her.'

'My friends and companions,' responded Mr Ryder, 'I thank you, one and all. It is the answer I expected, for I knew your hearts.'

He turned and walked toward the closed door of an adjoining room, while every eye followed him in wondering curiosity. He came back in a moment, leading by the hand his visitor of the afternoon, who stood startled and trembling at the sudden plunge into this scene of brilliant gayety. She was neatly dressed in gray, and wore the white cap of an elderly woman.

'Ladies and gentleman,' he said, 'this is the woman, and I am the man, whose story I have told you. Permit me to introduce to you the wife of my youth.'

1899

The Yellow Wallpaper

It is very seldom that mere ordinary people like John and myself secure ancestral halls for the summer.

A colonial mansion, a hereditary estate, I would say a haunted house, and reach the height of romantic felicity – but that would be asking too much of fate!

Still I will proudly declare that there is something queer about it.

Else, why should it be let so cheaply? And why have stood so long untenanted?

John laughs at me, of course, but one expects that in marriage.

John is practical in the extreme. He has no patience with faith, an intense horror of superstition, and he scoffs openly at any talk of things not to be felt and seen and put down in figures.

John is a physician, and *perhaps* – (I would not say it to a living soul, of course, but this is dead paper and a great relief to my mind) – perhaps that is one reason I do not get well faster.

You see he does not believe I am sick!

And what can one do?

If a physician of high standing, and one's own husband, assures friends and relatives that there is really nothing the matter with one but temporary nervous depression – a slight hysterical tendency – what is one to do?

My brother is also a physician, and also of high standing, and he says the same thing.

So I take phosphates or phospites – whichever it is, and tonics, and journeys, and air, and exercise, and am absolutely forbidden to 'work' until I am well again.

Personally, I disagree with their ideas.

Personally, I believe that congenial work, with excitement and change, would do me good.

But what is one to do?

I did write for a while in spite of them; but it *does* exhaust me a good deal – having to be so sly about it, or else meet with heavy opposition.

I sometimes fancy that in my condition if I had less opposition and more society and stimulus — but John says the very worst thing I can do is to think about my condition, and I confess it always makes me feel bad.

So I will let it alone and talk about the house.

The most beautiful place! It is quite alone, standing well back from the road, quite three miles from the village. It makes me think of English places that you read about, for there are hedges and walls and gates that lock, and lots of separate little houses for the gardeners and people.

There is a *delicious* garden! I never saw such a garden — large and shady, full of box-bordered paths, and lined with long grape-covered arbors with seats under them.

There were greenhouses, too, but they are all broken now.

There was some legal trouble, I believe, something about the heirs and coheirs; anyhow, the place has been empty for years.

That spoils my ghostliness, I am afraid, but I don't care — there is something strange about the house — I can feel it.

I even said so to John one moonlight evening, but he said what I felt was a *draught*, and shut the window.

I get unreasonably angry with John sometimes. I'm sure I never used to be so sensitive. I think it is due to this nervous condition.

But John says if I feel so, I shall neglect proper self-control; so I take pains to control myself — before him, at least, and that makes me very tired.

I don't like our room a bit. I wanted one downstairs that opened on the piazza and had roses all over the window, and such pretty old-fashioned chintz hangings! But John would not hear of it.

He said there was only one window and not room for two beds, and no near room for him if he took another.

He is very careful and loving, and hardly lets me stir without special direction.

I have a schedule prescription for each hour in the day; he takes all care from me, and so I feel basely ungrateful not to value it more.

He said we came here solely on my account, that I was to have perfect rest and all the air I could get. 'Your exercise depends on your strength, my dear,' said he, 'and your food somewhat on your appetite; but air you can absorb all the time.' So we took the nursery at the top of the house.

It is a big, airy room, the whole floor nearly, with windows that look all ways, and air and sunshine galore. It was nursery first and then playroom and gymnasium, I should judge; for the windows are barred for little children, and there are rings and things in the walls.

The paint and paper look as if a boys' school had used it. It is stripped off – the paper – in great patches all around the head of my bed, about as far as I can reach, and in a great place on the other side of the room low down. I never saw a worse paper in my life.

One of those sprawling flamboyant patterns committing every artistic sin.

It is dull enough to confuse the eye in following, pronounced enough to constantly irritate and provoke study, and when you follow the lame uncertain curves for a little distance they suddenly commit suicide – plunge off at outrageous angles, destroy themselves in unheard of contradictions.

The color is repellent, almost revolting; a smouldering unclean yellow, strangely faded by the slow-turning sunlight.

It is a dull yet lurid orange in some places, a sickly sulphur tint in others.

No wonder the children hated it! I should hate it myself if I had to live in this room long.

There comes John, and I must put this away, – he hates to have me write a word.

We have been here two weeks, and I haven't felt like writing before, since that first day.

I am sitting by the window now, up in this atrocious nursery, and there is nothing to hinder my writing as much as I please, save lack of strength.

John is away all day, and even some nights when his cases are serious.

I am glad my case is not serious!

But these nervous troubles are dreadfully depressing.

John does not know how much I really suffer. He knows there is no *reason* to suffer, and that satisfies him.

Of course it is only nervousness. It does weigh on me so not to do my duty in any way!

I meant to be such a help to John, such a real rest and comfort, and here I am a comparative burden already!

Nobody would believe what an effort it is to do what little I am able – to dress and entertain, and order things.

It is fortunate Mary is so good with the baby. Such a dear baby! And yet I *cannot* be with him, it makes me so nervous.

I suppose John never was nervous in his life. He laughs at me so about this wall-paper!

At first he meant to repaper the room, but afterwards he said that I was letting it get the better of me, and that nothing was worse for a nervous patient than to give way to such fancies.

He said that after the wall-paper was changed it would be the heavy bedstead, and then the barred windows, and then that gate at the head of the stairs, and so on.

'You know the place is doing you good,' he said, 'and really, dear, I don't care to renovate the house just for a three months' rental.'

'Then do let us go downstairs,' I said, 'there are such pretty rooms there.'

Then he took me in his arms and called me a blessed little goose, and said he would go down to the cellar, if I wished, and have it whitewashed into the bargain.

But he is right enough about the beds and windows and things.

It is an airy and comfortable room as any one need wish, and, of course, I would not be so silly as to make him uncomfortable just for a whim.

I'm really getting quite fond of the big room, all but that horrid paper.

Out of one window I can see the garden, those mysterious deepshaded arbors, the riotous old-fashioned flowers, and bushes and gnarly trees.

Out of another I get a lovely view of the bay and a little private wharf belonging to the estate. There is a beautiful shaded lane that runs down there from the house. I always fancy I see people walking in these numerous paths and arbors, but John has cautioned me not to give way to fancy in the least. He says that with my imaginative power and habit of story-making, a nervous weakness like mine is sure to lead to all manner of excited fancies, and that I ought to use my will and good sense to check the tendency. So I try.

I think sometimes that if I were only well enough to write a little it would relieve the press of ideas and rest me.

But I find I get pretty tired when I try.

It is so discouraging not to have any advice and companionship about my work. When I get really well, John says we will ask

Cousin Henry and Julia down for a long visit; but he says he would as soon put fireworks in my pillow-case as to let me have those stimulating people about now.

I wish I could get well faster.

But I must not think about that. This paper looks to me as if it *knew* what a vicious influence it had!

There is a recurrent spot where the pattern lolls like a broken neck and two bulbous eyes stare at you upside down.

I get positively angry with the impertinence of it and the everlastingness. Up and down and sideways they crawl, and those absurd, unblinking eyes are everywhere. There is one place where two breadths didn't match, and the eyes go all up and down the line, one a little higher than the other.

I never saw so much expression in an inanimate thing before, and we all know how much expression they have! I used to lie awake as a child and get more entertainment and terror out of blank walls and plain furniture than most children could find in a toy-store.

I remember what a kindly wink the knobs of our big, old bureau used to have, and there was one chair that always seemed like a strong friend.

I used to feel that if any of the other things looked too fierce I could always hop into that chair and be safe.

The furniture in this room is no worse than inharmonious, however, for we had to bring it all from downstairs. I suppose when this was used as a playroom they had to take the nursery things out, and no wonder! I never saw such ravages as the children have made here.

The wall-paper, as I said before, is torn off in spots, and it sticketh closer than a brother – they must have had perseverance as well as hatred.

Then the floor is scratched and gouged and splintered, the plaster itself is dug out here and there, and this great heavy bed which is all we found in the room, looks as if it had been through the wars.

But I don't mind it a bit – only the paper.

There comes John's sister. Such a dear girl as she is, and so careful of me! I must not let her find me writing.

She is a perfect and enthusiastic housekeeper, and hopes for no better profession. I verily believe she thinks it is the writing which made me sick!

But I can write when she is out, and see her a long way off from these windows.

There is one that commands the road, a lovely shaded winding road, and one that just looks off over the country. A lovely country, too, full of great elms and velvet meadows.

This wall-paper has a kind of sub-pattern in a different shade, a particularly irritating one, for you can only see it in certain lights, and not clearly then.

But in the places where it isn't faded and where the sun is just so, I can see a strange, provoking, formless sort of figure, that seems to skulk about behind that silly and conspicuous front design.

There's sister on the stairs!

Well, the Fourth of July is over! The people are all gone and I am tired out. John thought it might do me good to see a little company, so we just had mother and Nellie and the children down for a week.

Of course I didn't do a thing. Jennie sees to everything now.

But it tired me all the same.

John says if I don't pick up faster he shall send me to Weir Mitchell in the fall.

But I don't want to go there at all. I had a friend who was in his hands once, and she says he is just like John and my brother, only more so!

Besides, it is such an undertaking to go so far.

I don't feel as if it was worth while to turn my hand over for anything, and I'm getting dreadfully fretful and querulous.

I cry at nothing, and cry most of the time.

Of course I don't when John is here, or anybody else, but when I am alone.

And I am alone a good deal just now. John is kept in town very often by serious cases, and Jennie is good and lets me alone when I want her to.

So I walk a little in the garden or down that lovely lane, sit on the porch under the roses, and lie down up here a good deal.

I'm getting really fond of the room in spite of the wall-paper. Perhaps *because* of the wall-paper.

It dwells in my mind so!

I lie here on this great immovable bed – it is nailed down, I believe – and follow that pattern about by the hour. It is as good as gymnastics, I assure you. I start, we'll say, at the bottom, down in the corner over there where it has not been touched, and I determine for the thousandth time that I *will* follow that pointless pattern to some sort of a conclusion.

I know a little of the principle of design, and I know this thing was not arranged on any laws of radiation, or alteration, or repetition, or symmetry, or anything else that I ever heard of.

It is repeated, of course, by the breadths, but not otherwise.

Looked at in one way each breadth stands alone, the bloated curves and flourishes – a kind of 'debased Romanesque' with *delirium tremens* – go waddling up and down in isolated columns of fatuity.

But, on the other hand, they connect diagonally, and the sprawling outlines run off in great slanting waves of optic horror, like a lot of wallowing seaweeds in full chase.

The whole thing goes horizontally, too, at least it seems so, and I exhaust myself in trying to distinguish the order of its going in that direction.

They have used a horizontal breadth for a frieze, and that adds wonderfully to the confusion.

There is one end of the room where it is almost intact, and there, when the crosslights fade and the low sun shines directly upon it, I can almost fancy radiation after all – the interminable grotesques seem to form around a common centre and rush off in headlong plunges of equal distraction.

It makes me tired to follow it. I will take a nap I guess.

I don't know why I should write this.

I don't want to.

I don't feel able.

And I know John would think it absurd. But I *must* say what I feel and think in some way – it is such a relief!

But the effort is getting to be greater than the relief.

Half the time now I am awfully lazy, and lie down ever so much.

John says I mustn't lose my strength, and has me take cod liver oil and lots of tonics and things, to say nothing of ale and wine and rare meat.

Dear John! He loves me very dearly, and hates to have me sick. I tried to have a real earnest reasonable talk with him the other day, and tell him how I wish he would let me go and make a visit to Cousin Henry and Julia.

But he said I wasn't able to go, nor able to stand it after I got there; and I did not make out a very good case for myself, for I was crying before I had finished.

It is getting to be a great effort for me to think straight. Just this nervous weakness I suppose.

And dear John gathered me up in his arms, and just carried me upstairs and laid me on the bed, and sat by me and read to me till it tired my head.

He said I was his darling and his comfort and all he had, and that I must take care of myself for his sake, and keep well.

He says no one but myself can help me out of it, that I must use my will and self-control and not let any silly fancies run away with me.

There's one comfort, the baby is well and happy, and does not have to occupy this nursery with the horrid wall-paper.

If we had not used it, that blessed child would have! What a fortunate escape! Why, I wouldn't have a child of mine, an impressionable little thing, live in such a room for worlds.

I never thought of it before, but it is lucky that John kept me here after all, I can stand it so much easier than a baby, you see.

Of course I never mention it to them any more — I am too wise — but I keep watch of it all the same.

There are things in that paper that nobody knows but me, or ever will.

Behind that outside pattern the dim shapes get clearer every day.

It is always the same shape, only very numerous.

And it is like a woman stooping down and creeping about behind that pattern. I don't like it a bit. I wonder — I begin to think — I wish John would take me away from here!

It is so hard to talk with John about my case, because he is so wise, and because he loves me so.

But I tried it last night.

It was moonlight. The moon shines in all around just as the sun does.

I hate to see it sometimes, it creeps so slowly, and always comes in by one window or another.

John was asleep and I hated to waken him, so I kept still and watched the moonlight on that undulating wall-paper till I felt creepy.

The faint figure behind seemed to shake the pattern, just as if she wanted to get out.

I got up softly and went to feel and see if the paper *did* move, and when I came back John was awake.

'What is it, little girl?' he said. 'Don't go walking about like that – you'll get cold.'

I thought it was a good time to talk, so I told him that I really was not gaining here, and that I wished he would take me away.

'Why darling!' said he, 'our lease will be up in three weeks, and I can't see how to leave before.

'The repairs are not done at home, and I cannot possibly leave town just now. Of course if you were in any danger, I could and would, but you really are better, dear, whether you can see it or not. I am a doctor, dear, and I know. You are gaining flesh and color, your appetite is better, I feel really much easier about you.'

'I don't weigh a bit more,' said I, 'nor as much; and my appetite may be better in the evening when you are here, but it is worse in the morning when you are away!'

'Bless her little heart!' said he with a big hug, 'she shall be as sick as she pleases! But now let's improve the shining hours by going to sleep, and talk about it in the morning!'

'And you won't go away?' I asked gloomily.

'Why, how can I, dear? It is only three weeks more and then we will take a nice little trip of a few days while Jennie is getting the house ready. Really dear you are better!'

'Better in body perhaps – ' I began, and stopped short, for he sat up straight and looked at me with such a stern, reproachful look that I could not say another word.

'My darling,' said he, 'I beg of you, for my sake and for our child's sake, as well as for your own, that you will never for one instant let that idea enter your mind! There is nothing so dangerous, so fascinating, to a temperament like yours. It is a false and foolish fancy. Can you not trust me as a physician when I tell you so?'

So of course I said no more on that score, and we went to sleep before long. He thought I was asleep first, but I wasn't, and lay there for hours trying to decide whether that front pattern and the back pattern really did move together or separately.

On a pattern like this, by daylight, there is a lack of sequence, a defiance of law, that is a constant irritant to a normal mind.

The color is hideous enough, and unreliable enough, and infuriating enough, but the pattern is torturing.

You think you have mastered it, but just as you get well underway in following, it turns a back somersault and there you are. It slaps you in the face, knocks you down, and tramples upon you. It is like a bad dream.

The outside pattern is a florid arabesque, reminding one of a fungus. If you can imagine a toadstool in joints, an interminable string of toad-stools, budding and sprouting in endless convolutions — why, that is something like it.

That is, sometimes!

There is one marked peculiarity about this paper, a thing nobody seems to notice but myself, and that is that it changes as the light changes.

When the sun shoots in through the east window — I always watch for that first long, straight ray — it changes so quickly that I never can quite believe it.

That is why I watch it always.

By moonlight — the moon shines in all night when there is a moon — I wouldn't know it was the same paper.

At night in any kind of light, in twilight, candle light, lamplight, and worst of all by moonlight, it becomes bars! The outside pattern I mean, and the woman behind it is as plain as can be.

I didn't realize for a long time what the thing was that showed behind, that dim sub-pattern, but now I am quite sure it is a woman.

By daylight she is subdued, quiet. I fancy it is the pattern that keeps her so still. It is so puzzling. It keeps me quiet by the hour.

I lie down ever so much now. John says it is good for me, and to sleep all I can.

Indeed he started the habit by making me lie down for an hour after each meal.

It is a very bad habit I am convinced, for you see I don't sleep.

And that cultivates deceit, for I don't tell them I'm awake — Oh no!

The fact is I am getting a little afraid of John.

He seems very queer sometimes, and even Jennie has an inexplicable look.

It strikes me occasionally, just as a scientific hypothesis, that perhaps it is the paper!

I have watched John when he did not know I was looking, and come into the room suddenly on the most innocent excuses, and

I've caught him several times *looking at the paper!* And Jennie too. I caught Jennie with her hand on it once.

She didn't know I was in the room, and when I asked her in a quiet, a very quiet voice, with the most restrained manner possible, what she was doing with the paper – she turned around as if she had been caught stealing, and looked quite angry – asked me why I should frighten her so!

Then she said that the paper stained everything it touched, that she had found yellow smooches on all my clothes and John's, and she wished we would be more careful!

Did not that sound innocent? But I know she was studying that pattern, and I am determined that nobody shall find it out but myself!

Life is very much more exciting now than it used to be. You see I have something more to expect, to look forward to, to watch. I really do eat better, and am more quiet than I was.

John is so pleased to see me improve! He laughed a little the other day, and said I seemed to be flourishing in spite of my wall-paper.

I turned it off with a laugh. I had no intention of telling him it was *because* of the wall-paper – he would make fun of me. He might even want to take me away.

I don't want to leave now until I have found it out. There is a week more, and I think that will be enough.

I'm feeling ever so much better! I don't sleep much at night, for it is so interesting to watch developments; but I sleep a good deal in the daytime.

In the daytime it is tiresome and perplexing.

There are always new shoots on the fungus, and new shades of yellow all over it. I cannot keep count of them, though I have tried conscientiously.

It is the strangest yellow, that wall-paper! It makes me think of all the yellow things I ever saw – not beautiful ones like buttercups, but old foul, bad yellow things.

But there is something else about that paper – the smell! I noticed it the moment we came into the room, but with so much air and sun it was not bad. Now we have had a week of fog and rain, and whether the windows are open or not, the smell is here.

It creeps all over the house.

I find it hovering in the dining-room, skulking in the parlor, hiding in the hall, lying in wait for me on the stairs.

It gets into my hair.

Even when I go to ride, if I turn my head suddenly and surprise it — there is that smell!

Such a peculiar odor, too! I have spent hours in trying to analyze it, to find what it smelled like.

It is not bad — at first, and very gentle, but quite the subtlest, most enduring odor I ever met.

In this damp weather it is awful, I wake up in the night and find it hanging over me.

It used to disturb me at first. I thought seriously of burning the house — to reach the smell.

But now I am used to it. The only thing I can think of that it is like is the *color* of the paper! A yellow smell.

There is a very funny mark on this wall, low down, near the mopboard. A streak that runs round the room. It goes behind every piece of furniture, except the bed, a long, straight, even *smooch*, as if it had been rubbed over and over.

I wonder how it was done and who did it, and what they did it for. Round and round and round — round and round and round — it makes me dizzy!

I really have discovered something at last.

Through watching so much at night, when it changes so, I have finally found out.

The front pattern *does* move — and no wonder! The woman behind shakes it!

Sometimes I think there are a great many women behind, and sometimes only one, and she crawls around fast, and her crawling shakes it all over.

Then in the very bright spots she keeps still, and in the very shady spots she just takes hold of the bars and shakes them hard.

And she is all the time trying to climb through. But nobody could climb through that pattern — it strangles so; I think that is why it has so many heads.

They get through, and then the pattern strangles them off and turns them upside down, and makes their eyes white!

If those heads were covered or taken off it would not be half so bad.

*

I think that woman gets out in the daytime!

And I'll tell you why — privately — I've seen her!

I can see her out of every one of my windows!

It is the same woman, I know, for she is always creeping, and most women do not creep by daylight.

I see her on that long road under the trees, creeping along, and when a carriage comes she hides under the blackberry vines.

I don't blame her a bit. It must be very humiliating to be caught creeping by daylight!

I always lock the door when I creep by daylight. I can't do it at night, for I know John would suspect something at once.

And John is so queer now, that I don't want to irrirate him. I wish he would take another room! Besides, I don't want anybody to get that woman out at night but myself.

I often wonder if I could see her out of all the windows at once.

But, turn as fast as I can, I can only see out of one at one time.

And though I always see her, she *may* be able to creep faster than I can turn!

I have watched her sometimes away off in the open country, creeping as fast as a cloud shadow in a high wind.

If only that top pattern could be gotten off from the under one! I mean to try it, little by little.

I have found out another funny thing, but I shan't tell it this time! It does not do to trust people too much.

There are only two more days to get this paper off, and I believe John is beginning to notice. I don't like the look in his eyes.

And I heard him ask Jennie a lot of professional questions about me. She had a very good report to give.

She said I slept a good deal in the daytime.

John knows I don't sleep very well at night, for all I'm so quiet!

He asked me all sorts of questions, too, and pretended to be very loving and kind.

As if I couldn't see through him!

Still, I don't wonder he acts so, sleeping under this paper for three months.

It only interests me, but I feel sure John and Jennie are secretly affected by it.

Hurrah! This is the last day, but it is enough, John to stay in town over night, and won't be out until this evening.

Jennie wanted to sleep with me – the sly thing! but I told her I should undoubtedly rest better for a night all alone.

That was clever, for really I wasn't alone a bit! As soon as it was moonlight and that poor thing began to crawl and shake the pattern, I got up and ran to help her.

I pulled and she shook, I shook and she pulled, and before morning we had peeled off yards of that paper.

A strip about as high as my head and half around the room.

And then when the sun came and that awful pattern began to laugh at me, I declared I would finish it today!

We go away tomorrow, and they are moving all my furniture down again to leave things as they were before.

Jennie looked at the wall in amazement, but I told her merrily that I did it out of pure spite at the vicious thing.

She laughed and said she wouldn't mind doing it herself, but I must not get tired.

How she betrayed herself that time!

But I am here, and no person touches this paper but me – not *alive!*

She tried to get me out of the room – it was too patent! But I said it was so quiet and empty and clean now that I believed I would lie down again and sleep all I could; and not to wake me even for dinner – I would call when I woke.

So now she is gone, and the servants are gone, and the things are gone, and there is nothing left but that great bedstead nailed down, with the canvas mattress we found on it.

We shall sleep downstairs tonight, and take the boat home tomorrow.

I quite enjoy the room, now it is bare again.

How those children did tear about here!

This bedstead is fairly gnawed!

But I must get to work.

I have locked the door and thrown the key down into the front path.

I don't want to go out, and I don't want to have anybody come in, till John comes.

I want to astonish him.

I've got a rope up here that even Jennie did not find. If that woman does get out, and tries to get away, I can tie her!

But I forgot I could not reach far without anything to stand on! This bed will *not* move!

I tried to lift and push it until I was lame, and then I got so angry I bit off a little piece at one corner – but it hurt my teeth.

Then I peeled off all the paper I could reach standing on the floor. It sticks horribly and the pattern just enjoys it! All those strangled heads and bulbous eyes and waddling fungus growths just shriek with derision!

I am getting angry enough to do something desperate. To jump out of the window would be admirable exercise, but the bars are too strong even to try.

Besides I wouldn't do it. Of course not. I know well enough that a step like that is improper and might be misconstrued.

I don't like to *look* out of the windows even – there are so many of those creeping women, and they creep so fast.

I wonder if they all come out of that wall-paper as I did?

But I am securely fastened now by my well-hidden rope – you don't get *me* out in the road there!

I suppose I shall have to get back behind the pattern when it comes night, and that is hard!

It is so pleasant to be out in this great room and creep around as I please!

I don't want to go outside. I won't, even if Jennie asks me to.

For outside you have to creep on the ground, and everything is green instead of yellow.

But here I can creep smoothly on the floor, and my shoulder just fits in that long smooch around the wall, so I cannot lose my way.

Why there's John at the door!

It is no use, young man, you can't open it!

How he does call and pound!

Now he's crying for an axe.

It would be a shame to break down that beautiful door!

'John dear!' said I in the gentlest voice, 'the key is down by the front steps, under a plantain leaf!'

That silenced him for a few moments.

Then he said – very quietly indeed, 'Open the door, my darling!'

'I can't,' said I. 'The key is down by the front door under a plantain leaf!'

And then I said it again, several times, very gently and slowly, and said it so often that he had to go and see, and he got it of course, and came in. He stopped short by the door.

'What is the matter?' he cried. 'For God's sake, what are you doing!'

I kept on creeping just the same, but I looked at him over my shoulder.

'I've got out at last,' said I, 'in spite of you and Jane. And I've pulled off most of the paper, so you can't put me back!'

Now why should that man have fainted? But he did, and right across my path by the wall, so that I had to creep over him every time!

1895

OWEN WISTER
1860–1938

Specimen Jones

Ephraim, the proprietor of Twenty Mile, had wasted his day in burying a man. He did not know the man. He had found him, or what the Apaches had left of him, sprawled among some charred sticks just outside the Cañon del Oro. It was a useful discovery in its way, for otherwise Ephraim might have gone on hunting his strayed horses near the cañon, and ended among charred sticks himself. Very likely the Indians were far away by this time, but he returned to Twenty Mile with the man tied to his saddle, and his pony nervously snorting. And now the day was done, and the man lay in the earth, and they had even built a fence round him; for the hole was pretty shallow, and coyotes have a way of smelling this sort of thing a long way off when they are hungry, and the man was not in a coffin. They were always short of coffins in Arizona.

Day was done at Twenty Mile, and the customary activity prevailed inside that flat-roofed cube of mud. Sounds of singing, shooting, dancing, and Mexican tunes on the concertina came out of the windows hand in hand, to widen and die among the hills. A limber, pretty boy, who might be nineteen, was dancing energetically, while a grave old gentleman, with tobacco running down his beard, pointed a pistol at the boy's heels, and shot a hole in the earth now and then to show that the weapon was really loaded. Everybody was quite used to all of this – excepting the boy. He was an Eastern new-comer, passing his first evening at a place of entertainment.

Night in and night out every guest at Twenty Mile was either happy and full of whiskey, or else his friends were making arrangements for his funeral. There was water at Twenty Mile – the only water for twoscore of miles. Consequently it was an important station on the road between the southern country and Old Camp Grant, and the new mines north of the Mescal Range. The stunt, liquor-perfumed adobe cabin lay on the gray floor of the desert like an isolated slab of chocolate. A corral, two desolate stable-sheds, and the slowly turning windmill were all else. Here

Ephraim and one or two helpers abode, armed against Indians, and selling whiskey. Variety in their vocation of drinking and killing was brought them by the travellers. These passed and passed through the glaring vacant months – some days only one ragged fortune-hunter, riding a pony; again by twos and threes, with high-loaded burros; and sometimes they came in companies, walking beside their clanking freight-wagons. Some were young, and some were old, and all drank whiskey, and wore knives and guns to keep each other civil. Most of them were bound for the mines, and some of them sometimes returned. No man trusted the next man, and their names, when they had any, would be O'Rafferty, Angus, Schwartzmeyer, José Maria, and Smith. All stopped for one night; some longer, remaining drunk and profitable to Ephraim; now and then one stayed permanently, and had a fence built round him. Whoever came, and whatever befell them, Twenty Mile was chronically hilarious after sundown – a dot of riot in the dumb Arizona night.

On this particular evening they had a tenderfoot. The boy, being new in Arizona, still trusted his neighbor. Such people turned up occasionally. This one had paid for everybody's drink several times, because he felt friendly, and never noticed that nobody ever paid for his. They had played cards with him, stolen his spurs, and now they were making him dance. It was an ancient pastime; yet two or three were glad to stand round and watch it, because it was some time since they had been to the opera. Now the tenderfoot had misunderstood these friends at the beginning, supposing himself to be among good fellows, and they therefore naturally set him down as a fool. But even while dancing you may learn much, and suddenly. The boy, besides being limber, had good tough black hair, and it was not in fear, but with a cold blue eye, that he looked at the old gentleman. The trouble had been that his own revolver had somehow hitched, so he could not pull it from the holster at the necessary moment.

'Tried to draw on me, did yer?' said the old gentleman. 'Step higher! Step, now, or I'll crack open yer kneepans, ye robin's egg.'

'Thinks he's having a bad time,' remarked Ephraim. 'Wonder how he'd like to have been that man the Injuns had sport with?'

'Weren't his ear funny?' said one who had helped bury the man.

'Ear?' said Ephraim. 'You boys ought to been along when I found him, and seen the way they'd fixed up his mouth.' Ephraim explained the details simply, and the listeners shivered. But

Ephraim was a humorist. 'Wonder how it feels,' he continued, 'to have—'

Here the boy sickened at his comments and the loud laughter. Yet a few hours earlier these same half-drunken jesters had laid the man to rest with decent humanity. The boy was taking his first dose of Arizona. By no means was everybody looking at his jig. They had seen tenderfeet so often. There was a Mexican game of cards; there was the concertina; and over in the corner sat Specimen Jones, with his back to the company, singing to himself. Nothing had been said or done that entertained him in the least. He had seen everything quite often.

'Higher! skip higher, you elegant calf,' remarked the old gentleman to the tenderfoot. 'High-yer!' And he placidly fired a fourth shot that scraped the boy's boot at the ankle and threw earth over the clock, so that you could not tell the minute from the hour hand.

' "Drink to me only with thine eyes," ' sang Specimen Jones, softly. They did not care much for his songs in Arizona. These lyrics were all, or nearly all, that he retained of the days when he was twenty, although he was but twenty-six now.

The boy was cutting pigeon-wings, the concertina played 'Matamoras,' Jones continued his lyric, when two Mexicans leaped at each other, and the concertina stopped with a quack.

'Quit it!' said Ephraim from behind the bar, covering the two with his weapon. 'I don't want any greasers scrapping round here tonight. We've just got cleaned up.'

It had been cards, but the Mexicans made peace, to the regret of Specimen Jones. He had looked round with some hopes of a crisis, and now for the first time he noticed the boy.

'Blamed if he ain't neat,' he said. But interest faded from his eye, and he turned again to the wall. ' "Lieb Vaterland magst ruhig sein," ' he melodiously observed. His repertory was wide and refined. When he sang he was always grammatical.

'Ye kin stop, kid,' said the old gentleman, not unkindly, and he shoved his pistol into his belt.

The boy ceased. He had been thinking matters over. Being lithe and strong, he was not tired nor much out of breath, but he was trembling with the plan and the prospect he had laid out for himself. 'Set 'em up,' he said to Ephraim. 'Set 'em up again all round.'

His voice caused Specimen Jones to turn and look once more,

while the old gentleman, still benevolent, said, 'Yer langwidge means pleasanter than it sounds, kid.' He glanced at the boy's holster, and knew he need not keep a very sharp watch as to that. Its owner had bungled over it once already. All the old gentleman did was to place himself next the boy on the off side from the holster; any move the tenderfoot's hand might make for it would be green and unskilful, and easily anticipated. The company lined up along the bar, and the bottle slid from glass to glass. The boy and his tormentor stood together in the middle of the line, and the tormentor, always with half a thought for the holster, handled his drink on the wet counter, waiting till all should be filled and ready to swallow simultaneously, as befits good manners.

'Well, my regards,' he said, seeing the boy raise his glass; and as the old gentleman's arm lifted in unison, exposing his waist, the boy reached down a lightning hand, caught the old gentleman's own pistol, and jammed it in his face.

'Now you'll dance,' said he.

'Whoop!' exclaimed Specimen Jones, delighted. '*Blamed* if he ain't neat!' And Jones's handsome face lighted keenly.

'Hold on!' the boy sang out, for the amazed old gentleman was mechanically drinking his whiskey out of sheer fright. The rest had forgotten their drinks. 'Not one swallow,' the boy continued. 'No, you'll not put it down either. You'll keep hold of it, and you'll dance all round this place. Around and around. And don't you spill any. And I'll be thinking what you'll do after that.'

Specimen Jones eyed the boy with growing esteem. 'Why, he ain't bigger than a pint of cider,' said he.

'Prance away!' commanded the tenderfoot, and fired a shot between the old gentleman's not widely straddled legs.

'You hev the floor, Mr Adams,' Jones observed, respectfully, at the old gentleman's agile leap. 'I'll let no man here interrupt you.' So the capering began, and the company stood back to make room. 'I've saw juicy things in this Territory,' continued Specimen Jones, aloud to himself, 'but this combination fills my bill.'

He shook his head sagely, following the black-haired boy with his eye. That youth was steering Mr Adams round the room with the pistol, proud as a ring-master. Yet not altogether. He was only nineteen, and though his heart beat stoutly, it was beating alone in a strange country. He had come straight to this from hunting squirrels along the Susquehanna, with his mother keeping supper warm for him in the stone farm-house among the trees. He had read books in which hardy heroes saw life, and always triumphed with precision on the last page, but he remembered no receipt for this particular situation. Being good game American blood, he did not think now about the Susquehanna, but he did long with all his might to know what he ought to do next to prove himself a man. His buoyant rage, being glutted with the old gentleman's fervent skipping, had cooled, and a stress of reaction was falling hard on his brave young nerves. He imagined everybody against him. He had no notion that there was another American wanderer there, whose reserved and whimsical nature he had touched to the heart.

The fickle audience was with him, of course, for the moment, since he was upper dog and it was a good show; but one in that room was distinctly against him. The old gentleman was dancing with an ugly eye; he had glanced down to see just where his knife hung at his side, and he had made some calculations. He had fired four shots; the boy had fired one. 'Four and one hez always made five,' the old gentleman told himself with much secret pleasure, and pretended that he was going to stop his double-shuffle. It was an excellent trap, and the boy fell straight into it. He squandered his last precious bullet on the spittoon near which Mr Adams happened to be at the moment, and the next moment Mr Adams had him by the throat. They swayed and gulped for breath, rutting the earth with sharp heels; they rolled to the floor and floundered with legs tight tangled, the boy blindly striking at Mr Adams with the pistol-butt, and the audience drawing closer to lose nothing, when the bright knife flashed suddenly. It poised, and flew across the room, harmless, for a foot had driven into Mr Adams's arm, and he felt a cold ring grooving his temple. It was the smooth, chilly muzzle of Specimen Jones's six-shooter.

'That's enough,' said Jones. 'More than enough.'

Mr Adams, being mature in judgment, rose instantly, like a good old sheep, and put his knife back obedient to orders. But in the brain of the overstrained, bewildered boy universal destruction was whirling. With a face stricken lean with ferocity, he staggered to his feet, plucking at his obstinate holster, and glaring for a foe. His eye fell first on his deliverer, leaning easily against the bar watching him, while the more and more curious audience scattered, and held themselves ready to murder the boy if he should point his pistol their way. He was dragging at it clumsily, and at last it came. Specimen Jones sprang like a cat, and held the barrel vertical and gripped the boy's wrist.

'Go easy, son,' said he. 'I know how you're feelin'.'

The boy had been wrenching to get a shot at Jones, and now the quietness of the man's voice reached his brain, and he looked at Specimen Jones. He felt a potent brotherhood in the eyes that were considering him, and he began to fear he had been a fool. There was his dwarf Eastern revolver, slack in his inefficient fist, and the singular person still holding its barrel and tapping one derisive finger over the end, careless of the risk to his first joint.

'Why, you little —— ,' said Specimen Jones, caressingly, to the hypnotized youth, 'if you was to pop that squirt off at me, I'd turn you up and spank y'u. Set 'em up, Ephraim.'

But the commercial Ephraim hesitated, and Jones remembered. His last cent was gone. It was his third day at Ephraim's. He had stopped, having a little money, on his way to Tucson, where a friend had a job for him, and was waiting. He was far too experienced a character ever to sell his horse or his saddle on these occasions, and go on drinking. He looked as if he might, but he never did; and this was what disappointed business men like Ephraim in Specimen Jones.

But now, here was this tenderfoot he had undertaken to see through, and Ephraim reminding him that he had no more of the wherewithal. 'Why, so I haven't,' he said, with a short laugh, and his face flushed. 'I guess,' he continued, hastily, 'this is worth a dollar or two.' He drew a chain up from below his flannel shirt-collar and over his head. He drew it a little slowly. It had not been taken off for a number of years – not, indeed, since it had been placed there originally. 'It ain't brass,' he added, lightly, and strewed it along the counter without looking at it. Ephraim did look at it, and, being satisfied, began to uncork a new bottle, while the punctual audience came up for its drink.

'Won't you please let me treat?' said the boy, unsteadily. 'I ain't likely to meet you again, sir.' Reaction was giving him trouble inside.

'Where are you bound, kid?'

'Oh, just a ways up the country,' answered the boy, keeping a grip on his voice.

'Well, you *may* get there. Where did you pick up that – that thing? Your pistol, I mean.'

'It's a present from a friend,' replied the tenderfoot, with dignity.

'Farewell gift, wasn't it, kid? Yes; I thought so. Now I'd hate to get an affair like that from a friend. It would start me wondering if he liked me as well as I'd always thought he did. Put up that money, kid. You're drinking with me. Say, what's yer name?'

'Cumnor –. J Cumnor.'

'Well, J. Cumnor, I'm glad to know y'u. Ephraim, let me make you acquainted with Mr Cumnor. Mr Adams, if you're rested from your quadrille, you can shake hands with my friend. Step around, you Miguels and Serapios and Cristobals, whatever y'u claim your names are. This is Mr J. Cumnor.'

The Mexicans did not understand either the letter or the spirit of these American words, but they drank their drink, and the concertina resumed its acrid melody. The boy had taken himself off without being noticed.

'Say, Spec,' said Ephraim to Jones, 'I'm no hog. Here's yer chain. You'll be along again.'

'Keep it till I'm along again,' said the owner.

'Just as you say, Spec,' answered Ephraim, smoothly, and he hung the pledge over an advertisement chromo of a nude cream-colored lady with bright straw hair holding out a bottle of somebody's champagne. Specimen Jones sang no more songs, but smoked, and leaned in silence on the bar. The company were talking of bed, and Ephraim plunged his glasses into a bucket to clean them for the morrow.

'Know anything about that kid?' inquired Jones, abruptly.

Ephraim shook his head as he washed.

'Travelling alone, ain't he?'

Ephraim nodded.

'Where did y'u say y'u found that fellow layin' the Injuns got?'

'Mile this side the cañon. 'Mong them sand-humps.'

'How long had he been there, do y'u figure?'

'Three days, anyway.'

Jones watched Ephraim finish his cleansing. 'Your clock needs wiping,' he remarked. 'A man might suppose it was nine, to see that thing the way the dirt hides the hands. Look again in half an hour and it'll say three. That's the kind of clock gives a man the jams. Sends him crazy.'

'Well, that ain't a bad thing to be in this country,' said Ephraim, rubbing the glass case and restoring identity to the hands. 'If that man had been crazy he'd been livin' right now. Injuns'll never touch lunatics.'

'That band have passed here and gone north,' Jones said. 'I saw a smoke among the foot-hills as I come along day before yesterday. I guess they're aiming to cross the Santa Catalina. Most likely they're that band from round the San Carlos that were reported as raiding down in Sonora.'

'I seen well enough,' said Ephraim, 'when I found him that they wasn't going to trouble us any, or they'd have been around by then.'

He was quite right, but Specimen Jones was thinking of something else. He went out to the corral, feeling disturbed and doubtful. He saw the tall white freight-wagon of the Mexicans, looming and silent, and a little way off the new fence where the man lay. An odd sound startled him, though he knew it was no Indians at this hour, and he looked down into a little dry ditch. It was the boy, hidden away flat on his stomach among the stones, sobbing.

'Oh, snakes!' whispered Specimen Jones, and stepped back. The Latin races embrace and weep, and all goes well; but among Saxons tears are a horrid event. Jones never knew what to do when it was a woman, but this was truly disgusting. He was well seasoned by the frontier, had tried a little of everything: town and country, ranches, saloons, stage-driving, marriage occasionally, and latterly mines. He had sundry claims staked out, and always carried pieces of stone in his pockets, discoursing upon their mineral-bearing capacity, which was apt to be very slight. That is why he was called Specimen Jones. He had exhausted all the important sensations, and did not care much for anything any more. Perfect health and strength kept him from discovering that he was a saddened, drifting man. He wished to kick the boy for his baby performance, and yet he stepped carefully away from the ditch so the boy should not suspect his presence. He found himself standing still, looking at the dim, broken desert.

'Why, hell,' complained Specimen Jones, 'he played the little man to start with. He did so. He scared that old horse-thief, Adams, just about dead. Then he went to kill me, that kep' him from bein' buried early tomorrow. I've been wild that way myself, and wantin' to shoot up the whole outfit.' Jones looked at the place where his middle finger used to be, before a certain evening in Tombstone. 'But I never—' He glanced towards the ditch, perplexed. 'What's that mean? Why in the world does he git to cryin' for *now*, do you suppose?' Jones took to singing without knowing it. ' "Ye shepherds, tell me, have you seen my Flora pass this way?" ' he murmured. Then a thought struck him. 'Hello, kid!' he called out. There was no answer. 'Of course,' said Jones. 'Now he's ashamed to hev me see him come out of there.' He walked with elaborate slowness round the corral and behind a shed. 'Hello, you kid!' he called again.

'I was thinking of going to sleep,' said the boy, appearing quite suddenly, '– I'm not used to riding all day. I'll get used to it, you know,' he hastened to add.

' "Ha-ve you seen my Flo – Say, kid, where y'u bound, anyway?'

'San Carlos.'

'San Carlos? Oh. Ah. "Flo-ra pass this way?" '

'Is it far, sir?'

'Awful far, sometimes. It's always liable to be far through the Arivaypa Cañon.'

'I didn't expect to make it between meals,' remarked Cumnor.

'No. Sure. What made you come this route?'

'A man told me.'

'A man? Oh. Well, it *is* kind o' difficult, I admit, for an Arizonan not to lie to a stranger. But I think I'd have told you to go by Tres Alamos and Point of Mountain. It's the road the man that told you would choose himself every time. Do you like Injuns, kid?'

Cumnor snapped eagerly.

'Of course y'u do. And you've never saw one in the whole minute-and-a-half you've been alive. I know all about it.'

'I'm not afraid,' said the boy.

'Not afraid? Of course y'u ain't. What's your idea in going to Carlos? Got town lots there?'

'No,' said the literal youth, to the huge internal diversion of Jones. 'There's a man there I used to know back home. He's in the cavalry. What sort of a town is it for sport?' asked Cumnor, in a gay Lothario tone.

'*Town*?' Specimen Jones caught hold of the top rail of the corral. '*Sport*? Now I'll tell y'u what sort of a town it is. There ain't no streets. There ain't no houses. There ain't any land and water in the usual meaning of them words. There's Mount Turnbull. It's pretty near a usual mountain, but y'u don't want to go there. The Creator didn't make San Carlos. It's a heap older than Him. When He got around to it after slickin' up Paradise and them fruit-trees, He just left it to be as He found it, as a sample of the way they done business before He come along. He 'ain't done any work around that spot at all, He ain't. Mix up a barrel of sand and ashes and thorns, and jam scorpions and rattlesnakes along in, and dump the outfit on stones, and heat yer stones red-hot, and set the United States army loose over the place chasin' Apaches, and you've got San Carlos.'

Cumnor was silent for a moment. 'I don't care,' he said. 'I want to chase Apaches.'

'Did you see that man Ephraim found by the cañon?' Jones inquired.

'Didn't get here in time.'

'Well, there was a hole in his chest made by an arrow. But there's no harm in that if you die at wunst. That chap didn't, y'u see. You heard Ephraim tell about it. They'd done a number of things to the man before he could die. Roastin' was only one of 'em. Now your road takes you through the mountains where these Injuns hev gone. Kid, come along to Tucson with me,' urged Jones, suddenly.

Again Cumnor was silent. 'Is my road different from other people's?' he said, finally.

'Not to Grant, it ain't. These Mexicans are hauling freight to Grant. But what's the matter with your coming to Tucson with me?'

'I started to go to San Carlos, and I'm going,' said Cumnor.

'You're a poor chuckle-headed fool!' burst out Jones, in a rage. 'And y'u can go, for all I care – you and your Christmas-tree pistol. Like as not you won't find your cavalry friend at San Carlos. They've killed a lot of them soldiers huntin' Injuns this season. Good night.'

Specimen Jones was gone. Cumnor walked to his blanket-roll, where his saddle was slung under the shed. The various doings of the evening had bruised his nerves. He spread his blankets among the dry cattle-dung, and sat down, taking off a few clothes slowly. He lumped his coat and overalls under his head for a pillow, and, putting the despised pistol alongside, lay between the blankets. No object showed in the night but the tall freight-wagon. The tenderfoot thought he had made altogether a fool of himself upon the first trial trip of his manhood, alone on the open sea of Arizona. No man, not even Jones now, was his friend. A stranger, who could have had nothing against him but his inexperience, had taken the trouble to direct him on the wrong road. He did not mind definite enemies. He had punched the heads of those in

Pennsylvania, and would not object to shooting them here; but this impersonal, surrounding hostility of the unknown was new and bitter: the cruel, assassinating, cowardly South-west, where prospered those jail-birds whom the vigilantes had driven from California. He thought of the nameless human carcass that lay near, buried that day, and of the jokes about its mutilations. Cumnor was not an innocent boy, either in principles or in practice, but this laughter about a dead body had burned into his young, unhardened soul. He lay watching with hot, dogged eyes the brilliant stars. A passing wind turned the windmill, which creaked a forlorn minute, and ceased. He must have gone to sleep and slept soundly, for the next he knew it was the cold air of dawn that made him open his eyes. A numb silence lay over all things, and the tenderfoot had that moment of curiosity as to where he was now which comes to those who have journeyed for many days. The Mexicans had already departed with their freight-wagon. It was not entirely light, and the embers where these early starters had cooked their breakfast lay glowing in the sand across the road. The boy remembered seeing a wagon where now he saw only chill, distant peaks, and while he lay quiet and warm, shunning full consciousness, there was a stir in the cabin, and at Ephraim's voice reality broke upon his drowsiness, and he recollected Arizona and the keen stress of shifting for himself. He noted the gray paling round the grave. Indians? He would catch up with the Mexicans, and travel in their company to Grant. Freighters made but fifteen miles in the day, and he could start after breakfast and be with them before they stopped at noon. Six men need not worry about Apaches, Cumnor thought. The voice of Specimen Jones came from the cabin, and sounds of lighting the stove, and the growling conversation of men getting up. Cumnor, lying in his blankets, tried to overhear what Jones was saying, for no better reason than that this was the only man he had met lately who had seemed to care whether he were alive or dead. There was the clink of Ephraim's whiskey-bottles, and the cheerful tones of old Mr Adams, saying, 'It's better 'n brushin' yer teeth'; and then further clinking, and an inquiry from Specimen Jones.

'Whose spurs?' said he.

'Mine.' This from Mr Adams.

'How long have they been yourn?'

'Since I got 'em, I guess.'

'Well, you've enjoyed them spurs long enough.' The voice of

Specimen Jones now altered in quality. 'And you'll give 'em back to that kid.'

Muttering followed that the boy could not catch. 'You'll give 'em back,' repeated Jones. 'I seen y'u lift 'em from under that chair when I was in the corner.'

'That's straight, Mr Adams,' said Ephraim. 'I noticed it myself, though I had no objections, of course. But Mr Jones has pointed out—'

'Since when have you growed so honest, Jones?' cackled Mr Adams, seeing that he must lose his little booty. 'And why didn't you raise yer objections when you seen me do it?'

'I didn't know the kid,' Jones explained. 'And if it don't strike you that game blood deserves respect, why it does strike me.'

Hearing this, the tenderfoot, outside in his shed, thought better of mankind and life in general, arose from his nest, and began preening himself. He had all the correct trappings for the frontier, and his toilet in the shed gave him pleasure. The sun came up, and with a stroke struck the world to crystal. The near sand-hills went into rose, the crabbed yucca and the mesquite turned transparent, with lances and pale films of green, like drapery graciously veiling the desert's face, and distant violet peaks and edges framed the vast enchantment beneath the liquid exhalations of the sky. The smell of bacon and coffee from open windows filled the heart with bravery and yearning, and Ephraim, putting his head round the corner, called to Cumnor that he had better come in and eat. Jones, already at table, gave him the briefest nod; but the spurs were there, replaced as Cumnor had left them under a chair in the corner. In Arizona they do not say much at any meal, and at breakfast nothing at all; and as Cumnor swallowed and meditated, he noticed the cream-colored lady and the chain, and he made up his mind he should assert his identity with regard to that business, though how and when was not clear to him. He was in no great haste to take up his journey. The society of the Mexicans whom he must sooner or later overtake did not tempt him. When breakfast was done he idled in the cabin, like the other guests, while Ephraim and his assistant busied about the premises. But the morning grew on, and the guests, after a season of smoking and tilted silence against the wall, shook themselves and their effects together, saddled, and were lost among the waste thorny hills. Twenty Mile became hot and torpid. Jones lay on three consecutive chairs, occasionally singing, and old Mr Adams had not gone away either, but watched him; with more tobacco running down his beard.

'Well,' said Cumnor, 'I'll be going.'

'Nobody's stopping y'u,' remarked Jones.

'You're going to Tucson?' the boy said, with the chain problem still unsolved in his mind. 'Goodbye, Mr Jones. I hope I'll – we'll—'

'That'll do,' said Jones; and the tenderfoot, thrown back by this severity, went to get his saddle-horse and his burro.

Presently Jones remarked to Mr Adams that he wondered what Ephraim was doing, and went out. The old gentleman was left alone in the room, and he swiftly noticed that the belt and pistol of Specimen Jones were left alone with him. The accoutrement lay by the chair its owner had been lounging in. It is an easy thing to remove cartridges from the chambers of a revolver, and replace the weapon in its holster so that everything looks quite natural. The old gentleman was entertained with the notion that somewhere in Tucson Specimen Jones might have a surprise, and he did not take a minute to prepare this, drop the belt as it lay before, and saunter innocently out of the saloon. Ephraim and Jones were criticising the tenderfoot's property as he packed his burro.

'Do y'u make it a rule to travel with ice-cream?' Jones was inquiring.

'They're for water,' Cumnor said. 'They told me at Tucson I'd need to carry water for three days on some trails.'

It was two good-sized milk-cans that he had, and they bounced about on the little burro's pack, giving him as much amazement as a jackass can feel. Jones and Ephraim were hilarious.

'Don't go without your spurs, Mr Cumnor,' said the voice of old Mr Adams, as he approached the group. His tone was particularly civil.

The tenderfoot had, indeed, forgotten his spurs, and he ran back to get them. The cream-colored lady still had the chain hanging upon her, and Cumnor's problem was suddenly solved. He put the chain in his pocket, and laid the price of one round of drinks for last night's company on the shelf below the chromo. He returned with his spurs on, and went to his saddle that lay beside that of Specimen Jones under the shed. After a moment he came with his saddle to where the men stood talking by his pony, slung it on, and tightened the cinches; but the chain was now in the saddle-bag of Specimen Jones, mixed up with some tobacco, stale bread, a box of matches, and a hunk of fat bacon. The men at Twenty Mile said good day to the tenderfoot, with monosyllables and indifference, and watched him depart into the heated desert. Wishing for a last look at Jones, he turned once, and saw the three standing, and the chocolate brick of the cabin, and the windmill white and idle in the sun.

'He'll be gutted by night,' remarked Mr Adams.

'I ain't buryin' him, then,' said Ephraim.

'Nor I,' said Specimen Jones. 'Well, it's time I was getting to Tucson.'

He went to the saloon, strapped on his pistol, saddled, and rode away. Ephraim and Mr Adams returned to the cabin; and here is the final conclusion they came to after three hours of discussion as to who took the chain and who had it just then:

Ephraim. Jones, he hadn't no cash.

Mr Adams. The kid, he hadn't no sense.

Ephraim. The kid, he lent the cash to Jones.

Mr Adams. Jones, he goes off with his chain.

Both. What damn fools everybody is, anyway!

And they went to dinner. But Mr Adams did not mention his relations with Jones's pistol. Let it be said, in extenuation of that performance, that Mr Adams supposed Jones was going to Tucson, where he said he was going, and where a job and a salary were awaiting him. In Tucson an unloaded pistol in the holster of so handy a man on the drop as was Specimen would keep people civil, because they would not know, any more than the owner, that it was unloaded; and the mere possession of it would be sufficient in nine chances out of ten – though it was undoubtedly for the tenth that Mr Adams had a sneaking hope. But Specimen Jones was not going to Tucson. A contention in his mind as to whether he would do what was good for himself, or what was good for another, had kept him sullen ever since he got up. Now it was settled, and Jones in serene humor again. Of course he had started on the Tucson road, for the benefit of Ephraim and Mr Adams.

The tenderfoot rode along. The Arizona sun beat down upon the deadly silence, and the world was no longer of crystal, but a mesa, dull and gray and hot. The pony's hoofs grated in the gravel, and after a time the road dived down and up among lumpy hills of stone and cactus, always nearer the fierce glaring Sierra Santa Catalina. It dipped so abruptly in and out of the shallow sudden ravines that, on coming up from one of these into sight of the country again, the tenderfoot's heart jumped at the close apparition of another rider quickly bearing in upon him from gullies where he had been moving unseen. But it was only Specimen Jones.

'Hello!' said he, joining Cumnor. 'Hot, ain't it?'

'Where are you going?' inquired Cumnor.

'Up here a ways.' And Jones jerked his finger generally towards the Sierra, where they were heading.

'Thought you had a job in Tucson.'

'That's what I have.'

Specimen Jones had no more to say, and they rode for a while, their ponies' hoofs always grating in the gravel, and the milk-cans lightly clanking on the burro's pack. The bunched blades of the yuccas bristled steel-stiff, and as far as you could see it was a gray waste of mounds and ridges sharp and blunt, up to the forbidding boundary walls of the Tortilita one way and the Santa Catalina the other. Cumnor wondered if Jones had found the chain. Jones was capable of not finding it for several weeks, or of finding it at once and saying nothing.

'You'll excuse my meddling with your business?' the boy hazarded.

Jones looked inquiring.

'Something's wrong with your saddle-pocket.'

Specimen saw nothing apparently wrong with it, but perceiving Cumnor was grinning, unbuckled the pouch. He looked at the boy rapidly, and looked away again, and as he rode, still in silence, he put the chain back round his neck below the flannel shirt-collar.

'Say, kid,' he remarked, after some time, 'what does J stand for?'

'J? Oh, my name! Jock.'

'Well, Jock, will y'u explain to me as a friend how y'u ever come to be such a fool as to leave yer home — wherever and whatever it was — in exchange for this here God-forsaken and iniquitous hole?'

'If you'll explain to me,' said the boy, greatly heartened, 'how you come to be ridin' in the company of a fool, instead of goin' to your job at Tucson.'

The explanation was furnished before Specimen Jones had framed his reply. A burning freight-wagon and five dismembered human stumps lay in the road. This was what had happened to the Miguels and Serapios and the concertina. Jones and Cumnor, in their dodging and struggles to exclude all expressions of growing mutual esteem from their speech, had forgotten their journey, and a sudden bend among the rocks where the road had now brought them revealed the blood and fire staring them in the face. The plundered wagon was three parts empty; its splintered, blazing boards slid down as they burned into the fiery heap on the ground; packages of soda and groceries and medicines slid with them, bursting into chemical spots of green and crimson flame; a wheel crushed in and sank, spilling more packages that flickered and hissed; the garbage of combat and murder littered the earth, and in the air hung an odor that Cumnor knew, though he had never smelled it before. Morsels of dropped booty up among the rocks showed where the Indians had gone, and one horse remained, groaning, with an accidental arrow in his belly.

'We'll just kill him,' said Jones; and his pistol snapped idly, and snapped again, as his eye caught a motion – a something – two hundred yards up among the boulders on the hill. He whirled round. The enemy was behind them also. There was no retreat. 'Yourn's no good!' yelled Jones, fiercely, for Cumnor was getting out his little, foolish revolver. 'Oh, what a trick to play on a man! Drop off yer horse, kid; drop, and do like me. Shootin's no good here, even if I was loaded. *They* shot, and look at them now. God bless them ice-cream freezers of yourn, kid! Did y'u ever see a crazy man? If you 'ain't, *make it up as y'u go along!*'

More objects moved up among the boulders. Specimen Jones ripped off the burro's pack, and the milk-cans rolled on the ground. The burro began grazing quietly, with now and then a step towards new patches of grass. The horses stood where their riders had left them, their reins over their heads, hanging and dragging. From two hundred yards on the hill the ambushed Apaches showed, their dark, scattered figures appearing cautiously one by one, watching with suspicion. Specimen Jones seized up one milk-can, and Cumnor obediently did the same.

'You kin dance, kid, and I kin sing, and we'll go to it,' said Jones. He rambled in a wavering loop, and diving eccentrically at Cumnor, clashed the milk-cans together. ' "Es schallt ein Ruf wie Donnerhall," ' he bawled, beginning the song of 'Die Wacht am Rhein.' 'Why don't you dance?' he shouted, sternly. The boy saw the terrible earnestness of his face, and, clashing his milk-cans in turn, he shuffled a sort of jig. The two went over the sand in loops, toe and heel; the donkey continued his quiet grazing, and the flames rose hot and yellow from the freight-wagon. And all the while the stately German hymn pealed among the rocks, and the Apaches crept down nearer the bowing, scraping men. The sun shone bright, and their bodies poured with sweat. Jones flung off his shirt; his damp, matted hair was half in ridges and half glued to his forehead, and the delicate gold chain swung and struck his broad, naked breast. The Apaches drew nearer again, their bows and arrows held uncertainly. They came down the hill, fifteen or twenty, taking a long time, and stopping every few yards. The milk-cans clashed, and Jones thought he felt the boy's strokes weakening. 'Die Wacht am Rhein' was finished, and now it was ' "Ha-ve you seen my Flora pass this way?" ' 'Y'u mustn't play out, kid,' said Jones, very gently. 'Indeed y'u mustn't;' and he at once resumed his song. The silent Apaches had now reached the bottom of the hill. They stood some twenty yards away, and Cumnor had a good chance to see his first Indians. He saw them move, and the color and slim shape of their bodies, their thin arms, and their long, black hair. It went through his mind that if he had no more clothes on than that, dancing would come easier. His boots were growing heavy to lift, and his overalls seemed to wrap his sinews in wet, strangling thongs. He wondered how long he had been keeping this up. The legs of the Apaches were free, with light moccasins only half-way to the thigh, slenderly held up by strings from the waist. Cumnor envied their unencumbered steps as he saw them again walk nearer to where he was dancing. It was long since he had eaten, and he noticed a singing dulness in his brain, and became frightened at his thoughts, which were running and melting into one fixed idea. This idea was to take off his boots, and offer to trade them for a pair of moccasins. It terrified him – this endless, molten rush of thoughts; he could see them coming in different shapes from different places in his head, but they all joined immediately, and always formed the same fixed idea. He ground his teeth to master this encroaching inebriation of his will and judgment. He clashed his can more loudly to wake him to reality, which he still could recognize and appreciate. For a time he found it a good plan to listen to what Specimen Jones was singing, and tell himself the name of the song, if he knew it. At present it was 'Yankee Doodle,' to which Jones was fitting words of his own. These ran, 'Now I'm going to try a bluff, And mind you do what I do'; and then again, over and over. Cumnor waited for the word 'bluff'; for it was hard and heavy, and fell into his thoughts, and stopped them for a moment. The dance was so long now he had forgotten about that. A numbness had been spreading through his legs, and he was glad to feel a sharp pain in the sole of his foot. It was a piece of gravel that had somehow worked its way in, and was rubbing through the skin into the flesh. 'That's good,' he said, aloud. The pebble was eating the numbness away, and Cumnor drove it hard against the raw spot, and relished the tonic of its burning friction. The Apaches had drawn into a circle. Standing at some interval apart, they entirely surrounded the arena. Shrewd, half convinced, and yet with awe, they watched the dancers, who clashed their cans slowly now in rhythm to Jones's hoarse, parched singing. He was quite master of himself, and led the jig round the still blazing wreck of the wagon, and circled in figures of eight between the corpses of the Mexicans, clashing the milk-cans above each one. Then, knowing his strength was coming to an end, he approached an Indian whose splendid fillet and trappings denoted him of consequence; and Jones was near shouting with relief when the Indian shrank backward. Suddenly he saw Cumnor let his can drop, and without stopping to see why, he caught it up, and slowly rattling both, approached each Indian in turn with tortuous steps. The circle that had never uttered a sound till now receded, chanting almost in a whisper some exorcising song which the man with the fillet had begun. They gathered round him, retreating always, and the strain, with its rapid muttered words, rose and fell softly among them. Jones had supposed the boy was overcome by faintness, and looked to see where he lay. But it was not faintness. Cumnor, with his boots off, came by and walked after the Indians in a trance. They saw him, and quickened their pace, often turning to be sure he was not overtaking them. He called to them unintelligibly, stumbling up the sharp hill, and pointing to the boots. Finally he sat down. They continued ascending the mountain, herding close round the man with the feathers, until the rocks and the filmy tangles screened them from sight; and like a wind that hums uncertainly in grass, their chanting died away.

The sun was half behind the western range when Jones next moved. He called, and, getting no answer, he crawled painfully to where the boy lay on the hill. Cumnor was sleeping heavily; his head was hot, and he moaned. So Jones crawled down, and fetched blankets and the canteen of water. He spread the blankets over the boy, wet a handkerchief and laid it on his forehead; then he lay down himself.

The earth was again magically smitten to crystal. Again the sharp cactus and the sand turned beautiful, and violet floated among the mountains, and rose-colored orange in the sky above them.

'Jock,' said Specimen at length.

The boy opened his eyes.

'Your foot is awful, Jock. Can y'u eat?'

'Not with my foot.'

'Ah, God bless y'u, Jock! Y'u ain't turruble sick. But *can* y'u eat?'

Cumnor shook his head.

'Eatin's what y'u need, though. Well, here.' Specimen poured a judicious mixture of whiskey and water down the boy's throat, and wrapped the awful foot in his own flannel shirt. 'They'll fix y'u over to Grant. It's maybe twelve miles through the cañon. It ain't a town any more than Carlos is, but the soldiers'll be good to us. As soon as night comes you and me must somehow git out of this.'

Somehow they did, Jones walking and leading his horse and the imperturbable little burro, and also holding Cumnor in the saddle. And when Cumnor was getting well in the military hospital at Grant, he listened to Jones recounting to all that chose to hear how useful a weapon an ice-cream freezer can be, and how if you'll only chase Apaches in your stocking feet they are sure to run away. And then Jones and Cumnor both enlisted; and I suppose Jones's friend is still expecting him in Tucson.

1894

HAMLIN GARLAND
1860–1940

Under the Lion's Paw

Along this main-travelled road trailed an endless line of prairie-schooners, coming into sight at the east, and passing out of sight over the swell to the west. We children used to wonder where they were going and why they went.

I

It was the last of autumn and first day of winter coming together. All day long the ploughmen on their prairie farms had moved to and fro in their wide level fields through the falling snow, which melted as it fell, wetting them to the skin – all day, notwithstanding the frequent squalls of snow, the dripping, desolate clouds, and the muck of the furrows, black and tenacious as tar.

Under their dripping harness the horses swung to and fro silently, with that marvellous uncomplaining patience which marks the horse. All day the wild geese, honking wildly, as they sprawled sidewise down the wind, seemed to be fleeing from an enemy behind, and with neck outthrust and wings extended, sailed down the wind, soon lost to sight.

Yet the ploughman behind his plough, though the snow lay on his ragged great-coat, and the cold clinging mud rose on his heavy boots, fettering him like gyves, whistled in the very beard of the gale. As day passed, the snow, ceasing to melt, lay along the ploughed land, and lodged in the depth of the stubble, till on each slow round the last furrow stood out black and shining as jet between the ploughed land and the gray stubble.

When night began to fall, and the geese, flying low, began to alight invisibly in the near corn-field, Stephen Council was still at work 'finishing a land.' He rode on his sulky plough when going with the wind, but walked when facing it. Sitting bent and cold but cheery under his slouch hat, he talked encouragingly to his four-in-hand.

'Come round there, boys! Round agin! We got t' finish this

land. Come in there, Dan! *Stiddy*, Kate – stiddy! None o' y'r tantrums, Kittie. It's purty tuff, but got a be did. *Tchk! tchk!* Step along, Pete! Don't let Kate git y'r single-tree on the wheel. *Once* more!'

They seemed to know what he meant, and that this was the last round, for they worked with greater vigor than before.

'Once more, boys, an' then, sez I, oats an' a nice warm stall, an' sleep f'r all.'

By the time the last furrow was turned on the land it was too dark to see the house, and the snow was changing to rain again. The tired and hungry man could see the light from the kitchen shining through the leafless hedge, and lifting a great shout, he yelled, 'Sup*per* f'r a half a dozen!'

It was nearly eight o'clock by the time he had finished his chores and started for supper. He was picking his way carefully through the mud, when the tall form of a man loomed up before him with a premonitory cough.

'Waddy ye want?' was the rather startled question of the farmer.

'Well, ye see,' began the stranger, in a deprecating tone, 'we'd like t' git in f'r the night. We've tried every house f'r the last two miles, but they hadn't any room f'r us. My wife's jest about sick, 'n' the children are cold and hungry—'

'Oh, y' want a stay all night, eh?'

'Yes, sir; it 'ud be a great accom—'

'Waal, I don't make it a practice t' turn anybody way hungry, not on sech nights as this. Drive right in. We ain't got much, but sech as it is—'

But the stranger had disappeared. And soon his steaming, weary team, with drooping heads and swinging single-trees, moved past the well to the block beside the path. Council stood at the side of the 'schooner' and helped the children out – two little half-sleeping children – and then a small woman with a babe in her arms.

'There ye go!' he shouted jovially, to the children. '*Now* we're all right! Run right along to the house there, an' tell Mam' Council you wants sumpthin' t' eat. Right this way, Mis' – keep right off t' the right there. I'll go an' git a lantern. Come,' he said to the dazed and silent group at his side.

'Mother,' he shouted, as he neared the fragrant and warmly lighted kitchen, 'here are some wayfarers an' folks who need sumpin' t' eat an' a place t' snooze.' He ended by pushing them all in.

Mrs Council, a large, jolly, rather coarse-looking woman, took the children in her arms. 'Come right in, you little rabbits. 'Most asleep, hey? Now here's a drink o' milk f'r each o' ye. I'll have s'm tea in a minute. Take off y'r things and set up t' the fire.'

While she set the children to drinking milk, Council got out his lantern and went out to the barn to help the stranger about his team, where his loud, hearty voice could be heard as it came and went between the haymow and the stalls.

The woman came to light as a small, timid, and discouraged-looking woman, but still pretty, in a thin and sorrowful way.

'Land sakes! An' you've travelled all the way from Clear Lake t'-day in this mud! Waal! Waal! No wonder you're all tired out. Don't wait f'r the men, Mis'—' She hesitated, waiting for the name.

'Haskins.'

'Mis' Haskins, set right up to the table an' take a good swig o' tea whilst I make y' s'm toast. It's green tea, an' it's good. I tell Council as I git older I don't seem to enjoy Young Hyson n'r Gunpowder. I want the reel green tea, jest as it comes off'n the vines. Seems t' have more heart in it, some way. Don't s'pose it has. Council says it's all in m' eye.'

Going on in this easy way, she soon had the children filled with bread and milk and the woman thoroughly at home, eating some toast and sweet-melon pickles, and sipping the tea.

'See the little rats!' she laughed at the children. 'They're full as they can stick now, and they want to go to bed. Now, don't git up, Mis' Haskins; set right where you are an' let me look after 'em. I know all about young ones, though I'm all alone now. Jane went an' married last fall. But, as I tell Council, it's lucky we keep our health. Set right there, Mis' Haskins; I won't have you stir a finger.'

It was an unmeasured pleasure to sit there in the warm, homely kitchen, the jovial chatter of the housewife driving out and holding at bay the growl of the impotent, cheated wind.

The little woman's eyes filled with tears which fell down upon the sleeping baby in her arms. The world was not so desolate and cold and hopeless, after all.

'Now I hope Council won't stop out there and talk politics all night. He's the greatest man to talk politics an' read the *Tribune*. How old is it?'

She broke off and peered down at the face of the babe.

'Two months 'n' five days,' said the mother, with a mother's exactness.

'Ye don't say! I want 'o know! The dear little pudzy-wudzy!' she went on, stirring it up in the neighborhood of the ribs with her fat forefinger.

'Pooty tough on 'oo to go gallivant'n' 'cross lots this way—'

'Yes, that's so; a man can't lift a mountain,' said Council, entering the door. 'Mother, this is Mr Haskins, from Kansas. He's been-eat up 'n' drove out by grasshoppers.'

'Glad t' see yeh! Pa, empty that wash-basin 'n' give him a chance t' wash.'

Haskins was a tall man, with a thin, gloomy face. His hair was a reddish brown, like his coat, and seemed equally faded by the wind and sun. And his sallow face, though hard and set, was pathetic somehow. You would have felt that he had suffered much by the line of his mouth showing under his thin, yellow mustache.

'Hain't Ike got home yet, Sairy?'

'Hain't seen 'im.'

'W-a-a-l, set right up, Mr Haskins; wade right into what we've got; 'taint much, but we manage to live on it – she gits fat on it,' laughed Council, pointing his thumb at his wife.

After supper, while the women put the children to bed, Haskins and Council talked on, seated near the huge cooking-stove, the steam rising from their wet clothing. In the Western fashion Council told as much of his own life as he drew from his guest. He asked but few questions; but by and by the story of Haskins' struggles and defeat came out. The story was a terrible one, but he told it quietly, seated with his elbows on his knees, gazing most of the time at the hearth.

'I didn't like the looks of the country, anyhow,' Haskins said, partly rising and glancing at his wife. 'I was ust 't northern Ingyannie, where we have lots o' timber 'n' lots o' rain, 'n' I didn't like the looks o' that dry prairie. What galled me the worst was goin' s' far away acrosst so much fine land layin' all through here vacant.'

'And the 'hoppers eat ye four years hand runnin', did they?'

'Eat! They wiped us out. They chawed everything that was green. They jest set around waitin' f'r us to die t' eat us, too. My God! I ust t' dream of 'em sittin' 'round on the bedpost, six feet long, workin' their jaws. They eet the fork-handles. They got worse 'n' worse till they jest rolled on one another, piled up like snow in winter. Well, it ain't no use. If I was t' talk all winter I couldn't tell nawthin'. But all the while I couldn't help thinkin' of all that land back here that nobuddy was usin' that I ought o' had 'stead o' bein' out there in that cussed country.'

'Wall, why didn't ye stop an' settle here?' asked Ike, who had come in and was eating his supper.

'Fer the simple reason that you fellers wantid ten 'r fifteen dollars an acre fer the bare land, and I hadn't no money fer that kind o' thing.'

'Yes, I do my own work,' Mrs Council was heard to say in the pause which followed. 'I'm a gettin' purty heavy t' be on m' laigs all day, but we can't afford t' hire, so I keep rackin' around somehow, like a foundered horse. S' lame – I tell Council he can't tell how lame I am, f'r I'm jest as lame in one laig as t' other.' And the good soul laughed at the joke on herself as she took a handful of flour and dusted the biscuit-board to keep the dough from sticking.

'Well, I hain't *never* been very strong,' said Mrs Haskins. 'Our folks was Canadians an' small-boned, and then since my last child I hain't got up again fairly. I don't like t' complain. Tim has about all he can bear now – but they was days this week when I jest wanted to lay right down an' die.'

'Waal, now, I'll tell ye,' said Council, from his side of the stove, silencing everybody with his good-natured roar, 'I'd go down and *see* Butler, *anyway*, if I was you. I guess he'd let you have his place purty cheap; the farm's all run down. He's ben anxious t' let t' somebuddy next year. It 'ud be a good chance fer you. Anyhow, you go to bed and sleep like a babe. I've got some ploughing t' do, anyhow, an' we'll see if somethin' can't be done about your case. Ike, you go out an' see if the horses is all right, an' I'll show the folks t' bed.'

When the tired husband and wife were lying under the generous quilts of the spare bed, Haskins listened a moment to the wind in the eaves, and then said with a slow and solemn tone:

'There are people in this world who are good enough t' be angels, an' only haff t' die to *be* angels.'

2

Jim Butler was one of those men called in the West 'land poor.'

Early in the history of Rock River he had come into the town and started in the grocery business in a small way, occupying a small building in a mean part of the town. At this period of his life he earned all he got, and was up early and late sorting beans, working over butter, and carting his goods to and from the station. But a change came over him at the end of the second year, when he sold a lot of land for four times what he paid for it. From that time forward he believed in land speculation as the surest way of getting rich. Every cent he could save or spare from his trade he put into land at forced sale, or mortgages on land, which were 'just as good as the wheat,' he was accustomed to say.

Farm after farm fell into his hands, until he was recognized as one of the leading landowners of the country. His mortgages were scattered all over Cedar County, and as they slowly but surely fell in he sought usually to retain the former owner as tenant.

He was not ready to foreclose; indeed, he had the name of being one of the 'easiest' men in the town. He let the debtor off again and again, extending the time whenever possible.

'I don't want y'r land,' he said. 'All I'm after is the int' rest on my money – that's all. Now, if y' want 'o stay on the farm, why, I'll give y' a good chance. I can't have the land layin' vacant.' And in many cases the owner remained as tenant.

In the meantime he had sold his store; he couldn't spend time in it; he was mainly occupied now with sitting around town on rainy days smoking and 'gassin' with the boys,' or in riding to and from his farms. In fishing-time he fished a good deal. Doc Grimes, Ben Ashley, and Cal Cheatham were his cronies on these fishing excursions or hunting trips in the time of chickens or partridges. In winter they went to Northern Wisconsin to shoot deer.

In spite of all these signs of easy life Butler persisted in saying he 'hadn't enough money to pay taxes on his land,' and was careful to convey the impression that he was poor in spite of his twenty farms. At one time he was said to be worth fifty thousand dollars, but land had been a little slow of sale of late, so that he was not worth so much. A fine farm, known as the Higley place, had fallen into his hands in the usual way the previous year, and he had not been able to find a tenant for it. Poor Higley, after working himself nearly to death on it in the attempt to lift the mortgage, had gone off to Dakota, leaving the farm and his curse to Butler.

This was the farm which Council advised Haskins to apply for; and the next day Council hitched up his team and drove down to see Butler.

'You jest let *me* do the talkin',' he said. 'We'll find him wearin' out his pants on some salt barrel somew'ers; and if he thought you *wanted* the place he'd sock it to you hot and heavy. You jest keep quiet; I'll fix 'im.'

Butler was seated in Ben Ashley's store telling fish yarns when Council sauntered in casually.

'Hello, But; lyin' agin, hey?'

'Hello, Steve! How goes it?'

'Oh, so-so. Too dang much rain these days. I thought it was gon' t' freeze up f'r good last night. Tight squeak if I get m' ploughin' done. How's farmin' with *you* these days?'

'Bad. Ploughin' ain't half done.'

'It 'ud be a religious idee f'r you t' go out an' take a hand y'rself.'

'I don't haff to,' said Butler, with a wink.

'Got anybody on the Higley place?'

'No. Know of anybody?'

'Waal, no; not eggsackly. I've got a relation back t' Michigan who's ben hot an' cold on the idee o' comin' West f'r some time. *Might* come if he could get a good lay-out. What do you talk on the farm?'

'Well, I d' know. I'll rent it on shares or I'll rent it money rent.'

'Wall, how much money, say?'

'Well, say ten per cent, on the price – two-fifty.'

'Wall, that ain't bad. Wait on 'im till 'e thrashes?'

Haskins listened eagerly to this important question, but Council was coolly eating a dried apple which he had speared out of a barrel with his knife. Butler studied him carefully.

'Well, knocks me out of twenty-five dollars interest.'

'My relation'll need all he's got t' git his crops in,' said Council, in the same, indifferent way.

'Well, all right; *say* wait,' concluded Butler.

'All right; this is the man. Haskins, this is Mr Butler – no relation to Ben – the hardest-working man in Cedar County.'

On the way home Haskins said: 'I ain't much better off. I'd like that farm; it's a good farm, but it's all run down, an' so 'm I.

I could make a good farm of it if I had half a show. But I can't stock it n'r seed it.'

'Waal, now, don't you worry,' roared Council in his ear. 'We'll pull y' through somehow till next harvest. He's agreed t' hire it ploughed, an' you can earn a hundred dollars ploughin' an' y' c'n git the seed o' me, an' pay me back when y' can.'

Haskins was silent with emotion, but at last he said, 'I ain't got nothin' t' live on.'

'Now, don't you worry 'bout that. You jest make your headquarters at ol' Steve Council's. Mother'll take a pile o' comfort in havin' y'r wife an' children 'round. Y' see, Jane's married off lately, an' Ike's away a good 'eal, so we'll be darn glad t' have y' stop with us this winter. Nex' spring we'll see if y' can't git a start agin.' And he chirruped to the team, which sprang forward with the rumbling, clattering wagon.

'Say, looky here, Council, you can't do this. I never saw—' shouted Haskins in his neighbor's ear.

Council moved about uneasily in his seat and stopped his stammering gratitude by saying: 'Hold on, now; don't make such a fuss over a little thing. When I see a man down, an' things all on top of 'm, I jest like t' kick 'em off an' help 'm up. That's the kind of religion I got, an' it's about the *only* kind.'

They rode the rest of the way home in silence. And when the red light of the lamp shone out into the darkness of the cold and windy night, and he thought of this refuge for his children and wife, Haskins could have put his arm around the neck of his burly companion and squeezed him like a lover. But he contented himself with saying, 'Steve Council, you'll git y'r pay f'r this some day.'

'Don't want any pay. My religion ain't run on such business principles.'

The wind was growing colder, and the ground was covered with a white frost, as they turned into the gate of the Council farm, and the children came rushing out, shouting, 'Papa's come!' They hardly looked like the same children who had sat at the table the night before. Their torpidity, under the influence of sunshine and Mother Council, had given way to a sort of spasmodic cheerfulness, as insects in winter revive when laid on the hearth.

3

Haskins worked like a fiend, and his wife, like the heroic woman that she was, bore also uncomplainingly the most terrible burdens. They rose early and toiled without intermission till the darkness fell on the plain, then tumbled into bed, every bone and muscle aching with fatigue, to rise with the sun next morning to the same round of the same ferocity of labor.

The eldest boy, now nine years old, drove a team all through the spring, ploughing and seeding, milked the cows, and did chores innumerable, in most ways taking the place of a man; an infinitely pathetic but common figure – this boy – on the American farm, where there is no law against child labor. To see him in his coarse clothing, his huge boots, and his ragged cap, as he staggered with a pail of water from the well, or trudged in the cold and cheerless dawn out into the frosty field behind his team, gave the city-bred visitor a sharp pang of sympathetic pain. Yet Haskins loved his boy, and would have saved him from this if he could, but he could not.

By June the first year the result of such Herculean toil began to show on the farm. The yard was cleaned up and sown to grass, the garden ploughed and planted, and the house mended. Council had given them four of his cows.

'Take 'em an' run 'em on shares. I don't want a milk s' many. Ike's away s' much now, Sat'd'ys an' Sund'ys, I can't stand the bother anyhow.'

Other men, seeing the confidence of Council in the newcomer, had sold him tools on time; and as he was really an able farmer, he soon had round him many evidences of his care and thrift. At the advice of Council he had taken the farm for three years, with the privilege of re-renting or buying at the end of the term.

'It's a good bargain, an' y' want 'o nail it,' said Council. 'If you have any kind ov a crop, you c'n pay y'r debts, an' keep seed an' bread.'

The new hope which now sprang up in the heart of Haskins and his wife grew almost as a pain by the time the wide field of wheat began to wave and rustle and swirl in the winds of July. Day after day he would snatch a few moments after supper to go and look at it.

'Have ye seen the wheat t'-day, Nettie?' he asked one night as he rose from supper.

'No, Tim, I ain't had time.'

'Well, take time now. Le's go look at it.'

She threw an old hat on her head – Tommy's hat – and looking almost pretty in her thin, sad way, went out with her husband to the hedge.

'Ain't it grand, Nettie? Just look at it.'

It was grand. Level, russet here and there, heavy-headed, wide as a lake, and full of multitudinous whispers and gleams of wealth, it stretched away before the gazers like the fabled field of the cloth of gold.

'Oh, I think – I *hope* we'll have a good crop, Tim; and oh, how good the people have been to us!'

'Yes; I don't know where we'd be t'-day if it hadn't ben f'r Council and his wife.'

'They're the best people in the world,' said the little woman, with a great sob of gratitude.

'We'll be in the field on Monday, sure,' said Haskins, gripping the rail on the fences as if already at the work of the harvest.

The harvest came, bounteous, glorious, but the winds came and blew it into tangles, and the rain matted it here and there close to the ground, increasing the work of gathering it threefold.

Oh, how they toiled in those glorious days! Clothing dripping with sweat, arms aching, filled with briers, fingers raw and bleeding, backs broken with the weight of heavy bundles, Haskins and his man toiled on. Tommy drove the harvester, while his father and a hired man bound on the machine. In this way they cut ten acres every day, and almost every night after supper, when the hand went to bed, Haskins returned to the field shocking the bound grain in the light of the moon. Many a night he worked till his anxious wife came out at ten o'clock to call him in to rest and lunch.

At the same time she cooked for the men, took care of the children, washed and ironed, milked the cows at night, made the butter, and sometimes fed the horses and watered them while her husband kept at the shocking. No slave in the Roman galleys could have toiled so frightfully and lived, for this man thought himself a free man, and that he was working for his wife and babes.

When he sank into his bed with a deep groan of relief, too tired to change his grimy, dripping clothing, he felt that he was getting nearer and nearer to a home of his own, and pushing the wolf of want a little farther from his door.

There is no despair so deep as the despair of a homeless man or woman. To roam the roads of the country or the streets of the city, to feel there is no rood of ground on which the feet can rest, to halt weary and hungry outside lighted windows and hear laughter and song within – these are the hungers and rebellions that drive men to crime and women to shame.

It was the memory of this homelessness, and the fear of its coming again, that spurred Timothy Haskins and Nettie, his wife, to such ferocious labor during that first year.

4

' 'M, yes; 'm, yes; first-rate,' said Butler, as his eye took in the neat garden, the pig-den, and the well-filled barn-yard. 'You're gitt'n quite a stock around yeh. Done well, eh?'

Haskins was showing Butler around the place. He had not seen it for a year, having spent the year in Washington and Boston with Ashley, his brother-in-law, who had been elected to Congress.

'Yes, I've laid out a good deal of money durin' the last three years. I've paid out three hundred dollars f'r fencin'.'

'Um – h'm! I see, I see,' said Butler, while Haskins went on.

'The kitchen there cost two hundred; the barn ain't cost much in money, but I've put a lot o' time on it. I've dug a new well, and I—'

'Yes, yes, I see. You've done well. Stock worth a thousand dollars,' said Butler, picking his teeth with a straw.

'About that,' said Haskins, modestly. 'We begin to feel's if we was gitt'n' a home f'r ourselves; but we've worked hard. I tell ye we begin to feel it, Mr Butler, and we're goin' t' begin to ease up purty soon. We've been kind o' plannin' a trip back t' *her* folks after the fall ploughin's done.'

'*Eggs*-actly!' said Butler, who was evidently thinking of something else. 'I suppose you've kine o' kalklated on stayin' here three years more?'

'Well, yes. Fact is, I think I c'n buy the farm this fall, if you'll give me a reasonable show.'

'Um – m! What do you call a reasonable show?'

'Waal; say a quarter down and three years' time.'

Butler looked at the huge stacks of wheat which filled the yard, over which the chickens were fluttering and crawling, catching grasshoppers, and out of which the crickets were singing innumerably. He smiled in a peculiar way as he said, 'Oh, I won't be hard on yer. But what did you expect to pay f'r the place?'

'Why, about what you offered it for before, two thousand five hundred, or *possibly* three thousand dollars,' he added quickly, as he saw the owner shake his head.

'This farm is worth five thousand and five hundred dollars,' said Butler, in a careless and decided voice.

'What!' almost shrieked the astounded Haskins. 'What's that? Five thousand? Why, that's double what you offered it for three years ago.'

'Of course, and it's worth it. It was all run down then; now it's in good shape. You've laid out fifteen hundred dollars in improvements, according to your own story.'

'But *you* had nothin' t' do about that. It's my work an' my money.'

'You bet it was; but it's my land.'

'But what's to pay me for all my—'

'Ain't you had the use of 'em?' replied Butler, smiling calmly into his face.

Haskins was like a man struck on the head with a sandbag; he couldn't think; he stammered as he tried to say: 'But – I never'd git the use – you'd rob me! More'n that: you agreed – you promised that I could buy or rent at the end of three years at—'

'That's all right. But I didn't say I'd let you carry off the improvements, nor that I'd go on renting the farm at two-fifty. The land is doubled in value, it don't matter how; it don't enter into the question; an' now you can pay me five hundred dollars a year rent, or take it on your own terms at fifty-five hundred, or – git out.'

He was turning away when Haskins, the sweat pouring from his face, fronted him, saying again:

'But *you've* done nothing to make it so. You hain't added a cent. I put it all there myself, expectin' to buy. I worked an' sweat to improve it. I was workin' for myself an' babes—'

'Well, why didn't you buy when I offered to sell? What y' kickin' about?'

'I'm kickin' about payin' you twice f'r my own things – my own fences, my own kitchen, my own garden.'

Butler laughed. 'You're too green t' eat, young feller. *Your* improvements! The law will sing another tune.'

'But I trusted your word.'

'Never trust anybody, my friend. Besides, I didn't promise not to do this thing. Why, man, don't look at me like that. Don't take me for a thief. It's the law. The reg'lar thing. Everybody does it.'

'I don't care if they do. It's stealin' jest the same. You take three thousand dollars of my money. The work o' my hands and my wife's.' He broke down at this point. He was not a strong man mentally. He could face hardship, ceaseless toil, but he could not face the cold and sneering face of Butler.

'But I don't take it,' said Butler, coolly. 'All you've got to do is to go on jest as you've been a-doin', or give me a thousand dollars down, and a mortgage at ten per cent on the rest.'

Haskins sat down blindly on a bundle of oats near by, and with staring eyes and drooping head went over the situation. He was under the lion's paw. He felt a horrible numbness in his heart and limbs. He was hid in a mist, and there was no path out.

Butler walked about, looking at the huge stacks of grain, and pulling now and again a few handfuls out, shelling the heads in his hands and blowing the chaff away. He hummed a little tune as he did so. He had an accommodating air of waiting.

Haskins was in the midst of the terrible toil of the last year. He was walking again in the rain and the mud behind his plough; he felt the dust and dirt of the threshing. The ferocious husking-time, with its cutting wind and biting, clinging snows, lay hard upon him. Then he thought of his wife, how she had cheerfully cooked and baked, without holiday and without rest.

'Well, what do you think of it?' inquired the cool, mocking, insinuating voice of Butler.

'I think you're a thief and a liar!' shouted Haskins, leaping up. 'A black-hearted houn'!' Butler's smile maddened him; with a sudden leap he caught a fork in his hands, and whirled it in the air. 'You'll never rob another man, damn ye!' he grated through his teeth, a look of pitiless ferocity in his accusing eyes.

Butler shrank and quivered, expecting the blow; stood, held hypnotized by the eyes of the man he had a moment before despised – a man transformed into an avenging demon. But in the deadly hush between the lift of the weapon and its fall there came a gush of faint, childish laughter and then across the range of his vision, far away and dim, he saw the sun-bright head of his baby girl, as, with the pretty, tottering run of a two-year-old, she moved across the grass of the dooryard. His hands relaxed; the fork fell to the ground; his head lowered.

'Make out y'r deed an' morgige, an' git off'n my land, an' don't ye never cross my line again, if y' do, I'll kill ye.'

Butler backed away from the man in wild haste, and climbing

into his buggy with trembling limbs, drove off down the road, leaving Haskins seated dumbly on the sunny pile of sheaves, his head sunk into his hands.

1891

Whistling Dick's Christmas Stocking

It was with much caution that Whistling Dick slid back the door of the box-car, for Article 5716, City Ordinances, authorized (perhaps unconstitutionally) arrest on suspicion, and he was familiar of old with this ordinance. So, before climbing out, he surveyed the field with all the care of a good general.

He saw no change since his last visit to this big, almsgiving, long-suffering city of the South, the cold weather paradise of the tramps. The levee where his freight-car stood was pimpled with dark bulks of merchandise. The breeze reeked with the well-remembered, sickening smell of the old tarpaulins that covered bales and barrels. The dun river slipped along among the shipping with an oily gurgle. Far down toward Chalmette he could see the great bend in the stream outlined by the row of electric lights. Across the river Algiers lay, a long, irregular blot, made darker by the dawn which lightened the sky beyond. An industrious tug or two, coming for some early sailing ship, gave a few appalling toots that seemed to be the signal for breaking day. The Italian luggers were creeping nearer their landing, laden with early vegetables and shellfish. A vague roar, subterranean in quality, from dray wheels and street cars, began to make itself heard and felt; and the ferryboats, the Mary Anns of water craft, stirred sullenly to their menial morning tasks.

Whistling Dick's red head popped suddenly back into the car. A sight too imposing and magnificent for his gaze had been added to the scene. A vast, incomparable policeman rounded a pile of rice sacks and stood within twenty yards of the car. The daily miracle of the dawn, now being performed above Algiers, received the flattering attention of this specimen of municipal official splendour. He gazed with unbiased dignity at the faintly glowing colours until, at last, he turned to them his broad back, as if convinced that legal interference was not needed, and the sunrise might proceed unchecked. So he turned his face to the rice bags, and, drawing a flat flask from an inside pocket, he placed it to his lips and regarded the firmament.

Whistling Dick, professional tramp, possessed a half-friendly acquaintance with this officer. They had met several times before on the levee at night, for the officer, himself a lover of music, had been attracted by the exquisite whistling of the shiftless vagabond. Still, he did not care, under the present circumstances, to renew the acquaintance. There is a difference between meeting a policeman upon a lonely wharf and whistling a few operatic airs with him, and being caught by him crawling out of a freight-car. So Dick waited, as even a New Orleans policeman must move on some time – perhaps it is a retributive law of nature – and before long 'Big Fritz' majestically disappeared between the trains of cars.

Whistling Dick waited as long as his judgment advised, and then slid swiftly to the ground. Assuming as far as possible the air of an honest laborer who seeks his daily toil, he moved across the network of railway lines, with the intention of making his way by quiet Girod Street to a certain bench in Lafayette Square, where, according to appointment, he hoped to rejoin a pal known as 'Slick,' this adventurous pilgrim having preceded him by one day in a cattle-car into which a loose slat had enticed him.

As Whistling Dick picked his way where night still lingered among the big, reeking, musty warehouses, he gave way to the habit that had won for him his title. Subdued, yet clear, with each note as true and liquid as a bobolink's, his whistle tinkled about the dim, cold mountains of brick like drops of rain falling into a hidden pool. He followed an air, but it swam mistily into a swirling current of improvisation. You could cull out the trill of mountain brooks, the staccato of green rushes shivering above chilly lagoons, the pipe of sleepy birds.

Rounding a corner, the whistler collided with a mountain of blue and brass.

'So,' observed the mountain calmly, 'you are already pack. Und dere vill not pe frost before two veeks yet! Und you haf forgotten how to vistle. Dere was a valse note in dot last bar.'

'Watcher know about it?' said Whistling Dick, with tentative familiarity; 'you wit yer little Gherman-band nixcumrous chunes. Watcher know about music? Pick yer ears, and listen agin. Here's de way I whistled it – see?'

He puckered his lips, but the big policeman held up his hand.

'Shtop,' he said, 'und learn der right way. Und learn also dot a rolling shtone can't vistle for a cent.'

Big Fritz's heavy moustache rounded into a circle, and from its depths came a sound deep and mellow as that from a flute. He repeated a few bars of the air the tramp had been whistling. The rendition was cold, but correct, and he emphasized the note he had taken exception to.

'Dot p is p natural, und not p vlat. Py der vay, you petter pe glad I meet you. Von hour later, und I vould half to put you in a gage to vistle mit der chail pirds. Der orders are to bull all der pums after sunrise.'

'To which?'

'To bull der pums – eferybody mitout fisible means. Dirty days is der price, or fifteen tollars.'

'Is dat straight, or a game you givin' me?'

'It's der pest tip you efer had. I gif it to you pecause I pelief you are not so bad as der rest. Und pecause you gan visl "Der Freischütz" bezzer dan I myself gan. Don't run against any more bolicemans aroundt der corners, but go away from town a few tays. Goot-pye.'

So Madame Orleans had at last grown weary of the strange and ruffled brood that came yearly to nestle beneath her charitable pinions.

After the big policeman had departed, Whistling Dick stood for an irresolute minute, feeling all the outraged indignation of a delinquent tenant who is ordered to vacate his premises. He had pictured to himself a day of dreamful ease when he should have joined his pal; a day of lounging on the wharf, munching the bananas and cocoanuts scattered in unloading the fruit steamers; and then a feast along the free-lunch counters from which the easy-going owners were too good-natured or too generous to drive him away, and afterward a pipe in one of the little flowery parks and a snooze in some shady corner of the wharf. But here was a stern order to exile, and one that he knew must be obeyed. So, with a wary eye open from the gleam of brass buttons, he began his retreat toward a rural refuge. A few days in the country need not necessarily prove disastrous. Beyond the possibility of a slight nip of frost, there was no formidable evil to be looked for.

However, it was with a depressed spirit that Whistling Dick passed the old French market on his chosen route down the river. For safety's sake he still presented to the world his portrayal of the part of the worthy artisan on his way to labour. A stall-keeper in the market, undeceived, hailed him by the generic name of his ilk, and 'Jack' halted, taken by surprise. The vender, melted by this proof of his own acuteness, bestowed a foot of Frankfurter and half a loaf, and thus the problem of breakfast was solved.

When the streets, from topographical reasons, began to shun the river bank the exile mounted to the top of the levee, and on its well-trodden path pursued his way. The suburban eye regarded him with cold suspicion, individuals reflected the stern spirit of the city's heartless edict. He missed the seclusion of the crowded town and the safety he could always find in the multitude.

At Chalmette, six miles upon his desultory way, there suddenly menaced him a vast and bewildering industry. A new port was being established; the dock was being built, compresses were going up; picks and shovels and barrows struck at him like serpents from every side. An arrogant foreman bore down upon him, estimating his muscles with the eye of a recruiting-sergeant. Brown men and black men all about him were toiling away. He fled in terror.

By noon he had reached the country of the plantations, the great, sad, silent levels bordering the mighty river. He overlooked fields of sugar-cane so vast that their farthest limits melted into the sky. The sugar-making season was well advanced, and the cutters were at work; the wagons creaked drearily after them; the Negro teamsters inspired the mules to greater speed with mellow and sonorous imprecations. Dark-green groves, blurred by the blue of distance, showed where the plantation-houses stood. The tall chimneys of the sugar-mills caught the eye miles distant, like lighthouses at sea.

At a certain point Whistling Dick's unerring nose caught the scent of frying fish. Like a pointer to a quail, he made his way down the levee side straight to the camp of a credulous and ancient fisherman, whom he charmed with song and story, so that he dined like an admiral, and then like a philosopher annihilated the worst three hours of the day by a nap under the trees.

When he awoke and again continued his hegira, a frosty sparkle in the air had succeeded the drowsy warmth of the day, and as this portent of a chilly night translated itself to the brain of Sir Peregrine, he lengthened his stride and bethought him of shelter. He travelled a road that faithfully followed the convolutions of the levee, running along its base, but whither he knew not. Bushes and rank grass crowded it to the wheel ruts, and out of this ambuscade the pests of the lowlands swarmed after him, humming a keen, vicious soprano. And as the night grew nearer, although colder, the whine of the mosquitoes became a greedy, petulant snarl that shut out all other sounds. To his right, against the heavens, he saw a green light moving, and, accompanying it, the masts and funnels of a big incoming steamer, moving as upon a screen at a magic-lantern show. And there were mysterious marshes at his left, out of which came queer gurgling cries and a choked croaking. The whistling vagrant struck up a merry warble to offset these melancholy influences, and it is likely that never before, since Pan himself jigged it on his reeds, had such sounds been heard in those depressing solitudes.

A distant clatter in the rear quickly developed into the swift beat of horses' hoofs, and Whistling Dick stepped aside into the dew-wet grass to clear the track. Turning his head, he saw approaching a fine team of stylish grays drawing a double surrey. A stout man with a white moustache occupied the front seat, giving all his attention to the rigid lines in his hands. Behind him sat a placid, middle-aged lady and a brilliant-looking girl hardly arrived at young ladyhood. The lap-robe had slipped partly from the knees of the gentleman driving, and Whistling Dick saw two stout canvas bags between his feet – bags such as, while loafing in cities, he had seen warily transferred between express wagons and bank doors. The remaining space in the vehicle was filled with parcels of various sizes and shapes.

As the surrey swept even with the sidetracked tramp, the bright-eyed girl, seized by some merry, madcap impulse, leaned out toward him with a sweet, dazzling smile, and cried, 'Mer-ry Christ-mas!' in a shrill, plaintive treble.

Such a thing had not often happened to Whistling Dick, and he felt handicapped in devising the correct response. But lacking time for reflection, he let his instinct decide, and snatching off his battered derby, he rapidly extended it at arm's length, and drew it back with a continuous motion, and shouted a loud, but ceremonious, 'Ah, there!' after the flying surrey.

The sudden movement of the girl had caused one of the parcels to become unwrapped, and something limp and black fell from it into the road. The tramp picked it up, and found it to be a new black silk stocking, long and fine and slender. It crunched crisply, and yet with a luxurious softness, between his fingers.

'Ther bloomin' little skeezicks!' said Whistling Dick, with a broad grin bisecting his freckled face. 'W'ot d' yer think of dat, now! Mer-ry Chris-mus! Sounded like a cuckoo clock, dat's what she did. Dem guys is swells, too, bet yer life, an' der old 'un stacks dem sacks of dough down under his trotters like dey was common as dried apples. Been shoppin' fer Chrismus, and de kid's lost one of her new socks w'ot she was goin' to hold up Santy wid. De bloomin' little skeezicks! Wit' her "Mer-ry Chris-mus!" W'ot d' yer t'ink! Same as to say, "Hello, Jack, how goes it?" and as swell as Fift' Av'noo, and as easy as a blowout in Cincinnat.'

Whistling Dick folded the stocking carefully and stuffed it into his pocket.

It was nearly two hours later when he came upon signs of habitation. The buildings of an extensive plantation were brought into view by a turn in the road. He easily selected the planter's residence in a large square building with two wings, with numerous good-sized, well-lighted windows, and broad verandas running around its full extent. It was set upon a smooth lawn, which was faintly lit by the far-reaching rays of the lamps within. A noble grove surrounded it, and old-fashioned shrubbery grew thickly about the walks and fences. The quarters of the hands and the mill buildings were situated at a distance in the rear.

The road was now enclosed on each side by a fence, and presently, as Whistling Dick drew nearer the houses, he suddenly stopped and sniffed the air.

'If dere ain't a hobo stew cookin' somewhere in dis immediate precinct,' he said to himself, 'me nose has quit tellin' de trut'.'

Without hesitation he climbed the fence to windward. He found himself in an apparently disused lot, where piles of old bricks were stacked, and rejected, decaying lumber. In a corner he saw the faint glow of a fire that had become little more than a bed of living coals, and he thought he could see some dim human forms sitting or lying about it. He drew nearer, and by the light of a little blaze that suddenly flared up he saw plainly the fat figure of a ragged man in an old brown sweater and cap.

'Dat man,' said Whistling Dick to himself softly, 'is a dead ringer for Boston Harry. I'll try him wit de high sign.'

He whistled one or two bars of a rag-time melody, and the air was immediately taken up, and then quickly ended with a peculiar run. The first whistler walked confidently up to the fire. The fat man looked up, and spake in a loud, asthmatic wheeze:

'Gents, the unexpected but welcome addition to our circle is Mr Whistling Dick, an old friend of mine for whom I fully vouches.

The waiter will lay another cover at once. Mr W. D. will join us at supper, during which function he will enlighten us in regard to the circumstances that give us the pleasure of his company.'

'Chewin' de stuffin' ou 'n de dictionary, as usual, Boston,' said Whistling Dick; 'but t'anks all de same for de invitashun. I guess I finds meself here about de same way as yous guys. A cop gimme de tip dis mornin'. Yous workin' on dis farm?'

'A guest,' said Boston sternly, 'shouldn't never insult his entertainers until he's filled up wid grub. 'Tain't good business sense. Workin'! but I will restrain myself. We five – me, Deaf Pete, Blinky, Goggles, and Indiana Tom – got put on to this scheme of Noo Orleans to work visiting gentlemen upon her dirty streets, and we hit the road last evening just as the tender hues of twilight had flopped down upon the daisies and things. Blinky, pass the empty oyster-can at your left to the empty gentleman at your right.'

For the next ten minutes the gang of roadsters paid their undivided attention to the supper. In an old five-gallon kerosene can they had cooked a stew of potatoes, meat, and onions, which they partook of from smaller cans they had found scattered about the vacant lot.

Whistling Dick had known Boston Harry of old, and knew him to be one of the shrewdest and most successful of his brotherhood. He looked like a prosperous stock-drover or a solid merchant from some country village. He was stout and hale, with a ruddy, always smoothly shaven face. His clothes were strong and neat, and he gave special attention to his decent-appearing shoes. During the past ten years he had acquired a reputation for working a larger number of successfully managed confidence games than any of his acquaintances, and he had not a day's work to be counted against him. It was rumored among his associates that he had saved a considerable amount of money. The four other men were fair specimens of the slinking, ill-clad, noisome genus who carried their labels of 'suspicious' in plain view.

After the bottom of the large can had been scraped, and pipes lit at the coals, two of the men called Boston aside and spake with him lowly and mysteriously. He nodded decisively, and then said aloud to Whistling Dick:

'Listen, sonny, to some plain talky-talk. We five are on a lay. I've guaranteed you to be square, and you're to come in on the profits equal with the boys, and you've got to help. Two hundred hands on this plantation are expecting to be paid a week's wages tomorrow morning. Tomorrow's Christmas, and they want to lay off. Says the boss: "Work from five to nine in the morning to get a train load of sugar off, and I'll pay every man cash down for the week and a day extra." They say: "Hooray for the boss! It goes." He drives to Noo Orleans today, and fetches back the cold dollars. Two thousand and seventy-four fifty is the amount. I got the figures from a man who talks too much, who got 'em from the bookkeeper. The boss of this plantation thinks he's going to pay this wealth to the hands. He's got it down wrong; he's going to pay it to us. It's going to stay in the leisure class, where it belongs. Now, half of this haul goes to me, and the other half the rest of you may divide. Why the difference? I represent the brains. It's my scheme. Here's the way we're going to get it. There's some company at supper in the house, but they'll leave about nine. They've just happened in for an hour or so. If they don't go pretty soon, we'll work the scheme anyhow. We want all night to get away good with the dollars. They're heavy. About nine o'clock Deaf Pete and Blinky'll go down the road about a quarter beyond the house, and set fire to a big canefield there that the cutters haven't touched yet. The wind's just right to have it roaring in two minutes. The alarm'll be given, and every man Jack about the place will be down there in ten minutes, fighting fire. That'll leave the money sacks and the women alone in the house for us to handle. You've heard cane burn? Well, there's mighty few women can screech loud enough to be heard above its crackling. The thing's dead safe. The only danger is in being caught before we can get far enough away with the money. Now, if you –'

'Boston,' interruped Whistling Dick, rising to his feet, 't'anks for de grub yous fellers has given me, but I'll be movin' on now.'

'What do you mean?' asked Boston, also rising.

'W'y, you can count me outer dis deal. You oughter know that. I'm on de bum all right enough, but dat other t'ing don't go wit' me. Burglary is no good. I'll say good night and many t'anks fer –'

Whistling Dick had moved away a few steps as he spoke, but he stopped very suddenly. Boston had covered him with a short revolver of roomy calibre.

'Take your seat,' said the tramp leader. 'I'd feel mighty proud of myself if I let you go and spoil the game. You'll stick right in this camp until we finish the job. The end of that brick pile is your limit. You go two inches beyond that, and I'll have to shoot. Better take it easy, now.'

'It's my way of doin',' said Whistling Dick. 'Easy goes. You can depress de muzzle of dat twelve-incher, and run 'er back on de trucks. I remains, as de newspapers says, "in yer midst".'

'All right,' said Boston, lowering his piece, as the other returned and took his seat again on a projecting plank in a pile of timber. 'Don't try to leave; that's all. I wouldn't miss this chance even if I had to shoot an old acquaintance to make it go. I don't want to hurt anybody specially, but this thousand dollars I'm going to get will fix me for fair. I'm going to drop the road, and start a saloon in a little town I know about. I'm tired of being kicked around.'

Boston Harry took from his pocket a cheap silver watch, and held it near the fire.

'It's a quarter to nine,' he said. 'Pete, you and Blinky start. Go down the road past the house, and fire the cane in a dozen places. Then strike for the levee, and come back on it, instead of the road, so you won't meet anybody. By the time you get back the men will all be striking out for the fire, and we'll break for the house and collar the dollars. Everybody cough up what matches he's got.'

The two surly tramps made a collection of all the matches in the party, Whistling Dick contributing his quota with propitiatory alacrity, and then they departed in the dim starlight in the direction of the road.

Of the three remaining vagrants, two, Goggles and Indiana Tom, reclined lazily upon convenient lumber and regarded Whistling Dick with undisguised disfavor. Boston, observing that the dissenting recruit was disposed to remain peaceably, relaxed a little of his vigilance. Whistling Dick arose presently and strolled leisurely up and down keeping carefully within the territory assigned him.

'Dis planter chap,' he said, pausing before Boston Harry, 'w'ot makes yer t'ink he's got de tin in de house wit' 'im?'

'I'm advised of the facts in the case,' said Boston. 'He drove to Noo Orleans and got it, I say, today. Want to change your mind now and come in?'

'Naw, I was just askin'. Wot kind o' team did de boss drive?'

'Pair of grays.'

'Double surrey?'

'Yep.'

'Women folks along?'

'Wife and kid. Say, what morning paper are you trying to pump news for?'

'I was just conversin' to pass de time away. I guess dat team passed me in de road dis evenin'. Dat's all.'

As Whistling Dick put his hands into his pockets and continued his curtailed beat up and down by the fire, he felt the silk stocking he had picked up in the road.

'Ther bloomin' little skee icks,' he muttered, with a grin.

As he walked up and down he could see, through a sort of natural opening or lane among the trees, the planter's residence some seventy-five yards distant. The side of the house toward him exhibited spacious, well-lighted windows through which a soft radiance streamed, illuminating the broad veranda and some extent of the lawn beneath.

'What's that you said?' asked Boston, sharply.

'Oh, nuttin' 't all,' said Whistling Dick, lounging carelessly, and kicking meditatively at a little stone on the ground.

'Just as easy,' continued the warbling vagrant softly to himself, 'an' sociable an' swell an' sassy, wit' her "Mer-ry Chris-mus," Wot d'yer t'ink, now!'

Dinner, two hours late, was being served in the Bellemeade plantation dining-room.

The dining-room and all its appurtenances spoke of an old regime that was here continued rather than suggested to the memory. The plate was rich to the extent that its age and quaintness alone saved it from being showy; there were interesting names signed in the corners of the pictures on the walls; the viands were of the kind that bring a shine into the eyes of gourmets. The service was swift, silent, lavish, as in the days when the waiters were assets like the plate. The names by which the planter's family and their visitors addressed one another were historic in the annals of two nations. Their manners and conversation had that most difficult kind of ease – the kind that still preserves punctilio. The planter himself seemed to be the dynamo that generated the larger portion of the gaiety and wit. The younger ones at the board found it more than difficult to turn back on him his guns of raillery and banter. It is true, the young men attempted to storm his words repeatedly, incited by the hope of gaining the approbation of their fair companions; but even when they sped a well-aimed shaft, the planter forced them to feel defeat by the tremendous discomfiting thunder of the laughter with which he accompanied his retorts. At the head of the table, serene, matronly, benevolent, reigned the mistress of the house, placing here and there the right smile, the right word, the encouraging glance.

The talk of the party was too desultory, too evanescent to follow, but at last they came to the subject of the tramp nuisance, one that had of late vexed the plantations for many miles around. The planter seized the occasion to direct his good-natured fire of raillery at the mistress, accusing her of encouraging the plague. 'They swarm up and down the river every winter,' he said. 'They overrun New Orleans, and we catch the surplus, which is generally the worst part. And, a day or two ago, Madame New Orleans, suddenly discovering that she can't go shopping without brushing her skirts against great rows of the vagabonds sunning themselves on the banquettes, says to the police: "Catch 'em all," and the police catch a dozen or two, and the remaining three or four thousand overflow up and down the levees, and madame there' — pointing tragically with the carving-knife at her — 'feeds them. They won't work; they defy my overseers, and they make friends with my dogs; and you, madame, feed them before my eyes, and intimidate me when I would interfere. Tell us, please, how many today did you thus incite to future laziness and depredation?'

'Six, I think,' said madame, with a reflective smile; 'but you know two of them offered to work, for you heard them yourself.'

The planter's disconcerting laugh rang out again.

'Yes, at their own trades. And one was an artificial-flower maker, and the other a glass-blower. Oh, they were looking for work! Not a hand would they consent to lift to labor of any other kind.'

'And another one,' continued the soft-hearted mistress, 'used quite good language. It was really extraordinary for one of his class. And he carried a watch. And had lived in Boston. I don't believe they are all bad. They have always seemed to me to rather lack development. I always look upon them as children with whom wisdom has remained at a standstill while whiskers have continued to grow. We passed one this evening as we were driving home who had a face as good as it was incompetent. He was whistling the intermezzo from "Cavalleria" and blowing the spirit of Mascagni himself into it.'

A bright-eyed young girl who sat at the left of the mistress leaned over, and said in a confidential undertone:

'I wonder, mamma, if that tramp we passed on the road found my stocking, and do you think he will hang it up tonight? Now I can hang up but one. Do you know why I wanted a new pair of silk stockings when I have plenty? Well, old Aunt Judy says, if you hang up two that have never been worn, Santa Claus will fill one with good things, and Monsieur Pambe will place in the other payment for all the words you have spoken – good or bad – on the day before Christmas. That's why I've been unusually nice and polite to everyone today. Monsieur Pambe, you know, is a witch gentleman; he –'

The words of the young girl were interrupted by a startling thing.

Like the wraith of some burned-out shooting star, a black streak came crashing through the window-pane and upon the table, where it shivered into fragments a dozen pieces of crystal and china ware, and then glanced between the heads of the guests to the wall, imprinting therein a deep, round indentation, at which, today, the visitor to Bellemeade marvels as he gazes upon it and listens to this tale as it is told.

The women screamed in many keys, and the men sprang to their feet, and would have laid hands upon their swords had not the verities of chronology forbidden.

The planter was the first to act; he sprang to the intruding missile, and held it up to view.

'By Jupiter!' he cried. 'A meteoric shower of hosiery! Has communication at last been established with Mars?'

'I should say – ahem! Venus,' ventured a young-gentleman visitor, looking hopefully for approbation toward the unresponsive young-lady visitors.

The planter held at arm's length the unceremonious visitor – a long dangling black stocking. 'It's loaded,' he announced.

As he spoke he reversed the stocking, holding it by the toe, and down from it dropped a roundish stone, wrapped about by a piece of yellowish paper. 'Now for the first interstellar message of the century!' he cried; and nodding to the company, who had crowded about him, he adjusted his glasses with provoking deliberation, and examined it closely. When he finished, he had changed from the jolly host to the practical, decisive man of business. He immediately struck a bell, and said to the silent-footed mulatto man who responded:

'Go and tell Mr Wesley to get Reeves and Maurice and about ten stout hands they can rely upon, and come to the hall door at once. Tell him to have the men arm themselves, and bring plenty of ropes and plough lines. Tell him to hurry.' And then he read aloud from the paper these words:

TO THE GENT OF DE HOUS:
  Dere is five tuff hoboes xcept meself in the vaken lot near de road war de old brick piles is. Dey got me stuck up wid a gun see and I taken dis means of communikaten. 2 of der lads is gone down to set fire to de cain field below de hous and when yous fellers goes to turn de hoes on it de hole gang is goin to rob de hous of de money yoo gotto pay off wit say git a move on ye say de kid dropt dis sock in der rode tel her mery crismus de same as she told me. Ketch de bums down de rode first and den sen a relefe core to get me out of soke youres truly,

                                                    WHISTLEN DICK

There was some quiet, but rapid, manœuvring at Bellemeade during the ensuing half hour, which ended in five disgusted and sullen tramps being captured, and locked securely in an outhouse pending the coming of the morning and retribution. For another result, the visiting young gentlemen had secured the unqualified worship of the visiting young ladies by their distinguished and heroic conduct. For still another, behold Whistling Dick, the hero, seated at the planter's table, feasting upon viands his experience had never before included, and waited upon by admiring femininity in shapes of such beauty and 'swellness' that even his ever-full mouth could scarcely prevent him from whistling. He was made to disclose in detail his adventure with the evil gang of Boston Harry, and how he cunningly wrote the note and wrapped it around the stone and placed it in the toe of the stocking, and, watching his chance, sent it silently, with a wonderful centrifugal momentum, like a comet, at one of the big lighted windows of the dining-room.

The planter vowed that the wanderer should wander no more; that his was a goodness and an honesty that should be rewarded, and that a debt of gratitude had been made that must be paid; for had he not saved them from a doubtless imminent loss, and maybe a greater calamity? He assured Whistling Dick that he might consider himself a charge upon the honour of Bellemeade; that a position suited to his powers would be found for him at once, and hinted that the way would be heartily smoothed for him to rise to as high places of emolument and trust as the plantation afforded.

But now, they said, he must be weary, and the immediate thing to consider was rest and sleep. So the mistress spoke to a servant, and Whistling Dick was conducted to a room in the wing of the house occupied by the servants. To this room, in a few minutes, was brought a portable tin bathtub filled with water, which was placed on a piece of oiled cloth upon the floor. There the vagrant was left to pass the night.

By the light of a candle he examined the room. A bed, with the covers neatly turned back, revealed snowy pillows and sheets. A worn, but clean, red carpet covered the floor. There was a dresser with a beveled mirror, a washstand with a flowered bowl and pitcher; the two or three chairs were softly upholstered. A little table held books, papers, and a day-old cluster of roses in a jar. There were towels on a rack and soap in a white dish.

Whistling Dick set his candle on a chair and placed his hat carefully under the table. After satisfying what we must suppose to have been his curiosity by a sober scrutiny, he removed his coat, folded it, and laid it upon the floor, near the wall, as far as possible from the unused bathtub. Taking his coat for a pillow, he stretched himself luxuriously upon the carpet.

When, on Christmas morning, the first streaks of dawn broke above the marshes, Whistling Dick awoke, and reached instinctively for his hat. Then he remembered that the skirts of Fortune had swept him into their folds on the night previous, and he went to the window and raised it, to let the fresh breath of the morning cool his brow and fix the yet dream-like memory of his good luck within his brain.

As he stood there, certain dread and ominous sounds pierced the fearful hollow of his ear.

The force of plantation workers, eager to complete the shortened task allotted to them, were all astir. The mighty din of the ogre Labor shook the earth, and the poor tattered and forever disguised Prince in search of his fortune held tight to the window-sill even in the enchanted castle, and trembled.

Already from the bosom of the mill came the thunder of rolling barrels of sugar, and (prison-like sounds) there was a great rattling of chains as the mules were harried with stimulant imprecations to their places by the wagon-tongues. A little vicious 'dummy' engine, with a train of flat cars in tow, stewed and fumed on the plantation tap of the narrow-gauge railroad, and a toiling, hurrying, hallooing stream of workers were dimly seen in the half darkness loading the train with the weekly output of sugar. Here was a poem; an epic – nay, a tragedy – with work, the curse of the world, for its theme.

The December air was frosty, but the sweat broke out upon Whistling Dick's face. He thrust his head out of the window, and looked down. Fifteen feet below him, against the wall of the house, he could make out that a border of flowers grew, and by that token he overhung a bed of soft earth.

Softly as a burglar goes, he clambered out upon the sill, lowered himself until he hung by his hands alone, and then dropped safely. No one seemed to be about upon this side of the house. He dodged low, and skimmed swiftly across the yard to the low fence. It was an easy matter to vault this, for a terror urged him such as lifts the gazelle over the thorn bush when the lion pursues. A crash through the dew-drenched weeds on the roadside, a clutching, slippery rush up the grassy side of the levee to the footpath at the summit, and – he was free!

The east was blushing and brightening. The wind, himself a vagrant rover, saluted his brother upon the cheek. Some wild geese, high above, gave cry. A rabbit skipped along the path before him, free to turn to the right or to the left as his mood should send him. The river slid past, and certainly no one could tell the ultimate abiding place of its waters.

A small, ruffled, brown-breasted bird, sitting upon a dog-wood sapling, began a soft, throaty, tender little piping in praise of the dew which entices foolish worms from their holes; but suddenly he stopped, and sat with his head turned sidewise, listening.

From the path along the levee there burst forth a jubilant, stirring, buoyant, thrilling whistle, loud and keen and clear as the cleanest notes of the piccolo. The soaring sound rippled and trilled and arpeggioed as the songs of wild birds do not; but it had a wild free grace that, in a way, reminded the small, brown bird of something familiar, but exactly what he could not tell. There was in it the bird call, or reveille, that all birds know; but a great waste of lavish, unmeaning things that art had added and arranged, besides, and that were quite puzzling and strange; and the little brown bird sat with his head on one side until the sound died away in the distance.

The little bird did not know that the part of that strange warbling that he understood was just what kept the warbler without his breakfast; but he knew very well that the part he did not understand did not concern him, so he gave a little flutter of his wings and swooped down like a brown bullet upon a big fat worm that was wriggling along the levee path.

1899

EDITH WHARTON
1862–1937

A Journey

As she lay in her berth, staring at the shadows overhead, the rush of the wheels was in her brain, driving her deeper and deeper into circles of wakeful lucidity. The sleeping-car had sunk into its night-silence. Through the wet window-pane she watched the sudden lights, the long stretches of hurrying blackness. Now and then she turned her head and looked through the opening in the hangings at her husband's curtains across the aisle . . .

She wondered restlessly if he wanted anything and if she could hear him if he called. His voice had grown very weak within the last months and it irritated him when she did not hear. This irritability, this increasing childish petulance seemed to give expression to their imperceptible estrangement. Like two faces looking at one another through a sheet of glass they were close together, almost touching, but they could not hear or feel each other: the conductivity between them was broken. She, at least, had this sense of separation, and she fancied sometimes that she saw it reflected in the look with which he supplemented his failing words. Doubtless the fault was hers. She was too impenetrably healthy to be touched by the irrelevancies of disease. Her self-reproachful tenderness was tinged with the sense of his irrationality: she had a vague feeling that there was a purpose in his helpless tyrannies. The suddenness of the change had found her so unprepared. A year ago their pulses had beat to one robust measure; both had the same prodigal confidence in an exhaustless future. Now their energies no longer kept step: hers still bounded ahead of life, preëmpting unclaimed regions of hope and activity, while his lagged behind, vainly struggling to overtake her.

When they married, she had such arrears of living to make up: her days had been as bare as the white-washed school-room where she forced innutritious facts upon reluctant children. His coming had broken in on the slumber of circumstance, widening the present till it became the encloser of remotest chances. But imperceptibly the horizon narrowed. Life had a grudge against her: she was never to be allowed to spread her wings.

At first the doctors had said that six weeks of mild air would set him right; but when he came back this assurance was explained as having of course included a winter in a dry climate. They gave up their pretty house, storing the wedding presents and new furniture, and went to Colorado. She had hated it there from the first. Nobody knew her or cared about her; there was no one to wonder at the good match she had made, or to envy her the new dresses and the visiting-cards which were still a surprise to her. And he kept growing worse. She felt herself beset with difficulties too evasive to be fought by so direct a temperament. She still loved him, of course; but he was gradually, undefinably ceasing to be himself. The man she had married had been strong, active, gently masterful: the male whose pleasure it is to clear a way through the material obstructions of life; but now it was she who was the protector, he who must be shielded from importunities and given his drops or his beef-juice though the skies were falling. The routine of the sick-room bewildered her; this punctual administering of medicine seemed as idle as some uncomprehended religious mummery.

There were moments, indeed, when warm gushes of pity swept away her instinctive resentment of his condition, when she still found his old self in his eyes as they groped for each other through the dense medium of his weakness. But these moments had grown rare. Sometimes he frightened her: his sunken expressionless face seemed that of a stranger; his voice was weak and hoarse; his thin-lipped smile a mere muscular contraction. Her hand avoided his damp soft skin, which had lost the familiar roughness of health: she caught herself furtively watching him as she might have watched a strange animal. It frightened her to feel that this was the man she loved; there were hours when to tell him what she suffered seemed the one escape from her fears. But in general she judged herself more leniently, reflecting that she had perhaps been too long alone with him, and that she would feel differently when they were at home again, surrounded by her robust and buoyant family. How she had rejoiced when the doctors at last gave their consent to his going home! She knew, of course, what the decision meant; they both knew. It meant that he was to die; but they dressed the truth in hopeful euphuisms, and at times, in the joy of preparation, she really forgot the purpose of their journey, and slipped into an eager allusion to next year's plans.

At last the day of leaving came. She had a dreadful fear that they would never get away; that somehow at the last moment he would fail her; that the doctors held one of their accustomed treacheries in reserve; but nothing happened. They drove to the station, he was installed in a seat with a rug over his knees and a cushion at his back, and she hung out of the window waving unregretful farewells to the acquaintances she had really never liked till then.

The first twenty-four hours had passed off well. He revived a little and it amused him to look out of the window and to observe the humors of the car. The second day he began to grow weary and to chafe under the dispassionate stare of the freckled child with the lump of chewing-gum. She had to explain to the child's mother that her husband was too ill to be disturbed: a statement received by that lady with a resentment visibly supported by the maternal sentiment of the whole car . . .

That night he slept badly and the next morning his temperature frightened her: she was sure he was growing worse. The day passed slowly, punctuated by the small irritations of travel. Watching his tired face, she traced in its contractions every rattle and jolt of the train, till her own body vibrated with sympathetic fatigue. She felt the others observing him too, and hovered restlessly between him and the line of interrogative eyes. The freckled child hung about him like a fly; offers of candy and picture-books failed to dislodge her: she twisted one leg around the other and watched him imperturbably. The porter, as he passed, lingered with vague proffers of help, probably inspired by philanthropic passengers swelling with the sense that 'something ought to be done;' and one nervous man in a skull-cap was audibly concerned as to the possible effect on his wife's health.

The hours dragged on in a dreary inoccupation. Towards dusk she sat down beside him and he laid his hand on hers. The touch startled her. He seemed to be calling her from far off. She looked at him helplessly and his smile went through her like a physical pang.

'Are you very tired?' she asked.

'No, not very.'

'We'll be there soon now.'

'Yes, very soon.'

'This time tomorrow –'

He nodded and they sat silent. When she had put him to bed and crawled into her own berth she tried to cheer herself with the thought that in less than twenty-four hours they would be in New York. Her people would all be at the station to meet her – she pictured their round unanxious faces pressing through the crowd. She only hoped they would not tell him too loudly that he was looking splendidly and would be all right in no time: the subtler sympathies developed by long contact with suffering were making her aware of a certain coarseness of texture in the family sensibilities.

Suddenly she thought she heard him call. She parted the curtains and listened. No, it was only a man snoring at the other end of the car. His snores had a greasy sound, as though they passed through tallow. She lay down and tried to sleep . . . Had she not heard him move? She started up trembling . . . The silence frightened her more than any sound. He might not be able to make her hear – he might be calling her now . . . What made her think of such things? It was merely the familiar tendency of an over-tired mind to fasten itself on the most intolerable chance within the range of its forebodings . . . Putting her head out, she listened; but she could not distinguish his breathing from that of the other pairs of lungs about her. She longed to get up and look at him, but she knew the impulse was a mere vent for her restlessness, and the fear of disturbing him restrained her . . . The regular movement of his curtain reassured her, she knew not why; she remembered that he had wished her a cheerful good night; and the sheer inability to endure her fears a moment longer made her put them from her with an effort of her whole sound tired body. She turned on her side and slept.

She sat up stiffly, staring out at the dawn. The train was rushing through a region of bare hillocks huddled against a lifeless sky. It looked like the first day of creation. The air of the car was close, and she pushed up her window to let in the keen wind. Then she looked at her watch: it was seven o'clock, and soon the people about her would be stirring. She slipped into her clothes, smoothed her dishevelled hair and crept to the dressing-room. When she had washed her face and adjusted her dress she felt more hopeful. It was always a struggle for her not to be cheerful in the morning. Her cheeks burned deliciously under the coarse towel and the wet hair about her temples broke into strong upward tendrils. Every inch of her was full of life and elasticity. And in ten hours they would be at home!

She stepped to her husband's berth: it was time for him to take his early glass of milk. The window-shade was down, and in the dusk of the curtained enclosure she could just see that he lay sideways, with his face away from her. She leaned over him and drew up the shade. As she did so she touched one of his hands. It felt cold . . .

She bent closer, laying her hand on his arm and calling him by name. He did not move. She spoke again more loudly; she grasped his shoulder and gently shook it. He lay motionless. She caught hold of his hand again: it slipped from her limply, like a dead thing. A dead thing? . . . Her breath caught. She must see his face. She leaned forward, and hurriedly, shrinkingly, with a sickening reluctance of the flesh, laid her hands on his shoulders and turned him over. His head fell back; his face looked small and smooth; he gazed at her with steady eyes.

She remained motionless for a long time, holding him thus; and they looked at each other. Suddenly she shrank back: the longing to scream, to call out, to fly from him, had almost overpowered her. But a strong hand arrested her. Good God! If it were known that he was dead they would be put off the train at the next station—

In a terrifying flash of remembrance there arose before her a scene she had once witnessed in travelling, when a husband and wife, whose child had died in the train, had been thrust out at some chance station. She saw them standing on the platform with the child's body between them; she had never forgotten the dazed look with which they followed the receding train. And this was what would happen to her. Within the next hour she might find herself on the platform of some strange station, alone with her husband's body . . . Anything but that! It was too horrible – she quivered like a creature at bay.

As she cowered there, she felt the train moving more slowly. It was coming then – they were approaching a station! She saw again the husband and wife standing on a lonely platform; and with a violent gesture she drew down the shade to hide her husband's face.

Feeling dizzy, she sank down on the edge of the berth, keeping away from his outstretched body, and pulling the curtains close, so that he and she were shut into a kind of sepulchral twilight. She tried to think. At all costs she must conceal the fact that he was dead. But how? Her mind refused to act: she could not plan, combine. She could think of no way but to sit there, clutching the curtains, all day long ...

She heard the porter making up her bed; people were beginning to move about the car; the dressing-room door was being opened and shut. She tried to rouse herself. At length with a supreme effort she rose to her feet, stepping into the aisle of the car and drawing the curtains tight behind her. She noticed that they still parted slightly with the motion of the car, and finding a pin in her dress she fastened them together. Now she was safe. She looked round and saw the porter. She fancied he was watching her.

'Ain't he awake yet?' he enquired.

'No,' she faltered.

'I got his milk all ready when he wants it. You know you told me to have it for him by seven.'

She nodded silently and crept into her seat.

At half-past eight the train reached Buffalo. By this time the other passengers were dressed and the berths had been folded back for the day. The porter, moving to and fro under his burden of sheets and pillows, glanced at her as he passed. At length he said: 'Ain't he going to get up? You know we're ordered to make up the berths as early as we can.'

She turned cold with fear. They were just entering the station.

'Oh, not yet,' she stammered. 'Not till he's had his milk. Won't you get it, please?'

'All right. Soon as we start again.'

When the train moved on he reappeared with the milk. She took it from him and sat vaguely looking at it: her brain moved slowly from one idea to another, as though they were stepping-stones set far apart across a whirling flood. At length she became aware that the porter still hovered expectantly.

'Will I give it to him?' he suggested.

'Oh, no,' she cried, rising. 'He – he's asleep yet, I think –'

She waited till the porter had passed on; then she unpinned the curtains and slipped behind them. In the semi-obscurity her husband's face stared up at her like a marble mask with agate eyes. The eyes were dreadful. She put out her hand and drew down the lids. Then she remembered the glass of milk in her other hand: what was she to do with it? She thought of raising the window and throwing it out; but to do so she would have to lean across his body and bring her face close to his. She decided to drink the milk.

She returned to her seat with the empty glass and after a while the porter came back to get it.

'When'll I fold up his bed?' he asked.

'Oh, not now – not yet; he's ill – he's very ill. Can't you let him stay as he is? The doctor wants him to lie down as much as possible.'

He scratched his head. 'Well, if he's *really* sick –'

He took the empty glass and walked away, explaining to the passengers that the party behind the curtains was too sick to get up just yet.

She found herself the centre of sympathetic eyes. A motherly woman with an intimate smile sat down beside her.

'I'm real sorry to hear your husband's sick. I've had a remarkable amount of sickness in my family and maybe I could assist you. Can I take a look at him?'

'Oh, no – no, please! He mustn't be disturbed.'

The lady accepted the rebuff indulgently.

'Well, it's just as you say, of course, but you don't look to me as if you'd had much experience in sickness and I'd have been glad to assist you. What do you generally do when your husband's taken this way?'

'I – I let him sleep.'

'Too much sleep ain't any too healthful either. Don't you give him any medicine?'

'Y – yes.'

'Don't you wake him to take it?'

'Yes.'

'When does he take the next dose?'

'Not for – two hours –'

The lady looked disappointed. 'Well, if I was you I'd try giving it oftener. That's what I do with my folks.'

After that many faces seemed to press upon her. The passengers were on their way to the dining-car, and she was conscious that as they passed down the aisle they glanced curiously at the closed curtains. One lantern-jawed man with prominent eyes stood still and tried to shoot his projecting glance through the division between the folds. The freckled child, returning from breakfast, waylaid the passers with a buttery clutch, saying in a loud whisper, 'He's sick;' and once the conductor came by, asking for tickets. She shrank into her corner and looked out of the window at the flying trees and houses, meaningless hieroglyphs of an endlessly unrolled papyrus.

Now and then the train stopped, and the newcomers on entering the car stared in turn at the closed curtains. More and more people seemed to pass – their faces began to blend fantastically with the images surging in her brain . . .

Later in the day a fat man detached himself from the mist of faces. He had a creased stomach and soft pale lips. As he pressed himself into the seat facing her she noticed that he was dressed in black broadcloth, with a soiled white tie.

'Husband's pretty bad this morning, is he?'

'Yes.'

'Dear, dear! Now that's terribly distressing, ain't it?' An apostolic smile revealed his gold-filled teeth. 'Of course you know there's no sech thing as sickness. Ain't that a lovely thought? Death itself is but a deloosion of our grosser senses. On'y lay yourself open to the influx of the sperrit, submit yourself passively to the action of the divine force, and disease and dissolution will cease to exist for you. If you could indooce your husband to read this little pamphlet –'

The faces about her again grew indistinct. She had a vague recollection of hearing the motherly lady and the parent of the freckled child ardently disputing the relative advantages of trying several medicines at once, or of taking each in turn; the motherly lady maintaining that the competitive system saved time; the other objecting that you couldn't tell which remedy had effected the cure; their voices went on and on, like bell-buoys droning through a fog . . . The porter came up now and then with questions that she did not understand, but that somehow she must have answered since he went away again without repeating them; every two hours the motherly lady reminded her that her husband ought to have his drops; people left the car and others replaced them . . .

Her head was spinning and she tried to steady herself by clutching at her thoughts as they swept by, but they slipped away from her like bushes on the side of a sheer precipice down which she seemed to be falling. Suddenly her mind grew clear again and she found herself vividly picturing what would happen when the train reached New York. She shuddered as it occurred to her that he would be quite cold and that someone might perceive he had been dead since morning.

She thought hurriedly: 'If they see I am not surprised they will suspect something. They will ask questions, and if I tell them the truth they won't believe me – no one would believe me! It will be terrible' – and she kept repeating to herself: 'I must pretend I don't know. I must pretend I don't know. When they open the curtains I must go up to him quite naturally – and then I must scream.' . . .

She had an idea that the scream would be very hard to do.

Gradually new thoughts crowded upon her, vivid and urgent: she tried to separate and restrain them, but they beset her clamorously, like her school-children at the end of a hot day, when she was too tired to silence them. Her head grew confused, and she felt a sick fear of forgetting her part, of betraying herself by some unguarded word or look.

'I must pretend I don't know,' she went on murmuring. The words had lost their significance, but she repeated them mechanically, as though they had been a magic formula, until suddenly she heard herself saying: 'I can't remember, I can't remember!'

Her voice sounded very loud, and she looked about her in terror; but no one seemed to notice that she had spoken.

As she glanced down the car her eye caught the curtains of her husband's berth, and she began to examine the monotonous arabesques woven through their heavy folds. The pattern was intricate and difficult to trace; she gazed fixedly at the curtains and as she did so the thick stuff grew transparent and through it she saw her husband's face – his dead face. She struggled to avert her look, but her eyes refused to move and her head seemed to be held in a vice. At last, with an effort that left her weak and shaking, she turned away; but it was of no use; close in front of her, small and smooth, was her husband's face. It seemed to be suspended in the air between her and the false braids of the woman who sat in front of her. With an uncontrollable gesture she stretched out her hand to push the face away, and suddenly she felt the touch of his smooth skin. She repressed a cry and half started from her seat. The woman with the false braids looked around, and feeling that she must justify her movement in some way she rose and lifted her travelling-bag from the opposite seat. She unlocked the bag and looked into it; but the first object her hand met was a small flask of her husband's, thrust there at the last moment, in the haste of departure. She locked the bag and closed her eyes . . . his face was there again, hanging between her eye-balls and lids like a waxen mask against a red curtain . . .

She roused herself with a shiver. Had she fainted or slept? Hours seemed to have elapsed; but it was still broad day, and the people about her were sitting in the same attitudes as before.

A sudden sense of hunger made her aware that she had eaten nothing since morning. The thought of food filled her with disgust, but she dreaded a return of faintness, and remembering that she had some biscuits in her bag she took one out and ate it. The dry crumbs choked her, and she hastily swallowed a little brandy from her husband's flask. The burning sensation in her throat acted as a counter-irritant, momentarily relieving the dull ache of her nerves. Then she felt a gently-stealing warmth, as though a soft air fanned her, and the swarming fears relaxed their clutch, receding through the stillness that enclosed her, a stillness soothing as the spacious quietude of a summer day. She slept.

Through her sleep she felt the impetuous rush of the train. It seemed to be life itself that was sweeping her on with headlong inexorable force – sweeping her into darkness and terror, and the awe of unknown days. Now all at once everything was still – not a sound, not a pulsation . . . She was dead in her turn, and lay beside him with smooth upstaring face. How quiet it was – and yet she heard feet coming, the feet of the men who were to carry them away . . . She could feel too – she felt a sudden prolonged vibration, a series of hard shocks, and then another plunge into darkness: the darkness of death this time – a black whirlwind on which they were both spinning like leaves, in wild uncoiling spirals, with millions and millions of the dead . . .

She sprang up in terror. Her sleep must have lasted a long time, for the winter day had paled and the lights had been lit. The car was in confusion, and as she regained her self-possession she saw that the passengers were gathering up their wraps and bags. The woman with the false braids had brought from the dressing-room a sickly ivy-plant in a bottle, and the Christian Scientist was reversing his cuffs. The porter passed down the aisle with his impartial brush. An impersonal figure with a gold-banded cap asked for her husband's ticket. A voice shouted 'Baig-gage *ex*press!' and she heard the clicking of metal as the passengers handed over their checks.

Presently her window was blocked by an expanse of sooty wall, and the train passed into the Harlem tunnel. The journey was over; in a few minutes she would see her family pushing their joyous way through the throng at the station. Her heart dilated. The worst terror was past . . .

'We'd better get him up now, hadn't we?' asked the porter, touching her arm.

He had her husband's hat in his hand and was meditatively revolving it under his brush.

She looked at the hat and tried to speak; but suddenly the car grew dark. She flung up her arms, struggling to catch at something, and fell face downward, striking her head against the dead man's berth.

1899

The Bride Comes to Yellow Sky

I

The great Pullman was whirling onward with such dignity of motion that a glance from the window seemed simply to prove that the plains of Texas were pouring eastward. Vast flats of green grass, dull-hued spaces of mesquite and cactus, litte groups of frame houses, woods of light and tender trees, all were sweeping into the east, sweeping over the horizon, a precipice.

A newly married pair had boarded this coach at San Antonio. The man's face was reddened from many days in the wind and sun, and a direct result of his new black clothes was that his brick-colored hands were constantly performing in a most conscious fashion. From time to time he looked down respectfully at his attire. He sat with a hand on each knee, like a man waiting in a barber's shop. The glances he devoted to other passengers were furtive and shy.

The bride was not pretty, nor was she very young. She wore a dress of blue cashmere, with small reservations of velvet here and there, and with steel buttons abounding. She continually twisted her head to regard her puff sleeves, very stiff, straight, and high. They embarrassed her. It was quite apparent that she had cooked, and that she expected to cook, dutifully. The blushes caused by the careless scrutiny of some passengers as she had entered the car were strange to see upon this plain, under-class countenance, which was drawn in placid, almost emotionless lines.

They were evidently very happy. 'Ever been in a parlor-car before?' he asked, smiling with delight.

'No,' she answered; 'I never was. It's fine, ain't it?'

'Great! And then after a while we'll go forward to the diner, and get a big lay-out. Finest meal in the world. Charge a dollar.'

'Oh, do they?' cried the bride. 'Charge a dollar? Why, that's too much – for us – ain't it, Jack?'

'Not this trip, anyhow,' he answered bravely. 'We're going to go the whole thing.'

Later he explained to her about the trains. 'You see, it's a thousand miles from one end of Texas to the other; and this train runs right across it, and never stops but four times.' He had the pride of an owner. He pointed out to her the dazzling fittings of the coach; and in truth her eyes opened wider as she contemplated the sea-green figured velvet, the shining brass, silver, and glass, the wood that gleamed as darkly brilliant as the surface of a pool of oil. At one end a bronze figure sturdily held a support for a separated chamber, and at convenient places on the ceiling were frescos in olive and silver.

To the minds of the pair, their surroundings reflected the glory of their marriage that morning in San Antonio; this was the environment of their new estate; and the man's face in particular beamed with an elation that made him appear ridiculous to the negro porter. This individual at times surveyed them from afar with an amused and superior grin. On other occasions he bullied them with skill in ways that did not make it exactly plain to them that they were being bullied. He subtly used all the manners of the most unconquerable kind of snobbery. He oppressed them; but of this oppression they had small knowledge, and they speedily forgot that infrequently a number of travellers covered them with stares of derisive enjoyment. Historically there was supposed to be something infinitely humorous in their situation.

'We are due in Yellow Sky at 3:42,' he said, looking tenderly into her eyes.

'Oh, are we?' she said, as if she had not been aware of it. To evince surprise at her husband's statement was part of her wifely amiability. She took from a pocket a little silver watch; and as she held it before her, and stared at it with a frown of attention, the new husband's face shone.

'I bought it in San Anton' from a friend of mine,' he told her gleefully.

'It's seventeen minutes past twelve,' she said, looking up at him with a kind of shy and clumsy coquetry. A passenger, noting this play, grew excessively sardonic, and winked at himself in one of the numerous mirrors.

At last they went to the dining-car. Two rows of negro waiters, in glowing white suits, surveyed their entrance with the interest, and also the equanimity, of men who had been forewarned. The pair fell to the lot of a waiter who happened to feel pleasure in steering them through their meal. He viewed them with the manner of a fatherly pilot, his countenance radiant with benevolence. The patronage, entwined with the ordinary deference, was not plain to them. And yet, as they returned to their coach, they showed in their faces a sense of escape.

To the left, miles down a long purple slope, was a little ribbon of mist where moved the keening Rio Grande. The train was approaching it at an angle, and the apex was Yellow Sky. Presently it was apparent that, as the distance from Yellow Sky grew shorter, the husband became commensurately restless. His brick-red hands were more insistent in their prominence. Occasionally he was even rather absent-minded and far-away when the bride leaned forward and addressed him.

As a matter of truth, Jack Potter was beginning to find the shadow of a deed weigh upon him like a leaden slab. He, the town marshal of Yellow Sky, a man known, liked, and feared in his corner, a prominent person, had gone to San Antonio to meet a girl he believed he loved, and there, after the usual prayers, had actually induced her to marry him, without consulting Yellow Sky for any part of the transaction. He was now bringing his bride before an innocent and unsuspecting community.

Of course people in Yellow Sky married as it pleased them, in accordance with a general custom; but such was Potter's thought of his duty to his friends, or of their idea of his duty, or of an unspoken form which does not control men in these matters, that he felt he was heinous. He had committed an extraordinary crime. Face to face with this girl in San Antonio, and spurred by his sharp impulse, he had gone headlong over all the social hedges. At San Antonio he was like a man hidden in the dark. A knife to sever any friendly duty, any form, was easy to his hand in that remote city. But the hour of Yellow Sky – the hour of daylight – was approaching.

He knew full well that his marriage was an important thing to his town. It could only be exceeded by the burning of the new hotel. His friends could not forgive him. Frequently he had reflected on the advisability of telling them by telegraph, but a new cowardice had been upon him. He feared to do it. And now the train was hurrying him toward a scene of amazement, glee, and reproach. He glanced out of the window at the line of haze swinging slowly in toward the train.

Yellow Sky had a kind of brass band, which played painfully, to the delight of the populace. He laughed without heart as he thought of it. If the citizens could dream of his prospective arrival with his bride, they would parade the band at the station and escort them, amid cheers and laughing congratulations, to his adobe home.

He resolved that he would use all the devices of speed and plains-craft in making the journey from the station to his house. Once within that safe citadel, he could issue some sort of vocal bulletin, and then not go among the citizens until they had time to wear off a little of their enthusiasm.

The bride looked anxiously at him. 'What's worrying you, Jack?'

He laughed again. 'I'm not worrying, girl; I'm only thinking of Yellow Sky.'

She flushed in comprehension.

A sense of mutual guilt invaded their minds and developed a finer tenderness. They looked at each other with eyes softly aglow. But Potter often laughed the same nervous laugh; the flush upon the bride's face seemed quite permanent.

The traitor to the feelings of Yellow Sky narrowly watched the speeding landscape. 'We're nearly there,' he said.

Presently the porter came and announced the proximity of Potter's home. He held a brush in his hand, and, with all his airy superiority gone, he brushed Potter's new clothes as the latter slowly turned this way and that way. Potter fumbled out a coin and gave it to the porter, as he had seen others do. It was a heavy and muscle-bound business, as that of a man shoeing his first horse.

The porter took their bag, and as the train began to slow they moved forward to the hooded platform of the car. Presently the two engines and their long string of coaches rushed into the station of Yellow Sky.

'They have to take water here,' said Potter, from a constricted throat and in mournful cadence, as one announcing death. Before the train stopped his eye had swept the length of the platform, and he was glad and astonished to see there was none upon it but the station-agent, who, with a slightly hurried and anxious air, was walking toward the water-tanks. When the train had halted, the porter alighted first, and placed in position a little temporary step.

'Come on, girl,' said Potter, hoarsely. As he helped her down they each laughed on a false note. He took the bag from the negro, and bade his wife cling to his arm. As they slunk rapidly away, his hang-dog glance perceived that they were unloading the two trunks, and also that the station-agent, far ahead near the baggage-car, had turned and was running toward him, making gestures. He laughed, and groaned as he laughed, when he noted the first effect of his marital bliss upon Yellow Sky. He gripped his wife's arm firmly to his side, and they fled. Behind them the porter stood, chuckling fatuously.

2

The California express on the Southern Railway was due at Yellow Sky in twenty-one minutes. There were six men at the bar of the Weary Gentleman saloon. One was a drummer who talked a great deal and rapidly; three were Texans who did not care to talk at that time; and two were Mexican sheep-herders, who did not talk as a general practice in the Weary Gentleman saloon. The barkeeper's dog lay on the board walk that crossed in front of the door. His head was on his paws, and he glanced drowsily here and there with the constant vigilance of a dog that is kicked on occasion. Across the sandy street were some vivid green grass-plots, so wonderful in appearance, amid the sands that burned near them in a blazing sun, that they caused a doubt in the mind. They exactly resembled the grass mats used to represent lawns on the stage. At the cooler end of the railway station, a man without a coat sat in a tilted chair and smoked his pipe. The fresh-cut bank of the Rio Grande circled near the town, and there could be seen beyond it a great plum-colored plain of mesquite.

Save for the busy drummer and his companions in the saloon, Yellow Sky was dozing. The new-comer leaned gracefully upon the bar, and recited many tales with the confidence of a bard who has come upon a new field.

'– and at the moment that the old man fell downstairs with the bureau in his arms, the old woman was coming up with two scuttles of coal, and of course – '

The drummer's tale was interrupted by a young man who suddenly appeared in the open door. He cried: 'Scratchy Wilson's drunk, and has turned loose with both hands.' The two Mexicans at once set down their glasses and faded out of the rear entrance of the saloon.

The drummer, innocent and jocular, answered: 'All right, old man. S'pose he has? Come in and have a drink, anyhow.'

But the information had made such an obvious cleft in every

skull in the room that the drummer was obliged to see its importance. All had become instantly solemn. 'Say,' said he, mystified, 'what is this?' His three companions made the introductory gesture of eloquent speech; but the young man at the door forestalled them.

'It means, my friend,' he answered, as he came into the saloon, 'that for the next two hours this town won't be a health resort.'

The barkeeper went to the door, and locked and barred it; reaching out of the window, he pulled in heavy wooden shutters and barred them. Immediately a solemn, chapel-like gloom was upon the place. The drummer was looking from one to another.

'But say,' he cried, 'what is this, anyhow? You don't mean there is going to be a gun-fight?'

'Don't know whether there'll be a fight or not,' answered one man, grimly; 'but there'll be some shootin' – some good shootin'.'

The young man who had warned them waved his hand. 'Oh, there'll be a fight fast enough, if any one wants it. Anybody can get a fight out there in the street. There's a fight just waiting.'

The drummer seemed to be swayed between the interest of a foreigner and a perception of personal danger.

'What did you say his name was?' he asked.

'Scratchy Wilson,' they answered in chorus.

'And will he kill anybody? What are you going to do? Does this happen often? Does he rampage around like this once a week or so? Can he break in that door?'

'No; he can't break down that door,' replied the barkeeper. 'He's tried it three times. But when he comes you'd better lay down on the floor, stranger. He's dead sure to shoot at it, and a bullet may come through.'

Thereafter the drummer kept a strict eye upon the door. The time had not yet been called for him to hug the floor, but, as a minor precaution, he sidled near to the wall. 'Will he kill anybody?' he said again.

The men laughed low and scornfully at the question.

'He's out to shoot, and he's out for trouble. Don't see any good in experimentin' with him.'

'But what do you do in a case like this? What do you do?'

A man responded: 'Why, he and Jack Potter –'

'But,' in chorus the other men interrupted, 'Jack Potter's in San Anton'.'

'Well, who is he? What's he got to do with it?'

'Oh, he's the town marshal. He goes out and fights Scratchy when he gets on one of these tears.'

'Wow!' said the drummer, mopping his brow. 'Nice job he's got.'

The voices had toned away to mere whisperings. The drummer wished to ask further questions, which were born of an increasing anxiety and bewilderment; but when he attempted them, the men merely looked at him in irritation and motioned him to remain silent. A tense waiting hush was upon them. In the deep shadows of the room their eyes shone as they listened for sounds from the street. One man made three gestures at the barkeeper; and the latter, moving like a ghost, handed him a glass and a bottle. The man poured a full glass of whiskey, and set down the bottle noiselessly. He gulped the whiskey in a swallow, and turned again toward the door in immovable silence. The drummer saw that the barkeeper, without a sound, had taken a Winchester from beneath the bar. Later he saw this individual beckoning to him, so he tiptoed across the room.

'You better come with me back of the bar.'

'No, thanks,' said the drummer, perspiring; 'I'd rather be where I can make a break for the back door.'

Whereupon the man of bottles made a kindly but peremptory gesture. The drummer obeyed it, and, finding himself seated on a box with his head below the level of the bar, balm was laid upon his soul at sight of various zinc and copper fittings that bore a resemblance to armor-plate. The barkeeper took a seat comfortably upon an adjacent box.

'You see,' he whispered, 'this here Scratchy Wilson is a wonder with a gun – a perfect wonder; and when he goes on the war-trail, we hunt our holes – naturally. He's about the last one of the old gang that used to hang out along the river here. He's a terror when he's drunk. When he's sober he's all right – kind of simple – wouldn't hurt a fly – nicest fellow in town. But when he's drunk – whoo!'

There were periods of stillness. 'I wish Jack Potter was back from San Anton',' said the barkeeper. 'He shot Wilson up once – in the leg – and he would sail in and pull out the kinks in this thing.'

Presently they heard from a distance the sound of a shot, followed by three wild yowls. It instantly removed a bond from the men in the darkened saloon. There was a shuffling of feet. They looked at each other. 'Here he comes,' they said.

3

A man in a maroon-colored flannel shirt, which had been purchased for purposes of decoration, and made principally by some Jewish women on the East Side of New York, rounded a corner and walked into the middle of the main street of Yellow Sky. In either hand the man held a long, heavy, blue-black revolver. Often he yelled, and these cries ran through a semblance of a deserted village, shrilly flying over the roofs in a volume that seemed to have no relation to the ordinary vocal strength of a man. It was as if the surrounding stillness formed the arch of a tomb over him. These cries of ferocious challenge rang against walls of silence. And his boots had red tops with gilded imprints, of the kind beloved in winter by little sledding boys on the hillsides of New England.

The man's face flamed in a rage begot of whiskey. His eyes, rolling, and yet keen for ambush, hunted the still doorways and windows. He walked with the creeping movement of the midnight cat. As it occurred to him, he roared menacing information. The long revolvers in his hands were as easy as straws; they were moved with an electric swiftness. The little fingers of each hand played sometimes in a musician's way. Plain from the low collar of the shirt, the cords of his neck straightened and sank, straightened and sank, as passion moved him. The only sounds were his terrible invitations. The calm adobes preserved their demeanor at the passing of this small thing in the middle of the street.

There was no offer of fight – no offer of fight. The man called to the sky. There were no attractions. He bellowed and fumed and swayed his revolvers here and everywhere.

The dog of the barkeeper of the Weary Gentleman saloon had not appreciated the advance of events. He yet lay dozing in front of his master's door. At sight of the dog, the man paused and raised his revolver humorously. At sight of the man, the dog sprang up and walked diagonally away, with a sullen head, and growling. The man yelled, and the dog broke into a gallop. As it was about to enter an alley, there was a loud noise, a whistling, and something spat the ground directly before it. The dog screamed, and, wheeling in terror, galloped headlong in a new direction. Again there was a noise, a whistling, and sand was kicked viciously before it. Fear-stricken, the dog turned and flurried like an animal in a pen. The man stood laughing, his weapons at his hips.

Ultimately the man was attracted by the closed door of the Weary Gentleman saloon. He went to it and, hammering with a revolver, demanded drink.

The door remaining imperturbable, he picked a bit of paper from the walk, and nailed it to the framework with a knife. He then turned his back contemptuously upon this popular resort and, walking to the opposite side of the street and spinning there on his heel quickly and lithely, fired at the bit of paper. He missed it by a half-inch. He swore at himself, and went away. Later he comfortably fusilladed the windows of his most intimate friend. The man was playing with this town; it was a toy for him.

But still there was no offer of fight. The name of Jack Potter, his ancient antagonist, entered his mind, and he concluded that it would be a glad thing if he should go to Potter's house, and by bombardment induce him to come out and fight. He moved in the direction of his desire, chanting Apache scalp-music.

When he arrived at it, Potter's house presented the same still front as had the other adobes. Taking up a strategic position, the man howled a challenge. But this house regarded him as might a great stone god. It gave no sign. After a decent wait, the man howled further challenges, mingling with them wonderful epithets.

Presently there came the spectacle of a man churning himself into deepest rage over the immobility of a house. He fumed at it as the winter wind attacks a prairie cabin in the North. To the distance there should have gone the sound of a tumult like the fighting of two hundred Mexicans. As necessity bade him, he paused for breath or to reload his revolvers.

4

Potter and his bride walked sheepishly and with speed. Sometimes they laughed together shamefacedly and low.

'Next corner, dear,' he said finally.

They put forth the efforts of a pair walking bowed against a strong wind. Potter was about to raise a finger to point the first appearance of the new home when, as they circled the corner, they came face to face with a man in a maroon-colored shirt, who was feverishly pushing cartridges into a large revolver. Upon the instant the man dropped his revolver to the ground and, like lightning, whipped another from its holster. The second weapon was aimed at the bridegroom's chest.

There was a silence. Potter's mouth seemed to be merely a grave for his tongue. He exhibited an instinct to at once loosen his arm from the woman's grip, and he dropped the bag to the sand. As for the bride, her face had gone as yellow as old cloth. She was a slave to hideous rites, gazing at the apparitional snake.

The two men faced each other at a distance of three paces. He of the revolver smiled with a new and quiet ferocity.

'Tried to sneak up on me,' he said. 'Tried to sneak up on me!' His eyes grew more baleful. As Potter made a slight movement, the man thrust his revolver venomously forward. 'No; don't you do it, Jack Potter. Don't you move a finger toward a gun just yet. Don't you move an eyelash. The time has come for me to settle with you, and I'm goin' to do it my own way, and loaf along with no interferin'. So if you don't want a gun bent on you, just mind what I tell you.'

Potter looked at his enemy. 'I ain't got a gun on me, Scratchy,' he said. 'Honest, I ain't.' He was stiffening and steadying, but yet somewhere at the back of his mind a vision of the Pullman floated: the sea-green figured velvet, the shining brass, silver, and glass, the wood that gleamed as darkly brilliant as the surface of a pool of oil – all the glory of the marriage, the environment of the new estate. 'You know I fight when it comes to fighting, Scratchy Wilson; but I ain't got a gun on me. You'll have to do all the shootin' yourself.'

His enemy's face went livid. He stepped forward, and lashed his weapon to and fro before Potter's chest. 'Don't you tell me you ain't got no gun on you, you whelp. Don't tell me no lie like that. There ain't a man in Texas ever seen you without no gun. Don't take me for no kid.' His eyes blazed with light, and his throat worked like a pump.

'I ain't takin' you for no kid,' answered Potter. His heels had not moved an inch backward. 'I'm takin' you for a damn fool. I tell you I ain't got a gun, and I ain't. If you're goin' to shoot me up, you better begin now; you'll never get a chance like this again.'

So much enforced reasoning had told on Wilson's rage; he was calmer. 'If you ain't got a gun, why ain't you got a gun?' he sneered. 'Been to Sunday-school?'

'I ain't got a gun because I've just come from San Anton' with my wife. I'm married,' said Potter. 'And if I'd thought there was going to be any galoots like you prowling around when I brought my wife home, I'd had a gun, and don't you forget it.'

'Married!' said Scratchy, not at all comprehending.

'Yes, married. I'm married,' said Potter, distinctly.

'Married? said Scratchy. Seemingly for the first time, he saw the drooping, drowning woman at the other man's side. 'No!' he said. He was like a creature allowed a glimpse of another world. He moved a pace backward, and his arm, with the revolver, dropped to his side. 'Is this the lady?' he asked.

'Yes; this is the lady,' answered Potter.

There was another period of silence.

'Well,' said Wilson at last, slowly, 'I s'pose it's all off now.'

'It's all off if you say so, Scratchy. You know I didn't make the trouble.' Potter lifted his valise.

'Well, I 'low it's off, Jack,' said Wilson. He was looking at the ground. 'Married!' He was not a student of chivalry; it was merely that in the presence of this foreign condition he was a simple child of the earlier plains. He picked up his starboard revolver, and, placing both weapons in their holsters, he went away. His feet made funnel-shaped tracks in the heavy sand.

1898

PAUL LAURENCE DUNBAR
1872–1906

The Strength of Gideon

Old mam' Henry, and her word may be taken, said that it was 'De powerfulles' sehmont she ever had hyeahd in all huh bo'n days.' That was saying a good deal, for the old woman had lived many years on the Stone place and had heard many sermons from preachers, white and black. She was a judge, too.

It really must have been a powerful sermon that Brother Lucius preached, for Aunt Doshy Scott had fallen in a trance in the middle of the aisle, while 'Merlatter Mag,' who was famed all over the place for having white folk's religion and never 'waking up,' had broken through her reserve and shouted all over the camp ground.

Several times Cassie had shown signs of giving way, but because she was frail some of the solicitous sisters held her with self-congratulatory care, relieving each other now and then, that each might have a turn in the rejoicings. But as the preacher waded out deeper and deeper into the spiritual stream, Cassie's efforts to make her feelings known became more and more decided. He told them how the spears of the Midianites had 'clashed upon de shiels of de Gideonites, an' aftah while, wid de powah of de Lawd behin' him, de man Gideon triumphed mightily,' and swaying then and wailing in the dark woods, with grim branches waving in the breath of their own excitement, they could hear above the tumult the clamor of the fight, the clashing of the spears, and the ringing of the shields. They could see the conqueror coming home in triumph. Then when he cried, 'A-who, I say, a-who is in Gideon's ahmy today?' and the wailing chorus took up the note, 'A-who!' it was too much even for frail Cassie, and, deserted by the solicitous sisters, in the words of Mam' Henry, 'she broke a-loose, and faihly tuk de place.'

Gideon had certainly triumphed, and when a little boy came to Cassie two or three days later, she named him Gideon in honor of the great Hebrew warrior whose story had so wrought upon her. All the plantation knew the spiritual significance of the name, and from the day of his birth the child was as one set apart to a holy mission on earth.

Say what you will of the influences which the circumstances surrounding birth have upon a child, upon this one at least the effect was unmistakable. Even as a baby he seemed to realize the weight of responsibility which had been laid upon his little black shoulders, and there was a complacent dignity in the very way in which he drew upon the sweets of his dirty sugar-teat when the maternal breast was far off bending over the sheaves of the field.

He was a child early destined to sacrifice and self-effacement, and as he grew older and other youngsters came to fill Cassie's cabin, he took up his lot with the meekness of an infantile Moses. Like a Moses he was, too, leading his little flock to the promised land, when he grew to the age at which, barefooted and one-shifted, he led or carried his little brothers and sisters about the quarters. But the 'promised land' never took him into the direction of the stables, where the other pickaninnies worried the horses, or into the region of the hen-coops, where egg-sucking was a common crime.

No boy ever rolled or tumbled in the dirt with a heartier glee than did Gideon, but no warrior, not even his illustrious prototype himself, ever kept sterner discipline in his ranks when his followers seemed prone to overstep the bounds of right. At a very early age his shrill voice could be heard calling in admonitory tones, caught from his mother's very lips, 'You 'Nelius, don' you let me ketch you th'owin' at ol' mis' guinea-hens no mo'; you hyeah me?' or 'Hi'am, you come offen de top er dat shed 'fo' you fall an' brek yo' naik all to pieces.'

It was a common sight in the evening to see him sitting upon the low rail fence which ran before the quarters, his shift blowing in the wind, and his black legs lean and bony against the white-washed rails, as he swayed to and fro, rocking and singing one of his numerous brothers to sleep, and always his song was of war and victory, albeit crooned in a low, soothing voice. Sometimes it was 'Turn Back Pharaoh's Army,' at others 'Jinin' Gideon's Band.' The latter was a favorite, for he seemed to have a proprietary interest in it, although, despite the martial inspiration of his name, 'Gideon's band' to him meant an aggregation of people with horns and fiddles.

Steve, who was Cassie's man, declared that he had never seen such a child, and, being quite as religious as Cassie herself, early began to talk Scripture and religion to the boy. He was aided in this when his master, Dudley Stone, a man of the faith, began a little Sunday class for the religiously inclined of the quarters, where the old familiar stories were told in simple language to the slaves and explained. At these meetings Gideon became a shining light. No one listened more eagerly to the teacher's words, or more readily answered his questions at review. No one was wider-mouthed or whiter-eyed. His admonitions to his family now took on a different complexion, and he could be heard calling across a lot to a mischievous sister, 'Bettah tek keer daih, Lucy Jane, Gawd's a-watchin' you; bettah tek keer.'

The appointed man is always marked, and so Gideon was by always receiving his full name. No one ever shortened his scriptural appellation into Gid. He was always Gideon from the time he bore the name out of the heat of camp-meeting fervor until his master discovered his worthiness and filled Cassie's breast with pride by taking him into the house to learn 'mannahs and 'po'tment.'

As a house servant he was beyond reproach, and next to his religion his Mas' Dudley and Miss Ellen claimed his devotion and fidelity. The young mistress and young master learned to depend fearlessly upon his faithfulness.

It was good to hear old Dudley Stone going through the house in a mock fury, crying, 'Well, I never saw such a house; it seems as if there isn't a soul in it that can do without Gideon. Here I've got him up here to wait on me, and it's Gideon here and Gideon there, and every time I turn around some of you have sneaked him off. Gideon, come here!' And the black boy smiled and came.

But all his days were not days devoted to men's service, for there came a time when love claimed him for her own, when the clouds took on a new color, when the sough of the wind was music in his ears, and he saw heaven in Martha's eyes. It all came about in this way.

Gideon was young when he got religion and joined the church, and he grew up strong in the faith. Almost by the time he had become a valuable house servant he had grown to be an invaluable servant of the Lord. He had a good, clear voice that could lead a hymn out of all the labyrinthian wanderings of an ignorant congregation, even when he had to improvise both words and music; and he was a mighty man of prayer. It was thus he met Martha. Martha was brown and buxom and comely, and her rich contralto voice was loud and high on the sisters' side in meeting time. It was the voices that did it at first. There was no hymn or 'spiritual' that Gideon could start to which Martha could not sing an easy blending second, and never did she open a tune that Gideon did not swing into it with a wonderfully sweet, flowing, natural bass. Often he did not know the piece, but that did not matter, he sang anyway. Perhaps when they were out he would go to her and ask, 'Sis' Martha, what was that hymn you stahrted today?' and she would probably answer, 'Oh, dat was jes' one o' my mammy's ol' songs.'

'Well, it sholy was mighty pretty. Indeed it was.'

'Oh, thanky, Brothah Gidjon, thanky.'

Then a little later they began to walk back to the master's house together, for Martha, too, was one of the favored ones, and served, not in the field, but in the big house.

The old women looked on and conversed in whispers about the pair, for they were wise, and what their old eyes saw, they saw.

'Oomph,' said Mam' Henry, for she commented on everything, 'dem too is jes' natchelly singin' demse'ves togeddah.'

'Dey's lak de mo'nin' stahs,' interjected Aunt Sophy.

'How 'bout dat?' sniffed the older woman, for she objected to any one's alluding to subjects she did not understand.

'Why, Mam' Henry, ain' you nevah hyeahd tell o' de mo'nin' stahs whut sung deyse'ves togeddah?'

'No, I ain't, an' I been livin' a mighty sight longah'n you, too. I knows all 'bout when de stahs fell, but dey ain' nevah done no singin' dat I knows 'bout.'

'Do heish, Mam' Henry, you sho' su'prises me. W'y, dat ain' happenin's, dat's Scripter.'

'Look hyeah, gal, don't you tell me dat's Scripter, an' me been a-setting' undah de Scripter fo' nigh onto sixty yeah.'

'Well, Mam' Henry, I may 'a' been mistook, but sho' I took hit fu' Scripter. Mebbe de preachah I hyeahd was jes' inlinin'.'

'Well, wheddah hit's Scripter er not, dey's one t'ing su'tain, I tell you – dem two is singin' deyse'ves togeddah.'

'Hit's a fac', an' I believe it.'

'An' it's a mighty good thing, too. Brothah Gidjon is de nicest house dahky dat I ever hyeahd tell on. Dey jes' de same diffunce 'twixt him an' de othah house-boys as dey is 'tween real quality an' strainers – he got mannahs, but he ain't got aihs.'

'Heish, ain't you right!'

'An' while de res' of dem ain' thinkin' 'bout nothin' but dancin' an' ca'in' on, he makin' his peace, callin', an' 'lection sho'.'

'I tell you, Mam' Henry, dey ain' nothin' like a spichul named chile.'

'Humph! g'long, gal; 'tain't in de name; de biggest devil I evah knowed was named Moses Aaron. 'Tain't in de name, hit's all in de man hisse'f.'

But notwithstanding what the gossips said of him, Gideon went on his way, and knew not that the one great power of earth had taken hold of him until they gave the great party down in the quarters, and he saw Martha in all her glory. Then love spoke to him with no uncertain sound.

It was a dancing-party, and because neither he nor Martha dared countenance dancing, they had strolled away together under the pines that lined the white road, whiter now in the soft moonlight, He had never known the pine-cones smell so sweet before in all his life. She had never known just how the moonlight flecked the road before. This was lovers' lane to them. He didn't understand why his heart kept throbbing so furiously, for they were walking slowly, and when a shadow thrown across the road from a by-standing bush frightened her into pressing close up to him, he could not have told why his arm stole round her waist and drew her slim form up to him, or why his lips found hers, as eye looked into eye. For their simple hearts love's mystery was too deep, as it is for wiser ones.

Some few stammering words came to his lips, and she answered the best she could. Then why did the moonlight flood them so, and why were the heavens so full of stars? Out yonder in the black hedge a mocking-bird was singing, and he was translating – oh, so poorly – the song of their hearts. They forgot the dance, they forgot all but their love.

'An' you won't ma'y nobody else but me, Martha?'

'You know I won't, Gidjon.'

'But I mus' wait de yeah out?'

'Yes, an' den don't you think Mas' Stone 'll let us have a little cabin of ouah own jest outside de quahtahs?'

'Won't it be blessid? Won't it be blessid?' he cried, and then the kindly moon went under a cloud for a moment and came out smiling, for he had peeped through and had seen what passed. Then they walked back hand in hand to the dance along the transfigured road, and they found that the first part of the festivities were over, and all the people had sat down to supper. Everyone laughed when they went in. Martha held back and perspired with embarrassment. But even though he saw some of the older heads whispering in a corner, Gideon was not ashamed. A new light was in his eyes, and a new boldness had come to him. He led Martha up to the grinning group, and said in his best singing voice, 'Whut you laughin' at? Yes, I's popped de question, an' she says "Yes," an' long 'bout a yeah f'om now you kin all 'spec' a' invitation.' This was a formal announcement. A shout arose from the happy-go-lucky people, who sorrowed alike in each other's sorrows, and joyed in each other's joys. They sat down at a table, and their health was drunk in cups of cider and persimmon beer.

Over in the corner Mam' Henry mumbled over her pipe, 'Wha'd I tell you? wha'd I tell you?' And Aunt Sophy replied, 'Hit's de pa'able of de mo'nin' stahs.'

'Don't talk to me 'bout no mo'nin' stahs,' the mammy snorted; 'Gawd jes' fitted dey voices togeddah, an' den j'ined dey hea'ts. De mo'nin' stahs ain't got nothin' to do wid it.'

'Mam' Henry,' said Aunt Sophy, impressively, 'you's a' oldah ooman den I is, an' I ain' sputin' hit; but I say dey done 'filled Scripter 'bout de mo'nin' stahs; dey's done sung deyse'ves togeddah.'

The old woman sniffed.

The next Sunday at meeting someone got the start of Gideon, and began a new hymn. It ran:

> 'At de ma'ige of de Lamh, oh Lawd,
>   God done gin His 'sent.
> Dey dressed de Lamb all up in white,
>   God done gin His 'sent.
> Oh, wasn't dat a happy day,
> Oh, wasn't dat a happy day, Good Lawd,
> Oh, wasn't dat a happy day,
>   De ma'ige of de Lamb!'

The wailing minor of the beginning broke into a joyous chorus at the end, and Gideon wept and laughed in turn, for it was his wedding-song.

The young man had a confidential chat with his master the next morning, and the happy secret was revealed.

'What, you scamp!' said Dudley Stone. 'Why, you've got even

more sense than I gave you credit for; you've picked out the finest girl on the plantation, and the one best suited to you. You couldn't have done better if the match had been made for you. I reckon this must be one of the marriages that are made in heaven. Marry her, yes, and with a preacher. I don't see why you want to wait a year.'

Gideon told him his hopes of a near cabin.

'Better still,' his master went on; 'with you two joined and up near the big house, I'll feel as safe for the folks as if an army was camped around, and, Gideon, my boy,' – he put his arms on the black man's shoulders – 'if I should slip away some day – '

The slave looked up, startled.

'I mean if I should die – I'm not going to run off, don't be alarmed – I want you to help your young Mas' Dud look after his mother and Miss Ellen; you hear? Now that's the one promise I ask of you – come what may, look after the women folks.' And the man promised and went away smiling.

His year of engagement, the happiest time of a young man's life, began on golden wings. There came rumors of war, and the wings of the glad-hued year drooped sadly. Sadly they drooped, and seemed to fold, when one day, between the rumors and predictions of strife, Dudley Stone, the old master, slipped quietly away out into the unknown.

There were wife, daughter, son, and faithful slaves about his bed, and they wept for him sincere tears, for he had been a good husband and father and a kind master. But he smiled, and, conscious to the last, whispered to them a cheery goodbye. Then, turning to Gideon, who stood there bowed with grief, he raised one weak finger, and his lips made the word, 'Remember!'

They laid him where they had laid one generation after another of the Stones and it seemed as if a pall of sorrow had fallen upon the whole place. Then, still grieving, they turned their long-distracted attention to the things that had been going on around, and lo! the ominous mutterings were loud, and the cloud of war was black above them.

It was on an April morning when the storm broke, and the plantation, master and man, stood dumb with consternation, for they had hoped, they had believed, it would pass. And now there was the buzz of men who talked in secret corners. There were hurried saddlings and feverish rides to town. Somewhere in the quarters was whispered the forbidden word 'freedom,' and it was taken up and dropped breathlessly from the ends of a hundred tongues. Some of the older ones scouted it, but from some who held young children to their breasts there were deep-souled prayers in the dead of night. Over the meetings in the woods or in the log church a strange reserve brooded, and even the prayers took on a guarded tone. Even from the fulness of their hearts, which longed for liberty, no open word that could offend the mistress or the young master went up to the Almighty. He might know their hearts, but no tongue in meeting gave vent to what was in them, and even Gideon sang no more of the gospel army. He was sad because of this new trouble coming hard upon the heels of the old, and Martha was grieved because he was.

Finally the trips into town budded into something, and on a memorable evening when the sun looked peacefully through the pines, young Dudley Stone rode into the yard dressed in a suit of gray, and on his shoulders were the straps of office. The servants gathered around him with a sort of awe and followed him until he alighted at the porch. Only Mam' Henry, who had been nurse to both him and his sister, dared follow him in. It was a sad scene within, but such a one as any Southern home where there were sons might have shown that awful year. The mother tried to be brave, but her old hands shook, and her tears fell upon her son's brown head, tears of grief at parting, but through which shone the fire of a noble pride. The young Ellen hung about his neck with sobs and caresses.

'Would you have me stay?' he asked her.

'No! No! I know where your place is, but oh, my brother!'

'Ellen,' said the mother in a trembling voice, 'you are the sister of a soldier now.'

The girl dried her tears and drew herself up. 'We won't burden your heart, Dudley, with our tears, but we will weight you down with our love and prayers.'

It was not so easy with Mam' Henry. Without protest, she took him to her bosom and rocked to and fro, wailing 'My baby! my baby!' and the tears that fell from the young man's eyes upon her gray old head cost his manhood nothing.

Gideon was behind the door when his master called him. His sleeve was traveling down from his eyes as he emerged.

'Gideon,' said his master, pointing to his uniform, 'you know what this means?'

'Yes, suh.'

'I wish I could take you along with me. But – '

'Mas' Dud,' Gideon threw out his arms in supplication.

'You remember father's charge to you, take care of the women-folks.' He took the servant's hand, and, black man and white, they looked into each other's eyes, and the compact was made. Then Gideon gulped and said 'Yes, suh' again.

Another boy held the master's horse and rode away behind him when he vaulted into the saddle, and the man of battle-song and warrior name went back to mind the women-folks.

Then began the disintegration of the plantation's population. First Yellow Bob slipped away, and no one pursued him. A few blamed him, but they soon followed as the year rolled away. More were missing every time a Union camp lay near, and great tales were told of the chances for young negroes who would go as body-servants to the Yankee officers. Gideon heard all and was silent.

Then as the time of his marriage drew near he felt a greater strength, for there was one who would be with him to help him keep his promise and his faith.

The spirit of freedom had grown strong in Martha as the days passed, and when her lover went to see her she had strange things to say. Was he going to stay? Was he going to be a slave when freedom and a livelihood lay right within his grasp? Would he keep her a slave? Yes, he would do it all – all.

She asked him to wait.

Another year began, and one day they brought Dudley Stone home to lay beside his father. Then most of the remaining negroes went. There was no master now. The two bereaved women wept, and Gideon forgot that he wore the garb of manhood and wept with them.

Martha came to him.

'Gidjon,' she said, 'I's waited a long while now. Mos' eve'ybody else is gone. Ain't you goin'?'

'No.'

'But, Gidjon, I wants to be free. I know how good dey've been to us; but, oh, I wants to own myse'f. They're talkin' 'bout settin' us free every hour.'

'I can wait.'

'They's a camp right near here.'

'I promised.'

'The of'cers wants body-servants, Gidjon – '

'Go, Martha, if you want to, but I stay.'

She went away from him, but she or someone else got word to young Captain Jack Griswold of the near camp that there was an excellent servant on the plantation who only needed a little persuading, and he came up to see him.

'Look here,' he said, 'I want a body-servant. I'll give you ten dollars a month.'

'I've got to stay here.'

'But, you fool, what have you to gain by staying here?'

'I'm goin' to stay.'

'Why, you'll be free in a little while, anyway.'

'All right.'

'Of all fools,' said the Captain. 'I'll give you fifteen dollars.'

'I do' want it.'

'Well, your girl's going, anyway. I don't blame her for leaving such a fool as you are.'

Gideon turned and looked at him.

'The camp is going to be moved up on this plantation, and there will be a requisition for this house for officers' quarters, so I'll see you again,' and Captain Griswold went his way.

Martha going! Martha going! Gideon could not believe it. He would not. He saw her, and she confirmed it. She was going as an aid to the nurses. He gasped, and went back to mind the women-folks.

They did move the camp up nearer, and Captain Griswold came to see Gideon again, but he could get no word from him, save 'I'm goin' to stay,' and he went away in disgust, entirely unable to understand such obstinacy, as he called it.

But the slave had his moments alone, when the agony tore at his breast and rended him. Should he stay? The others were going. He would soon be free. Everyone had said so, even his mistress one day. Then Martha was going. 'Martha! Martha!' his heart called.

The day came when the soldiers were to leave, and he went out sadly to watch them go. All the plantation, that had been white with tents, was dark again, and everywhere were moving, blue-coated figures.

Once more his tempter came to him. 'I'll make it twenty dollars,' he said, but Gideon shook his head. Then they started. The drums tapped. Away they went, the flag kissing the breeze. Martha stole up to say goodbye to him. Her eyes were overflowing, and she clung to him.

'Come, Gidjon,' she pled, 'fu' my sake. Oh, my God, won't

you come with us – it's freedom.' He kissed her, but shook his head.

'Hunt me up when you do come,' she said, crying bitterly, 'fu' I do love you, Gidjon, but I must go. Out yonder is freedom,' and she was gone with them.

He drew out a pace after the troops, and then, turning, looked back at the house. He went a step farther, and then a woman's gentle voice called him, 'Gideon!' He stopped. He crushed his cap in his hands, and the tears came into his eyes. Then he answered, 'Yes, Mis' Ellen, I's a-comin'.'

He stood and watched the dusty column until the last blue leg swung out of sight and over the gray hills the last drum-tap died away, and then turned and retraced his steps toward the house.

Gideon had triumphed mightily.

1900

BIOGRAPHICAL NOTES

AMBROSE BIERCE (1842–1913?) was a journalist, a poet and a short story writer. He served in the American Civil War and drew on his detailed knowledge of that war in a number of his stories. Born in Ohio, he travelled to San Francisco and established his reputation as a book reviewer and editor. His first story, 'The Haunted Valley', appeared in *The Overland Monthly* in 1871. The following year he left for what turned out to be a three-year stay in England, and while there he published several books of sketches and epigrams, including *The Fiend's Delight* (1872) and *Cobwebs from an Empty Skull* (1874).

He returned to San Francisco where he remained working as a columnist until 1896, when he moved to Washington. He published his *Collected Works* in twelve volumes, between 1909 and 1912. In 1913 he disappeared, it is believed, somewhere in Mexico. His best known works are *Tales of Soldiers and Civilians* (1891), retitled *In The Midst of Life* in 1898, and *The Devil's Dictionary* (1911).

GEORGE WASHINGTON CABLE (1844–1925) left school at the age of fourteen and joined the Confederate Army four years later. His first success as a writer came in 1879 with *Old Creole Days*, a short story collection that includes 'Café des Exilés.' This was followed in 1881 by an extended short story, *Madame Delphine*.

Despite his southern background and his war service for the confederacy Cable was liberal in his attitude to former slaves and to working people. A collection of his articles, *The Silent South* (1885), like many of his articles, found little favour in the South. Partly as a result he moved north and settled in Massachusetts where he produced *The Negro Question* (1888) and *The Southern Struggle for Pure Government* (1890).

Thereafter he largely returned to fiction, producing a series of books from *Bonaventure* (1888) and *Strange Stories of Louisiana* (1889) to *Gideon's Band* (1914) and *Lovers of Louisiana* (1918).

CHARLES CHESNUTT (1858–1932) was the first successful black novelist in America. Born in Ohio, he was by turns a teacher, a journalist and a court stenographer. His first book, *The Conjure Woman*, was published in 1899. He followed this with *The Wife of His Youth and Other Stories of the Color Line* (1899), *The House Behind the Cedars* (1900) and *The Colonel's dream* (1905).

LYDIA MARIA CHILD (1802–1880) was an innovator who, in 1826, created the first monthly especially for children, the *Junior Miscellany*. She wrote the first anti-slavery book to advocate immediate emancipation of slaves and the legalisation of miscegenation, *Appeal in Favor of That Class of Americans called Africans* (1833), and she campaigned for women's rights. publishing in 1835 *A History of the Condition of Women in Various Ages and Nations*. Her espousal of the black cause led to a boycott of the *Junior Miscellany* which foundered as a result. She became editor of the *National Anti-Slavery Standard* and published a reader for ex-slaves called *The Freedman's Book* (1865). In her novel *Hobomok* (1924) she told the story of an Indian's marriage to a white woman. Few writers showed her awareness of the needs and, indeed, the lives and experiences of those marginalised by American society and excluded from its myths no less than its supposed benefits. In 1828 she published *The First Settlers of New England* and began a campaign against the dispossession of Indians which culminated in 1868 with her *Appeal for the Indians*. Her final novel, *A Romance of the Republic*, appropriately enough, featured a series of inter-racial marriages.

KATE CHOPIN (1851–1904) was born in St Louis, Missouri and moved to Louisiana when she married. Her interest in the area led to a short story collection called *Bayou Folk* (1894). She followed this with a second collection, *A Night in Acadie* (1897). Her last novel, *The Awakening* (1899) dealt with miscegenation and extra-marital love, a combination that provoked a scandalised response.

STEPHEN CRANE (1871–1900) was the son of writers and brother to two reporters. He began writing early, producing *Maggie: A Girl of the Streets* while still at university and publishing it, privately, when he was twenty-two. That same year he began working on *The Red Badge of Courage*, which appeared in *The Philadelphia Press* in 1894 and in book form in 1895. A collection of stories called *The Little Regiment and Other Episodes of the American Civil War* appeared in 1896.

Crane wrote 'The Bride Comes to Yellow Sky' while in England, in 1897. He travelled widely as a reporter, writing dispatches from Greece and Cuba. In increasing financial difficulties he wrote a series of stories and poems to raise cash. His novel *Active Service* appeared in 1899, along with his second collection of poetry, *War Is Kind*. Crane died of tuberculosis in Germany on June 5, 1900.

REBECCA HARDING DAVIS (1831–1910) was born in Pennsylvania and was an early realist still best known for the story that she published in the *Atlantic Monthly* in 1861, 'Life in the Iron Mills'. Subsequent novels included *Margaret Howth* (1862), *Waiting for the Verdict* (1868) and *John Andross* (1874). Her work deteriorated as she began to contribute uninspired stories to *Peterson's Magazine*, with which her husband had a working relationship. It was a move she later regretted. Her reputation was in some ways eclipsed by that of her son, Richard Harding Davis.

PAUL LAURENCE DUNBAR (1872–1906), like his fellow black novelist Charles Chesnutt, was born in Ohio. A poet and novelist, he was influenced by the southern writer Thomas Nelson Page, particularly in his use of dialect, and by Robert Burns, though at times he chafed against the pressure to produce dialect poetry.

The son of a slave, Dunbar was fully aware of the nature of slavery, though he had no direct experience in the South. He published a series of verse collections: *Lyrics of Lowly Life* (1896), *Lyrics of the Hearthside* (1899), *Lyrics of Love and Laughter* (1903) and *Lyrics of Sunshine and Shadow* (1905). His novels included *The Uncalled* (1898) and *The Sport of the Gods* (1902).

HAROLD FREDERIC (1856–1898). A sophisticated journalist who was, for a time, the London correspondent of *The New York Times*, Frederic brought to his fiction writing a sense of social realism that challenged many contemporary conventions. Among his novels are *Seth's Brother's Wife* (1887), *The Copperhead* (1893), and, most famously, *The Damnation of Theron Ware* (1896), a story about the collapse of religious orthodoxy. In 1894 he published an edition of his stories: *Marsena, And Other Stories*.

MARY ELEANOR WILKINS FREEMAN (1852–1930) was born and raised in New England (Massachusetts and Vermont), and her first book was a collection of poems, *Decorative Plaques* (1883). Spurred on by financial need she began to write short stories. Her first collection, *A Humble Romance and Other Stories* (1887), was followed by a second, *A New England Nun and Other Stories* (1891). A third collection, this time of ghost stories, appeared in 1903, *The Wind in the Rosebush*. Her novels included *Jane Field* (1893), *Pembroke* (1894) and *The Heart's Highway* (1900).

Her early books appeared under the name of Mary Wilkins. Following her marriage, in 1902, she continued to publish, though little reached the standard of her early work.

HAMLIN GARLAND (1860–1940). Born in Wisconsin, Garland knew the life of the settler; following his family from Wisconsin to Iowa and then homesteading in South Dakota. He subsequently moved east where he largely educated himself and got to know some of the leading writers of his day, including William Dean Howells whose realistic fiction influenced his own writing.

In 1891 he published *Main-Travelled Roads*, following this with *Prairie Folk* (1892) and *Wayside Courtships* (1897). In these works he offered a portrait of rural life at odds with myths of rural innocence or heroic endeavour.

He subsequently transferred his attention to the question of political corruption – *A Member of the Third House*, *Jason Edwards* and *A Spoil of Office*, all of which appeared in 1892 – before returning to a rural setting for *Rose of Dutcher's Cooly* (1895). Later he became in effect a writer of westerns, producing novels about cattlemen and Indians before, late in his career, producing a series of books about pioneer life: *A Son of the Middle Border* (1917), *Trail-Makers of the Middle Border* (1926) and *Back-Trailers from the Middle Border* (1928).

CHARLOTTE PERKINS GILMAN (1860–1935). A great niece of Harriet Beecher Stowe, Charlotte Perkins Gilman was born in Connecticut and raised in Rhode Island. In 1890 she moved to California, following the collapse of her marriage, and gave lectures on political and economic freedom for women. Her concerns for women are reflected in *Women and Economics* which she published in 1898. She was the author of novels, stories and poems. 'The Yellow Wallpaper', based on her own experiences, appeared in *The New England Magazine*, in May, 1892, having been rejected by *The Atlantic Monthly*, despite the support of William Dean Howells. Twenty-eight years later he reprinted it in *Great Modern American Stories*.

BRET HARTE (1836–1902) was a journalist, poet, novelist, dramatist and editor. Born in Albany, New York, he moved to California in his late teens and drew on his experiences of that state in many of his stories. In 1867 he published *The Lost Galleon and Other Tales* and followed it with *The Luck of Roaring Camp and Other Stories* (1870). In 1877 he collaborated with Mark Twain on a play, *Ah Sin*, though his relationship with Twain proved a strained one. He was one of the few writers to show any interest in California's Chinese population. Though his reputation declined, he remained prolific and he did have lasting influence on the development of the western story and thereby, perhaps, on the western film.

NATHANIEL HAWTHORNE (1804–1864) destroyed as many copies of his first novel, *Fanshawe* (1828), as he could find, as he did the manuscript of a book of short stories. In 1837, however, came *Twice-Told Tales* and its success restored his confidence. In 1846 he published *Mosses from an Old Manse*, from which 'The Birthmark' is drawn. In 1850 he followed the collection with a novel that established him as America's leading writer: *The Scarlet Letter*, the story of Hester Prynne and her adulterous relationship with the reverend Arthur Dimmesdale. Later works included *The House of the Seven Gables* (1851), *The Blithedale Romance* (1852), *The Marble Faun* (1860) and *Our Old Home* (1863)

O. HENRY (WILLIAM SYDNEY PORTER: 1862–1910). Born in North Carolina, Porter moved to Texas where he worked in a number of jobs, including that of bank clerk. He began writing pieces for newspapers and founded his own magazine. He was then charged with embezzlement and fled south of the border, only returning when his wife was dying. He was tried, sentenced and spent three years in a state penitentiary. While there he began submitting stories to some of the leading magazines, and on his release he went to New York where he was hailed as an outstanding short story writer. He published a number of collections, including *The Four Million* (1906), *The Trimmed Lamp* (1907), *Heart of the West* (1907), *The Gentle Grafter* (1908), *Roads of Destiny* (1909), *Options* (1909), *Strictly Business* (1910) and *Whirligigs* (1910). Further volumes appeared after his death.

WASHINGTON IRVING (1783–1859). Irving's first work appeared under the pseudonym of Jonathan Oldstyle, Gent. In 1807–8 he collaborated with his brother William and James Paulding to write and publish a series of essays entitled *Salmagundi*, and in 1809, again under a pseudonym (Diedrich Knickerboker) published *A History of New York*, which quickly established his reputation. His best known book, however, appeared in 1820. *The Sketch Book of Geoffrey Crayon,*

Gent., which includes 'Rip Van Winkle', was first published in England where Irving lived for a number of years.

Irving, whose later work included *Bracebridge Hall* (1822), *Tales of a Traveller* (1824), *The Legends of the Alhambra* (1832), and *A Life of Oliver Goldsmith* (1849), was, in effect, America's first professional writer and the first with a genuinely international reputation.

HENRY JAMES (1843–1916). One of the greatest writers of the nineteenth century, Henry James was profoundly influenced by Europe, where he eventually found his home, becoming a naturalised British subject. In Europe he encountered a density of cultural experience, and a sense of the complexities of the past, which he could play off against his notion of the new American. His first book was a novel, *Watch and Ward*, serialised, like many of his later works, in *The Atlantic Monthly* magazine. He followed this with *A Passionate Pilgrim and Other Tales* (1875) a collection of short stories, and he remained a master of that genre throughout his career.

His first novel of substance, *Roderick Hudson*, was published in 1876 and this ushered in a remarkably productive period with *The American* (1877), *Washington Square* (1880), *The Portrait of a Lady* (1881), *The Bostonians* (1886) and *The Princess Casamassima* (1886).

In the 1890s he wrote some of his best short stories, including 'The Real Thing', along with *What Maisie Knew* and *The Awkward Age*, both 1899. The early years of the twentieth century, meanwhile, saw the publication of *The Sacred Fount* (1901), *The Wings of the Dove* (1902), *The Ambassadors* (1903) and *The Golden Bowl* (1904). The New York edition of his works, which he prepared for publication between 1907 and 1909, eventually expanded to twenty-six volumes. The prefaces he wrote for these volumes are not only interesting for the light they throw on individual texts but also their important commentary on the nature of fiction.

SARAH ORNE JEWETT (1849–1909) was born in South Berwick, Maine, and drew on that area for many of her short stories. Her collections include *Deephaven* (1877), *A White Heron* (1886), *The King of Folly Island* (1888), *A Native of Winby* (1893), *The Life of Nancy* (1895) and her best known, *The Country of the Pointed Firs* (1896). She wrote three novels: *A Country Doctor* (1884), *A Marsh Island* (1885) and *The Tory Lover* (1901)

HERMAN MELVILLE (1819–1891). At the age of twenty Melville went to sea and the sea proved a rich resource for his fiction. *Typee* (1846) and

Omoo (1847), his first novels, were both set in the South Seas, as was *Mardi and the Voyage Thither* (1849), though this was less an account of his journeys than a philosophical work about the search for truth. *Redburn: His First Voyage* (1849) was in part based on Melville's own voyage to England, while *White Jacket* (1850) drew on his experiences in the Navy. It was with *Moby-Dick* (1851), however, that he achieved his greatest work, though its popular reception hardly suggested as much. Indeed, in many ways it marked the decline of Melville's reputation, a decline accelerated by the publication of *Pierre; or the Ambiguities* in 1852. Even so the 1850s proved very productive as far as short stories were concerned, the *Piazza Tales* (1856) containing some of his best, including 'Bartleby the Scrivener'.

Melville continued to write both poetry and prose. Ahead lay *The Confidence-Man* (1857) and *Billy Budd*, whose publication had to await Melville's death. His reputation was not restored until the 1920s.

THOMAS NELSON PAGE (1853–1922) was raised on a Virginia plantation and absorbed many of the assumptions that went with that fact. He set out on a career as a lawyer but the appearance, in 1884, of the dialect story 'Marse Chan' prompted a career as novelist and short story writer. His first collection of stories, *In Ole Virginia or Marse Chan and Other Stories*, appeared in 1887 and his first novel, *Red Rock*, which romanticised the revolt against the Reconstruction that gave birth to the Ku Klux Klan, was published the following year.

Further novels included *Gordon Keith* (1903), *John Marvel, Assistant* (1909) and *The Red Riders*, completed by his brother and published in 1924. Page was also an historian and spent six years as American ambassador to Italy.

In his work Page celebrated the values of the Old South and was resistant to many aspects of the New South.

EDGAR ALLAN POE (1809–1849) was orphaned at the age of two and raised by John Allan, a wealthy merchant with whom he had a stormy relationship. In 1827 he published, anonymously, *Tamerlane and Other Poems*. It was not until he moved to Baltimore, however, that he began to make his way as a writer and critic. As editor of the *Southern Literary Messenger* he wrote both poems and short stories and began serialisation of a novel, *The Narrative of Arthur Gordon Pym*, which he eventually published in New York in 1838. This was followed, in 1840, by *Tales of the Grotesque and Arabesque* and in succeeding years he wrote a string of short stories of genuine originality. He can be seen as the originator of the modern detective story, with such works as 'The Murders in the Rue Morgue' (1841) and became an outstanding exponent of the gothic tale.

In his own eyes he was primarily a poet and certainly his reputation was enhanced by the publication, in 1845, of *The Raven*. His poetry was much admired in Europe, by Tennyson and Baudelaire (his French translator) in particular, but it was through his short stories that he became internationally respected.

ELIZABTH DREW STODDARD (1823–1902) was born in Mattapoisett, Massachusetts, and moved to New York on her marriage. Ironically, she established her reputation as a journalist through a column she contributed to the *Daily Alta California*, reporting on the New York scene. She wrote three novels: *The Morgesons* (1852), *Two Men* (1865) and *Temple House* (1867). These works were well received by critics but increasing poverty forced her into hack work. Besides her stories for adults she also published a collection for children called *Lolly Dinks' Doings* (1874).

HARRIET BEECHER STOWE (1811–1896). The daughter, sister and wife of clergymen, Harriet Beecher Stowe was acutely alive to moral issues, especially those posed by slavery. Incensed by the Fugitive Slave Act she eagerly broke the law by sheltering a slave, and she wrote a book that Abraham Lincoln saw as playing a role in provoking the Civil War.

Her first story won a competition in 1834, beating one submitted by Edgar Allan Poe. Her first, and most famous novel, *Uncle Tom's Cabin*, was serialised in *The National Era* and published as a book in 1852. It sold 300,000 copies in its first year. She capitalised on that success, travelling to Europe and writing many more books, including *Dred* (1856), another attack on slavery, *The Minister's Wooing* (1859) and *Oldtown Folks* (1869). Her work was collected in the year of her death; it amounted to sixteen volumes. 'The Ghost in the Cap'n Brown House' is from her 1872 collection, *Sam Lawson's Oldtown Fireside Stories*.

MARK TWAIN (SAMUEL LANGHORNE CLEMENS 1835–1910). A newspaperman and a licensed Mississippi pilot, Mark Twain decided to become a writer while working on the *Territorial Enterprise* in the then Nevada Territory. His early success with a short story, 'The Celebrated Jumping Frog of Calaveras County', originally written for the San Francisco *Sunday Press*, in 1865, confirmed his decision. His first book, which incorporated that story, appeared two years later. He followed this with the hugely successful *The Innocents Abroad* (1869) and a series of books that established his reputation as America's leading humorist: *Roughing It* (1871), *The Gilded Age* (1873), *The Adventures of Tom Sawyer* (1876), *Life on the Mississippi* (1883), and his masterpiece, *The Adventures of Huckleberry Finn* (1884).

Twain was a prolific author, a popular lecturer, an enthusiast for the theatre and a sceptical observer of American values and human affairs. 'The Man That Corrupted Hadleyburg' (1899) exemplifies a pessimistic strain in his work that was the darker side of the humour for which he was otherwise celebrated.

EDITH WHARTON (1862–1937) was a child of wealthy and sophisticated parents. She began writing early but her first published book was about interior decoration. Dissatisfied with this she turned first to short stories – publishing a collection, *The Great Inclination*, in 1899 – and then to the short novel, with *The Touchstone* (1900). Her real subject was the brittle New York society she knew so well. This was the soil that produced *The House of Mirth* (1905), *The Custom of the Country* (1913) and *The Age of Innocence* (1920) as New England prompted *Ethan Frome* (1911) and *Summer* (1917).

In 1907 Edith Wharton moved to France and stayed there throughout the war, later writing two novels that reflected her experiences at that time: *The Marne* (1918) and *A Son at the Front* (1923).

A great admirer of Henry James, she, like he, regarded the novel as ideally suited to an exploration of psychological truth and moral complexities.

OWEN WISTER (1860–1938) was the grandson of the actress Fanny Kemble, and a novelist, essayist, biographer and short story writer. Born in Philadelphia and educated at Harvard, he went west to Wyoming to recover from illness. Impressed by what he found he set most of his work in that state. His most famous work was *The Virginian* (1902), dedicated to Theodore Roosevelt, a personal friend. Among his books are *Red Men and White* (1895), *Lin McLean* (1898), *Lady Baltimore* (1906), and *When the West Was the West* (1928).

THE SHORT STORY AND THE CRITICS

Henry James on being an American writer:

[. . .] we young Americans are (without cant) men of the future. I feel that my only chance for success as a critic is to let all the breezes of the west blow through me at their will. We are Americans born – *il faut en prendre son parti*. I look upon it as a great blessing; and I think that to be an American is an excellent preparation for culture. We have exquisite qualities as a race, and it seems to me that we are ahead of the European races in the fact that more than either of them we can deal freely with forms of civilization not our own, can pick and choose & assimilate and in short (aesthetically &c) claim our property wherever we find it. To have no national stamp has hitherto been a regret & a drawback, but I think it not unlikely that American writers may yet indicate that a vast intellectual fusion and synthesis of the various National tendencies of the world is the condition of more important achievements than any we have seen. We must of course have something of our own – something distinctive & homogeneous – & I take it that we shall find it in our moral consciousness, our unprecedented spiritual lightness and vigour. In this sense at least we shall have a national *cachet*. I expect nothing great during your lifetime or mine perhaps; but my instincts quite agree with yours in looking to see something original and beautiful disengage itself from our ceaseless fermentation and turmoil. You see I am willing to leave it a matter of instinct. God speed the day. [Henry James to T. S. Perry, September, 1867]

William Dean Howells on 'A National Literature':

From time to time there comes a voice across the sea, asking us in varied terms of reproach and entreaty, why we have not a national literature. As we understand this voice, a national literature would be something very becoming and useful to us as a people, and it would be no more than is due the friendly expectation of the English witnesses of our destitution, who have denied from the beginning that we ever could have a national literature; and proved it. The reasons which they still address to our guilty consciousness in demanding a national literature of us are such and so many that the American who reads their appeals must be a very hardened offender if he does not at once inwardly resolve to do all he can to have one. For our own part, we scarcely know how to keep our patience with the writers who have as yet failed to supply us with it. We are personally acquainted with a dozen Americans who could any one of them give us a national literature, if he would take the pains. In fact, we know of some Englishmen who could produce a very fair national literature for us. All they would have to do would be to write differently from those American authors whose works have failed to embody a national literature, and then they would create for us a literature of unmistakable nationality. But with a literature of their own to maintain, it is too much to ask this of them, and we should not hope for help from English writers, except in the form of advice and censure. We ought to be very glad to have so much, but whether we are glad or not we are likely to have it, for there is nothing mean about Englishmen when it comes to advice and censure; and if we cannot get them to make a national literature for us, we had better learn from them how to make it ourselves.

II

We do not understand the observers of our literary poverty to deny that in certain qualities and colors we have already something national in literature. Perhaps if they were to extend the field of their knowledge a little in the direction of their speculations they might discover that we had something more positive than these colors and qualities; but it never was necessary for an Englishman to know anything of American affairs before writing about them. Here and there an Englishman, like Mr Bryce, takes the trouble to inform himself, but we do not fancy he is the more acceptable or edifying to his countrymen on that account; and the fact remains that he really need not do it. In treating of American literature the English critic's great qualification is that he should be master of the fact that Mr Walt Whitman is the only American who writes like Mr Walt Whitman. It must be owned that the English critic works this single qualification very hard; he makes it go a long way; but we do not blame him for his thrifty use of it; and we should be sorry to quarrel with the simple economy of the inference that we have not a national literature in the proportion that we do not write like Mr Whitman. If this will serve the turn of the English writer with the English public, why should he be at any greater pains in the matter?

Usually the English writer is not at any greater pains, and the extravagance of knowing something more than what is necessary to such an inference is rare. Even Mr Watts, who has lately exposed our literary lack to the world in *The Nineteenth Century*, and Mr Quiller-Couch, who has blamed our literary indifference to the working-man in *The Speaker*, do not go much beyond this inference in their philosophization of our case. Yet, if we were to allow ourselves to bandy words with our betters, we think we might make a suggestion in the interest of general criticism which would perhaps advantage them.

III

In the first place we should like to invite observation to the fact that for all æsthetic purposes the American people are not a nation, but a condition. They are the old, well-known Anglo-Saxon race, affected and modified by the infusion of other strains, but not essentially changed by these, and not very different from the English at home except in their political environment, and the vastness of the scale of their development. Their literature, so far as they have produced any, is American-English literature, just as the English literature is English-European, and it is as absurd to ask them to have a literature wholly their own as to ask them to have a language wholly their own. In fact, we have noted that where our language does differ from that of the mother English, or grand-mother English, the critics who wish us to have a national literature are not particularly pleased. They call our differences Americanisms, and they are afraid of their becoming the language of the whole race.

They ought to be very careful, then, not to chide us too severely for our lack of a national literature. If ever we should turn to and have one, there might be a serious risk of its becoming the literature of the whole race. There is no great danger of an event so mortifying at present, and we merely intimate its possibility as a warning to our critics not to press us too hard. If things should ever come to that pass, we notify them that not only will the American parlance become the English language, but it will be spelled according to Noah Webster. The 'traveller' will have to limp along on one *l*, and the man of 'honour' will no longer point with the pride of long descent to the Norman-French *u* in his last syllable.

IV

In the mean time we wish to ask our critics if they have not been looking for American literature in the wrong place; or, to use an American expression which is almost a literature in itself, whether they have not been barking up the wrong tree. It appears to us that at this stage of the proceedings there is no such thing as nationality in the highest literary expression; but there is a universality, a humanity, which is very much better. There is no doubt, judging from the enterprising character of our people in other respects, that if we had not come upon the scene so very late in the day we should have had a literature of the most positive nationality in form as well as spirit. It is our misfortune rather than our fault to have arrived when all the literary forms were invented. There remained nothing for us to do but to invent literary formlessness, and this, we understand, is what the English admire Mr Whitman for doing; it is apparently what they ask of us all. But there is a curious want of variety in formlessness; the elements are monotonous; it is their combinations that are infinitely interesting; and Mr Whitman seems to have exhausted the resources of formlessness. We cannot go on in his way without servile imitation; the best we can do, since we cannot be national in form, is to be national in spirit and in ideal, and we rather think that in many good ways we are unmistakably so. This is evident from the comparison of any American author with any English author; the difference of qualities is at once apparent; and what more of nationality there might be would, we believe, come of error. There may once have been a time in the history of literature when nationality was supremely desirable: the nationality which expressed itself in the appropriation of forms; but in our time this is not possible, and if it were we think it would be a vice, and we are, above all, virtuous. The great and good things in literature nowadays are not the national features, but the universal features. For instance, the most national fiction at present is the English, and it is the poorest, except the German, which is not at all; while the Russian and the Spanish, the Norwegian and the Italian, the French and the American, which are all so much better, are distinguished by what they have in common rather than by what they have in severalty. The English, who have not felt the great world-movement towards life and truth, are national; those others who have felt it are universal; and perhaps the English critics could be more profitably employed in noting how much the American fiction resembles the Continential fiction than in deploring its want of that peculiarity which renders their own a little droll just now.

Besides, it seems to us that even if we were still in the dark ages when nationality seemed a valuable and admirable thing in itself, they would not find it in our literature in the way they have taken. In any research of the kind we think that the question is not whether this thing or that thing in an author is American or not, but whether upon the whole the author's work is such as would have been produced by a man of any other race or environment. We do not believe that any American writer of recognized power would fail to be found national, if he were tried by this test; and we are not sure but the general use of such a test would result in the discovery of an American literature commensurate in weight and bulk with the emotions of the warmest patriot. The distinctive character of a man's face resides in that complex called his looks; and the nationality of a literature is embodied in its general aspect, not in its particular features. A literature which had none of these would be remarkable for their absence, and if it were produced by one people more than any other would be the expression of their nationality, and as recognizable from its negativity as if it abounded in positive traits.

We do not know, however, that our censors reproach our literature for a want of positivity. Their complaint seems rather to be that it is inadequate to a people who are otherwise so prodigious and original. It strikes them that it is but a small and feeble voice to be the utterance of such a lusty giant; they are listening for a roar, and they hear something very like a squeak, as we understand them. This disappoints them, to say nothing worse; but perhaps it is only our voice changing, and perhaps it would not sound like a squeak if it came from a less formidable body, say San Marino, or Andorra, or even Switzerland. We ought to consider this and take comfort from the possibility, while we taste the tacit flattery in their expectation of a roar from us; from a smaller republic our comparatively slight note could very well pass for a roar, and from a younger one for a mature utterance.

What it is, it is; and it is very probably the natural expression of our civilization, strange as the fact may appear. Our critics evidently think that the writers of a nation can make its literature what they like; but this is a fallacy: they can only make it what the nation likes, involuntarily following the law of environment.

It has been noted that our literature has always been distinguished by two tendencies, apparently opposite, but probably parallel: one a tendency toward an elegance refined and polished, both in thought and phrase, almost to tenuity; the other a tendency to grotesqueness, wild and extravagant, to the point of anarchy. The first has resulted in that delicate poetry which is distinctively American, and in that fiction which has made itself recognized as ours, wherever it is liked or disliked. The last has found its outcome in our peculiar species of humor, which no one can mistake for any other, not even for the English imitations of it. Our literature has these tendencies because the nation has them, and because in some measure each and every American has them. It would take too long to say just how and why; but our censors may rest assured that in this anomalous fact exists the real nationality of our literature. They themselves have a half perception of the truth when they accept and advance Walt Whitman as the representative of our literature. With a supreme passion for beauty, and impatient of all the trammels and disguises of art, he is eager to seize and embrace its very self. For the most part the effort is a failure; the divine loveliness eludes him, and leaves only a 'muddy vesture of decay' in his grasp. He attains success often enough to make good his claim to the admiration the English yield him, and he misses it often enough to keep the more intelligent American observer in doubt. We understand better than they how and why Walt Whitman is; we perceive that he is now and again on the way to the way we should all like to find; but we know his way is not the way. At the same time we have to own that he is expressive of that national life which finds itself young and new in a world full of old conventions and decrepit ideals, and that he is suggestive if not representative of America. But he is no more so than the most carefully polished writer among us. He illustrates the prevalence of one of our moods, as Longfellow, say, illustrates the other. No one but an American could have written the poetry of Whitman; no one but an American could have written the poetry of Longfellow. The work of both is a part of that American literature which also embraces the work of Mark Twain and of Lowell, of Artemus Ward and of Whittier, of Bret Harte and of Emerson, of G. W. Cable and of Henry James, of Miss Murfree and of O. W. Holmes, of Whitcomb Riley and of T. B. Aldrich.

V

The great difficulty with America is that she has come to her consciousness at a moment when she feels that she ought to be mature and fullgrown, the Pallas among the peoples, with the wisdom of a perfectly trained owl at her bidding. It will not do to be crude when the farthest frontier has all the modern improvements, and the future is penetrated at every point by the glare of an electric. If we are simple we must know it; if we are original, it must be with intention and a full sense of originality. In these circumstances we think we have done not so badly in literature. If we listen to our censors, in general we shall probably do still better. But we do not think we shall do better by heeding them in details. We would not have any considerable body of our writers set about writing novels and poems concerning the life of toil, which Mr Quiller-Couch says we have neglected; because in the first place Mr Quiller-Couch seems to speak from rather a widespread ignorance of the facts; and because in the last place the American

public does not like to read about the life of toil; and one of the
conditions of producing an American literature is that it shall
acceptably address itself to the American public. Nearly all the
Americans are in their own persons, or have been in those of their
fathers or grandfathers, partakers of the life of toil; and anything
about it in literature is to them as coal is to Newcastle, or corn- bread
to a Kentuckian. They have had enough of it. What they want is
something select, something that treats of high life, like those English
novels which have chiefly nourished us; or something that will teach
us how to escape the life of toil by a great stroke of business, or by a
splendid marriage. What we like to read about is the life of noblemen
or millionaires; that is our romance; and if our writers were to begin
telling us on any extended scale of how mill hands, or miners, or
farmers, or iron-puddlers really live, we should very soon let them
know that we did not care to meet such vulgar and commonplace
people. Our well-to-do classes are at present engaged in keeping their
eyes fast shut to the facts of the life of toil, and in making believe that
the same causes will not produce the same effects here as in Europe;
and they would feel it an impiety if they were shown the contrary.
Our finest gentilities do not care anything about our literature; they
have no more concern in it than they have in our politics. As for the
people who are still sunk in the life of toil, they know enough of it
already, and far more than literature could ever tell them. They know
that in a nation which honors toil, the toiler is socially nothing, and
that he is going from bad to worse quite as if the body politic had no
interest in him. What they would like would be some heroic
workman who superhumanly triumphs over his environment and
marries the boss's daughter, and lives idle and respected ever after.
Almost any class of readers would like a hero of that mould; but no
class, and least of all his fellows, would like the life of a workman
shown in literature as it really is, and his condition painted as hopeless
as the condition of ninety-nine workmen out of every hundred is. The
life of toil will do very well for nations which do not honor toil, to
read about; but there is something in the very reverence we have for it
that renders the notion of it repulsive to us. This is very curious; we do
not attempt to explain it; but we can promise the foreign observer
that he need not look for American literature in that direction. The
life of toil! It is a little too personal to people who are trying to be
ladies and gentlemen of elegant leisure as fast as they can. If we have
had to dig, or if we are many of us still digging, that is reason enough
why we do not want the spade brought into the parlor. [Harper's
Monthly, November, 1891]

Edgar Allan Poe on 'the tale' and Hawthorne:

The tale proper, in our opinion, affords unquestionably the fairest field for the exercise of the loftiest talent, which can be afforded by the wide domains of mere prose. Were we bidden to say how the highest genius could be most advantageously employed for the best display of its own powers, we should answer, without hesitation – in the composition of a rhymed poem, not to exceed in length what might be perused in an hour. Within this limit alone can the highest order of true poetry exist. We need only here say, upon this topic, that, in almost all classes of composition, the unity of effect or impression is a point of the greatest importance. It is clear, moreover, that this unity cannot be thoroughly preserved in productions whose perusal cannot be completed at one sitting. We may continue the reading of a prose composition, from the very nature of prose itself, much longer than we can perservere, to any good purpose, in the perusal of a poem. This latter, if truly fulfilling the demands of the poetic sentiment, induces an exaltation of the soul which cannot be long sustained. All high excitements are necessarily transient. Thus a long poem is a paradox. And, without unity of impression, the deepest effects cannot be brought about. Epics were the offspring of an imperfect sense of Art, and their reign is no more. A poem *too* brief may produce a vivid, but never an intense or enduring impression. Without a certain continuity of effort – without a certain duration or repetition of purpose – the soul is never deeply moved. There must be the dropping of the water upon the rock. De Béranger has wrought brilliant things – pungent and spirit-stirring – but, like all immassive bodies, they lack *momentum*, and thus fail to satisfy the Poetic Sentiment. They sparkle and excite, but, from want of continuity, fail deeply to impress. Extreme brevity will degenerate into epigrammatism; but the sin of extreme length is even more unpardonable. *In medio tutissimus ibis.*

Were we called upon, however, to designate that class of composition which, next to such a poem as we have suggested, should best fulfil the demands of high genius – should offer it the most advantageous field of exertion – we should unhesitatingly speak of the prose tale, as Mr Hawthorne has here exemplified it. We allude to the short prose narrative, requiring from a half-hour to one or two hours in its perusal. The ordinary novel is objectionable, from its length, for reasons already stated in substance. As it cannot be read at one sitting, it deprives itself, of course, of the immense force derivable from *totality*. Worldly interests intervening during the pauses of perusal, modify, annul, or counteract, in a greater or less degree, the impressions of the book. But simple cessation in reading, would, of itself, be sufficient to destroy the true unity. In the brief tale, however, the author is enabled to carry out the fulness of his intention, be it what it may.

'During the hour of perusal the soul of the reader is at the writer's control. There are no external or extrinsic influences – resulting from weariness or interruption.

A skilful literary artist has constructed a tale. If wise, he has not fashioned his thoughts to accommodate his incidents; but having conceived, with deliberate care, a certain unique or single *effect* to be wrought out, he then invents such incidents – he then combines such events as may best aid him in establishing this preconceived effect. If his very initial sentence tend not to the outbringing of this effect, then he has failed in his first step. In the whole composition there should be no word written, of which the tendency, direct or indirect, is not to the one pre-established design. And by such means, with such care and skill, a picture is at length painted which leaves in the mind of him who contemplates it with a kindred art, a sense of the fullest satisfaction. The idea of the tale has been presented unblemished, because undisturbed; and this is an end unattainable by the novel. Undue brevity is just as exceptionable here as in the poem; but undue length is yet more to be avoided.

We have said that the tale has a point of superiority even over the poem. In fact, while the *rhythm* of this latter is an essential aid in the development of the poet's highest idea – the idea of the Beautiful – the artificialities of this rhythm are an inseparable bar to the development of all points of thought or expression which have their basis in *Truth*. But Truth is often, and in very great degree, the aim of the tale. Some of the finest tales are tales of ratiocination. Thus the field of this species of composition, if not in so elevated a region on the mountain of Mind, is a table-land of far vaster extent than the domain of the mere poem. Its products are never so rich, but infinitely more numerous, and more appreciable by the mass of mankind. The writer of the prose tale, in short, may bring to his theme a vast variety of modes or inflections of thought and expression – (the ratiocinative, for example, the sarcastic, or the humorous) which are not only antagonistical to the nature of the poem, but absolutely forbidden by one of its most peculiar and indispensable adjuncts; we allude, of course, to rhythm. It may be added here, *par parenthèse*, that the author who aims at the purely beautiful in a prose tale is laboring at great disadvantage. For Beauty can be better treated in the poem. Not so with terror, or passion, or horror, or a multitude of such other points. And here it will be seen how full of prejudice are the usual animadversions against those *tales of effect*, many fine examples of which were found in the earlier numbers of Blackwood. The impressions produced were wrought in a legitimate sphere of action, and constituted a legitimate although sometimes an exaggerated interest. They were relished by every man of genius: although there were found many men of genius who condemned them without just ground. The true critic will but demand that the design intended be accomplished, to the fullest extent, by the means most advantageously applicable.

We have very few American tales of real merit – we may say, indeed, none, with the exception of 'The Tales of a Traveller' of Washington Irving, and these 'Twice-Told Tales' of Mr Hawthorne. Some of the pieces of Mr John Neal abound in vigor and originality; but in general, his compositions of this class are excessively diffuse, extravagant, and indicative of an imperfect sentiment of Art. Articles at random are, now and then, met within our periodicals which might be advantageously compared with the best effusions of the British Magazines; but, upon the whole, we are far behind our progenitors in this department of literature.

Of Mr Hawthorne's Tales we would say, emphatically, that they belong to the highest region of Art – an Art subservient to genius of a very lofty order. We had supposed, with good reason for so supposing, that he had been thrust into his present position by one of the impudent *cliques* which beset our literature, and whose pretensions it is our full purpose to expose at the earliest opportunity; but we have been most agreeably mistaken. We know of few compositions which the critic can more honestly commend than these 'Twice-Told Tales.' As Americans, we feel proud of the book.

Mr Hawthorne's distinctive trait is invention, creation, imagination, originality – a trait which, in the literature of fiction, is positively worth all the rest. But the nature of originality, so far as regards its manifestation in letters, is but imperfectly understood. The inventive or original mind as frequently displays itself in novelty of *tone* as in novelty of matter. Mr Hawthorne is original at *all* points. [Graham's Magazine 1842.]

D. H. Lawrence on Edgar Allan Poe:

[In] *The Fall of the House of Usher* . . . the love is between brother and sister. When the self is broken, and the mystery of the recognition of *otherness* fails, then the longing for identification with the beloved becomes a lust. And it is this longing for identification, utter merging, which is at the base of the incest problem. In psychoanalysis almost every trouble in the psyche is traced to an incest-desire. But it won't do. Incest-desire is only one of the modes by which men strive to get their gratification of the intensest vibration of the spiritual nerves, without any resistance. In the family, the natural vibration is most nearly in unison. With a stranger, there is greater resistance. Incest is the getting of gratification and the avoiding of resistance.

The root of all evil is that we all want this spiritual gratification, this flow, this apparent heightening of life, this knowledge, this valley of many-colored grass, even grass and light prismatically decomposed, giving ecstasy. We want all this *without resistance*. We want it continually. And this is the root of all evil in us.

We ought to pray to be resisted, and resisted to the bitter end. We ought to decide to have done at last with craving.

The motto to *The Fall of the House of Usher* is a couple of lines from Béranger.

> *Son cœur est un luth suspendu;*
> *Sitôt qu'on le touche il résonne.*

We have all the trappings of Poe's rather overdone, vulgar fantasy. 'I reined my horse to the precipitous brink of a black and lurid tarn that lay in unruffled luster by the dwelling, and gazed down – but with a shudder even more thrilling than before – upon the remodeled and inverted images of the gray sedge, and the ghastly tree stems, and the vacant and eyelike windows.' The House of Usher, both dwelling and family, was very old. Minute fungi overspread the exterior of the house, hanging in festoons from the eaves. Gothic archways, a valet of stealthy step, somber tapestries, ebon black floors, a profusion of tattered and antique furniture, feeble gleams of encrimsoned light through latticed panes, and over all 'an air of stern, deep, irredeemable gloom' –this makes up the interior.

The inmates of the house, Roderick and Madeline Usher, are the last remnants of their incomparably ancient and decayed race. Roderick has the same large, luminous eye, the same slightly arched nose of delicate Hebrew model, as characterized Ligeia. He is ill with the nervous malady of his family. It is he whose nerves are so strung that they vibrate to the unknown quiverings of the ether. He, too, has lost his self, his living soul, and become a sensitized instrument of the external influences; his nerves are verily like an æolian harp which must vibrate. He lives in 'some struggle with the grim phantasm, Fear,' for he is only the physical, post-mortem reality of a living being.

It is a question how much, once the true centrality of the self is broken, the instrumental consciousness of man can register. When man becomes selfless, wafting instrumental like a harp in an open window, how much can his elemental consciousness express? The blood as it runs has its own sympathies and responses to the material world, quite apart from seeing. And the nerves we know vibrate all the while to unseen presences, unseen forces. So Roderick Usher quivers on the edge of material existence.

It is this mechanical consciousness which gives 'the fervid facility of his impromptus.' It is the same thing that gives Poe his extraordinarary facility in versification. The absence of real central or impulsive being in himself leaves him inordinately, mechanically sensitive to sounds and effects, associations of sounds, associations of rhyme, for example – mechanical, facile, having no root in any passion. It is all a secondary, meretricious process. So we get Roderick Usher's poem, *The Haunted Palace*, with its swift yet mechanical subtleties of rhyme and rhythm, its vulgarity of epithet. It is all a sort of dream-process, where the association between parts is mechanical, accidental as far as passional meaning goes.

Usher thought that all vegetable things had sentience. Surely all material things have a *form* of sentience, even the inorganic: surely they all exist in some subtle and complicated tension of vibration which makes them sensitive to external influence and causes them to have an influence on other external objects, irrespective of contact. It is of this vibration or inorganic consciousness that Poe is master: the sleep consciousness. Thus Roderick Usher was convinced that his whole surroundings, the stones of the house, the fungi, the water in the tarn, the very reflected image of the whole, was woven into a physical oneness with the family, condensed, as it were into one atmosphere – the special atmosphere in which alone the Ushers could live. And it was this atmosphere which had molded the destinies of his family.

But while ever the soul remains alive, it is the molder and not the molded. It is the souls of living men that subtly impregnate stones, houses, mountains, continents, and give these their subtlest form. People only become subject to stones after having lost their integral souls.

In the human realm, Roderick had one connection: his sister Madeline. She too, was dying of a mysterious disorder, nervous, cataleptic. The brother and sister loved each other passionately and exclusively. They were twins, almost identical in looks. It was the same absorbing love between them, this process of unison in nerve-vibration, resulting in more and more extreme exaltation and a sort of consciousness, and a gradual breakdown into death. The exquisitely sensitive Roderick, vibrating without resistance with his sister Madeline, more and more exquisitely, and gradually devouring her, sucking her life like a vampire in his anguish of extreme love. And she asking to be sucked.

Madeline died and was carried down by her brother into the deep vaults of the house. But she was not dead. Her brother roamed about in incipient madness – a madness of unspeakable terror and guilt. After eight days they were suddenly startled by a clash of metal, then a distinct, hollow metallic, and clangorous, yet apparently muffled, reverberation. Then Roderick Usher, gibbering, began to express himself: *'We have put her living into the tomb!* Said I not that my senses were acute? I *now* tell you that I heard her first feeble movements in the hollow coffin. I heard them – many, many days ago – yet I dared not – *I dared not speak.'*

It is the same old theme of 'each man kills the thing he loves.' He knew his love had killed her. He knew she died at last, like Ligeia, unwilling and unappeased. So, she rose again upon him. 'But then without those doors there *did* stand the lofty and enshrouded figure of the Lady Madeline of Usher. There was blood upon her white robes, and the evidence of some bitter struggle upon every portion of her emaciated frame. For a moment she remained trembling and reeling to and fro upon the threshold, then, with a low moaning cry, fell heavily inward upon the person of her brother, and in her violent and now final death-agonies bore him to the floor a corpse, and a victim to the terrors he had anticipated.'

It is lurid and melodramatic, but it is true. It is a ghastly psychological truth of what happens in the last stages of this beloved love, which cannot be separate, cannot be isolate, cannot listen in isolation to the isolate Holy Ghost. For it is the Holy Ghost we must live by. The next era is the era of the Holy Ghost. And the Holy Ghost speaks individually inside each individual: always, forever a ghost. There is no manifestation to the general world. Each isolate individual listening in isolation to the Holy Ghost within him.

The Ushers, brother and sister, betrayed the Holy Ghost in themselves. They would love, love, love, without resistance. They would love, they would merge, they would be as one thing. So they dragged each other down into death. For the Holy Ghost says you must *not* be as one thing with another being. Each must abide by itself, and correspond only within certain limits. [*Studies in Classic American Literature*, 1923.]

William Dean Howells on Charles Chesnutt:

The critical reader of the story called 'The Wife of his Youth' [. . .] must have noticed uncommon traits in what was altogether a remarkable piece of work. The first was the novelty of the material; for the writer dealt not only with people who were not white, but with people who were not black enough to contrast grotesquely with white people, – who in fact were of that near approach to the ordinary American in race and color which leaves, at the last degree, everyone but the connoisseur in doubt whether they are Anglo-Saxon or Anglo-African. Quite as striking as this novelty of the material was the author's thorough mastery of it, and his unerring knowledge of the life he had chosen in its peculiar racial characteristics. But above all, the story was notable for the passionless handling of a phase of our common life which is tense with potential tragedy; for the attitude, almost ironical, in which the artist observes the play of contesting emotions in the drama under his eyes; and for his apparently reluctant, apparently helpless consent to let the spectator know his real feeling in the matter. Anyone accustomed to study methods in fiction, to distinguish between good and bad art, to feel the joy which the delicate skill possible only from a love of truth can give, must have known a high pleasure in the quiet self-restraint of the performance; and such a reader would probably have decided that the social situation in the piece was studied wholly from the outside, by an observer with special opportunities for knowing it, who was, as it were, surprised into final sympathy.

Now, however, it is known that the author of this story is of negro blood – diluted, indeed, in such measure that if he did not admit this descent few would imagine it, but still quite of that middle world which lies next, though wholly outside, our own. Since his first story appeared he has contributed several others [. . .] and he now makes a showing palpable to criticism in a volume called *The Wife of his Youth, and Other Stories of the Color Line*; a volume of Southern sketches called *The Conjure Woman*; and a short life of Frederick Douglass, in the Beacon Series of biographies. The last is a simple, solid, straight piece of work, not remarkable above many other biographical studies by people entirely white, and yet important as the work of a man not entirely white treating of a great man of his inalienable race. But the volumes of fiction *are* remarkable above many, above most short stories by people entirely white, and would be worthy of unusual notice if they were not the work of a man not entirely white.

It is not from their racial interest that we could first wish to speak of them, though that must have a very great and very just claim upon the critic. It is much more simply and directly, as works of art, that they make their appeal, and we must allow the force of this quite independently of the other interest. Yet it cannot always be allowed. There are times in each of the stories of the first volume when the simplicity lapses, and the effect is as of a weak and uninstructed touch. There are other times when the attitude, severely impartial and studiously aloof, accuses itself of a little pompousness. There are still other times when the literature is a little too ornate for beauty, and the diction is journalistic, reporteristic. But it is right to add that these are the exceptional times, and that for far the greatest part Mr Chesnutt seems to know quite as well what he wants to do in a given case as Maupassant, or Tourguénief, or Mr James, or Miss Jewett, or Miss Wilkins, in other given cases, and has done it with an art of kindred quiet and force. He belongs, in other words, to the good school, the only school, all aberrations from nature being so much truancy and anarchy. He sees his people very clearly, very justly, and he shows them as he sees them, leaving the reader to divine the depth of his feeling for them. He touches all the stops, and with equal delicacy in stories of real tragedy and comedy and pathos, so that it would be hard to say which is the finest in such admirably rendered effects as 'The Web of Circumstance,' 'The Bouquet,' and 'Uncle Wellington's Wives.' In some others the comedy degenerates into satire, with a look in the reader's direction which the author's friend must deplore.

As these stories are of our own time and country [. . .] They are new and fresh and strong, as life always is, and fable never is; and the stories of *The Conjure Woman* have a wild, indigenous poetry, the creation of sincere and original imagination, which is imparted with a tender humorousness and a very artistic reticence. As far as his race is concerned, or his sixteenth part of a race, it does not greatly matter whether Mr Chesnutt invented their motives, or found them, as he feigns, among his distant cousins of the Southern cabins. In either case, the wonder of their beauty is the same; and whatever is primitive and sylvan or campestral in the reader's heart is touched by the spells thrown on the simple black lives in these enchanting tales. Character, the most precious thing in fiction, is as faithfully portrayed against the poetic background as in the setting of the *Stories of the Color Line.*

Yet these stories, after all, are Mr Chesnutt's most important work, whether we consider them merely as realistic fiction, apart from their author, or as studies of that middle world of which he is naturally and voluntarily a citizen. We had known the nethermost world of the grotesque and comical negro and the terrible and tragic negro through the white observer on the outside, and black character in its lyrical moods we had known from such an inside witness as Mr Paul Dunbar; but it had remained for Mr Chesnutt to acquaint us with those regions where the paler shades dwell as hopelessly, with relation to ourselves, as the blackest negro. He has not shown the dwellers there as very different from ourselves. They have within their own circles the same social ambitions and prejudices; they intrigue and truckle and crawl, and are snobs, like ourselves, both of the snobs that snub and the snobs that are snubbed. We may choose to think them droll in their parody of pure white society, but perhaps it would be wiser to recognize that they are like us because they are of our blood by more than a half, or three quarters, or nine tenths. It is not, in such cases, their negro blood that characterizes them; but it is their negro blood that excludes them, and that will imaginably fortify them and exalt them. Bound in that sad solidarity from which there is no hope of entrance into polite white society for them, they may create a civilization of their own, which need not lack the highest quality. They need not be ashamed of the race from which they have sprung, and whose exile they share; for in many of the arts it has already shown, during a single generation of freedom, gifts which slavery apparently only obscured. With Mr Booker Washington the first American orator of our time, fresh upon the time of Frederick Douglass; with Mr Dunbar among the truest of our poets; with Mr Tanner, a black American, among the only three Americans from whom the French government ever bought a picture, Mr Chesnutt may well be willing to own his color.

But that is his personal affair. Our own more universal interest in him arises from the more than promise he has given in a department of literature where Americans hold the foremost place. In this there is, happily, no color line; and if he has it in him to go forward on the way which he has traced for himself, to be true to life as he has known it, to deny himself the glories of the cheap success which awaits the charlatan in fiction, one of the places at the top is open to him. He has sounded a fresh note, boldly, not blatantly, and he has won the ear of the more intelligent public. [*The Atlantic Monthly*, May, 1900.]

William Dean Howells on Hamlin Garland's *Main-Travelled Roads*:

At present we have only too much to talk about in a book so robust and terribly serious as Mr Hamlin Garland's volume called *Main-Travelled Roads*. That is what they call the highways in the part of the West that Mr Garland comes from and writes about; and these stories are full of the bitter and burning dust, the foul and trampled slush of the common avenues of life: the life of the men who hopelessly and cheerlessly make the wealth that enriches the alien and the idler, and impoverishes the producer. If anyone is still at a loss to account for that uprising of the farmers in the West, which is the translation of the Peasant's War into modern and republican terms, let him read *Main-Travelled Roads* and he will begin to understand, unless, indeed, Mr Garland is painting the exceptional rather than the average. The stories are full of those gaunt, grim, sordid, pathetic, ferocious figures, whom our satirists find so easy to caricature as Hayseeds, and whose blind groping for fairer conditions is so grotesque to the newspapers and so menacing to the politicians. They feel that something is wrong, and they know that the wrong is not theirs. The type caught in Mr Garland's book is not pretty; it is ugly and often ridiculous; but it is heart-breaking in its rude despair. The story of a farm mortgage as it is told in the powerful sketch 'Under the Lion's Paw' is a lesson in political economy, as well as a tragedy of the darkest cast. 'The Return of the Private' is a satire of the keenest edge, as well as a tender and mournful idyl of the unknown soldier who comes back after the war with no blare of welcoming trumpets or flash of streaming flags, but foot-sore, heart-sore, with no stake in the country he has helped to make safe and rich but the poor man's chance to snatch an uncertain subsistence from the furrows he left for the battle-field. 'Up the Coulé,' however, is the story which most pitilessly of all accuses our vaunted conditions, wherein every man has the chance to rise above his brother and make himself richer than his fellows. It shows us once for all what the risen man may be, and portrays in his good-natured selfishness and indifference that favorite ideal of our system. The successful brother comes back to the old farmstead, prosperous, handsome, well dressed, and full of patronizing sentiment for his boyhood days there, and he cannot understand why his brother, whom hard work and corroding mortgages have eaten all the joy out of, gives him a grudging and surly welcome. It is a tremendous situation, and it is the allegory of the whole world's civilization: the upper dog and the under dog are everywhere, and the under dog nowhere likes it.

But the allegorical effects are not the primary intent of Mr. Garland's work: it is a work of art, first of all, and we think of fine art; though the material will strike many gentilities as coarse and common. In one of the stories, 'Among the Corn Rows,' there is a good deal of burly, broad-shouldered humor of a fresh and native kind; in 'Mrs Ripley's Trip' is a delicate touch, like that of Miss Wilkins; but Mr Garland's touches are his own, here and elsewhere. He has a certain harshness and bluntness, an indifference to the more delicate charms of style; and he has still to learn that though the thistle is full of an unrecognized poetry, the rose has a poetry too, that even over-praise cannot spoil. But he has a fine courage to leave a fact with the reader, ungarnished and unvarnished, which is almost the rarest trait in an Anglo-Saxon writer, so infantile and feeble is the custom of our art; and this attains tragical sublimity in the opening sketch, 'A Branch Road,' where the lover who has quarrelled with his betrothed comes back to find her mismated and miserable, such a farm wife as Mr Garland has alone dared to draw, and tempts the broken-hearted drudge away from her loveless home. It is all morally wrong, but the author leaves you to say that yourself. He knows that his business was with those two people, their passions and their

probabilities. He shows them such as the newspapers know them.
[*Harper's Monthly*, September, 1891.]

SUGGESTIONS FOR FURTHER READING

Albright, Evelyn May, *The Short Story: Its Principles and Structure* (New York, 1931).

Ford, Richard, Introduction to *The Granta Book of the American Short Story* (Harmondsworth, 1992).

Grabo, Carl, *The Art of the Short Story* (New York, 1913).

James, Henry, *The Art of the Novel: Critical Prefaces* (New York, 1962).

O'Brien, Edward J., *The Advance of the American Short Story* (New York, 1923).

O'Connor, Frank, *The Lonely Voice* (London, 1977).

Pattee, E.W., *The Development of the American Short Story: An Historical Survey* (New York, 1923, rep. 1966).

Reid, Ian, *The Short Story* (London, 1977).

Rhode, Robert D., *Setting in the American Short Story of Local Color 1865–1900* (The Hague, 1975).

Voss, Arthur, *The American Short Story: A Critical Survey* (Norman, Oklahoma, 1973).

Wharton, Edith *The Writing of Fiction* (New York, 1925, rep. 1966).

SHORT STORY COLLECTIONS
IN EVERYMAN

A SELECTION

The Secret Self 1: Short Stories by Women

'A superb collection' *Guardian* **£4.99**

Selected Short Stories and Poems

THOMAS HARDY
The best of Hardy's Wessex in a unique selection **£4.99**

The Best of Sherlock Holmes

ARTHUR CONAN DOYLE
All the favourite adventures in one volume **£4.99**

Great Tales of Detection Nineteen Stories

Chosen by Dorothy L. Sayers **£3.99**

Short Stories

KATHERINE MANSFIELD
A selection displaying the remarkable range of Mansfield's writing **£3.99**

Selected Stories

RUDYARD KIPLING
Includes stories chosen to reveal the 'other' Kipling **£4.50**

The Strange Case of Dr Jekyll and Mr Hyde and Other Stories

R. L. STEVENSON
An exciting selection of gripping tales from a master of suspense **£3.99**

The Day of Silence and Other Stories

GEORGE GISSING
Gissing's finest stories, available for the first time in one volume **£4.99**

Selected Tales

HENRY JAMES
Stories portraying the tensions between private life and the outside world **£5.99**

EVERYMAN

THE SECRET SELF
Short Stories by Women

Edited by
HERMIONE LEE

£4.99

AVAILABILITY

All books are available from your local bookshop or direct from
**Littlehampton Book Services Cash Sales, 14 Eldon Way, Lineside Estate,
Littlehampton, West Sussex BN17 7HE.** PRICES ARE SUBJECT TO CHANGE.

To order any of the books, please enclose a cheque (in £ sterling) made payable to
Littlehampton Book Services, or phone your order through with credit card details (Access,
Visa or Mastercard) on 0903 721596 (24 hour answering service) stating card number and
expiry date. Please add £1.25 for package and postage to the total value of your order.

In the USA, for further information and a complete catalogue call 1-800-526-2778.

CLASSIC FICTION
IN EVERYMAN

A SELECTION

Frankenstein
MARY SHELLEY
A masterpiece of Gothic terror in its
original 1818 version **£3.99**

Dracula
BRAM STOKER
One of the best known horror stories
in the world **£3.99**

The Diary of A Nobody
GEORGE AND WEEDON
GROSSMITH
A hilarious account of suburban life
in Edwardian London **£4.99**

Some Experiences
and Further Experiences
of an Irish R. M.
SOMERVILLE AND ROSS
Gems of comic exuberance and
improvisation **£4.50**

Three Men in a Boat
JEROME K. JEROME
English humour at its best **£2.99**

Twenty Thousand Leagues
under the Sea
JULES VERNE
Scientific fact combines with
fantasy in this prophetic tale of
underwater adventure **£4.99**

The Best of Father Brown
G. K. CHESTERTON
An irresistible selection of crime
stories – unique to Everyman **£4.99**

The Collected Raffles
E. W. HORNUNG
Dashing exploits from the most glam-
orous figure in crime fiction **£4.99**

£5.99

AVAILABILITY
All books are available from your local bookshop or direct from
**Littlehampton Book Services Cash Sales, 14 Eldon Way, Lineside Estate,
Littlehampton, West Sussex BN17 7HE.** PRICES ARE SUBJECT TO CHANGE.

To order any of the books, please enclose a cheque (in £ sterling) made payable to
Littlehampton Book Services, or phone your order through with credit card details (Access,
Visa or Mastercard) on 0903 721596 (24 hour answering service) stating card number and
expiry date. Please add £1.25 for package and postage to the total value of your order.

In the USA, for further information and a complete catalogue call 1-800-526-2778.